ANNIHILATION

THE DARKNESS DEEPENS

2

J F MACDONOGH

CW01475183

ANNIHILATION
Book Two
THE DARKNESS DEEPENS

Copyright © Text Jeremy F. Macdonogh

This is the first edition.

The author asserts the moral right under the Copyright, Designs and Patents Act 1988 to be identified as the author of this work.

Arts Council England

(feedaread.com/Lightning Source)

All rights reserved. No part of this publication may be reproduced, stored in a retrieval system, or transmitted, in any form or by any means without the prior written consent of the author, nor otherwise circulated in any form of binding other than that in which it is published and without a similar condition being imposed on the subsequent publisher.

Also by J F Macdonogh

*

A GAP YEAR OR TWO
Adventures in Europe between 1970 -1974
2007, Athena Press
reedited 2012 by Arts Council England
(feedaread.com/Lightning Source)

*

THE LAST IRISHMEN
A Family's Defiance, Struggle and Passion
2012 by Arts Council England
(feedaread.com/Lightning Source)

I first went to Kanturk, a town in the 'barony' of Duhallow, County Cork, a little over twenty years ago. I was a little shocked by what I saw. Or, more exactly, by what I didn't see.

I went there to see if the family from which my line supposedly derives had left any evidence. I felt bound to find masses of information there.

Aside from a ruinous mansion, however, near which a sign declared it to have been the seat of the MacDonagh-MacCarthys (*sic*), there was no tangible trace of the clan that had ruled Duhallow as princes for so many centuries. Of their subordinate clans, the O'Callaghans, the O'Keeffes, the MacAuliffes, there was rather more. Shops, bars, garages all bore those names, but not even a bookmaker called 'MacDonogh's' was to be seen on the little town's charming streets.

It was becoming clear that some mass eviction or shocking disaster must have overtaken the race I was investigating. Somewhere in the past there had been a dislocation in history.

The National Library in Dublin came to the rescue. There I learned the story of the extinction of the County Cork branch of this family and its relationship to its surviving septs. The name is rare but still alive in Counties Sligo, Galway and Roscommon.

In fact, the North Cork clan was never MacDonagh-MacCarthy. It was MacDonogh Carty, the last word signifying both a distinction from the MacDonoghs of Tyrerill and of Corran, and a recognition that these MacDonoghs were princes under the paramountcy of the MacCarthys.

Due to the paucity of hard fact, I have to tell the story as a novel, a dramatic reconstruction, the crossing point of history and fiction. This is the tale of a grand and native Irish family when Oliver Cromwell felt the urge to pay Ireland a visit.

The few substantial facts I have gleaned from an almost barren field have caused characters, dead these four hundred years, to rise from Ireland's soil, ready as ever to defend their traditions and their religion. Their epic tale has sprung into life.

While this is the tale of just one Irish family, by extension it is the story of all Ireland. My hope is that the reader will find it a cracking yarn.

Jeremy Macdonogh, Winter 2014
Hoxne, Suffolk

CHRISTENDOM IN THE EARLY SEVENTEENTH CENTURY
(in a nutshell)

In the early seventeenth century, the primordial forces of religion, politics, power and naked ambition coalesced into a philosophical and spiritual tornado. Nations sundered, frontiers shifted, Christianity fractured, heretics united and families divided.

'Empire' was the thing, and everyone wanted one.

For some it was already too late. Spain's Golden Age was drawing to an end. At the start of this tale, her dominions wrapped the world, as far as the Philippines. In the Americas she flourished. In the north, California, Colorado, Nevada, Florida, Arizona and Mexico were all hers. She contested Central America with the Dutch. The three largest islands in the Caribbean - Hispaniola, Cuba and Jamaica – flew her flag and her *conquistadores* had long brought most of South America under her protection. As for South America, her only rival was the Portuguese.

Portugal's colonies straddled the world. Her imperialists busied themselves in Macao, Goa, Bombay, Angola, Tangiers, the Cape of Good Hope and Brazil.

France, runner-up, had trained her colonial sights on the Lowlands, Canada, the Caribbean and the newly discovered Mississippi basin to the west of Virginia, yet to be named Louisiana.

So too the Grand Duchy of Muscovy, about to take possession of Alaska. The Czars also trained their sights on the northern reaches of the Subcontinent.

The Sublime Porte and her vassal Kingdoms of Greece, Albania and Bulgaria looked enviously at Austria and the Holy Roman Empire's Mediterranean countries, Serbia, Bosnia and Slovenia. Sundry viziers drew arrows on maps of Central Europe, stretched out across the ottomans and divans of the Topkapi Palace.

Charles V had governed a Holy Roman Empire of a dozen countries; among them Bohemia, Moravia, Silesia, Flanders and Brabant, many of which had once been the patrimony of the Dukes of Burgundy. The greatest German principalities, Saxony, Brandenburg and the Kingdom of Bavaria were now under the Imperial yoke, as were the bishoprics of Rhine, Mainz, Trier and Cologne. Charles's successor, Rudolf, now governed them all.

Lutheran Sweden, the Protestant superpower, ruled Norway, Denmark and Finland, and had expansionist designs on Poland, Latvia, and Estonia - even Russia.

A quieter and shrewder route to glory was adopted by Calvinist Holland's East India Company, building monopolies, protecting trade routes and harvesting its settlements from New Amsterdam to Cape Town and as far as Indonesia.

Even the Helvetic Confederation of Switzerland had designs on the Calvinist nation of Geneva, only recently 'liberated' from Burgundian Catholicism.

England was reduced to a walk-on part in this manifold Imperial drama. Under the arrogant and extravagant Tudors, the rich English provinces of the Pas de Calais, Normandy, Aquitaine and Gascony were lost. Yet to acquire Jamaica and Barbados from the Spanish, India would not see English influence until after the Restoration, still half a century away. True, the Tudor Rose flew over Elizabeth's only American possession, Virginia, but the colony was almost lost to starvation, disease and resentful Powhatans. Its only crop, tobacco, had been harvested with such single-mindedness that the soil could no longer grow vegetables.

Even if Guido Fawkes' 1605 attempt to blow up the Houses of Parliament had failed, the clear-sighted had already discerned the auguries of Civil War.

England's client Kingdom of Ireland, always dreaming of rebellion, was only kept from going its own way by the enforced settlement of countless Protestants onto its Catholic soil. Such strategies would eventually cause Nationalism and Catholicism to merge. Countless unsuccessful wars against their large and single-minded aggressor brought only repeated defeat and divided innumerable families and clans. While some ancient Irish families ignored that danger, others chose to side with the English, often becoming 'Anglican'. Still others found shelter abroad.

Those exiles dreamed of and plotted a glorious return to their immemorial hearths and beloved emerald hills.

ACKNOWLEDGEMENTS

The author would like to thank the painter Brian Whelan – a great scholar - for having the patience to read the first draft. Brian, I hope you will see that every one of your suggestions has been incorporated.

So, too, Paul Hrynaszkiewicz, for doing the same to this one.

Daniel Catignani has had to endure my reading excerpts to him, often over a pint.

John Bawtree painted the original picture of the Old Court at Kanturk, which now serves as a front cover.

Tony Diamond, my Ultonian friend, despite being a Baptist, has swallowed his distaste for Catholicism and helped give my religious expositions some restraint. He has also made many useful suggestions as to the prose.

Finally, my deepest gratitude is to my wife Helen, for her tireless editing of the typescript as it fell out of the printer.

The ultimate dedication is to my son Felix, who will learn the stuff of which his family is, or was, made.

ANNIHILATION
THE DARKNESS DEEPENS

PROLOGUE
Leicester House, London.

The king had repeatedly told Lord Leicester that the late and 'much missed' Lord Strafford had spoken highly of Lord Ormonde. The earl was not surprised, therefore, to find himself reading a military commission, drawn up by some impatient palace clerk, passed to him for comment or signature. Lord Leicester gave it a few brief moments of his valuable time. It was addressed to The Right Trusty and Honourable Cousin the Marquess of Ormonde, Uncommon Courtier, Gallant Soldier and Countryman.

"Countryman' indeed!' he snorted. For him, the countryside conjured dogfights, hayricks, buxom landladies and wildfowling, none of which appealed. "Rustic', would seem a better term.' He had never been tempted by the celebrated outdoor life of the Irish.

His secretary was fussing about, tidying some documents.

'This deplorable age is unnecessarily given to 'manliness',' Leicester pronounced. ''Manliness' is wholly unnatural. Rising from a comfortable bed at some ungodly hour, traipsing about in filthy weather, up to one's knees in mud, wearing unutterably coarse cloth, enduring rude winds and boorish rain, all to shoot defenceless rabbits. What room is there left in such a life for Terpsichore, Erato and Euterpe to make their grand entrances *si charmantes?'*

He paused, while his clerk stood silently ready. The secretary was well accustomed to his master's tirades.

'Still, if Lord Ormonde must dress up as a soldier, at least Strafford's uniforms are indeed quite fetching.'

From his magnificent house in St Martin's Fields, London's 'West End', the Lord Deputy of Ireland watched carelessly as his clerk poured molten wax onto the parchment, anticipating the application of the noble earl's sealing fob.

Lord Leicester did not disappoint. He applied his imprimatur to the Marquess of Ormonde's commission, instating him as Lieutenant-General of the King's Army in Ireland.

'Call me sceptical if you must, but I don't believe the Irish Army actually exists.' The secretary had the temerity to raise an eyebrow, but Lord Leicester simply passed him the sealed commission. It would in turn be passed to a courier.

While Leicester had once served the Crown in Holland, he was utterly unimpressed by all things military. Nothing would please him more than to delegate those duties to such a man as Ormonde. A sickening journey over the water was not for him. Nor was waving his sword about in the air like a stage Dervish.

'I have already shared my views on the subject of the Irish with the talented thespians who are to perform for me and my sensitive guests in the ballroom tonight. They all agreed with my every word.'

'They always do, my lord,' said his secretary, by way of agreement.

The letters patent sailed across the Irish Sea in a diplomatic bag. Eventually Lord Howth placed them directly into the Earl, or Marquess, of Ormonde's hands, together with a word of explanation.

'I am sorry about the accidental marquisate, my lord. I presume some scribe in Whitehall has carelessly promoted you, or failed to notify your distinction to *The Gazette*? I hope it won't nullify the commission?'

Lord Ormonde was untroubled.

'I shouldn't think it will. As for the marquisate, there has been some talk. Nothing formal as yet but it can only be a matter of time. Thank you for delivering the letters to me in person, Lord Howth. Now, do go and find something to eat downstairs. My chef will look after you, my lord. I would join you but I had better take this document to Dublin directly.'

With that, Ormonde set off from his favourite house at Carrick-on-Suir, there and then, carrying his appointment, its seal unbroken, to Dublin Castle. He had heard the rumours of a Rebellion as clearly as every other Irishman. His commission was timely. Remarkably, it had arrived before it was too late.

*

ANNIHILATION
The Darkness Deepens

Being an account of the near extinction of the Macdonoghs of Kanturk

Places mentioned in the narrative

17

CHAPTER ONE
TROUBLE BREWS

Dermod Oge MacDermod MacOwen MacDonogh Carty, ninth Lord of Duhallow, had received two letters, both dated October 14, 1641.

The first was a 'round-robin' from the Lords Justice in Dublin. It called upon all Catholic Gentry to rally to the defence of Ireland. It besought them 'to support the Lord Deputy in keeping the peace, and to afford all succour and provision in men and arms that the royal government in Ireland might need to call upon'. Dermod Oge deduced that rumours of an incipient rebellion had finally reached the duumvirate that ruled Dublin.

The second was rather more interesting. It was from Rory O'More, a Liex[i] chief, saying that an insurrection was planned but that no details at this stage could be shared with those beyond the Pale. It disclosed only the tantalising confidence that Ireland was about to regain its identity and purpose. It suggested that the old families of Eire should ready themselves for whatever was to come.

Dermod Oge, Mayor of Kanturk, called a Council at his castle at Dromsicane. Some even muttered that he had been taking his time over it. The truth, had they but known it, would have amazed them. It had been his wife Cliona who had talked him into it.

'Let me tell you', a worked-up Seamus O'Callaghan roared at his employer. 'Let me tell you, that bastard Lord Cork is nothing less than the Prince of Darkness himself. Oh! My deepest apologies, Madam MacDonogh. I didn't see you there!'

He bowed to an almost invisible figure who sat away from the light in a corner of the hall. Since her husband was centre stage - not at her side - Sir Philip de Perceval had offered to sit beside her, his sword at her service.

'Sorry for that. On occasion I get a little carried away. Off on the wrong foot, to coin a phrase.' He pressed on anyway. 'I promise to speak less intemperately, Madam, Gentlemen. Going back to that swine Cork, the earl has done us more harm than anyone. People here want payment and revenge for the way the slubberdegullion captured O'Mahony's castle and destroyed his clan, for the way he bombarded O'Sullivan Beare's castle until he'd reduced it and its occupants to bloodstained stones. That's not all! I want to taste his blood for the way he salted the earth and empted the south west of the county of living beings. Jackdaw Cork is lining his nest with our land, stooping to the same methods as his role model, the late and unlamented Lord Strafford. Once Cork was just a humble Clerk to the Court. Plain Richard Boyle, his name was then, fresh over from England with twenty-seven pounds in his pocket. He may have amassed a vast fortune but his true character hasn't changed. Do we not remember how this base and greedy lordling started out? The 'great gentleman' paid a mark for the privilege of taking the news of our defeat at Kinsale to the Virgin Queen, who thanked him 'for his valour' with the abbey-castle at Lismore, the one she had just confiscated from Sir Walter Raleigh! Valour my arse! For being good-looking, more likely, but it was the making of him. No doubt he discharged his debt to the old queen in her bedchamber. Just three years later he had enough money to buy another 40,000 acres at Youghal and entertain the President of Munster, Sir George Carew, to dinner. Since then they have become old chums.'

'That's a fact,' interrupted an elderly Gnogher O'Mahony. 'Boyle is our real enemy. When he built his townland, near Bandon Bridge - on my family's land, mark you - that place became Munster's Londonderry. Its walls are nine feet thick, fifty feet high and, just as at the Prod city in the north, Catholics are denied entry.'

Dermod Oge looked around at the lesser chiefs and richer merchants he had brought together at Dromsicane. A motley crew, he thought. Not that there were too many of them.

'Thank you O'Mahony. You would drive us all to war, but we must consider the consequences of revolt,' he said, his tone level, unexcitable, deliberate. 'If we rebel we can expect no mercy from the English, not even a soldier's death. Let me remind you all that after Kinsale, with 30,000 prisoners to deal with, rounded up all over Ireland, the English disposed of half of them as cannon fodder to Sweden's Gustavus Adolphus. Most of those were dead in months. The other half were sold as slaves, indentured labourers in Central America.'

The gathering listened carefully. They had not yet worked out whether they were being asked to fight or not.

'Back then,' Dermod Oge continued, 'some of our leaders exiled themselves to the Continent, the English making it easy for their clans to follow. Exile, however, whether compulsory or otherwise, was not enough for Lord Deputy Falkland. King James I continued to sell Irish rounded-up woodkerne[1] as slaves to planters and settlers in the New World. Falkland had some work in Newfoundland and, in 1612, yet more

---

[1] Bandits, sometimes called 'tories', living rough and wreaking havoc.

Irishmen were sold to a settlement on the Amazon River[ii], their women serving the African slaves as breeding stock.'

'It's not all Boyle's fault,' said O'Keeffe, the pork butcher. 'What about Captain Freke? He also fought against us at Kinsale. He got nearly 14,000 acres in the Barony of Carbury for his pains. His family's house at Rathbarry is now an enormous fortress. Castlefreke, he calls it.'

'What about the Scots?' asked Mr O'Leary, the Ulsterman. 'I hope no Scots number among your neighbours.'

'Such settlers as we have in north east Cork are mainly English and Welsh,' Dermod Oge replied. 'Unlike you Ultonians, we haven't suffered wholesale eviction. At least yet. Saying that, many of the undertakers have built themselves fortified houses, only permitting the Irish to remain as sub-tenants, servants or labourers.'

'In Ulster the policy amounts to nothing less than the systematic purging of every square inch of habitable land,' persisted O'Leary. 'There, the settlers are Lowland Scotch. They are like locusts. Believe me, their towns are well defended. May God keep and save Sir Phelim and his friends.'

'Amen', several murmured.

'We live in County Cork. All our clansmen want to fight for the cause of Ireland,' said Dermod Oge. 'As Lord of Duhallow I can raise and arm two thousand men. My *tanist*, Bryen, has been formally trained as an officer, somewhat ironically by the Saxon Wentworth.'

'Very good, but how many men can the Prods raise?' asked O'Leary. 'What about Bandon Bridge? That is one big, ugly enemy stronghold.'

'It certainly is,' confirmed O'Mahony.

'At least Bandon Bridge is one of the very few Protestant towns in Munster,' persisted O'Leary.

'Thank heaven for small mercies!' O'Dwyer sarcastically exclaimed.

'So far,' added a sceptical O'Leary. 'Kinsale and Youghal could easily go the same way. They have English garrisons. So has Cork City.'

'I don't really understand why we need a Dublin Parliament at all. When we have evicted the Saxons we should build one of our own. Not at Swords. Well away from the Pale,' suggested Mr Kevin O'Grady.

'The problem with Dublin is…?' O'Keeffe began to query.

'…that too many Prods live there.' O'Grady could complete the sentence for him.

O'Malley also had twopence of his own to toss in the pot.

'What's more,' he said with a phlegmatic shrug, "Poynings' Law" means that a Dublin Parliament has to be subservient to the English one, even in purely Irish matters. Whenever Dublin tries to pass a law to protect us from the Sasanach it is straight away overruled in Westminster.' His tone epitomised resignation.

'Times are changing,' said Dermod Oge, 'and O'Grady is right. A new Parliament, a home-grown one of our own, would be fully justified. The presumption of the Protestants of the Pale to govern doesn't merely irritate us, the Catholic Irish majority. It is also beginning to annoy the Old English. That is all to the good. It means that our Anglo-Norman friends, many of whom we have tolerated for fully five hundred years, recognise that they are as Irish as any of us and are at last preparing to come in with us.'

'Like Sir Philip de Perceval. You two have long been as thick as thieves,' said Dr Dempsey, the apothecary who had been to the new College in the capital. He did not approve of Perceval. 'What is he doing here?'

Sir Philip was sitting with Madam MacDonogh in the corner of the room where there was least light. He stood up. A dozen Irishmen stared at him. The atmosphere was brittle: Sir Philip was not only English, he was an Anglican. For many of them this combination was Ireland's most deadly enemy.

Before he could speak a bristling O'Malley was on his feet.

'May I ask the President of this Council why exactly is Sir Philip de Perceval has to be here? He is hardly a native.'

'He is not a Milesian,' Dermod Oge replied easily. 'My father-in-law is not a Catholic, either, but he is a proud Irishman. Old English and pure Irish will be pulling together, so get used to it, O'Malley. Sir Philip, would you care to answer the question yourself.'

'Thank you, MacDonogh Carty of Duhallow.' Sir Philip cleared his throat. 'Gentlemen, Madam, the leopard you see on his feet has changed at least some of his spots. Many of you loathed my father, and that I understand. The taxes he raised were unjust. He had little choice, I realise, but I have never carried his torch. I hardly knew him, as he died before my tenth birthday. I never had the chance to argue the matter with him. I was old enough, however, to make a choice. Mine was harmony with my fellow landowners and tenantry, here in Duhallow and on my estates at Egmont. Some of you will have heard the expression *Hiberniores Hibernis Ipsis* - more Irish than the Irish. For some time it has labelled a particular breed of Old English families in Ireland. We are proud of this soubriquet. My father was successful in his dealings with the English, but I have made it my privilege to stand beside your Lord of Duhallow, amongst others. I claim the honour of having rescued some Irish families financially from the certain ruin that would surely have overtaken them had I not. When I first met your chief his pockets were empty, his castles half-ruined. Restoration of a noble family cannot be achieved with courage alone; this great hall, here at Dromsicane, represents to me a very considerable risk to my capital, and my duty is to protect that investment.' He paused thoughtfully. 'No, please allow me to correct myself. It is Ireland itself that is my investment. I have spent too much time in Dublin in recent months to see how the country will turn out if such men as Borlase, Parsons and Coote are to gain real power. It is our task to sweep our country free of these villains and prevent a civil war.'

He sat down to reserved if polite applause.

'Thank you, Sir Philip,' said Dermod Oge. The room fell silent and the chief looked around to see if hands were raised. No one had anything to say. That makes a change, he thought.

Cliona had surprised some when they saw she was a member of this 'cabinet' but since she had first learned of a planned Rebellion she had determined to play her part. Now she stood and moved into the light.

She was not wearing the day-dress that a woman of her rank would normally wear. Instead, she moved to stand beside her husband's chair in a light riding habit, her athletic form plainly discernible

'May I ask my husband's permission to address the meeting?'

'Please do,' said Dermod Oge, a light smile on his face. 'I am confident that everyone here would like to hear the feminine side of these arguments.'

'Thank you, husband mine, though whether I shall oblige you with domestic femininity and ladylike charm I am far from certain.'

The councillors laughed good-naturedly. Curiosity, or gallantry, made them grow quiet for her little speech. They respected her husband the chief too much to voice their collective thought out loud; that the subject of today's discussion was man's business.

'We should be grateful to the Saxons,' she began, her voice heavy with irony. 'For thousands of years we Irish liked to fight one another – Celts against Formorians and Danaans, Owenians versus Dalcassians, Normans against Milesians – but with this redoubled Saxon threat, we have at last found a foe to unite against. We expect the English to be surprised to see us revolt. Any nation less conceited than the Saxons would have seen it coming long ago.

'They should have noticed that most Old English lords spoke the Gaelic – witness Sir Philip here. They wholly failed to foresee that such men would read, enjoy and even write our poetry and music. Since the Battle of Kinsale, it is striking - at least to me - that, fully a generation ago, intermarriage between Celt and Norman became almost commonplace. We have at last become one nation.

'Saxon obduracy, greed and their strange religious impositions have shown us that our clan divisions of dateless antiquity no longer serve. Their arrogance, hubris and confiscations, serve no cogent purpose other than to make room for their surplus population. If they continued, Ireland would become a peasant nation, with no leaders but priests, and with no sympathisers but the enemies of the Crown.

'King Charles may be a little more pleasant than his predecessors, Elizabeth and James, but even he mistakes the uneasy quiet for peace. Only for so long can our every petty disobedience of the Saxons - and their Dublin puppets - be rewarded with a seizure of our lands. Their readiness to inculpate every member of a particular clan, whose chief they have pronounced guilty, has made Dublin the enemy of the greater part of Ireland.

'It is hard to swap prosperity for penury. To watch our neighbours and friends so miserably reduced breaks my heart. The Saxons have to learn that some sort of reprisal will follow every confiscation. We are still too meek. The continual, relentless, pitiless eviction of Catholic smallholders and minor landowners is nothing less than a *casus belli*. Nor is it only a quarrel over land. It is just as much a struggle over faith.

'While the settlers attempt to peddle their scriptural certainties, they are met all over Ireland with the unbridled zeal of the counter-reformation; teams of courageous friars are illegally teaching your children the rudiments of the true faith. Many of you here will have had your education at the hands of these brave men, who have spread resistance. Our self-confidence grows wherever they go. Every so often, the English murder a few of them. About a dozen a year. May their souls know eternal peace.'

She lowered her head to make the Sign of the Cross.

'Since the summer the Dominicans and Franciscans have been joined by Jesuits, the cleverest of men. Gentlemen, may I ask you a question? Do the Saxons believe simple barbarity is in itself enough to cower us? If they ever did, they can do so no longer. These hints of Rebellion give you the answer; far from collapsing, our resolve is stiffening, day by day, night by night, hour by hour.

'I have heard tell that some of you say that my husband, your mayor, your lord, your chief, sits on the fence. Let me answer you; you know who you are. You would not have a Catholic chief today if he had been as hot-headed as he was sorely tempted. At best you would now be tolerated tradesmen in a brave new Saxon world. At worst, you would be slaves in some American plantation. Your holdings and businesses, however modest, would have been parcelled out to 'deserving' Protestants. My husband's long suffering endurance has paid you all a dividend. Up to now, that is. The Irish nation is at last on the point of rising. There will be a new dawn.

'If my husband, my boys, choose to go to war they will have my absolute support. More than that. Gentlemen, I resolve to fight this war alongside them.

'I will challenge Boyle, St Leger, Freke, Coote, Inchiquin, Borlase and Parsons; all the other bullies and tyrants who believe the future of our nation is for it to be debased into a collection of English feudal ties.

'I will fight. I can ride as well as any man. I have learned to use a sword. If forced, I shall fight the enemy with my fists.

'Gentlemen, every woman in Duhallow feels the same way as I. If you are not prepared to risk your necks, we of the supposedly gentler sex will leave you to your councils and take our war to the enemy ourselves.

'After centuries, at last, Ireland has a chance of belonging to the Irish, as once it did, five hundred years or so ago. Build our own Irish Parliament? Yes! Let's fly our golden harp above it and raise the tribes,' she commanded. 'And in case your courage fails you on the field of battle, look behind you. You will see me there, the cutting edge of my sabre sharpened to rival the razor of a fractured flint.

'My fight, our fight, is for Ireland and for God. Even if some of us fall, all of us will live in a better world.'

She stopped speaking. Her fists were still clenched, and her determination continued to radiate into the silence around her.

Slowly all in the stone hall at Dromsicane rose to their feet. They began to cheer and applaud her. The roar of approval continued for many minutes.

A goose drover in the castle yard muttered to his lad, 'something's got 'em going'.

'Gentlemen,' said Dermod Oge, rising to his feet, his face stern. He signalled that the meeting should quieten. 'Only once we have our own legitimate assembly, sanctioned by the heads of other European states and in alliance with those friendly powers, then and only then should we embrace this struggle. The Scots found the legal strength to defy the English Government. As Cliona says so passionately, let's have our own Parliament; that's when we take our government back, just as Scotland has. If the English insist on using force, we should not shrink from returning the compliment. They will discover this family ready for them.'

He raised his sword in front of him, the way he had been taught to salute at La Flèche, in younger days in France.

'*Eireann go brach!*' he cried. 'Who will be ready to fight alongside us, when the time is right?'

'I', said forty voices in unison.

*

CHAPTER TWO
THE GREAT REBELLION

A dusty horseman dismounted outside a modest half-timbered house in Little Abbey Street, North Dublin. Being summer, he was lightly dressed; a thin linen doublet, kid leather breeches, a short sword. His lace jabot flapped about in the breeze.

He paused for a moment before tugging at the bell-pull but even as he did the door opened.

The darkness of the room forced him to peer awkwardly inside, almost bumping into the man in front of him. A familiar voice put the traveller at ease.

'Ah, there you are, dear Cousin. Thank you for treating my request so urgently.' Colonel MacMahon laughed in that easy way of his. 'Goodness me! Owen O'Connolly, will you just look at yourself! You must have ridden every one of those sixty miles from Monaghan without bothering to breathe! That mare of yours looks half dead. Hurry now, take her around to the mews and have my man wash her down. Then come into the parlour the back way join me in a glass. A great game is afoot!'

Hugh Òg MacMahon's guest, O'Connolly, was indeed his kinsman. O'Connolly was a stiff unbending fellow, but still the sort who would benefit greatly from that glass or, better yet, its successor.

The two had known each other since childhood and, unlike some of the other conspirators, MacMahon was disposed to overlook the many errors of judgement O'Connolly had made in his life to date. It was widely agreed that the greatest had been to accept employment from the infamous Sir John Clotworthy – now Lord Massereene - one of Ulster's most bigoted Puritans. The second, in MacMahon's opinion at least, was almost as grave. He had married a very plain and deeply priggish Englishwoman. In this, MacMahon stood alone. To the other rebels his wife didn't matter; it was the Massereene connection that they meant to exploit.

MacMahon himself was nothing less than a grandson of the Great Tyrone, Hugh O'Neill, the Ulster earl who had fought so hard to liberate Ireland at Kinsale in 1601. Until quite recently, MacMahon had been a distinguished half-colonel in *el Tercio Irlanda*, but at last he had returned from serving the Spanish Crown in the Netherlands. At the time he declared that he was in Ireland to save what was left of his demesne at Clones.

As O'Connolly reappeared, the Colonel showed him where to rest his sword. He waved his guest at a chair, sat down opposite and leaned forward.

'My dear fellow, I hope you are ready for this. I have something quite astonishing to share with you. It's of historical importance, a matter of which the not-yet-born will talk about to their grandchildren. By sunset this night, half our band of heroes will have arrived in Dublin. They will disperse in small groups to a number of private and public houses and await my signal. Those who are not already here will arrive during the night or, at the latest, daybreak. Don't worry, they will be safe; the fair on the morrow will give them cover. Owen O'Connolly, just picture it! Hundreds of sound and pious Irishmen in Dublin - thousands throughout the country – all about to play their part in our momentous drama!'

'Can it be that you have really managed it, Hugh Òg? You have truly prepared a full-scale insurrection in the capital itself under the noses of Lords Justice Borlase and Parsons? You are a marvel!'

'Goodness, Cousin, I can hardly take all the credit myself. There's Maguire of course, Rory O'More, many others besides. And, now that I have let you into our secret, there's you. Owen, you are to join us at the very highest level. Your connections with your Puritan master and his important friends make you key to our takeover of Dublin and the nation. Let's shake hands. There, well done! Now, go and brush yourself down, we are off to call on his lordship!'

'The Lord Justice?'

'Think straight, man! We are off to find Connor Maguire, the dashing Lord Enniskillen. Tonight he is merely our chief conspirator. Tomorrow he will be the first Irishman to rule from Dublin Castle.'

*

'So tell me, Sir Phelim?' Lord Caulfield brought insatiable curiosity to his dining table at Charlemont, Co Armagh. 'Evidently, you were cast from the same heroic mould as your famous relation. That theatrical rig of yours tells me that. So please, explain the paradox to me if you will, of how a Catholic can be both a warrior and disposed to turn the other cheek?'

Sir Phelim and Lady O'Neill were his principal guests. Their arrival, to much applause, had forcibly reminded everyone of the Celtic chieftains of old. The chief and his outriders were dressed *cap-à-pié* like Elizabethan *bonnacht*[iii], caped and armed with broadswords, a costume outlawed since the Desmond rebellions, half a century ago. The dowager

28

Lady Caulfield and her son - who had recently succeeded to his father's title - welcomed them hospitably, despite their fancy dress.

O'Neill's soldiers were sent to the garrison's mess where they were sat in front of generous trenchers while, upstairs, Sir Phelim O'Neill looked up from a pewter dish of broken botargo a footman had just put before him. Lord Caulfield, who had made the flattering comparison with The Great O'Neill (and the more improbable one with Jesus Christ), was the Governor of the sizable fortress. It had been designed to protect the Ulster Plantation.

'If we Catholics were not able to turn the other cheek your conscripts would not be still in Ulster,' Sir Phelim replied lightly. 'I saw the exercise yard. Presumably you command your men to march to-and-fro five times a day?'

Caulfield, and most of the other guests, including the captain of his Household Guard, laughed easily. In his own seat, surrounded by his soldiers - waiting at table or standing by the doors – Lord Caulfield could afford to relax. It was hard for any of them to see a man with such elegant manners as a dangerous revolutionary. Besides, Sir Phelim had sided with the English in the Nine Years War. That was why he had been permitted to hang on to Kinnard Castle and keep some token privileges. And again, on a personal level, Caulfield found Sir Phelim's company congenial, even if he suspected that this Catholic landowner was not housetrained. Here, in this garrisoned castle at least, his guest could do no harm.

Caulfield and his mother were certainly dining in style and the dowager was a generous hostess. Her son the Governor had begun to suspect his mother of having conceived a fondness for the Irish fellow.

'I? March my men about? You impute my character with some sort of martial quality, Sir Phelim. I am merely a Protestant politician, not a great warrior like yourself. Personally, I would never try to win an argument with a sword. Words and reason are my weapons.'

'I have heard some of your speeches, my lord.' Sir Phelim smiled graciously. 'One stands out. You denounced Catholics as dupes of the antichrist. I must disclose you aroused some displeasure in my people.'

'Those were words! The building blocks of politics, dear Sir Phelim! Only when politics fail do swords leap from scabbards. You of all people know I don't mean a word I say. The wise know that merely being a gentleman is enough to transcend that religious hocus-pocus that so diverts our peasantry.'

Lord Caulfield was one of Monaghan's members of Parliament. He certainly knew his politics. Rather more engagingly, Lady Caulfield knew her food, the Irishman thought as his platter was exchanged for another, this time charged with fillets of pike. Sir Phelim didn't really care for pike. He pushed it around the plate a little.

'I have decided to reserve my appetite for the sirloin of beef that is bound to arrive,' he confided to the lady on his left.

'It's remarkable how quiet this great castle is,' Lady O'Neill observed. 'I should have thought I might hear all sorts of military merriment from the men's quarters.'

'They are unusually quiet, Lady O'Neill,' Lady Caulfield agreed. She looked across the room to the little orchestra. 'Fergus, be a good man and strike up a *planxty*.'

The band had been waiting for the off. Its leader, from his harp, struck up a jig. Somehow such Irish music in this most Protestant of households sounded odd, even provocative.

*

Few Dubliners would have guessed from his reputation, or even from his appearance, that the second Baron Enniskillen or, more plainly, Connor Maguire, was only twenty-two years old. His father, Sir Brian Roe Maguire, had been ennobled Lord Enniskillen in gratitude for his loyalty to the English crown, but his mother was Owen Roe O'Neill's sister.

Connor Maguire's particular cragginess, combined with wild hair and a red beard, vividly implied a life where tapestried walls and plastered ceilings could be painlessly swapped for rain and open skies.

An active man of military bearing, he was also an attentive listener, always the outward sign of innate intelligence. He had been educated at Magdalen College, Oxford. He spent three years there, studying reasonably conscientiously but, as a Catholic, he could neither matriculate nor graduate. It hadn't worried him. The combination of academic supervision – for which he was forced to pay around twice the going rate - and the astonishing libraries were enough. He was never going to be a lawyer or a doctor and a formal degree mattered little.

When he returned to Ireland he married Mary Fleming, the Anglo-Irish heiress of Castle Fleming in Queen's County. He was bound to do so; she had already borne him a son.

As for the time-honoured question of an occupation, once he had succeeded to his peerage he would nobly condescend to attend the Dublin House of Lords from time to time.

O'Connolly took in Maguire's aristocratic Castle Street town house. Somehow, some Catholic lords had kept their possessions through thick and thin.

Maguire, meanwhile, was studying MacMahon's cousin.

'So you're O'Connolly. The colonel here has sung your praises so often that I feel I know you already. I hereby claim the privilege of shaking your hand.'

'That privilege is entirely mine, my lord,' O'Connolly replied, mightily pleased, offering his hand.

MacMahon laughed. He sat down easily, pushing his sword to one side.

'O'Connolly, I hope you will excuse my caution but you will forgive me for asking you to make a formal oath of secrecy? The same oath we all have made?'

'Of course, my lord. I expected no less.'

'Then, good. If you would read out loud the words on this little card?'

O'Connolly took the proffered piece of paper into his hand and looked at it carefully. Reading skills were not his chief talent but he was determined to overcome his difficulties.

> In the Holy Name of God the Creator, and under the watchful eyes of Christ the Judge who sees into our hearts; the Virgin Mary who loves mankind for what it is; and the Holy Ghost who inspires our greatest enterprises; I do solemnly swear that I shall never disclose any secret or confidence that I may learn of the Rebellion or of the Confederacy to any person, friendly or not, whom I have not personally witnessed make this same oath. I do of my free will, without coercion. I pray to Saints Michael and Patrick, my witnesses, alongside the Confederates I am now amongst, that the fires below be fuelled by my body at the smallest hint of my transgression.

O'Connolly looked up. The rebels were staring at him. Then he made the Sign of the Cross.

'I so swear,' he said almost noiselessly.

'Amen. The saints be praised! Thank you, O'Connolly, from the bottom of my heart. Secrecy is by its nature fragile; news of our imminent Rebellion must never break.'

Maguire looked at his candidate for high office with an analytical eye.

'MacMahon tells me that as boys you went to church together and learned your catechism side-by-side.' He smiled, and stood. 'You should know that MacMahon and I believe that a native Irishman and kinsman can only be in favour of the repatriation of Ireland to the Irish people. So, welcome to the Cause.'

'I shall make it my mission, now and forever, to serve Ireland as best I am able,' O'Connolly replied dutifully, his head bowed.

*

Dinner at Charlemont was long over. Sir Phelim and Lady O'Neill listened appreciatively to yet another ballad. Caulfield's concert of Irish music was a delight.

A knock at the door made Lord Caulfield frown and turn to his right. 'I'm so sorry, Lady O'Neill. I gave orders that nothing was to disturb us. I'm afraid it must be urgent.'

The band halted their song and the footmen opened the double doors that led from the castle's hall.

What was revealed caused Lady Caulfield to gasp. Even Lord Caulfield's jaw, famously rigid, dropped the smallest fraction.

An Irish warrior, clad in the long-banned battle dress that had once so characterised his nation, held an immense and bloodied two-handed sword.

'As you predicted, general,' the Celtic warrior coolly informed Sir Phelim from behind. 'Merely token resistance. Only the Constable...'

Lord Caulfield rose to his feet, glaring at Sir Phelim. 'Is this how my hospitality is repaid?'

'*Mea culpa*, Lord Caulfield,' answered a calm Sir Phelim, still seated, his back to the door. 'I know that you are a keen student of history. You will therefore remember how O'Docherty's rebellion began. I have simply drawn from his example.'

'I remember how it ended,' said Lord Caulfield. If he meant to say more, his speech was temporarily interrupted by forty armed Irish warriors who filed into the room and started to bind the hands of the footmen.

'O'Docherty's head on a spear, decorating one of Dublin Castle's gates,' Caulfield finished.

'Times have changed, my lord. By now Dublin Castle will be in Irish hands. Lady Caulfield, you are of course free to do as you please. Our quarrel is not with you; my men need not detain you. But you, sir, are my prisoner. Do not despair; you have made history. You are the first prisoner of war of what I believe will be called the Confederate Government of Ireland. Lord Caulfield, before surprising you here at Charlemont I had but a barrel or two of gunpowder and a few swords. Your armoury will henceforward serve my regiment. Your people will find me a force to be reckoned with, I think. Lady Caulfield, may I thank you for a most pleasant dinner. Should we meet again it will be my privilege.'

Lady Caulfield was less affable in her reply.

'Were I a young man and not a frail old lady I would run you through, ruffian!'

Sir Phelim only smiled. He turned to his subaltern. 'Arm half of our men with whatever you find and lead them to Fort Mountjoy.' Turning back to his wife, he continued. 'My darling, I apologise for not having told you in advance what I had planned. At the time I felt it might have unduly alarmed you, even put you at risk. At last I can speak freely. Our nation has risen. Ulster will be returned to its former owners.' He glanced at Lord Caulfield's fine longcase clock. 'It is late. We may have overstayed our welcome. Sweetheart, do you remember telling me that when you were a girl you once dined at Dungannon Castle as a guest of the Great O'Neill and his Miss Magennis? Would you care to visit that great house again? Or perhaps you would prefer to return to the safety of Kinnard?'

'Dungannon is nearer, I think, husband mine. Just five miles away, while our house is nearer eight.'

'Then Dungannon it is. Come, we have much to do.'

*

In Little Abbey Street, Dublin, Maguire had risen to his feet.

'Listen, O'Connolly, and listen well. Lord Strafford stored arms for 30,000 men in the Castle while preparing to fight the Scots. That's enough to liberate Ireland. You have been a slave of that Puritan Clotworthy, or Massereene as he is now, for far too long. Soon you shall have an equally good man as yourself to wait upon you.'

'How can I serve, my lord colonel?'

'For the moment, just be with us. Our primary duty is to encourage the others. Come, let's meet some of them, at the Lion in Wine Tavern Street.'

They joined a group of young men who acknowledged the newcomers with brisk military bows, telling the waiter who had just arrived with a great jug of shrub[iv] to leave the room. Once the door was locked, they began a series of toasts to a reborn Ireland, the resurrection of an historic nation's oldest customs and the success of the next day's work.

O'Connolly had spread a heavy napkin over his lap. Now he appeared to swallow glass after glass. He even proposed a few healths of his own, keen as he was to maintain his cover as a ruffling squire, the sort who liked to attach themselves to the coattails of gentlemen of fortune, expressly to pocket the generous fees that such labours always earn.

MacMahon and Maguire seemed neither hungry nor thirsty. They commanded O'Connolly to join them for a light supper in Kerfoot's Dining Rooms, next to the New Theatre. There, they told him, Colonels Plunkett, Byrne and O'More would join their table. O'Connolly blew his nose and put the soaking cloth into his pocket.

Ostler Kerfoot distinguished himself that night with a crown rack of hogget.

While the waiters were putting plates in front of the diners, no one talked business. It was not until everyone had eaten their fill that the doors to the private room were closed and the conversation turned to the events of a momentous day for Irish history.

'Are we all set for ten o'clock tomorrow morning?' asked O'More.

'My men will be at the Ship Street Gate, mingling with the crowd, ready for your signal. Some of them will be armed. When they hear Connor Maguire fire the Castle cannon they will dispatch the guard and move inside.' Colonel Plunkett was an Anglo-Irishman, one of the Catholic Lords of the Pale that O'More had been so keen to bring on board. His palace at Trim doubled as a fort and had protected the Pale long before being English had become synonymous with being Protestant.

'Mine will be at the Cork Gate. Once inside the Castle they will capture the ordnance.' Colonel Byrne had also seen service under Colonel Owen Roe O'Neill.

'I'll have disarmed the Castle before you get there,' said a confident MacMahon. 'My grand entrance will be through the small gateway in the wall by the tower where the city wall joins the Castle.'

'You will be awful wet, Hugh Òg, when you get there. You and your men will have just swum the moat. It is October and you will be cold...'

'...and you will have caused the distraction that will allow us do just that. Not that we will easily be seen from anywhere at all. That is the gateway through which the Great Tyrone rescued Lord Tyrconnell from the Stanyhurst Tower, all those years ago. That will serve as a noble precedent.'

O'Connolly, apparently befuddled by all those bumpers, thought it wise to keep quiet. It was all a little unreal, or too real, which amounts to the same thing. In his self-imposed silence he was beginning to realise that his fellow conspirators might actually capture Dublin Castle. He put his empty whiskey glass on the table, but so clumsily it fell over.

Now he had the knowledge he needed, he had to report what he knew.

'Gentlemen, I must leave you for an instant,' he said.

'Ach, use the pisspot in the corner.' Byrne felt that, in male company at least, people could be too prissy.

'I need to go outside. A lot to drink. Don't worry about me. I'll leave my sword here. I won't be a minute, only 'till until my head quits a-turning.' He walked unsteadily to the door, opened it carefully and closed it over-firmly behind him.

Then he ran.

*

Lady O'Neill rode her favourite mare, side-saddle, alongside her husband's stallion, on the road from Charlemont to Dungannon. If she was commonly thought of as being delicate, even frail, throughout that squally night she seemed to possess the strength of Queen Maeve of Celtic legend. It was in the small hours of the early morning when she and her husband rode through the battered walls of Lord Tyrone's former seat. Their men had not yet slept, but none showed the faintest sign of exhaustion. In the late and Great O'Neill's one-time fortress, and while O'Neill painlessly disarmed Dungannon's soldiers and collected their arms, it was Lady O'Neill who accepted the mayor's unconditional surrender.

'Ni dhiolann dearmad fiacha', she told him. Even a forgotten debt needs repaying. 'This settles an old score. We are even.'

Not completely, however. The grand and beautiful castle she remembered from forty years before was charred and ruined. Only the garrison blocks were habitable and they sat, ingloriously, among the sad remains of the Great O'Neill's stately tower-house. It was now a Spartan barracks, and its English conquerors had renamed it 'Fort Dungannon'.

Ordinary Catholics had long been banned from their town. Sir Phelim offered Dungannon's new Protestant citizens - men, women and children - a stark choice.

'You must leave Ulster now. Seek safety in the Pale. No one will stop you. If you stay behind you will probably die.'

A cold night, a colder season. Drogheda, the nearest sizeable Protestant townland, was fully sixty miles away. Some citizens would never make it. Even so, it was apparent that the Irish were in no mood to take prisoners. A long file of Protestants, having packed a few possessions, headed south towards the protection of their coreligionists in the Pale.

A mordant wind had risen, determined to turn the pages of history.

Charlemont had only been the beginning of this adventure. Sir Phelim's Irish regiment took fort after fort. After every raid its numbers increased.

By dawn the O'Quinns had taken Mountjoy and the O'Donnellys had seized Castlecaulfield. By noon, O'Neill's stores included seventy barrels of black powder from Newry. Magennis's men had also carried away wagon-loads of pikes and muskets.

Now all Ulster knew that Fort Mountjoy had fallen, its soldiers disarmed and sent 'packing'; carrying the wherewithal of survival. Some of the men they found there, probably not the most committed Protestants in Ireland, defected and swelled the Irish ranks. A growing Irish army went on to take several more Protestant strongholds. Mostly there was little resistance; the English were largely unprepared for defence. As MacMahon had already boasted to the Justices, 'the Rebellion was now beyond the Power of Man to prevent'.

On the first day, Sir Phelim O'Neill and his closest lieutenants had taken a dozen Protestant forts by stratagem and surprise. Further victories would need force, but every time a fort fell the Irish were better armed. The omens for the liberation of Ireland were good.

*

In the smokey world of intrigue that was North Dublin, no one yet knew that Owen O'Connolly was a traitor to Ireland's fragile dreams of independence. That was about to change.

O'Connolly's motive was zealotry. He knew as a fact that he would be proved right. He was one of God's 'elect'. Not only would his fundamentalist faith return the strength to his limbs that heroic amounts of beer, shrub and whiskey had taken away, but the Lords Justice would reward him handsomely for his intelligence.

He ran like a steeplechaser! Clearing fences and palings, he made his way across the city, only pausing at the Brazen Head in Bridge Street, to imbibe a little more liquid courage. He would need it before ringing the bell to the door of Lord Justice Parsons' house on Merchant's Quay.

Finally, an unsteady O'Connolly pulled at the Lord Justice's bell.

Parsons, however, was not at first inclined to believe a word of the confused and strange tale he was hearing. For one thing, the informer

36

was tight. The Irishman admitted to refreshment on the way but Parsons could see he was intoxicated. This was not encouraging behaviour from a supposedly good Calvinist. Yet while O'Connolly persisted with his rambling narrative, Parsons slowly became convinced of its truth. Not from O'Connolly's self-serving account so much as from his own unswerving trust in Lord Massereene, O'Connolly's employer.

'Thank you, O'Connolly. You will be well rewarded – money and a pension - but before that happens, you must go back and get more information from MacMahon.' He wrote a list for O'Connolly. 'I take it you can read and write? We'll need names, arms, numbers, locations.'

O'Connolly stumbled into the fresh air, bent on fulfilling his treacherous mission. Lord Justice Parsons decided to consult his colleague, fellow fundamentalist and friend.

Lord Justice Borlase lived at Chichester House on College Green, and it took Parsons but a minute or two to walk there.

When Borlase heard Parsons tell O'Connolly's story he sent for as many of the Council as could be found, commanding them to wait on him in the Castle. It was now very late; most good Protestants rose at dawn and took to their beds at sunset. God had not invented night for pleasure. Only two of the Privy Councillors were not yet asleep.

The first to heed the summons was Dublin's Lord Mayor who, as soon as he heard the report, directed the Castle's Constabulary to stop and question every stranger. If their excuses were not immediately plausible they were to be imprisoned without further ado pending interrogation. Of course, O'Connolly had to fall into the hands of the night watch. Luckily for him, Borlase's own men, performing an identical task to the Constable's, rescued him from summary imprisonment. O'Connolly, shaken, dutifully returned to his errand.

Borlase, to Parson's great annoyance, actually fell asleep while the latter read O'Connolly's statement. 'Not altogether surprising', Parsons commented tartly, 'given his age'.

Lord Justice Parsons gave orders to strengthen the Castle's defences further, to double the guard. Officers were dispatched to arrest MacMahon at his lodgings.

The colonel was at home, utterly unaware that the plot had been discovered, when the Guards burst in and beat him insensible. That preliminary achieved, their search revealed arms in every room. This alone was quite enough to hang him.

Now, in the small hours of the morning of October 24, he was brought to be examined before the Council.

Realising he was finished, MacMahon's back stiffened. Though he could no longer stand, he was his old self again. He proudly acknowledged his part in the plot and declared the Rebellion irreversible.

'You are too late,' he said. 'Every garrison in Ireland has already been surprised. Even while I am in your hands, this unpleasantness is wasted on me. Deal with me as you must. I care not. My death will be avenged.'

Parsons shrugged. He beckoned the soldiers from the door.

'Take the bogtrotter away. Chain his arms and legs and cast him into the most dismal cell in the very Castle that the idiot presumed to command. Let hubris be his torturer.'

Further members of the Council arrived, one by one, and debated, deliberated throughout the night. By daybreak the Privy Councillors had swelled in number to eight.

Eventually the Lords Justice, the Lord Mayor and sundry Privy Councillors issued a joint proclamation.

> A most disloyal and detestable conspiracy, intended by some evil-minded Papists to impose idolatry upon the righteous subjects of the king, has been uncovered.

Copies of the document were quickly circulated through the country, posted onto trees, tavern doors and a few surviving village crosses. Borlase also ordered the proclamation to be handed to the town crier and sung out to the people of Dublin.

Soldiers were sent to arrest the rebel leaders. Lord Maguire was discovered hiding in his cockloft in Cook Street. He was thrown in to share Colonel MacMahon's depressing little oubliette.

Maguire's first reaction was to deny everything. Unfortunately MacMahon's proud confession had fatally wrong-footed him.

In the way of compensation, Colonels Plunkett and Byrne had managed to get clear of the capital.

So too had Rory O'More. He escaped by rowing up-river to Islandbridge, from where he made his way to his daughter's house at Lucan. She had married a Sarsfield, and she and her husband welcomed a terrified but proud revolutionary.

*

The newly appointed Lieutenant-General of the Royal Irish Army, whose letters patent had him styled as the Marquess of Ormonde, had reached Dublin Castle, riding hard from his house at Carrick-on-Suir. When he heard from the Lord Mayor the first accounts of what Sir Phelim had been up to in Ulster he determined on an immediate campaign. He demanded access to the Lords Justice and presented them with his royal commission, signed and sealed by the Lord Deputy, absent as always in his palace in Leicester Square.

'It has to be this very moment,' said Lord Ormonde, after the briefest of pleasantries. 'I am determined to deprive the Irish of the time they need to get their pike poles made and their blades sharpened. Today they are only lightly armed. That will not be the case tomorrow. Speed, Sir John, Sir William, is as always of the essence.'

'We shall order all foreigners˅ to leave the city. If any remain we shall hang them. We are not slowcoaches here in the Castle, my lord,' Sir William Parsons declared with some impatience. 'I may venture further. MacMahon's declaration has rung in our ears as would an alarm clock. Be confident; we are awake.'

'Yes, Lord Ormonde, we are. We have already declared Dublin to be in a state of siege...'

'...we have established courts martial...'

'...we have arranged for all the redundant arms stored here by the late Lord Strafford to be distributed to the Godfearing citizenry...'

'You have the matter well in hand, I see clearly, Sir John, Sir William. Have you entrusted the Castle to a new Constable?'

'We have,' said Sir William Parsons. An old friend of his, Sir Francis Willoughby, currently Governor of Galway, had been sent for the moment O'Connolly had revealed the conspiracy. 'Sir Francis will soon be here.'

'No doubt you have appointed a Military Governor to take charge of the defence of the city?'

'We have, Sir! Sir John has asked Sir Charles Coote, currently Provost-Marshall of Connacht, to fill that role.'

'Coote? When the Irish hear whom you have chosen they will run for cover like rabbits. Coote even scares me.'

Ormonde may have had little time for Coote but his reaction to the news was disingenuous. In his private opinion, the Lords Justice were making a colossal mistake. Coote's appointment would drive the insurgents near mad with anger. The more so when they learned that

Coote and the likeminded President of Munster, Sir William St Leger[2], would be licensed to hang 'insurgents' at will.

'Coote is a pious and scriptural Christian, Lord Ormonde. An Anabaptist, I fancy. Did you intend to say otherwise?' asked Sir William.

'Sir Charles Coote may be cruel but he is a bright and skilled soldier,' confirmed Sir John. 'He has mellowed since his, ah, resolute youth. He is now in his sixties, after all. On his horse he is uninhibited by the wooden leg he won at the Battle of Kinsale.'

'The loss of that leg still irritates him. A barbarian chief had the better of him. That was shortly after he had been dispatched to suppress a Rising in Wicklow. The O'Byrnes and the O'Tooles had raised their clans and were happily evicting the settlers. Obviously, their punishment would have to be extreme, and Coote obliged.'

'The Irish still loathe him,' said Ormonde. 'They remember just how extreme that punishment was. The young Captain Coote had his soldiers begin by dispatching the male rebels. He then ordered his men to spear their children in front of their mothers, even those that had not yet left the breast. On his orders, the infants were carried, writhing, on the pikes of his amused soldiers. Only then did they hang their mothers. None was spared. The worthy commander confessed that he liked to let his men 'enjoy such frolics'. When asked about this decision, he explained to Lord Mountjoy, then Lord Deputy, that 'nits grow into lice'.'

Coote, the only son of a smallholder, had first come over to Ireland during the Nine Years War, set on making his name and fortune. To pay for his Commission he sold his land, burning his bridges, so to speak.

After the Flight of the Earls, in 1607 - the dismal postscript to the Nine Years War with England - King James I deployed Coote in Connacht as his Provost-Marshall and Vice-Governor. Coote celebrated his elevation and generous stipend with the purchase of a baronetcy. Out in the west, the acres he contrived to possess and the privileges he was rapidly accumulating made very wealthy. Large grants of land, principally in Connacht, now netted him £4,000 a year, a colossal sum. Coote, colonel and baronet, had estates to suit a prince.

Not the kindest of princes, however. Native 'tories', or brigands, had caused damage to his iron smelting works and had vandalised his great estate. In his own inimitable style, he 'chastised' the culprits, their associates, their kin and casual acquaintances. In short, everyone.

Stories of his astonishing severity reached Carrick-on-Suir. Lord Ormonde had heard many times, after the ladies had withdrawn, of how

---

[2] Pr 'Sellinger'

Coote did not concern himself with the nice distinction between innocence and guilt. Something about acts of cruelty thrilled him, perhaps because his violence transcended every law of every land. It suited the Lords Justice to the ground. From the Castle's perspective, after all, the only victims of his departure from the rules of civilisation were Irish.

'He cuts a striking figure.' Sir William was clearly well-disposed to the man.

Lord Ormonde frowned. 'A little compassion would make him more illustrious.'

'You need to see him in a more generous light, Lord Ormonde,' Sir John persisted.

'His use of the lash is perhaps a trifle overenthusiastic,' sighed Sir William, 'but if it causes his men to hate him, they also fear and obey him.'

'I have to say, speaking in my personal capacity, his lash doesn't bother me overmuch,' said Sir John. 'He is hardly likely to use it on me.'

Everyone laughed.

'I will concede, Lord Ormonde,' Sir William continued, his tone emollient, 'that we find his blasphemy and barrack room language somewhat difficult to stomach. We wish he would not take our Lord's name quite so lightly.'

Lord Ormonde was finding this strand of conversation pointless. 'Well, I expect you want me to take a brigade to Ulster and put an end to O'Neill's shenanigans?'

Sir William was examining Ormonde's letters patent.

'One moment, Lord Ormonde. There seems to be a problem with your Commission. While its purpose is wholly clear, it's not exactly in your name, is it.' Sir William Parsons looked up over his pince-nez. 'It refers to you as the most honourable Marquess of Ormonde. You are I think the right honourable Earl of Ormonde. Can that be quite right? I have read nothing of your elevation in *The Gazette*?'

He passed the parchment to Sir John, who looked at it carefully.

'The commission is not in your name, Lord Ormonde,' he said, as he passed it to the noble earl. 'We cannot in all honesty let you run an army on a mistaken premise. What are we to do?'

'I have an idea,' said Sir John. 'Why don't we write to the king? If we request that the earl before us be raised a marquess then his commission will then be in order, if retrospectively. It will only take a few days if we get on to it straight away. At most a month or two. Sir Phelim can't do that much harm in so little time.'

'You're quite right, Sir John. I'm confident the king will approve your marquisate, Lord Ormonde, and we both offer our sincere congratulations on what will surely, and soon, be confirmed. You deserve it. You are after all the richest man in Ireland.'

'I believe that privilege belongs to the Earl of Cork.'

'Well then, the noblest.'

'And that honour will belong to a native Irishman. The O'Connor Don, perhaps?'

'Here in the Castle we do not recognise any native claims to nobility, Lord Ormonde.'

'I think you may have to adapt that attitude. The Irish may insist.'

'Let us not bicker. In the meantime, Lady Ormonde will enjoy the capital. All the latest London frippery is to be found in Grafton Street. Lord Ormonde, take some time to enjoy Dublin. Being an Anglican, Lord Ormonde, you will discover the taverns and inns are doing a roaring trade. The mood in the capital is quite exuberant. Sir John and I would join you but our Reformed Religion forbids it. We have taken a vow.'

'A promise,' added Sir John. 'Never to sully the pure delight in loving God with the base satisfaction of physical pleasure.'

'The same with eating,' continued Sir William. 'We eat only to live. We eat as fast as we are able and never thank anyone for catering to such base needs.'

'Nor would we even think of writing a letter to thank a hostess,' Sir John continued.

'The carnal delights are not exempted.' Sir William was leaning back, a half smile lighting his usually stern face. 'We are resolved never to make love to our wives but instead to procreate as simply and as briefly as possible. That way we may avoid delight and focus only on the firm purpose of creating children in God's image.'

'While some people,' Sir John assured Lord Ormonde, 'exploit sexual congress as a recreation!'

'This, and in Ireland too!' sighed Sir William.

James Butler, Earl of Ormonde, whose formal elevation to marquess was in fact gazetted that very morning, may have had notional control of the army in Ireland, such as it was, but the Lords Justice trusted almost everyone else rather more.

While Ormonde was widely acknowledged to have the potential to be an illustrious statesman, he was still young. He had just turned thirty-one and, so far, the only remarkable thing in his political career so far was that unlikely friendship with Lord Strafford. It had been useful; a general fear of upsetting the Lord Deputy had made it easier for him to restore and re-unite the estates of his own family, the Butlers, putting them all under his personal protection. It had been no easy task, since these demesnes were all over the south of Ireland and many of them had already been awarded to King James' early colonists. As for Strafford, that ill-fated English earl, he had seen in Ormonde many qualities; intelligence, drive and diplomacy, skills which combined with affection for the king. For Strafford, Ormonde had been a friend and ally in a hostile world.

It was dawning on some inhabitants of that world that Ormonde's extraordinary ability to be accepted by all sides would be indispensable, even to the Lords Justices. In the general mayhem that followed the Rebellion, he made the Castle very uneasy. Only those with the ability to stand apart from the dogmas of the day saw clearly that Ormonde, a royalist and an Anglican, would not be able indefinitely to subordinate himself to such men as Parsons, Borlase and Coote.

There were many reasons why the Lords Justice would search for the means to remove an unctuous Ormonde from the ointment. First, he was a liberal, sympathetic to the Irish. His face could not fit into any Puritan frame. He had served the House of Stuart as a courtier which strongly suggested that he was far too close to the king.

In the circumstances, Borlase and Parsons resolved that Ormonde would be best employed well away from the comfort and safety of the Pale. Above all, he should not be allowed any chance of a military triumph. Their War Cabinet would remain under the consular direction of the Lords Justice, to which Coote and Willoughby were already suborned. Borlase and Parsons would reluctantly draft the king's man Ormonde into it, but before they did they would deploy some artful prevarication to keep him ineffectual.

Of course, once the 'error' in his title was corrected, the Lords Justice could no longer exclude him.

Colonel Sir Charles Coote, bart., arrived at the Castle in full armour on a huge battlehorse. The Lords Justice jointly awarded the breathless Provost of Connacht the command of the Dublin Garrison. In reply the baronet trooped the garrison's colours in the Castle yard, to much applause.

Everyone was left a little uncomfortable, however. The new Commander seemed to live in a furious temper. He was observed to be quite beside himself with rage, at all times, seven days a week.

He would stay that way for many months. Until May the following year, in fact.

*

In Ulster, Sir Phelim's campaign was going well. If he knew his victory was far from inevitable, he was the only one. His men, all of them, thought he held the winning ticket. His attention was currently directed to the garrison at Enniskillen. By cover of night his army had quietly surrounded it, even if an heroic Protestant horseman had galloped through the darkness of the night to warn its governor Sir William Cole and gain him some valuable time.

When the Irish general attacked, at first light on the 23rd, its gates were already shut. Its terrified settlers had safely retreated behind its thick stone walls. Many of them were on their knees, in its brand new chapels.

Carrickfergus and Coleraine also found time to concentrate their cattle and townsmen within their curtilages.

No matter, a fatter target was in Sir Phelim's sights. Early in November, the Protestant Mayor of Londonderry had, in the name of security, summarily evicted every Catholic family that lived within his jurisdiction. In the other direction, Nonconformist refugees, fleeing Sir Phelim, immediately filled the vacated places - servants' quarters, attics, shacks and cabins – of the evicted Derry Catholics. The city's population doubled overnight and the incomers felt safe. Sentries were posted everywhere and the town's circumvallation was thick and tall. The town boasted a large number of useful fighting men. Surely Sir Phelim would not chance his luck here?

*

The king directed the Lords Justice to furnish the Earl of Leicester, their absentee Lord Deputy, with copies of each and every one of their orders in council. The Castle had accordingly done so, but on this occasion they attached an account of the Rebellion. Instead of depending on the government courier, they appointed Lord Massereene's manservant Owen O'Connolly 'special envoy' and entrusted him to carry the mail.

O'Connolly arrived in London late on Sunday October 31. Shortly after daybreak, having banked a few hours' sleep, he went to see Lord Leicester. His lordship would be at home, he supposed. The Upper House, of which Lord Leicester was an active member, would not sit on Monday Nov 1, as it was All Saints' Day which the Lords still kept holy. The Parliamentarians in the Lower House would hardly revere the legions of Catholic saints and martyrs, but then O'Connolly's business was not with them.

'So you're a cousin of the traitor MacMahon,' Lord Leicester remarked. 'How very droll! Such a different pedigree to that of my usual guests. Massereene must have used all his considerable influence and more to have the Castle employ you as a 'special envoy'. Do you speak the local language?'

'The Gaelic? I can, Your Lordship, Sir, if for the most part I choose not to.'

'Good man. Listen carefully, O'Connolly. For my sins, I am required to receive a number of Irishmen here in Leicester Square. Can't understand a word most of them say and, when I can, I don't care to. I imagine you won't be returning to Ireland in any hurry. I can offer you a post, if you'll have it. You will receive my visitors from that westerly Kingdom, distil their over-elaborate utterances into a few short sentences and tell me what they actually mean, or want. That way there will be no need for me to meet them in person. Rest assured, for this useful service you will be handsomely rewarded.'

*

CHAPTER THREE
A GOOD FIRST WEEK

The Irish Rebellion had got off, at least in Ulster, to a good start. Its lengthening list of successes reassured the insurgents that God was on their side. A litany of minor successes also attracted many previously unconvinced into the threadbare Irish army. That army, however, was about to suffer a terrible setback.

Ormonde's elevation was now official. In the first week of November, 1641, Parsons and Borlase could no longer prevaricate and handed the marquess his baton. The Lords Justice now began to round up every fit working man in the Pale for a Protestant army.

While his valet brushed the Lieutenant-General's hair, Ormonde gloomily considered the calibre of the men the Lords Justice were delivering to his command. He reflected that in Munster he had only a single troop of horse, the same in Connacht. Both had been raised as a household guard by their respective Provincial Presidents, St Leger and Willoughby. In Kilkenny, Dublin and some of the midland counties, he wondered if both the Catholic gentry might raise volunteers for their own defence. Surely they would respond to his call?

Yet even if they did, manpower would remain a challenge. In Dublin, the Castle militia had rounded up 1,500 of Strafford's old infantry. Despite being unpaid and resentful, Ormonde inspired a little enthusiasm in them with promises of compensation. Ormonde's word, or fortune, was sufficient to let him add six new regiments of foot and thirteen volunteer companies to its overall strength, each a hundred strong. In the Castle there were arms and ammunition, but nothing like enough for the 30,000 the Lords Justice had set as a target. He had eight thousand pikes, a thousand muskets and a fine train of field artillery, courtesy of the decapitated Lord Lieutenant, originally intended for use in the Scottish 'Bishops War'. Nevertheless, in the northern counties alone, where the Rebellion was at its most acute, the Irish had 30,000 men in the field.

Ormonde shrugged this off. The figure was misleading. Two thirds of them had neither arms nor ammunition. Barely one in ten had shoes, and only one in fifty had any military training. It was a poor beginning to Ireland's loyal army.

Another problem was that they were not conveniently housed in the Castle's barracks. Far from it; they were dispersed throughout the entire Kingdom of Ireland.

Hard and ugly facts conspired to undermine the Lieutenant-General's more optimistic presentiments. Before surprising Forts Charlemont and Mountjoy, Sir Phelim O'Neill could only have had a barrel or two of gunpowder. The stores in those forts, added to the seventy barrels taken at Newry by Magennis, and those added to the swords and muskets they had acquired on the way, was beginning to amount to a significant arsenal.

'Significant, yes, but not yet a real threat to the Castle,' said Lord Ormonde. 'Time is the real issue.'

Ormonde again requested the War Cabinet for leave to launch an immediate campaign in the North.

'I am making the reasonable presumption that Sir Phelim lacks even the most basic weapons.'

'Our thanks, Noble Lord, but we the Lords Justice of Ireland must say no.'

On the Irish side, there was another problem, one that Ormonde had not factored into his military strategy. In his civilian past, Sir Phelim had been a lawyer. Neither he nor Rory O'More had ever seen military service. While this would be remedied when Colonel Owen Roe O'Neill and the other overseas officers finally appeared, a conspiracy of circumstances – mostly bad weather – was preventing the exiles from coming home.

Sir Phelim had no chance to fill the break himself. He grandly assumed the title of 'Lord General of the Catholic Army in Ulster'. He also adopted the even more historic title, to the Gaelic-speaking population at least, of 'The O'Neill', chief of his name.

*

The king had yet to learn of the Rebellion. The Lords Justice sent a messenger to Carrickfergus, who crossed the Irish Sea to Dunbarton. He made his way to Musselburgh, a golf course near Edinburgh, to find the King of the Scots at the fifteenth hole. His Majesty read Sir William and Sir John's letter in silence and then returned, without comment, to his game. There were three more holes beyond this one, after all.

The communication had not bothered the King. In his northern Kingdom to appease the Scottish Covenanters, he may have seen something in the contents of the dispatch that suggested the crisis in Ireland might actually help him.

In fact, the Lords Justice's letter begged him to send a Protestant force to Ulster. They knew that resourcing such an army in London would be impossible, but given that he was in Scotland, His Majesty might find a way to send a token army, say 1,500 Lowlanders, to reinforce Carrickfergus. It had been under siege for a week. Parsons and Borlase quite plausibly pointed out that the Ulster settlers and the lowland Scots shared a religion and, being of the same race, were devoted to the House of Stewart.

The Lords Justice had successfully gambled on a favourable response. They had already authorised Lords Chichester, Ardes and Clandeboy - Ulster Protestants all - to raise new regiments from their own purged tenantry.

Within two days the king's Scottish army put into Lough Belfast. It was welcomed and garlanded by Chichester and his fellow peers. Ulster's Protestant force now amounted to five thousand foot and five hundred horse, a glorious sight under its proud Saltire, supported by the flags of Sts George, Michael and Andrew. The soldiers were more than keen to crack a few Papist skulls. They set off on a jaunty march towards the fort they meant to relieve.

A scout reported their progress to Sir Phelim. He was well prepared. He detached some men from his siege works to lure the combined relief force along the causeway away from Carrickfergus onto the supposedly sparsely inhabited Island Magee. Sir Phelim felt that the Protestants could do little harm in that remote and peaceful place. There they could march about like the toy soldiers they were, as much as they pleased.

'They may get bored on Island Magee,' he casually observed, 'but I have more important things to do than worry about entertaining humourless Puritans. If they find the place too dull, perhaps they'll find the time to play skittles?'

Skittles were all the rage.

'Shall we follow the heretics onto the island?' asked one of Sir Phelim's commanders.

'No,' came the firm reply. 'Keep up the pressure on Carrickfergus,'

Having crossed onto Island Magee, after being misdirected and outmanoeuvred, the tide turned the promontory back into an island. An infuriated Protestant army raged around in a risen red mist, their barbarity brutish and unconfined. They murdered the Catholic inhabitants they found there, all of whom were unarmed and none having anything at all to do with the Rebellion. They did not sheath their swords until they had cleared that innocent island of all its terrified human souls. Those who courageously stood their ground, and those whose feet were simply riveted to the ground, were cut down where they were. Those hapless souls who ran, terrified, hoping to hide, were driven over the cliffs into a furious, fathomless Atlantic.

True, Sir Phelim could not have known how many desperate Ultonian smallholders and their families had fled to that island from the mainland, across the sea-lough at low tide when it was dry. He had also basked in the mistaken presumption that his enemy was not pointlessly vindictive. On both counts he had miscalculated. The enemy zealots wanted to make sure their otherwise wasted time on Island Magee would provide the Catholics with an object lesson; that Protestants were to be feared. The Covenanters murdered the poor defenceless islanders with genocidal determination. In this cruel school they were the teachers.

Cruelty on one side spurs savagery in the other. This is the 'vicious circle' of renown. The massacre on Island Magee ushered in a new phase of the war.

Sir Phelim O'Neill was no longer in the mood for compromise. At the outset of the insurrection, Rory O'More had issued an edict that the Rebellion was to be conducted by the rules of the ancient *Cáin Adomnáin*[ii], declared at the Synod of Birr in 697 AD. Sir Phelim was no longer in the mood to obey such an order. The Protestants had chosen to abandon the Augustinian code, and it only stiffened his resolve.

*

Two Catholic 'tories' were looking forward to an adventure, the first of their lives. These two gentlemen were rich enough to own enough clothes to lend them modesty, but not quite enough for a pair of shoes.

'Patrick O'Farrell, have you ever seen with your own eyes inside a Saxon town?'

'And just what would I be doing in such a place, Malachy O'Dea? They are places of sin, where sacraments are not observed, and where unmarried men and women sit side by side in worship!'

'Then you'll never have seen a street of terraced houses? They have nothing to do with our cabins. They have windows and fireplaces, sometimes more than one! Some have attics for their servants, would you believe it?. Their owners drink fresh milk and eat meat every Sabbath!'

'And who pays for such indulgence, I'd like to know?'

'Who d'you think, Patrick? It is us, the Irish. Them it is what sells the food we farm for them, or the chairs we build. We work all day, 'cepting the Sabbath of course, and then go home to sleep in our cold, dark huts.'

'And just how would I have seen such palaces, Malachy O'Dea? We are banned from entering the cities of Ulster.'

'Very true. I told you all that so you'd know the holy fathers will absolve us for taking a little revenge.'

'By which I think you'll be meaning the torching of the settlers' houses?'

'Well put, Patrick. Any gentlemen would find it easy to forgive.'

*

At noon, on the third day of the Rebellion, a proclamation appeared as if by magic, on trees, walls and church doors. It allowed no doubt that the whole nation was in full scale revolt. Dated October 23 and signed 'P. O'Neill', it claimed to have been written within the fortress town of Dungannon itself.

It set out the rebels' 'true intent and meaning'. They had not, it declared, risen out of hostility to His Majesty.

> We do not intend any enmity to any of his subjects, neither English nor Scotch; but only for the defence and liberty of ourselves and the Irish natives of this his westerly kingdom.

Later that same day the quill of Rory O'More delivered another, longer and more passionate manifesto. The oppression that had caused the Irish to rise was broken down into key points. The king's long promised 'Graces' - pro-Catholic reforms - were acknowledged but the frustration caused by the malice of the Puritans was explained with equal clarity. O'More suggested that the Reformed Church posed as much danger to the Anglicans of the Episcopal Church as they did to the Catholic people. He asserted in the strongest terms the constant devotion of the Catholics to the Crown. The insurrection was never treason, never directed against His Majesty.

While political philosophers may ponder the nice point that rebellion need not be treason, repeated Irish successes concentrated the Saxon mind at a less academic level. In the first three days of the Rebellion, 'English' towns and forts fell one after the other. The MacMahons conquered Castleblaney and Carrickmacross. The O'Hanlons took Tandragee. Philip O'Reilly razed the fort at Cavan, while Roger Maguire burned the fort at Fermanagh to the ground and in front of its terrified and suddenly homeless denizens.

Worse still, right on the border of the Pale with Ulster, Newry surrendered to Sir Connor Magennis.

It was patently obvious that however loyal to the Crown they claimed to be, the rebels' argument was with the Lords Justice in Dublin. These powerful men were supported with money and munitions by the

King and Parliament of England. No analysis was likely to give either Monarchists or Anglicans much comfort.

All over Ulster, the undertakers – settlers - were at last reading the small print on the price ticket of living apart from their neighbours. In their hour of greatest need, no Catholic countryman would take them in. Every door was slammed in their faces. *In extremis* they saw that with hindsight it might have been wiser not to treat the natives with such contempt. On their march towards the Pale, hundreds perished by a hostile roadside. It killed them with a mortal concoction of exposure, famine and exhaustion. The condition of the few survivors who finally arrived in Drogheda, and the handful who reached Dublin, told their sorry tale to an appalled, aghast but receptive audience. Worn out, frozen, creeping along on hands and knees, they were all at the point of death. Some died within sight of shelter. No witness would ever forget the dreadful spectacle.

In the beginning was the Word, and the Word was God. The Word, for some, was the rubric of Science, of 'natural law'. It explained the consistency of nature. Others took it to mean grammar and articulacy; the logical process that communicates one man's thought to another. On this definition, Word must include *metaphor*, and presumably it was this usage that permitted the Castle to describe the mass evictions as a 'massacre'. Not every Protestant could understand such nuance – many of whom had adopted the practice of speaking literally. Did Our Lord avail Himself of metaphors? The parables would evidence that He did, yet when He took bread at the Last Supper, and gave thanks, and brake it, and gave unto them, saying, 'This is my body which is given for you: this do in remembrance of me', it was the Protestants who thought Him speaking metaphorically, while the Catholics took His words literally.

Two confused but opposing schools of philosophy had locked horns in battle, just as they had in France nearly a century before and, just as in France, this subtle debate would cost tens of thousands of lives.

How the Protestant presses rolled! The pamphleteers of the City of London redoubled their fortunes by inflaming Protestant opinion with the grizzly details.

One semi-literate Puritan leaflet detailed how…

…Sir Patrick Dunstan's wife was ravished, while the unfortunate gentleman was slowly cut to pieces. They cut off his ears and nose, teared [sic] off both his cheeks, after cut off his arms and legs, cut out his tongue and after ran a red-hot iron through him.

The possibility that some Protestants, who had supposedly 'seen the light', would choose to join the Irish Army when offered the chance, if only to be fed and housed, was just too awful to contemplate; it was therefore not reported. It might imply that some would choose their religion, less through revelation or the authority of the scriptures and more on the basis of material comfort. That would be an inconvenient truth indeed.

> Many persons of high quality covered only with old rags –
> mothers with their children, ministers and others that had escaped
> with their lives, sorely wounded – all frozen up with cold, ready to
> give up the ghost in the street.
> Many empty houses in the city were taken up for them, barns,
> stables and outhouses filled with them; yet many lay in the streets
> and others under stalls where they miserably perished.[vii]

A small number were billeted with townsmen. The Marchioness of Ormonde had herself rushed from Carrick-on-Suir, deep in Waterford, for Dublin. She relieved...

> ...to the uttermost the many distressed English[viii] and took over the
> perpetual charge of twelve poor distressed English children.

The Catholic natives were neither devils nor angels, but they were Christian. They could reasonably plead innocent to most of the charges against them.

The truth was, most of the tales of wholesale massacres, so widely and industriously circulated, were invented and composed within the cold stone walls of Dublin Castle.[ix]

*

Sir Connor Magennis's sights were set on County Down.

'There can't be too many Sasanach troops left there,' his ADC opined. 'They will have turned tail for the safety of Enniskillen. Why don't we simply storm the town?'

'Because, if we do, we will lose too many of our men to musket and cannon. No, siege warfare is our best weapon, even if I have never cared for it. Find me pen and paper. I shall offer the enemy terms.'

He wrote to request the town's surrender and his letter contained a threat.

To the Officer Commanding, Down.

> We convey our greetings to you from our Catholic fortress at
> Newry.

Our military engagements are for our lives and liberties, not for any other end. The paramountcy of these our aims override Peace itself. Please believe us, we desire no blood to be shed. Be very aware, however, if you intend to shed our blood, we shall be as ready as you for that purpose.

Our cause is holy. If it is besmirched with barbarism we will be fighting on your terms, not our own.

You will be given clear passage to the Pale if you surrender quietly and immediately.

Your servant,

Connor Magennis

'Now, take this directly to the enemy under a white flag,' Magennis told his messenger.

Down surrendered bloodlessly. That fall suited the Parliamentarian administration not at all. Their chief anxiety was that the Irish might appear fair, or worse yet, civilised. Violence would have suited them far better. They desperately needed more troops, powder and weapons. If only the Irish could be a little more bloodthirsty, England might ride to their rescue!

Then, right on cue, the Pale had a stroke of luck; yet another wave of asylum seekers from recently liberated Tyrone reached the walls of Drogheda, telling horrible and distressing stories to the Protestant administration. Hordes of armed and caped savages, they heard, had dragged honest Protestants out of their houses, stripped them almost to the skin, and had driven them into the wintry weather. Tales of the terrible hardships of their gruelling trek were taken down verbatim, all telling the same harrowing tale. Ulster could no longer provide asylum to Calvinists or Puritans.

Parsons' and Borlase's prayers had been answered. The Irish were seen to have a progrom, a vile scheme to rid a nation of its Christian immigrants. The horrid accounts of these poor people's dispossession and extinction would reverberate well, both in England and Scotland. Loosely bound copies of the witness statements were sent to London's publishers in Pater Noster Alley or Ave Maria Lane, who printed them as pamphlets.

At last the Lords Justice were confident that the king and Lord Leicester (the absentee Lord Deputy) would now be forced to react.

*

Sir William St Leger was at home in Doneraile House, Co. Cork, where he generally held his Court of Presidency. Long ago he had been an Irish

53

hero. In 1607, while still a Catholic, he had joined the 'Flight of the Earls', in which the cream of the Gaelic and Catholic Resistance had fled to Europe.

After spending twenty years abroad, he received the offer of a pardon from King James I, in exchange for his apostasy. When he returned, King Charles appointed him President of Munster. The post came with extensive grants of confiscated land. He had become a respected convert.

He built an Anglican church close to his mansion. Settler families also rejoiced that to clear the site he had to tear down an oratory and two rude Catholic churches, despite being paleoChristian temples of untold antiquity.

When Ireland caught fire, that October 23, St Leger took the responsibility for dealing with Munster's insurgents, even though the militia he had at his disposal was utterly inadequate to the task. He saw that martial law, and of the greatest severity, was necessary to make any impact whatsoever.

Wherever he could, he cemented relations with the few Protestant Gaels in the province. He married one of his six children to Murrough Inchiquin, son of the Anglican Earl of Thomond.

In Dublin, Parsons and Borlase - the beleaguered Lords Justice - had only the remnants of Strafford's standing force to rely on. Despite the failed attempt on the Castle, it had shown a mite too pointedly just how poorly the Saxon fortress had been garrisoned. Naturally enough, the instinctive reflex reaction of the government was to withdraw almost every garrison from Munster and concentrate their soldiers on safeguarding the Pale and Castle. One of the more remote was at Cappoquin, in Co Waterford. That garrison, with many others, was abandoned.

St Leger sat at a desk that commanded an unrivalled view of the magnificent gardens that he had built on his patiently drained bogs. He dipped his plume in an inkwell and, in an elegant hand, began to inscribe on a clean sheet of parchment. He needed to explain how there was only one man who could rescue Munster from itself, from fomenting Papists. Himself, of course, and he would need material assistance, in the form of treasure.

His letter, therefore, was addressed to the Earl of Cork, who shared, with the detested Lord Ormonde, the reputation of being the richest man in Ireland.

To the Right Honourable Earl of Cork, please admit a humble Knight Bachelor's petition.

Munster, the inflammable Province of which Your Lordship is chief ornament, desperately needs your help. The Army which I raised for Lord Strafford, so long before the Rebellion, was disbanded years ago without Wages. I worry that disgruntled, discharged Soldiers are tinder for the Flames, and their manifold Grievances may provoke them to turn coats.

My Conscience, my Faith, my King and the Lords Justice all ask me to defend every English Settlement throughout this Province, an enormous Challenge. I cannot but fail to acquit myself without the Means to pay these unhappy men their back pay.

It is now my intention to follow the Example of the late Thomas Wentworth and to levy such Numbers as will one day serve the King and restore Natural Order. I am ready to hang the Rebels and will do so in all Conscience – in good Faith – until the Rebellion is quelled. If, sometimes, this may be with only token Trials and with little in the way of Proof of Guilt, it is to be regretted, of course, but these are the real Rules of War.

My lord, my overarching Duty is to put Munster's Fires out.

I know that you care for the Region that houses so much of your Fortune and so many of your Castles. I observe that you have sent your Kinsmen Joshua and William to be Recorder of Youghal and Sheriff of Cork respectively.

Your Purpose will be to protect both English and your own Interests, a Stand I respect wholeheartedly. It is therefore a Stratagem I must similarly adopt, which is why I, in my capacity of Lord President of Munster, have asked my cousin Lord Dungarvan to serve as Governor of Youghal.

Together, dear Lord Cork, our Stroll in the Darkening Day may be unsteady, but if we divide we shall undoubted stumble. The Help you may offer me must be of the practical kind, for in the end it will guarantee our shared Ambitions for our Kin and Countrymen.

Before I replace my pen in its familiar groove, may I reassure Your Lordship you have no more faithful Servant than the undersigned
Wm St Leger

The urgent tone of his letter somewhat disguised the fact that the Irish had not yet risen in Munster, but St Leger had seen that it was only a matter of time before the northern conflagration would blaze a path along the inflammable roads that led south and west from Dublin and Ulster.

Despite his protestations, St Leger's personal fortune was already considerable, yet it could become truly sizable if he snuggled up closer to the Lords Justice in the Castle.

He put himself up for election to Parliament. It would give him an excuse for frequent trips to Dublin.

As predicted, he was duly elected, unopposed, by Co. Cork's property-owning constituents.

In Dublin, Borlase and Parsons had been deeply unnerved by the Rebellion. When they pronounced a 'state of emergency' throughout Ireland, it gave Lord Ormonde the power to deal with captured 'tories' as he pleased, a right which the Lieutenant-General delegated to his officers in all four provinces. In practice, this meant that Irish prisoners-of-war could be hanged without trial.

This was soon to be put to the test. In early November, Sir William saw a valuable opportunity to demonstrate his resolve. He heard that William Kingsmill, incidentally his brother-in-law, had had his house near Silvermines plundered by 'tories'. St Leger led a punitive expedition into Tipperary. He decided that there was too little time for the awkward, time-consuming process of law. Instead, he and his militia rounded up every unfortunate Irishman who happened to be near the scene of the crime, whether they were rebels, common criminals or even innocent bystanders, and ordered his Godly and Protestant militia to execute them all. It took a couple of days for the two officers and their private companies of horse and foot to destroy six hundred of the rebels without the loss of one man of their own. As there were too few trees in the area, the mass execution was conducted in shifts. St Leger's noose was worked so hard it frayed.

Nevertheless, St Leger knew his force was too small to impose a Protestant peace on a Catholic nation. Even Lord Cork, who was wont to praise the Lord President, was aware that Sir William had neither men nor munitions. In the circumstances, the earl declared that 'enthusiastic use of the noose would overcome any such difficulty'. St Leger had gained his support.

Informal, ill-disciplined rebel bands were, by now, increasingly infesting Co Waterford. Lord Inchiquin was pleased to accept Sir William's kind invitation to accompany him in hot pursuit of one of these raiding parties

Having been warned of one such rebel expedition, St Leger's and Lord Inchiquin's horse made an audacious sortie over the mountains towards Carrick-on-Suir, near Lord Ormonde's favourite country residence. When they arrived they found some distressed 'English' gentlemen who had been outwitted by Irish 'tories'.

Lord Inchiquin was amazed by what he saw there.

'What in the name of all that's holy have we here?'

'It is exactly how it looks. In Lord Ormonde's absence, the rascals have robbed and pillaged every settler in town,' a distressed householder replied.

'We have clearly not adequately impressed the Irish, St Leger. A showy deployment, don't you think?'

'I have the very plan,' responded St Leger, 'and I've already tested it at Silvermines. We will round up and corral the Irish just as sheepdogs do sheep. We shall concentrate the Irish into an enclosure and, without the palaver of a court martial, they will be sent to meet the ultimate Judge.'

'Then let's not waste time, Sir William; we need to concentrate their minds. If any liberal lawyer turns up, hoping to interfere, you may count on my support.'

The operation, as it turned out, was painfully slow. The herded villagers were successfully confined in a field but the English had only brought one portable, disposable gallows. The Irish had to be executed one at a time and its rope was already frayed from its hard work at Silvermines. There was a tradition that survivors of capital punishment would not have to suffer twice. St Leger sadly realised that some rebels might earn a reprieve.

'Retie the noose towards the end of the rope, St Leger. We will shift the knot when we must.'

Among the captives were children. St Leger's men watched indifferently as one after another their mothers pulled on their choking children's twitching legs, hoping to ease the pain of their 'journey'. Barely an hour later those same mothers would replace their offspring on the working end of the rope.

It was a tedious business. Whenever the old hemp rope gave way, the noose was retied and the exercise repeated. The macabre reduction of those supposedly sympathetic to the Rebellion took nearly a week.

'Mitigation and mercy only give rise to false hopes', St Leger commented as he filled in a docket for fifty lengths of 'hempen collar'.

'That is why I hang the children in front of their mothers, and the mothers before their rebellious husbands and fathers. Women and children first. One must be seen as decisive and single-minded to instil the fear of our Protestant God.'

'Quite right,' Lord Inchiquin agreed. 'There are so few government troops in Munster that the Irish, were they better organised, could easily take Munster back to Rome. That must never happen.'

*

My dear Lord Ormonde,

You have said to me, and I heartily concur, that in these dark days the terms of Magna Carta need not be insisted upon. Far more important to us, in our current predicament, is that we must leave no weapon in the hands of the Romishly affected. To achieve this, I beg you to supply me with three thousand stand of arms, for I can find here more Protestants to wear and fight with us than all those come out of England.

Your most obedient and humble servant, William St Leger, waits impatiently for your favourable response.

The response that came by return was nothing if not terse.

Dear and right trusted Lord President,

Let me promise, Sir William, that I shall do what I can, even if there are those around me who think me too favourable to the Irish.

I remain &,

Ormonde

As he kept telling everyone, Sir William had far too few men to keep the whole of Munster untainted by the Rebellion. He returned to stately Doneraile to celebrate Christmas with his family, always hoping for good news from the Castle.

Despite a single troop of horse and the irregulars that his neighbours had mustered, he was on the brink of despair before, after some agonising days, Lord Cork came to the rescue. St Leger's dealings with Lord Cork were not always cordial, but common danger had brought them together. Cork added two companies to St Leger's one.

Even so, the enemy's horse, regathered in Cashel, was superior in number and skills to his own. There were now said to be ten thousand of them! Cashel, arguably Christianity's chief seat on Ireland, would be a tough nut to crack.

*

Having delayed too long, Borlase and Parsons finally announced from Dublin Castle their explicit orders concerning the Catholics of Dublin.

'If not absolutely and demonstrably beyond reproach, they are to be presumed guilty, disarmed and put to the rack until their complicity is confirmed. Let us waste no more time. Massereene has suggested that the king himself may himself be implicated in our issues. We want to know how, when and with whom.'

'Have we also concluded that the hedgerow priests are also involved?'

'Good point, Sir William. Of course they are. Gentlemen of the Guard, the cleansing of Dublin is to be extended to priests, of the hedgerow or cassocked varieties. Seek them out, chase them down and expel or imprison them.'

'Will they need to be tried, my lord?' asked a naïve young captain. 'It makes a difference to how we treat them first.'

'There will be no trials. They don't need a platform for their idolatrous mouthings. All persons of that religion are either traitors already or on the brink of becoming so. Sir William, have we missed anything?'

'The magistrates will not be happy with imprisonment without trial,' remarked his fellow Lord Justice. 'It's their livelihood, after all.'

'You're right. We must extend the state of emergency to all of the Pale. Impose martial law on Dublin! That will silence the lawyers. Sir William, we should identify some trustworthy clerks to watch everyone known to be sympathetic to the Papists.'

'They should also note the behaviour of families with Popish servants.'

'Good point, Sir William. We shall follow the example of the illustrious Walsingham. He knew everything in Queen Bess's day. What did he say? He was 'the Palace's ear'. There are two of us. The Castle should grow a pair.'

The two consuls laughed easily.

'And eyes, Sir John. We need more eyes. As many as a bee.'

'And a thousand lorgnettes to go with them, Sir William.'

Quelling the insurrection, the Lords Justice calculated, would need a lot more money. The English House of Commons obliged with £50,000 in the form of a gilt-edged bond from the merchants and guilds of the City of London. Out of this princely sum, Lord Leicester deducted £500 for Owen O'Connolly, whom he also awarded a pension of £200 a year, 'until an estate of greater value can be provided'.[xi]

By mid-November, 1641, the number of Protestants who had actually died, whether from exposure or directly at the hands of the mob, had become incalculable. The truth, however, was never as sordid as the rumour. The numbers in circulation were fuelled by panic and fear. They grew tenfold in every hostelry, every inn. Four thousand murdered swelled to forty thousand; eight thousand dead of exposure to eighty thousand. People heard whatever suited their purpose or cause.

When these reports of Protestant deaths reached England, one particularly austere Parliamentarian heard them. His heart filled with rage. In the name of his pure and scriptural faith he resolved to have his revenge. At that time he was forty-two years old, and in his prime, but his time was not yet come.

Oliver Cromwell needed a purpose. His personal fortune had long been in decline. His family had once been rich and he felt the decline in that fortune very personally. Ten years before he had had to sell nearly all his property around Huntingdon and lease a farmstead at St Ives. There he had performed the backbreaking work of a yeoman farmer for five years, always looking for a way to blame his situation on the king and his royal cronies. He nurtured a smouldering resentment against what he saw as a swaggering court.

Only when Cromwell's childless and widowed maternal uncle Sir Thomas Steward departed this world did his fortune change. He now had a substantial inheritance. Even so, on his return to prosperity, if anything, his mood became still darker.

Following midnight that October 22, Sir Phelim's sword had seldom been in its scabbard. The fields of Ulster were steeped in gore, let from the wounds of mostly innocent people, caught in the eye of the storm. Well-tempered Toledo and Sheffield blades clashed noisily and long. The balm of that most divine force of humanity, that Christianity that both sides invoked and claimed as their own, no longer had the power to assuage any knighted horseman or colonel of foot. From here, the recording angel would see that both sides had embraced Satan's mistress, dressed in her scabrous robes of malice and atrocity, her vile form glimpsed obscurely, occasionally, through a veil of flies.

To Chichester and his ilk, Godless Catholics, devotees as they were of the scarlet whore of Babylon (as it pleased them to call the Pope) had nothing to look forward to but the burning brimstone of hell. Death could only shorten their cruel unequal struggle; their mortal end was at least kinder than their immortal damnation.

The Irish view was markedly different. If they had their own savage streak, it was less to do with self-righteousness. It was more to do with fifty years of progressive dispossession. Every man, woman and child in Ulster had some reason to feel they had lost a house, or land, or cattle, or tradition, or faith. Even a member of their family. Everyone who ever frequented a *sibín* heard stories of someone's eviction, sometimes at swordpoint. Anger welled in their beakers, and such sustained fury would pervert the generous character of the Celts, perhaps forever.

Especially Sir Phelim O'Neill. Incandescent after the cynical massacre on Island Magee, he was more enraged than anyone. For fifty years, the English had focussed their fury on his clan, more than any other, and he had difficulty restraining his men. Since Island Magee, sinful though it was, he had let them have their head.

Maguire and MacMahon's failure to take Dublin Castle had left him embittered. When Monro's invading army found its way to the stronghold of Carrickfergus and rendered it impregnable, Phelim O'Neill was appalled at the inability of his men to take the fortress. Bile and frustration tore his heart in two. He told his men to quit their siege and sharpen their swords.

In Ulster the Irish had still failed to take Enniskillen, the garrison at Derry, the Castles of Killeagh and Crohan in Cavan, or Lisburn, or Belfast.

O'Neill redirected his army to the city of Armagh. It was here where a great Catholic delinquency occurred.

The Protestant citizens of Armagh had levelly assessed the mood of the twenty thousand Irish soldiers whom they had seen encircle their town. Never before had any of them seen such a vast and threatening multitude. They knew they had too little provender to sit out a siege. Believing they had no real choice, they put their lives in the hands of their enemy, laying down their arms and opening the gates to their town, whence they emerged under a white flag. It brought them nothing. As they came out, on their knees or with their hands raised in supplication, they were butchered in cold blood. Even those that ran away were almost casually cut down.

Sir Phelim had always acknowledged his mercurial temper. If the storm he had unleashed at Armagh had stained an otherwise honourable character, his crime was not typical of his confederates. It was also an act that stood alone in O'Neill's life and demeanour. Those who chose to speak up for him never ceased to remember he had always been brave to the point of foolhardiness.

It was, however, a deplorable way to launch a Great Rebellion.

*

'Sir John, I think we should up the ante.'

The Lords Justice had called a meeting of their War Cabinet in Dublin Castle.

61

'I agree, Sir William. Shall we awaken our Kraken?'

'The very man. We should license Coote to use his famous negotiation skills.'

'The Catholic priests will be in trouble if we do!'

'Now, there's a pity, to be sure, Sir John.'

Sir Charles Coote, Commander of the Dublin Garrison, chose this timely moment to push his way noisily into the room. As usual he was in armour. He sat on a stool, not waiting for an invitation, his spurs noisily spinning. The startled footmen, recognising him, resumed their places by the doors where they stood more stiffly to attention than ever their customary wont.

Neither Sir William and Sir John were used to dramatic entrances but, once their nerves had settled, they explained that it had been decided that County Dublin was to be made secure, its Popish citizens disarmed or expelled.

Through the huge window, Lord Ormonde had been absently watching Coote's 'lambs', as Sir Charles wittily referred to his troops, drilling in the Castle yard. He turned away.

'Are you aware, Sir Charles,' he asked in his easiest tone, 'that the so-called Godless Franciscans and Jesuits of Cashel are protecting Dr Pullen, the Anglican Chancellor of that Cathedral with some other Protestant prisoners? That Lord Muskerry has also offered some Protestants safe refuge in Munster?'

'Lord Ormonde, these people you refer to so kindly are Popish traitors. You are showing signs of sentimentality.'

'Sir Charles, you do not have to remind me that this is a war. Yet it is not merely a war; it is the preamble to a history. We should take care not to be recorded in some future textbook as monsters. Some Catholics, at immense personal risk, are behaving very decently.'

'Yes? Such as who? As if I care.'

'Such as those at Cloughouter Castle in Cavan, Bishop Bedell's residence. It's crowded with Protestant refugees and the Catholic Philip O'Reilly is chivalrously protecting them all.'

Ormonde wondered, yet again, why he bothered. Coote lacked a crucial component. Was it a soul? He sighed and returned to the window. Little light was likely to break through the dark clouds outside. Not for quite a while.

As if to prove the marquess right, the very next day, Coote handed Fr Higgins and Fr White of Naas, Kildare, to his 'lambs'. They wasted little time. Both priests were peremptorily hanged in the transept of their almost unpurged church from the very hook that until the Reformation had hung the representation of Christ on the Cross. This, despite Lord Ormonde's granting them both safe conduct out of the country.

Though Coote knew this, he had condoned both murders. His explanation?

'I've nothing to be ashamed of. It was my duty. They were agents of a foreign power. Spies, in short.'

*

It was already clear that Ireland's Rebellion was no mere flash in a pan. The Lords Justices, preferring to act with their carefully chosen quorum of Privy Councillors, prorogued the Irish Parliament. The Kingdom of Ireland would be perfectly safe without politicians for a while.

Back in October, the Castle had asked the Catholic Lords of the Pale to arm their clansmen, believing them to be loyal. Now came a change of heart; these same lords were now ordered to disarm their clans and remit their arms to the Castle.

Some irritated members of the Dublin Upper House had asked the Irish Lords Dillon and Taaffe, both committed royalists and Anglicans, and therefore unlikely to be obstructed by the Castle, to convey their grievances to the king in person. Such upright and blameless peers would be respected by the Protestants on their journey over the Irish Sea and on to Whitehall Palace.

They were wrong. Lord Massereene warned his English Parliamentary friends that they were bearing some Popish message. As a result, English Puritans seized the peers as they set foot on English turf. Their papers were burned and the couriers were thrown into the gaol in Ware.

Only after pressure from the English House of Lords, were they peremptorily deported without an audience. Whatever they had to say was never heard by the King of Ireland.

Meanwhile, Rory O'More's clansmen had recovered their chief's old seat at Dunamase, together with other strongholds in his patrimony. This happy event persuaded the chief to redouble his efforts to recruit. He marched south with an army bristling with enthusiasm but, yet again, when he attacked Lisburn he lost heavily.

'You can't win them all,' he pronounced philosophically. Happily, his troops still backed him. A few days later, he took Mellifont Abbey, which made amends. The former abbey was locked into the Irish heart. It had been there where Lord Tyrone had surrendered to a dead queen, thirty-seven years before.

From Mellifont his legion advanced on the Pale. Colonel Plunkett, now promoted general, joined him. It was a godsend. Plunkett was at this time the only properly experienced commander in the Irish army.

O'More's two thousand pitched their camp between Ardee and Dundalk. While there, he found time to continue his natural calling, that of a recruiting sergeant. His task was easy. The Castle's threat to Catholics was on such a scale he discovered hundreds of farming men queuing to join his army.

The Protestant menace had left the Irish utterly uncowed. The Catholics were ready for action in the open field and had already been far more successful than anyone would have dared predict.

News spread rapidly that one of Sir Phelim's detachments had defeated a force of Government soldiers at a bridge between Dublin and Belfast. His army cut off five of the six companies marching from Dublin to reinforce *Baile Iúiliáin*, or Julianstown.

*

Within a few weeks of October 23, much of Counties Tyrone, Armagh and Down was in rebel hands.

The struggle was degenerating into a war between every native Irishman and every uninvited settler. The first help the beleaguered Covenanters in Ulster received was, predictably, from the Scots. Now the English Parliament authorised the conscription of troops in England and Wales to assist in the suppression of the Irish. The Catholic gentry, many reluctant to rise with their tenants, were under mounting pressure to take sides.

Much of the resulting violence was driven by revenge. Catholics robbed Protestants, drove them off their land, torched their farms and houses, stealing their cattle. Less publicised, at least in England, was that the Protestants were not slow to take their own counter-measures. Their weapon was the lynch mob. Everywhere were trees, bowed with strange fruit. Violence, as always, fed on itself.

The reciprocal massacres that began in 1641 would polarise Irish politics along sectarian lines forever. The thesis of the old Earl of Tyrone, the Great O'Neill, that Catholicism and Nationalism could harness each other, was proved.

The Irish Rebellion was described in contemporary England as an attempted *coup d'état* by the Irish Catholic gentry. What is sure is that if only Dublin Castle had been taken, it would have been relatively bloodless, all over in a matter of months. Instead, the resentment felt by the natives of Ulster towards the Castle ensured the violence would escalate.

When reports of the Rebellion were carried back to Oliver Cromwell, the member for Cambridge in the English House of Commons, he learnt of massacres of gentle English and Scottish Protestants at the hands of Irish savages. Anyone with a level head would have known that such tales were bound to be exaggerated, the perspective distorted, especially so in Parliamentarian circles, but Cromwell, reminded of the treatment that had been meted out to French Huguenots on St Bartholomew's Day, 1572, felt that such wanton cruelty had to be quashed with remorseless efficiency, and on an epic scale.

Cromwell's social standing had improved dramatically after his recent inheritance. His re-election delivered him connections with the more important Puritans of his constituency. On grateful recognition of his being made a freeman of the borough of Cambridge he made a passionate, brilliant - if clumsy - speech, drawing attention to the unfair incarceration of the popular Puritan, anti-Anglican John Lilburne.

Cromwell's self-confidence grew daily.

In Parliament he chose to focus his venom on the episcopy. If at first his speeches veered between the populist and the inarticulate, he amply supplied his oratorical deficiency with passion. He had discovered in himself a rising taste for speechifying, always drawing on self-righteousness. Tales from the Old Testament were exploited to disguise or legitimise outrageous bigotry.

His efforts were well-received, When he was brought to Sir John Pym's attention as a cousin of John Hampden, the 'ship money martyr', the old statesman publicly and emotionally adopted Cromwell as his protégé.

With this kind of support, Cromwell was ready to lobby for a Parliamentarian army and for a systematic cleansing of Ireland.

*

CHAPTER FOUR
THE RISE OF SIR PHELIM O'NEILL

In late November, Parsons and Borlase fearfully concluded that the Irish might take the capital. If they did, their timing would be immaculate. The capital was ill-defended and the Irish Sea too rough, too dangerous, for English reinforcements to cross.

Leinster, slow to adopt the Irish cause, had at last begun to accept Rory O'More's exhortations. His ineffectual siege of Protestant Julianstown, near Drogheda, in Leinster's County Meath, still continued, but Sir Phelim and his 'wild rovers' were closing in on it. The city's mayor begged the Castle to intervene, but while the army was notionally under Ormonde's command, the Lords Justice were still not prepared to cut the courtier loose. Dubliners had, at all cost, to be prevented from admiring their royalist Lieutenant-General.

Instead the Lords Justice acted independently. They levied Ulster's Protestant refugees, now dwelling in Dublin's poor houses, and sent an untrained force to relieve the besieged.

This unenthusiastic militia was intercepted by Sir Phelim O'Neill. The two sides met at the bridge outside that ill-fated townland, where the Irish rebels charged the Castle's soldiers, shouting their warcries. For a while, the Lords Justice's soldiers held them off, even firing a few volley, but all too soon they panicked. Seeing the rebels bearing down on them, most of them simply threw down their muskets and ran.

The rebels soon captured the English deserters. They spared the Irishmen among them but hanged every Saxon and Scot. Only then did they collect the discarded weapons.

The consequences were far greater than Julianstown's surrender might suggest. Sir Phelim's victory made him and his men seem far more dangerous than they actually were, and their bloody victory fanned the flames of insurrection in every Irish province.

*

A third conspirator in the plot to take the Castle had been arrested and thrown into Maguire's and MacMahon's dismal cell, deep under Dublin Castle.

The Castle's net had landed a very small fish – a bewildered and furious lad, probably in his teens or at most in his early twenties. His name was Reade. He had wanted to take Dublin Castle 'for Ireland', he said.

Coote made much use of his rack on all three prisoners. Sometimes he turned the wheel himself. More typically he delegated such delights to the professionals, euphemistically known as 'magistrates'.

Maguire had already stated his ambitions for Ireland, freely and without torture, at the time of his arrest. He seemed quite sincerely not to know the numbers, whereabouts or strength of the rebels. Eventually his torturers believed him and relented.

Colonel MacMahon, however, took a different view. He was taken to the rack every day, always refusing to say a word to the magistrates, let alone name his fellow travellers.

The third 'arch conspirator', Reade, quite obviously knew nothing.

When the magistrates reported MacMahon's obduracy and Reade's ignorance to Sir William Parsons, the Lord Justice was all for hanging all three of his prisoners, there and then in the Castle yard.

'Patience, Sir William, is a virtue,' Borlase warned him. 'Maguire, or perhaps I should call him Lord Enniskillen, is a peer of the king. You can't hang him like a common blackguard!'

'No, you're right, Sir John, but his is an Irish peerage, isn't it? In England, Maguire will be a commoner. Over the Irish Sea he will have no special privileges.'

'Quite right, Sir William. You make an excellent point, Sir, and one that I think was settled long ago. You will be recalling the case of Leonard Grey? Viscount Grane over here but plain old Mr Grey in the Kingdom of England.'

'I was. Grey was accused of allowing his sister Elizabeth's son, the young Earl of Kildare, and escaped to France in 1539. When he returned, as criminals always do, he was arrested. He strenuously denied all charges. Nevertheless Grey was tried and attainted of high treason. King Henry VIII had him executed in the Tower of London.'

'Well, let's keep our prisoners a little longer. Justice should not be rushed. Coote and his magistrates will no doubt be able to extract a little more useful information even now. We'll send them all to be hanged in England in the spring when the shipping lanes reopen.'

*

It was now six weeks since the Irish volcano had erupted. English authority in Ireland overall was breaking down. Everywhere, but most especially in Ulster, small groups of newly landless Irish launched uncoordinated, unpredictable and sporadic attacks on those urban aggregations of English and Scottish settlers known as townlands.

In Dublin Castle, the conversation was mostly on O'More's latest siege; Drogheda.

'If O'More is to pull it off, he will need more than his two thousand men,' said Lieutenant-General Ormonde. 'He will need siege guns and sappers, not merely his brand of mad Irish courage, to defeat it. He will need Sir Phelim, but our knighted friend has taken his tribe back to Ulster.'

Ormonde had a point. Drogheda was a strongly walled town, right on the border of Leinster and Ulster, a little upstream on the Boyle. Its warehouses were full. It was well governed and, during more favourable months, easily provisioned from the sea.

'Never mind Drogheda,' Ormonde told the War Cabinet. 'Let the Irish waste their time. It's a distraction. My considered advice is that we subjugate the rebel leaders in the North before our other Provinces become as badly infected. We need to make an advance on Dublin quite impossible. An Ulster campaign would pay dividends, even as late as this. While they are all divided we can far more easily defeat them.'

'Is that entirely wise, dear Marquess?' asked Sir John Borlase. 'Our men have little training.'

'We should restrict our ambitions to the defence of the Pale,' Sir William Parsons persisted. 'Our soldiers don't like marching, y'know. They're not very good at it.'

'Leave that to the natives. Let the Irish savages march as much as they wish over their endless bogs.' Sir Charles Coote was phlegmatic. 'That is, after all, what they've always done.'

'Our duties lie here in Dublin,' confirmed Sir William.

In December, 1641, however, Sir Phelim O'Neill's 'rag-tag-and-bobtail' army - now made up of ten thousands 'veterans' - arrived outside Drogheda to reinforce O'More's less-experienced two thousand.

Such numbers forced the Dublin War Cabinet to reassemble.

Lord Ormonde wanted to liberate the Drogheda but the collective will of the Dublin Cabinet again overruled him. On seeing the anger on his face, however, the Lords Justice permitted the Lieutenant-General to revisit his case.

'I have an army, notionally 10,000 infantry and around 1,000 horse, at my disposal. It is the former standing army of Lord Strafford, put into my command by His Majesty, King Charles and the Lord Deputy, the Earl of Leicester. Since October I have been training its pikemen, have formed endless squares in the Castle yard, and coached the cavalry in their lancework.'

Unvoiced was the matter of a shortage of powder and ball. The Palesmen's muskets would have to serve as clubs.

The king's name sharpened Sir John's thoughts a little.

'We have had intelligence that Sir Phelim has swollen O'More's siege army at Drogheda. The Irish clearly mean to use it as a bridgehead for an invasion of the Pale,' Sir John pronounced.

Sir William heard his cue.

'We hereby authorise you, General, to take reinforcements as far as the border with Ulster,' he said, his voice sober. 'We anticipate the king's Long Parliament in London will sanction us. We are also confident that the town's governor, Sir Henry Tichburne, will be his usual vigilant self. Ormonde, relieve the town!'

'Were the Irish siege of Drogheda to succeed it would cause the citizens of Dublin to panic; and that would cause an exodus from the Pale,' Sir John added. 'They would run to England, ready to criticise ourselves.'

'We can't have that, can we now?' asked Sir William rhetorically.

Clearly, the Lords Justice had at last recognised that as Lieutenant-General, Ormonde was indispensable. If he failed he would take the blame. If he succeeded, the Lords Justice had been wise enough to employ his skills. It was also all too evident that Ormonde, a royalist and an Anglican, would not share a platform, at least not forever, with such devoted Puritans as Parsons, Borlase, and Coote.

Especially not if he ever had to chose between king and Parliament.

*

'We are in mortal danger.' Cliona told Dermod Oge in the grand gallery of Kanturk's Old Court. 'Husband, we cannot wait forever for you to join Rory O'More. Many of our people have already gone off to join the Rebellion. Why don't you?'

'Darling wife, I know, I know. The danger to us in Kanturk is real. I have just learned that the greedy old Earl of Cork has sent a thousand indictments to the Speaker of the Long Parliament in London. Everyone named in it is an Irishman of property. He has asked for the authority to dispossess the 'outlaws'.'

'Are we on that list?'

'Cliona, I don't quite see how we could be, but I have to say the chances are high that we are.'

There was a moment's silence. Cliona looked out of the window and watched Bryen taking Fingal over the traces. The avenue of leafless Irish oaks was darkly dramatic in the winter sun.

'One positive result of the Parliamentarians' strategy, at least,' she said at last, 'is that as every day passes it brings forward the day that unites Catholics of all our Irish races.'

'True, but I counsel caution. That may even be what Cork wants. The more men rebel, the more estates there are to confiscate.' Dermod Oge rose to his feet and moved to sit beside Cliona. He took her hand and together they watched Bryen. He was a remarkable horseman.

'You can't stay out of it forever,' said Cliona. 'You're a Catholic landowner, and a major one. They're simply not going to leave us in peace. It can only be a matter of time before there are cannons parked on our lawns. Kitty tells me that in the south of the county the President of Munster is already directing murderous raids on the peasantry.'

'He and St Leger like killing people,' admitted Dermod Oge. 'They make no distinction between men and women. Not even children.'

'I've been told that Lord Muskerry, with many other prominent recusants, has at last decided to take a leading role in the Rebellion. Dermod Oge, he has even more to lose than we do.'

They watched together as Bryen swung in the saddle to touch one foot and then the other, all while riding at a rising trot.

'And, then these thousand indictments...' Cliona prompted.

'I did hear that Philip O'Dwyer has captured the ancient city of Cashel. He has announced the 'Rising of the South'. Waterford has opened its gates to Colonel Butler. Wexford has declared for the Catholic cause and Kilkenny has surrendered to Lord Mountgarrett.'

'All that? If now you still refuse to join the Confederacy, then I shall join without you.'

'You? You are a woman!'

'Perhaps, but I'm a better horseman than you. I can use a sword better than any of your men. If I do, don't try to stop me, Dermod Oge. If I must, I am not afraid to disobey you.'

*

Sir Charles Coote, having heard what Lord Cork had done in Munster, issued four thousand similar indictments of his own. It took him just two days. In every case he submitted an accusation of treason, sometimes evidenced, mostly not. Witnesses had been encouraged to report all subversive behaviour, even conversations. Their tongues had been loosened with a cocktail of small coins and a dose of Coote's mobile rack. The former Provost-Marshall of Connacht and now the Commander of the Dublin Castle Garrison was no respecter of standing or age. Sir John Read, an officer of the King's Bedchamber, and a Mr

Barnwall of Kilbrue, a centenarian, were among the many who endured the excruciating pain of having their joints slowly and systematically dislocated.

Some wondered, if this were how Coote's 'tribunals' were conducted in full view of the authorities, the excesses of his soldiery, in the backwoods and bayswaters of the open country, must be truly unimaginable.

*

No Protestant in the Pale had really expected the general contagion to spread within the ruling class, but the Catholic Lords of this most Anglicised region of Ireland began to share the hurt of their oppressed populace. They were slowly coming to the conclusion that they had long been too submissive.

On December 8, 1641, the Lords Justice, sensing the changing mood, invited the recusant Lords of the Pale to attend them in Dublin. Suspecting a trap, the Catholics sent their regrets to the Lords Justice. Attached to their refusal was their reason: the proposed 'safe-conduct' into the lions' den was at best implausible.

The Justices replied with a proclamation. They denied the Catholics' allegation and converted their request into an order. Lords Fingal, Gormanston, Slane, Dunsany, Netterville, Louth, and Trimleston should attend them in Dublin Castle, a week later. Failure to obey would be deemed an act of treason.

To show they meant business, Borlase and Parsons removed Coote's muzzle and pointed him at the flourishing villages of Fingal. The burning thatch of the tenantry's cottages, kindled by his men, was easily seen by the Catholic lords from Swords's round tower, just ten miles away. Rather too close for comfort.

The recusants regathered on Crofty Hill in County Meath. While they debated the best course of action, a party of armed horsemen, accompanied by a guard of musketeers, approached them. The Catholic peers sent their militia to investigate, but the newcomers proved to be none other than the Celtic chiefs Rory O'More, Philip O'Reilly, Colonel Byrne, Captain Fox and Costelloe MacMahon, brother of the famous prisoner in the Tower.

Lord Gormanston rode in front of his friends and formally addressed the Irish.

'Why have you come, armed as you are, into the Pale?' he called out.

Rory O'More replied very clearly, projecting his voice so all could hear.

'We understand how the king has been compromised by his Parliament. We are here for the freedom and liberty of our consciences and the maintenance of His Majesty's prerogative. Our purpose is to make the subjects of this Kingdom of Ireland as free as those of England.'

Lord Gormanston wheeled his horse around and spoke for a few moments with his friends. He then rode up to O'More. Many recorded his words.

'Seeing these be your true ends, we will likewise join with you.'

O'More wheeled his horse around.

'Capital! *Pro Deo, Rege et Patria, Hibernia Unanimis*[3], he cried. Thus was first uttered the motto of the fledgling Irish Confederacy.

The two leaders dismounted and embraced. Their followers roared their approval while O'More and Gormanston retired to their tented quarters to agree and write down what they called, in the language of the old religion, a *modus vivendi operandumque*.[xii] They were of one mind, *unanimis*, as one. They then drew up a warrant authorising the Sheriff of Meath to summon the gentry of the county to a convocation on the Hill of Tara on Christmas Eve, coincidentally the fortieth anniversary of the Irish defeat at the Battle of Kinsale.

*

That same day, in London, saw fierce anti-Catholic demonstrations in Smithfield Market. They were enough to persuade King Charles to make yet more concessions. This time the Cockney Puritans were not only carrying banners. They bore dead cats on poles, symbolising or satyrising the 'familiars' of Catholics. Their Preachers, Pastors, Presbyters and Divines exhorted the Londoners to accuse the Papists of witchcraft.

Enough's enough, thought the king. Give them a little of what they want. That should keep them quiet.

Unfortunately, Charles was consistently wrong. Every concession, every accommodation served only to encourage the rabble to riot more volubly. Then, to exacerbate the king's dilemma, Parliament presented him with their 'Grand Remonstrance'. They had passed it, by a paltry eleven whipped votes, but it was enough. The demands on the House of Stuart were now in writing and the authors spoke of themselves as successors to the Runnymede barons.

The Remonstrance was really a list of 'enemies of the state'. At first glance, one could have been forgiven for thinking that every subject's

---

[3] For God, King and Country, One Ireland.

name was on it. All those who Parliament wanted imprisoned or exiled were there. According to the House, those responsible for 'subverting the fundamental laws and principles of government' were 'mostly Jesuits, Papists, bishops, the 'Romanised part' of the Anglican clergy, surviving Benedictines or Franciscans and those courtiers who had even once volunteered their services to a foreign prince'. Again, for 'foreign prince' read 'Pope'.

The Commons, moreover, called for a Synod of Divines from England - and other Protestant countries - to regulate the Church in a way that conformed to the pure and primitive faith, without the egregious and repellent accretions that Rome had introduced over the last millennium. Again and again they denied that anything had been learned from all the councils and synods in which the Universal Church had disputed lengthily and studiously for these last thousand years.

Above all, Parliament demanded that the existing laws against Popery be more officiously persecuted. The Remonstrance, subject of course to His Majesty's royal approval, would permit the king only to appoint only such ministers in whom Parliament had confidence.

If the king did not see fit to assent to these 'modest' demands, Parliament would no longer allot 'His Majesty such supplies for support of the Crown estate, nor such assistance to the Protestant party beyond the sea, as is frequently desired'.

*

It was Christmas Day in Blarney Castle, Lord Muskerry's seat in Co. Cork, and the clock above the fireplace in the dining parlour struck nine o'clock. Despite some issues with Queen Elizabeth, who had wanted the pile for her Irish residence, a portrait in oil of King Charles - a spaniel at his feet - hung on a wall.

Now that dinner was over, the females who had eaten at table could withdraw and relax.

The dining room, on the first floor of the MacCarthy's great seat, had been extended into space, in a manner of speaking, during the time of the Tudors. This had been done by building an oriel window in solid stone and supporting it as if it had been an Italian *balcone*. The imposing glazed windows, in daylight at least, looked for miles over the valley. At night, it was hoped the torches of any approaching army would have been clearly seen by the family.

'You've actually dined with Sir William, Mr Bellings?' Bellings was the local Member of Parliament, although a committed recusant.

73

'I have had that privilege, Lord Muskerry. St Leger is a brave and prudent gentleman, a tolerant Protestant with a taste for theological controversy. When I was at his table, so was our Catholic Dean of Cork!'

'He fought in the continental wars, but on the side of the Dutch.' Muskerry's tone was even, avoiding any criticism. He had known the knight for years. 'He is certainly a man of huge experience and enjoys a good reputation with his men. He knows the rules of war and makes his best efforts to adhere to them. His severity, I believe, is designed to deter the wilder rovers that continue to infest our forests and *clachans*. His problem is that his exemplary punishment is applied, how shall we put it, confusedly. Some wholly innocent labourers and husbandmen have suffered unjustly and, when that occurs, it enflames the generalised Irish despair. Mark my words, unrest will follow, as night follows day.'

'Well! A paean worthy of lyric verse! Brave and prudent he may be, but in your excellent summation you have embedded a coded message that the Lord President is too rough in his practice, too fiery in his method,' Bellings commented.

Garret Barry was even less inclined to be generous.

'I see his method as vindictive,' he declared. 'He strikes terror into rebelling peasants with constant harrying. That, combined with a policy of hanging them without mercy, gives much offence to the Catholic gentry of the country. They are, after all, bound by blood, history and tradition to protect their peasants. They think his manner both crude and hasty.'

'Don't forget he has to uphold martial law,' said Lord Muskerry.

The hour required the servants to put pewter mugs and a jar of whiskey on the table.

'All true,' said Richard Bellings, 'but the last thing the Castle can possibly want is the remaining Irish landowners to rise against the English. I feel that it will soon be necessary for Dublin to censure him and issue a posthumous pardon under the Great Seal for all he has slain.'

'I doubt that it's only the President's stern ways that are causing the revolt to spread.' Lord Muskerry pushed back his chair and stood. The men at his table did likewise.

'He is not alone in hanging our peasants by the tumbrilful. So have many other of the Castle's officers. This filthy work began in Ulster. Gentlemen, it is late and I still have a letter to write. St Leger's daughter Elizabeth is affianced to Murrough O'Brien, Lord Inchiquin's boy. It's here, in The Gazette.' He tapped the newspaper. 'So, I hope you'll excuse me. Do feel free to join the ladies, or to remain here, as you please. Gentlemen, God save the King of Ireland.'

The table raised its tumblers to the royal portrait.

'God keep and save His Majesty' rang out in a clarion and loyal echo.

*

Ulster's long-smouldering bracken had finally taken light. By early January, 1642, it had become a firestorm and threatened to ignite the whole of Ireland.

The country at large was losing all sense of direction. Fearing an invasion of anti-Catholic forces, sent by an over-mighty English Parliament and the Scottish Covenant, Dublin was at last facing the prospect of street-fighting; in short, civil war.

The authorities had it that Ulster remained manageable. So long as England's traditional allies, the Old English and Anglo-Irish, remained tame. The Castle declared at every opportunity, and from every pulpit, that a full blown, country-wide rebellion was unlikely.

'Less of a prophesy and more of a resolution,' Ormonde told his wife.

In England, Parliament urged the king to denounce his 'Irish rebels'. To general astonishment, Charles did as he was bid. He actually asked Parliament to send arms and men.

'We shall never tolerate Popery in that Kingdom', he repeatedly declared. 'If Parliament consents, we shall lead our army in person.'

With such words the poor beleaguered monarch satisfied neither his friends nor placated his enemies; worse, by such craven offers he dishonoured himself. Many very senior English families were still of the old faith. They were disgusted. Up to now, they had been far from hostile.

Yet it was true that the violence in Ireland was spiralling out of control. It threatened to outwit those men of peace, Protestant or Catholic, who still hoped to contain it. The first reaction of the English authorities in Dublin was therefore both too excited and too lofty. Castle officials dismissed the rebels' purpose as being a simplistic ploy to exact a bloodthirsty revenge on a wave of usurping immigrants, while Parsons and Borlase convinced each other that a single, awesome shock of force would 'put the flames out, as gunpowder can be used to stop the spread of a fire.'

January would see them wake up to reality.

Rory O'More had decided to rid Swords Castle of its Huguenots. The Lords of the Pale needed a safer place to meet than the open air. The castle, only ten miles north of Dublin, had been, in pre-Reformation Ireland, the country residence of the Archbishops of Dublin. Now it was in Protestant hands. In 1583 Sir Henry Sydney, then Lord Deputy, had settled some French refugees, mostly master craftsmen, into the castle where they had repaired, extended and redecorated its noble apartments and built battlements to make it defensible again. Last, but not least, it boasted a serviceable great hall on the east side of its bawn.

O'More considered a short siege would soon deliver it to Ireland's aspirant ruling class.

When Sir Charles Coote learned of Rory O'More's ambitions he attacked and raised the Irish siege. He did this easily, but the Irish merely regrouped without significant losses.

O'More repaid the compliment with an attempt on the capital. His incursion into the Dublin suburbs, however, found Coote waiting for him. He was beaten back by the baronet's bayonets. It was O'Mpre's turn to shrug. Such an outcome was not unanticipated. He had sent a message to the Dubliners that their capital was not as secure as the Lords Justice constantly proclaimed.

He returned directly to Swords and expelled Coote's sentinels. The Anglo-Irish Lords of the Pale now had a defensible place in which to meet.

For political reasons, the Castle's masters continued to underestimate the seriousness of the Rebellion. Their complacency was compounded when they chose to declare the Lords of the Pale 'self-declared rebels', after their courteous refusal to talks in Dublin. Borlase and Parsons ordered Coote to storm and this time destroy the enemy's new base. His fee, willingly paid, was that when he had finished he would be free to deploy his legendary compassion on the Catholic land-holdings in the Province at large.

In Lord Leicester's absence, Parsons and Borlase were running the government of Ireland. Neither cared overmuch for Lord Ormonde, their Anglican Lieutenant-General. Perhaps the marquess was too much of a gentleman. They could not exactly sideline the distinguished nobleman, given that he had been appointed by the king and endorsed by the Lord Deputy, but wherever they could they gave Ormonde the most dangerous and especially, distant commissions. The Castle felt more confident that he would come to a sticky end and that their zealous Puritan knights errant, Sir Charles Coote and Sir William St Leger, had the requisite ruthlessness to subdue the excitable natives of that westerly kingdom.

This was yet another mistake. Licensing Coote and St Leger had the opposite effect; it drove the insurgents into a frenzy of resentment, the more so when Coote and St Leger appeared to be condoning indiscriminate murder. Reports of their reprisals provoked many Catholic Irish landlords, whether or not they had already lost their estates, to join the Rebellion and sack the townlands of neighbouring Protestant settlers.

In the meantime, O'More took Naas.

Parsons and Borlase sent Ormonde to deal with the matter. He did so successfully.

O'More was not put off by these minor reversals of fortune. He knew they were temporary. Almost every day he discovered leading families, all keen to confront the invading settlers. Soon his army had strength enough to lay siege to almost every fortified borough in the Pale. Some of these settlements had been walled from the times of the first Geraldines who, all those centuries ago, had had the foresight to protect themselves from the aboriginal Irish. These battlements had mostly decayed, however. Time after time O'More gained their surrender.

The gallant lawyer would always begin his sieges with a proposal to spare any Protestant citizens who surrendered their arms. They were promised safe conduct to Dún Laoghaire whence they might take ship for England. A surprisingly large number took up O'More's offer and returned across a stormy Irish Sea as refugees. Of those left behind, the most obdurate settlers were simply slain.

By itself, this should have been worrying enough. Worse still, like Chinese whispers, the rumours became detached from their basis in fact. Once heard on English shores, wild tales of horrible massacres spread like wildfire through Protestant England's and Calvinist Scotland's chapels, meeting houses, parlours and ale houses. They reinforced all earlier rumours.

In this climate, the Lords Justice issued a statement that the rebel prisoners in the Castle would get the hearing they deserved. Reade, Maguire and MacMahon were dispatched to London, chained and on board a heaving warship, to await the tender mercies of the Court of the King's Bench. After that, doubtless, they would be hanged from a common gibbet.

*

Dublin had not been ready to go on the offensive before the New Year. Coote recommended to the War Cabinet that the countryside surrounding Dublin – especially its townlands - be cleared of large houses or castles where rebels might concentrate.

This work, cruel in itself, was enthusiastically performed with Coote's characteristic style. In Wicklow, Coote's 'lambs' especially distinguished themselves. Their atrocities far exceeded the Norsemen's fabled essays in carnage.

His soldiers joyously revived the English baronet's 'frolics'. Neither youth nor sex would earn the victims any mercy.

It was often said that Sir Charles had no sense of humour. Perhaps to prove the contrary, on one occasion, Coote, standing proudly beside his son, was watching his men evict a threadbare family from its cabin in County Dublin. Coote's son, who had uncritically inherited his father's every trait, suggested that his old man should demonstrate that the Crown's business could have an amusing angle.

The baronet rose to the challenge. He called on the tearful head of the soon-to-be homeless family to approach him. He told the peasant that his nightmare could be ended if he would just blow into the barrel of an English pistol. When the simple fellow obeyed, Coote shot him dead in his absurd position.

*

In Dublin itself, paranoia increasingly provoked the authorities to persecute the Catholics, but to do so it needed much more money. Assessments of the wealth of notable citizens were ordered, in order to raise taxes for fires, lanterns, candlelight and other necessaries for Coote's Court of Guards as they defended the city and suburbs. Loyal citizens were commanded to bring in their silver to be turned into coin. This drive raised the terrific sum of £2000.

Dublin needed every penny. It may have been capital of the 'Pale' but O'More had successfully raised its Catholic Lords. This put him in a position to prevent any food from arriving from outside the walls. The seas were still too high to allow meaningful relief from England, so he directed his ten thousand Irishmen and put Dublin under siege.

The city's 'crazy old walls' were of little use as a defence. During the centuries of peace they had been neglected. Now, at their time of greatest need, when people from the suburbs flowed around and over them to the supposed safety of the city, the walls were trampled further down under desperate thousands of unshod feet.

Many citizens thought that rather than stay in an undefended Dublin they would escape by boat. It was an unwise choice. The dismal season was as stormy 'as in the memory of man had ever been recorded'. Half their ships would founder in the high seas.

Even at this terrible hour, tyranny (in the menacing form of Sir Charles Coote) stalked the Pale.

One astonishingly callous act has survived the redaction of Whig historians. Coote ordered the Catholic suburb of Clontarf to be torched. Most of its citizens died horribly, but fifty-six men, women and children had somehow crowded into boats and rafts to flee the flames. Coote ordered their simple crafts boarded and their Catholics shackled and thrown into the churning waters to drown.

Yet even this cruel act of state-sponsored terrorism was counter-productive. It only succeeded in hardening the resolve of the Catholics, transforming hitherto law-abiding and peaceful folk into desperados.

In Dublin itself, the famine in land and the storms at sea looked set to bring the Castle to its knees. Luckily a heavily laden merchantman from Bristol miraculously made harbour.

Even so, for the first time in living memory, the eerie sound of wolves could be heard in the suburbs as the slavering beasts searched for easy pickings.

*

In London, that January, the Puritans were rioting again. The damage they caused only heightened the tension between Crown and Legislature. A desperate king attempted to seize and impeach five MPs and one peer on the grounds that they (repeating the words of the Grand Remonstrance) had attempted to undo the laws of the kingdom. Forewarned, the men had absented themselves from Parliament. When the loyal Yeomen of the Guard arrived for them, the Speaker told them to look for the accused in Old Sarum, the Chiltern Hundreds and Dunwich.

Unfortunately, the Yeomen had too little education to realise that these rotten boroughs had not actually boasted a resident politician for a century or more.

*

The Court, Kanturk, was bound to find itself involved, no matter how hard its master tried to keep it neutral.

'Ah, Bryen, there you are,' Cliona told her son. 'What a delight to see you! You are a sight for sore eyes!'

'You're back from your holidays on Sherkin Island, a couple of days early', agreed his father. 'Was there some problem?'

'How were the twelve days of Christmas? Or was it ten?'

'Come on, we want reports, details. Your godfather O'Driscoll? His lads? Their health?'

'Mama, Papa, something came up. I've just had an over-exciting ride home on one of Fineen's bolting stallions. I would rest, but first I have something important to tell you. On New Year's Eve Lord Castlehaven told us that he had decided to join the Rebellion. Then, on the feast of the Epiphany, St Leger's militia arrived in Baltimore and arrested him. News travels fast, even in the west. One of O'Driscoll's servants must be an informer. Well, the soldiers took Castlehaven prisoner. They tied his hands and feet and put him in a cart. He will already be well on the road for Dublin, where he'll face a charge of treason. He won't stand a chance; they'll hang him after a mock trial.'

'Am I supposed to feel sorry for him just because he changed sides? Last October he was loudly volunteering to suppress the Irish. He deserves all he gets.'

'That's not how I see it, Papa. He may be English but he's a Catholic. Generations of his family have paid the mounting fines for recusancy without flinching. Now he needs our help and when he has it he will see the world as we do.'

'Our help?'

'Mine and Finbar's. Yours if possible. Donal O'Donovan – '

'You are thinking of rescuing him from Dublin Castle? You are either stark staring mad or insanely reckless. I won't have you sacrifice yourself for the scion of an unnatural pervert!'

'Papa, I have passed wonderful days and elegant evenings with him and with the others at Castlehaven, Sherkin and Baltimore. Lord Castlehaven is a gentleman. It was his father, not the man himself, who was the criminal in the sad case you are thinking of, all those years ago. Besides, if O'Driscoll and O'Donovan are willing to put their heads above the parapet, why shouldn't I? Not only are those two as Irish as I am; they are his next door neighbours. Castlehaven bought O'Driscoll's ruined castle and poured money and love into it. O'Donovan is in his family's seat across the bay. They have watched him at close quarters for years. They trust him totally. If we succeed we shall have gained another Old English ally, and this time a rich one.'

'His grandfather fought my father at Kinsale.'

'A lot of water has flowed in and out of that pretty harbour since then, Papa. If we don't succeed he will pass to oblivion through the same strait gate as Lord Strafford. We must try, or the Old English will stay aloof from our Rebellion.'

'Well, Bryen, I suppose you and Finbar have a plan?'

'Yes, Father, we have. It should work. This is what we intend to do.'

*

In Ulster the war was becoming so bitter that even O'More, O'Reilly and Magennis had problems managing it. They desperately needed a field commander, one who could harness the anarchic violence of the rebel tories and turn it into a manageable weapon of war.

The supposed leader of the Great Rebellion, Colonel Owen Roe O'Neill, had not yet been able to return to Ireland. Every time the Irish thought he was on his way, some mishap in Flanders held him back. Mostly the weather.

The south of the country had remained at peace until the President of Munster, Sir William St Leger, began his murderous raids on the defenceless peasantry of South Cork. The reaction was predictable. Lord Muskerry and other leading recusants were driven to combine; more than a thousand dispossessed families, all of whom owed their unhappiness to Lord Cork, instantly swelled their ranks.

The same anger, the one the outraged clans of the Pale had long known, now began to infuse the remaining Catholic Lords. They were waking to the fact they had been submissive for far too long, that they had endured too much in a well-meant but ultimately vain hope of peace.

*

In Dublin, it took but a simple bribe for Donal O'Donovan and Finbar O'Driscoll to take the place of the drovers on a delivery wagon and enter the Castle's Great Court. Dressed as farmers, they drove to the kitchen block, unloaded their merchandise and turned their cart around. It was raining in the castle yard and nobody wanted to be in the open air any longer than necessary. Bryen, looking for all the world like an English gentleman in his doublet, a rapier on his hip and a pistol in his sash, had long released himself from the cart's undercarriage and vanished nimbly into the shadows.

All the vital information concerning Lord Castlehaven's cell had been learned in the Bridge Tavern the previous night. The Castle Guards liked to drink there. Their quarry, Bryen, Donal and Finbar soon discovered, was in the Bermingham Tower. That was a lucky break, as at the base of this tower was that little gate above the moat that had, a generation before, been the path to freedom for Red Hugh O'Donnell. There was a chance, of course, that the portal had been closed off, or that extra sentries might have been posted. The latter was unlikely. No escape had been attempted through the moat in forty years. In January the Poddle water was icy. It was said that just four minutes' immersion would be lethal.

That door would neither be locked nor bricked up, the Irishmen reasoned. The castle servants still had to clear the green, reportedly poisonous algae from the moat. The Poddle water had to be readied for drinking.

Then there was the inescapable fact that the Castle did not consider Castlehaven to be a sinister or even a real danger to the English *imperium*. While he had been on their side, volunteering to support English interests in Munster while Sir Phelim was ravaging Ulster, he had not been paid the compliment of a command. The Lords Justice had simply not taken him seriously. Now they had him, ready for export to London and the axe. Lazily they had posted a tired guard to his chambers in the tower and even that guard was not always there. His noble prisoner regularly sent the Castle servant into Dublin to fetch provisions, often of an alcoholic nature, enticing the exchange with a small coin.

No one in the Castle suspected for an instant that the Irish would be idiotic enough to attempt a rescue. Everyone knew that the Old English and the Gaels could barely bring themselves to speak to one another and, if no Gael would dare attempt the Castle, the Old English were loyal to their supposed home country.

They had not reckoned on Captain Bryen MacDonogh. He was a twenty-five year old with Old English connections to his Celtic line. He was also extremely agile.

At the bottom of the Bermingham Tower, Bryen stopped to ask a sentry a question.

'This is the right address for Lord Castlehaven, my good fellow?' he asked in English.

'It certainly is, Sir,' came the reply.

'I have a package for his lordship. A game pie from Mr Bellamy. His favourite.'

'You'd better take it up, sir. His apartments are on the first floor. You can give the package to his guard, or leave it by the door to his rooms.'

'Thank you, my man. Here's sixpence for your trouble.'

'Thank you, Sir, and may Providence himself bestow His blessings upon you.'

Bryen arrived at the door to Castlehaven's 'apartments' but found it secured with a bolt and padlock. There was a chair for his guard but no sign of its occupant. He was probably negotiating some wine in the city, far beyond the Castle walls.

Bryen reflected for a moment on the ironic certainty that the prisoner was more comfortably housed than his warden. His 'cell' was a suite of well-furnished rooms.

'Please stand well away from the door, Lord Castlehaven.'

'Is that you, Bryen?'

'Yes, Sir. Are you standing clear? This will take a few minutes. In the meantime, put on your warmest clothes. We have to do a little swimming.'

Bryen took the gunpowder charges from his parcel – each in the pre-weighed cartouches used to load the business end of a musket – and pressed them all around the door, beneath it and, especially, close to the hinges.

He then opened a couple more and poured a trail of black powder to the top of the stairs where he could safely shelter from the blast.

A tinderbox lit the trail.

The next second, a hiss and a flame moved at lightning speed across the floor, followed by percussion as the flame leapt from charge to charge. The landing filled with sulphurous smoke, and Bryen heard cheers from the captives below and above.

The front door to the tower had opened, and the guard was running up the stairs.

'Are you all right, Sir?' asked the unsuspecting and kindly fool, before going to the prisoner's door. Bryen stepped aside and behind the soldier, from where he could bring his flintlock down smartly on the crown of a hapless head. The blow broke the poor man's skin and his blood flowed freely. That meant he was still alive, but the poor fellow was in for the worst of headaches when he recovered his wits.

Bryen moved back to Castlehaven's door. The charge has done its work.

As he pulled it open, Lord Castlehaven pushed from the other side.

'Don't bother talking to me,' said the earl as his door fell crashing down. 'I won't hear anything for a week! Why didn't you just call a locksmith?'

'There's no time for banter. My God, your clothes!'

'I didn't have time to pack, Bryen. That kindly warden asleep over there lent them to me…'

'… and that beard of yours! You haven't shaved since your arrest? Hang on, our Lord didn't shave, did he? I don't recall any mention of shaving in the scriptures. You look exactly like a Puritan…'

Bryen had had an idea. He really didn't fancy a swim in the icy moat.

'Grab one of your books, my lord, a small one, one of those designed to fit in a greatcoat pocket. Read it to me while we walk. There is no-one about in any case and we will look like a gentleman and his preacher. Our friends are waiting for us outside the Cork Gate. Just look relaxed as we walk past the guards. They'll suspect nothing. People here are checked on the way in, not on the way out.'

James Castlehaven did exactly as he was told. Plausibly imitating a bearded Parliamentarian lecturing a pious student on some arcane spiritual issue, the couple weren't even challenged. They walked clear of the castle to find O'Donovan and O'Driscoll just below the gate, exactly where they were supposed to be.

As they drove off towards Laragh, deep in the Wicklow Hills, where friends would give them food and shelter, O'Donovan and O'Driscoll listened to the story of the Great Escape from Ireland's most secure dungeon and fell about with laughter.

They were well clear of Dublin before the alarm was even raised.

Once rested and fed, the party would break up. The two west coast Irish chiefs would return to their castles beside the ocean. Lord Castlehaven would make his way to the Waterford town of Kilkenny. That town had already declared for the insurgents and he would be safe there.

Bryen would return to Kanturk. He had a great tale to share with his parents.

*

'The Earl of Castlehaven escaped from Dublin Castle?' Cliona put down her copy of *The Spy Glass*. 'Was not Finbar O'Driscoll's old house called Castlehaven?'

'It was, yes, but it's not Finbar's old house any longer.' Her husband, the ninth Lord of Duhallow, had been completing his correspondence. 'Not for the last forty years or so. Between the Saxons and the Spanish it was lucky that any of the fabric survived the Battle of Kinsale. A year or so after that, a semi-piratical English Sea captain tried to take the slighted castle from O'Driscoll Mór, and by force. 'For the queen', that's what he said. Finbar's father put up quite a struggle, not quitting until the naval guns had so damaged the place it had become uninhabitable. Only then did the sea-captain back off, but it was too late. Finbar was forced to auction the wreck, in London. It was bought, unseen, by an elderly, rich Englishman. A certain George Touchet, the eleventh Lord Audley, who soon became the first Earl of Castlehaven.'

'That name rings a bell?'

'So it should. When you were a very little girl, and while I was at school in France, Audley was Governor of Kells. He fought us at Kinsale, was wounded, and both Lords Mountjoy and Cork endorsed his gallantry. He did well out of it. The O'Driscolls, on the other hand, were reduced to a clutch of castles, at Baltimore and on the three nearby islands of Cape Clear, Sherkin and Heir.'

'Is that the man that Bryen has rescued?'

'No. Bryen has rescued his grandson, James. This Castlehaven is around thirty-five years old.'

'Why does this James Castlehaven not live in the land of his ancestors, Dermod Oge?'

'He had to come here, to the sporting estate he already owned in County Meath. Then he sold all he had in England. A great part of his considerable fortune was ploughed into the wrecked pile on the coast.'

'He was exiled here? Is that what you're saying?'

'The reason you do not know the story is that it is too shocking to have been told to you. James's father Mervyn was convicted of, how shall we say, indecent acts with a stableboy and found guilty of a torrid crime. He was beheaded on Tower Hill. The charges against him were brought by that very James whom Bryen has rescued.'

'That's awful!'

'The tale has the flavour of Greek tragedy. It gets worse, too. The unnatural page testified under oath that the Countess of Castlehaven 'was the wickedest woman in the world, and had more to answer for than any woman that lived'.'

'Was the charge justified?' Cliona asked her husband, her hand over her mouth.

'The severity of the sentence on the second earl reflected the countess's extravagant and flagrant adultery. She was at least her husband's equal in immorality. Fear of scandal and ridicule is why James could never return to England.'

'And Bryen is now close to the product of such sin?'

'Charity, dear Cliona. James is wholly innocent of his parents' crimes. The high court could see that. Just two years after his father's execution, James Touchet had the English Barony of Audley and its associated estates restored to him and his heirs for ever.'

'And he is a Catholic, an Irish patriot? Can we call him an Irishman?'

'A real Catholic yes, but a convert Irishman. I'm not sure how far we should trust him. After all, it was his own indiscretion that led to his arrest.

*

CHAPTER FIVE
MUNSTER RISES

In February, 1642, the proud castle at the heart of the City of Kilkenny, was arguably the strongest fortress in Ireland. It was staffed and surrounded by Irishmen who owed their lives and livelihood to the Butler clan, as they had for centuries. It never had and never was going to fall to any threat.

Its incumbent, at this time, was the Catholic chief, Lord Mountgarrett.

His lordship was all too well aware that elsewhere in his province, fellow Catholics were being harassed by armed Puritan zealots, carrying out 'punitive' raids. He was convinced that the wind that blew over the Catholics of Ireland was from the east, where the chill wind of Calvary arose.

He ached to teach these vigilantes a lesson, knowing that the Lord President of Munster's ability to fight a war was gravely compromised by its chronic lack of men and ordnance.

That evaluation was tested when he marched his Irish army west from Kilkenny, in a show of force, to a people who desperately needed reassuring.

When news of this expedition reached Doneraile, thirty miles west of Cork City. St Leger dashed off a panicky message to the Earl of Cork in his own great seat at Lismore.

> May it please your lordship,
> We face a clear and present danger.
> I have to question our ability to oppose Lord Mountgarrett.
> Our foot are inconsiderable and of wretched composure. Their condition is so dire that I dare not adventure anything upon them. All that we have to rely upon are the corralling skills of our horse.
> Your practical support is needed more than ever, if only to supplement our divine purpose and realise the loyal ambitions of your servant and friend,
> Wm St Leger

Lord Broghill could not withhold a smile as he read Sir William's letter out loud to his father, the Earl of Cork, in Lismore's great dining hall.

Broghill had in military skill all that his famous father had in political. He was confident that if he completed the dismantling of the remaining Popish landholdings, the English government would handsomely reward him, just as it had his father.

His father had ensured his elevation to his barony. Of his wits, no one had any doubt. The boy had attended Trinity College, Dublin, was articled at Gray's Inn in London and had completed his demanding education in France and Italy. He even lodged in Geneva with Giovanni Diodati, the Calvinist theologian and *quondam* translator of the Bible.

On his return to England, his elder brother Richard, the first Earl of Burlington, arranged for his presentation at Court. Broghill arranged to attend the king at Berwick, during the first Bishop's War and was awarded command of a troop of horse under Lord Northumberland.

In keeping with his courtly pretensions, in January 1641, Broghill married Lady Margaret Howard, a daughter of the Earl of Suffolk. It was a hugely advantageous marriage and brought him a substantial dowry, sufficient to allow him to buy an estate at Marston Bigod in Somerset. The fact that Lady Margaret was Catholic must have lent a bitter sweetness to his wedding bed.

'How cunningly the fox phrases his begging letter', Lord Cork exclaimed. If Broghill thought St Leger a fool, his father analysed its contents more thoroughly. 'Realistically, we have no choice but to help.'

Dinners at Lismore were always events – Lord Boyle was not merely a potentate, he had fourteen children after all, but Lismore Castle's dining hall, in which the Boyles were now gathered, was truly splendid. Boyle's chief seat was the doyen of Ireland's 'grand old places'.

The castle was almost impossibly old. Monks had built their first refuge there in the eighth century after Christ. Nearly four hundred years later, in 1185, King John had castellated it. It became a palace-monastery until the Dissolution.

When the Benedictines were evicted, the demesne awarded to Sir Walter Raleigh by his grateful queen. From the outset, Raleigh meant to impress. Chapter houses and dorters, the abbot's lodgings - these appurtenances made for an easy conversion into the stateliest of mansions. Nor during the intervening centuries, was its fabric neglected.

On Raleigh's fall, Richard Boyle, the first Earl of Cork, acquired it for a song. He celebrated immediately by hiring a regiment of landscape gardeners to lay out the eight acres that lay within its outer defensive walls. They were now mature and had become the finest gardens in Ireland.

Lismore's principal apartments were not just decorated with tapestry hangings, embroidered silks and velvet. Over every head, elaborate fretwork plaster ceilings reminded every guest of Boyle's rise to riches.

The men in the party eschewed military dress, even though it was becoming the fashion. Lismore's house rules required every man to dress as for the country. Linen and silk, from hose to doublet, reinforced their peaceful message. Their women demurely wore damask and lace.

Those peaceable women were, however, not afraid to voice their opinions.

'St Leger is grossly overrated', said Lady Margaret, 'and he's clumsy on a horse.'

'I'd say he is a brave and martial man, well able to act all the parts of a governor,' the earl stiffly replied.

'Nevertheless,' Lady Broghill continued, 'St Leger hasn't the force to silence his enemy with the sword. His cunning plan, 'attrition' he calls it, is to round 'em up and string 'em up. Without an army, this form of war will eventually lose the day unless, of course, he executes every Catholic in Ireland. Mark my words, 'attrition' will lead to so much revulsion, here and abroad, that in the long run it will be the undoing of the Anglo-Irish.'

'He'll certainly need a helping hand if he is to confront Lord Moungarrett's five thousand. I'll persuade Lords Barrymore and Dungarvan to follow suit and join him.' While Broghill appeared to agree with his wife, she felt he had missed the subtlety of her point.

'By all means, Husband. You have my blessing. Take all our men. But do be careful: Mountgarrett is a dangerous enemy and on his own turf he can only win.'

The two sides met at Killmallock. In more of a minor skirmish than a classic set-piece battle, St Leger's Protestant captains came through the day victorious. The losses were negligible on either side. After the engagement, Lord Mountgarrett returned safely to his seat at Kilkenny, where the Catholic nobleman was impregnable. He had seen the need to reorder his army.

In the meantime, England would be still. Reports of the Catholic nobility's support for the enemy spurred Parliament into action. The Long Parliament decided rescue Protestant Ireland. A thousand English foot soldiers made the dangerous crossing and arrived in Dublin's docks, under the reliable Sir Simon Harcourt. Then, in February, the port of Wexford saw Sir Richard Grenville arrive with four hundred horse. Towards the end of the month, Lieutenant-Colonel George Monk[xiii] would join the fray, commanding Lord Leicester's personal regiment of fifteen hundred men.

The mercury was rising.

*

The mounting numbers of Protestant English soldiers encouraged vast numbers of Catholic 'rebels' to rise. Warriors emerged from who knows where. They were sufficient to put every English station on the Cork coast under siege simultaneously, and such co-ordination threw all Protestant Ireland into a place between consternation and panic.

One such coastal garrison was Youghal, where the Recorder, Joshua Boyle, had his head in his hands.

'We are surrounded by rovers, tories and woodkerne,' he told a distinguished gentleman who had just arrived by sea. 'If that weren't bad enough, Lord Dungarvan has just brought us a hundred and forty English soldiers, whom he rounded up on a hill outside Cork City. The soldiers are penniless, starving and unarmed. They appear to have deserted, but Dungarvan spared their lives and deposited them on us.'

'I'm not sure I understand your complaint, Sir. Is that you will have to feed them?'

Sir Charles Vavasour, to whom he was pouring out his heart, had brought with him a rather fitter complement: a thousand fresh and rested English soldiers and some modest supplies.

'It is exactly that, Sir Charles. We now have fifteen companies to feed, and no food other than salt beef, a little barrelled butter and some bread. All there is to drink is cold water. Our buttermilk long ago ran out. Such meagre rations make for a rich churchyard and a weak garrison.'

'I have barely enough for my own men, Mr Boyle. How long do you believe it will take the Lord President, or your uncle the Earl of Cork, to come to our aid?'

'I cannot say. A week, perhaps? Then we will be safe and sound. Two weeks and we shall no longer be sound. Three and we'll be dead.'

In the event it would take rather longer than that. In late March Youghal was at last relieved.

To every citizen's surprise and delight, St Leger had fought his way into Youghal, scattering the Catholic besiegers in all directions. The siege was over. The starving Protestant inhabitants cheered their Lord President to the rafters.

St Leger was formally received by Joshua Boyle, Sir Charles, and the town council. They selected the tastier elements of the general relief and used them to throw a banquet.

90

'My apologies for being a little late for this excellent repast. I had to pause my journey at Dungarvan, take the Fort and hang its occupiers - at least those that failed to run bare-arsed into the forests.'

'You know, my dear fellow,' Sir Charles declaimed to St Leger, 'that was a stout effort. I am delighted to meet such a grand and gallant fellow. Mind you, the way the ground lies round here is purpose-built for soldiering. It may interest you to know that before setting sail from Bristol, I made it my business to study Youghal and its topography. Only then did I agree to come and save you all. I'll wager you didn't know, by way of example, Youghal's name derives from two Irish words: *eo*, which signifies a yew, and *cahu*, a wood. It's where the River Avonmore, or Broadwater, or Blackwater, or whatever, drains into the sea. Apparently this river was anciently called *Nemh*, or *Niamh* in the Irish idiom. Now, admit it. Ain't that interesting?'

'Utterly fascinating, Sir Charles,' said St Leger. 'Mr Boyle, how are you faring here in Youghal?'

'Youghal's coffers are almost empty, my Lord President. During the siege we paid greedy Irish sea-borne merchants far too much for their goods from our depleted treasury. Such extortion has drained us dry.'

'Yet you possess warehouses full of corn. Couldn't you have paid them from there?'

'Let me make a suggestion, gentlemen.' Sir Charles had had another idea. 'If you lack the means to secure the wine I need to wash down my supper, or some small beers to keep up the spirits of my men, you should ease the pressure with a quantity of freshly minted coin. That's what we'd do in England. Strike some 'siege pieces'.'

Joshua Boyle was amazed. Vavasour had actually made an intelligent suggestion. He immediately agreed.

Crude 'farthings of necessity' were struck. A few were made of silver; most were of copper, brass, lead or pewter. While mostly circular, those that weren't were octagonal, square or triangular. They bore a date, 1642, the name of Youghal and the city's armorial bearings.

'Impressive. They'll be collectors' pieces one day,' said Sir Charles, proud of himself. 'I'll take a few pounds' worth back home with me when my business here is done.'

There was indeed plenty to do.

Runners brought the news that the Catholics had reassembled at Killeagh, William Boyle's seat, yet another member of Lord Cork's extensive family and Joshua's cousin. Lord Cork had appointed him

91

'famine commissioner' for Co. Cork. With the position came the right to warehouse the county's foodstuffs, for a fee, and a very profitable deal it was too. William did his job diligently and, in recognition of his services, he was promoted to sheriff, a post that actually carried a salary to even out his variable commission. He spent his money wisely, constructing an enormous castle, only slightly less imposing than Lismore. Unfortunately, its very existence seemed to annoy the natives.

At last, his long run of good fortune ran out. Now all William Boyle had to do was to look out of his mullioned windows to see Lord Castlehaven's tents and a determined army of two thousand rebels.

*

That Easter, Dromsicane Castle caught Dermod Oge with something on his mind. Perhaps it was the article he had just read in *The Spy Glass*, for he put the paper down and crossed to an oak table to pour himself a whiskey. He then, almost as an afterthought, poured one for his eldest son, Bryen.

He carried it over to the fireplace, where Bryen had been warming himself. Spring had started with a frost and the 'little ice age', as local people liked to call it, looked likely to last a lot longer.

'Bryen, did you ever notice any changes in Lord Inchiquin? I mean, while you were in England together. You mentioned the two of you were comrades-in-arms, but since your return he rather seems to have embraced Coote's rather muscular brand of Protestantism.'

'No, father, at the time I can't say I did. Like his father, he was an Anglican went he went to England. Not especially devout, I thought, like most Anglicans. Mind you, looking back, while we were facing the Scots he found time to talk to the Calvinist chaplain. Aside from one telling remark I thought little of it.'

'A telling remark?'

Bryen concentrated.

'Yes. Just the one. He said that he thought that Almighty God was working with him. I told him that Lord Jesus loves each and every one of us, but he replied that he meant God the Creator, not our Lord and Judge, and that the Grace of His love had chosen the vessel of his very own heart to work upon. Other than being an odd turn of phrase, I thought little of it at the time. Only later did I realise that it was slightly heretical. God's Grace does not select particular individuals, we are all His children and it shines equally upon us all. Our choice is only to see it.'

'Quite so. Do you esteem him as a soldier? As an officer? A Grecian?'

'A Grecian? Odd that you should use that word. Yes father, I do. He is a brilliant soldier. Strategic and decisive. But a Grecian? If so, it is because he is a committed player in our national drama. He will now attempt to destroy families like ours. My tragedy is that he should have been one of my greatest friends and will instead become one of my most bitter enemies.'

*

In the Palace of Westminster, the Long Parliament passed and the king signed an 'Act for the Reduction of Ireland'. Adventurers were invited to submit money to suppress the Rebellion. In exchange they would be guaranteed land, just as soon as it could be taken from the natives. Private soldiers, too, would earn a shilling a month. If they served long enough, they would also be permitted to dispossess an Irish family, even two. That should be incentive enough. Accordingly, but slowly, this band began to gather in Bristol Harbour. Lord Wharton was awarded its command, but the order to embark seemed to take its time. Wharton paced up and down the hard, eagerly awaiting his chance in Ireland. He meant Parliamentary mischief.

Meanwhile the House of Commons was drafting a Militia Bill, designed to allow Parliament to nominate a Lord Lieutenant in every county of England, Scotland and Ireland. This would be a rival to the Royal appointee. Every such parliamentarian would be required to raise a county regiment in the defence of Protestant interests.

On Tuesday March 1, a courier brought the Bill to the palace for Royal Assent. The king glanced at it and snorted. In his later response to the Commons the hostility of his immediate refusal was not even thinly veiled.

Pym soon saw a way around the royal obstacle. Parliament passed it as a 'Militia Ordinance', a law without royal assent. The obstinacy of the king had been side-stepped. It occurred to some that the monarchy itself might be similarly bypassed. Parliament had taken something semi-mystical from its sacred institution.

That same afternoon, Pym called into Speaker's House. He congratulated the Commons on a splendid decision, but he had admonition on his mind.

'Sir John, you cannot order Wharton to set sail!' the speaker said plainly.

Sir William Lenthal, the Speaker of the House, was beside himself. 'The king has issued his own version of our 'Commissions of Array' to the gentlemen of the shires. He has ordered your Militia Ordinance set aside. He has begun to muster forces for a new Royal Army. Our army cannot go to Ireland, not yet in any case! It may yet be needed at home to serve against His Majesty.'

The possibility of unspeakable catastrophe, nothing less than Civil War, had at last been voiced. That dawn saw the raw and bloody fingers of a new and unpredictable age draw back the night.

'I think we had better exercise our rights as Privy Councillors and have an audience of the king. It's time we insisted on our Nineteen Propositions,' said Sir John Pym.

'He'll never sign,' Sir William Lenthal replied. 'He has already refused to acknowledge the mildest one, the one which requires the king to place his children's upbringing and marriages into Parliament's care.'

'He'll have to. Do you believe he has not noticed Wharton's army? If it sailed for Ireland he would be tempted to do something right royally rash in England.'

'We could perhaps sacrifice our demands on the succession if he'll sign the others?' agreed the Speaker.

'Good idea. After some pretended reluctance, I'll agree to drop it - provided the others are agreed.'

The strategy was sound, and the king was duly outwitted. He did as he was told.

*

As her husband and eldest son came into the curtilage of Dromsicane Castle, Millstreet, Co Cork, Cliona put her basket down and her hands on her hips. Freshly cut aconites, bluebells and croci for the dining parlour would have to wait a moment longer.

'Dermod Oge,' said Cliona in her most disapproving voice, as they went into the small parlour, 'my kinsman Donogh MacCarthy and his wife Lady Margaret are due to arrive here this morning, stay for a whole week, and both you and Bryen look like you've been digging potatoes.'

Dermod Oge kissed his supposedly cross wife on her brow.

'We have been wildfowling. Just how should we look?'

'Go and put on your best clothes immediately, the both of you. Donogh will be dressed as befits a prince and I would like you to provide him with some competition. He is called the *Buchaill Bán*, the fair-haired boy, at least by his kin. He's immensely good-looking.'

'Good-looking, is he? So we must put on our finery? To avoid his feeling overdressed?'

'He is entitled to respect. He is a viscount nowadays. Lord Muskerry no less. As a peer of the king he needs to be treated appropriately.'

'I liked him better when he was plain old Donogh MacCarthy.'

'Rightly, and he should have stayed that way. Things changed when his elder brother died a couple of years ago and he succeeded to his title. His mother will tell you soon enough.'

'His mother is coming too? Things are getting better. No doubt she has some English title?'

'His mother, Lady Eleanor, is Lord Thurles's daughter.'

'Right. That makes her important then?'

'It does make her the sister of James Butler, the Marquess of Ormonde. Donogh Muskerry, therefore, is nothing less than Lord Ormonde's nephew. The Lieutenant-General of England's army in Ireland, in case the name is unfamiliar.'

'Phew.' Dermod Oge smiled teasingly. 'And his wife, whom you say is called Lady Margaret. Remind me?'

'Lady Margaret is Ulrick Clanrickarde's daughter. He is the chief of the Burkes. That's why you must both get dressed. I don't want her to think we are threadbare peasants.'

'What you are really thinking about, my darling, is that Muskerry is bringing his daughters. Will you forgive me for observing that we have two sons, Bryen and Donogh, who need marrying off?'

Cliona blushed. 'Dermod Oge MacDonogh,' she declared, 'may I not be permitted to scheme a little in my own house?'

'May I join your pleasant little chat?' came a voice from the window.

Bryen was naturally averse to the role of a shuttlecock in someone else's game of badminton.

'In no way am I averse to marriage but I will have some say as to when and with whom,' he declared. 'Besides, Muskerry's daughters may be hideous. I intend to love my wife for all of my life and with all of my heart. Beauty is vital to convert an affectionate man into a lover. I cannot marry otherwise, no matter how well-connected my bride.'

'Well said, Bryen MacDermod Oge,' said his father, while slipping an arm around his wife. 'You are a chip off an old block. If they are hideous, as you put it, we shall just have to tell them to take their dubious charms elsewhere.'

*

The king had resumed residence in Whitehall Palace. His unruly Parliament was, as usual, in need of royal management.

95

'Find the queen and beg her to wait on us at her convenience', the king told his Gentleman of the Wardrobe. The rather aristocratic footsteps of the 'servant' padded gracefully into the distance. She could be anywhere in this maze of buildings they called a palace.

In the meantime, the king paced up and down the gallery.

His affection for his Parliament came and went. Mostly the latter. Perhaps it could still be rekindled? Perhaps if he enacted Sir John Pym's Adventurers Bill, Parliament might warm to him. That would be a start. The bill had been before him for months.

The door was opened by two footmen and the petite person of Queen Henrietta-Maria came into the room. As she saw her husband she curtseyed, but not to the ground. More of a bob, in fact. He, for his part, bowed with cavalier swagger.

'Hen, there you are; prettier than ever. Hen, darling, I hope you've been eating fox sandwiches like dad's Steenie used to - I need you to be at your brainiest. Here's today's question; why won't Parliament simply do my bidding?'

'It may be, King of Angels, that you alternate between magnanimous royal concession and stubborn Stuart intractability. At least, that's what they say. Perhaps you should do more of the first and less of the second.'

'You win. I'll sign Pym's wretched bill. The one designed to bring Ireland in on Parliament's reel.'

'If you do that you'll astonish everybody, even your supporters. I mean, they'll respect your wisdom even more than they do now. My English is so poor.'

'I do intend to mollify Parliament. Pym says I am too headstrong to heed well-meant advice, by which he means his. I will make him eat his words.'

'What would Buckingham have said, were he still with us?'

'He'd have told me that Pym's abominable Act was an essay in tyranny. It promises huge estates in Ireland, still to be confiscated from their legitimate owners, and for whom? To any speculator willing to finance a company of men. All civilisations since the dawn of time have condemned licensing greed as a political tool, all correctly considering it an act worthy of savages. This has been the consensus among the educated since the days when the British painted themselves in wode. Saying that, every one of them has done it.'

'Husband mine, you must think more carefully than ever. My servants, when they think I'm out of earshot, speak of the danger of Civil

War. In that awful event, all your peoples would be forced to take sides and, *faut de mieux*, kill each other.'

'Hen, these are desperate times. No one knows that as well as I. Our three Kingdoms – Ireland, England and the Scots - are at daggers drawn. The nightmare of mutual slaughter is depriving six million men, women and children of their sleep.'

'You must comfort them. In France we have had such wars. Neighbours, fathers and sons engaged each other in battle, and only a few generations ago. Whether on the right or wrong side, in a civil war half the population has to be defeated.'

'Hen,' the king said sadly, his voice lowered, 'can it really be that Parliament, Monarchy and the Church are so useless that they could allow the British Isles to tear its own heart to pieces?'

'The Church?'

'The Anglican Church. Currently useless. Since Parliament impeached Laud of Canterbury and imprisoned him in the Tower, we have no archbishop.'

'So what are your plans?'

'I intend to drum up support in the east and the midlands, despite the protests of Parliament. No one can know if I will carry the day, but I mean to do my best. You must know that both Houses have agreed a motion that the 'kingdom should be put in a posture of defence'.'

'What can that mean?'

'It means, Hen, that Parliament believes itself to be morally superior, to both King and Church. It believes it has the right – the duty, even – to manage every strand of public life. Instead of concerning itself with raising taxes it has come to believe it should legislate on every and any subject. It denies the Church's ownership of morality and believes itself justified in listening to people's hearts, even punishing them when they transgress. It has extended the definition of a crime from the act to the thought that preceded it.'

'Darling King, you must harness the mystery attaching to the notion of royalty. You must enhance it with your charm, your erudition, the sheer force of your personality. Do that and add in a few well-targeted threats as well.'

With his queen's words ringing in his ears, the first leg of his charm offensive took him to Newmarket and thence to Royston. The plan was to continue on to the Midlands.

Mercifully the King was very well received, wherever he went. Hundreds (though not thousands) of loyal subjects told him their lives were his to dispose of as he saw fit.

Among his admirers, however, the local Members of Parliament were conspicuous by their absence.

Parliament had sent the counties a 'declaration'.

It listed a dozen reasons why they should thenceforward ignore royal authority. It bore Sir Edward Coke's signature and, predictably, at the top of that list was *Magna Carta*. The liberty they enjoyed, the paper argued, was due to Parliament, the real sovereign in England. That was its repeated phrase. Parliament is sovereign.

When the King heard of their declaration, he denounced it. His language was exquisite in its rhetoric, its turns of phrase and its consummate eloquence. It was, however, wasted on many and, of course, the rift with Parliament only deepened.

*

If the Irish felt that danger was knocking at the door, in England it had already forced its way inside.

The boundary between the north and south had long been decreed to be at Stamford, Lincolnshire. When the king and his court had progressed as far as Burghley House, seat of the Governor of the North, the king warned his subjects not to obey Parliament's illegal Militia Ordinance. His message was gloomily received.

To calm his host's delicate Protestant nerves (and to defuse the ubiquitous rumours that the king was some sort of covert Catholic – the charge that had led to Laud's impeachment) he again proclaimed that the laws against recusant Catholics were to be applied unbendingly.

By March 19 the king had progressed to the walled and royalist city of York. He planned to rule his kingdoms from here, at least until the storm clouds blew over.

His wife's words bore in his head. 'Wars are not won by surrendering', she had told him, 'but by staying at the helm.'

He summoned the Northern Council of Nobles to York's Merchant Adventurers' Hall, a magnificent building close by the Shambles. A throne had been placed at one end of the hall and faced the standing nobles who had gathered to pay their sovereign homage. The hatchment of every northern family hung from the walls, as they had since the chamber had been built in 1357. Here and there, a shield remembered a family who had gone extinct; the Black Death and the

Wars of the Roses had taken a terrible toll on the aristocracy of old. Some other families, unknown in the fourteenth century, had been ennobled by the Tudors. Their coats of arms, however, were not yet there. No one had thought to change the escutcheons; families with pedigrees of merely a century's antiquity were *arriviste*.

The Sheriff of York, bowing like mad to everyone there, indicated that the nobles present 'should attend His Majesty with their ears'. Then he bowed to the king, so deeply that a gust of wind might have toppled him. Then, as he backed away, His Majesty King Charles had the floor.

'Noble cousins,' the king began. 'We are grateful for your courtesy in receiving us in this your fine hall, built, we are told, in the time of our forebear King Edward III.

'The reason why we have commanded your presence before us today will be obvious. War threatens our kingdoms and we are bent on peace.'

The king was rewarded with a burst of loyal applause.

'Our reading of the Florentine philosopher Machiavelli,' Charles pressed on, 'has taught us that if we wish for peace we must prepare for war. Parliament has passed the 'Adventurers Act', pledging Irish land to those who raise money to suppress them. We believe that this Bill, while we were constrained to enact it, will guarantee that the contagion that provoked the Irish into rising, will spread throughout this Kingdom too. Parliament has become an *agent provocateur*. Indeed, we have learned this day that in our Irish Kingdom, the borough of Galway has declared for the rebels. Nevertheless, even Galway has made an arrangement with our trusty cousin the Earl of Clanrickarde, most loyal to our person, that he should retain control and discourage attacks on our soldiers.

'Further to our peaceful purpose, we always try to be conciliatory in our answer to Parliament's 'declaration'. We call it our 'Repudiation'. We are grateful to our secretary Edward Hyde for his skills in penmanship. We believe the publication of our Repudiation will encourage wavering royalists to view us in a more favourable light. We also hope they will finally see that it is Sir John Pym whose ambition will destroy this kingdom. This knight, so much a beneficiary of our nation's largesse, has espoused the marble-hearted fiend of legend, Ingratitude Incarnate.'

A door at the back of the hall had been opened quietly. A boy, gorgeously dressed, came into the room. He wore gloves, spurs, a sword and a great hat with a wide brim, a vast cockade of feathers tucked into its band.

When the lad raised it to the king, magnificent dark curls fell over his shoulders and his handsome young face. It was fleshier than his father's, and caught the light.

'We are pleased to welcome our younger son James to our court. He is duke of this City, Shire and County of York. In the literal sense, therefore, we are his guest, not he ours. It is sweeter than a sugarloaf to have a handsome loving child, and the prince brings the welcome news that Parliament has just received a petition from Lancastershire or, as its people will have it, Lancashire, rejecting the Parliamentarian Lord Wharton's appointment as Lord Lieutenant of that county. Instead, they have chosen our friend and trusted cousin Lord Strange. We also welcome to our gathering our right honourable friend William Seymour, Marquess of Hertford. Lord Hertford is one of our most influential landowners in the West of England and has the practical means of preserving its loyalty.'

Hertford stood, bowed to the king and acknowledged the applause of the northern nobility.

'God bless you all,' the king continued. 'Lord Hertford will move among you and agree your contributions to our divinely appointed realm. Go in peace, love God and fear thy king.'

*

Cliona's curtsey took her to the stone floor of Dromsicane Castle's hall. Only her gaze did not dip. Just inside the Great Door of the vast tower house at Dromsicane was a tall and striking blond man in extravagant court dress, bearing a French, basket-handled rapier, making a splendid entrance. A little over forty years old, he was younger than either Dermod Oge or Cliona.

'The Lady of Duhallow,' Lord Muskerry surmised silkily. 'My all-time favourite chatelaine! How grand it is to see you again.' He took her hand and drew her back to her feet.

'Dear noble cousin,' replied Cliona, now at her full height. Without letting Muskerry release her hand, she twisted slightly and addressed the woman on his arm. 'Lady Eleanor. How privileged we all are!'

Lady Eleanor Clancarty leant forward and let Cliona kiss her cheek. To her right, Dermod Oge nodded his court bow. To her left, Bryen and Donogh bowed from the waist. Their sister Caitlín bobbed gracefully.

Lady Margaret Muskerry and her four children came up behind.

'Thank you, cousin,' said Lady Margaret, kissing Dermod Oge, Cliona, Bryen, Donogh and Caitlín in formal order of precedence. 'Thank you so much for allowing us to stay in your charming little castle. I do hope so large a company will not prove an uncomfortable drain on your resources?'

It was indeed a large party.

Twelve horsemen had brought the Muskerrys to Dromsicane, not from their fortress at Blarney but from Carrigadrohid, their magical castle on a bridge. Some of their horses looked fit for any purpose. Their captain, Eoghan MacEgan, they were instructed, would also join the household for the week.

'Bryen,' commanded Dermod Oge. 'You are to show Lord Muskerry's escort the stables. Once their chargers are boxed, find his men suitable bedding in the soldiers' quarters. Oh yes, be back as soon as you can.' He turned to Muskerry. 'It may be a little crowded but I'm sure your guards will manage.'

Lord and Lady Muskerry handed their capes and hats to Kevin O'Grady, the MacDonogh's factotum. The Muskerrys looked around as they passed into Dromsicane's stately stone hall. None of them had been there before. Behind them, Lord Muskerry's mother, Lady Eleanor, followed with the *lenteur* that only great age may indulge and escape censure.

Then came the Muskerry children, happily chattering to one another.

They took in the carved lozenges, the scrolls, the gilded Jacobean 'stalactites', the linenfold wainscoting, the suits of armour, the picturesque arrangements of pikes.

'Take a look at that ceiling, how fine is that…' said one.

'…and just take a peek at those tapestries,' said another.

'Welcome to our house, dear cousins,' said Cliona, gratified to have impressed.

Viscount Muskerry's two daughters – every bit as pretty as the boys had hoped – admired Caitlín's frock and made some sweet remarks about her complexion. They asked her to show them her room, the door to which led to the secret world of girls on the brink of womanhood.

The Muskerry brothers were not far off Bryen's age. Their dress suggested their purpose was more for the hunt than the military; they wore breeches, boots, short riding coats but no swords. And yes, hunting had indeed been arranged for the following day.

Cliona, a MacCarthy of Carrigaphooca and Drishane, was a cousin several times over of the MacCarthys of Blarney, Carrigadrohid, Mahallagh, Rathonoane and Knockavollig castles. The two lines had intermarried with almost unhealthy frequency since the Middle Ages, even before. They had also fought the Old English Fitzgeralds in periodic disputes over the Kingdom of Desmond. All that, however, that was all in the past.

Since the Rebellion there was no surviving rivalry, let alone enmity, between those clans. Common danger had quite blown the clouds away.

*

Pope Innocent X received a plea, delivered to the Quirinale Palace in Rome by the French ambassador to the Holy See. It was in Queen Henrietta-Maria of England's elegant hand.

'Your Eminences', the Pope told the Curia at a semiplenary meeting in the Sistine Chapel. 'We are asked by Her Majesty of England to help the Irish in their hour of need. In this letter we are begged to restore and re-establish the public exercise of our Catholic religion in the Kingdom of Ireland.'

He looked at the sea of cardinals ranged before him in that loveliest of chambers. Nothing could be read into their expressions. Perhaps they were wondering how many warships, how many legions the Holy Father might conjure up?

'We are advised that her husband and sovereign lord, Charles, is seeking to endear himself to the Puritans. Monsignor, please read out the list of sects in England.'

'Yes, Holiness. We have listed Ranters, Baptists, Libertiners, Calvinists, Adventists, Diggers, Zwingliists, Anabaptists, Sabbatarians, Millenniarists, Seventh Day Adventists, Fifth Day Monarchists, Bedel Brethren, Presbyterians, Zoroastrians, Congregationalists, Shakers, Unitarians, Quakers, Dissenters...'

'Thank you, Monsignor.' His Holiness impatiently interrupted his secretary with a sigh. 'To accommodate the deranged, the king is actively promoting a penal suppression of the sane in his westerly kingdom. All these sects you list for us hve in common is their driving and inflexible devotion to their protest *against* the liberty of conscience and the gift of free will. They share a contempt for that conjoined sacrament of confession, forgiveness and redemption that Our Lord bequeathed to us, as the way and the light that led Man to sublimate from the previous era, that of Moses. Forgive us our trespasses, He taught us, as we must forgive those who trespass against us.

'Our Lord was, is and will be the way. Following Him is the only key to the Kingdom of Heaven, if mankind is to be rescued from the ninth circle of the inferno, the torturing abyss that is the absolute absence

102

of love. We must extirpate these Protestant heresies for the sake - not of our Faith, the Word itself - but for the everlasting life of the human soul.

'From our pulpits we must demonstrate how insidious the danger of heterodoxy truly is. Encourage your priests to use local and relevant examples. They register better with the masses than does theology. Permit us to share one such example with you. Some twenty years ago, a worrying development occurred among the schismatics. Our saintly predecessor, Pope Paul V, heard of a number of little sailing craft crossing the great Spanish Main to the northern shores of the New World. While the Society of Jesus successfully ensured the southern continent remained faithful to our Holy Writ, our Doctors of the Faith and to our Triple Crown, an area equal in extent to the rest of Christendom itself has turned heretic. All can see in North America how seemingly infertile latitudinarianism eats at our flesh like a cancer. Now the Queen Consort of England entreats us to lead the Irish People to safety, but not as tributaries to the Holy See, as they were five centuries ago. Simply she begs us all in her petition to call for their prayers to be answered, that they may have the grace to submit to our divine yoke. Only in this way, she argues, will their souls achieve the incalculable, unknowable glories of Paradise.

'Your Eminences, we shall address our prayers to the Holy Spirit. We pray that we are able to communicate the divine spark that distinguishes mankind from the lower beasts, whose purpose God has restricted to loyalty, food, shelter and procreation. If Divine Will chooses to answer our prayers, as we believe He will, then the patriarchs and metropolitans, the archbishops and archimandrites of Christendom will collectively encourage the congregations of their humblest parishes to provide such mites, *denarii* or tokens which, when aggregated, shall furnish Queen Henrietta-Maria of England with considerable treasure. She is willing to take it upon herself to pass it to the appropriate pontifical ministers for local distribution.

'Your Eminences, Ireland is a Catholic country. It may even be among the most Catholic nations on Earth. As such, it merits the complete and uncompromising support that we command.'

He clapped his hands.

'Now we shall recite together the prayer that Our Lord gave us on the Mount.'

*

103

CHAPTER SIX
ST PATRICK'S DAY, 1642

It took less than an hour to show the Muskerrys and their tribe to their allocated rooms deep within Dromsicane's keep but, before anyone was quite ready, the longcase clock in the hall struck noon. Typically, O'Grady went too far, enthusiastically striking a very noisy gong, and for far too long, in an effort to hurry the guests along. Given the circumstances it was time for them to return to the stone hall where a number of trestle tables had been covered in white linen and laid for dinner, the MacDonogh's midday meal. It was St. Patrick's Day, after all. Huge efforts had been made. O'Grady had polished every last piece of MacDonogh silver until it gleamed with an intense, almost inner light. To lend charm to this impressive sight, Caitlín and Cliona had spent an hour earlier that morning arranging spring flowers, naturally including shamrocks, to decorate the spine of the table.

Four of MacDonogh's garrison would wait at table in their household livery, as would four of Muskerry's. As the guests appeared and looked for their names, the footmen had distributed themselves around the hall where they patiently stood 'stock-still', inasmuch as that word had an Irish translation.

By way of Grace, Father Boetheus declaimed a Latin salute to the national saint. Three long minutes of heartfelt piety tested their patience. At last, and after the word 'amen', they gratefully sat.

In providing her 'French' feast, Cliona had delved into her husband's past and his boyhood in France, but it was her cook who had contrived the menu from that enticing archive of memories, imagination and fine ingredients. She had delegated the choice of wines to Millot and the seasoned sea captain had expertly chosen and brought them to Dromsicane from his cellars in Honfleur.

Continental practice was adopted, though it caused some initial confusion. The meal was divided into courses. Leek and potato soup, enriched with poached oysters, was followed by slices of slow-cooked venison. The meat had been steeped overnight in sherry, or 'sack' as they called it, a wine that many remembered when Spanish customs still dominated the south and west coasts. Bowls of yellow kale, mixed with pine nuts and sesame seeds were placed as garnishes on the table, together with pea and scallion champ.

Finally, a home-grown masterpiece. Plates of a rhubarb, ginger, whiskey and custard tart were placed by the serving men in front of every guest.

Following continental practice, the guests had been required to eat their meal with a knife and fork. For most of them this was an ordeal. For the less travelled, they were difficult to manage. Warned not to eat directly from the knife, the party tried its hardest. After a struggle, and as the third course ended, they pushed them together with relief, as they had been discreetly warned to do.

It would be an economical use of English to declare it all greatly appreciated.

A gesture told the servants they had finished.

Into a satisfied murmur an ornate and enamelled silver spoon was sharply if riskily struck against a fragile hand-blown glass.

'This house is proud to welcome Lord Muskerry and his extended family', a standing Dermod Oge told his family and his guests. 'Kinsman Muskerry is the brightest star in our Munster constellation. Do you really need to know how he earned his qualifications for such an accolade? Let me give you an abbreviated account. Not in any particular order, he is my cousin, a soldier, a hero and a diplomat. We Catholics of property selected and begged the eloquent owner of the Blarney Stone to present our grievances to King Charles, the year before last. Once our case had been made, Lord Muskerry went further. He personally warned the king of the likelihood of our Rebellion.'

Lord Muskerry raised a hand to silence the applause.

'I did too,' he said. His infectious grin spread among his fellow diners. Muskerry was flattered that his reputation and history was well known, but it was time for modesty. 'It was all useless, however. His Majesty took no notice of me whatsoever.'

'Yet you ended up protecting Protestant refugees from the Catholic furies?' interjected Dermod Oge.

'Scholars term that 'dramatic irony', I believe. Not being a scholar, I should call it common humanity.' He rose to his feet. 'May I too be permitted to say a couple or words, Dermod Oge?'

Dermod Oge readily agreed. He gave way to his guest and sat down to listen.

'Madam MacDonogh, my lords, ladies and gentlemen,' said Muskerry, 'this meal has been utterly delicious. Sequencing the dishes in this way has been the stuff of genius, even if these modern *forchettes* take a little handling. Lady Margaret, please take note, we may also adopt this

French idea. Mark my words, these little dining tools will catch on, and by the time the rest of Ireland joins in we shall have outpracticed everyone except, of course, the MacDonoghs themselves.

'My visit, of course, is not merely to indulge your hospitality, exemplary as it is. It is more about the immediate danger we all face. I shall explain why presently but, before I do, I should rejoice that we, as a race, a breed and a family, have finally acquired a purpose. In truth, such a thing has eluded us since Strongbow disrupted our ancient and convivial way of life. I believe our unity to be the only means of preserving or recovering the Catholic Church in Ireland, together with the king's prerogative and the rights of our Irish nobility. Together with Garret de Barrye, a fellow veteran of the Irish Legion in Flanders, I have assumed command of the Rebellion in Munster.'

Dermod Oge's eyebrow advanced a little north across his brow.

'Even before we have created our Confederacy?' he asked, but if he was unimpressed, his family were enthusiastic. They celebrated Donogh Muskerry's braggadoccio.

'The reason, MacDonogh of Duhallow, why we need your help is because we believe we are about to be attacked with all the spite and fury the Saxon hordes can muster. We hope to enlist every Catholic Irishman, including some of you, to defend us all in our hour of need. Danger, my dear Dermod Oge, is no respecter of timetables.'

'Who may join you?' asked Cliona.

'Any Irishman. Catholic, Gaelic, Old English, Anglo-Irish, you name it. If an aggrieved Jew should be inclined to join us, I should welcome him too. Just no Protestants.'

'What about a woman?'

Cliona had asked an unexpected question.

'A woman? Cliona MacTeige, why on earth should a woman want to join us?'

'Perhaps because she believes in the Rebellion as much as you do?'

'Well, there's a thought. It's a noble cause, surely, but you should warn your female friend that the life of a soldier is mostly boring, always squalid and only occasionally interrupted by moments of terror. Any woman who wants to share that with us would be a remarkable one indeed, Madam MacDonogh. Do you really know such a woman?'

'I do know a young man who will join you.'

'Yes, you do,' cried Bryen. 'Here I am!'

'So am I,' said Donogh.

'No, Donogh, the Rebellion is not for you.' Dermod Oge was adamant. 'You have your studies to complete.' He turned to Lord

Muskerry. 'He is studying for the priesthood with the brothers of Maynooth. They are employees of the Prince of Peace.'

'Donogh MacDonogh of Duhallow,' Lord Muskerry pronounced. 'You have heard your father speak. I will have no boy soldiers in my army without their fathers' express permission, though I confess I am loathe to disappoint you.

'Everyone should know, before making a rash or disobedient decision, that Lord Ludlow, alongside Lord Broghill and Sir Hardress Waller, are campaigning in South Munster as we speak. We are not talking of princely militias, nor yet arrays of *bonnacht*, *kern* and *galloglass* as there were in our grandfathers' time. St Leger has four thousand foot and two hundred horse. My castle at Carrigadrohid may be small but since it is one of just four bridges across the Lee, it has become a very strategic target.'

He turned to speak directly to Cliona.

'Our bridge straddles a natural reservoir on the river. Unless the enemy controls it they will be unable to march from their Saxon barracks outside the walls of Cork City to Tralee or Macroom, Limerick or Kilkenny. No one can without our consent.'

He redirected his speech to Dermod Oge.

'My friends in Cork have told me the English intend to remove us. It seems we are an obstacle to the onward march of their Christian soldiers.'

Dermod Oge devined what Muskerry was asking of him.

'And you would like our support, Donogh Muskerry?' While Dermod Oge still smiled the table could hear the steel in his voice. 'Support that would compromise us in the eyes of Parliament? You want me to wager our patrimony?'

'Carrigadrohid is certainly less of a palace than here, but our own heritage matters greatly to my family. The late queen already tried to take Blarney. We have had English title to our castles and manors since 1578. My grandfather Cormac MacTeige surrendered and it was re-granted by Good Queen Bess. Your grandfather, I believe, did much the same for you.'

'The MacDonoghs will not formally join any war in Ireland unless it is legal. That is final. To do otherwise would cost our lives, and our lands would be taken by the Saxons in attainder.'

'You said 'formally', Dermod Oge?'

'Yes. I, as chief of my name, cannot accept your invitation, but should Bryen wish to join you I cannot stop him. He is a grown man and has been trained in the arts of war. Nor can I send a regiment, but if

Bryen has any friends who wish to join him in such an adventure I should not oppose him. Bryen, have you any such friends?'

'Yes, father. I have a thousand such friends.'

The table burst into applause. Donogh Muskerry walked up to Bryen and shook his hand.

'That concludes the formal part of my business here. From now, let us restrict our conversation to sweeter, pleasanter matters.'

By which he meant the hunt.

The Duhallow had scheduled one last foxhunt before preparing for the cubbing season. Bryen, as Master of Foxhounds, installed Donogh Muskerry as 'Guest Master' with a pleasant 'round' of knockabout swordplay.

The Duhallow met at the Court in Kanturk. Although the sun had burned off the scents, and the hunt did not kill, it was destined to be an astonishing day. Fully a thousand men had turned out to follow the hounds, of which sixty were mounted. It seemed that every able man in Duhallow had turned out.

No one had ever seen such a thing, ever before. It was a spectacle to match no other.

Curiously, it resembled an army on the brink of war.

*

'Carrigadrohid may be smaller than MacDonogh Court, Bryen,' Lord Muskerry remarked with a sweep of his hand, engaging his newly appointed captain in light conversation. The two of them nursed a pair of pewter noggins in front of the flaming logs. 'You will soon discover it's built on a rocky outcrop in the middle of a river. Yet in some other ways it is quite similar. Like Kanturk, we use it as a hunting lodge and it is a fine one, though in our case the sports in question are fishing and wildfowling.'

'It must bask in sunlight all the months of the year.'

'It's not the garden of Eden, Bryen, and for my sins I must confess it's haunted by the memory of a dreadful disgrace. It is where Sir James of Desmond, the White Knight, unfurled the Catholic standard on the Ballyhoura hills in the November of 1579, hard by the castle.'

He looked levelly at Bryen.

'You are so very young, Sir. Have you even heard of the Desmond Rebellions?'

'Yes, Sir. We are not so very far from West Cork. We have often spoken of that time at table. There are those who say your family remained aloof.'

'Aloof? My grandfather was not aloof. Hesitant, perhaps, like your father is now. Then, as now, there was a lot to play for.'

'He changed his mind?'

'His indecision was exacerbating the problem he was so anxious to solve. When August came, the White Knight James Desmond led a great army into Muskerry, where we engaged him at a ford on the Glashgariff tributary of the Lee, east of Carrigadrohid near Aghavrin.'

'Did you win, Sir?'

'In the military sense, yes, we did. We took Desmond, desperately wounded, to Carrigadrohid Castle. The ford where he was captured has since been bridged but still bears the name, *Aharuddera* - the knight's ford.'

'I have been there. A melancholy spot.'

'Then you probably know that when the queen's officials in Cork heard of Desmond's capture, they demanded that our prisoner be handed over to them. My grandfather, Cormac MacTeige, prevaricated for a while, but it is said that he was swayed by his wife, Joan Butler. He drove the White Knight from Carrigadrohid to Blarney and handed him over to the queen's commander, the old Earl of Ormonde. The knight was summarily tried at Shandon Castle, hanged near Cork's Northgate Bridge and, after he was taken down, decapitated. The knight's severed head was sent to Queen Bess in an earthenware pot. We Muskerrys must live with this shameful legacy. My chief bard, Constantius MacEgan of Aghinagh, has put the sorry saga to verse. The words never fail to admonish me. All my life I have sought to make amends,'

'How did you survive the purge after Kinsale,?'

'Well, truth be told, it was a close run thing. My grandfather was suspected by the Lord President of Munster, Sir George Carew, of plotting with Spain for another invasion. Carew, therefore, determined to get him into his power and acquire his stronghold. My grandfather was seized and brought before the Lord President.'

'I know how the story ends. Your MacEgans, are kin to the MacEgans of Duhallow. They were all pardoned by Sir George Carew, alongside your forebear Cormac MacTeige MacCarthy of Blarney and all his kinsmen and dependants, in May 1602.'

'You do know your history. I am impressed.'

During the Muskerry week, the observant Cliona noticed how Bryen had sought every opportunity to sit next to Sorcha[xiv], or to ride his Caliban beside her mare and show her the magnificent Duhallow country. Cliona also observed that Sorcha, while never offering false hope, did little to discourage her eldest son from gallant attentions.

'Have you seen Bryen?' Cliona asked her husband, late that night, when at last she had Dermod Oge to herself.

'Do you mean, have I seen how he has put a fern in his hatband?'

'I fear for him. I would take his place in the war if I could.'

'We would all do that. It is a fruitless hope. Nothing will stop him, now that he's made up his mind.'

'And you, Dermod Oge? Are you to join in the Rebellion?'

'No. Or, at least, not yet. St Leger and Cork are issuing warrants for the confiscation of the property of the 'rebels'. For the time-being I intend to protect our inheritance. The English have had their eye on it for too long.'

'You are either sitting on your hands or the fence.'

'I am securing our future. It's not quite the same thing. I have publicly 'forbidden' Bryen from enlisting. If he does, it is against my orders. I have witnesses who will swear that is the case.'

'Without your permission, he may do as he chooses?'

'Let us pray that Muskerry roundly defeats Inchiquin and his cohorts. Muskerry still lacks a legal cause. So do I. Cliona, I long for a Confederacy of the Irish and, sooner or later, it will happen. I don't believe it will be housed in Swords, so close to Dublin Castle, but it will be somewhere. When it does, I pray it will commission me and our race. Then we will do what we can for Ireland in the name of the king.'

*

The rebels' siege of Protestant Drogheda, on the Boyne, was leading nowhere, yet still it continued. O'More was not even tempted to give up. Sir Phelim had joined him and the governor was bound to seek terms. All Leinster, Catholic and Protestant, desperately sought for a decisive outcome, either way. If the Protestants surrendered the Catholics would be ready to join the uprising. Some of the more far-sighted Lords of the Pale had already realised that they had no choice but to commit to the Rebellion, whether their hearts were in it or not. They had come to the sober realisation that even if they did not declare for the Irish, Dublin and the English Parliament would assumed they had, in any case.

In the circumstances, they might as well enlist.

Spring was leisurely unfurling like a wokn cat; the weather eased and the days lengthened. Ferns unfurled and the rising sap provoked new daring. The Marquess of Ormonde told the Lords Justice he would relish the chance to limber up and stretch his military muscles.

The siege of Drogheda was going badly for those inside its walls. Rory O'More and Sir Phelim O'Neill had the place surrounded and for three long months the siege had continued its deadly work. The citizens were in desperate need of food and water.

The Lords Justice ordered the Lieutenant-General to march on the beleaguered port. They secretly hoped the marquess would not be able to relieve it. Their wish looked likely to be granted. Sir Phelim and O'More, between them, outnumbered Ormonde, which suited Parsons and Borlase. Ormonde needed taking down a peg or two.

'You are absolutely certain he won't be able to manage it, Sir John?'

'Sir William, if the Irish are angry, they are also frustrated. As soon as they see Lord Ormonde, Sir Phelim will lead them in attack. With no back-up and seeing their general has only daring as a weapon, the marquess's men will turn tail. Victory will be ours.'

'Ours? Well, certainly not Lord Ormonde's, in any case.'

In Sir Phelim's camp a very different conversation was taking place.

O'More had had a change of heart.

'Sir Phelim, my men have been regularly attacking these walls. Every time we do the governor, Sir Henry Tichburne, drives us back. The siege is going nowhere.'

'True, but my men will make a crucial difference.'

'Really? Nothing much has happened since you joined us. Remember, only a few weeks ago, you made your own desperate attempt to break the defences. Tichburne saw you off with ease. We left hundreds of dead comrades beneath the walls. We are weak, depleted and almost as hungry as the citizens of that noble city.'

'Well, we have but little food, I'll give you that. Chin up!' Sir Phelim was not ready to retreat. 'Come on, let's give it one more try.'

They regrouped.

They were about to attack when a scout brought news of Ormonde's approach.

'The Lieutenant-General has four thousand fresh troops and a squadron of artillery,' the breathless messenger reported.

O'Neill reconsidered the matter.

'Rory, because we lack artillery we can't engage Lord Ormonde. We can't attack the garrison for want of powder to mine the walls. I have no choice but to recommend retreat.'

'Not such an impetuous soldier-lawyer, then, Sir Phelim?'

'My impetuosity, Mr O'More, ran out last week.'

The 'rebels' abandoned their siege and withdrew orderly into the safety of the hills and forests. Their carts, now filled with muskets and pikes, were made invisible with a top layer of straw. When it drove away, the Irish, not in uniform, simply blended into the everyday landscape.

As he grew close, Lord Ormonde immediately saw that the Irish had fled. The day was his.

Ormonde sent the courier back to the Castle for leave to chase O'Neill into the bogs and glades, but he correctly guessed he would be denied permission. His written orders expressly forbade him to follow his enemy in hot pursuit. Parsons and Borlase had planned for the unlikely eventuality that Ormonde might somehow win, and they had no intention of letting Lord Ormonde have any credit in the victory.

Instead, the Lords Justice sent in Lord Moore with a sizeable army. He was followed by wagonloads of food. Ordered to join Sir Henry Tichburne, together they were to drive any loitering rebels away from Drogheda and out of Ardee and Dundalk. Those two townlands had been the Catholics' most glittering prizes.

As for Lord Ormonde, he was recalled to the capital.

The Castle was beginning to discover some very able soldiers among its own ranks. It even flirted with the idea of asking the king to replace Lord Ormonde, despite his inconvenient victory at Drogheda. Sir Henry Tichburne and Lord Moore were clearly Borlase's and Parsons's candidates.

The Castle had a second try at engineering a defeat for Ormonde. This time they sent him towards Athy.

The marquess reread his orders.

You are to engage Lord Mountgarrett at Kilrush.

He would be hopelessly outgunned. This battle, surely, he could not win.

Yet fate was to side with Lord Ormonde. This was the moment when, very much to Sir Phelim's and O'More's regret, the rebels of

County Cork elected Lord Muskerry as their general. It impressed them that he had served with distinction in Flanders as colonel of an infantry regiment. His appointment, however, was to Mountgarrett's cost, since it duplicated his command and divided the rebel strength in the south west between the two generals.

Lord Muskerry's promotion meant that Mountgarrett had just half the men the Castle had calculated. Ormonde won his set-piece engagement with ease and Mountgarrett was again forced to withdraw to his fortress in Kilkenny, this time with his tail between his legs. His losses were not so slight.

And, to the resentment of the Lords Justice, Ormonde came through with his reputation enhanced. The king wrote to him to thank him, in his own hand, and the Castle had to grimace and bear it. They even felt constrained to award him a triumphal banquet in the Castle.

The Irish had no choice but to fight – they knew how merciless were the Lords Justice. But Ormonde? Unlike Coote, he was a gentleman. Once his objectives were achieved, to the chagrin of the Lords Justice, he allowed his adversaries to live. Perhaps it was a matter of breeding. Could there be grounds for optimism in that? Was a change in the style of conflict heralded?

What was certain was that Ormonde's repeated victories, combined with his clemency, undermined the will of the Irish to resist. They began to peg their hopes on some sort of post-war reconciliation, if at least it could be negotiated with Lord Ormonde.

Ormonde's victorious return produced offers of submission from many of the Pale's rebel gentry. Some of them, who had previously been occupied making sure that little food or provisions could reach Dublin from the interior, relented and attended Ormonde's meetings at Crofty and Tara. Lord Dunsany and Sir John Netterville capitulated in person on the marquess's personal guarantee of their safety. They were sent to Dublin, on their own parole, there to await a pardon. Lords Gormanston and Slane offered by letter to follow their example, but by contrast they would wait a fortnight. They were keen to see what would happen to Dunsany and Netterville.

They were wise to be cautious. When Dunsany and Netterville reached the capital, they were immediately thrown into the Castle's darkest dungeons. Gormanston's written proposals were not casually tossed aside, however. They were hurled aside with contempt.

In London, that March, the Long Parliament was able to declare two and a half million acres of recusant Irish property forfeit to the State. With this substantial holding 'banked', they could parcel it out to every 'adventurer' in proportion to the scale of their donation or the length of their military service.

The Bill was sponsored by the Parliamentarian Lord Essex. He duly carried it to the king for royal assent.

'Tell us, noble Essex, what will become of the Irish after their reduction and ruin?' asked the king, enabling the Act with the Great Seal of England.

'My personal recommendation, Sire, is that in any future conflict, every captured recusant should be transported in chains to the West Indian Colonies, under penal indenture, where they might focus on producing sugar and molasses alongside their West African colleagues.'

The Act's contents, gazetted a few days later, effectively put paid to any negotiations between the opposing factions in Ireland.

*

Bryen set off on Caliban for Carrigadrohid. He wore the uniform he had worn in the war with the Scots under Lord Conway; the one that the late Lord Strafford had designed. He had tucked a snaplock pistol into his belt and let a rapier hang usefully at his side. A packhorse, roped to his saddle, tramped behind him, carrying his field tent, some medical provisions, clothes, stoppered flasks of small beer, a cured ham and similar vital matters. His mother had also insisted he should carry a flask of *potín*, lest he need to disinfect a wound.

Close behind him was his company of horse. All of them were seasoned Duhallow 'huntsmen'. Following these - marching, walking or shuffling, despite the brisk pace being asked of them - came more than nine hundred foot, stooped under the weight of their backpacks, joking and swapping their nervous banter. They pretended to be unaware that for some, at least, this would be their last adventure.

A hundred or so held pikes. Only a tenth of even that small number – twelve in all - had swords, mostly antique broadswords. A slightly larger number carried javelins, a form of flighted spear attached to a reel of linen thread. They could be reused if they failed to find a target. Some likely lads had slingshots. As for the rest, they carried farm tools; here a scythe, there a pitchfork. Most were barefoot, and none wore armour; even their commander wore only a simple helmet and a leather breastplate.

One distinguishing feature separated them from their Saxon enemies. Since pre-Christian times, some of the Celts were scarified with elaborate, war-inspired black aand red representations of the Virgin, her great cloak coloured with dark blue woad.[xv]

If an English spy had seen this 'warlike' rabble he might have laughed, but what it lacked in technology it made up for in will and determination. Unlike the Saxons, their stake in the deadly game was everything they believed in, loved, owned, even ate.

Bryen would only add that he was there for his king and his Kingdom of Ireland.

To those who watched developments in England, it was becoming inescapably clear that kingdom was about to split in two. It was worrying. Wherever England went, Ireland usually followed.

News had reached Dublin that Parliament had impeached three of the king's closest supporters, and that the Church of Ireland was in free fall. The Archbishop of Canterbury was in the Tower. What would happen to him was far from obvious but Lord Strafford's head, on a pole at the south end of London Bridge, set commentators a dreadful example.

Another poor soul was none other than the Attorney General. This man, loyal to his king, had dared to resist Pym's Militia Bill. The king had directed him to charge five members of Parliament - John Pym, John Hampden, Denzil Holles, Sir Arthur Hesilrige and William Strode - with treason. Lord Mandeville (the future Earl of Manchester) was also to be arrested. That they were a concert party was not in doubt. The accused openly admitted – even boasted – that they meant to wrest control of the armed forces from the Crown.

The king suspected that these were the prominent Calvinists who had fomented the Bishops' Wars. He had seen evidence that they had persuaded the Scots to invade England. He had also learned that they had been busy stirring up riots and tumults against him in London. Worse still, it appeared they were conspiring to impeach Her Majesty the Queen, alleging her complicity in unspecified Catholic plots.

Parliament rallied to support its Five Members. It refused to hand them over, claiming parliamentary privilege.

Charles was furious. He marched to Westminster at the head of a body of soldiers and retainers, intent on arresting them himself. Leaving the soldiers at the door, he strode into the House of Commons and sat in the Speaker's chair, ignoring the fact that no other monarch in English history had ever done such a thing.

Meanwhile, the Five Members had escaped.

The king pointed his finger at William Lenthall, the Speaker of the House, standing in front of his chair.

'Mr Speaker, do you see any of them present? Or, do you know where they are?'

'I have neither eyes to see nor tongue to speak in this place but as this House is pleased to direct me.'

The king had no choice but to leave. Angry shouts of 'Privilege, Privilege!' followed him to the door.

The Five Members had been hidden in the City by another militant Puritan Isaac Penington[xvi]. The mood became so brittle that the king and his family thought it best to leave Whitehall and return to Hampton Court for a few days, until the dust had settled.

As for the Five Members, they made their triumphal return to Westminster the following day.

Quite another was Lord Digby. His lordship was incriminated in letters from Catholics in what had been the Spanish Netherlands. His servant - a Dissenter in the pay of Parliament - had opened them. On the basis of that interception he was charged with a brand new crime, unknown in common law or in any statute book: Parliament declared he had been 'singularly and personally waging war on the nation'.

Institutional paranoia was running wild. The House of Lords, usually rather better disposed than the Commons towards their king, was maintaining that any man who advised King Charles to reject the Militia Bill was an 'enemy of the state'. This charge was destined to become associated with the confiscations, executions and tyranny which were about to corrupt Ireland's future history.

Meanwhile, over in Ireland, the Castle's response to the Rebellion was made crueller by a refusal to differentiate between the 'rebels' and the wider population. A negotiated settlement looked most unlikely, especially when power was owned by that most sinister of cabals; Coke, Massereene, Parsons, Borlase and Coote.

Bryen could hear his father's judgement ring in his ears.

'If the Castle squares up to the king, Bryen, then Ireland will have its very own Thirty Years War, its villages trampled by opposing armies as they range to and fro under their different banners.'

'Papa,' he remembered replying, 'Lord Muskerry is committed to the Rebellion. He told us at dinner that it was the only means of preserving Catholicism, the King's Prerogative and the rights of the Irish nobility.'

'And, Bryen, you will serve him and our cause with my blessing. Now may even be the right time for you, while Lord Cork and your old friend Inchiquin and are vying with each other for control of the Munster Protestants.'

'Papa, I believe that Lord Inchiquin will emerge as their military commander. He is a true soldier, Cork is merely a rich man.'

'How true, Bryen. You should remember, however, that Lord Cork is an Englishman. He is bound to suspect the Irish Lord Inchiquin. No matter how much the Saxons need friends, they would never appoint a Gael, even an O'Brien, to their high table. The good news is that you, and especially you, know what you're up against. Donogh Muskerry has appointed Garreth de Barrye, or plain Garret Barry as he seems to prefer, to be general of the Munster brigades. He, too, is a good soldier and a veteran of Spain's Flemish army.'

While Bryen rode on, his thoughts turned on the chances of success.

There was as yet no 'confederacy' of the Irish tribes, clans, races, and provinces. No overall chief or 'high king' was in place to coordinate their Rebellion. Irish progress could, therefore, only be agonisingly slow. The chiefs were still waiting for the great Owen Roe O'Neill's famous fighting machine to appear from the Continent and save the day; *machina ex Deo,* his father had joked. While England was distracted by events at home, surely the time to strike was right now? At least the Church was doing all it could. A fortnight before, the Primate of All Ireland had called a synod of Ulster's Catholic clergy. They had met at Kells and called for the scattered Catholic rebels to unite. Unfortunately, even they could not decide under whom.

The Irish commanders generally favoured guerrilla warfare. They liked to make intermittent and unpredictable raids, particularly on Protestant townlands. These tactics, without a strategy for their permanent nationalisation, meant victory was never to be permanently gained from the settlers.

The Rebellion needed a subtler vision.

As Bryen MacDonogh led his thousand 'friends' the thirty miles due south from Duhallow to Carrigadrohid, the land grew very difficult. Beyond Knockanroe, less than ten miles into their march, the *claghans*

117

almost ceased to exist. This was not because of enemy action. It was because the waterlogged soil would barely support even the humblest cabin. There were paths, of course, but all but invisible to the untrained eye. All Bryen's men, however, had ridden with the Duhallow Hunt, or followed it on foot. No one knew better how to read the turf.

In consequence, the men made good speed over the boggy ground. They had set off at dawn and fully expected to be at their destination before sunset. The route they took, however, caused the Thousand to make its way in single file a mile long. Bryen had two prayers; that St Luke would hear him and that a stray English musketeer never caught sight of this long and strange procession.

Not that many of his soldiers had an interest in architecture, military or otherwise, but Bryen had watched his father restore two castles. He was keen to see what his father had described as a remarkable structure, set in the middle of the river on a stone bridge. 'It's a place of sublime and outstanding beauty,' Dermod Oge had told him.

'It's an old place, is it, Papa?' Bryen had asked.

'It was begun at least two hundred years ago, Bryen, but the MacCarthys have never neglected it. It has three floors and a wonderful and spacious spiral staircase, a stone waterfall.' Dermod Oge's eyes focussed on his eldest son. 'It also boasts two rather beautiful daughters.'

'It's really on the bridge?'

'Its main door lets onto the bridge, right in the middle. No one crosses the river without Muskerry's consent.'

Dermod Oge's quip about Lord Muskerry's daughters was well aimed. Bryen was looking forward to seeing Sorcha again. At fifteen she was nubile and astonishingly pretty. Her shape was filling out nicely and her blonde hair crowned a sweet and innocent face, and one with cheeks like apples.

Bryen's men, on the other hand, were probably more interested in where they could be accommodated. A thousand of them, and twice as many again of Muskerry's, would need a canvas townland. Happily the weather was fine.

It didn't have to be. The men, simple farming folk, were well inured to hardship. Had the weather been torrential, it would not have deterred them.

*

Bryen's army had ridden to within a few miles of Carrigadrohid when Muskerry intercepted him. His Lordship rode up at the head of his bodyguard, six horsemen armed and uniformed, like a European army.

118

When they saw Bryen and his Thousand they drew their swords and saluted like Spaniards.

'Bryen, what a gorgeous spectacle you make!' exclaimed Lord Muskerry, dismounting. Bryen similarly swung out of his saddle and the two men embraced, kissed and shook hands. 'You promised me a thousand men and you have delivered! Just look at them all! They will have to camp on the north bank of the Lee for the night. Tomorrow we are to head east and march on Cappoquin.'

Bryen's face showed well enough that he had no idea where Cappoquin was.

'It's a few miles north of Youghal, Bryen, in County Waterford. Relax; we will feed your men tonight. Come on home and reacquaint yourself with my family. You really do have a thousand men, by God! Remount, dear fellow, and follow me. I shall tell you our plans as we ride home.'

As Bryen's Thousand came over the Carrigadrohid hill, the light was beginning to fail but, even in the gloaming, they could still make out the river Lee beneath them, draining the bogs to either side of their surplus moisture, and pouring it slowly into the ocean.

Even in the dusk, Bryen could see the famous stone bridge that crossed the river, directly ahead. As promised, it boasted a great stone fortress halfway across.

'We had originally thought to meet the enemy on the southern part of our bridge. There, without artillery, they would have been defenceless and we have two cannons trained on the south bank. Alas, your old friend Inchiquin anticipated our plans. He persuaded Lord Cork to let him march on us from Youghal, which will mean his approach is from the north. Our friends there have let us know that the Saxon army will not set off until the day after tomorrow, as they are awaiting a brigade from Bristol to bring up their numbers. Normally, to reach us from Youghal would need at least fifteen hours' forced march but the intelligence we have has put our boot on the other foot, if you follow. I plan to spike his wheels at Cappoquin. The spot is ideal; discreet and readily defensible. Its English fort was in use until last November, when the Castle called its garrison back to Dublin. Inchiquin will wander into our trap without any idea we are waiting for him, and now, with your Thousand, we shall even outnumber him.'

It was a tired Bryen MacDonogh Carty who finally stood behind his chair at the Muskerry table in the vaulted dining hall at Carrigadrohid. Sorcha and her younger sister Rioghnagh[4] joined the diners. Lady Muskerry took the end of the table opposite her husband, and Fr Benedict O'Connell was on his host's right hand. General Garret Barry stood on his left, while Muskerry's two sons took their place to either side of his wife Ellen. Other places were taken by Bryen's uncles, Thadeus and Aidan MacCarthy, whom Muskerry had engaged to manage his army, now three thousand strong and cooking itself a splendid supper over hot coals in the braziers of their camp.

Bryen was twenty-three years old. He had held the King's commission. He had served His Majesty in the second Bishops' War. Now he was leading a thousand loyal countrymen to war against the king's enemies. He felt very lonely, scared and young.

Looking around he realised that everyone there was technically a rebel. It was astonishing to think that men so loyal to their king could be 'rebels'. Not merely that; they might not even win their war. If their Rebellion failed they would surely all be hanged, or exiled in irons, or left to scavenge with the tinkers and the dispossessed. He watched Muskerry's sons chatter easily with one another while they waited to sit, a thin veneer of excitement and optimism colouring their cheeks. Within a couple of days, one or both might be dead upon a field, cut down carelessly as collateral damage in a battle over whether the Irish might maintain their old faith and their older ways.

Across the table Bryen caught Sorcha's eye, who blushed and lowered her gaze. Then she looked up at him directly. Had she been thinking the same about him? That he and his future might be extinct before the week was out?

Father O'Connell stretched out his arms in prayer. '*Oremus*', he said. All bowed their heads. Some elaborate Latin followed before they all sat and the servants brought in the meal.

'MacDonogh,' began General Barry, 'I understand you served alongside Lord Inchiquin in the King Charles's recent disagreement with the Scots?'

'I did that, Sir,' replied Bryen.

'I'm told Lord Thomond's boy is a young and noble-spirited commander. Would that be your own opinion?'

'Yes, sir. I know we are on opposite sides in this conflict but I was pleased for him when he was made Governor of Munster. A great honour for a man only five years or so older than me.'

---

[4] Pr Riona. It means 'descended from Kings'.

'Then it's perhaps fortunate that his lack of money hampers him so badly.'

'Can't Lord Cork meet the shortfall?' asked Muskerry.

'Lord Cork is interested in hoarding money, not in spending it,' answered Barry.

Lady Margaret stepped into the conversation, rescuing it from the vulgar direction it was threatening to take.

'We did so enjoy our stay in Duhallow, didn't we, Sorcha? Such a lovely part of Ireland. So many lovely things to see.'

Bryen glanced across the table but Sorcha was studying her plate.

'Thank you, Lady Margaret,' he said. 'I shall pass on your compliments as soon as I can.'

'Thank you Bryen. Please tell my sister-in-law that she is most welcome to bring her tribe to visit us here or in Blarney. Before you leave I shall give you a choice of dates to offer her.' She turned to her husband. 'Blarney would be a more comfortable place to receive them than here, do you not think, Lord Muskerry?'

'Whatever you say, my darling,' the Catholic commander agreed. He returned to his conversation with Garret Barry. 'You were telling me, General, about the natural amphitheatre at Cappoquin?'

'Quite, General Lord Muskerry. We have to get there before the enemy, that is all. Then we can surprise Cork's army just where the road leads through it. We shall have the advantage of the hills and woods to give us cover and shelter. If Inchiquin attempts to attack us it will be up hill.'

'Our men will be tired after a long march. You're sure the English soldiers at Cappoquin have been recalled?'

'Certain. The old fort is deserted. Its troops are in Dublin, protecting the capital from Sir Phelim. Our men will not be tired. They won't even be sleepy. Take a closer look at them. They are farming folk. They would walk thirty miles for a decent alehouse. Their arms and legs are of Irish oak.'

Muskerry's oldest son Tierney[5] spoke to his father.

'May I ride with MacDonogh, Sir?'

'You must ask Captain MacDonogh for that privilege.'

'Captain?' interrupted General Barry. 'MacDonogh, now you are fighting for your country you had better bear the rank of major.'

'Well said,' said Lord Muskerry. 'I heartily agree.'

---

[5] He pronounced it 'Terny'. It means 'lordly'.

121

'Then that's done. Looking forward to tomorrow's little adventure, Major?'

'I am, Sir, but not without a little sadness. Some of us may never return.'

'Any we lose will swell the numbers petitioning the angels for an Irish victory. Is that not the case, Father O'Connolly?'

'The angels never refuse Paradise to a Catholic soldier who has died in a holy war, Lord Muskerry', replied the priest. 'I shall ensure our warriors' sins are absolved before they begin their march tomorrow.'

'Good. Thank you, Father. Lady Margaret, as we agreed, you are to take our daughters and servants to the safety of Blarney Castle. General Barry will accompany you and provide your escort. As for this house, I have arranged for fifty trusted men to remain behind and have left instructions for the bridge to be mined. If the English should arrive here, despite our efforts at Cappoquin, the bridge the enemy wishes to secure will cease to exist. This lovely house, hopefully, will remain.'

Muskerry glanced up and down his table.

'I see we have all finished our supper,' said Lord Muskerry, 'May I humbly suggest that we thank the Lord our God for what we have received and repair to our beds? We have work to do. Grave and serious work, on behalf of our great great grandchildren and all who come after us in the long centuries ahead.'

Major Bryen had been given a room to himself, on the second floor. Its window overlooked the bridge below but more critically, as it looked east, the early morning light would stream in through its stone mullions. At its first hint, Lady Muskerry had assured him, a servant would fetch him a bowl of hot water. He would be able to shave before he joined his men to make sure they had rubbed the dust from their eyes, placed a fresh fern for a cockade in their simple hats and were eager and ready to march.

He knelt beside the bed.

'Gentle Mother of the God of power and mercy,' he began, 'mother of the Maker and Lover of peace. Blessed Mary, be my protection in our great battle against evil. Let the days ahead help us put this war behind us and promote love, and justice, among all men. May Jesus Christ our Lord grant this through your intercession.'

He pulled back the eiderdown. Linen sheets! It would be grand to feel them next to his skin. He took his clothes off carefully to climb into bed as naked as the day he was born.

He then fell into a wonderful sleep, provoked by his great hike across some very hard country. He did not propose to dream that night. No *incubus* would dare disturb his slumbers.

Yet it was no more than half an hour later when woke. A gentle tapping had found its way into his consciousness.

He sat up in bed and lit the candle. The tapping had stopped. It was probably nothing at all. How strange! He lay back, puzzled. What could it have been?

Then it came again. It was a soft knock at his door. How could he answer it? He had no clothes on.

'Who is it?' he said clearly.

'It's Sorcha,' came the familiar Cork lilt. 'Can I come in for a moment? It's important.'

'What if someone sees you?'

'Everyone's asleep. Except you and me.'

'Well you'd better not stand out there talking to me through an oak door. Come in then, but you can't stay. We could both be in terrible trouble.'

Bryen had his sheets pulled up to his chin. Sorcha came in. She had changed into her nightclothes. She looked nervous but determined.

'Move your feet', she said, sitting at the foot of Bryen's bed. 'I have something most particular to say to you.'

'Could you not have said it when we said goodnight?'

'Other people might have heard. What I have to say is only for you.'

'I must be mad to let you stay, Sorcha. But since you're here…'

'Bryen, listen to me. Everyone in the house is asleep. You should be too. Tomorrow you go to war. You will face a Sasanach army and not even my father knows how great a number. If Lord Cork is a ruthless man, his men are even more so. Lord Inchiquin will never shed a tear for any Catholic. He is a clever man and I think he may be cleverer than my father. He may even be cleverer than you.'

'We shall have surprise working for us and he may have fewer men than us.'

'His men will have muskets, cannons, pistols. How many of those do you have?'

'We have courage and purpose. We fight for our faith. All Cork's men want is to go home.'

'Bryen, I am not a soldier. Look at me. Look at a simple girl, hopelessly in love with a brave man whose heart is the size of a crock of gold.'

There was a brief, charged silence.

'Why hopelessly? I shall come back, Sorcha, and I shall seek your father's permission to court you. You must have seen that I love you too?'

'Bryen, if you die, I vow to remain a spinster for the rest of my life. No other man shall I ever let approach me. This I swear by the blessed Virgin. I mean to hold you in my arms, dear Bryen, just for a while before you go. I have never even kissed a boy, or a man, but if you go without letting me kiss you the way a wife kisses her husband, then I shall die the saddest maiden in the world.'

'Sorcha, I shall come back and marry you. Let St Luke witness this promise. I shall ask your father's permission first thing in the morning.'

Sorcha had taken Bryen's hand, somehow without his realising. Some strange alchemical energy was running up his arm.

'Bryen, by your promises we are married already. All that is missing are earthly witnesses. Do you mean to cherish me forever, to let me bear your children and champion your heart in any crowd?'

'I do.'

'God and all the saints have seen and heard our vows. Let me into your bed.'

'Sorcha!' Bryen's head was spinning. 'Let me speak to your father in the morning?'

'I should prefer to keep our secret until you are safely home.'

Sorcha had somehow found her way between the sheets. If she was surprised to find that he was naked, she was too busy showering him with kisses to say.

What happened to the night?

The maid that brought Bryen his hot water a few minutes before dawn found Sorcha folded into Bryen's arms, the both of them fast asleep. She yelped with surprise and alarm, dropping the china bowl that noisily smashed into a thousand pieces.

Even worse was that this was the moment Lord Muskerry, wondering why his new Major was tardy, chose to come into the room.

'What do I see? Do my eyes deceive me? MacDonogh, seducer, you are banned from this house. I never want to see your face again. Take your men back to Duhallow this minute. Get out of my sight.'

Before Bryen could speak, Sorcha was at her father's feet.

124

'Papa, we are married. We said our vows before God last night. You cannot separate a married couple. You are not capable of such cruelty.'

'Is this true?' The hurt and anger on Muskerry's face was plain to see.

Bryen was rather more than simply awake now.

'Every word, sir. I intend to look after Sorcha for all of my life, long or short. I hope to do so with your blessing, but I offer her a fair living with or without it.'

'MacDonogh, she may be with child!'

This observation caused Sorcha to react,

'Please Papa, I hope so. Bryen may die in this war. If I am to carry his child, then I will love that precious person as much as I love you, and mama, and its father.'

Lord Muskerry had run out of argument.

He turned to the maid, still in the room, still shocked and speechless.

'Mairead, go and fetch Lady Margaret and Father O'Connolly directly. Do not speak to anyone else of this. Do you understand?'

The maid vanished like a scalded cat.

Lord Muskerry seemed to have mellowed. He even sat on the edge of the bed.

'What you did was very wrong. Yet there is a way we can make it right. I had intended, when we married Sorcha to the right man, to have his parents join us in the celebration. Not just his parents but every tenant on our estates. The whole of Munster, perhaps, but you have denied me that pleasure. The priest will be here in a moment. Neither of you will leave this room. He will hear your confessions and, if he sees fit to absolve you from the sin of, let's see, wilfulness, then he, Lady Margaret and I will hear your wedding vows. As for your father, Bryen, I may be lost for words but he won't be. Now, Bryen, I shall turn my back. Put some clothes on for goodness sake.'

*

CHAPTER SEVEN
CAPPOQUIN

It was the eve of battle.

It was March, 1642, and the ground was still pliable, not yet hard. It was the favourite season of farmers.

To reach Cappoquin with time enough to set their ambush, General Lord Muskerry drove his army, three thousand foot and a hundred horse, at some speed. Despite their forced pace, they only arrived at the hamlet as light began to fade.

Cappoquin turned out to be a pleasant spot. Even in the twilight the soldiers saw that the rolling hills to the north rippled easily upwards and, some way beyond a gentle ridge, the sinister stony mass of the Knockmealdown Mountains rose high above the plain like a tidal wave.

The plain to the south had been levelled over centuries by the river Blackwater.

'I calculate that Lord Inchiquin will ferry his army across the river at Youghal, twenty miles away to the south. From there he will lead his imported English soldiers across the southern hills, over the plain, going due north along the east bank of the great river, as far as Aglish, where the river has carved a pass. There his army will turn west towards Cappoquin,' Lord Muskerry told his subalterns. 'Their route in all likelihood will be confined to the firm but narrow strip between the foothills and the river, taking them past the old English fort and beyond, into this 'amphitheatre' where you will hide this army.'

He smiled.

'Inchiquin is nothing if not a strategist. He will aim for the relative safety of Fermoy. From Youghal, it lies roughly halfway to Carrigadrohid. There he thinks he will camp for a night before surprising me and ridding my bridge of its annoying fortress. Everything in his plan is based on the reasonable assumption that I am expecting his Protestants to arrive from the south, from Cork City. He will think I am concentrating my defences on the southern approach, and that I will have left the northern approaches almost undefended. That is why the English lines, forced between the Blackwater and the hills, will be stretched thin. That will not trouble Lord Inchiquin in the least. He will think it unlikely that his army disturb a single woodkerne. The weakness in his strategy lies in not understanding that I have countless eyes and ears in both Cork and

126

Youghal and an officer who was close to him in the king's 'Bishops' Wars'.'

He swept his arm across the landscape in a grand gesture,

'They will pass beneath our lines, just down there,' Lord Muskerry continued. 'Since they are hauling cannons and siege engines they'll make slow progress. Artillery is not easy to pull uphill.

His tent, pitched high in the foothills, gave him a view over the whole battlefield. He had immediately realised that if his men encamped on the plain through which the enemy would come, they would be bound to leave some visible advance warning. The darkening sky silhouetted some low hills. Muskerry ordered his army to pitch camp, behind them, well set back from the road in the approaches to the mountains of County Waterford.

The men made their way carefully up the gentle slopes. The sponginess of the ground was a godsend; it would help them leave no tracks.

'We have the twin advantages of height and surprise,' the general told his adjutants. 'The possibility that we may be outnumbered should not be allowed to gnaw at our determination. When we attack they will scatter like dust, leaving us their baggage train, payroll and field pieces.'

'Do you have our battle stations, General?'

'Your final dispositions will wait 'till the morning. I expect Lord Inchiquin's army to set off from Youghal at first light. That means they physically cannot arrive here before nine. Before then would be impossible. You may, and should, enjoy a good night's sleep.'

He slowly took in each of his officers, looking them in the eye.

'I hope you all realise what that means,' he said. 'In case you do not, it means that every tent, every brazier, every indication that three thousand warriors have been here must vanish in the hour that follows daybreak. Only that way will the Saxons fall into our trap. At first light my officers and I will give you your final orders. Gentlemen, you have time to feed, rest and hide your men. God bless and save you all.'

A few of Bryen's Thousand, mostly his musket and horse, had joined Muskerry's, but his foot remained under his direct command. The men received their incomplete orders in good heart. They were farmers, it was true, but many were also huntsmen, thanks to the Duhallow. If a farmer is a colonist by instinct, a huntsman is a force of nature, one who understands and protects his landscape. If such philosophical niceties were wasted on these simple folk, the general principal was not.

Before supper, Bryen drilled his men. They would need to close in on the Saxon soldiers, to confine them and to cut off their retreat.

No soldier enjoys drill but they acquiesced with some grace. Few of them had ever seen action and they all knew that only in rehearsed obedience did they have a chance of defeating Lord Inchiquin's army from across the Irish Sea.

Finally, Bryen dismissed them. The men set about their supper with martial gusto.

They lit no fires – their supper was bread, cheese and small beer – and by dawn evidence of their camp would be invisible. It would be as if they had never existed.

Unfortunately, some of Muskerry's other regiments pitched camp more carelessly. A few even lit fires.

While Bryen had no authority to interfere with units not under his command, he thought that if he were planning a raid so deep into enemy country, he would send a squadron of scouts ahead, well in advance of his army. That way, every ten miles or so, a scout could peel off and report to the army that the road was safe, at least as far as he had seen.

If the idea had occurred to him, the same might have occurred to Inchiquin? Blast those fires.

Some distance away he heard a group of men break into a boisterous song. In the still of the night they sounded very close. How far would that sound travel?

Relax, Major, he told himself. Inchiquin has not even started out. The sound might carry but it was twenty miles to Youghal. It wouldn't carry that far.

Before he himself turned in, Bryen revisited his men. They were in small groups, eating and talking quietly amongst themselves. None had ever fought a battle before but they trusted their commander.

Bryen assured them that the Protestant army would also have had very little training. They could do nothing at all on Irish soil at night and even by day could only move at half speed. They could not read the land like an Irishman and their massive weapons would slow them down. Nor had they saints to pray to or to watch over them – except perhaps St George – and they were not moved by love but only by money and promises of confiscated land.

'Those of you with weapons', Bryen told them, 'will form the front line. Javelins first. Pikes will advance behind them. Swords and axes will protect the unarmed. Slingshots will fire from the hills. Those of you without arms, you will be protected. Your job is to attend the injured and take up any fallen weapons. In that way the heroism of those who fall in battle will live on.'

That night, Fr O'Connolly heard their confessions, giving them absolution for their sins. Behind him, Bryen circulated with pen and paper. He encouraged his troops to give their wives, lovers, children or parents some message on the eve of battle. For the most part they had never learned to read or write. Bryen took dictation and promised their messages would get home, even if the soldier did not.

What he found himself writing down was, for the most part, simple and affectionate. A sentence or two, mostly of the 'go with God' or 'I love you' variety. There were one or two of his men who had much longer messages. Bryen wrote these down, uncomplainingly. He was his men's notary; their sentiments were under something akin to the seal of the confessional. It had to be that way; alarmingly, one of his soldiers confessed to having murdered a lover's husband before marrying the widow.

An owl startled the camp with its war cry, swooping low over them. Time for sleep. The better rested they were, the safer they would be and the greater a danger they would be to their enemy.

Bryen made his way to his tent – unlike his men he would sleep under cover – where he lit a lamp and wrote a letter to his bride of a few hours.

It was bound to be a trifle more poetic than the love letters of his men, but its theme was as simple and as affectionate. In round numbers, it too started with 'I love you' and finished with 'Go with God'.

Cappoquin, Co. Waterford
Eve of battle
March 26, 1642

Dear, dearest little Sorcha, darling bride of a mad and joyful night, though I prepare for war I need to tell you that I will always love you.

If you have been given this letter, it is because my body has been left on the field. They may tell you your Bryen is dead, but a part of me still lives. That is the part of me that loves you and cannot die.

A soldier needs a purpose to go to war. Mine was not Ireland, nor even the Church. It was you. You, our future children, and I; we have been chosen somehow to give each other succour, happiness and peace. To make that happen, our enemy needs to go home, back across the Irish Sea. So that our many children may grow up safely, sheltered by our love and the love of God, I have no choice but to remove the threat that hangs on a thread, like that famous Greek sword, above our heads.

It has only been a day, just one short day, since I set off for Cappoquin. I saw those tears in your eyes and felt that sad, shy wave of yours batter my heart. Over the day, I have realised a thousand times how much less than whole I am without you. Without you, my witty, wonderful, wilful Sorcha, my life is only a purposeless sounding brass. Out here I have no work of art to gaze at, no timeless melody to hear. If I have known happiness, my life now can only be depicted in shades of grey, all its glorious colours now fading.

Without your complete comfort, even that great and generous love of yours would not be enough to let me laugh aloud and delight in your kisses, as we did at Carrigadrohid on our wedding night. Those tender moments we had together will remain forever fresh, however much is left of my life. You are embedded in my enraptured heart, whether it beats or not.

It is late and I am tired. Now I must sleep. Half the night have I spent talking to our soldiers, trying to reassure them of our Lord's clemency. I have used up all my best words. Now, only the Judge knows my innermost feelings.

Sorcha, I shall wait for you in Elysium. Please know that you could never have had a more constant or more affectionate admirer and lover. Consider me unalterably yours, my lovely girl. My love, the memory of which I know to be locked away in the secret depths of your soul, will be there for you forever. Whenever you think of me, my face, my arms around you, my heartfelt vows, all this will echo in your heart.

No more. The battle is tomorrow. I expect a sharp and short adventure. When the time comes we shall meet again, to the joy of every choir in heaven but, before that happy day, if you ever need to summon up some warm recollection, it will suffice for you to dwell for an instant on your absent but adoring Bryen.

Bryen carefully folded his letter. In the morning he would give it to Lord Muskerry, his father-in-law. In the unhappy case that he fell in battle, the general would hand it on to his daughter.

Bryen slept surprisingly well in his military tent. At five thirty he was dressed, though not exactly for a ball. He had more important things to do than shave. He had to ready his men for battle.

Three thousand Milesians in the hills were similarly beginning to stir. As they peered around they saw the mist upon the fateful field. The light was thin and it was still a good few minutes before sun up, but these men would otherwise have been tending their fields. They had their own strange way of knowing the time. In fact, their alarm call was the birdsong and in March it is particularly loud and cheerful.

Behind him, here and there, hungry soldiers lit fires to warm black pudding or rashers of bacon. He decided to ignore them. They were in the hills. Their smoke would not alert the enemy if they were extinguished early enough. He ordered his men to use water from the streams to put them out when they had finished eating. This was done. No one wanted to serve as a beacon to Lord Inchiquin.

The new day was well on its way. Painterly streaks of salmon pink lit the grey of the early sky and the birdsong had become quite deafening. On the eastern horizon, Bryen watched a bright light, like a fire, appear on the horizon. Within what seemed like seconds a flattened orange ball had fought its way from the earth into the sky. In the plain the sun began its urgent daily task of burning off the mist and dew.

A little before six, Fr O'Connolly, the chaplain, made another wholesale round. He had a pious constituency; the ground was unconsecrated and he declined to say mass, but he had taken hours to write out the *ave Maria* a large number of times. He pronounced its holy words to every man among them and handed out a copy to all who could read. These were precious slips of paper, written as they were by a priest whose ordination descended by apostolic succession from Christ and Peter. The men gained comfort from them, secreting these sacred strips of paper in their pockets or purses.

The river below lapped noisily at its shores. The dozens of streams that drained into it slithered and gurgled. This natural orchestra was made more operatic by a chorus of masculine banter and laughter. For a day that would send a number of their company to meet their Maker, the first act was remarkably cheerful.

To the east, Captain Thaddeus MacCarthy busied himself with making sure that the troops had left no traces of their rustic sojourn that could be espied from the road. His men picked up stoppered jugs, crusts of bread, litter of every kind. Some used garden rakes - the soldiers had brought them to fight the enemy - to raise the turf and restore its pristine innocence.

A messenger came up to Bryen and saluted.

'General Lord Muskerry would like to see his captains now, sir, and give his final instructions on the conduct of the battle.'

131

'First, the javelins. They are to take out the cavalry,' Bryen relayed to his men. 'Second, you pikemen will march into the valley and block the path of their infantry. As the enemy tries to find a way around, you slingshooters will attack them from the hills. Do not fear, Muskerry's musketeers will aim at the artillery. When the Saxon bombardiers flee for cover, that's the time for you swordsmen, you axemen, to chase the scattered Sasanach and pacify them. Gentlemen, pacify them as hard as you can. This is war.'

By nine o'clock, however, there was absolutely no sign of the English.

Lord Muskerry had a spyglass but a persistent low mist floated off the river and obscured the road. If anything the wretched mist was rising. Unless it lifted, the enemy might come undetected within a few hundred yards of the Irish emplacements.

Bryen looked up at the sky. The clouds were gathering, lowering, darkening. It might even rain.

Muskerry, for strategic reasons, had added Bryen's muskets to his fusiliers. Bryen was left with only his swords, axes, pikes and catapults, but he took great pride in all of these. Some gorse, close to the road, to the east of the battlefield, would provide his javelins with cover.

The rest of his men he had still to position.

What would be the enemy order of battle? Muskerry had said they would be led by their horse. All of them? Would not half of their cavalry be at the rear? How did Saxons deal with stragglers, or deserters for that matter? Would they be rounded up? Or would Lord Inchiquin station marksmen at the rear?

No, thought Bryen. Inchiquin might be on the wrong side, but was a civilised man. He would round up his strays. Not that there would be many. His army was uniformed, after a manner of speaking, and deserters would not get far in those boots, with those badges. They would be safer staying with their officers.

On his own side, the men were dressed in simple country clothes. They knew that if they ran away they could vanish without trace. All they need do was discard the ferns from their hats. It wouldn't happen. Everything they loved came into battle with them.

Another half hour had passed. Bryen walked a hundred yards to the west. There he inspected his pikemen. Their sergeant presented them with pride.

Bryen walked along their line, offering a word here, a little praise there. He shook his sergeant's hand.

'A fine body of men. My congratulations.'

He beckoned the pikemen to gather around.

'Men,' said Bryen, privately wondering where his own *sang froid* sprang from, 'first blood belongs to our javelins. There may be time for two or even three flights. When I judge the moment good, you will hear me cry *'fag an bealach'*, my family's ancient war cry. That is your signal. Pikemen, march briskly onto the road, directly into the path of the Saxons. They will be confused after the javelin attack, their horses will be frightened. Arrange yourselves in a line, two deep as we have rehearsed, across the road, your pikes heeled, your barricade absolute.

'Then, while you stand fast, Muskerry's musketeers will have their time. Those Sasanach who flee to the hills will be cut down by our sword and axe. Those who stay on the road will remain there until the day of judgement. Your own position will be defended by our horse.

'Courage, my brave and gallant men. On your side is Right and Truth. Your last prayers before the battle, in an hour or so, might usefully be directed to St Michael. Mine will be. In battle you are to be honourable. We are not barbarians. Now, men, are you ready for war?'

'We are, sir,' came a baritone chorus.

'Then the blessings of Almighty God be upon you all.'

To Bryen's surprise, two hundred pikemen, in unison, cried out that famous war cry.

'*Fag an bealach.*'

Clear the road.

Major Bryen MacDonogh Carty had now spoken to every soldier under his command.

He had just given his words of encouragement to his slingshots. This tribe of likely lads were used to supplementing their family meagre diets with some very effective poaching. If they were only around fourteen years old, in many ways these were the deadliest of his men. One of them, his voice far from broken, could infallibly kill a hare at fifty yards. Each of them had a bag of stones in a bag, tied to a belt with a hempen cord. These stones, the 'Irish crown jewels' one of their company had called them, were the size of plovers' eggs. Against a man, a good shot could deliver oblivion, blindness, even death.

The lads seemed happily indifferent to what was about to happen to them. Let's leave it that way, thought their commander.

Bryen's young swordsmen were few in number, but accepted the grimmest of duties. One of their tasks was to ensure that no wounded English arose to rejoin their ranks. When their commander reached their

133

positions, he saw that they were sharpening their weapons on leather strops. They had already been as sharp as a barber-surgeons blade. The men were all clean shaven and Bryen realised for the first time the significance.

The axemen, and those who carried other deadly farming tools, were the strongest of his men, giants with legs that could be mistaken for the trees of the Duhallow forests. These men could run down any enemy if they tried to flee. Whenever they did, the Saxon enemy would first drop his sword or musket, and the Duhallow garrison would add another weapon for its three hundred or more unarmed men. By that evening, the men of Duhallow might be slightly fewer in number but it would be far better armed.

On his round, Bryen met Thady MacCarthy.

'Almost ten thirty. Still no sign of them. Inchiquin must have given them a lie in,' his uncle stated.

'They're on their way,' Bryen replied. 'I can sense it. So can the men.'

The mist still carpeted the flood plain. Waiting was hard.

Lord Muskerry gave the order for absolute silence. This was not directly to protect his men, or even to spring his trap more effectively. It was because he wanted to listen for the enemy's arrival.

The sun told everyone it was midday.

Muskerry had been worrying that too long a delay might undo his men. As a veteran of the war in Flanders he knew that over-prolonged excitement will exact a toll. A soldier cannot stay in a state of readiness for ever. If he does, something like recklessness, a state akin to drunkenness, sets in.

Just how long could it take for the English to walk twenty miles?

The sun had cleared the middle of the sky.

Muskerry had spent an hour with his rosary. The numbing rhythm of those prayers had brought him an hour of calm.

It was Fr O'Connolly who broke into his reverie.

'Do you hear something, General?'

'No. What can you hear, Father?'

'General, with respect, stand up and listen. I think it's some kind of marching song.'

Sure enough, a whisper came from the southeast, through the mist. The song was unrecognisable, but the beat was not. It was driven by a side drum.

It was coming from an army, one of many thousands, now less than a mile away.

It had started to rain, but the hushing whisper of a shower did not disguise the arrival of the moment of reckoning.

Bryen, who was standing by the road, could still see nothing but now he too could hear Inchiquin's army.

The enemy marched in step. The sound of their boots on the earth was a vast rhythmic pulse, louder with each beat. While they marched, they were singing what seemed to be a version of the psalms. A side drum kept time. Bryen had never heard such a choir. Every Protestant was singing with all his heart.

A line of verse became distinguishable.

'He is trampling out the vintage where the grapes of wrath are stored.'

Bryen faced his javelins.

'Any moment now they will be in front of us,' he said to their sergeant.

'I've seen Him in the watchfires of a hundred circling camps.'

'We are ready for them, Sir. God bless and save you, Sir.'

'Thank you, O'Flaherty. May the Lord send you home to Mrs O'Flaherty, sound in wind and limb.'

'Amen', said O'Flaherty. No one would doubt his sincerity.

'He hath loosed this fateful lightning of His terrible swift sword.'

As the English drew closer, one of the young soldiers thought he knew the song.

'Let us die to make men free'.

'It's not a psalm, this one. It's called 'Canaan's wedding, I think,' he said, pleased as punch with himself. 'It's a hymn, specially written for war!'[xvii]

'His day is marching on.'

'A hymn for killing and fighting?' He would never understand the Protestants. 'Sergeant, are your men ready?'

'They are, Sir.'

'Then wait for my command. Any moment now.'

*

General Lord Muskerry, from his superior vantage, saw what Bryen could not. At first he saw the tips of the enemy's pikes, carried vertically above the ground-hugging mist. There were around a thousand of them.

He could also see their cavalry vanguard, at least a hundred horses, lances held erect, soldiers in wet armour. Was it leather, was it steel? Even with his spyglass he could not be sure.

It was too late to worry in any case.

There would be a mounted rearguard, of course, and yet more musketeers. Maybe twice as many muskets as pikes? That alone took the enemy to five or six thousand. On this single-track road, marching four abreast, the file would stretch at least a thousand yards. It could well exceed a mile.

Half the Irish army was effectively unarmed. Was Ireland in store for a catastrophic defeat?

The enemy vanguard was now almost level with Major MacDonogh's javelins.

Muskerry watched the whole thing unfold. A fine lad, his new son-in-law, he thought. He checked his pocket. The letter the lad had entrusted to him was there. Please God, let it be redundant.

The enemy horse was now so close that his glass could reveal the expressions on their riders' faces. They sang, looked happy and resolute, not anticipating any difficulty. Behind them were their thousands, marching on their roundabout journey to Carrigadrohid. They had marched some twenty miles already without a break. They would be tired. Perhaps the Saxon troopers among them were fantasising about Cork, its pubs, its beakers of good Saxon ale.

The vanguard drew level with a curious stone, a pagan menhir. None of them gave it any particular attention.

Their complacency, however, was shattered by an extraordinary cry from the roadside, an ancient war cry that even made Muskerry's hair stand on end, the cry the Gaels had used in battle when they too were a conquering power, taking Ireland from its aboriginal Firbolg, Danaan and Fermorians.

Muskerry watched as what looked like a flight of spears flew from the hills that rose from beside the roadside.

These were no ordinary spears. These were flighted javelins.

A hundred of them hit a target; here a horse, there a man. Then, the most uncanny sight, one that even Muskerry had never seen before; half the spears wriggled like startled snakes across the ground back to where they had come from. Sometimes they were even yanked from writhing soldiers.

The crackle of Protestant muskets could now be heard. Muskerry saw the little palls of smoke rise from the English ranks.

Bryen's pikemen had blocked the English advance but the Saxon vanguard was useless against them; Inchiquin's musketeers would have to be brought to the front.

As the horses turned in confusion, the reeled-in javelins came raining down again. They took a ghastly toll. Twenty or thirty cavalry and a dozen horses were impaled on the second volley.

While the English cavalry regrouped, that terrible war cry came again from the foothills to their right.

Muskerry could hear cries of pain over the yells of command, the snap and zing of the musketeers and the whoosh of the stones the slingshots rained on the English. The lads were every bit as accurate as Bryen MacDonogh had promised.

The general gave the order for his shot to advance to behind the kneeling pikemen and defend them.

Some of Inchiquin's horse had drawn their swords and were attempting to climb the hills. The streams and yesterday's rain made the soil especially treacherous. Muskerry watched horse after horse trip and fall. Here and there an Irish swordsman would step out from behind the trees and dispatch an aggressor.

Unable to advance, the English horse turned and rode back along the river's edge. One of them, in steel armour, was particularly vigorous in his orders and encouragement.

That will be Lord Inchiquin, thought Muskerry, lowering his spyglass. He issued an order to be sent to his Saxon musketeers. 'Fire at will', it said.

The Irish obediently delivered a lethal fusillade.

A number of the enemy, out of desperation, leapt into the river, but there was no safety there. Even this far inland the Blackwater was still tidal. A strong tide came upstream from the sea to meet a torrent of water from the hills, heading for the isthmus. The men who thought it might provide an aqueous shelter found that the opposing currents turned them over and over and that they could not find the surface. None of them would again breathe air.

A bugle could be heard. It was the retreat! Inchiquin had ordered his men to retreat!

Muskerry collapsed his spyglass. The day was his.

'Take a message to our captains,' he told his ADC. 'There is to be no pursuit. Only the muskets are to continue their action while their targets are still in range. Tell the men they are to be congratulated. We have had this day a great victory for our Irish nation.'

The Irish moved among the fallen. Six hundred men, sixty horses, all dead. One solitary Irish casualty, a great man with an axe. He had been run through. He must have died quite instantly: he still had a beatific smile on his face.

Lord Muskerry came down from his command post and accepted the salute of his captains.

'What have we captured, Major MacDonogh?'.

'Four 32-pound cannons and eight haulage oxen. The barrel on the second cart contains around half-a-ton of black powder. On the third are beers and foods of various descriptions. Permission to offer them to the men?'

'Go ahead, Major. The men deserve a beer or two. We are in no hurry. What's on the first?'

'Two very cumbersome chests. I think they may be the army's payroll.'

'Break them open. Half is to arm and shoe the army. I shall administer that. The remainder should be divided among the officers. Spoils of war. Any armour, Major?'

'Yes Sir. We have collected around a hundred cuirasses and rather more steel helmets. And we have two torsion siege engines.'

'Trebuchets? Really? Let me see.'

'They're over here, sir.'

The officers inspected the medieval catapults. Such devices were seldom used; cannons had made them redundant. When used to raze a castle, however, they were as effective as cannons and much lighter to transport.

'Inchiquin must have been thinking of using them to slight Carrigadrohid. Well, we shall turn the tables on him. MacDonogh, when the men have eaten, we shall return to our bridge upon the Lee.'

Lord Muskerry turned to address all his captains. 'Men, the day is ours, praise the Lord. Let the heretics vanish from sight as they carry their wounded back to Youghal. You will be hungry. Eat now, before we begin our journey home.

'We have won a battle, but not a war. Gentlemen, be aware that Inchiquin will not take his defeat lying down. He will retreat to Youghal, reform and continue on to Cork and to the English garrison there. Then, having licked his wounds, he will come for us again, this time from the south. That is why we will go to Cork ourselves. We will wait for him to enter the walls, and then we shall make sure no food goes in and no men come out.'

His arm swept over the cannons and siege engines.

'This time we may even ruffle Lord Inchiquin's fine head of hair.'

*

CHAPTER EIGHT
THE BALANCE OF POWER

By the spring that year, 1642, in the battle between King, Parliament, Catholic and Protestant, there were tectonic shifts in the imperium. The Parliamentary forces were slowly recapturing territory in Ulster, Leinster and Munster, and the Irish Rebellion had seemed to falter.

The whole issue had been greatly exacerbated by the quarrel between the king and his Long Parliament. The mere fact that the Irish Lieutenant-General was a king's man made the Irish Parliament both defensive and aggressive.

In the west, the rebels had begun a long siege of the stubborn Earl of Clanrickarde in Galway, but when Lord Ormonde defeated the Kildare rebels at Kilrush, the rebels in Galway began to quaver.

The Irish mood would perk up, however, when Randal MacDonnell, Marquess of Antrim, deserted his official post to rejoin his rebellious Ulster clan.

*

Muskerry had his own reasons for challenging Inchiquin, and not all were defensive. He remembered and resented that, the previous December, Inchiquin had accompanied St Leger in a murderous expedition, and he had a debt to repay.

He had reflected on the first chapter of the Munster Rebellion. It began with the Catholics skirmishing with the Protestant militias of Waterford and Tipperary. The Protestant expedition to Carrick-on-Suir saw Inchiquin and St Leger summarily executed their every prisoner.

Lord Muskerry kept the details of this outrage from his men; there was a significant risk they would desert him *en masse* in order to take their private revenge on Lord Thomond's heir. The consequences would have been unimaginably disastrous, and for them – not for Inchiquin.

Yet 'tis an ill wind that blows no one any good. Inchiquin's crime drove the O'Sullevans, the O'Donovans, and dozens of other clans to fight on the side of the king. By the time the news of the infamy had become common knowledge, most of the able-bodied of Munster had volunteered for Muskerry or Mountgarrett.

Now, the God-sent victory at Cappoquin told the soldiers that they were better off in a well-commanded army than by taking the matter into their own hands. They were ready to submit to command.

A message reached Bryen MacDonogh that he should ride beside his general for a while.

'Ever set foot in our 'rebel city', Major?'

'I've been to Cork once or twice,' MacDonogh admitted. 'My father sends our produce there to sell.'

'He doesn't go himself?'

'The city is dependent on produce from such hinterland regions as Duhallow, but Milesian farmers are not made very welcome in Cork's English Market[xviii]. We have had an uneasy relationship with the burgesses since way back, two or three centuries ago.'

'Why then, particularly? Bad blood?'

'That was the time of the Gaelic resurgence. There was a parting of the ways. From that time the city severed most of its links with people like us and forged new alliances with the Geraldines. That was when it discovered its modern role of defending the Old English.'

'Even so, trade is still Cork's lifeblood. The English Market is justifiably famous. I think you'll find it far less hostile than you have been led to believe. Might I suggest, Major, that you take your wife there, when the time is right? You'll find your way around very easily. The city walls enclose two islands with a single separating strip of water. It has one fine street, the Grand Parade, which runs in a straight line between the South and North Gates. You'll find all the dress and shoe shops in the world, I think, in the lanes and alleys that run off it. Sorcha likes to spend her allowance there.'

'Just when would I do that, General? Before or after we have reduced the city to rubble?'

Muskerry laughed.

'Well, not immediately. We will spend a few days at Carrigadrohid first. General Barry will bring my wife home from Blarney, with some additional troops. Only after that, will we rescue Cork from the forces of darkness. Barry and I have agreed to content ourselves with their surrender, their weapons and their payroll. Especially the last. We don't want them recruiting another army just as soon as our back is turned, do we? There may also be a hostage or two worth taking, I think you know whom I mean. An old friend of yours, and mine. That job done, Sorcha and you can soon enough go shopping.'

'I'm looking forward to being back at Carrigadrohid, Sir.'

'Of course you are, and so will be little Sorcha. If I'm not mistaken she will have bitten her fingernails to the quick.'

They rode on in silence for a while. Their minds were on different matters.

Then the general reached into his pocket.

'I don't need this any more.' He handed Bryen his letter to Sorcha. 'You may want to give it to her anyway. We had a memorable action, Bryen. I will be writing a letter myself, to your father. I have been too busy to write to him up to now. Have you told him you are married yet?'

'I have to confess I have not. There really hasn't been an opportunity. I'm not even sure how to go about it.'

'Tell him the truth, but write you must. If you prefer, write to your mother instead. She will be nearly mad with worry. I half expected to see her at the front, looking after you. She will certainly understand your marriage and will heap her blessings on you. We all have to remember, Bryen, that we were young once. Not always, of course, in such a hurry.'

*

Lord Muskerry's 'big tent', outside Cork City, was far from a typical campaign headquarters. It had had to serve as such on several occasions, but now there was little for the officers to do, not now that the siege had started. Routine checks ensured that the walls were not breached from the inside and that the merchants were not buying food and smuggling it into the city to sell to the hungry at extortionate prices.

Reasoning that he would find Muskerry alone, Bryen MacDonogh sauntered in.

He found his father-in-law smoking a pipe. His doublet was unbuttoned and the earl looked relaxed.

The younger man saluted.

'Come in, Bryen' said Lord Muskerry, 'and sit down. Let's talk rubbish for an hour or so.'

'You have selected my favourite subject, Sir.'

'I don't think so. This is your second war. How are you finding it?'

'It doesn't feel like a war, Sir. More like a series of fairly deadly scuffles. I suppose I had anticipated set-piece battles.'

'We haven't the men to fight a war the way your grandfather did at Kinsale.'

'Is that why you pressed my father to raise our tenants, Lord Muskerry?'

'I asked him to raise his clan, Bryen, because the English response to the Rebellion has been so been brutal. Everyone of Irish origin is suspected of 'treason', a self-fulfilling prophecy if ever there was one. We also have to prevent our tenants' cattle from being plundered in what they laughingly call 'punishment raids'. Cynical opportunism is not the recipe for a negotiated settlement. Sadly, war is our only defence. Your father has other ideas. If I disagree with him, I do respect his judgement.'

'Why are the English so aggressive here in Munster? The Rebellion is hundreds of miles away, in Ulster. Here in the south we have always tried to live in peace with all our neighbours.'

'Bryen, it's the same everywhere. Even in faraway Connacht. Lord Clanrickarde says that if the Castle's anti-Catholic policy is adopted by the king, Ireland will become like the Holy Roman Empire, riven by religious wars. The king needs to settle this unfortunate business as a matter of urgency.'

'He will have other things on his mind. How is the situation in England?'

'Bad, and getting worse. Parliament is trying to impeach His Majesty's closest supporters. The Commons and the Lords have jointly declared that all those who advised the king to reject the Militia Bill are enemies 'of the state'. When the most loyal men in that kingdom are called such names, civil war is inevitable.'

'We will be far worse off than the recusants are in England. No one at all in Dublin defends us. In England, there is a House of Lords, a third of whom are Catholics.'

'The clergy of Armagh assembled a synod at Kells, only weeks ago. They are calling for unity among the scattered rebels.'

'That is supposed to reassure me, Lord Muskerry?'

'It is at least something, Major.'

*

In early April, 1642, the Marquess of Ormonde freed three towns from the 'rebels'; Borris, Birr, and Knockmenease.

Scotland's Covenant Assembly, an exclusively Calvinist body, celebrated these victories by sending three regiments to Ireland from Stranraer - two and a half thousand men under Colonel Sir Robert Monro. They would reinforce their compatriot Ulster Scots and be based in the fort at Carrickfergus, whence they would be able to ride out safely and engage the Catholic militias of O'More and O'Neill.

Monro left the west coast of Scotland, sailed through the North Channel, crossed a stormy Irish Sea and landed in Belfast Lough. Colonel Chichester handed him the fortress and informed him that the Scottish Assembly had promoted Monro to general.

'Yours is a soldier's posting; the fortress is by far the strongest in Ulster,' Chichester told him.

Monro smiled but what he didn't know was that he would remain there for the next six years.

The ambitious General Monro opened his campaign on three fronts; Armagh, Newry and Down. His numbers and firepower totally eclipsed Sir Phelim's. When Newry was seized, the Protestants were at last close to striking Catholic hopes a fatal blow. Indeed, Monro's Scots engaged Phelim O'Neill's Catholic insurgents at Kilwarlin Wood, near Lisburn, County Down, with vastly superior numbers and weaponry and, inevitably, completely routed the Irish.

Protestant stars were again in the ascendant.

Miles to the south, the rebels had experienced another serious defeat. It had been in the disputed, war-torn village of Kilrush, about four miles from Athy in the heart of Leinster. Lord Ormonde had been reinforcing Naas, the town where the late Lord Wentworth had built himself a swaggering mansion.

The marquess had an army of four thousand men and, that April, he confronted the Catholics, who flew the colours of Lords Mountgarrett, Ikerrin, Dunboyne, Sir Morgan Cavenagh, Rory O'More and Hugh O'Byrne.

Eight thousand Catholics tried to block Ormonde's progress. The character of the marquess's commanders - Lord Brabazon, Sir Richard Grenville, Sir Charles Coote and Sir Thomas Lucas – guaranteed the battle would be short and murderous. Inevitably, the rebels were decimated; more than seven hundred men, including Sir Morgan Cavenagh and some other officers, were left dead upon the field, the remainder retreating in chaos.

Lord Ormonde, having scarcely lost a man, returned in triumph to Dublin. For this heart-warming victory the Long Parliament, in a rare moment of enthusiasm, voted the Lieutenant-General a jewel worth £500.[6]

The Lords Justice even condescended to offer their own congratulations.

*

Hull is no great distance from York. It was strategically important to both warring parties. It had a Royal Arsenal, filled with the weapons the king believed he might have to use one day, and its ancient castle was, formally at least, the seat of His Royal Highness the Duke of York.

---

[6] Possibly £500,000 today?

144

Kingston-upon-Hull's town walls had four main gates, several posterns and thirty towers. The castle, on the river's west bank, protected the river's harbour. Henry VIII had ordered two blockhouses to be enclosed in a curtain wall, and James I had made the complex the core of a citadel, nothing less than a bastioned star fort.

The nine-year-old prince was certainly good-looking. The king's sympathisers acclaimed the lad the best-favoured boy in Europe. His mentor prevented the prince from issuing edicts or threats in his royal father's name, so he confined his role to being an advertisement for grace and style. Even Parliament could not object too violently to such restraint. They put up with the irritation that he would always dress as a cavalier, in glorious robes complete with a scaled-down sword.

That mentor in question was the faithful and intelligent courtier, Lord Digby. This royalist peer had sought and obtained royal protection and lived safely from Parliament's undesirable attentions in the castle. Digby commanded a troop of loyal cavalry, which he garrisoned within the town. That too reassured the handsome princeling.

This comfortable arrangement might have gone on forever, were it not for the king's rash decision to appoint his friend and confidant, the Earl of Newcastle, to be Hull's governor.

This irritated Parliament. It suggested that the city's muskets and cannons could fall into the prince's father's hands. The House of Commons revoked the Crown appointment and nominated its own man to secure the town. This man was Sir John Hotham, a Parliamentarian with a fierce and particular grudge against the king.

Sir John Hotham came from a grand Yorkshire family. He had fought for the Protestant cause in Europe during the early part of the Thirty Years' War. He had bought his baronetcy in the 1620s and had been a Member of Parliament in five parliaments. He had risen to be High Sheriff of Yorkshire but, in 1639, he attracted the king's displeasure when he refused to pay ship-money.

He was relieved of his post by royal command, only to slither resentfully into a seething nest of Parliamentarian vipers. To an impressed audience he liked to boast his readiness to kill the king with his bare hands.

In January, Parliament rewarded Hotham. Both Houses invested the baronet with full authority to maintain and retain the guns and ammunition in all circumstances, no matter what the king might say.

He accepted his commission and went with his son, the able and young Captain Hotham, engaging a regiment of foot out of his own deep pockets to form a northern wing of the Parliamentary Army.

Sir John commandeered Ye Olde White Hart Inn, in the centre of town, as his gubernatorial residence. Within days it was known as 'The Plotting Parlour'.

It wasn't long before Sir John Hotham and the likeminded Corporation of Hull found for Parliament and declared Lord Newcastle *non grata* within the City walls. Open conflict between the forces of Parliament and those of the Royalists suddenly ratcheted up from likely to probable. Lord Newcastle, who had not yet taken up his duties, rode to York where he reached his king.

'Parliament did this? *'Non Grata'*? That is our royal prerogative. Hotham has persuaded Parliament to carry out its old threat and declare itself 'sovereign'?' the king asked him. 'How very droll. What does Hothead think that makes us?'

'You should visit him, king-husband,' said his queen when she heard the news. 'Not just to retrieve the prince our son. Let him see the gravity of his error. Take a detachment of foot with you, to make sure he gets the point.'

'No, Hen, the offensive should be couched in charm. I shall wear my best, most kingly, smile.'

'That should scare them even more, my king.'

The king arrived at Hull's Beverley Gate in early April, 1642. He was at the head of a large party that included the Palatinate brothers - Prince Rupert and his elder brother the *Elektor* Karl-Ludovic, Frederick's sons. The older one was better known in England as Charles-Louis.

The Elector's father had married James I's daughter Elizabeth.[xix] The highlight of that reign had been the year he had spent as King of Bohemia, before being forced to flee to The Hague in Holland. He had lived there for the rest of his life, in exile with his wife and family, dying in 1632. Charles-Louis succeeded him as Palatine Elector.

The royal party had taken five days to travel between York and Hull. Each night the king stayed in a royalist household, generously accepting his loyal subjects' elaborate homage *en route*.

Now, drawing close, they saw that the gates were open. The last few hundred yards were lined with the household division that was stationed there. The Duke of York was on a well-groomed pony, ready to receive his father. It all looked very promising.

Not for long, however.

Unknown to almost anyone, Governor Hotham was determined to hold the city and, more importantly, its magazine, for Parliament.

As the king and his company drew close they saw, with alarm and astonishment, the doors to the city slammed shut from within.

Outside, the handful of courtiers who had been preparing to welcome the monarch turned their horses around and demanded access. The Duke of York was of their number. To royal amazement and courtly horror they witnessed the Puritan governor appear in person on the walls with a voice trumpet.

'Sire,' he began to explain, 'it is by a mass vote that the people of Hull have commanded me to close the gates of this city to Your Majesty. I have no choice but to obey.'

This was *lese majesté* – in itself a form of treason.

Such a display of civil disobedience showed all too plainly that the cities of England would take sides. This moment of defiance marked for many the start of the Civil War in England.

What could the royal party do? Insulted, humiliated, King Charles, his son and the royal party was forced to withdraw to York, from where the king dispatched two regiments of foot. Hull was under siege.

'If they will not allow us in, then we shall not allow them out,' said the king with a bitter smile. 'They will soon find themselves in 'Hull on earth'.'

*

The Royalist siege of Hull had begun.

Hotham sought out Lord Digby, effectively his hostage, promising him that he would surrender the town to the king. Digby was duly released to convey the Governor's message to the Royal Army under a white flag but, when Charles tried a second time to gain admittance, the city gates remained closed.

The Duke of York, Prince Rupert and the Elector Charles-Louis rejoined the king. Beneath a display of good humour, Charles was livid. He charged Sir John Hotham with high treason, but Parliament refused to issue the warrant. The king then asked Sir Richard Lovelace to persuade Parliament and loyalists in Kent to present a petition to Parliament. Again it was rejected.

The House of Commons had ostentatiously lost the will to honour its king.

*

CHAPTER NINE
CIVIL WAR

That England was now in a Civil War could no longer be denied. All that was missing was the bloodshed.

They didn't have long to wait. Royalist and Parliamentary forces clashed violently in Manchester and, on July 15, the Royalists, under Lord Strange, were forced out of the city.

Meanwhile, Hull was completely encircled by the royalist army. Famine soon began to make its persuasive arguments. Many members of the Town Council now saw that they had been rash to take on the Crown without thinking about the consequences and their mood was ugly. When the first of its citizens died of malnutrition or dysentery, it seemed like a good time to take action. The first to escape, under cover of darkness, was Sir John Hotham.

It took little time for the king's brigade to discover him, hiding in a priest's hole with his son in their manor house in Scarborough. They were arrested and taken to London on board 'The Hercules'. On arrival, and in order to avoid any parliamentarian attempts at rescue, Sir John and his son were imprisoned in the Tower of London, a royal palace.

The Commons had no further use for them either, somewhat disloyally charging them both with desertion. Parliament then issued an *ad hominem* order that Sir John's and Captain Hotham's specie, estates, cattle and goods were to be seized and sold to fund the back pay of Hull's Puritan infantry.

The king had lost a great deal of face in the episode. He was still in York, as were the Palatinate brothers, and now, more than ever, it was the time to make certain of their support. He arranged for Prince Rupert and the Duke of York to be invested Knights of the Garter. Sadly, the Elector Charles-Louis declined the honour, believing that he was being used as a pawn. Every attempt to mollify him failed.

Worse than that: he abandoned King Charles and returned to the Palatinate. His younger sibling Prince Rupert, on the other hand, became the king's most devoted companion.

The Hothams, now paupered, would spend years in miserable confinement. They had no longer the means to secure any comfort in their sordid cell. Relief only came when they were beheaded.

In the meantime, outright Civil War in England seemed to have been momentarily averted. In all the general panic at home, no one seemed to notice that the Irish rebels had taken the city of Waterford.

*

On April 10, 1642, Cork City was still under siege. That was because the city served as Parliament's and the Protestants' GHQ in Munster. In its walls, its grandees swapped strategies.

'Well met, Lord Inchiquin! How is our little emergency coming along?'

'Not too badly, Lord Barrymore. You will have heard that three Scots regiments have just landed at Carrickfergus?'

'Scots? Are they Catholic? MacDonald's redshanks back in Ireland?'

'Catholics! You must be joking! Sir Robert Monro's Scots are are Covenanters, Calvinists. They would gladly put all Catholics to the stake.'

'Interesting, but how does that help us, Lord Inchiquin? They are in Ulster. Miles away. What is our condition in Munster? What, if anything, is St Leger doing to relieve this siege? The Dykeside warehouses are nearly empty. We have already emptied Ronayne's. I'd be surprised if we could survive another whole month.'

'It rather seems that down here, at least, the Irish Catholics are gaining the upper hand. Most of this province has fallen, except here and those few other towns on the south coast with English garrisons.'

'So, who exactly is in command? Who has our destiny in his grasp?' asked Lord Barrymore.

'Of us? St Leger. It's William St Leger, even though he is supposed to share it with the Earl of Cork.'

'If it's St Leger, he hasn't long to live. That's what I hear. When he dies, what will happen then? Most people think that after the President's death, you and Lord Cork will vie for control of the province's Protestants. My money is already on you.'

Inchiquin laughed modestly.

'The Catholics? Do they have leaders?' he asked.

'Yes, my lord, they do. Garret Barry is competent, but since Lord Muskerry joined the insurgency he looks the more promising of the two. You had dealings with him at Cappoquin, I believe?'

Inchiquin stopped smiling.

'How committed is Muskerry to the rebel cause?'

'He says that the Rebellion is the only way of preserving Catholicism, the king's prerogative and the rights of the Irish nobility.'

'Lord Muskerry said that? Well, he has successfully confined us to barracks, here in Cork. A temporary setback, however. The rebels cannot not keep us trapped for long.'

*

As it turned out, Muskerry's siege of the City of Cork confined Inchiquin for nearly two months. By the early summer, general shortages forced Inchiquin to consider re-engaging Muskerry.

The River Lee, on which Cork had been founded, served the city as a moat. The town was also protected by walls. Ordinarily, it housed two regiments of 'English' foot, mostly housed in the Entrance Fort, with a few other companies sheltered in several others. They had been built to defend the two thousand original Corkonians, mostly of Danish or Viking ancestry, from the Gaels and Anglo-Normans - the 'Old English' - who would have otherwise happily attacked it. Many of these men had now joined Inchiquin's army, after his defeat at Cappoquin, and the town's defences had swollen. Altogether, the city housed two companies of horse, three hundred musketeers and three thousand foot, who had found a billet of sorts in Cork's Holly Rode Fort. Their commander resided in Forts Gate, built over the river-moat at the east end of the island.

The additional strength came at a cost. It was a great drain on the town's resources, and in a siege that was far from good.

The Irish, meanwhile, had pitched camp clear of the city's perimeter. Four thousand Gaels patrolled the fields and suburbs. No one was going in or coming out of Cork City.

The Irish generals, and some senior officers, shared a 'big tent'.

One of those was Major Bryen MacDonogh.

'I remember Lord Inchiquin well,' Bryen told his father-in-law. 'He will attempt the unexpected.'

'Thank you, Major, for so generously sharing that insight with me,' Lord Muskerry replied. 'What else d'you think might not have occurred to me?'

'Night time? A diversion? A red herring of some kind? He knows we are provisioned and he is not. Perhaps he is expecting relief from the sea, from Bristol? I do know he's not the type to sit down quietly and watch the citizens go wanting.'

'Thank you for your kind advice, Major. Night time, you think. I shall double the watch. Tell the officers that if Inchiquin successfully liberates his Vikings and heretics we shall withdraw to Blarney.'

A redoubled nightwatch was tedious but since the nights were short, the men need not suffer too much discomfort.

Just how much grain could Inchiquin have secreted in those huge warehouses? The Protestants would have to make a break for it at some point. Muskerry was ready for the unexpected but, when it actually happened, it left him and his officers wrong-footed and astonished.

It came on a Sunday. It hadn't rained for a week and the going was easy under hoof and foot. The air was clear and bright and the Irish could see for miles. Inside Cork City the bells of Shandon Church called the pious to prayer. The bells of St Mary's Church, which had resisted the Reformation, had long been silent.

 The Protestants of Cork City had never trusted their county. The locality was so 'infested with evil Irish rovers' that many had never ventured beyond the security of their gates. Outside their walls the world was hostile and Catholic. Few of the neighbouring hamlets and townlands could boast a Protestant temple. The result was that the citizens of Cork had to marry each other. For nearly a century they had become steadily more interbred, and with the passing of each generation they became ever more of a race apart.

Not that it affected Muskerry's army. His soldiers made their own way to any of the dozen slighted Catholic churches surrounding Cork on every hill and in every ancient settlement.

Bryen had been to the earliest mass, as he had the day-watch detail.

Though half of his men were still at prayer, he felt safe. Only an idiot would start a war when their troops could be seen for miles, and Inchiquin was no idiot.

Bryen was both overconfident and wrong.

He was not even looking towards Cork when the doors of the Fort Bridge were thrown open and Lord Inchiquin and his two regiments of horse thundered out at speed, aiming themselves at Muskerry's captured cannons, whose gunners were wholly taken by surprise. Faced with two hundred sabre-brandishing cavalrymen charging straight for them, they abandoned their artillery and fled.

Meanwhile, the English and their fellow travellers had been mobilised. They emerged from the numerous garrisons beside the walls, some carrying muskets, others flaming torches. Their musket volleys sang out lethally while their foot, bearing pikes, marched on the Irish in squares.

Their 'sally' lasted for an hour at most, while they set fire to the Irish camp. Any Irishman who stood his ground was cut down.

The Irish were routed and the English planned a long wanted dinner.

Lord Muskerry was back in Blarney Castle, his chief seat.

'Expect the unexpected, Bryen, you advised me. And what happens? A double bluff. Lord Inchiquin emerges by day, to face a reduced guard as we thought he would attack by night. He finds our men mostly in church, breaks up our camp, steals our baggage, provisions and field pieces.'

'They were mostly his in the first place.'

'That is hardly the point, Major.'

'What will he do with the artillery?'

'He is already attacking our Irish castles to the west of Cork harbour.'

'Can he justify such naked aggression?'

'Our friends had been harrying the English relief vessels. Preventing them from reaching Cobh and landing their provisions or reinforcing the Protestants. Inchiquin's raids are about revenge.'

So now Cork is his and re-established. So what is Inchiquin's next move?'

'General Barry's siege of Limerick will be worrying him, of that I'm certain. I think he will try to raise it.'

'Shall we follow him?'

'Not directly. We have suffered a setback, not a defeat. We shall reapply ourselves to the south coast. Let us free Kinsale and Youghal from Inchiquin's lightning sword.'

*

The Rt Hon the Earl of Castlehaven,
Care of Lord Mountgarret
Kilkenny Castle.

June 1642

Before I explain the purpose of my letter, dear Lord Castlehaven, let me add my name to the long list of people congratulating you on your military commission in our new Catholic Confederacy. Your name is and will be inscribed in the hearts of scholars already born and yet to come.

152

We have never met, but we have a mutual friend in Finbar O'Driscoll; now, I am told, commissioned major and serving under you. I am confident that he will both vouch for me and, when he can, present me to you.

Similarly I have the privilege of having the acquaintance of Generals Lord Muskerry and Garret Barry. The former is my son's father-in-law. The above will, I believe, serve to reassure you as to my character and resolve.

Then, last but not least, you know my son Bryen. You may feel you owe him something, a debt of gratitude perhaps. I can tell you that it is not a debt that he would ever consider calling in.

It falls to me, the absent parent, to ask that favour in his stead.

Before I disclose what it is, my dear general, I must tell you that it is vitally important that my lord and husband, Dermod Oge MacDonogh Carty of Duhallow, knows nothing of what I am about to ask. Dear Lord Castlehaven, if you cannot submit to this request, please read no further. Simply feed this letter to your flames or pigs, now, and of course do not respond.

If, however, you are still reading, it must mean you have assented to my request.

Lord Castlehaven, it is common knowledge that your regiment is heavily engaged in our Rebellion. Rumours have reached Duhallow that you intend to free Youghal, Kinsale and Cork to Ireland from their presumptuous English masters.

I should like to play my part in these adventures and I beg you to offer me a secret commission in your regiment.

I am fit, a good horsewoman, barely forty years old, and for more than half my life I have hunted the Duhallow. As for my martial skills, I have learned my swordcraft from soldiers as skilled as my husband. I have also commissioned a lightly armoured suit which hides my sex and my identity. Wearing it I pass for a young man.

The crisis in Ireland provokes me to put myself, and the twenty men who have secretly bound themselves to me, at your disposal.

Youghal is not so very far from Duhallow. Its liberation will need all the help it can find. I would be honoured beyond any order of gallantry if you would let me ride alongside you, anonymously, outside the walls of that occupied town, in order to help you with your siege until you lose patience with my womanly ways.

I am not afraid to come face to face with my enemy. My family is grown and my conscience is easy. I am ready to do my duty.

If you have read this far, please write as soon as you are able, Lord Castlehaven, to your most loyal servant, Cliona MacDonogh of Duhallow.

In Ulster, things continued badly for Sir Phelim O'Neill. His enemy's army was better furnished, better trained and, above all, larger than his.

All told, and with Chichester's forces thrown in, General Monro commanded a very significant force - 19,000 troops, regulars and volunteers - in the garrison or in the field. He quickly recovered Newry. In the process Monro hanged seventy men, ten women and two priests. The Rebellion was only eight months old, and already the Catholics had become inured by such savagery.

Magennis had had to abandon Down, and McMahon thought it best to let Monaghan go too. Rather than surrender Dungannon, Sir Phelim torched it. When Monro heard, he set out in hot pursuit, casually slaughtering O'Neill's men where he confronted them, first at Kilwarlin Wood, then at Loughbrickland. When he realised that a handful of survivors was hiding in the woods behind him, he turned back, seized the cattle he found there as a fee and killed any Irish man, woman and child he found in his way.

The Ulster Catholics considered capitulation. Sir Phelim, desperate to restore his countrymen's morale and to resist the Covenanter general from across the water, determined to take a stand at Charlemont. There he faced Sir Robert and Sir William Stewart. He showed his usual courage and was rewarded with more than his recent luck. The Scottish advance was reversed, at least for a while. His victory did a lot for Irish morale.

Elsewhere, Catholic landowners needed little persuasion to raise their clans and tenantry. Such conscripts had to be drilled into *ad hoc* militias. Small-holders saw their farms were torched, their cattle rustled, it was no use pretending there wasn't a problem, and their chiefs had to harness the whirlwind of anarchic, self-righteous anger that was threatening to engulf the country.

Not all Catholics chiefs were prepared to stake their lives on the outcome. Some were too cautious, and in some cases their tenants were too over-agitated to submit to martial discipline.

There was also a generalised conspiracy theory to disprove. The fact that some of the lesser chiefs still had land suggested to many of their tenants that some sort of a deal had been struck with the Castle. This circular suspicion provoked some chiefs to fear that after the settlers had been evicted, a vengeful people might turn on them.

The general anxiety was compounded by the English Parliament's timely declaration that *all* Irish Catholics, regardless of any infirmity, complicity, age and sex, were responsible for the Rebellion. The martyrdom of Protestants would be punished accordingly. An eye for an eye, as in the Holy Writ.

This was interpreted by all Irishmen as a threat to every life, merely on the basis of being a native of that country and adhering to the faith of their ancestors. Had anywhere in Christendom ever seen such a comparable sin? Could the Puritan English really countenance the extermination of a race, of a faith? It was hard to believe, yet some Protestants had already shown their readiness to do such an awful thing.

O'More's rebels' defeat of Dublin's forces at Julianstown caused many relieved chiefs to gain confidence and sign up. Inevitably, the pendulum chose this moment to change direction, and when the rebels staged another attempt to take nearby Drogheda, and failed, Catholic confidence subsided a little.

The inescapable fact was the rebels lacked officers. The few that had military skills had gained them on the Continent. Overall, when faced with men of St Leger's calibre, they desperately needed training, experience, money and a Government.

Before a national organisation, with a senate, executive, treasury, army, ships and diplomats could come into being, the Catholic Irish had three steps to take.

The first was to involve every county outside the Pale.

The second challenge, far harder, was to inveigle the Lords of the Pale into enlisting. It was not impossible, however. Some of the more far-sighted Lords of the Pale, however, had realised that they had no choice but to commit to the Rebellion, whether their hearts were in it or not.

These ambitions were already being realised, if slowly.

The third step, now being taken, was to secure the support of the bishops.

These mitred gentlemen met in great secrecy at their Provincial Synod in Kells. With just one abstention - the Bishop of Meath - they pronounced 'the hitherto *de facto* war just and, consequently, *de jure*', solemnly condemning all acts of private vengeance. They indicted all those who, under cover of conflict, sought to expropriate other people's lands. Lastly, they issued an invitation to all the lords of Catholic Ireland, spiritual and temporal, to gather in Kilkenny Castle in May.

*

CHAPTER TEN
ANTIPOPERY

In England, within the confines of the Palace of Westminster, Sir John Pym spoke at any and every opportunity, in his customary and expansive rhetoric, of an international Popish plot.

'Any dullard can see that the scarlet succubus of Rome has seduced the idolators of Paris and Madrid. Even our king has fallen under his sway. Especially the king. He is in the thrall of his Papist wife and the Pope. Between them, every foreign prince is engineering a war in Ireland. We must hold them to account for every drop of Protestant blood they spill. Let me tell you, good gentlemen, honourable members, the king's closest advisors are each as guilty as the next, and that the King of England is succumbing to their contagion.'

In similar vein he contrived to present every initiative of the Counterreformation in such a way that proved to many he was right. Papists could commit murder on a Saturday and their priests would absolve them on Sunday. He talked of the cruelty of the Holy Inquisition. He dwelt on the menace of the Jesuits. Catholics were inherently evil; they had the atavistic bloodlust that led to the death of good free-thinking and righteous men and women, today in Ireland and, a few years before, in France.

'Is there anyone in this House who can hear the dreadful date 'St Bartholomew's Day' and not shudder?'

Pym's Puritan connections ensured that his scurrilous assertions would be repeated from every lectern and pulpit in England. His primary insinuation - that the king himself was not to be trusted with control of an army, nor even to quell the Rebellion - fell on fertile and well-prepared ground. Many of the voting (and property-owning) public began to believe that only Parliament should be entrusted with power.

Observers speculated that Pym's very personal attack on the King's Person might hasten or even bring about a terrible contest between the king and Parliament. Was this Pym's secret purpose? Might he actually want a Civil War? Maybe he did. Only then would MPs, all with private means and uniformly elected by the property-owning middle class, gain sovereign power. The 'new rich', heirs to the Tudor kleptocracy, lived on and profited from the lands that monasteries had once tended for God. A little is never enough. They wanted everything.

Pym's speeches spread fear and loathing. He presented the fighting in Ireland as being between rival foreign monarchs, not between small bands or militias, raised by Catholic or Protestant lords from their local people. Privately, he didn't think that Catholics were evil. He thought them stupid. Could they not see the way the wind was blowing? He actually laughed when he learned that the Old English chiefs, the 'Geraldines', were joining the Rebellion *on the wrong side*.

Then, Sir Phelim O'Neill, who as a lawyer should have known better, played into Pym's hands. He did something so sublimely idiotic as almost to award a victory to his enemies.

He forged a letter from the monarch. It appeared to authorise the Irish *in the royal name* to rise against the English Parliament and its Dublin puppet in defence of their liberties. Once copies of Sir Phelim's letter had begun to circulate in England the king lost even more support. Sir Phelim's support for the throne was entirely counterproductive.

The stakes had always been high. Now they looked set to break the bank.

Rory O'More and Sir Phelim O'Neill still controlled the roads in and out of the capital and Dublin was under siege. The Irish Sea was too choppy to permit relief from England. Within a couple of weeks the less fortunate were already becoming horribly hungry. They could not afford to buy what they needed. The prices of staple commodities had rocketed, and despair and disease had begun to undermine the resolve of the capital's population.

Wolves began to descend the Wicklow hills into the suburbs, and their eerie howls were plainly heard in Trinity College on the south-eastern edge of the town. As their brutal ambitions grew, they began to stalk the dying. For the first time in more than a century, long domesticated wolfhounds were assembled into a second-rate pack and huntsmen were ordered to rid the capital of these opportunistic predators.

The Castle's inability to do anything useful undermined its authority. Borlase and Parsons had long recalled their outlying garrisons to the defence of the Castle; this while ungoverned, resentful and angry Ulstermen freely savoured their revenge on the settlers, English and Scottish.

When they torched Armagh, Dubliners saw plainly that the indigenous people of Ireland were fervid with hatred. The rebel leaders pleaded by letter and via the priests for the Catholic tenantry to desist from their uncoordinated, opportunist and savage attacks on the Protestants. It was to no avail. Calm was not in season.

In England, Pym and Coke, supported from the wings by Lord Massereene, had at last found the courage to defy the king in the open. Having persuaded the English Parliament to raise forces of its own, under the Militia Ordinance, they told the Speaker, the king was today 'a mere sounding brass'.

In Ireland, too, cracks in the social fabric looked like the precursor to disaster.

*

To General Monro   Londonderry, 27
Carrickfergus   April 1642

We of this loyal city of Londonderry must have either been forgotten or given over for lost. All other parts of the Irish Kingdom are plentifully supplied and, while we have made our wants and miseries known divers times to Dublin, to England and to Scotland, no relief has ever come to us. We have had just thirty barrels of powder, brought by Captain Boulton from Dublin long before Christmas. The lack of powder and arms here hath been our ruin. It is due only to the great providence and goodness of God that we are still alive. We have nothing but old decayed calivers which we have trimmed up and made work to our great and personal charge.

We have but seven hundred men for the defence of the city, again at our own expense, while we wait for money and supplies. There are not one hundred good swords among them and the city's own arms are mean. Sir William Stewart, Sir Robert Stewart and Sir Ralph Gore were commissioned by His Majesty in November to raise three regiments and two troops of horse. They are somewhere in County Tyrone and have been all this winter, to oppose the enemy. Without food, shelter or money, however, they are of little use. Our powder is almost gone, our victuals are failing, and these three regiments would have long since starved if we had not relieved them with beef, butter, herrings and other necessaries, again at great cost. We have not now enough for our own men in the city. If a ship from Bristol had not arrived here with peas, meal and wheat, we should surely have perished. Even what we have will not last the regiments a fortnight. The provision of the country is destroyed by the enemy, or devoured by our own men; we are enforced to feed multitudes that are fled hither for relief. If the enemy's sword spares us, famine will dispatch us, except God in mercy provide for us. This is not all. Sir Phelim O'Neill has gathered from all parts a great army of horse and foot at Strabane, a mere ten miles of this city.

Sir Phelim is on the one side of the river, we are on the other. We are in sight of each other. We have to join with them, unfurnished and with no powder. To relieve our fainting spirits, God hath provided for our relief. He hath sent this bearer Captain Strange into Lough Foyle who, being in His Majesty's service, sent for the comfort of His Majesty's distressed subjects into those parts. We have told him of our desperate estate and the great peril we are in. We pray that for the love of God and honour of our King, and the safety of this place and people, ye will dispatch him back again to us with a good and large proportion of powder, match and lead, muskets, swords, pikes, some spades and shovels, whereof we have not any; and of these or what else may be had, as much as ye can possibly spare us; for we want all things fit to defend a distressed country and offend a desperate enemy.

We also pray that you will restore the captain the six barrels of powder we have borrowed of him; and if there be any biscuit, cheese, or any other victuals to be spared, to spend us some good proportion thereof. So being at present in great haste and perplexity, with our service presented to your honour, we remain your humble servants, &c.,

Mayor Robert Thornton, Henry Osborne, John Vaughan

*

May, 1642, was showing signs of evolving into a hot Summer. Tempers rose still further in the quickening heat.

Despite Westminster's generous support, the 'New Irish' - undertakers and settlers - were far from complacent. The growing catalogue of Protestant deaths served as a mallet to smash their protective shell of self-confidence. In Ulster in particular, many planters came to the bitter conclusion that no Catholic could ever be trusted. The rich minority's hatred of the poor majority led them to inflict lethal, pre-emptive reprisals on Catholics, whenever they had the chance. Feeling the Papist worm was bound to turn, their best recourse was to stamp on it before it did.

The rebels knew this and they armed themselves accordingly. They were ready; their ordnance ranged from arquebuses to pitchforks, hitherto hidden in their haylofts.

The Rebel forces were divided into four main concentrations. Sir Phelim O'Neill commanded in Ulster. Around the Pale, Rory O'More and Viscount Gormanston had divided the command between them. In the southeast, septs of the Butler family led the rebels, mostly under Lord Mountgarrett. In Munster, Lord Muskerry held the reins.

The Protestants of Cork, Dublin, Carrickfergus and Derry had originally raised their own militias in self-defence, but now they thirsted for action.

Months of deadly chaos would scourge all Ireland.

Across the Irish Sea the Long Parliament had taken fright. It levied 16,000 men to subdue Ireland. Disturbingly, unconstitutionally, this was done without royal assent. Lord Wharton was commissioned as chief-designate of the expeditionary force and the Earl of Warwick was appointed the Parliamentary commander of the fleet. Lord Essex, a noble Parliamentarian, was made their Lord General and one of his captains was his coreligionist, Oliver Cromwell, gent., honourable Member for Cambridge.

From the moment the Parliamentarians raised their own army, Charles and his Parliament were divided by the sword.

Wharton waited impatiently on English shores for orders to weigh anchor.

From the Irish perspective, the military prognosis was improving. Now the English were bickering amongst themselves as well as with those who honoured their king. Anyone denouncing those who thought Parliament sovereign was deemed a royalist. An English Civil War would make the Irish Rebellion seem insignificant. The expedition would have to be postponed or cancelled.

The Irish had gained the breathing space they needed.

Their leaders profited from Saxon indecision and prepared to renew their war on the Heretics. There may not have been an Irish 'nation' but there was a common faith, and it included the monarchy. In this matter, at least, Ireland would find for the king.

*

CHAPTER ELEVEN
THE KILKENNY CONFEDERACY

While the Rebellion, and Dublin Castle's reaction to it, continued to carve a murderous swathe up and down Ireland, something both unpredicted and utterly unprecedented was happening. It was a little marvellous, everyone said. By the May of 1642 the Irish were beginning to think like a single nation.

Its first iteration was somewhat pompous. The First National Synod of the Irish Confederacy was called to Lord Mountgarrett's seat, Kilkenny Castle. This was a vast and majestic fortress, looming above a bend on the river Nore, deep in the very heart of its eponymous county. The castle was the mightiest seat of the warrior FitzWalter dynasty, which in the twelfth century had adopted the English-sounding surname of 'Butler'. This great and Catholic Old English family had gained pre-eminence after its original owners, the indigenous O'Carrolls, had been unseated, their lands taken in honest conquest and their tenants rents transferred to new masters.

Despite the savage skirmishing and innumerable sieges up and down the country, almost every Catholic invitee managed to make his way there, safely and from the four corners of the Irish kingdom. Everyone had had four weeks' notice of the Assembly. Some would need all that time to make the journey. Ordinarily, early summer would be a fine one for travel and nowhere in Ireland is much more than a few weeks' brisk march from anywhere else, but the country was panicked and some of it was in tumult.

Dublin's troops were busy trying to raise the sieges and quell the frequent risings in Ulster and in the Pale. The issue in the south west was Lord Muskerry and General Barry. The Catholic 'Powers-in-Waiting' knew that the heretics still had plenty of opportunities to ambush their delegates at any time, and more often than not in the realistic hope of a ransom.

Nevertheless, following the call to Kilkenny, and to the thrilled amazement of the country folk, every route south began to fill with stately, colourful traffic, mounted companies and solitary horsemen, all making their way in varying degrees of discomfort along the ill-made roads. Trains of ancient covered wagons, hauled by pairs of emaciated oxen; noble carriages with their teams of fine horses, stately phaetons, dog carts pulled by recalcitrant mules, and rickety chariots of every era, shape and roadworthiness; all these and more rattled noisily by.

Crowds of curious children ran behind or beside the conveyances. Women dropped to their knees to make the sign of the cross if they thought the passenger within could be an anointed and consecrated bishop. Here and there the carriages would mire in the clay and local labourers saw a profitable chance to pull the vehicles from the mud. Local dogs barked happily, following the cavalcade until they risked forgetting the trail of the scents that would lead them home.

Every Roman bishop, with the exception of Dease of Derry, had consented to be at Kilkenny's Synod. O'Reilly, Archbishop of Armagh and Primate of Ireland, was already there. So too was Bishop Butler, the 'rival' tutelary of Cashel. Also arriving, in a proud display of faded archiepiscopal purple, were O'Kealy of Tuam, Rothe of Ossory and the bishops of Clonfert, Elphin, Waterford, Lismore, Conor, Kildare and Down.

To this brave if anachronistic convocation came the soberly gowned figures of the proctors of Dublin, Limerick and Killaloe, their elderly chargers flanked by their 'bulldogs'. Since the days of the Tudors their hereditary offices had been reduced to the purely ceremonial. In the Pale, 'English' militias had inherited the workload that the proctors once had. If Dublin Castle's authorities had witnessed their procession, they would have been astonished and not a little unnerved to see that these supposedly extinct offices had been discreetly maintained and that they were, that day, distinguished with so much splendour.

Sixteen heads of religious orders, walking in their long-banned white, brown or black habits, accompanied by their incense-swinging acolytes, had joined the extraordinary throng. Such a sight had been unseen since the Reformation.

Neither last nor least, the 'chiefs of their names', the heads of the great families of Celtic history, chose to flaunt the capes and broadswords of ancient tradition. Doublets were not for them this day. As they rode through the huge outer doors of Kilkenny Castle, making their way across the *bawn* to the great hall, they added much colour to an excited throng.

Clearly the native peoples of Ireland had no local word or phrase for 'beyond repair.' Most of their clothes were so much restored that it would have challenged a seasoned antiquary to know the year in which this cloak or that pair of trews had once been new. It was enough that someone somewhere had thought to make do and mend these antique garments.

The faded apparel of prelates and nobles, officials and other Irish office-holders, particularly their patched pantaloons, the coarse fisher-

stitching, the frayed lace of their cuffs; none of these brought the assembly into the slightest disrepute nor encouraged the ridicule of the worldly-wise. On the contrary, the people unanimously invested their new but overdue National Assembly with the highest conceivable moral purpose. That it had met at all seemed like a miracle.

The Holy Spirit Himself had summoned the Ghost of Ireland Past.

The Irish were about to have their own Assembly. They would require it to establish order among the more chaotic elements of the Rebellion. Seeing the delegates arrive in their awesome panoply, all the witnesses knew that instant that their Confederacy could not fail.

*

In Northern Ireland, Sir Charles Coote was not going to come to the aid of any Protestant. Especially not in Londonderry. For one thing the rebels had made it enemy territory. For another he was just too damn busy. In the Pale he seemed invincible. The merciless saberer, following yet another a murderous skirmish at Kilrush, was again triumphant. He might have an attempt at liberating Birr Castle from a rebel siege. Instead, he allowed it to suffer. At least Birr, in Co Offaly, was not in 'bow-and-arrow' country, as he liked to call the parts of Ireland that remained Catholic.

News now came from Geashill that the lawyer O'More had persuaded the O'Dempseys, a neighbouring Catholic tribe, to lay siege to the Anglican Letitia Lady Digby, the owner of Offally's recently converted abbey. Coote wasted no time. He set off on his rescue mission immediately, despite being advised of the difficulties he would certainly face, should he ever need to retreat through the mountain passes on the way.

The O'Dempseys had written to the 62-year-old baroness.

Honourable Lady Digby,

We, his Majesties loyal subjects, being at present employed in his Highnesses Service for the taking of this your Castle, you are therefore to deliver unto us free possession of your said Castle, promising faithfully that your Ladyship, together with the rest in the said Castle restant shall have reasonable composition; otherwise upon the not yielding of the Castle, we do assure you that we will burn the whole town, kill all the Protestants, and spare neither man, woman, nor child, up to taking the castle.

Consider, madam, of this our offer, and impute not the blame of your own folly unto us; think not that we brag. Your Ladyship upon submission shall have a safe convoy to secure you from the hands

163

of your enemies, and to lead you where you please. A speedy reply is desired with all expedition, and thus we surcease.

To the Honourable, and thrice virtuous Lady, the Lady Digby, Henry O'Dempsy and others of his name.

Lady Digby had replied.

I received your letter, wherein you threaten to sack this my Castle, by His Majesty's authority. I am, and ever have been, a loyal subject, and a good neighbour amongst you, and therefore cannot but wonder at such an assault. I thank you for your offer of a convoy, wherein I hold little safety, and therefore my resolution is, that being free from offending his Majesty, or doing wrong to any of you, I will live and die innocently, and will do my best to defend my own, leaving the issue to God. And though I have been, and still am desirous to avoid the shedding of Christian blood, yet being provoked, your threats shall no whit dismay me.

For her cousin Henry Dempsy and the rest,
Lettice Offalia

While the O'Dempseys built great wooden siege engines, they never expected a headlong charge from Coote's horse. Abandoning their catapults and trebuchets, they turned tail to vanish into the forest. There they soon found a glade and regrouped. Coote would comb the woods but he found the clannish nut hard to crack. It would take weeks before her ladyship's castle of Geashill was successfully relieved.

Coote's victory had been delayed by a lack of local knowledge. His most deadly weapons had always been his skewed courage, his tirelessness and his single-minded thoroughness, but on thisocassion at least even those qualities had not been quite enough.

Now, having at last raised the siege, the baronet launched a lightning campaign on his way home, scattering the 'woodkerne' though the Montrath woods as he went. He returned to his base camp without the loss of a single man. Coote had shown his customary talent to rout the Irish and amaze everyone, yet he felt somehow outwitted.

By the time he climbed into his tent, where as usual he would sleep armed and propped up, he had spent forty-eight hours in the field without a break, and in the saddle. When the news reached the Lords Justice they thought his feat prodigious, as well they might. He was their kind of general, and as he re-entered Dublin's gates, he was treated to the triumphal acknowledgement of the entire capital.

'I protest. I was facing an incoherent rabble,' he told his commanding officer, the Marquess of Ormonde, while having an order of chivalry bestowed on him, 'I have never thought of retreat in my life. Nor have I ever failed by forcing my way. I always consider how to do my business and when done I go home again, as best I can.'

His boast had the benefit of being true. Coote slept remarkably little during a campaign. When he closed his eyes he would be leaning in armour against a wall or a tree, always ready for a scrap.

Ormonde now sent Coote on another expedition, this time to tame the Irish townland of Philipstown[xx]. Coote interpreted his orders literally and enthusiastically, depopulating the settlement and ending the passage into the future of a thousand pointless families in the process.

He had no time for furlough. Within a week of the Philipstown carnage he led a foray against a significant Catholic force around Trim. The Confederates' Colonel Plunkett had housed his men in his immense castle in the centre of town. Trim Castle was easily the largest Anglo-Norman castle in Ireland. Back in the old days, Hugh de Lacy and his son Walter had taken thirty years to build it in an effort to put a brake on Strongbow. The massive twenty-sided keep, cruciform in shape, was protected by a ditch, a curtain wall and moat. Surely it was impenetrable?

Coote occupied the town and proceeded to surround the castle.

Then, in the dead of night, three thousand armed Irishmen emerged from the fortress to surprise the English. One of Coote's lookouts gave the alarm. The baronet, with a bodyguard of just seventeen horse, sallied straight at the hugely superior force, his sword held high in the air. His foot followed his horse, and very nearly as fast. The Irish, amazed and dazzled by his daring, broke up. The Protestants were able to wheel around and regain their safety before the Catholics could reform.

Despite his readiness to let his men 'frolic', as he liked to put it, with the native women and children, Coote's affection for the cat had ensured he could never be popular. On the contrary, and in almost every campaign, a poor wretch or two would be flogged, flayed or hanged.

On a dark night in May, while leading yet another sally against the Catholics of Trim, an unidentified musketeer took Coote's life. The ball was later shown to be of English manufacture, but whether the general's demise was the work of the enemy or one of his own troopers was never determined. What is sure is that the violent death of that most ruthless and arguably deranged enemy gave the Catholics some grim satisfaction and put fear into the hearts of the Lords Justice.

*

The General Assembly of the Confederacy, now securely based in Kilkenny Castle, saw eleven bishops and fourteen lords represent the Irish peerage. Two hundred and twenty-six commoners spoke for the constituencies. Kilkenny Castle had only one great hall, so both bodies sat in the same chamber, divided by a raised dais.

The first meeting began in a truculent mood. By forcing the Gaels and the Anglo-Irish to sing from the proverbial hymn sheet, it was all too predictable that their deliberations might be fractious.

The respect that everybody accorded to the venerable Archbishop O'Reilly, underwritten by the sharp crack of his crook on the hall's stone floor, quietened the querulous opening session.

'Gentlemen, I would like to welcome you all to this great castle, chief seat of the Butlers. You have had a difficult journey, all of you. The epic stories I have already heard of your travels should have made my hair turn grey, except that the Maker has already made that revision to my pristine good looks.' He waited patiently for applause and was modestly rewarded. 'I should particularly like to welcome to this historic gathering the dignitaries of Connacht.'

He was again the beneficiary of a round of applause, but when he resumed his tone was darker.

'Your presence here is truly remarkable. We are all aware that west of the Shannon, the pain of Strafford's reign of terror is fresh and, as yet, unavenged. The Earl of Clanrickarde, who should know better, is still trying to oppose or contain the general conversion to the Confederacy.'

There were many angry murmurs.

'Before we even begin, we must swear to an Oath of Association. I insist. It is designed to bind our Confederacy. We have spent much time and energy on this oath and now, at long last, I should like to put it behind us. I shall read it out. Please confirm the words I read aloud and make sure that the men to your either side are doing the same.' He took a sheet of paper from a curate.

> In the name of the Father, Son and Holy Ghost, I, a member of this Confederacy of Irish Catholics, do solemnly declare that I shall bear true faith and allegiance to my sovereign lord King Charles and to his lawful successors.

With a roar of 'I so swear', the crowd heartily declared that they did.

> I, a follower of this Confederacy of Irish Catholics, shall maintain the fundamental laws of Ireland and the free and unrestrained exercise of our Apostolic faith and religion.

166

'I so swear', blazed the new constituency.

I hold this war to be just and lawful.

'I so swear.'

I condemn the internecine rivalry that has long polluted Ireland, and any other unwanted distinction of race, such as 'new' and 'old' Irish.

'I so swear', the convocation dutifully murmured. If this time the response were a little muted, it was perhaps because the gathering were finding the swearing-in ceremony a little wordy.

I declare the Confederacy's watchword to be 'tolerance'.

'I so swear.'

I request my bishop to anathematise the acridity that has arisen from the contested ownership of Truth.

This time there was a noticeable pause, before the delegates replied, 'I so swear.'

They may not all have understood that last oath, but at least they were minded to agree.

The bishop folded his papers and handed them back to his curate.

'Thank you, Gentlemen. Let us offer one another the sign of the only true peace, our Lord's. *Pax nobiscum.*'

All there shook hands or kissed, the older tradition, muttering the words '*pax tecum*' to each other.

Lord Gormanston now rose to his feet.

'Thank you, my lord Bishop,' he said. He nodded a stiff bow to the Primate of All Ireland and returned to the Assembly.

'Gentlemen, our purpose today is greater than merely to debate current affairs. We are here in Kilkenny to transform our Confederacy into a Government, a legislature in time of war. Your Committee must settle the question we have all been asking each other. Who will preside over us? Lord Mountgarrett, may we hear your ideas on this subject?'

'Is it absolutely out of the question to invite or persuade my kinsman the Marquess of Ormonde to accept the post?' asked Lord Mountgarrett by way of reply. 'He may be an Anglican but his every pore is Irish. If he came over to us the Castle would lose its greatest soldier. The others depend on cruelty, a satanic creature that can never command loyalty or affection. Ormonde is no Puritan and he is as loyal to the king as are we.'

'The Lieutenant-General? I won't say no, but I will not say yes, Lord Gormanston. We are a Catholic Association. True, 'tolerance' is our watchword but in due course. Let's say 'perhaps'. Sir Phelim, your hand is raised?'

'So Ormonde is out. Gentlemen, let it be his noble cousin Mountgarrett, here, on the platform to my right. It was Lord Mountgarrett who had the courage to risk escorting Ormonde's wife and children from here to Dublin. Mountgarrett is chief of the Catholic Butlers. As a younger man he fought alongside Tyrone at Kinsale, which by itself would make him a hero. What's more, it's Mountgarrett's ancient claims on this stronghold that makes our occupation legitimate. What is your considered opinion, Lord Gormanston?'

'I completely concur.'

'Well then, we should vote. Will anyone second the motion, that this house elect Lord Mountgarrett to be our captain-general?' asked Bishop Roche.

There was an enthusiastic show of hands.

'Carried, then.'

'Thank you, Confederates.'

The Primate of All Ireland rose to his feet. His brow was knit.

'Pray silence for the Archbishop of Armagh', Mountgarrett commanded.

When the priest spoke his tone was very solemn.

'I should like you to bear witness to the fact that we, the Bishops of Ireland, have resolved to excommunicate any man who takes the oath, the one you have all taken, and later violates it, whether their crime be murder, or violence, or looting, even if disguised as honourable under the pretext of war. May I ask you to raise your hands again?'

The Assembly 'witnessed' the Bishops' decision with the same uncompromising enthusiasm they had agreed all previous matters.

Then the chair was ceded to Lord Gormanston.

'Your acting committee, comprising Lord Castlehaven, Sir Phelim O'Neill, Sir Richard Belling, Mr Patrick Darcy and myself, wishes to promote the creation of a Supreme Council. To ensure it is representative and can wield sufficient power to be effective, we ask you to confirm that it should be composed of six members from each of our Irish provinces. Twenty-four in all. We submit that, in addition, the Archbishops of Armagh, Dublin and Tuam, the Bishops of Down and of Clonfert, Lords Mountgarrett, Roche and Mayo, myself and fifteen of our most eminent commoners should join this council. May I ask for another show of hands? All those in favour?'

A sea of raised hands guaranteed the carriage of the motion. There were however a few abstentions. The Assembly itself had not had time to short-list its candidates. Some would have structured the Supreme Council a little differently.

'Thank you, Gentlemen. The Supreme Council will be asked to write our Constitution.'

Bishop Roche passed Lord Gormanston a note. The peer read it carefully.

'I have an amendment to this last point before me, from my lord Bishop Roche. He suggests that to conduct the Assembly's ordinary business a quorum of nine will be sufficient. May I see your support for this?'

Again the crowd obliged.

'We have a number of appointments for which we need your approval. The first is the celebrated lawyer, Mr Patrick Darcy, currently a member of the Dublin Commons, as our nation's Chancellor. The second is Sir Richard Belling, to whom we have already offered the role of Secretary.'

They were duly elected.

'We also feel that a permanent guard of honour of five hundred foot and two hundred horse should protect this House and your Supreme Council.'

The motion was likewise carried.

'Now, your *ad hoc* Committee seeks your permission to resign, to be replaced by the *de jure* Supreme Council which you have already designed.'

The hands had it.

'Any other business?'

'I have a matter I should like to put to the Assembly, Lord Gormanston.'

'Please, Lord Mountgarrett. The floor is yours.'

'I may be your general officer but our Assembly is not a military council. In fact, most of us - Irish chiefs and Anglo-Irish noblesse alike - lack soldierly experience. This will change. Day-by-day, battle-hardened Irish soldiers are responding to our call. Slowly they return from Europe, willing to volunteer their arms and lives. Today we have built a bicameral Parliament; a General Assembly and a Supreme Council. You have generously voted me supreme, if temporary, command of our armed forces – but only until the day our émigrés have returned. When the appropriate soldier returns, I shall submit to him.'

'Very well,' said an irritated Lord Gormanston. 'The minutes will record that Lord Mountgarrett has numbered his own days in high office. Now, to matters of government. Do we have any proposals?'

'Your lordship will need an administration to direct and finance the military,' said Mr Darcy.

'Yes. You will need money,' said the Archbishop of Cashel, the throneless prelate. 'Rather a lot of it.'

'True, Gentlemen. We shall collect some silver from our more prosperous citizens and strike some coins,' said Mountgarrett. 'That, and a small revenue from taxation, should suffice.'

'What about diplomatic relations with foreign powers? France? The Papal States? Spain?' asked Lord Muskerry. 'And how shall we accommodate their envoys?'

'Yes, milord, you have a point. We shall send emissaries to all those places, charged with persuading those friendly powers to come to our aid.'

'Our envoys should also ask for money. Foreign powers may provide the resources and weapons we need. Our war looks likely to continue for quite a while,' declared Mr Darcy. 'Perhaps one of our landowners has a spare castle, ready to house a *nuncio* or ambassador?'

'The Parliament will need teeth,' remarked Sir Phelim O'Neill. 'We will need four regional military commands; Ulster, Leinster, Munster and Connacht.'

'And we need you to direct the war in Ulster, Sir Phelim,' confirmed Lord Mountgarrett.

Sir Phelim laughed modestly.

'Only until my kinsman, Colonel Owen Roe, reaches Ireland,' he said. 'I am only a lawyer, but I shall do my best until he comes.'

Patrick Darcy's draft constitution was carried as law. It concluded the first General Assembly. Twenty-four of its members were elected to the Supreme Council. Ormonde's cousin, Lord Mountgarrett, was sworn in as president and a gown was placed over his stooped shoulders.

'Gentlemen,' said the old soldier, 'for the sacred trust you have placed in me I thank you from the bottom of my heart. I shall not fail you. Nor shall we fail each other. This concludes our Confederacy's first full Assembly. Our next General Assembly is hereby set for October 23, the anniversary of the Ulster rising, to be known henceforward as 'Lord Maguire's day'. Go from here in peace, in the love of God, and prepare for war and a wingèd victory. Peace, our Lord's greatest gift to man, will follow. Such intentions, should He provide, and if matched with earthly vigilance, will guarantee the return of Ireland to its ancient peoples and to the rule of true Irish law.'

The Confederation's Oath was sworn enthusiastically. Four Provincial Councils were elected. Lord Muskerry was confirmed as President in Munster. General Barry became his Commander-in-Chief.

*

Following Coote's death, in Dublin, the Lords Justice saw at last that they had little choice but to give the Marquess of Ormonde a little more space. He repaid them with the recapture of Newry, just over the Leinster border into Ulster. If this were a great victory for Dublin Castle, in Catholic minds, the marquess's Anglican halo slipped a little that day; he chose to obey the Lords Justices' orders and executed his prisoners of war.

Swift and lethal reprisals made the Catholics fearful, doubtful, questioning. When, further north, the Covenanters recaptured Forts Mountjoy and Dungannon, the flame of the Rebellion flickered back to life in easterly wind.

*

CHAPTER TWELVE
AN EPITAPH FOR MAGUIRE AND MACMAHON

That same June, Maguire, MacMahon and Reade were moved to the impregnable Tower of London. In keeping with the *mores* of the times, Maguire's and MacMahon's bankers were permitted to allow the prisoners a very reasonable allowance, a shilling a day. With that they could rent a comfortable suite in the Beauchamp Tower and buy quite reasonable food and wine. They even employed a cook. Their confinement was not too arduous.

Such comfort at His Majesty's pleasure would soon end. Eleven months later they were transferred to Newgate Gaol like common felons. There too, if a prisoner had money, some modest ease could be purchased, but they still had to endure the sobering hangings, every Sabbath in the prison yard. Only pastors, chaplains and executioners worked without censure on the Lord's Day in an increasingly Puritan England.

Two years' imprisonment passedin that squalid gaol before, in August 1644, the Irishmen saw a chance to escape. They bribed a guard and ran through a tradesman's door to hide in a friend's house in Drury Lane.

England was too dangerous. Every road to Ireland was monitored by Parliamentary eyes. Maguire and MacMahon decided that they had to find a way to France. Unfortunately, on October 20, MacMahon rashly called from a top window to an oyster seller in the street. The street vendor recognised the accent; they were shopped, recaptured and in two hours were back in the Tower, this time in chains.

The oysterman was suitably and generously rewarded.

If the walls of Newgate were notoriously porous, not so the Tower. Reade, still in Newgate, chose this moment to escape himself. He was never seen again. History does not reveal whether he liked oysters or not.

Maguire told his gaolers that he and Colonel MacMahon would prefer to be tried in the Star Chamber. That court was famous for being partial to the king, against whom, they maintained, they had committed no treason. Therefore, Maguire reasoned, they might stand a slim chance of acquittal.

It was not to be. They were a matter of months too late.

The Council of the Star Chamber could inflict any punishment short of death, and frequently sentenced the objects of its anger to the pillory, to a whipping or to mutilation. The judicial cutting-off-of-ears was one such favourite. In 1641, Pym and Massereene, inflamed by the harsh treatment of John 'Freeborn' Lilburne, the Puritan agitator, saw that the *Habeas Corpus* Act of 1640, which the king had reluctantly enacted, could be used to rid the king entirely of his not-so-secret weapon, his infamous court.[xxi]

As a youth, 'Freeborn' had been apprenticed to the extreme Puritan John Hewson and, together with a Dr Bastwick, had penned a large number of inflammatory pamphlets, mostly railing against the existence of bishops. Inevitably, agents of Archbishop Laud had him arrested and mutilated for his pains.

The Puritans might not get the verdict they wanted if the Irishmen were tried in a court that so favoured the king and archbishop. It was decided to try them before the King's Bench of learned magistrates who would serve as a jury.

After many delays, some of a legalistic nature, in February 1645 Maguire and MacMahon were brought for arraignment and trial before Mr Justice Bacon.

Throughout his trial Maguire was scrupulously addressed as Lord Enniskillen. The question of his being a peer had caused, at first, a little difficulty for Mr Justice Bacon, but he had several precedents for trying Irish traitors in England. After the legitimacy of the court was established it was easy to show that the Irish lord was a commoner in England, just as Parsons and Borlase had predicted. Many points of law were raised, but the facts were clear from the off.

The star witness for the prosecution was Mr Owen O'Connolly, formerly the servant of the ennobled Sir John Clotworthy and of upright and good character. He was heard by a packed courtroom. The gallery included an up-and-coming politician and soldier, Captain Oliver Cromwell.

O'Connolly insisted that he had warned MacMahon against engaging in plots of any kind from the very depths of his heart. He had, he swore, advised the colonel to report whatever he knew to the Lords Justice. If he did this, O'Connolly had told his Colonel, such 'betrayal' would 'redound to his great honour'.

'Lord Maguire', O'Connolly revealed to Bacon's expert probing, 'pretended he knew nothing of any plot. There he made another mistake.'

'I can guess what that was', said Bacon, addressing the jury. 'He had underestimated Lord Massereene's skills as a missionary. The simple-minded idiot before you had assumed that the good man's faith and loyalty would have remained constant since his childhood, as his had.

Neither the trusting Colonel MacMahon nor Lord Enniskillen could never have known that O'Connolly went directly to tell the Lords Justice of Ireland all he had heard.'

In a regular court the accused would not be permitted to speak. Justice was the property of a jury, twelve good men and true, who listened only to the evidence. A desperate man accused of a capital crime made an unreliable witness.

Bacon had found a way around this awkward rule. Each of the accused had been charged with a slightly different capital crime. In this way, while not permitted to defend themselves, they could give their evidence of the other's ignominy.

Colonel MacMahon's trial came first. It lasted just two hours. After a unanimous verdict of guilty he was sentenced to be hanged by the neck until dead. No leave to appeal was granted. The sentence was executed the following Sunday at the fair on Tyburn Hill[xxii]. By the time Maguire appeared in the dock Colonel MacMahon was already dead, hanged with a hempen rope alongside the highwaymen, common murderers, thieves of goods valued at more than a shilling and other such rapscallions.

Proud Maguire cut a lonely, tragic figure at the bar of the court. His appearance even brought the hardened Parliamentarians, who had long since decided the verdict, some sadness. The mere fact that Maguire was just twenty-four years old made them realise quite forcibly that not every youth had been wholly convinced that a world without ornament, without music, without celebration, a world that studiously kept the Sabbath a day of rest, would of necessity be a better world. Thank God that in His infinite mercy most men who saw fit to disagree were confined to that treacherous nation across the Irish Sea.

Mr Francis Bacon, the President of the Court, invited 'Lord Inniskillen' to reveal who it was that had induced him into the conspiracy. Maguire mentioned the name of Rory O'More. Would he repeat that name? The court had a little trouble understanding him. Despite his slow and dignified speech, he had trouble speaking. His unfamiliar Irish accent had been rendered nearly unintelligible when his jaw had been broken, somewhere between the Tower of London and the Middle Temple.

'O'More pointed out the mess that I was in.' Mr Bacon relayed the accused's words to the jury, verbatim. 'He reminded me over and over again, how I was overwhelmed by debt, the smallness of my estate and the greatness of the estate my ancestors had enjoyed, and how I should be sure to get it back or at least a large part of it and, moreover, how the welfare of the Catholic religion, which, he said, the Parliament now in England will suppress, doth depend on it.'

Treason! He was fighting to have the land that had been lawfully awarded to Protestants returned to him. Convicted by his own words! Just how brilliant was Mr Justice Bacon?

It was not necessary for the jury to withdraw. They gave their unanimous verdict on demand. Guilty of High Treason, they solemnly told the bench, and Lord Enniskillen was duly sentenced to be hanged, drawn and quartered on Tyburn Hill.

Had the Irishmen been undone by their trusting friendship in O'Connolly? Affection had perhaps overridden MacMahon's natural caution. Had not O'Connolly himself told MacMahon that in its own interest, a 'conquered people' must submit? Since neither thought of Ireland as a conquered country, neither the peer nor the colonel had taken that throwaway line too seriously. Enniskillen's only reply had been to hope that Ireland would soon be delivered from the slavery and bondage under which, and for the time being, it laboured.

That conversation should have been a warning to the conspirators but clues are always easier to detect after the event.

The fact was that the pious and 'elect' Lord Massereene had discovered a useful idiot in his valet. Knowing the man's connections, he had groomed him over decades, calculating that they would be useful one day. By the time MacMahon confided in O'Connolly, he was taking an inimical convert into his confidence. This was the error that broke the camel's back. News of the plot to take the Castle had been brought to Lord Justice Parsons on the very eve of its execution, at the eleventh hour.

After his conviction, the branded William Prynne, a member of the prosecuting counsel, urged the prisoner to 'confer with some godly ministers,' but Maguire would have only a Catholic priest. This was not allowed. Indeed, the only Catholic priests in London that the court knew of were some embassy chaplains and Père Robert Philip who confessed the queen, Henrietta-Maria.

Lord Massereene himself was in the gallery to witness his fellow alumnus receive his sentence. He had attended the same school as Lord Enniskillen, though some years previously. Perhaps that was why he was moved to do what he could? When the accused requested the consolation of holding some 'curious' papers in his hand while he was taken to the place of his execution, Massereene addressed Mr Bacon directly and his intercession was granted.

Those papers were clutched in his hand when Maguire was tied to a sled, almost nude, and dragged through the streets of London to Tyburn Hill. All manner of waste was thrown at him, or poured over him from overhanging windows, while Cockneys taunted him cruelly about his faith. Maguire remained stoic, unmoved.

From the carnificial platform he declared to a hushed crowd, quite audibly, that he forgave his 'enemies and defenders, even those that have a hand in my death.'

The grim work of the executioner began. A long hour later it was over.

After his passing, the crowds could no longer be restrained. They burst upon the charnelled altar, anxious to rid the remains of the lordly corpse of its gold teeth, its earrings, its signet ring. Some dipped their handkerchiefs in Maguire's blood. Such mementos, even a lock of his golden hair, would serve as a protection against evil spirits, even in a devoutly Protestant house. They might also fetch a good price. The advertising bills, notifying Londoners of the execution and which had been nailed to every tree in London, were ripped down and wrapped around these macabre relics to serve as provenance.

In the scramble, the papers that Massereene had arranged for him to carry fell from a stiffening hand, onto the blood-soaked sawdust below. A spectator, perhaps wondering if they had some value, took them away from the ghastly scene to read.

They were partly of a devotional character, written in clerical script. A touching paragraph in his own hand, were his directions to himself as to how he should bear himself *in extremis*. They included a line or two from Shakespeare.

> Nothing in his life
> Became him like the leaving it; he died
> As one that had been studied in his death,
> To throw away the dearest thing he ow'd,
> As 'twere a careless trifle.

The chieftainship of Fermanagh fell to his younger brother Rory, who would fight for the Confederacy. For the rest of his days he carried a lock of his brother's hair in a silver medallion, next to his heart. Its inscription read,

> If you can look into the seeds of time, and say which grain will grow, and which will not, then speak.[xxiii]

176

CHAPTER THIRTEEN
MUNSTER FIGHTS BACK

In late June, 1642, St Leger showed considerable mettle in marching his army from Dungarvan through hostile country, bravely passing fairly close to several Irish sieges, before making his way into the liberated county town of Cork.

The morale of the people of that Atlantic city was greatly lifted by the courage and example of the Lord President in their time of need. Lord Inchiquin awarded him a formal reception, replete with fireworks.

This noble gesture, however, ignored the fact that the open country was still the preserve of the enemy. Lords Mountgarrett and Muskerry effectively confined St Leger and Inchiquin to their towns and castles, even though the Protestants had given the Irish a good run around and taken to the field whenever they could.

It had been a punishing season, however, and the toll on the Lord President of Munster began to show worrying symptoms. His chest pains were recurring a little too frequently. He had other problems too - back pay was one – and to keep his men from revolting he had to borrow £4,000 from the banker Sir Robert Tynte, who considered a Protestant victory an unsecured loan and charged the Lord President an inordinate rate of interest.

> While I am writing to you, dear Lord Ormonde, to congratulate you on your several victories over the rebels, in your triumph you continue to neglect me. I have received no money for twelve months. The Dublin government will not even give me a few small field-pieces, even if they are not needed elsewhere. If they have not wholly deserted me and bestowed so much of the government of this province on my Lord of Cork, you might yet persuade them to unburden themselves of so much artillery as they cannot themselves employ.
>
> I look to you, my lord, to give me the practical assistance without which there is a grand likelihood that the English garrisons at Youghal, Bandon Bridge, Cork and Kinsale will fall to brutes, void of reason or understanding. The Irish must be so or they would never hasten to join such a herd of unclean beasts.
>
> Your servant,
> Wm St Leger

Clearly this intemperate letter worked. Further reinforcements arrived and St Leger took to the field again. His illness, however, grew daily worse and, on July 2, he died in his bed in Cork, having carefully bequeathed his duties to his vice-president, Viscount Inchiquin.

Inchiquin had returned to Limerick City. There he learned of St Leger's death. He was very surprised, and all the more so when also discovered that his own promotion had been announced in Dublin Castle and confirmed above the Great Seal of the Kingdom of Ireland.

This should have been grounds for celebration but he was currently being besieged by General Barry. Still, he would be no pushover. While young and still a Catholic he had studied war at close range in the Spanish service. Later, as an Anglican, he had served Lord Wentworth in the Bishops' Wars. Since then he had become a Calvinist. Whatever his religion, he was always a soldier.

On his return to Ireland he was happy to fight the Catholics. By the spring of 1642 he had achieved some minor victories but he too was encumbered by a lack of money.

When he heard that Alexander Forbes, the 11th baron of that name and darling of the English Parliamentarians, had landed at Kinsale with his Puritan chaplain, Hugh Peters, and with a thousand 'adventurers', he thought his luck had changed. He was to be disappointed. Forbes paid no attention at all to his pleas for help. The fact was that Inchiquin was still loyal to his king had queered his pitch.

Catholic prisoners cost food and money to keep alive. In Youghal, the situation was desperate. Inchiquin, in Limerick, sick of reading Lord Dungarvan's pleas for aid, ordered the lordly commandant at Youghal to hang all his Catholic soldiers and civilians. While fighting was the only industry in town, and such men had been seen as the raw material of soldiery, times had changed. The shopkeepers and Irish seafarers had begun to refuse Vavasour's 'siege pieces' and Youghal no longer had the means of paying anyone anything. Something somewhere had to give. Inchiquin too thought to turn to Ormonde.

> I trust that my continual petitioning of the Almighty, Lord Ormonde, has been to some effect, yet I feel obliged to trespass on your lordship's patience yet again. You are surely aware that the English Parliament is still sending men to our many garrisons in County Cork without arms or payroll. What can be its purpose? Unless of course it be that these men shall talk the rebels to death?
>
> I remain confident that the succour that England will send her ragged sister Ireland in her hour of need will relieve the manifold sieges that enclose our cities and release your humble and loyal servant Inchiquin from his enforced captivity.

Ormonde would send no succour. On the other hand, the Earl of Cork, with his sons, actively supported English interests in Cork and Waterford. Cork co-operated with Inchiquin, if not particularly cordially. If the earl's son, Lord Broghill, was ready and happy to suppress the Irish, his chariot also had brakes. His issues were mostly financial. Support for an army is always costly. Desperate times need desperate measures, but when Inchiquin seized the tobacco from Cork's merchants' licensed warehouses, to sell it on to Cork's own tobacconists with a surcharge to pay for his militias, every shopkeeper in Cork cried out in pain. Undaunted, he then expropriated the cattle and corn in every district under his control.

'Force majeure,' he wrote to Cork's mayoralty. 'The king has not the money we need and the English Parliament has neither the time nor the inclination to attend to this Kingdom of Ireland. Nor is it ready to grant money into what it calls 'unsafe hands'. There will be compensation for the sequestered tobacco, I promise. Be patient and pray God that we shall be victorious.'

Lord Inchiquin was at Doneraile when Muskerry recaptured Limerick. The latter's feat was applauded throughout the Catholic world, yet in the context of the Rebellion the saga was neither an Irish nor an English victory. The whole story would recur, again and again, all over the country. Here the Catholics would lose, there they would win, bowing or being bowed to, almost as in the preordained sequence of a holy mass.

*

When King Charles attended a State Opening of the Westminster Parliament he liked to wear St Edward's crown, the one that the Confessor had commissioned half a millennium before. In his hands he would hold the Orb and Sceptre, symbols of celestial and earthly power. He held the Sceptre in his right hand and Orb in his left.

The *globus cruciger* was a heavy golden orb topped with a cross. It had been fashioned in the eleventh century.[xxiv] By itself it symbolised Christ's dominion over the world, but when held by the sovereign it implied the sovereignty of an earthly ruler, representing the Monarch's role as Defender of the Faith and Supreme Governor of the Church of England.

The sceptre, essentially an ornamental club, represented the king's authority to make law and to inflict punishment on his subjects if they did not submit. Law, the king liked to say, was the true sovereign in

England, and had been since King Arthur had unified its warring petty kingdoms.

That year the king thought it best to be firm with the elected members of his House of Commons. This he did from his throne in the House of Lords.

'It gives us sadness to be constrained to reject the Nineteen Propositions you so recently submitted to us,' he began, 'but for us to cede more power to our Parliament would be to upset the fragile balance of power between the Commons, the Church, the Lords and ourself. Our role is not just to provide our kingdom with military might. We bear a moral obligation to supply the checks, balances and advice that popular enthusiasm so often ignores.

'The Commons exists to speak for the ordinary freemen of the realm, but not Everyman. It doesn't govern the Aristocracy, the Church or the Monarchy; it merely shares power with them. Only if these four work in harmony will one not come to dominate the others. A lack of balance would, in the fullness of time, lead to tyranny. We divide with you our sovereign purpose, to govern jointly and wisely. It has to be thus. If too much power is held by the people, laws will be generalised, conformity will be exacted, mediocrity will become the defining feature of our nation. High taxes and redistribution of wealth will be the handmaidens of such polity. You, the noble Commons, will find yourselves bribing your constituents with their own money, merely to secure the survival of your party. You will find yourselves obliged to plunder the Aristocracy, harnessing that vein of envy that is part of our sinful fabric, dismissing as negligible the role of such grandees in maintaining the pride and tradition of a nation. That would be a crime against all men, for it is within the means of the fortunate to ensure that ancient wisdom is handed down to future generations. That august fraction of society also serves to entice the more successful men of the people to be accepted into its ranks in exchange for its civilising grace. Aristocracy is the ladder of ambition and the purpose of industry.

'Nor should the Church, which guides us to God, find its role diluted. The Anglican fellowship exhorts us to love our neighbours as ourselves and demands that we are guided by our Lord's precepts of faith, hope and charity.

'The experience and wisdom of your, our, ancestors orchestrated this form of government. Its overture blends the background hum of the people with a medley of noble melodies, the serene siren of the truth of the Church and the whispered, thoughtful guidance of an hereditary monarchy. Do not underestimate the incontrovertible fact that every crowned head in history, in Christendom, has been raised from birth to his lonely office. It is this sacred and mystical combination that gives this kingdom the conveniences of all, without the inconveniences of any. Each of these Estates shall keep the other three in check.'

The king's address was met with loyal applause, but at the debate that followed the king's departure, the speech was pronounced a bad one. Some important members of the Commons pronounced themselves slighted. In their own opinion they, not the king, were sovereign.

Pym, predictably, led the protests.

'The king's formula is unconstitutional. Since *Magna Carta*, Parliament should be an absolute ruler, deferring neither to Throne nor Canterbury nor, least of all, the marble halls of the elite in the other place.'

Pym's ovation trumped the king's by a quarter hour.

Everywhere in Ireland, the natives had already seen the tendrils of English authority, housed in Dublin Castle, slowly severed. Before the reins of law and power could be reattached, the Irish were clearly willing to murder their oppressors. Sir Phelim, with the other insurgent leaders, tried to sweeten the native bile but his honeyed words fell on stony ground. The Celts would not listen; the people had never really grasped the idea that woken dogs should lie still. Too much dispossession had stoked their resentment.

Nor had they foreseen the extent to which their latent savagery would soar to new heights of atavism. Whenever Sir Phelim successfully surprised a walled settlement in Ulster, his troops rewarded its Protestant inhabitants with the pent-up and bitter fruits of their subjugation. Some towns, recently built, had excluded the natives on pain of death (of course except as domestic servants). In these attacks many Protestants died quickly from a merciful sword or, more probably, slowly from a cruel exposure to the elements.

Irish Catholics controlled two thirds of the country. They, and the Protestants of the British enclaves of Ulster, Dublin and around Cork in Munster, faced each other across an abyss of distrust and rival pieties.

Better armed, but vastly outnumbered, the Protestants' surrender in the long term was surely inevitable. It might take centuries, but Ireland would one day unite; of that few if any had any long term doubts. What was important was that this hypothetical unification should not happen for many generations.

If the Confederacy were to bring peace, such choler had to be harnessed, and untutored guerrilla warfare would need to end. To be recognised by the world, a Confederate victory would need to have been won through a legitimate and conventional war.

*

Only a month later, two old soldiers sat together in the observation chamber that the Butlers had built atop Kilkenny Castle's south tower. It had first been designed to scour the horizon for marauding Vikings. Now it was converted for studying the heavens.

The servants had long been let go; their dismissal had left the generals free to plan their campaign and impress one another with their soldiers' tales.

In truth, Mountgarrett and Barry had little in common. They were great men but in different ways. One important difference was racial. Mountgarrett was Old English. Barry was a thoroughbred Milesian.

Back in October 1641, when news of the Rebellion first reached Lord Mountgarrett, he had not been sure which path to tread. The overarching goal was peace in Ireland. He shrewdly calculated it would come sooner if he backed the winner. On the eruption of hostilities in Ulster, he had at first espoused the Government side. In gratitude, the Lords Justice appointed him, with his Anglican cousin Lord Ormonde, joint Governors of their castle. He was required to raise a defensive militia. Now – barely six months later - he had changed his mind. He had clearly seen the Irish cause as the better prospect.

During those months he had realised that the lives and liberty of the Irish would be fatally compromised if England's Protestant Parliament won the day. He explained to his cousin - the Marquess of Ormonde - that his pragmatism had been outranked by his principles. Ormonde was listening. He discreetly invited his kinsman to take possession of the Butler clan's vast and heroic residence, Kilkenny Castle, in the name of the Confederacy. For the duration, Ormonde himself would make do with his only slightly less magnificent country house near Carrick-on-Suir and an appropriate mansion in Dublin.

Mountgarrett, when questioned, would always say his purpose was to secure a better deal for the overwhelming mass of Irishmen. He could not, he would say, be expected to protect the lives and property of legions of settlers, planters, undertakers and adventurers. When he sent a task force to secure a neighbouring town, he met with so much passion and so many recruits that within a week every single fortress in Kilkenny, Waterford and Tipperary was under his control.

This was when - or why - the Confederacy chose him as their captain-general. The Catholics of County Cork, however, insisted on a Corkonian. They chose the MacCarthy chief - Lord Muskerry. It was written into their Hibernian souls to prefer the Milesians to the Anglo-Irish. The unfortunate consequences were that the Catholic armies in Munster were divided and Mountgarrett's strength was commensurately reduced.

To repair such division, Mountgarrett was making an overture, a charm offensive, to General Garret Barry. He stood and fetched a decanter from a sideboard. With 'noble condescension' the senior of the two filled the glass of his commoner guest.

'You might care to tell me how you secured Limerick for our cause? I always appreciate such accounts.'

For his part, General Barry appreciated a fine whiskey. He was in no particular hurry to answer. He had already forged a close alliance, and it was not with Mountgarrett. It was with Lord Muskerry.

Barry was a soldier through and through. He had first seen action in the service of Spain as an officer in the fleet and later in the army. During the Thirty Years' War he had twice escaped with his life, from both the Spanish Netherlands and the Empire.

'A few months after my return from Spain, Lord Mountgarrett, four thousand men and I put Limerick Castle to siege. It took us a good while before Captain George Courtenay, the governor, capitulated. This victory secured us some valuable heavy artillery. The mere sight of such huge weapons was enough to reduce every castle in County Limerick, even including noble Askeaton.'

'You still have those weapons? Well done, Barry. That was a job well done.'

'Thank you. For my part, I should very much like to know how you managed to survive St Leger's ambush in Co Cork,' General Barry retaliated, drawing on his pipe.

Lord Mountgarrett had moved to the window and looked out beyond the River Nore, now in torrent, and to the fields and forests beyond. The scene seemed to compel a sweet and sad nostalgia.

'From the outset, I too had thought to march on Cork,' he replied. His tone declared that this was not a happy memory. 'I had planned to take both city and county, choosing to enter Co. Cork through the Ballyhoura Mountains at Barnderg Pass. That was where Sir William St Leger ambushed me. His spies must have given him word of my plans. Mercifully, mine had word of his. I turned west to Killmallock and was joined by the chief lords and gentlemen of County Limerick. They came with their clansmen and, having heard of St Leger's action, rallied to my standard.'

'You certainly turned the tables on the Protestants!' Barry had a taste for understatement.

They both laughed, but Mountgarrett's chuckle was less than merry.

'I did have a victory of sorts, and St Leger was indeed routed, but the sad truth is that I barely dented his pride. My men had to return through Ballyhea, on their way to Buttevant. The enemy, meanwhile, withdrew to the castle in Mallow, not so far from Doneraile.'

'Were you were lucky that Inchiquin hadn't yet joined forces with the President?'

'I was. At the time, Inchiquin was in England. Is he a royalist? A Parliamentarian? Who knows? Then he was offering Parliament his undying loyalty. He persuaded the Commons to award him a regiment of foot and some horse and, a few weeks later, he landed his brand new psalm-singing regiment in Youghal. They went straight to Mallow to join St Leger. When Lord Inchiquin's father-in-law died, during that visit, the military command of the province passed to Lord Thomond's son. That, as you know only too well, just happens to be Murrough Inchiquin.'

*

Lord Inchiquin, supported by Lords Barrymore, Dungarvan, Kynalmeaky and Broghill, found shelter in Mallow Castle, almost a hundred miles away.

In the old days, they would have found the old place extremely comfortable.

Mallow was nothing if not a modern and stately pile. It had been twice rebuilt. Its first version was primordial, belonging to the time of forests and waterfalls. Its second incarnation coincided with King John's brief stewardship of Ireland. That was when the Roches, a Norman family, had displaced the native O'Keeffes from their own fortress and driven them west. The O'Keeffes had later resettled at Dromsicane.

The castle fared badly during the Desmond uprising, being referred to as 'the ruinous house of Mallow'. Its then owner, described as a brave soldier, was brutally murdered. Dublin ordered his dismembered body to be hung for a month or two from the gates of Cork. That had been back in 1581, when his lands stretched north for about three miles, almost to Caherduggan, and south to the O'Callaghans' castle of Dromore.

Its heyday ended with the Elizabethan confiscations. Mallow was set aside for Sir William Pelham, but it was Sir John Norreys who, as Munster's Lord President, succeeded in taking it over. He argued that Mallow, in its strategic position in the middle of the county, should be allocated to him.

Thomas's daughter, Elizabeth, was a godchild of Queen Elizabeth. She was presented with 'The Castle and Town of Mallow and Short Castle, alias Castle Garr' by a patent of James the First. She then married Sir John Jephson, a modest army officer.

In 1636 Lord Cork, who by that time owned a considerable part of the rest of Munster, offered the unimaginable sum of £15,000 for Mallow. Elizabeth Jephson refused him.

When that Sir John died, in 1587, the property – and his office - passed to his brother, Sir Thomas, who in turn transmitted it to his eldest son, John. His ownership was realised in the grant of the Seignory of Mallow, an estate of 6,000 acres. With it, he felt able to erect the grand and fortified house that Lord Inchiquin's close friend, Sir John Jephson, now occupied.

On the outbreak of the Confederate War, the Jephsons declared for Parliament. Unfortunately, much of Mallow town was burned following the Catholic march there in February of 1642.[xxv] Its castle, however, was largely undamaged.

*

In Kilkenny, Barry and Mountgarrett were still exploring ways of working together.

'Now that St Leger's augmented forces and their new general are ensconced at Mallow, you are proposing that I should give them a suitable reception? Who will be my captains?'

'All Duhallow. The Roches, the MacCarthys of Drishane, the Magners. Add to that last, the Lord of Duhallow's eldest son, Bryen. He has raised a thousand men - including the bulk of the O'Callaghans, MacAuliffes and O'Keeffes - and they have already had some experience of fighting Inchiquin. Even the Burgats of Fantstown have contributed a militia. The Fitzgeralds, led by the Knight of Glin[xxvi], are providing a great part of our Confederate force in Munster. All these gallant men will rendezvous with you at Two-Pot-House. Sadly for us, MacDonogh Mór, Bryen's father, has not yet been persuaded that remaining neutral and loyal to the king is no longer an option. His son, however, has wholeheartedly embraced the cause.'

Mountgarrett paused to recharge his glass.

185

'When you meet Inchiquin you must expect bitter fighting. Remember you will outnumber him. If you have to lay siege to Mallow Castle, its Constable, Lieutenant Williamson, won't hold out long. Offer generous terms and let him see your artillery. He'll surrender.'

'Thank you. And after we have dealt with Lord Inchiquin?'

'Don't rush your fences, Barry. There is an important task that comes first. If we are to be sure of success against Inchiquin, and if we are to disembarrass the Boyles of Co Cork's Saxon and Viking towns - Youghal, Kinsale, Cork, Dungarvan, Bandon Bridge - we will need to train and house your great army. For this you will need a substantial base. Your army already numbers more than six thousand. With the Duhallow contingent you will further increase that figure. I estimate you'll have seven thousand foot and five hundred horse.'

'You can't be thinking of Kilkenny? The country round here is already secure and your own garrison protects you. It would tie up an army where it wasn't needed.'

'True, but aside from your great force, the rest of Munster's warriors, real or potential, are all over the province. I hate to admit it, but they are mostly a hotchpotch of small and semi-independent bands. They will need to be brought together under one general, under one roof. No Barry, I am not thinking of here. We are nearly a hundred miles from the action. I am proposing Liscarroll.'

'Yes. Of course, Lord Mountgarrett, I follow. Liscarroll Castle is deep in prosperous, peaceful Duhallow, a region almost free of settlers. You have remembered I know Liscarroll castle well.'

'I have. Then we are agreed. There is one drawback, however. You will be aware that Liscarroll is at present in enemy hands? It's up to you, General Barry. Go, collect your captains and take it back. You have *carte blanche*.'

*

It was true. Barry knew Liscarroll all too well. His ancestors, once known as 'de Barras', or 'de Barrye', had built the castle in the 13th century, on a bend in the Awbeg river. As a young man he had lived there himself. It had been conceived from its very outset as a residence-cum-fortress.

In 1637, however, while he was still in the Spanish Netherlands, the Lords Justice had sequestered the fortress and granted it to Sir Philip de Perceval. Possibly the considerable fee that changed hands had something to do with it. The banker had immediately rebuilt it to a luxurious specification, intending it for his principal seat but, five years later, it had regained its martial purpose. Sir Philip had felt he had no choice but to take the English side and thereby dismiss his many

186

friendships with the Irish. His lease obliged him to, and otherwise he would lose his palace-fortress. Now that the pipes and drums of war had driven the birds from the trees and unsilted the trout in every stream he needed a fortress to protect his other houses, most especially Burton Court. He put Liscarroll under the command of his trusted sergeant, Thomas Raymond.

Liscarroll was a large, elegant rectangular structure, 240 by 120 feet, filled with restored staterooms and bedchambers. At each corner the castle had a rounded tower, with two further square towers set into the north and south facades. The bawn in which it stood was itself inside a curtilage, some thirty feet tall. Its principal entrance was via a portcullis.

Legend had it that the fortress was impregnable. Now this was to be challenged, and by its former owner.

Perhaps Raymond had the wherewithal to save it? By all accounts he was a very stubborn sergeant and had no intention of giving it up.

At least, that is, until he had to.

General Barry, however, was of a contrary disposition. He was determined to have his castle back, and was ready to be very persuasive.

In the process of taking Limerick, Barry and Muskerry had acquired an artillery train. Now Barry had transported his bronze cannons to a rocky hill, south-east of Liscarroll Castle, within easy ballistic range. The place was known as St Stephen's Rock. It had not been easy work. Between them they weighed more than three tons, which meant a gun carriage had to be built of timber, hewn hollow, its wide wheels drawn by twenty five yoke of oxen.

Barry's unrivalled knowledge of the country let his men travel over bogs where wheels should have sunk and where no carriage had ever been known to pass.

On Tuesday August 20, 1642, Barry told his men to present themselves, ready for action.

There had been a change of plan. He had previously intended to march on Mallow and Doneraile.

'Unfortunately,' he told Bryen MacDonogh, 'your father's news is that Sir Charles Vavasour occupies the late Lord President's seat at Doneraile and is resolved to fight to the end. With Inchiquin rattling around Mallow Castle, it means we must postpone that pleasure. At least those two are well out of harm's way. No, our immediate task is to restore Liscarroll Castle to its rightful owners.'

From St Stephen's Rock, Barry's Irish army looked over great plains and a quilt of fruitful fields, stretching as far as the eye could see. To the north and east, however, the camp was bounded with woods, bogs and barren ground.

On the far side of a screen of ash and oak lay Liscarroll, where Sir Philip's Sergeant Raymond was in command. Irish estimates of his strength were somewhat exaggerated. In fact he had just thirty men, though it was also rumoured he had a generous quantity of food and ammunition.

General Barry ordered Major Bryen MacDonogh to form half his thousand into marching squares and station them outside the castle gates. There he was to parade them, letting Raymond see a modest show of strength, but also allowing the Constable to think the Irish army was *smaller* than it was in reality.

'Perceval's Constable cannot have more than a hundred men in there. Your least disciplined soldiers, Major, may inspire him with misplaced confidence.'

'Tempt him out for a scrap, General?'

'Exactly. That would be a faster victory. I shall make sure the rest of my army takes care to be invisible. If the Constable saw them he'd never emerge. That would leave me no alternative but to starve him out, which might take weeks. I have ordered the field pieces to be trained on the well tower. The Constable will soon deduce that I know his base better even than him. He'll come through those doors soon enough, mark my words, most probably under a white flag.'

It didn't take long for Inchiquin, billeted in his friend Captain Sir John Jephson's castle at the heart of Mallow, to hear that General Barry had put Liscarroll under siege. His view hardly differed from Barry's. Without relief, and with a garrison to feed, he thought the castle could not hold out for more than a few days. He had no idea how many men reported to Sergeant Raymond. Nor even did Sir Philip de Perceval, and it was his fortress.

'My sergeant will have taken an adequate number of men-at-arms with him, but while my wife and children remain at Egmont, the number won't be huge,' he said unhelpfully.

The smaller the number, if it came to it, the longer the siege would last. The food would go further.

Nor was anyone in the Irish camp any wiser as to the garrison's strength.

'Every Protestant in Duhallow, I expect,' said General Barry.

'Well, that won't be many,' Bryen replied.

*

Lord Inchiquin, together with Lords Barrymore, Dungarvan, Kynalmeaky and Broghill, had been cajoled and pressured by Sir Philip de Perceval to liberate his fine fortress at Liscarroll – the house he was still hoping to make his family's principal seat - and, at the same time, put paid to Garrett Barry's army in the doing.

Inchiquin had accepted the challenge.

Mallow Castle was Inchiquin's HQ. By the standards of Irish castles, it was small; a gabled building about 80 by 30ft, with a turret at all four corners. It had three courtyards. One of these was a forecourt which admitted its owners and visitors to pass into the house through a doorway with a semi-elliptical[xxvii] head. Its thatched roof made it pretty rather than handsome. It had four projecting wings, one of which contained the stairs and the others the garderobes. Its mullioned windows had square and hooded heads. The whole building was built in red sandstone, with contrasting facings of cut limestone, much of which must have been salvaged from the older castles on the site. The clock tower in the stable yard was said to be the oldest in Ireland,[xxviii] and only the slits in the towers were expressly defensive.

The interior was not at all uncomfortable. In an extension to the main building was housed its great kitchen. Its floors, beds, wainscotting and other furniture were all in oak.

'I'll be sorry to leave this place,' said Sir Philip told Sir John a little wistfully. 'Your house has a lot of rustic charm. Yet leave we must. If Garrett Barry succeeds in taking Liscarroll, Munster will remain Irish forever.'

'We shall march overnight to Ballybeg,' Inchiquin directed. 'We have already sent a messenger on to Doneraille to winkle Sir Charles Vavasour out of his fastness. He should join us tomorrow. Once they're there we shall rest before marching over the following night on Liscarroll. There are clear skies. Like Argonauts, we shall steer by the stars.'

Inchiquin called for an archer.

'Cartwright, have you still got your crossbow hidden somewhere?'

'I have, my lord.'

'Then find it, and a fast horse. I want you to fire a letter this night into Liscarroll. Approach from the north and make sure you arrive before dawn. You won't want to be seen by General Barry. Your message tells Raymond to hold out, wait for us and that we're on our way. That's why it's vital you get through. If you are taken, you are to eat it before they hang you.'

Murrough Inchiquin marched his men out of the heart of Mallow at a gruelling pace.

Half his 'English' army was made up of suborned English or English-speaking riffraff, the other half from English settlers, obliged by the terms of their leases to serve their former nation whenever demanded. They had no formal dress, but badges and standards helped give them a uniform appearance. Their officers wore armour, of leather and, very occasionally, steel.

Their numbers were doubled by four Boyle lords: Lord Broghill, the Earl of Orrery, the Earl of Cork and Lord Kynalmeaky, Cork's eldest son. They had all ordered their households and tenantry to ride with Viscount Inchiquin.

'The Confederacy must not take Liscarroll. A victory is essential. If we fail, our Saxon army will starve while the Irish gather the harvest. Duhallow is the breadbasket of Cork and the fate of the entire province rests on the harvest,' Lord Inchiquin told Sir Philip de Perceval and the Earl of Cork. 'It's not far. It will only take two nights. Liscarroll is barely fifteen miles from Mallow's walls. We should expect to find the Confederates waiting for us. I am not in the least concerned with their useless footsoldiers. The intelligence that concerns me is that they have at least five hundred horse.'

'Who commands such a splendid regiment?'

'An Anglo-Irishman called Stephenson.'

'Not a Celt, then?' Lord Cork observed. 'He should be with us!'

'I know him,' said Sir Philip. 'He is an acquaintance of mine. He may be a descendent of Elizabethan settlers but he's also a recusant, a devout Catholic. They say he has courage.'

'What a premium the Irish put on courage! What they really need are brains!' said Lord Cork.

'On occasion, courage has some value.' Inchiquin's delicate irony was not wasted. 'Brains seldom encourage us to put our lives at risk.'

What no one needed to say was that in Irish circles, breeding was considered a greater virtue than skill.

At eleven in the morning of Friday September 2, Inchiquin's artillery, escorted by his cavalry, arrived in Buttevant, seven long miles from Mallow. His foot numbered seventeen hundred and was escorted by six

190

companies of horse. There they pitched camp, carefully out of the way, in order to rest after a testing march.

Inchiquin then sent Captain Bridges and forty of his horse on ahead to Liscarroll but they returned without having even seen the enemy.

'What? All I asked you to do was assess the Irish deployment, yet you failed to see thousands of barefoot ruffians, armed to the teeth? They are there, you know, or do you think I have an overwrought imagination? Next time, try opening your eyes,' he told them angrily. He turned to Sir Charles. 'This lack of intelligence is extraordinarily vexing. We still have no clear idea of the size of the Irish force.'

He snorted with anger, turned on his heel, left the room and slammed the door behind him. Murrough Inchiquin was an O'Brien, a notoriously short-tempered breed. He was splenetic with rage. Some said he sourced his energy from Fury herself.

It was now Saturday September 3, 1642, and early in the morning. It was cold but the weather upset no one in Inchiquin's army. The excitement and terror of war made them impervious to the chill.

When the Protestants drew within hailing distance of Liscarroll, still around half-a-mile mile distant, they halted. Inchiquin himself rode on, accompanied by a small personal guard. An hour and a half after day break, while the sun was gathered strength over Ballyhoura's heathery hills, Inchiquin and his men had their first glimpse of the stately fortress. His reconnoitre revealed his quarry to be a formidable Irish army, drawn up in perfect order. Barry was clearly ready to blast Liscarroll into folklore, he observed, and his army occupied what could well serve as a set-piece battlefield.

It was also clear that the Protestant army had not been detected and that Barry had posted no look-outs.

Rather than make an ill-considered charge against a superior force, Inchiquin rejoined his army to discuss tactics and strategy with his senior commanders. He would let the men rest before readying them for battle, scheduled for dawn the following day.

Inside Liscarroll, at 2 o'clock that afternoon, Raymond watched in mounting panic as the massive weapons of the Irish artillery began to fire on the castle. The bombardment was leisurely, as if the aggressor didn't want to cause too much damage. Even so, the debris had blocked off the well and there was only beer and wine to drink.

That was not good news for the trapped garrison. Most had taken the pledge.

The sporadic rain of cannonball continued until dusk. It was then that a terrified Raymond, who had loudly boasted his undying loyalty to Perceval, decided it best to surrender on terms. He had delayed as long as he dared, even though he had just received the news, attached to a crossbow bolt, that Lord Inchiquin was on his way with an army of two thousand foot and four hundred horse. The fact that Raymond could see that the Irish general was going to take the castle, there and then, concentrated his mind. He would surely take no prisoners, and Raymond wasn't yet prepared to meet his Maker.

In any case, it was pointless to remain steadfast. His master's castle would be destroyed within another day, his thirty men with it. Being hanged, in the cruel balance of war, would be kinder than being crushed by tumbling masonry.

Major Bryen MacDonogh, at the head of a hundred horse, rode up to Liscarroll's great gate under a white flag. It was a very frightened Constable who opened and rode out, also under a white flag, to negotiate terms with the enemy.

The Irishman flashed a piece of paper at the English sergeant.

'You must surrender and depart. If you can read, these are our terms in writing. Obey and you, your family, your men and their families will not be harmed. In the name of Ireland's future, the Confederacy claims this castle.'

'What? By what right? This is not yours to play games with! It is the legal and rightful property of Sir Philip de Perceval!'

'Relax, Sergeant. This is not a sporting matter but a military one. No need to get excited. You are a good Protestant, by all accounts, but you were never trained for war. We need to borrow Liscarroll for a while. Sir Philip, my godfather, is in Mallow. Go there. When you next see him, please present him with my compliments. You may tell him that you and your brave thirty men surrendered to Bryen MacDonogh of Duhallow and seven thousand Confederate soldiers. He will know that I am a man of my word. He will know that when I say you will be unharmed, that is a statement of pure and simple fact.'

Bryen smiled and reached for his startled enemy's hand.

'Cheer up, Sergeant. The odds were always against you. Liscarroll was formerly the property of our General Garret Barry. Tell Sir Philip we're not invading his fortress. We are simply coming home.'

With that the plucky defenders were off in the direction of Mallow.

With Raymond's surrender, Liscarroll ought to have become the headquarters for the military arm of the Confederacy. General Mountgarrett's greater purpose seemed to have been achieved. The President of the Confederacy and General Barry had calculated that Irish custody of Liscarroll would entice the English out of Mallow.

Inchiquin would now have to be dealt with first, and he would have to face a vast army and a massive artillery range. What the Irish had not predicted was that Inchiquin was already upon them.

The officers in the Irish Army were invited to join their general for celebratory dinner in Liscarroll's fine hall. The cellars, pantries and larders had been explored and a gourmet's fantasy had been realised. There were Rieslings from the banks of the River Mosel, imported from the northern reaches of the Empire. There was Rioja wine in abundance from the kingdoms of Navarra and Aragon. There was French wine from the ancient vineyards of Gaillac and Bordeaux. There was cured ham and a hard dry cheese from Parma and ham hocks from Saxony. There were live Stiltons in their wheels, begging to be eaten, and there was salt cod from Portugal. Sacks of rice from the Camargue littered the floor. The only thing missing was fresh water.

The meal would be unorthodox, but it would be a shame to let such comestibles go to waste.

Soon the wine had worked its magic and the officers had found in it the means to endure another of General Barry's speeches. That done, it was time for the victorious army to swap their true, or mostly true, stories.

Bryen's concerned on Mallow.

'There is a story my father likes to tell. Captain Jephson's father was addicted to pleasure. He had not sufficient fortune to supply his craving and his debts grew oppressive. One night, many years ago, a well-dressed stranger called unannounced. Placing a large bag of gold on the dining table, he asked Jephson if he would like to be free of his debts. Jephson eagerly agreed. At that, the gentleman produced a white rat and said that he could have the gold, provided that he agree to have the rat with him at all meal times, and sitting on his right. Somewhat bemused, Jephson agreed. He was the object of some merriment for years, until one night, he grew tired of endless, repetitive banter and threw the wretched animal out of the window.

'That night, after the guests had gone, the well-dressed stranger was again ushered into the room by the frightened servants.

'"Have you fulfilled your promise?'

"Yes, until this night.'

"The promise was forever'.

'The stranger then whisked Sir John's ancestor out of the window. The white rat, in later years, appeared before the death of every head of the family.' [xxix]

All too soon, dawn was ready to break.

Much wine had been consumed. Barry's commanders, accordingly, seemed a little slow-witted.

They would have appreciated a little time to relax, but this was when the Confederate sentries reported that they had detected the vanguard of a Saxon army in the woods.

Barry mobilised his army.

He divided his foot soldiers into three divisions, each of two thousand men. The right wing was sent to the top of St Stephen's rock where there was a well manned earthwork with a good store of shot.

His left wing was sent to a post nearer the castle, well within defensive musket range of Stephen's Rock and its artillery.

Between the two, and a little behind, the third part consisted mostly of pikes. Barry's horse was left free to advance in one lethal front, drawing up on their right.

Inchiquin watched attentively. He quickly grasped the Irish strategy. He similarly divided his foot into three. Eight hundred pike and musket stood on lower Knockbarry, alongside their own artillery. Vavasour's six hundred musketeers marked the Irish left wing. A smaller left wing, also made up of musketeers, faced the Irish right. On his left, the English horse on the slopes of Lower Coolbane marked the Irish cavalry. A small squadron of musketeers was positioned in the rear, primed to shoot the deserters.

For a moment, no one breathed. Dawn rose in utter silence,

The opposing commanders, without conferring with one another, had laid out a battlefield on sloping ground a quarter of a mile to the east of the castle, a field-of-honour twenty or thirty yards in width and many hundreds in length.

The day looked set to be Barry's; he had every advantage, after all. He outnumbered the English three to one, far more than Inchiquin had been led to expect. He had two small forts and Liscarroll castle on his half of the field, to any of which his men could retreat. Even the sun was in his favour. His right wing occupied a hill near a long-disused fortification, while the left wing stood closer to the palace-fortress. His artillery, those huge captured guns, was close by. His horse, concentrated on the brow of the hill, gave his chargers the advantage of the slope.

In common with the English, his officers were in half-armour, breastplates in steel or leather, helmets all crested. His men proudly wore a fern in their caps and had rapidly confessed their sins.

Unfortunately, his men were not in peak condition. His foot complained they were weak after the hardships they long endured. A few had red eyes from too little sleep, or too much wine. Others had fainted on their route march to Liscarroll. That should have been a warning. Still, it was too late to play nursemaid to an army.

Barry tested the water. Leading a company of horse, he charged through the park, almost cutting off the English vanguard, and advanced along an avenue already lined with Irish musketeers.

Inchiquin's opposing horse was forced to retreat, which it did slowly, making frequent stands, turning around as it withdrew to express how little they feared their opponents, seemingly pressing forward while actually retreating.

The two great armies were only on the brink of battle; so far there were no injuries. This benignity would not last, however.

The English were distinguished by their sober clothing and their standards. They were spurred by their conviction that God was on their side. The Catholics, on the other hand, knew that God does not favour Caesar's might. Each individual would have to account for himself, explain his conduct, on the Day of Judgement.

The excitement was extreme, and it would shortly be over. No matter how much time it took to assemble the men, few battles ever lasted much more than an hour.

General Barry's artillery barked an announcement that battle was joined in earnest.

The balls missed their targets and, in the relief that followed, Lord Inchiquin, seeing that the rebels[xxx] had been ordered to remain at their posts, decided to attack them where they stood. He detached some competent musketeers to direct their fire on Barry and his vanguard, and then ordered his men to advance.

'Only when your piece has been discharged with mortal purpose are you to rejoin us. Once you hear the crackle of musket fire peter out, this is your signal to advance towards Barry; the horse as one body, the foot in three great squares.'

Unfortunately for Inchiquin, the Irish proved useful. Their musketeers came ahead, running from bush to bush, ditch to ditch, holding their weapons low. Their horse followed in perfect order.

The English shot was forced back and their commanders had difficulty in protecting their men. The sight of seven thousand Irish provided such a formidable spectacle, as they pursued the retreating English westwards to Knockbarry Hill, that only Inchiquin still believed the English stood a chance of winning.

General Barry tried to make a little mischief with his artillery, but it was planted too high to do much damage.

Nevertheless, Barry also believed he had all but won the battle. He disregarded the constant need for vigilance and discipline and let his right wing seize the advantage and advance against the English foot. There they were gallantly received but determinably driven back. The horse, helped by three hundred musketeers, were recovered by Major MacDonogh and his men, who galled the enemy's horse and obstructed their advance.

Inchiquin dismounted. Shouting his orders from Knockbarry Hill, he began the English counter-attack, which his enemy received very bravely. What happened next should have been fatal. When the first and second ranks of his troop had fired, as directed, they wheeled off to the rear, which the hindmost ranks mistook for a retreat. They began to fall off in great confusion.

Assisted by sixty musketeers from Sir John Browne's company, Barry gradually regained some sort of control. Soon the whole Irish army had retreated to its original positions near the castle and took advantage of its fortifications.

One noble soldier, Lord Oxenbridge, an aristocrat whose ancestor had fought at Agincourt, rode out to suppress the retreating Irish vanguard. Sadly, he was so carried away he went too far. He had to be rescued by a hastily scrambled squadron. He was shaken but unharmed.

His venerable cuirass had a dozen dents the size of plover's eggs where Irish musket balls had tried to find his heart.

Lord Inchiquin led his vanguard but General Barry found it easy to drive him back. The English muskets, however, denied the Irish horse the chance to end their action satisfactorily.

Inchiquin's army was in trouble. It was actually retreating when an extraordinary event occurred.

Inchiquin himself, sword in hand, his pistol tucked into his sash, came up against his cousin, Captain Oliver Stephenson, commanding the Irish horse. His men had the English general at their mercy. They had only just failed to take the Earl of Cork as well. They were about to kill him – they had already wounded Lord Inchiquin in the hand and face - when the Irish Captain intervened and saved him.

'My Lord Inchiquin!' Stephenson exclaimed. 'It's your lucky day. I have promised my mother, your aunt, not to harm a hair of your head, should we ever meet in battle. Meet me half way, dear boy, and drop that sword, will you?'

Inchiquin obliged.

This extraordinary gesture completely flummoxed the Irish in the lower Coolbane sector of the battle.

'Ha, Sir! Ha! You are my prisoner!' bellowed the triumphant Stephenson, glancing at the fallen sword and not quite believing his own eyes. 'What d'you think to that, Sir?'

Stephenson rode around his noble prisoner.

'This day will take fully two years off this ludicrous struggle. Had I captured your fellow usurper Lord Cork we might even have brought this war to an end!'

Stephenson raised his visor, the better to look his haughty captive up and down.

'Well, you are an ugly looking brute,' he declared, as if he were an artist describing a rebarbative model. 'I could always disobey my mother. Should I make the world a better-looking place by hanging you?'

Around the captain and his prisoner, the formation of horse was collapsing in confusion. No one was obeying any orders. Horses' hooves, flying in every direction, showered the footsoldiers with clods.

Yet Stephenson's triumphant laughter was premature. Blood began to flow from his right eye. The soldier stiffened and began to sway on his mount. Then, almost as if in slow motion, he toppled from his saddle, onto the ground. He hit the turf clumsily and never moved again.

Inchiquin, seizing his chance, had plucked his snaplock from his sash and killed his cousin, who had just saved his life, by shooting him through his open visor, planting a pistol round into Stephenson's brain.

Left among his enemy, Inchiquin could expect no mercy. He would surely have followed Stephenson's fate, if he had not been saved by Captain Jephson's troop of horse, riding into the fray at the gallop, swords slicing the air and any unfortunate Irishman who got in the way.

When they saw their commander fall the Irish cavalry lost heart. Jephson forced them back, giving Murrough Inchiquin the chance to regain to his own lines, tie his sash around his hand as a tourniquet, rally his men and deliver a cavalry charge of his own.

The Irish infantry lacked the training and discipline to withstand the English. Indeed, while the Gaels were mostly armed with pikes, many were only armed with pitchforks or scythes. When the Saxons attacked, many dropped these unwieldy weapons and took flight, leaving the gates to the castle open, the portcullis raised.

Musket-fire ripped and shredded the sky. The English musketeers had formed themselves into ranks; marching, crouching, firing and reloading. The air sang and hissed. Sometimes a ball would drive through a soldier's body with such energy that the small coins he had in his purse were driven out behind as shrapnel, wounding those comrades who followed.

Now Inchiquin launched a full-scale attack upon the whole body of the Irish horse. The Gaels stood firm for a good while, but when they saw their right wing of foot take to its heels, they fell back.

Sir Charles Vavasour and his six hundred men chose this moment to attack, drive back the Irish and pick up any fallen muskets to pass them down their lines. He attacked the rebels' left wing and a sharp action ensued, until they saw their captured artillery was of little use.

Elsewhere, the Irish infantry was doing creditably, at least as far as it could. Their horse was scattered and the English took advantage. Sir Charles Vavasour and Sir Philip de Perceval rallied their men and moved in.

Some Irish musketeers began to fire on the English ranks but they had too few ready weapons; the English had three times as many. Unsurprisingly, the first Irish attacks were easily repulsed. The English shot, however, had little effect. The English decided to charge from their position in lower Coolbane. Inchiquin led the onslaught and, on his right, came Dungarvan and his brother Broghill. Brother-in-law Barrymore brought up the rear.

During these sorties, the Confederates lost their formation. Some fled in chaos, believing their battle lost.

Everywhere they fell, their cavalrymen spinning crazily from their saddles to earth, while infantrymen, as they ran, were shot in flight, ploughing headlong into the soft boggy soil in front of them.

The unluckiest were not killed outright. Not so far from the south gate an Irish javelinist sat upright, dazed and bewildered, his arm hanging uselessly by his side. The only word he said, over and over, each time more quietly, was 'ma'. Then he too lay down, as if to sleep.

Between the two armies was a little meadow. At the upper end of this field, where the English horse had to pass in order to charge, was a *clachan* bristling with Irish musketeers. Sixty English horse charged those miserable cabins. The Irish had time to retreat to the security of their main body but, in doing so, cleared a path for their enemy.

Lieutenant Oxenbridge pursued the small body of Irish. This time the ruse almost succeeded. Yet it failed. Oxenbridge rode too far and cut himself off from his own side. The English had to fight hard to rescue their man, but they did.

Inchiquin now had the advantage in the way the battlefield fell. He was still outnumbered so, to draw the Irish down from their hilltop, he advanced with a party of horse, against which the Irish ordered a party of musketeers to line the hedges. From there they could fire on the English while, with a body of horse, they steadily advanced against them. The English were forced to retreat.

Vavasour, meanwhile, was happily slaughtering those guarding the ordnance on Stephen's Rock, who had been holding out bravely. The surviving Irish, seeing that they were no longer protected, deserted their posts in droves to flee in the direction of Glenfield.

Now the battle entered its pitiless final phase. The Saxons gave no quarter. Their horse now surrounded the thick woodland north of Liscarroll and their foot marched confidently in.

Inchiquin rode behind his troopers. Having seen off the enemy's horse, he had now reached the farthest part of the bog, where many rebels remained. His foot marched on it in good order, to surround it, leaving no means of escape. Unfortunately, his Lordship, not knowing that the rebel's right wing had fled, mistook his own men for enemies. Ordering a retreat he reversed almost a mile before he realised he was deceived. That error let many Irishmen escape, but fifteen hundred had to stay where they were. They were already dead.

While the Saxons returned to their posts, Lord Kynalmeaky, Lord Cork's son, was shot by an Irish marksman. He would die alongside Captain Stephenson. A jubilant Irish shout of 'Kynalmeaky is down, death to the heretics' was heard by ten thousand men. His horse was recaptured by Francis Boyle but, try as he might, he could not get to his elder brother in the raging mêlée. His conspicuous courage in the heat of battle was recognised when he was later ennobled Viscount Shannon.

Nevertheless, the Irish left wing was routed. It quit the fort and retired to Killbolan bog. Their example was immediately followed by their third division of foot. It had, up to then, remained out of musket range but now it fled for safety to the same bog where it was impossible to follow them, half a mile distant from the battlefield.

If they had not abandoned the fight, they considered, few of their number would have escaped.

Lord Inchiquin had only twenty men killed in the Battle of Liscarroll, with around twenty more wounded, most of them horse, including young Lord Kynalmeaky, the first of the Earl of Cork's five sons to die in the war.

Of the Irish, about two thousand were slain, mostly in the prolonged hail of musket balls and the swish of Sheffield steel. Three pieces of artillery, fourteen colours, three hundred muskets, thirty wagons and three barrels of powder were taken that day.

Despite the fact that little quarter had been given, save to Colonel Richard Butler, Lord Ikerrin's son and two or three other officers, the English still had fifty prisoners of quality. Normally, the officers would be ransomed, but Inchiquin had other ideas.

It had been a very long battle - seven hours – and fortunes had fluctuated throughout. Contrary to all expectations, it had ended with an English victory.

The English army tried to follow the Irish in hot pursuit but were forced to abandon the trail when faced with impenetrable bogs and the thickest of woods.

The Irish death roll was not confined to junior ranks. The Catholic gentry suffered horribly in the battle. The valiant Burgats lost two uncles and a nephew, whose remains were later carried away to Kilmallock Abbey to be interred.[xxxi] The Old-English Fitzgeralds lost eighteen senior members of their race.

The next morning, a final, chilling denouement was played out by the victors.

Inchiquin had his engineers erect a huge extemporary gallows. Two great beams, almost thirty feet across, were roped together and raised some twelve feet above the ground, supported by three trees that suited his grim purpose. This dark engine was erected on the very hill that the Irish had held so valiantly and its fatal shape framed a gate into the infinite.

His men tied fifty nooses and tossed them over the beams.

Inchiquin was driven by anger – that emotion coloured his every fibre. Those fifty captured Irish officers, their hands now tightly bound, were prodded with bayonets and made to climb the hill. There, the collars were put in place. Two soldiers pulled each prisoner a foot or so into the air, and the other end of these hempen ropes was secured with stakes driven deep into the ground.

Many of these doomed young men were the sons of chiefs, who had thought to take their country back into the care of their ancestors. Others were talented boys promoted from the ranks by virtue of their talent. One was a priest.

Fr O'Flaherty had been captured on the battlefield while giving a fallen soldier the last rites. Now he tried to offer the same solace to his forty-nine companions. He got as far as saying '*in nomine Patris et Filii et Spiritus Sancti*' before the rope choked off his speech.

Death came at Inchiquin's invitation, but not punctually. The reaper was in no hurry. He selected his dancing companions in a leisurely way. There had been no drop, no broken necks to hasten this last journey. As the dangling forms tried to shake themselves free, or even to tighten the knot, the Saxon witnesses laughed. Some of the condemned soiled themselves, which provoked much merriment.

Inchiquin gave his men the time they needed to enjoy the spectacle before ordering the captured cannons to be turned on Liscarroll itself.

His logic was impeccable. The woods and bogs would have filled with angry Irishmen. The lovely old seat of the Barrys – and the present seat of the Percevals – needed to be made uninhabitable.

The castle had been built in an age before artillery existed. The gunners did their demolition work in no time at all. The place-fortress, said by many to have been the most beautiful castle ever erected on Irish soil, became a picturesque ruin before their eyes.

Though their defeat threw the Irish into a terrible consternation but, since Lord Inchiquin had neither pay nor food for his soldiers, he could not follow up his victory. He sent some men to raid the local farms, but found nothing, not even a pig. The country was wasted, and the 'English' general was forced the next day to march back to Mallow and disperse his army into garrisons.

Nearly every Irishman had been from Duhallow. Slowly, mothers and sisters, wives and children emerged from the *clachans*, the townlands and townships, which once had been the proud characteristic of this lovely part of Ireland. It first they searched in silence for someone who had mattered to them in life. When they identified some bullet ridden or decapitated corpse, they began to weep, and from there the melancholy fed on itself. The women began to keen, an eerie and distressing call to the infinite, or to the Virgin in her blue cloak, begging her to intercede so that the agony of the fallen could be rewarded with joy in heaven.

It took a further fortnight before the Irish thought it safe to bury their dead. They ended in a collective grave, just outside Kilmallock Abbey.

'I have written something for the headstone,' said Bryen. 'A testament.'

'Well, Major, let's hear it.' General Barry liked to indulge his protégés.

> O'er valley and hill lies a soul-crushing gloom
> When the war mangled corpses are awaiting a tomb.
> The Gael's gushing blood has stained the Puritan sword
> As they gave up their lives for the cause they adored.
> The women came weeping and wailing that night,
> To search for their menfolk, who fell in that fight;
> The moan of their keening spreads through the air
> Like the sigh of a nation sunk deep in despair.

It had been a great victory for the Protestant/Parliamentarian coalition. Inchiquin loudly boasted that Cork would remain a God-fearing and British stronghold for the next thousand years.

*

CHAPTER FOURTEEN
INCHIQUIN, A PROTESTANT HERO

The Lords Justice in Dublin learned of the victory soon enough. They were delighted that Lord Ormonde could not claim the credit and began to refer to Lord Inchiquin as a promising young man.

'How should we celebrate, Sir William?'

'By settling North Munster. Let's begin by evicting the Irish and selling the land to the highest bidder. Even after our commission, the balance should prove useful to our brothers in the Westminster Parliament.'[xxxii]

*

In Dublin Castle, Lord Ormonde's continuing success in Leinster still conspired to irritate Sir William Parsons and Sir John Borlase, the Lords Justice. It did not suit them to allow Lord Ormonde any triumph or credit. Like an ungodly heathen, he occasionally took a glass of wine. The tailoring of his mind was not of their sober stuff.

Yet, as a king's man, they had neither the authority nor the will to sack him. Their treasury was empty and the king was still sending treasure and troops. For their part, the Commons sent the Justices £11,500 pounds, with two thousand worthless, ill-disciplined troops. Even that colossal sum was insufficient since the new soldiers were semi-mutinous and more trouble than they were worth.

Lord Ormonde saw things differently. He sought out the relics of Wentworth's once proud army and settled their back-wages from his own pocket. He then took them to relieve Athlone. Even so, this astonishing generosity was not good enough for Parsons and Borlase. Far too many were Catholic for comfort.

The Castle's army grew daily more unmanageable. Castle intrigues and subversion from across the Bristol Channel undid it. The English Parliament sent over ever more Commissioners with orders to pen a report on the affairs of Ireland, make recommendations and, as always, ensure that lessons would be learned. The Lords Justice exploited this opportunity to draft and submit a new penal code to the Commissioners. It contained laws that would affect only Catholics. The Commissioners went away impressed. One even joked, admiringly, that Parsons and Borlase were Draco and Dionysus[xxxiii] reborn.

In Ulster, where the Catholics had struck the first blows, things were also growing worse. The talented Covenanter General Monro had defeated the Catholic Lord Antrim and taken Dunluce with the same ploy by which Sir Phelim had used to take Charlemont. He had invited himself as a guest and arrested his host at his own table.

*

The Confederacy, based in Kilkenny, was reasonably well positioned to direct the war in Leinster, Munster and the Pale. The castle was close to Dublin, Cork and Limerick and most of the southern and south-western roads met there. Within the town's walls was a trading centre[xxxiv], the seat of the Butlers and the palace of the Bishop of Ossory. An ideal headquarters, just as the ancient 'Half-Kingdom' had seen.

It was, however, difficult to manage the war in the north and northwest from so southerly a city. Poor communications made it hard - if not impossible - to impose authority or strategy on a general or army on the Erne or the Bann.

The confederates remembered that in England, many years before, the same problem had led to the creation of the Presidency of the North, with its council and headquarters in the city of York. Lord Strafford was the last to hold that office.

The Confederation resolved to divide itself into northern and southern groups. One of these would revolve around Kilkenny, the other would take its law from wherever Sir Phelim laid his hat.

*

Flaming Ulster put no one in a flattering light.

While Cole, Hamilton, the Stewarts, Chichester and Conway scoured the province for rebels, they met little opposition and gave less quarter. The Protestant commanders of Enniskillen, Deny, Newry and Drogheda found themselves almost unopposed. An outright Puritan victory was only held off by the lack of agreement between the Scottish commanders and the settled Undertakers. Catholics were no longer providing any serious resistance. Half of the tens of thousands who had risen less than a year before were now weak and disorganised. The other half was dead.

The Protestants began to gloat. Sir William Cole, among his many claims of service to the State, cheerfully reported seven thousand 'of the rebels famished to death' within a few miles of Enniskillen.

Some of the disheartened Irish had considered emigrating to the Catholic Scottish islands and highlands, when a magic phrase was whispered from one native ear to every other.

'Colonel Owen Roe O'Neill has arrived!'

The famous veteran of the Thirty Years War had made land on the Donegal coast. His ferry was a huge French warship.

Nor did he arrive empty-handed. His great ship bore treasure; French muskets, great casks of powder and shot, not to mention a hundred officers and many Irish veterans of the Thirty Years War.

Once on land, Owen Roe took his men the short distance to Doe Castle, near Creeslough. For the Irish rebels the castle had its own sacred memories. It was the principle seat of the MacSweeney family and it had been at Doe Castle that Sir Cahir O'Dogherty had set up his headquarters before he sacked Derry in 1608. The MacSweeneys joyfully and tearfully welcomed Owen Roe and his men to Ireland. They also welcomed his money, munitions and raised their hats to Richelieu. When they were told the Cardinal was dead, they said prayers for him.

News of this kind travels fast. Sir Phelim heard it in somewhere in County Antrim. He immediately delegated command to his ADC, mounted his horse and rode like the wind to Doe. On arrival, he offered his cousin command of the Ulster Confederates.

Barely an hour later, Rory O'More was himself at Doe. He too swore allegiance to Owen Roe, telling him that Ulster was unquestionably where Irish anger was at its keenest. It was where the colonel's skills were needed most, he said.

Owen Roe was unimpressed with suggestions that he was in mortal danger from the Calvinists.

'I think we'll manage,' he said succinctly.

*

In England, meanwhile, King Charles raised his standard at Nottingham, where he reciprocally declared the English Parliament to be treasonable. The English Civil War was now official.

*

The Irish Rebellion, at last, had reached Galway.

The mere presence of a rebel army was an insult in the eyes of the Protestant Governor of Connacht, Sir Francis Willoughby. He sent for reinforcements, and they arrived under the fanatical Lord Forbes.

Forbes at once set Clanrickarde's truce aside and, in revenge for the attacks he had endured on his journey. He burned Galway City's poorer, mostly Catholic suburbs, and sacked the Popish Churches. He imposed a reign of terror.

It had an unintended effect. Risings took place in Sligo, Mayo and Roscommon and with so much violence that the Lord President of the Province, Lord Ranelagh, had to lock himself in his own castle.

*

In Wexford, James Touchet, Earl of Castlehaven, had proffered the Cause his considerable fortune. In return, he was offered and accepted the leadership of the Leinster army.

While addressing the Supreme Council at Kilkenny, news came that three French frigates - towing around a dozen transports – had put into Wexford. Colonel Preston, widely lauded as the defender of the city and university of Louvain from the French, unloaded siege guns, field pieces, muskets, ammunition and some edible comestibles - mostly vile-smelling cheeses that apparently his men could not do without. They had been abroad a long time. He had also brought five hundred veterans and a number of highly qualified siege engineers.

Colonel Tomás Preston and Colonel Owen Roe O'Neill were about to revolutionise the poorly equipped and largely untrained Confederate army.

Up to this time the Confederates had mostly relied on guerrilla, hit-and-run raids. Both sides had been trying to visit economic ruin on the other by destroying crops, killing or stealing cattle and burning the other's settlements. In Ulster, especially, both the Covenanters' violent plundering and the savagery of the Catholic retaliations were becoming infamous as far away as England and the Continent, if the stories were adapted to suit widely different audiences. In the noble salons of Vienna, Paris and Rome, one spoke of Irish courage and derring-do in the face of mountainous odds. In the elegant drawing rooms of London, Amsterdam and Stockholm hostesses spoke of Irish 'barbarities', claiming to be unable to understand their cause.

The Confederate leaders knew that their war had descended into a suite of defeats and licensed murders. That would end, now that two truly strategic generals, Preston and O'Neill, could at last take charge.

Sir Phelim gave his kinsman a day's briefing at Charlemont, from where they collected their army before moving it to Clones, in Monaghan. There the fighting men of the northern clans had gathered to greet them. The army was asked to elect Owen Roe O'Neill 'General-in-

206

Chief of the Catholic Army of the North', Sir Phelim resigning in his favour. They obliged.

Owen Roe favoured the shorter formula, 'President of Ulster', a title that an Elizabethan Lord Essex had once wanted for the Great O'Neill himself.

To business. Owen Roe insisted the Catholic Confederation should temper the popular uprising. The Supreme Council of the Assembly of Kilkenny responded well to his suggestions. The litany of spontaneous, anarchic Irish uprisings would from now on be governed by humane rules of engagement. The Gaelic Irish and the 'Old English' aristocracy painlessly coalesced into an unprecedented alliance. By the late summer the Rebellion had metamorphosed into the Confederate War of Independence.

Owen Roe O'Neill ordered the Catholic war effort to be directed against the remaining British armies in Ireland; no longer against Protestants *per se*. Owen Roe wanted to deter a full-scale English or Scottish re-conquest of the country.

Colonel O'Neill put Irish Catholic nobles into regional commands. These men immediately armed and committed their own tenantry to the Confederacy and began to persuade other landowners to join in.

Between them they brought the widespread killing of innocent Protestants under control. Owen Roe had to hang several rebels for attacks on civilians but, from this time, the war, while still brutal, was fought under the civilised code of conduct that both O'Neill and the Scottish commander Robert Monro had practiced as professional soldiers in the Spanish Netherlands.

At the same moment Lord Lieven arrived from Scotland with the remainder of the ten thousand that the Scottish Parliament had voted. He had known O'Neill abroad and had a high opinion of his abilities. He wrote to him. It was not a long letter.

Colonel Owen Roe O'Neill

I take this occasion to express my surprise that a man of such a reputation as yours should be engaged in so poor a cause.

On reading the brief message, Owen Roe called for writing paper.

I believe, my dear Lord Lieven, that I have a better right to come to the relief of my own country than your lordship has to march into England against his lawful king.

The Civil War in England was turning ugly. Lieven, before returning home at Parliament's behest to prepare for war, urged Monro to act promptly.

> Your lordship may expect a severe lesson if the new commander succeeds in training and equipping his army.

Yet Monro was deaf to such well-meant advice. He had concluded that the Scottish and English forces in the Province would amount, if united, to twenty thousand foot and a thousand horse. That would carry the day. He dismissed all advice to the contrary.

Monro's inaction allowed O'Neill enough time to man, officer, drill, and arm a force not to be despised by one twice its size.

Now that professional soldiers were on the case, Confederate plans for Ireland could at last be realised, if slowly. Confederate gains were coming thick and fast. Loughgar and Askeaton followed Limerick.

Lord Inchiquin, unaware that Bryen was serving under Garrett Barry and Lord Muskerry, had the courtesy to send a missive to his old friend Bryen MacDonogh at Kanturk.

> Our paths may have diverged. I am well aware, that while today I am your friend and comrade, should you pick up a Catholic and Confederate sword, I shall have no qualms in hanging you from a common gibbet.

*

The General Assembly met in Kilkenny, on Maguire's Day, October 23, 1642, following the agreement that had been made that May.

The first plenary meeting of the newly constituted Supreme Council of Ireland coincided with the second General Assembly of the Confederacy. Each of the twenty-four councillors had a servant behind him. Standing just behind the Catholic Archbishop of Cashel, Fr Butler[xxxv], was a young man, dressed in the surplice and cassock that were his uniform at the hedgerow seminary of St Mary's, Maynooth.

Donogh MacDonogh looked serious but not troubled. Though a promising seminarian he sensed that his vocation might be tested in the near future. The confession of faith or the profession of arms? The more he heard, as he took notes for his employer, the more convinced he was that Ireland needed his sword.

The sixteen-year-old was a long way from his home in Kanturk. He was in Kilkenny, at a meeting packed with great lords and bishops.

Donogh knew that the huge castle he was standing in was owned by the Anglican Marquess of Ormonde and was currently the seat of his Catholic cousin, Lord Mountgarrett.

He looked at the noble figure seated at the east end of the great hall. Pride of place had of course been awarded to Lord Mountgarrett. Urgency permeated the air. The war in Ireland was daily more desperate and there was a chance that Lieutenant-General Lord Ormonde would attack his own first cousin.

Donogh thought Richard Mountgarrett's father an Irish hero in his own right, not least because he was related to the warrior O'Neills. His first wife, Margaret, had been the great Earl of Tyrone's eldest daughter. He had joined Tyrone's Nine Years War, distinguishing himself in his defence of the castles of Balyrahet and Cullihill. His vast estates would have been seized by attainder and the old man beheaded, but he was saved such ignominy by 'natural causes' in 1605. The attainder not having been served, his 'innocent' son was confirmed in the family's estates and demesnes the following year.

His son, the enthroned Mountgarrett, was for Donogh MacDonogh almost a demigod.

When the Rebellion first looked likely to oppose the Lords of the Pale, the best way to defend the Butler interests, Mountgarrett and Ormonde had agreed, was to take possession of Kilkenny in the name of the Catholic rebels. That at least would secure their castle from attack from the Irish. Mountgarrett already relied on his cousin's connections in the Castle to keep Dublin off his back.

'When we first gathered in this noble hall,' Mountgarrett was saying, 'you all swore an oath to reunite Ireland under the holy canopy of the Catholic Church. Patrick Darcy, our lawyer, drafted that Oath of Association, that Bishop Roche made you all swear. Each and every member of our Assembly is loyal to the Faith, the King's Rights and the Liberty of Ireland. Some of you may think it ironic that Darcy drew on the Scottish National Covenant for precedent and inspiration, but Scotland needed to determine its own customs, as befits a kingdom in its own right. She won its liberty. With these words, and with our lives, we too find for the Crown. Our enemy is not the King of England but those treacherous servants of his who seek to pollute our conscience with heresy and seize our land for their fellow bigots.

'As his majesty's loyal Catholic Irish subjects, our motto shall be *Pro Deo, Rege et Patria, Hibernia Unanimis*.'

There was applause for this.

'We still have to find some way of regaining legitimate and peaceable control of our Confederacy,' Archbishop Butler told the delegates. 'We need to be a Parliament: one that will give us national unity against heretics, schismatics and invaders.'

'We'll need a High King. Or an emperor,' Lord Muskerry mused, loudly enough for Donogh to hear him and write his comment down.

'We already have a king', said Lord Mountgarrett sternly. He had clearly heard Muskerry's observation too. 'His Majesty King Charles is our lawful anointed sovereign. Any other choice would be to bring God's wrath upon us.'

'I fear the king's loyal Parliament more,' said Muskerry to himself.

Many Gaelic Irish distrusted Mountgarrett and the presiding Supreme Council. It was dominated by the Anglo-Irish and Old English. The Celts thought them too moderate and wanted to take the gloves off. Some of the more radical delegates were already lobbying for a complete reversal of the plantations and the enforcement of Catholicism as Ireland's only religion. They wanted the king to accept a self-governing Catholic Ireland before formally allying with him. Failing that, they would seek an independent alliance with France or Spain.

Everyone, Celts and Normans alike, would agree, after some debate, that support for King Charles was central to their strategy, and without preconditions. They felt no need to press for radical political or religious reforms. They had not forgotten that English Parliament and the Scottish Covenanters had threatened to invade Ireland before the war, promising to destroy the Catholic religion and the Irish land-owning class forever.

The king, by way of contrast, repeatedly attempted concessions. In their negotiations with English Royalists, the Confederates decided that royal promises could wait to be ratified in a post-war Irish Parliament; one which would resemble the Confederate General Assembly but would be open to all Royalists. There was a rumour abroad that the king himself might even convert to his ancestral faith. Some Puritans were claiming he was already almost a Catholic. Possibly, some said, he secretly worshipped at the same altar-rail as his wife.

The Confederate Association of Ireland never actually claimed to be a formally independent government. Darcy advised it not to; only the king could declare it a Parliament. That irritating detail aside, no one could prevent it from acting like one; it was now the *de facto* government of most of Ireland beyond the Pale. Its General Assembly was democratic to an unusual degree for the time, at least for its day. It believed in elections. Its elective constituency was made up of Catholic Irish landowners and Catholic clergy. This body, the Assembly, in turn elected the Executive, the Supreme Council.

The first act of the Supreme Council was to confirm Colonel Owen Roe O'Neill as Captain-General and Commander-in-Chief in Ulster. It promoted Tomás Preston to General and gave him command of Leinster, over Castlehaven's head. General Barry got Munster. The supreme command in the West was held over for Clanrickarde, who, it was still hoped, might yet be coaxed into the Confederacy. Sir John Burke, his kinsman, became the Confederate Lieutenant-General in Connacht.

Owen Roe O'Neill, nephew of The Great O'Neill, used his prestige and military experience to stiffen the sinews of his Irish ranks.

'As I see it,' he told the Supreme Council, 'my task is to create a unified nation. It will be hardest for the Ultonians among you. I understand your anger at the cynical colonisation of your province - I am one of you, after all. When I left Ulster forty years ago, and after the punishment meted out to it by the Saxons, it looked like a desert. This Confederation will restore the nation we all love and may die for, by force. After our war there will be peace. All of us will have to forgive our enemies, particularly those who never took up arms against us. Your Supreme Council may want to allow a few of them to keep a little property, a few possessions. Keep that in your hearts; our cause is righteous, not vengeful.

'Gentlemen, you should know that, in England, the Puritans maintain that Queen Henrietta-Maria incited our Rising. They cite the fact that she invited the Pope to send an envoy to England, as proof. They are trying to imply that their Anglican monarch is secretly Catholic. Such distractions are helpful to our Confederacy. Extremists lose educated support whenever they make such preposterous assertions.

'That's enough political philosophy. For now, we have to address our want of money. Our need is very great and the Cardinal's generosity, splendid as it was, will not see us through the long campaign that is bound to follow.'

Mountgarrett replied that he would order an extensive system of taxation, to finance the war, to be set up.

'May I see a show of hands in support of Captain-General O'Neill's suggestion?' he asked.

The Synod heard and raised its collective hand.

The Kilkenny Assembly had been conducted with a dignified solemnity. All agreed that the Civil War in England was a fact. They considered their options carefully. For how long would the English Civil War last? Who would win? Some Geraldines had been considering staying apart from the Rebellion until Parliament formally declared war on the sovereign. The way they saw it, their Oath of Association had bound them together and asserted their rights as loyal subjects. When the Old English declared themselves for King Charles, Parliament had had to treat them as *de facto* revolutionaries, and now that the War in England was real, when they swore their new and formal Oath, in the eyes of Parliament they became rebels *de jure*.

Preston and Owen Roe, and all of the returning heroes, were affected by adversity at home, but they brought to the struggle an extraordinary knowledge of foreign and domestic politics. Particularly the secret of what the Spanish called the *guerilleros*. They had spent years on the Continent; in wars, schools, seminaries. They had learned how the Huguenots had held their hundred 'cautionary towns'. They could learn from these brave men, from the way they had set up 'leagues' and 'associations', just as much as they had from the way that Catholic resistance was organised in the Netherlands and in some Lutheran parts of the Holy Roman Empire.

Nor were the events occurring in their next-door island unknown or unweighed by that solemn Assembly. The extent and intent of the Scottish and English insurrections were by this time clear to every one.

'Even before king and Parliament declared war on each other,' Owen Roe O'Neill told the Synod, 'you had established a national government, this Confederacy of the Clans, here at Kilkenny. I have witnessed rebel Gaelic and Anglo-Irish noblemen join together in what had previously been considered an impossible alliance.

'Ireland has embarked on the boulder-strewn road to freedom. It will not be easy but we shall overcome. Once we have reached our goal, we shall govern ourselves as we have not done for almost a thousand years. Not since our High Kings ruled from Tara itself.'

*

CHAPTER FIFTEEN
AN ORMONDE PEACE

'Nobody wants to export our war to Ireland.' Oliver St John, the Attorney General and successor to Sir Edward Coke, was nothing if not adamant. 'The king can't afford a full-blown intervention over there; his slender resources are needed here. By the same token, nor should we in Westminster concern ourselves overmuch with that overseas kingdom.'

'Hear hear,' said several English MPs around the table.

'We will have to solve the Irish issue. Since no solution is immediately obvious, however, let us focus on those domestic matters that are worrying both the Presbyterians in our Parliament and the Puritans in our army.'

*

FROM THE RECORDER OF CORK

Cork City,   To the Most Noble Marquess of Ormonde
4 Dec, 1642.   His Majesty's Lord Lieutenant in Ireland

May it please Your Lordship, Lord Inchiquin commands me to write to you on the subject of Youghal. I shall try not to stray from this directive.

The news from that Protestant and enlightened enclave is provoking, but I am pleased to relate to Your Lordship that Youghal holds out very stoutly, considering its straits.

It was Richard Boyle who first attempted to defend poor weak Youghal from the Papists with a garrison. Have you been told, Sir, that the Irish there are three of them to one of us? If the town be lost, it is not defeatist but realistic to predict that all the hope of every English port in the Province shall likewise be lost.

Over the last few weeks, Parliament has sent us a number of English royalists, captured in Manchester and other Parliamentary towns. At first we took this as a vote of confidence, a great encouragement; we used them to augment our companies in arms. What appeared a benison, alas, quickly become a curse when the new men ran over to the enemy. I devoutly wish the Parliamentarians would send us no more prisoners. Common English royalists must be void of reason or understanding, or they would never defect to the horde of superstitious idolaters, men that worship the dead, that threatens us.

Does my pen run ahead of my reason? Perhaps you mean to ask me if the Irish have simply been maddened by our clumsiness? The news of your heroic efforts to achieve a lasting peace may not have penetrated the mud walls of their sties!

If this be so, you will tolerate a correction. The Irish are well led and disciplined. Around the beginning of this month, General Preston came with his Leinster Army to reinforce Lord Castlehaven in his long siege of our 'rebel' City of Cork, wherein we are once again trapped.

Over in Youghal, our plight is even greater. The Papists have placed ordnance on both sides of the harbour, six mines on Passagepoint and as many on our side, by the nunnery at Ferrypoint. The Irish Battery of three guns threatens the town but has not sufficient wherewithal to prevent ships landing at the port itself.

Joshua Boyle, Youghal's Recorder, may have fourteen hundred fighting men but he also has the care of six thousand women. As for provisions, he is presently reduced to a hundred barrels of wheat. Until he is relieved he can only allow a pound of bread a day for every soul.

Last Saturday morning, Sir Charles Vavasour led a gallant attempt to break into Youghal through the siege. When his soldiers saw the enemy ordnance and small shot play before them, their hearts failed and they fled, but not here to Cork where we could have put them to use but to nearby safe-havens - newly Protestant forts outside the walls. His efforts, while well meant, have further reduced our fighting strength.

Some of his men have since been discovered. We found them in a desperate condition, wandering through the county, begging, fearful for their lives.

That worthy man Lord Inchiquin himself has done what he can to provide food and ships and has been an exceeding great help to every garrison in this province. We too would like to help the people of Youghal, since grain here in Cork City is plentiful; our numerous wheat barrels each contain five Winchester bushels. Without this, we too should have long since been lost. But transporting it through enemy lines? No sir. That would be fatal.

Your Lordship should also know, that if you would be pleased to make stay of that iron ore you are sending to the English parliament, you could sell it here for much dearer rates; in Cork City it yieldeth fully 20/- a ton. Lord Inchiquin desires you will reserve him six tons, for which he will pay Your Lordship handsomely.

Your servant, Wm Boyle, is most sincerely yours to command.

*

In Carrickfergus, far away in the north, the Scots' Major-General Robert Monro had settled comfortably into Carrickfergus's vast fortress. In his ample private quarters he was not the least hemmed in by the tens of thousands of odiferous Covenanters who shared his castle and its neighbouring fields. Some might have resented the rigours of such a posting, but Monro relieved the tedium with hunter-killer raids against the Irish.

Despite the cruel winter of January 1643, Ulster proved the perfect place for a manhunt. Despite the major-general's efforts, the Province continued to seethe with 'maddened' Catholics. As the weeks went by, the Presbyterian general's mood slowly turned sour. He ordered that none of these pitchfork-waving clowns was to be taken prisoner. Obediently his soldiers killed every shovel-brandishing peasant they found in Kilwarlin woods, on Rathlin Island, at Glenmaquinn...

'In the end it's for their benefit. The Irish are delusional,' Monro added. 'Anyone who still believes he might yet get his land back is insane.'

His enemy, the Confederate General Tomás Preston, commanded 6,000 foot and six hundred horse, most of whom he had personally trained. Some had even served under him on the Continent.

Preston chose to avoid Monro. The Scotsman hugely outnumbered him. Instead, he engaged the Protestant General Monk at Tymahoe and again at Ballinakil. He suffered some losses, but by January he had cleared Birr, Banagher, Burris and Fort Falkland of their Protestant militias.

1643 saw the Confederacy master half of Ireland, roughly from the Shannon in the west to the Barrow in the north.

The war in Ireland, however, was about to take an unexpected turn. The Marquess of Ormonde had received secret letters from his sovereign, brought to him covertly. In them came orders to begin negotiations with his first cousin, Lord Mountgarrett, President of the Confederacy.

> This Irish savagery has to cease. You are to engineer a cessation of arms. We desire to fetch our loyal troops back from Ireland. We have need of them in England.
>
> Carolus R

Up to then, Ormonde's overtures to the Supreme Council of the Confederacy had remained unanswered. Now, to everyone's astonishment, Mountgarrett replied. The Confederates of Kilkenny would, at last, talk.

The parties could not meet directly. It would have to be an elaborate process, conducted via an exchanges of letters. Ormonde was not safe in Confederate country. Nor did Mountgarrett trust the Castle in Dublin. Clearly, the proposed 'Cessation of Arms' was not going to happen overnight.

For his part, Owen Roe found the attitude of the Munster gentry, whether Old English or Gaelic, frustrating. They seemed almost to enjoy sitting on the fence. Could they not see that if Cork and Ulster did not expel their settlers, the war would deliver no one a victory?

A young scribe in Kilkenny had the gift of a fair script. He had volunteered to take dictation and, overnight, translate both English and Irish into Latin. O'Neill asked for him to be presented. He soon learned that the lad was the nephew of Cormac Macdonogh, whom he remembered so well from Arras. Deciding to take advantage of the relative peace, he sought out Donogh's father, the Lord of Duhallow, hoping that way he might bring Celtic Ireland more deeply into the war.

*

Broghill's Protestant forces arrived outside Youghal's walls, armed to the teeth, determined to raise Lord Castlehaven's siege.

Castlehaven's scouts saw them as soon as the English vanguard came into view. They reported the enemy's numbers to be so great that Castlehaven wisely decided to abandon his siege.

At this, there was much rejoicing. During the Catholic siege, such food as there was had been restricted to good Protestants. Now every citizen could be relieved.

Retreat, perhaps, but Castlehaven was not going to leave his great guns behind.

The Irish commander and his ADC, a secretive youth of noble family, always in his light armour, galloped off in the direction of the fortress of Carrigaphooca, having directed the remainder of the army to load their guns onto wagons and, keeping an eye open all the way, return General Preston to the MacCarthy stronghold at Blarney.

Inchiquin wanted to hang the captured rebels for treason, but Broghill dissuaded him.

'We have won the battle for the south; there is room for magnanimity.'

This was not typical of the Boyles, but Inchiquin, curious, stayed his hand.

Yet it was true. Youghal raised the cross of St George. The other English garrisons – Kinsale, even Cork itself - followed suit. Lord Broghill had turned the clock back to a peaceful time before the Rebellion.

*

One day, in mid-February, 1643, Kevin O'Grady led Owen Roe O'Neill and Tomás Preston up the steps to the front door of The Court. Kanturk

Footmen opened the door with appropriate deference and the Confederate generals found Dermod Oge, Cliona and their three children waiting for them in the hall, in front of one of the two carved blue-grey limestone fireplaces. Their elaborate wooden overmantles told the family's version of the Garden of Eden.

'Welcome to my house,' said Dermod Oge, bowing from the waist. Cliona curtseyed elegantly and her children did as noble custom demanded. O'Neill and Preston reciprocated.

'We are honoured and appreciative of this interview,' said Owen Roe, while he and General Preston handed their capes to O'Grady. 'I know your brother well. We met in Arras.'

'We have heard much of your courage and steadfastness at that dreadful time,' rejoined Cliona, indicating that her guests should sit.

'I had little choice, truth be told,' said Owen Roe modestly.

'That's not as I understand it! You could have surrendered months before. Yet you stayed fast, tying the whole of France in knots for six long months!' said Cliona.

'And then you persuaded the Cardinal Infante and Cardinal Richelieu to back our cause,' said Dermod Oge.

'Well, now I have the honour to ask the Lord of Duhallow to do the same.'

Cliona raised a hand.

'You gentlemen will not need Caitlín and me for your grand affairs. Nor even Donogh, even though he will soon be off to Oxford to help Richard Mountgarrett negotiate with the king. It is better he hears nothing that may compromise him.' She caught a puzzled frown on O'Neill's face. 'General, you should be aware that Lord Ormonde has agreed to let some Confederate representatives travel to Oxford in England, in order to pen terms for a permanent peace. Donogh has been selected to be one of that team.'

The student, suddenly in the limelight, stood and bowed to his guests.

'With your permission, mama, I shall remain.'

'As you wish,' said his mother. 'Then I leave you and your chinwag a bright young celibate, together with a husband who was once a captain in the King of France's Guards and my son Bryen, once a captain in Lord Wentworth's Foot and now a major in Lord Muskerry's regiment. Gentlemen, given the hour, I shall have some wine sent in. Or would you prefer buttermilk?'

Cliona and her daughter stood, and the others all rose and bowed again. Then the ladies were gone.

Dermod Oge sat, leading the way by example, and his sons and distinguished guests did the same.

'You pay me the deepest of compliments, gentlemen, but now that Lords Ormonde and Mountgarrett look likely to agree a Cessation, I do not see exactly why you should wish me to take my clans to war?'

'Dermod Oge, this war may slow, even pause, but it will never cease. The English still own the north, the Dublin Pale, Cork City, various vassal townlands and a number of smaller garrisons. Without Cork, Dublin or Ulster what sort of victory would we have? Ormonde's peace is merely an expediency, occasioned by the dreadful war in England, a struggle between an anointed king and his rebel Parliament. Once that war is won, and the king safely returned to his throne, he will return to his old ways and tax us for the privilege of our faith. Don't look for or expect support from Lord Ormonde once the war is over. Lord Ormonde will remember he is at heart a Anglican and will revert to type.

'Lord Inchiquin, on the other hand, has supped with the devil. Regardless of his birth, his heart is now with the Parliamentarians. Whatever Ormonde, or Mountgarrett, may say now, there will be no permanent peace, Dermod Oge, not in Ireland. Not while Protestants and Catholics share these fields and while 'Poynings' Law' remains unrepealed.'

'Poynings' Law?' Dermod Oge had spent his childhood in France.

'Poynings' Law lies at the heart of the English oppression of the Irish,' Owen Roe explained, without the smallest hint of irritation. 'Poynings made the Irish Parliament subservient to the English one, even in the simplest domestic matters. It is the reason why our Parliament must never return to Dublin. All Ireland should be governed from Kilkenny. Whenever Dublin tried to pass a law to protect us from English 'ambition', as they call it, or 'greed', as we call it, it has always been overruled. It is not Gaels who suffer humiliation before the Saxons. Poynings' Law also humiliates the Anglo-Normans and has done so since medieval times. At last, despite the historic differences between Gaels and Normans, Kilkenny has united us all.'

Now it was General Preston's turn to lean forward in his chair.

'Once upon a time, the areas the English have settled, especially within the Pale, were fortified against raiding Gaelic clans. Back then, Milesians seldom spoke to the Anglo-Irish. Now, at last, the lust for power of the English has bridged the chasm between us all. Especially you, Dermod Oge of Duhallow, and your fellow chiefs at the highest level of society.'

'We have all been building bridges,' said Dermod Oge. 'Even here in our quiet backwater, those of Norman stock learned to speak our Gaelic tongue long ago. It is no longer uncommon for my Old English neighbours to patronise our poetry and music. Mixed marriages, once rare, have become almost commonplace.'

Owen Roe was serious. He absently thumped his fist on the arm of the chair.

'That, Sir, is precisely my point,' he said. 'Many Anglo-Irish and Old English are *hiberniores hibernis ipsis* - more Irish than the Irish. Intermarriage is our future - and we fight for it, that and the Faith. Only the blending of our races will create a true island nation. Divided, we fall.'

'That is why we must liberate Cork from its Saxon suzerainty, once and for all time. We must defeat the turncoat Inchiquin. We must expel Lord Monro from Carrickfergus and send him limping home to Galloway. We must starve the Protestants out of Dublin.'

He paused for breath and waited for calm to reinhabit his bearing. Then, in a quieter voice, he resumed.

'Dermod Oge, will you come with us on this hard and dangerous journey? The Confederacy needs colonels who have been formally trained in the arts of war. We need chiefs, such as yourself, who can raise thousands of men by personal command. If Ireland is not to wait for the arrival of a de Sales[xxxvi] and his Counter-Reformation, without you, without men like you, we can never hope to govern our own country.'

Tomás Preston tried to sum it all up.

'Lord Mountgarrett and the Lords Justice in Dublin have had, in their different ways, to deal with the same problem. They have to manage a people which has no national cohesion. Some English, even some Scottish colonists, long settled, have preserved the ancient faith. We should support these people. We have not as yet the strength to be sufficiently magnanimous to schismatics and apostates, even if that should be our long-term plan. Dermod Oge MacDermod, we need your help to reach a finer place.'

219

Rue des Deux Ponts, Paris
16 May, 1643

My dear brother Dermod Oge, I hope this missive finds you well.

I have to admit I feel as though I have reached the end of a cul-de-sac .

Have you yet have heard that the King of France has died? Two days ago! France has been in such turmoil it is only now that I have found the peace to write to you.

The late Louis was a great king. I am in mourning both for a friend and for a man who led France against the House of Habsburg for so many years. He made France the greatest power in the world. I shall miss serving him in court and in battle. I shall also miss the hunting and hawking on which I was sometimes privileged to accompany him.

As I wrote to you last December, Cardinal Richelieu is also dead. Without these two great men, I have precious few allies left at Queen Anne's court.

To cap it all, when Maman died last month, the moorings that kept my little ship in harbour were severed. Were it not for my lovely Isobel I should be quite alone.

All Paris rejoices in the news from Ireland that a Confederacy of the Clans has finally been achieved. We have also learned, if only lately, that it is Parliament - not England - that is emerging as the enemy. Your Lords Muskerry and Ormonde are technically opposed, while both claim to fight for the King of England. No one here can quite understand it.

Our new king, now renamed Louis after his saintly forebear, is just five years old. He is the fourteenth of that name. When his father realised that his own death was imminent he prepared for his son's impending rule by decreeing that a Regency Council should rule on the Boy-King's behalf, for the duration of his minority. With others, I advised him not to make Anne the sole regent despite her having given birth to the young princes. Anne has few political skills but I rather fear my well-meant advice has cost me the Presence. I hope not permanently.

Dearest brother, the late King Louis made her the head of a Regency Council on his deathbed. I only hope she will do little harm.

My worst fears, however, look set to be realised. Anne has already had her husband's will annulled by the Parlement. Yesterday she abolished the Council and declared herself sole regent. Appallingly, this very morning, she vested all her power in Cardinal Mazarin!

It was Richelieu who made France rich. Mazarin is an unknown. This morning I presented my sword to the Cardinal at his extravagant new palace overlooking the Louvre and, as I backed down the steps onto the Quai Mazarin, I saw a couple of urchins, armed with those slingshots they call *frondes*, trying to break a few of his windows. It gave me the most evil portent for the future of my adopted country.

I am not alone. The death of the king and his faithful cardinal has cost Ireland two great friends. Had the late King Louis been alive I should have begged him to let me take a real force to Ireland and reinforce all Duhallow in its hour of need. Richelieu, I am confident, would have sanctioned my request. All this is now pointless speculation. *Nil desperandum.*

To these great names a modest one will soon be added. I have decided it has been too long since I set foot in the country of my birth. Perhaps it is this bereavement that has led me to think of paying you a visit. Ireland is deep in my soul; placed there through the tales and legends so carefully inculcated into us by both our father and mother.

I have already written to your friend, the good Captain Millot, anticipating your favourable response. I have hired a small and private band of musketeers – fifty Gascon sharpshooters – and we shall take Millot's little ship from Honfleur to Bantry within a few days. My men will arm and train as many soldiers as Duhallow can spare.

I an not so proud as to expect to influence the outcome of your war to any perceptible degree. My life – or death - may prove a futile sacrifice, *absit omen*, but I cannot stand by and quietly watch you and my countrymen fight for our country without playing a part.

Expect me within the month. I shall stay some weeks.

Dear Brother, somehow I am a general, but I shall be yours to command. I only hope I may prove worthy to serve the elder brother of the undersigned,

Cormac MacDonogh Carty.

*

It would take most of the year for Kilkenny's patient secretariat to distil a manifesto from the angry torrent of shouts and rants. While they fought over the small print, however, Protestant on Catholic violence was dwindling. Finally, an elegant document, a one-year truce called the 'Cessation of Arms', was sealed in Kilkenny's great hall by every member of the Supreme Council. Hostilities were formally suspended between the Confederate's Catholics and Ormonde's Anglican Royalists and fireworks were set off in Kilkebby's extensive grounds.

Murrough Inchiquin, however, anathematised the peace treaty. He wrote to Ormonde, bitterly objecting, refusing to submit. Furious with its sponsors, he found for Parliament, abandoning the royal cause.

'The king's dealings with the Catholic Confederacy are both blasphemous and treasonable', he shouted to the cheers of his mutinous soldiery, who similarly disavowed Ormonde and the king, swearing allegiance to the Parliament in Westminster.

It had especially disgusted Inchiquin that the Cessation had been amended to allow any English troops in Ireland to return to England and defend their sovereign, and to do so without facing a charge of desertion. The terms also required President Mountgarrett to send money and supplies to the Royalist war machine in England. In exchange, Ormonde would allow the Confederates to govern the land they had captured so far with the full force of law. The king also undertook (again) to repeal the harsher penal laws and grant the Catholics the freedom of worship they had so long desired.

*

Dermod Oge MacDonogh sent for his son Bryen, who arrived at Kanturk within the week.

'Bryen, help me here. I have had reports of Inchiquin's intransigence. I presume that it's because the king has refused to ratify Inchiquin's position as Lord President of Munster?'

'You may be right, Papa. Inchiquin's adventures on the Scottish borders would seem to have turned his head', Bryen gravely declared. He shook his head sadly.

'To think that man was once my closest friend,' he murmured.

*

Elsewhere, when Massereene and his fellow Puritans learned the details of the Cessation, they were apoplectic with rage. So were the Lords Justices, so too the Irish Protestants.

Parliament perceived a way to exploit the situation. It flatly (and fraudulently) declared that the Anglican or Episcopalian troops who took advantage of the Cessation to return home were bloodthirsty Irish papists. Despite the soldiers' denials, the dry pamphlets of English Dissenters did their mendacious work. Homecoming Protestant soldiers were hissed at English ports by their own countrymen.

At the same time, the Scottish Covenanters allied with the English Parliament against the king. The Edinburgh Assembly similarly refused to recognise the Cessation, leaving Munro in Ulster with orders to remain active and to continue to suppress any 'tories' that emerged from their sylvan lairs.

*

CHAPTER SIXTEEN
A PARISIAN IN DUHALLOW

Captain Millot let the French general, Cormac MacDonogh, ashore in Bantry together with his elite squadron of musketeers. Their black tabards, emblazoned with a huge red cross, startled the sailors and fishermen of Bantry. They looked like the Irish Knights Templar must have done before the demolition of their preceptories in the early fourteenth century.

The *Magdala* had towed a transport. Millot had agreed, after a purse had changed hands, to bring fifty men and their horses from Honfleur to Bantry. He owed it, he had said, to the horses.

The long road to the MacDonogh castle at Dromsicane would take Cormac's men through some wild country and the townlands of Macroom and Millstreet. As for Millot and the general, they travelled in the sea-captain's 'calash'. The open carriage had forward-facing seats and a raised coachman's seat above its shallow body, making it look like a miniature galleon. Its four wheels made it adequately comfortable. As the company progressed across the south of Ireland, villagers cheered them on, pointing at the grizzled, unshaven sea-captain, his short grey hair mostly covered with a bicorn hat, and the gorgeously apparelled soldier beside him, with his curled reddish hair falling fully six inches below his collar. The passengers waved back, grateful and relieved. Cormac had been assured their route they would pass no English garrisons but he ordered his men to be vigilant, just the same. One never knew…

Their road lay as a string might idly fall. On the Continent, the Romans had left a legacy of roads as straight as the path of an arrow. Here in Ireland, the company took winding, circuitous and precarious routes through bogs and forests, between fields and, to make matters worse, their guides took detours to avoid sacred sites and fairy rings.

The horses that Captain Millot had brought with him to Ireland in his *Magdala* thought they had died and found themselves in a green and lush, grass-fuelled paradise. Far too often they would halt, unbidden, and taste the Irish ambrosia. Somehow they knew that in high summer, at least in France, the pastures would be dry and the grass would taste like straw.

Gluttonous horses aside, the ride was pleasant enough.

Near Millstreet, Cormac noticed the great fortress of Drishane, raised on a hill within a valley, protected by a great circumvallation. Its purpose was uncompromisingly military, not domestic. The French

Musketeers were familiar with such *chateauforts* and *donjons* in France, but where were the aristocratic palaces that the French nobility and clergy had favoured for so long? The men felt transported back to a time when the Franks had to defend their country against marauding Huns, Burgundians, Cathars, Longobards, Normans and, of course, the English.

Dromsicane lay some three miles due north of Millstreet but, unfortunately, the River Blackwater had to be crossed. The ford was at Dooneens.

Musketeers do not like fords. Horrible things happen there. Powder gets wet. More terrible yet; their lovely and expensive boots can be ruined. Every soldier had to pay for his *souliers* out of his meagre wages.

Mercifully, their horses were surefooted and the musketeers could cross, if carefully. Anxious to keep their weaponry dry, they carried it above their heads.

Once the far bank, back again on dry land, they were suddenly upon the curtain walls of the MacDonogh stronghold.

'Dromsicane', in the Irish, means 'the Ridge of the Seat'; the 'seat' in question being the MacDonogh's principal residence. Not that it had always been. The O'Keeffes had built it, long before the MacDonoghs had come to Duhallow from Lixnaw and beyond, so many centuries before. The MacDonoghs had taken it by conquest. Since then the MacDonoghs had had to defend it several times. When it changed hands, it had had to be retaken.

The castle consisted of a large walled quadrangle with a substantial rounded tower at each corner. This enclosed a walled *bawn,* at the centre of which was a keep. Cormac's soldierly assessment was that it was stout, and would resist almost any attack, always provided that artillery played no part.

As Cormac and his men made their way inside, trumpeters blew a military salute from the battlements. Cliona and her husband had arranged to give Cormac and his men a splendid reception.

As Cormac and his troop entered, they saw that their hostess had laid out the hall in the old way – a top table and three shorter tables beneath it. If this was the style of the middle ages, it suited the old place to the core.

'How was your journey?' was the first question Cliona out to her brother-in-law after Grace.

'Quiet, pleasant, dear Cliona. The channel was smooth, Millot talked too much, but fine weather came with us all the way. Our slow pace over your roads us the chance to take in the scenery. I should confirm that yours is a very different landscape to ours, my dear Sister. You must have thought the same about our countryside on your way to Paris, all those years ago.'

'There we saw castles everywhere we looked, and so many inns and churches.'

'So did we, as we would in France, but noticed fewer inns and the older churches were falling down, unloved. My my men were struck by countless ruined oratories and monasteries, ranging around tall and circular towers, all in an unfamiliar style. So many ruins. Your war has been a very long one, the longest in history. It has been fought for centuries and little of Ireland's past seems to have survived intact.'

'That's the land of your forebears, in a nutshell.'

'It is, but even your fields are different to ours. Most of your fields are unfenced. Where there are cattle they are mostly roped to a tree or a post. We even passed one where the owner had dug a huge ditch, which presumably helped drain the field and prevent or hinder his cattle from escaping.'

'And the roads? Were they kind to your horses?'

'The roads were good, but this is summer. Their compacted earth must turn to mud in the autumn making travel very hard indeed. Perhaps when the ice of winter arrives it is easy again?'

'This is Ireland, Brother. Even that cannot be guaranteed.'

Cormac would dine with his brother's family every evening, while every day he and his fifty-strong company trained a hundred Duhallow clansmen. Hard work only improved his appetite.

Cormac also introduced a military innovation; a new one to Ireland in any case. Cormac's men were trained to fight from the saddle without dismounting. The local blacksmiths made stirrups, in their hundreds. English cavalry had them, of course, but for ordinary Irishmen they were rare, almost a Saxon secret weapon.

'Your clansmen can now remain mounted and fight alongside the your cavalry,' Cormac told his brother Dermod Oge. 'We call these mounted footsoldiers 'dragoons' [xxxvii], after the soldiers of a generation before who had to drag or haul field artillery to the front line. Your armies will have the potential to cross country very much faster.'

'These 'dragoons' can even fight on horseback, you say?'

'Yes, but rather more than that. They can ford streams, swim in loughs, haul a baggage train, and all this from the saddle.'

'The horses will need training themselves not to panic on the field of battle,' said Dermod Oge doubtfully.

'I have kept your horses as close to the firing ranges as I dared, while teaching our craft to your hundred prospective marksmen. We are making good progress. If at first the horses were startled by the sound of gunfire, familiarity is now breeding a very handy indifference.'

Indeed, Dermod Oge's horses were trained as diligently as his men. They would kneel when ordered. A few select Irish marksmen were allowed to use the horses' saddles as support for their carbines, lending them a hundred feet or more to their customary accuracy.

Cormac had also had the means and presence of mind to bring a hundred such weapons to Ireland, and these were by no means simple military muskets. They had been expressly made by the Parisian gunsmith, *Francotte & Fils*, on the île St Louis. They had more in common with sporting pieces than military ones. With the sort of training the marksmen were now gaining, their rifling of their muskets ensured they could kill at four hundred yards.

After just three weeks, Cormac's work was almost done.

There could be no realistic end to a training programme but, at last, he allowed himself the relaxation of a day's hunt with the Duhallow. The hounds drew well. Two foxes were returned to the dust whence they came, and a hundred tenants breathed, on behalf of their hens and geese, a collective sigh of relief.

Dermod Oge and Cliona gave a dinner in the general's honour. The meal was as French as Dermod Oge and Cliona could manage, and (with Kitty's help) they made a fair fist of it. Certainly the wine, always a precious commodity, flowed easily.

The guests included two Anglo-Irishmen, Sir Philip de Perceval, the banker, and Lord Castlehaven, the Confederate general. Sir Philip was now, notionally at the very least, a Parliamentarian, but his presence, however, was on the basis on long and reciprocated friendship, not politics. His presence demonstrated the stoical side of his character, for he had lost his pride and joy, Liscarroll Castle, in a set piece battle a year before. While Bryen had been a conspicuous member of General Barry's army, Perceval's anger was reserved for Lord Inchiquin. It had been his order to deploy the cannons – not Barry's – and he had seen his reduction of the palace-fortress. Diplomatic relations with the MacDonoghs had survived.

The Ireland of chiefs was represented by Terence O'Rourke, Chief of his Name and son of that chief who had welcomed the O'Sullevans to his castle in Bréifne after Sir George Carew had destroyed his race, and by Fineen O'Driscoll, too, who had come over from his west coast fastness on Sherkin Island. The MacCarthy boys, Aidy, Thady and Hadey, were proudly of the party.

Dermod Oge's wife, two sons and daughter ornamented high table. So too did Sorcha, Bryen's wife, looking ravishing.

Beneath the salt, Kanturk's merchant class was well represented. It included Dr Dempsey, Eamonn Dunphy and O'Keeffe, the butcher, who saw Dermod Oge as Mayor, rather than chief. Sitting beside them was old Seamus O'Callaghan, field master of the Duhallow, with many other officers of the hunt.

Captain Millot and his wife Anya would take Cormac and his dragoons away the following day, but they had first persuaded their girls, Roisin and Grainne, to sing to the illustrious company after dinner.

No less a prelate than Fr Boetheus MacEgan had ensured the foods were blessed and that the diners were truly grateful. Kevin O'Grady, who did not sit, took it upon himself to see that everyone was served in the right order.

Dinners like this one were and always will be the stuff of legend.

At first, at high table, the conversation turned on the hunt, but politics could not long be kept out of the picture. Not while the civil war blazed in England.

'This Ormonde Peace, or whatever you call it, has rather let us down.' Cormac sounded wistful. 'My timing was wrong. I had supposed I should see action but it seems I am to be disappointed.'

'Personally, I rejoice in the fact. Our estates look likely to survive another dozen generations.' Dermod Oge's unpopular neutrality was clearly vindicated. 'I have watched the estates of too many others who have rebelled being forcibly cleared, only to be awarded to settlers without lineage or standing. If the Parliamentarians had triumphed outright, all of us would be in the same boat. As it is, the Cessation has allowed me to avoid opposing either them or the king, either of which would have been treason and guarantee an attainder.'

'You leave Bryen, Donogh and me out of your reckoning, my husband?'

'Not even a Chief can bind his wife, Cliona. Indeed, there is no power on earth that can confine a headstrong lass. The established fact that I do not take sides should protect us all. In these difficult circumstances, you and Bryen must do as your consciences direct. All I ask is that you think before you act.'

Cliona smiled sweetly at her husband but turned to her brother-in-law.

'Cormac, you will returning to France?'

'Alas, Cliona, it must be so. Isobel has only allowed me this brief window into my past, my heritage. I leave behind a hundred well-trained men, as fit for purpose as any in Europe, while I pray they will never have to demonstrate their skills. If brother Dermod Oge's analysis is correct, Ireland has or will soon have resolved its issues with England.'

'I really believe that,' said Dermod Oge, more optimistically than truthfully.

'I for one should like to. I pray for that,' said Fr Boetheus.

'So do we all,' Donogh MacDonogh responded piously.

'Amen,' resounded the company.

*

Bantry is seventy miles from Kanturk as the crow flies. It's therefore a journey of at least three days, even on sound roads and in a four-wheeler as fine as the one that Millot had hired. Behind the vehicle came Cormac's musketeers, relieved that they had not been asked to join in what they considered a private quarrel.

Every village or township they went through on their return was bedecked with flowers and garlands. News of their departure was as widespread as the news of their arrival had been secret.

Peace, or at least the Cessation of Arms, had brought joy to South West Ireland. Girls had threaded flowers through their hair. Landsmen and women emerged from their cabins to press posies into Millot's carriage and to wish the noble travellers a safe journey. In every market square small orchestras played folkloric melodies. While the horses rested the enchanted soldiers would watch the lasses perform their step-dances.

Millot's driver made good and steady progress. Captain Millot, being French, needed to whisper a *bon mot* to some of the prettier girls who blushingly peered into the open vehicle, murmuring their kind words and little prayers to the gentlemen within. 'God bless and save you all' was their favoured blessing.

The musketeers would stop overnight in Macroom, a draughty pile, said to have been built by the hated King John. Since those cruel days it had been given rather more than a lick of paint, and Hady MacCarthy was generosity itself.

The next morning, on the final leg of their journey, if any of the soldiers claimed he had not a headache then he was a liar.

The *Magdala*, bless her, was bobbing untroubled at the capstan where she had been tethered.

Cormac was leaving Ireland to his elder brother Dermod Oge, and the prospect for a lasting peace looked better than at any time since the Rebellion.

*

Lord Ormonde, in armour and looking like a Roman emperor, swept grandly into Dublin Castle's great Audience Chamber, spread his scarlet cloak behind him and sat on the throne, supposedly reserved for a visiting monarch or for the Lord Lieutenant. The crowded room, astonished by this impertinence, fell silent.

'Good morning, gentlemen,' he began, 'I won't waste your time. By the king's orders I have raised two thousand loyal men from Leinster and have subsumed a further two thousand, to Lord Inchiquin's annoyance, from his overmighty army in Munster. These men have been shipped to Bristol from Dublin and from Cobh harbours. They will be received by His Majesty as heroes.'

'Ha!' exclaimed Sir William Parsons, assuming he had leave to speak. 'So we are Royalists, are we?'

'Good question, Sir William,' rejoined Sir John Borlase. 'Ormonde, you think you have done well by such a daring move?'

'Sir John, since you ask, my actions have proved to be shrewd.' Ormonde clicked his fingers and an equerry stepped forward with a sheaf of papers. 'These letters patent confirm my appointment as His Majesty's Lord Lieutenant of Ireland. This time, Sir William, Sir John, my noble title has been correctly given. You will find that my men have already moved some modest possessions of mine into Vice-Regal Lodge.'

'You are Lord Lieutenant? No longer Lord Leicester?' the Lords Justice gasped in tandem.

'Yes. I am head of the Irish Executive and you will henceforward do my bidding. I do not expect my elevation to cause many tears to be shed, except perhaps by you. With my appointment come great duties, if few pleasures, but I will freely admit that allowing you both, Sir William and Sir John, to leave the castle is definitely one of the latter. It gives me unequalled joy to bid you both farewell.'

Sir William Parsons and Sir John Borlase were appalled, but speechless. They put their papers together without a word.

'Come, Sir John,' said Sir William, 'Let us return to our stewardship of the king's Four Courts.' They left together, taking with them whatever dignity they could muster.

Ormonde had indeed taken up residence in the Vice-Regal Lodge before he summoned his predecessors' administration to wait on him.

Now he told his clerks, stewards and assorted functionaries that henceforward their chief task was to prevent the Parliamentarians from reinforcing their ranks from Ireland and to deliver more troops to fight for the Royalist side in England. Dublin would restrict and contain both the Scottish Covenanter army in the north of Ireland and the Catholic Confederacy in Kilkenny. Mountgarrett could no longer engage the Parliamentarians, for if he did war would certainly return to Ireland. He had been directed by the king's Privy Council to prolong, at all costs, the 'Cessation of Arms'.

'I have taken the liberty of submitting my latest draft of the treaty to the Supreme Council of the Confederacy. It has the same purpose, to prevent an English Civil War from spreading to our shores. To gain Kilkenny's agreement I have had to abandon some long promised Graces. This concession has been very well received. I have the word of my cousin Lord Mountgarrett, the President of the Kilkenny Confederacy, that the revised treaty, which Mountgarrett refers to as the 'Ormonde Peace', will be scrupulously observed to the letter.'

There was polite if uneasy applause from the assembled dignitaries.

'Thank you. This should mean that we can now address some of the larger questions. Munro and Inchiquin will continue to mount their punitive raids. Barry and Castlehaven will no doubt maintain their revolving sieges of every Protestant garrison in Co Cork. Those irritations aside, I anticipate a period of relative calm in Ireland.

The applause was redoubled.

'My two priorities,' Lord Ormonde told his functionaries, 'are, first, to prevent English roundheads from being reinforced from Ireland, and second, to deliver the king more soldiers to fight for him in England. To these ends, I shall do all in my power to keep General Monro and his Dissenters in check and distracted. The king's inevitable victory will bring his kingdoms to heel.'

Everyone knew that Ormonde disliked Dissenters even more than Catholics, and his civil servants were unruffled. Unlike the Lords Justice, but like Ormonde, they were Anglicans, after all.

'Do not misunderstand me. The king's authority underwrites my deal with the Confederacy. It will allow their troops to be concentrated against Massereene's zealots, the true enemy.'

*

The 'Ormonde Peace' of June 1644 heralded in a time of relative calm. Lord Ormonde sought to take advantage of it with an audacious ploy. He decided to help Randal MacDonnell, the Catholic Marquess of Antrim, mount an Irish Confederate expedition into Scotland and reinforce the Scottish Royalists. The expedition's commander would be Alasdair MacColla. This *beau geste* would effectively export the English Civil War into Scotland. All three kingdoms would have a stake in the game.

In Scotland, the royalist camp – mostly Jacobite highlanders - was divided between the Marquesses of Hamilton and Montrose, who weakened their own effectiveness by contesting the leadership. The Kirk and the Assembly exploited the division and formally allied with the English Dissenters; the English Parliament was largely Presbyterian, after all. Royalists, under James Graham, Marquess of Montrose, would form the core of his army. Not that Ormonde could really spare them.

Antrim's Irishmen quit Ireland for Scotland to join the King of Scots' troops in June. On arrival they fought a spectacular campaign against the Covenanters, but it was the spark that the dry inflammable landscape of Scotland really did not need. Almost inevitably, Scotland followed England's example and declared war on itself.

As Ormonde had calculated, the Covenanters felt obliged to recall around half their kin from Ulster to fight Montrose and his loyalists. Those left behind were now not as much of a deterrent to the rovers, tories and woodkerne as they had been. Suddenly the Irish had hopes of driving the heretics out of Ulster; it was a unique opportunity. Unfortunately, the propitious moment could not be exploited. Lords Antrim and Castlehaven were too busy quarrelling over who should command the other to take advantage of the hiatus.

Raiding and skirmishing continued. Strongholds occasionally changed hands but neither the Confederates nor the remaining Covenanters were strong enough to deal each other a killer blow.

*

Donogh MacDonogh, in that January of 1645, was in Oxford. However scholarly his contributions to the protracted deliberations, Donogh watched gloomily as the Catholic Confederacy failed to deliver their Anglican king a clear road ahead.

So too the king. He was becoming persuaded that Ormonde was too partisan, too Irish. In desperation, he ordered the Catholic Earl of Glamorgan to Kilkenny.

Lord Glamorgan's family had contributed handsomely to the Royalist war-effort. Perhaps this was the reason why the king chose the scientist-earl to conduct his secret negotiations with the Confederates.

He certainly was not as a soldier. Back in 1643, his lordship had been commissioned lieutenant-general of the Royalist forces in south-east Wales and its marches. He had mustered a force of 1,500 foot and 500 horse and marched on the Parliamentarian stronghold of Gloucester. Unfortunately, the Parliamentarian Sir William Waller had surprised the Royalist encampment at Highnam and had captured or killed his enemy. Lord Glamorgan, who was not present, successfully laid the blame for the disaster on his deputies and retained command.

The king, in desperate need of more troops, saw an Irish role for the Welshman. Glamorgan was told to promise some serious concessions to the Catholics – even including a thorough implementation of the Graces – on condition they supplied the king with soldiers.

This was a confusing tactic. The Marquess of Ormonde was simultaneously negotiating a permanent peace treaty with the Confederates. To make it worse, the new Lord Lieutenant had no idea of Glamorgan's secret dealings. He certainly never suspected his king of duplicity. That was not a quality one could associate with an anointed monarch of the House of David.

*

Sir Richard Bellings, once the Speaker of the Dublin Commons, was now the Confederacy of Ireland's Secretary of State for Foreign Affairs.

On his first official mission, he arrived in Rome's Quirinale Palace to discover an enthroned Pope Innocent X in the audience chamber, having his likeness transferred to canvas by the King of Spain's court painter, Diego Velasquez.

As he knelt before the Holy Father, Fr Luke Wadding (one of the Pope's two protonotaries apostolic) put a finger to his lips. Bellings already knew Fr Luke. He was the Irish Franciscan who had explained to His Holiness that Irish Catholics regarded their Confederacy as the only way of restoring the Catholic Church to its former ascendency in Ireland.

Standing next to Fr Luke was Fr Bonavventura Baron, Wadding's own protégé and nephew. Fr Bonavventura was a Clonmel man, arguably as gifted academically as anyone in Rome.

A silent Bellings watched for a quarter of an hour while one of the greatest masterpieces in the history of portraiture drew more form and inspiration from both its artist and its subject. Eventually the painter said '*basta!*' Enough! He knelt before the Pope and kissed the papal signet. '*Una mezzoretta, Santità*', he said, backing from the room. Half an hour.

It was a time for words. Pope Innocent listened carefully to Richard Bellings and his sponsor Fr Luke. Innocent was already a strong supporter of the Confederacy. He would remain so, despite the shifting sands. Ireland's most valuable asset. however (Sir Richard thought, anyway) was Fr Luke.

At last, Wadding's exposition was over. Very quietly, the man who so recently had been an artist's model disclosed, apparently irrelevantly, that the Curia was minded to accredit Sir Richard with the letters patent of a formal ambassador.

These words were significant. They let Wadding, Baron and Bellings know that the Pope had become the first Head of State in the world to recognise Confederate Ireland as a sovereign state.

History had been made.

The Irishmen were overjoyed with the success of their lobbying, but it was still not enough. Above all they needed an exchange of envoys. The Pope should send Ireland a *nuncio straordinario*, an ambassador, to a country where such diplomats were not routinely sent.

*

'We have anticipated this request. We have a candidate in mind; Giovanni Battista Rinuccini. He is currently our Archbishop of Fermo. He already knows the requirements but it will be his decision, of course.'

His Holiness had been, until his election, a papal *nuncio* to two kingdoms; first the Two Sicilies and then Spain. He knew the form.

'Rinuccini is a genial man, a safe pair of hands,' the Pope told Bellings decisively. The turn of phrase let the Irishmen know that the archbishop would get the job, whatever the College of Cardinals might think.

*

CHAPTER SEVENTEEN
RINUCCINI

Sir Richard Bellings, now Confederate Ireland's Ambassador to the Holy See, converted his journey home into a grand tour. His newly elevated standing gave him access to the two most important crowned heads in Europe, the Kings of France and Spain, from both of whom he asked, and obtained, some valuable financial aid for his fledgling nation. Both these great powers had long been keen to recruit Irish troops – the Irish had distinguished themselves in the past – and both felt it oppertune to fly their standards over Kilkenny Castle.

When, that May, Bellings addressed the Supreme Council, he told Lord Mountgarrett's Grand Assembly of the Confederacy that Ireland's international status had changed.

'My Lord President,' he pronounced in his engaging lilt, 'it is my joyous duty to inform you, and this noble Assembly, that the Ghost of Tara has at last been invited to sup at Christendom's high table.'

When the tumultuous applause faded, Lord Mountgarrett proposed a vote of thanks to his Secretary of State Plenipotentiary. The Assembly's gratitude was of the practical sort; it would allow the diplomat the purchase of a significant country house and a significant residence on Rome's Palatine Hill.

'Gentlemen, we should also act upon the splendid tidings that Sir Richard has brought us. It seems to me, at least, wholly appropriate that our Confederate Assembly should ratify the parliamentary system we have agreed upon, and begin to govern the part of Ireland, its people, faith, laws and administration that we administer.

'I therefore suggest that the tricky and delicate business of giving birth to nationhood should begin here in Kilkenny. We shall vote on it here, in this very chamber, tomorrow morning at ten o'clock.'

In Rome, Archbishop Rinuccini of Fermo's formal appointment took place in the Vatican's palatial Curia, more widely known as the Sistine Chapel,[xxxviii] under Michelangelo's hundred-year-old ceiling.

Directly after the Pope had concluded a private audience with Cardinal Mazarin, the archbishop was received by the Pope and a protonotary. Judging by the way the Frenchman swept by, that meeting had been less than satisfactory.

The Pope, however, when he permitted the archbishop to approach him, looked happy and relaxed.

'*Figlio nostro*, we thank you from the bottom of our heart for accepting the weighty yoke of being our *nuncio* in Ireland. *I tuoi doveri*, your mission, most reverend child, will take you from your hilltop fastness in Fermum Picenum, where you have spent twenty happy and successful years as our chief pastor. You are bound for an even more remote place. It lies on the edge of our Old World. It is called Kilkenny. It has recently become the capital of the newly independent and Apostolic nation of Ireland. There you shall find the means to forgive and absolve the people in the name of Jesus Christ our Lord, to secure the free and public exercise of our Universal faith, to restore the altars of our churches that the people may celebrate His sacrifice, to sustain their king, to rescue them from their penalties and punishments and to restore them to their ancient rights and property.'

The Pope's clear Italian was amplified by the astonishing acoustics of the Sistine Chapel.

'Holiness, am I to achieve this through the intercession of the Prince of Peace? Or might there be also assistance of a more practical kind?'

Innocent laughed. It was a slow, lugubrious and humourless sound, made hollower so by the motionless and unamused Swiss Guards behind. Perhaps it wasn't laughter? Could it be indigestion? Unconvinced of his ground, Rinuccini permitted himself what he hoped was an ambiguous smile.

Perhaps his expression encouraged the Holy Father? In any even, the Pope continued.

'The church in that poor country is literally militant.' Innocent accepted a piece of parchment from his protonotary and pushed his pince-nez onto the bridge of his nose. 'You shall take with you, let me see, two thousand muskets and cartouche-belts, four thousand swords, two thousand pike-heads, four hundred brace of pistols and twenty thousand pounds of gunpowder. Oh yes, and a significant amount of treasure.'

He passed the paper to the archbishop, who read it carefully.

'That is treasure indeed. Your Holiness wants me to cross France with such a cargo? If news leaks out it will tempt every bandit in Western Europe from his cave or lair. Will not His Eminence Cardinal Mazarin object to such a convoy traversing his country? *Non sum dignus*, pontifex Maximus!'[7]

---

[7] I am not worthy [of your confidence], Greatest of Priests.

236

'*Non sei digno? Calmati, caro Rinuccini!* We have already informed the Cardinal that we intend to overrule his objections. Indeed, you will break your journey in Paris itself. There you will seek out Queen Henrietta-Maria, who has petitioned us to let her distribute such largesse herself. You will reassure her, but that task will be performed by you. You are presumably aware that she is now resident in Paris, for her safety's sake?'

'I am to make the journey overland, Your Holiness? I have never even held a pistol!'

'Two dozen of our Swiss Guards, two of their officers and a number of gallant Irishmen, currently resident here in Rome, will form your retinue. They will escort you to Paris and on to France's Atlantic coast. You will take ship from La Rochelle. Efforts are being made to find a ship's master who knows the west coast of the 'pagan isle'. For company on board, you will find His Excellency Richard Bellings an excellent and charming mentor. He may even teach you a little Irish. When, eventually, you land at some rustic and no doubt picturesque harbour you will be met by a suitable body of nobles. They will have found appropriate lodgings for you and will ensure your new life is passably comfortable.' The Pope looked carefully at his emissary. 'We understand you have never sworn a vow of poverty.'[8]

Rinuccini nodded while he thought. It occurred to him that the bearer of such supplies would be received as a hero. His name would be engraved in history.

'When should I depart, Most Holy Father?'

'That's the spirit. Put your affairs in Fermo in order, Gian-Battista. Read and study Irish matters. While England fights its domestic war there is a fragile peace in Ireland. *Ci racommandiamo figlio nostro; non tardar.* Be careful, and do not tarry. The weather will make your crossing most unpleasant if you leave it until the winter.'

'I shall begin my preparations immediately, Your Holiness.'

'*Bene. Andatene in Jesú.*'

Rinuccini knelt before the Pope to receive his blessing. The Holy Father let his half-closed left hand turn outwards. The archbishop took it, kissing an enormous ring on which an emerald the size of a quail's egg bore, intaglio, the Pamphilj coat-of-arms. It had been exquisitely carved early in the ninth century, when that family had been merely an ambitious if not yet house-trained barony.

Rinuccini then backed from the holy presence.

---

[8] The Pope was referring to the fact that Rinuccini had never been a member of a monastic order.

In March 1645, Archbishop Rinuccini began would be a very long journey. It began in a land where the warmth of the sun teased the earth into sending up vines to celebrate the warm joy of Spring, to the windswept north where the frozen or rain-drenched natives had only fermented cereals to delight them.

His route took him to Paris, where he spent six months trying to massage the strained relations between Cardinal Mazarin's government and the Holy See. With both a queen and a cardinal to pacify, he could not yet sail for Ireland. His stiff, authoritarian manner, moreover, discouraged easy agreement, especially from princes, and when he finally departed little had been settled.

A general, of Irish extraction, was presented to him in the Palace of the Louvre. Yes, he knew of a way of arriving unobserved on Ireland's west coast. He knew just the ship's captain to engage.

The little ship, *La Magdala*, was in La Rochelle as arranged. The archbishop saw an agile trading vessel, around fifty years old, armed with two dangerous-looking canons. Very fitting, he thought.

It was to be an epic voyage. Almost immediately after they had set sail *La Magdala* was spotted and pursued by a squadron of English warships. The Creator sent squalls and storms, forcing the English privateers to put about, and the Holy Virgin heard their prayers and protected ship, crew and cargo with her azure cloak. The ship's captain, a wind-tanned Millot, seemed indifferent to hostile craft or violent weather.

'*C'est pas grave*,' he said with classic maritime indifference to great danger. 'I've known worse.'

Rinuccini, to his own surprise, was discovering his sea-legs. He found himself enjoying the crossing, passing as much time swapping stories with the old sea dog as he did with Ambassador Bellings.

'The two men had somewhat different approaches to theology,' Rinuccini would later recount, 'but between them they gave me a precious insight into the Irish soul'.

Rinuccini had not yet left Paris when, in August, King Charles's royal emissary Lord Glamorgan met the Confederates in Kilkenny.

Glamorgan's second marriage, to Lady Margaret O'Brien, the Earl of Thomond's sister and Lord Inchiquin's aunt, brought him important contacts within the Irish nobility. Margaret may have died but the connections had not.

Glamorgan had every motivation to conclude a treaty. The king had offered the same incentive once used on Wentworth. Success would be rewarded with a dukedom and, since the earl was once again a widower, he would throw in the hand of his eldest daughter, the Princess Elizabeth.

The Welshman sailed for Ireland but from the outset his journey was jinxed. He was shipwrecked off the coast of Lancashire. Many were lost in the wreck. He did not arrive at Wexford until the end of June, and made his way to Kilkenny with a substantially reduced retinue.

'These letters will show that I am acting on the express behest of King Charles. In return for ordering the Castle to desist from attacking any Catholics, I humbly ask the Confederacy to train, equip a large number of their soldiers, prior to letting them support His Majesty in his hour of need.'

The terms were extremely secret. Many Confederates were so surprised, even appalled by them that they were leaked immediately.

*

Lord Castlehaven's Confederate army had now grown to five thousand. The general was on a roll. He had taken most of the English strongholds in County Cork by October and, when he arrived at Liscarroll, now an English garrison housed within the ruins of a once magnificent pile, the site of an appalling Catholic defeat three years before, his reputation was so strong that only some desultory musketfire was directed from the battlements. The 'English' shooting was erratic but did claim a victim. A helmeted, lightly armoured Irish officer, who had been riding recklessly around the damaged curtain walls with his sword drawn, waving it above his head, was shot through his cuirass unerringly into his heart. He fell, quite dead, from his startled horse, driving a long groove into the turf.

Before the body could be recovered and interred, the English in the castle needed to be disarmed and taken prisoner. This would not be a drawn out affair. Liscarroll could no longer defend itself from an army.

As it turned out, the sight of Castlehaven's immense force was enough. The English surrendered without further argument. Castlehaven ordered Captain Raymond, the recently promoted Commander of Liscarroll, to take the news of the Irish victory to Cork. This was not an honour. Predictably, when he arrived, Lord Inchiquin had him arrested. A peremptory trial for desertion in the face of the enemy was conducted and Raymond was condemned to death.

As for the single Irish casualty; when his armour was taken off he was found to be a woman. She was found to be wearing a wedding ring. In an effort to identify the fallen Amazon, the soldiers removed it from her finger and examined it for a clue.

They found some enigmatic words. Her husband must have engraved his wedding vow onto the inner surface of the band. Regrettably, not his name.

'I live if I marrye you; understand if noe I dye.'

That was all it said.

*

Rinuccini's vessel made landfall, in November, 1645, in a near-deserted fishing village in County Kerry. Dermod Oge MacDonogh Carty brought him a suitable escort. *'Deo placet, iter terramarique terribilis erat,'* Rinuccini told him, offering an ostentatious ring for the Irish chief to kiss.

Derreennamucklagh, their final port of disembarkation, could offer no discernable creature comforts.

As the owner of the *nuncio*'s future residence in Ireland, Dermod Oge had been encouraged to manage the Confederacy's delegation, a duty he readily completed. He brought 500 foot. A cousin of Lord Mountgarrett was also involved, none other than Lord Ormonde's Catholic brother Richard, who brought two companies of horse, replete with banners and pennants. Captain Millot had managed to bring the *Magdala* alongside the hard, and when the guard of honour saw the *nuncio* descend the gangplank they cheered. Dermod Oge MacDonogh Carty did so too, despite his deep mourning for Cliona. So did his son Bryen and his young and beautiful wife Sorcha.

'We have missed your summer. I deduce from this constant rain we have also missed your autumn,' Rinuccini pronounced. He had no English. His Irish was limited to the few words that Bellings had patiently taught him on board, but his Latin was more or less comprehensible.

Dermod Oge tried to steer the archbishop towards his reception committee but the *nuncio* took Dermod Oge's arm, drew him aside and spoke earnestly.

'The seas were mountainous, Lord Duhallow. We were only just spared extinction at the hands of some English buccaneers who, mercifully, neither knew our purpose nor our cargo. I must say your compatriots, Ambassador Bellings and Captain Millot, are great sailors. They have the courage of lions and we are now staunch friends. So this is Derreennamucklagh. It's a ridiculous little place, just as His Holiness warned me to expect, if in his tactful way he used the word 'picturesque'! What on earth happened to its houses? They are all new, poorly fashioned and they number fewer than a dozen! There's no church! Even the smallest port in all of Italy is better furnished!'

'The English happened to them, Your Excellency. Sir George Carew laid waste to County Kerry forty years ago.' Dermod Oge's Latin was more than competent. He had had the noble tongue beaten into him by the Jesuits at La Flèche, his childhood school.

Bellings and he walked a little behind the *nuncio*, who blessed the ground they stood on and reviewed his guard. Bellings quietly briefed Dermod Oge on the archbishop.

'If you were expecting a highly educated and distinguished gentleman; you were right. Rinuccini, the son of a Florentine patrician, was schooled in Rome and finished at the universities of Bologna, Perugia and Pisa, the last of which honoured him with a doctorate. It may have helped that his mother was the sister of a Cardinal. When the *nuncio* returned to Rome he became a cannon lawyer before, in his early twenties, becoming Archbishop of Fermo. That way he mercifully avoided the tedium of a curacy, priesthood and its associated parish duties. For the last twenty years his purpose has been to manage his local archidiaconate but now, through the mysterious workings of God, he is destined to be the spiritual leader of an entire nation.'

Dermod Oge looked his distinguished guest over. The *nuncio* was fifty-three years old. Despite his trying journey he was utterly unruffled. His general appearance was unimpressive, however. His hair was grey. If he was short – barely five feet tall – and he supplied the deficiency in inches with an enormous Roman nose. Since he resembled a kindly buzzard, it prevented him from being good looking. His body, however, looked fit.

The mutual inspection was over.

'They tell me, Duhallow,' the *nuncio* observed while they watched a valuable and explosive cargo unloaded, 'that your countrymen are maddened by oppression and have taken up arms. My people have graciously allowed me to bring you some useful bagatelles to help you in your struggle.'

'So I see, Your Excellency. Ireland thanks you, and your people, from the bottom of her heart.'

'Bellings here has told me you have a legislative assembly - an executive government, no less - and you have bound yourselves by oath not to cease fighting until you have undisputed possession of your lands. Good men. What about your religious liberty? Have you achieved it yet?'

'You are certainly well-informed.' The trio had reached the other dignitaries. 'Excellency, this is Richard Butler, Lord Ormonde's youngest brother. He is now a major in our Confederate Army. May I also present the Bishop of Ardfert to you? This gentleman with the purple stole is Monsignor Boetheus MacEgan. Father Boetheus was until recently my family's confessor. He is now chaplain to the Confederate Army. Trust him. He knows this country well. These two gentlemen will be your closest assistants.'

The Bishop of Ardfert and the recently consecrated Boetheus MacEgan duly presented themselves with all customary clerical humility.

The journey to Kilkenny resembled the leisurely progress of a medieval monarch, but it was less its stateliness and more the light drizzle that kept it slow.

Their first stop was the huge castle at the heart of Macroom.

Thadeus MacCarthy of Drishane greeted him at the great gate. After his father's untimely passing, Thady - his heir - had made the great Norman keep his principal seat.

At dinner, the *nuncio*'s host sought to make his distinguished visitor feel at ease.

'*Maigh Chromtha*', Thady told the Archbishop, 'or Macroom as the colonial cartographers would have it, means 'meeting place of followers of the god Crom'.'

Catching the look on the prelate's face he thought it might be best to back-track.

'As always, there are scholars who disagree. These say it translates as 'warped plain'. The area was thought to once have been the rendezvous for Munster's Druids, and folklore has it that Macroom is 'the town that never reared a fool'.'

The *nuncio* smiled. His *arrière-pensée* was that he had met an exception to the rule.

Thady, while Anglican, was to be Rinuccini's host for four days. He dutifully rested the *nuncio*'s horses, warmed and dried his men. The *nuncio* ostentatiously disapproved of him. Ireland had honoured a heretic with his presence? Even Thady's conversion of a small room into a Roman chapel failed to appease him.

Dermod Oge was not tempted to comment on these religious matters. Instead, he encouraged his daughter Caitlín to play him Irish songs on her late mother's virginal and Donogh, briefly home from Oxford, served Rinuccini as 'first gentleman', which in practice meant both 'altar boy' and 'valet'.

*

As soon as it could, the grand procession resumed. It took the road to the east, towards Millstreet and thence north, to Dromsicane, the principal residence of the MacDonoghs.

There he was welcomed by Bryen and Sorcha.

'Serving the Church is the outward manifestation of God's Grace. Your family is graciousness itself,' he told the young couple. 'Making this fine castle over to my *nunciatura*, my good sir, our 'embassy' if you will, is most generous. It may take me a few days to settle my staff, install myself and my retinue at your fine seat here at Dromsicane, allocate rooms, hang the odd tapestry, embellish the altar of your little chapel, deploy some chattels of my own. Only when that is done will I pay Lord Mountgarrett my compliments. I hope, Major, that your father will not concern himself if, on my eventual departure, I leave this delightful residence a little more lavish and elaborate than it is today?'

'Our castle meets with your approval, I surmise?'

'Dromsicane is perfect. I understand it to be barely day's ride from the capital of Ireland at Kilkenny. I do not ride hard, so a day with a pause in a tavern, perhaps? Your former confessor, Bishop Beotheus has agreed to stay behind as *capo degli affari*. *Chargé d'affaires* as some will have it. He will enable any synod I may convene and serve as my amanuensis.'

'The bishop has agreed to this?'

'To quote him, Major, he says he is glad to be home.'

*

When, in late November, he at last arrived in Kilkenny, Rinuccini was received with full honours. The president's guard met the *nuncio*'s carriage and escorted it into the courtyard above the town where soldiers in tabards had lined his route, playing tuneless fanfares on their trumpets.

Once inside the great hall, Rinuccini was in time to experience a plenary Assembly of the Confederation of Ireland.

He was greeted to a long and sincere standing ovation. President Mountgarrett knelt to kiss his guest's archiepiscopal ring and Archbishop Rinuccini returned the gesture by bowing deeply, first to the President and then to the Assembly.

The *nuncio* was then led to a smaller room to be briefed by the Supreme Council while, outside, the Assembly eagerly waited to hear his words.

When the confidants emerged, Lord Mountgarrett invited Rinuccini to speak to the 'legal government of Ireland' and then to take his permanent place on Mountgarrett's right hand. Rinuccini could speak no English or Irish, yet his Latin, spoken in the church's particular style, was widely understood.

'Now I am arrived in Ireland,' he began, 'I find to my astonishment that your Supreme Council and a Count Glamorgan are already entrenched in negotiations. I have learned that this count can bind the king. Through your noble interlocutors he is to promise you bigger, greater concessions. Since this is what I have prayed for all these months, I have especial cause to congratulate you.'

The applause lasted a long time.

'Please be aware that your President has invited me to join these sacred discussions. He knows, as should you, that I have the power to unleash the power of the Church, tantamount to the potency of God. My intentions in these discussions shall be to extract even more concessions from this Lord of Glamorgan. I brought from the Holy Father in Rome some negotiating tools in the copious hold of my ship, and even that military muscle is dwarfed by the authority vested in me by the Holy Father. Rather more power than needed to bind a king.'

An ovation, led by Owen Roe O'Neill, greeted this resolute declaration.

The archbishop raised his hands for silence.

'My instructions are not negotiable. They are set in stone,' he continued. 'They have been given to me by none other than the Vicar of Christ, the Fisher of Man, the Servant of Servants. I am commanded to strive for nothing less than the expulsion of all Protestants from Ireland. Only then can the faultless diamond of our faith be restored to its emerald setting. I strongly suggest that any parallel negotiations with Lord Ormonde should be minimal. Our Catholic friend, Lord Glamorgan, shares our faith and understands our passion.'

Owen Roe and Tomás Preston rose to their feet to lead another ovation.

'I second that,' cried Owen Roe O'Neill.

'So do I,' declared Tomás Preston.

Rinuccini raised his hands again.

'His Holiness has entrusted me with a mission to strengthen you against the schismatics in the English Parliament and their allies amongst the Scottish heretics. My overriding objective is to secure your freedom to worship the one true God, in the manner prescribed by the Holy Council of Trent. It is not to sustain your divinely appointed king. Ours is not a war on England or Scotland, but to defend our Universal Church from heresy. Above all we wish to help all Irish Catholics restore their divine and secular traditions. Any lingering claims that some may have to

244

former abbatial property, however, will have to be abandoned. Monastic lands have long been sold off. Their forcible return would involve an unsupportable number of evictions and provoke another Civil War.' He took in a sea of glum faces. 'Come, be of good cheer! The rest of my news is good.'

*

Only a few days later, in early December, a copy of Rinuccini's remarks was handed to the Marquess of Ormonde in his Castle in Dublin, together with Glamorgan's terms for a permanent peace. To say that the Lord Lieutenant was unimpressed would have been an understatement.

Nowhere was the consternation greater than in the Castle. Ormonde's officials had not even been aware of Lord Glamorgan's role as a peacemaker. The Anglican reaction was so furious that the king was forced to repudiate Glamorgan's treaty, even before the seals were attached.

'My opinion is that if Glamorgan's hugely partisan treaty were actually enacted, no Protestant Irishman would support the king in his hour of need. Protestant Ireland might very well transfer its allegiance to Parliament.'

*

The mood was very different in Kilkenny. Rinuccini had taken to Glamorgan in a big way. The fact that earl was a devout Catholic certainly helped.

Matters grew even worse when Glamorgan's most secret instructions were revealed in Westminster. Ormonde publicly disassociated himself from the royal envoy, going so far as to denounce him as a traitor, in that Glamorgan's concessions would undermine the Royalist cause.

By drawing the Puritan fire onto Glamorgan, the Lord Lieutenant went a long way to sparing the king any embarrassment.

Poor Glamorgan was deeply upset about the way his brilliant scheme had gone so badly wrong. To receive the king's displeasure, to be despised by the Lord Lieutenant, to be awarded no dukedom and to remain a widower! It was not the result he had foreseen. It seemed he had just one friend, it seemed; a diminutive Italian archbishop who resembled a vulture.

In despair, Glamorgan contemplated abandoning the royal cause altogether and seeking a commission in the French army, but the papal *nuncio* Archbishop Rinuccini persuaded him to stay on in Ireland. He appointed Glamorgan to the Confederate Supreme Council. In return

Glamorgan supported Rinuccini's denunciation of Ormonde's attempt to pour oil on troubled Irish waters.

Rinuccini decided to overlook Glamorgan's poor track record as a soldier in the first Civil War. He appointed the Catholic earl to be his Commander of Confederate forces in Munster.

This was, however, a step too far. The soldiers themselves rejected Glamorgan's authority and declared for their former commander Lord Muskerry.

Hearing that not even the Irish could support his envoy, an exasperated king publicly disavowed him and, to keep the Protestants sweet, conceded yet more Ulster plantations to the Scots.

This was a maddening setback indeed.

Since the Flight of the Earls, the Irish of Ulster were undefended by their old chiefs. People of low birth and pietistic faiths, Calvinists, Baptists, Unitarians, Quakers, Covenanters and the like, were again to settle what was left of tribal lands.

It was a red rag to a bull.

This time, that bull had a name. It was Owen Roe O'Neill.

*

CHAPTER EIGHTEEN
BENBURG

The French Cardinal was showing Queen Henrietta-Maria around his new library. With forty-five thousand books he could justify his overweening pride. It was superb.

It was January. His almost complete Palais de Mazarin soared in stone from the muddy left bank of the Seine. It was so close to the royal palace of the Louvre – a stately walk across the pont Neuf – that the Cardinal could be at the king's door in five dignified minutes. Its glorious dome, loosely copied from St Peter's, was designed to reinforce Mazarin's status as a Roman in Paris. It already dominated the area. The central building was oval, while Le Vau's rudimentary wings led back towards the ancient university that Abelard had founded nearly six centuries before. They were as yet unfinished but they were set on capturing eight or nine crowded medieval houses and levelling them into an heroic courtyard.

In a bid to earn some badly needed popular support, the cardinal had announced that his palace, after his death, would serve France as a college, part of the University of Paris. It would educate sixty gentlemen from the remoter regions of France.[xxxix]

'Your Majesty.' Cardinal Mazarin was pure silk when he spoke to his royal guest. They paused before a magnificent atlas, opened onto a map of Ireland, 'the Pope has graciously condescended to finance the Irish Confederacy directly, though not through our offices. He has also sent them a *nuncio*. It may be time for us to change tack, since as we're not yet certain that peace in that kingdom, while in itself and overall a good thing, of course, should be at the expense of the kingdom itself.'

'The king, my husband, needs concerted help. More than ever, in fact. General Cromwell's victory at Naseby strongly suggests that Parliament may yet win the day. Ormonde's Peace has Ireland in a narcotic grip and its royalists need to be woken and mobilised in my husband's greatest hour of need.'

'I agree. But the Pope has proposed and Rinuccini has disposed.'

'Yet, Eminence, I think I know someone who may help.' The Queen of England had in her head the acorn of a very big idea.

The queen had uncovered in Madame Rambouillet's salon a sharply-tuned ear in Sir Kenelm Digby. Sir 'Nelm' was a highly regarded Catholic philosopher and leading Blackloist. The quen, when she

247

discovered his gravitas and profound intellect, called him a 'warehouse' of all the arts.

'Sir Nelm, you come highly recommended,' she told him. 'Can it be beyond our combined wits to devise an alternative treaty to the Ormonde Peace? That one merely provides an armed neutrality. Between them, Rinuccini and Ormonde have brought Ireland to a complete standstill!'

'Your Majesty, we will need the Holy Father to communicate with Monsignor Rinuccini. It would be self-defeating, even pointless, to impose stasis on a kingdom at the cost of its king. Without a ruler the forces of darkness would quickly close in. We shall write our version and call it the 'Roman Treaty'. His Holiness may want to take the credit.'

'Would you agree, Sir Nelm, that the cause of all our anguish has been the rise of the Puritans; all these weird cults and all these heretic Dissenters? Without such people there would be no war? Anglicans and Catholics would get on with each other as they used to, if not in friendship but at least without murderous intent.'

When Cardinal Mazarin saw the first draft of the 'Roman Treaty', he initialled every clause and dispatched 'Nelm' directly to Rome to obtain the pope's imprimatur. The queen's gamble paid off when, against all the odds, Sir Kenelm succeeded.

*

In Ireland, Rinuccini, in receipt of the new treaty, was now obliged to play his tune in a different key. He had no choice but to promote it. Between them, the queen, the cardinal and the knight had changed everything.

*

Yet Queen Henrietta-Maria still worried for her husband. His situation was dire and the Civil War still looked likely more and more to be won by the Puritans, especially as they appeared to have discovered a brilliant and utterly ruthless general within their ranks.

The prospect of victory, Sir Nelm suggested, might provoke the Presbyterians in Parliament into an act of magnanimity. There were few Puritans in their House of Commons, after all. That sort was largely in the army.

The king planned to regain a stable base by consolidating the English midlands. In the spring he tried to form an axis between Oxford in the south and Newark-on-Trent in the north. Both of these were fortress towns which had always proved reliably loyal.

Royal resources were exhausted, however. Without Parliament, the king had no way of replenishing them. In May, having no clear idea where to turn, the King of Scots sought shelter among a Scottish army which had found its way to Nottinghamshire. It was a mistake. His northern subjects arrested him. The soldiers were Calvinist. For a while he was confined to Dunfermline Palace before, eventually, the Scottish Assembly handed him over to the English Parliament. He ended up under house arrest in his royal palace at Hampton Court.

*

'You should know the king of Ireland is confined in our palace on the Thames, Cardinal Wolsey's old seat,' the queen told Cardinal Mazarin.

'Is he now? That does not bode at all well. You must be strong, and for all of our sakes. If the Dissenters do what I most fear, it will have horrific consequences for us in France, and for all of us in Europe.'

*

It was there that news was brought to the king of the Parliamentary victories. The Puritan general had inflicted a particularly devastating defeat on the royalists. His name, Oliver Cromwell, was not yet widely known in political circles, especially internationally, but among his soldiers, many of whom were Levellers, it was spoken in hushed tones. His men carried a bible, paid for by their general out of his own pocket. Their enemy, mostly Anglicans, were destined to eternal damnation, he had explained before the battle. They were not to be spared, and nor were they.

*

By now, Covenanters ruled Scotland, just as Calvinists ruled England. Puritans, more and more, controlled the army. The royalists were forced to regroup and reform. Ireland was the last thing on their mind, except - that is - as a potential source of troops.

While relatively comfortable in his enormous palace, the inescapable truth was that the king had lost at least the first round of the English Civil War. His confinement had unleashed the Parliamentarians from any purely domestic agenda. Somehow he would have to cast off his gilded chains if the Civil War were to return a royalist victory.

*

Peace of a sort now reigned. The suspension of hostilities in England freed many Dissenters to defend their coreligionists in Ireland, mostly in the North. More than ever the Irish needed to devise a plan to support the king in his hour of need. King Charles had become their only means of containing a renewed Protestant threat. Unfortunately, all the king could do was pace the Renaissance chambers and corridors of his ornamental cage.

Could some sort of compromise between Anglicans and Catholics actually be achieved? Ormonde certainly said it could and, probably, thought so, too. The Confederate assembly looked as though it might gravitate to an irreligious compromise. Had everyone forgotten that it had to reinstate, embrace the True Faith if its lost souls were ever to find Paradise?

While Rinuccini reluctantly embraced the 'Roman Treaty', Owen Roe was less than impressed by this *volte face*. Talk to Ormonde? It was unthinkable. The man was a viper in a silk doublet.

Owen Roe began to contemplate a great set-piece battle, the sort his legion had fought so often in the Thirty Years War.

'I beseech you all,' he told the Assembly. 'Do not resume negotiations with Ormonde. We are trained and now, at last, we are armed. We can and shall win complete independence. Our purpose is to defeat General Monro!'

Owen Roe had a point. Rinuccini's supplies had raised the potency of the armies of Ulster and Leinster to European standards, for the first time. The scion of the O'Neill dynasty was not just a general; he was a man of uncompromising, unswerving faith. He besought the Assembly to listen carefully to the *nuncio* during the wordy, fulsome debates on the Confederacy's internal politics. Rinuccini saw immediately that he had O'Neill's support and came to depend on it.

When, however, Rinuccini, apparently acting on a Papal directive, encouraged the Irish Catholics not to strive so particularly for national independence but instead to concentrate on the defence of their anointed monarch from the Puritans, not everyone was equally impressed.

The treaty split Ireland. While the Old English and the Anglo-Irish were well disposed to be loyal to their king, there were many Celts who simply wanted the freedom to worship according to their tradition and missal. This group included most of the Catholic clergy, many Milesians and the best part of the exiles who had returned to Ireland. Most particularly Owen Roe O'Neill.

The Supreme Council at Kilkenny, however, was dominated by the Anglo-Irish. Their chief spokesman was emerging in the shape of Ormonde's brother-in-law, Lord Muskerry. Muskerry favoured a negotiated peace treaty with Parliament, the king's liberation from his stately confinement and looked to Ormonde for guidance. It was by far the most ambitious if, in all probability, the least likely bid to succeed.

There was even a third, more moderate, faction. It was led by the distinguished Anglo-Irish lawyer Nicholas Plunkett. It was simply to preserve the unity of the Confederacy while still protecting Ireland's political and religious interests. This was so boringly sensible it was almost completely overlooked.

*

After months of protracted negotiation, on March 28, 1646, Lord Ormonde successfully concluded his new treaty with the Confederates, acting on behalf of his king. It was an admixture of religious concessions, of which the most important was the legal right for Catholics to admit and practice their faith. It remained, as previously, behind closed doors. It meant fewer raids on illegal 'mass-houses' and removed some other long-standing grievances, but this time Rinuccini wanted the Confederates' General Assembly in Kilkenny to throw it out. To Owen Roe's clear approval, Rinuccini begged the Confederates' General Assembly in Kilkenny to reject the deal.

'You must brook no such compromise', he fulminated. 'No Ormonde Peace is good enough for us. Is the worship of God to be 'in private'? Hidden in a consecrated larder, perhaps? Relegated to an sacred earth closet? Gentlemen, we are debating the finer points of sacrilege. This is not why our constituencies have sent us here. You are a disappointment not just to me, not just to Ireland, but to the Creator, the Judge and Inspiration of all things.'

Rinuccini was able, successfully, to dissuade the Catholics from observing Ormonde's 'Peace'. He actually arrested those among their number who had signed the marquess's treaty.

The Puritans, however, felt that the Catholic rite belonged indeed in that earth closet. Their leader, Lord Massereene, would not take peace for an answer.

He tried to persuade the Royalist commander Ormonde to surrender Dublin to Parliament. His case was plausible enough. It was all too clear that the king had lost the English Civil War.

Yet this was Ireland. Massereene was reckoning without Owen Roe and the stiffening resolve of his Army of Ulster.

*

All of Rinuccini's precious cargo, except of course the money, had long been divided between the Confederacy's generals. O'Neill in Ulster and Preston in Leinster had the lions' share of the military wherewithal. Lord

Muskerry, General Garret Barry and Lord Castlehaven were allowed a useful portion. As for the gold, mostly it underwrote the *nunciatura* and the Confederacy, and in that order.

In Ulster, Catholic smallholders and tenants were still enduring Monro's predations. The ancient gentry had long been evicted.

The Confederacy was divided. Rinuccini wanted to conquer Dublin, while the President, Lord Mountgarrett, argued that the war should be taken to the north, where Monro and his Scots were paying scant attention to the Cessation. The Protestants of Ulster continued to rustle Catholic farms for cows and sheep, raid their barns for corn, and cynically strip Ulster of its precious forage for their cavalry. Attack, after all, is how a Scot defines defence.

It was not a practice designed to last.

Ordinary Irishmen had not yet the means to resist this implacable enemy. The Scots were trained, equipped and enthusiastic for action. The Irish had to put their faith in Owen Roe O'Neill and his field army. They prayed he would surprise and defeat the Covenanters.

O'Neill declared himself ready. 'Let Monro know we're open for business', was how he put it to the Confederate Assembly.

His advantage was manoeuvrability. He had rejected artillery – it tied an army down, he claimed – and was certainly more capable of spontaneity than was Monro. Nor was his army that much smaller than the Scot's.

He had hand-picked his grand army from those loyal to the Confederacy. In the South, peace of sorts reigned and his recruitment sergeants had a big pond to fish in. They collected seven thousand men.

O'Neill's army was made up of five thousand foot, three of which of which now served under Colonel O'Farrell as pikemen. Major Bryen MacDonogh Carty contributed a thousand fusiliers, a logical gesture since they were mostly drawn from his family's own militia. He also commanded a company of fifty mounted musketeers, or dragoons, who boasted some very particular talents. Lieutenant-Colonel Brien Roe O'Neill had five hundred horse, most of whom were lancers.

Owen Roe O'Neill had wanted a set-piece battle. Now he thought he could provoke one. Wasting no time, he set off with his men towards the north. Kilkenny to Ulster would cost him, and his men, ten days march.

By the end of May, his forces had reached at Galangal, near Lough Sheelin, on the Cavan-Westmeath border. His Catholic soldiers were trained, armed, very keen and waiting to be marched over the provincial border into enemy territory. Before that they would rest.

After Owen Roe had given them an heroic address, he sent in Fr Boetheus to hear their confessions and give them the absolution they needed before the battle.

The chaplain-general, from his capacious saddlebag, produced an altar stone, a square of consecrated marble set into a gilded frame. Secreted within it were some boney relics of Saint Abán, a fragment of Saint Bairrfhionn's vestments, a morsel of Saint Ciarán's index finger. This altar stone was large enough to rest the chalice and permitted the priest to celebrate holy mass where there was no church. Every soldier at his command attended that open-air service. The soldiers were about to march into Ulster and some might die. To have a chance of the Kingdom of Heaven they would need to be in a state of grace, pure in thought and mind before their holy crusade against the Heretic.

*

Major-General Monro had control of two distinct armies, housed in Down and Antrim. He had been planning to use his forces to extend his raids into the Confederate territory that surrounded Dublin. A smaller army, currently billeted in the Foyle valley, was to do the same in Connacht. When he heard how many Irish were coming his way, he decided to merge his forces. Messages were sent to every squadron, brigade, column and regiment in Ulster.

Monro marched west. His six thousand men were composed of six Scottish and four English regiments of foot and some six hundred horse. Two hundred and forty musketeers, and another hundred horse, were commanded by his cousin and son-in-law, Colonel George Monro. His infantry, under Viscount Montgomery, was two-thirds musket and one-third pike. Like O'Neill, his cavalry employed a large number of lancers. Monro also possessed a mighty weapon the Irishman wilfully lacked: artillery, in the form of six field pieces. He planned to launch a surprise attack on the Confederates' flank.

The Puritan general marched onwards with the confidence of the Elect, God's mission in his heart.

On June 4, General Monro reached Poyntz Pass, a little to the north of Newry. He pitched camp, sending his son-in-law with a cavalry detachment to discover exactly where the overdue Scottish column from Coleraine might be.

Colonel George Monro was fortunate. He came across some of O'Neill's scouts near Armagh. A captured horseman was persuaded to reveal the strength of the approaching Irish. After a stern interrogation

253

the man had little energy or purpose left in him; in the circumstances it seemed only fair to hang the wretched fellow from the nearest tree.

On learning the battle order of the Irish, General Sir Robert Monro decided that his better-armed Covenanters should approach O'Neill's army from the east. Surprise should combine well with greater numbers and he ordered a forced march towards Armagh. This was his chance to deal the Confederates the decisive blow that the English and Scottish Parliaments never ceased to demand.

*

What actually happened was rather different. The Presbyterians were surprised by the Confederates. On July 5, Monro's army's confidant progress was interrupted by the Confederates near the River Blackwater, at a little village called Benburb. Owen Roe O'Neill had been all too aware that the British forces were converging on him.

Early, on June 5, the Confederates had drawn up on the west bank of the Blackwater. Owen Roe ordered his scouts to cross the river and take their positions. He deployed these troops as commandos, camouflaged and hidden where boulders, furze bushes and soft ground would hamper the Scottish attack.

His army had been fuelled with holy purpose by their priests and the Rosary was declaimed every night. Threats from their sergeants also kept their strength up.

O'Neill sent companies to defend every ford within five miles. That way the river would shield him from Monro's main force. If, somehow, a tactical retreat were needed, the Confederate stronghold of Charlemont lay less than a mile behind.

Fording a river is always slow and dangerous, and would leave him horribly exposed to musket fire. Monro made a hard decision. Rather than attempt to cross the river directly into the Confederate army, he forced himself to wheel his troops around and cross the Blackwater six miles upstream, by Caledon's unprotected ford. From there he would return along the north bank and engage his enemy. The only drawback was that it meant another ten miles or so of route march for his tired, wet, cold and heavily armed men.

If Monro were concerned about his Coleraine column, O'Neill was equally so. He ordered his kinsman Lieutenant-Colonel Brien Roe O'Neill to take most of the Irish cavalry and a small party of foot northwards towards Dungannon. There they were to intercept George

Monro's army and draw first blood. Brien Roe O'Neill's detachment would have the time it needed to deal with the Coleraine column before it could merge with Monro's and reinforce the enemy's numbers.

For this strategy to bear fruit, the bulk of Monro's army would need to be delayed.

O'Neill sent Major Bryen MacDermod Oge MacDonogh Carty and a selected company of twelve of his dragoons to delay or obstruct the Scottish general's advance; until, at least, Brien Roe had returned.

Bryen set off along the north bank of the river, upstream. He was on Caliban, his favourite stallion, armed with a rapier and two flintlock pistols. His men carried muskets of a French design across their backs. They were all crack shots. They had been well trained.

Bryen and his men would have to appear to be a rather larger force than they actually were.

The good news was that the spongy soil beside the Blackwater made their advance on the British quite silent. Though it was early morning, the light was good. By wearing traditional clothes the Irish blended into the Irish colourscape. Their green ferns worked particularly well.

Half an hour would pass before Bryen first saw a unit of Covenanter cavalry. He raised a hand; his men dismounted silently and their horses knelt. They were now invisible and they lay in wait.

The British scouts - also a dozen – were riding about a thousand yards ahead of the army for whom they were pathfinding.

Bryen's men laid their muskets across the saddles of their horses. That way they would have a lethal range of around three hundred yards; at least when fired by these marksmen. Now all they had to do was wait patiently for their quarry to come into range. It took a few minutes. Then, on Bryen's signal, they discharged a volley of ten rounds. Every musket ball hit its target. The two surviving Scottish horsemen turned and flew for safety.

Pride would force them to report that they had been fired upon by a company of at least fifty musketeers. It would have to be at least that number to have killed ten men at that distance. Firearms were just not that accurate. Fewer than fifty would be miraculous, and it would not do at all to report that miracles favoured the Catholics.

The Scottish army ceased its advance while its officers conferred. They then resumed their march on O'Neill. Again, scouts were sent ahead, and again Bryen saw them off. It would take until early evening before Monro's troops were able to approach O'Neill's army from the east.

The forced marches from Poyntz Pass and Armagh, and their continued guerrilla skirmishes with Irish sharpshooters, exhausted the British troops. The skies were already considering putting the sun to bed as a tired Protestant army crossed the Blackwater. Monro was expecting O'Neill to fall back to Charlemont as soon as the main Scottish force and the Coleraine column converged on him, but he was reckoning without O'Neill's determination to meet the enemy in a set-piece confrontation.

Monro deployed his infantry in two lines, five brigades in each. Because of the poor ground and a small stream between the two armies that fed into the river, the Scottish cavalry had to draw up behind the infantry, ready to charge through the gaps between the squares. The field guns would normally take the high ground, but there wasn't any. Monro had to place his six cannons in front of his infantry.

On the other side, O'Neill had organised his army in two lines. Four infantry brigades made up the vanguard; three comprised the second line, arranged in files six to nine men deep. Half of Major MacDonogh's musketeers formed a rearguard; the remaining cavalry were on the wings in squadrons three or four deep. The Irish position cleverly restricted Monro's deployment to a small hill where there was little room to manoeuvre between, the river on their right and boggy ground to their left.

Only now did General O'Neill give the order for his infantry to advance.

The curtain of this theatre of war rose to a cannonade from Monro's artillery.

Monro's second-in-command, Viscount Montgomery, led his horse and musketeers to control the ford across a brook that separated the two armies. Bryen's commandos contested the crossing. The stream ceased to flow, dammed as it was with fallen Scottish soldiers. The resulting lake slowly filled with blood

Now O'Neill's horse drove Montgomery back in a classic cavalry charge.

Unable to deploy his men as he wanted, Monro turned to his big field guns and trained them on the Irish. For two long and gruelling hours, the Scottish guns continued to fire into the ranks of the Irish.

The Confederates lay flat during Monro's deadly onslaught, waiting for Brien Roe's cavalry to return. O'Neill's men were protected by the rocks, but they still had to endure Monro's musket and cannon fire.

Happily, Owen Roe's kinsman Brien Roe had surprised and routed the Coleraine column near Dungannon. Rejoining the Irish army, his men completed O'Neill's lines. Without the Coleraine column there was no longer any danger of Scottish and English reinforcements.

Bishop Boetheus, the chaplain-general of the Confederate Army, stood on his altar-stone and delivered a plenary indulgence. This was a holy war, he reminded them.

O'Neill rode among his men, exhorting his men to wreak havoc on the Scottish. The Heretics had, as if they needed to be reminded, forbidden them the Eucharist and driven them from their ancestral Ulster homelands. He invoked the most feared word of all. Dispossession.

This was at about eight o'clock in the evening. The light was faint when Monro's cavalry charged O'Neill's foot in a desperate attempt to break up the Irish lines before nightfall. Unfortunately, their horses were almost lame with tiredness after their long marches of the previous days; the local spongy ground slowed them, tripping them and throwing many soldiers to the ground. When the Covenanter foot approached from the east, they passed enormous boulders left there by prehistoric glaciers, hampering the kilted 'red-shanked' Scots. Many of these were picked off by patient marksmen.

Despite the difficult situation the English stood their ground, waiting or hoping for orders which never came. For an hour or more, grim and lethal hand-to-hand fighting took its toll. The muskets never ceased their clatter. Slowly, the Irish squares closed in on the English. A second cavalry charge failed to disrupt the Irish and O'Neill ordered Colonel O'Farrell to work around and attack Monro's left flank.

Outmanoeuvred, the shocked Covenanter cavalry fell back. As it did, the whole line slewed around, forced back towards the river.

What began as an orderly withdrawal rapidly became a rout. The Scottish cavalry and infantry collided with each other in the gathering gloom before they fled for their lives. They were the lucky ones. The tightly packed Scottish infantry began to form piles, corpse on corpse.

The Irish advance began in the gloaming. Monro had charged, hoping to break the Irish lines, but his cavalry was ineffective.

The Irish horse was fresh and repaid the compliment. This time their advance was pitiless.

Squares of Irish pikes marched on until they came face to face, pike to pike, with Monro's front line, and still they continued. Bryen MacDonogh's marksmen took careful aim at the English foot soldiers. There was a percussive rhythm to their mortal machine and the enemy pikes parted for their remorseless advance. The musketeers took two steps forward, the front line firing, then falling back to reload; the second line taking two steps forward, firing, before the process began again. Monro's squares were devastated. When the Irish infantry overran the artillery emplacements, they found the Scottish gunners equally demoralised.

Monro's position had collapsed and, as darkness fell, his cavalry took to its hooves.

Three thousand of Monro's men were killed in the battle and rout that followed. The Major-General himself was lucky to escape the slaughter. He lost his artillery – all six pieces - most of his pikes and muskets, his payroll and his baggage train. Irish losses were around three hundred men, mostly killed in Monro's early strafing of their ranks.

Owen Roe O'Neill had inflicted a major defeat on the enemy. This was the formal battle that he had for so long waited; a triumph for the Confederates and a major setback for the Ulster Covenanters. The Scots, though they had outnumbered the Irish, were wholly overwhelmed.

It was to be the greatest and most resounding victory the Irish ever won.

*

Yet Owen Roe missed his chance to finish the business. He should have driven the remnants of settler forces from the north.

It was not his fault. The *nuncio* had sent a messenger. The courier had orders to wait until the battle was over. If victorious, he had orders for O'Neill to return to Kilkenny, at once, to receive the plaudits of the Assembly.

In a romantic gesture, Rinuccini revealed to the Confederacy that he had brought the late Earl of Tyrone's sword from Rome and now he presented it to the victor. In this way the sword cascaded, as it had for so many centuries, from chief to chief, from prince to prince. Forbthe final leg of its journey it had had the distinction of being carried by an archbishop.

News of the victory travelled like lightning around Europe. It was celebrated everywhere with votive masses; at Kilkenny by Archbishop Rinuccini, and in Rome's Santa Maria delle Vittorie by Pope Innocent himself. Both *nuncio* and Pope confidently expected it to lead to the complete liberation of Ireland.

Now that the Confederacy had shown its metal, Rinuccini held all the trump cards. The 'Roman Treaty' was now a reality. The defeat of the Scots translated into support for the anointed king, the Defender of the Faith.

As for O'Neill, he was unstoppable. Leaving Kilkenny he returned to Clones and chased the enemy back to its impregnable strongholds in Derry, Donegal and Tyrone.

Owen Roe O'Neill now had the only army in the field, and he was Ireland's ablest general.

*

CHAPTER NINETEEN
THE EXILE OF THE PRINCE OF WALES

In June, 1646, Captain-General His Royal Highness Charles, Prince of Wales, joined his mother, Queen Henrietta Maria, in the gardens of the *château de Saint-Germain-en-Laye*, not too far west of Paris.

Wonderful 'Italian' gardens descended in three vast terraces from the middle of the palace's façade, a near symmetrical cascade of parterres, fountains, gravel walks, formal basins and bosquets. Everything was coming into a delightful, manicured maturity, and so it should. The landscape had been laid out fifty years before for Henri IV, and it was now in its showy prime.

'Particularly trying journey, *fils aîné?*'

'Agonising, *chère maman*. It has taken me four long months to be by your side.'

The prince kissed his mother affectionately. She sat on a *bergère*, gesturing that her son should sit on a matching chair beside her.

'In February I set sail from Cornwall,' he continued easily, 'with most of the king's Privy Council and some other loyal courtiers. We sheltered in the Scilly Isles after the Parliamentarians sent a fleet after us. Through prayer and God's mercy it was dispersed in a storm. After that we went to Jersey, praise God a profoundly royalist island. There your envoy, Lord Jermyn, found us and between us we managed to overrule the Council's understandable caution to join you here.'

He looked up, beyond his mother, at the vast palace above.

'Very good of the King of France to put his hunting lodge at your disposal, close as it is to Paris.'

'Will you present your companions, Charles? No need to introduce the Earl of Newcastle, of course. You are well, we trust, dear cousin?'

The earl had been the prince's governor during his early schooling. He answered the royal enquiry with a courtly bow.

'*Madame la Reine*', her son announced with regal formality, 'I have the honour to present George Goring, the Earl of Norwich.' The earl bowed low. 'This trusty gentleman, on my left, in whom I confide absolutely, is Marmaduke Langdale, whom my father recently made a baron. This learned fellow on my right is Dr Brian Duppa, a protégé of Archbishop Laud - though he has of late preferred to keep quiet about that - and is currently the Dean of Christ Church, Oxford.'

The queen acknowledged their courtly English deference.

'How long will you all be able to stay with us in France?'

'Until Father sends for us, *maman*. Until our war is won.'

*

In Dublin, Lord Ormonde conferred by letter with the Anglo-Irish lords on the Council and with Lord Muskerry. His latest initiative would tolerate just two streams of Christianity in Ireland, the Catholic and the Anglican. To Lord Massereene's disgust it was the turn of the Dissenters to lose out. Their chapels were closed and in no time small boys had smashed their windows.

By March, 1646, the Supreme Council of the Confederates had reached an agreement with Ormonde. Under its terms Catholics would again be allowed to hold public office and found schools. The Roman rite would be permitted in 'mass houses' – churches in all but tower, steeple, cross, or any other symbol that might advertise their purpose. Their priests were still banned from wearing vestments or even the banns that distinguish a clergyman, but Ormonde sweetened the bitter pill, combining a verbal promise of future toleration with a declaration that he would draw a veil over any treasonable acts committed in the Rebellion of 1641. That, and that no more Irish Catholic land would be seized.

Unfortunately, the Catholic wing of the Confederacy was not that easy to placate. Mass houses were not the answer. Aside from the offensive, humbling requirement for religious buildings to be nondescript, as soon as each one was identified it was vandalised. The suspects, of course, were the Dissenters in particular and the English in general.

Lord Muskerry had especially good grounds to be angry, almost beyond reason, when Lord Inchiquin's Protestant army reached Cork. In nearby Blarney Castle, his servants and garrison had had to make a last stand. Their courage brought them naught. After starving the castle half to death in a long siege,[xl]Inchiquin and Broghill had the inhabitants blasted out of Blarney Castle with Parliamentarian cannons and summarily hanged.

Owen Roe was, if anything, even more implacably opposed to the latest Ormonde plan for peace. His views on religious practice were profoundly Spanish and, if possible, reinforced when the news reached Mountgarrett and Rinuccini that Tomás Preston had captured the great castles at Roscommon and Bunratty, enabling the west of Ireland to be regarrisoned.

Nevertheless, in Kilkenny, the mood grew fractious and Rinuccini had to tread carefully. On the one hand, the Anglo-Irish and the Old English wanted peace and coexistence with the Milesians, involving some sort of equality of treatment for the Catholic and Anglican religions. They were largely in favour of the new treaty. Not so the Confederates. Their version of the 'reformed' church had no time for Puritan or Dissenter.

Perversely, perhaps, Preston's growing list of victories irritated Owen Roe and Gian-Battista Rinuccini. O'Neill and the *nuncio* had convinced themselves that the Catholics were capable of conquering the whole of Ireland without the need for compromise. Both became steadily more strident in their opposition to the Ormonde Peace.

Not just in Kilkenny was opinion divided. The Castle in Dublin had also split. Ormonde, a diehard royalist, was a courtier born and bred. He had done everything possible for his king but it was looking as though he, and Ireland, had backed the wrong horse.

It came as a great surprise, not to say relief, therefore, when the Confederate Supreme Council overruled Rinuccini and adopted his Peace. Ormonde himself was amazed. It was with some pride that he publicly proclaimed his diplomatic victory to an elated and grateful Dublin on July 30, 1646. This, though he knew in his heart it was all too late.

His Treaty was really a triumph for the Anglican Church and England. It contained no repeal of Poynings' Law, the ancient statute which subordinated the Irish Parliament to the English one. Nor was there any reversal of the Protestant domination of Parliament, nor any unstitching of the patchwork quilt of plantations in Ulster and Munster. Buried deep in the small print, Confederate lawyers discovered that the churches reclaimed by Catholics in the war would have to be returned to the Anglican rite. Indeed, even the limited toleration of Catholicism was not guaranteed indefinitely.

When this was pointed out to Archbishop Rinuccini, his reaction was predictable and immediate: beside himself with wrath he summoned the religious leaders of Irish Catholics to a synod to discuss the treaty's inherent implications and to expose its contradictions. It met at his *nunciatura*, Dromsicane Castle, that August 12, 1646.

After spending a few minutes blessing the assembled curacy, the *nuncio* set about the treaty in a fury atypical of a priest.

'Brothers in Christ; by agreeing Ormonde's poor compromise in return for some paltry concessions to the Catholic people of Ireland, The Lieutenant-General has the temerity to demand that Irish troops be sent to England to fight for and free an imprisoned king. This we cannot accept. Nor, I confidently predict, will it be acceptable to our military chiefs – notably Owen Roe O'Neill and Tomás Preston. Nor indeed should it be acceptable to this Holy Synod. Lord Mountgarrett, in signing this treaty, has acted unilaterally and unconstitutionally. He neither enjoys nor deserves the undiluted adherence of his electorate. Fathers, none of you, nor I, were party to this unholy treaty, one that utterly neglects Christ's purpose. Here is my protest!' He waved a sheet of paper in the air. 'Will any of you mitred churchmen append your seals to my protest?'

'Yes. I shall,' said the notional Bishop of Cashel.

'So shall I,' said another eight Irish bishops.

'This house believes the Ormonde Peace a mere manifesto of Ormonde's personal ambition,' declared the unthroned bishop. 'Those who sign it are breaking their Oath of Association. Let any town that adopts it face interdiction.'

The Bishop of Limerick spoke up angrily.

'Interdiction? Is that enough? Let us excommunicate every Ormondist in Ireland. Heresy should never be tolerated,' he said, his fists clenched by his side.

'First of all, we need to sweep our own stables,' said the Bishop of Cork. 'There are some among us who cannot be trusted. I propose we arrest and imprison those among our number who have appended their signatures to Ormonde's grubby piece of paper.'

'Why stop there? We must go further,' said Rinuccini. 'We should pronounce anathema upon all Confederates who favour an Anglican Peace.'

'Will the exiles support us?' asked a dubious Archbishop of Armagh.

'They're no more impressed with the Ormonde Peace than we are. It's not what Owen Roe and Tomás Preston came home to Ireland to achieve. I think you'll find we have the full military backing of our two great generals,' said a confident *nuncio*.

It was agreed that they all should be resolute.

Those Confederates who had signed the Ormonde Peace were duly arrested and imprisoned. That was around half the Supreme Council. It was left too sparse to wield authority. The synodic clergy appointed a rival body, in which they installed Archbishop Rinuccini as Lord President of All Ireland.

Rinuccini's first act at Dromsicane was nothing if not logical. He declared Ormonde's treaty null and void, giving the Confederate generals immediate leave to unite and launch a joint offensive against the walled city of Dublin.

Owen Roe felt the chance to rid Ulster of the Scots was being passed up but Preston disagreed. After some heated exchanges, the generals declared their support for the priests and proclaimed their readiness to put Dublin under siege, but only until the Pale had been sufficiently softened up to be taken by force.

Rinuccini's presidency emphasised and exploited the racial rift that had faced Kilkenny's Supreme Council. Many Gaels suspected the *de facto* senate of an inherent bias; many of its members were Anglo-Irish, bound to Ormonde by immemorial intermarriage. Indeed, many of its officers were actually quite closely related to him.

The *nuncio* eloquently summed up his views, that the English Civil War had come to an end in armed neutrality, but in Parliament's favour, and that sending Irish troops to England to bolster the remaining royalists would be a waste of lives and treasure.

O'Neill's Ulster army, Rinuccini declared, having defeated the Scots at the battle of Benburb, would soon add Dublin to its colours. Then the *nuncio* would reunite the entire Irish nation.

It was heady but persuasive stuff. Even the most cautious noted the need for money, and that Rinuccini held the strings to a heavy purse.

The *nuncio* would tolerate no more bickering. He made his opinion and support very clear to the delegates in Kilkenny, and the General Assembly voted by a large number to reject Ormonde's pacific overtures, even though Lord Mountgarrett had already agreed them. All those who opposed the Peace were generously backed, spiritually and financially, by the envoy.

Rinuccini, with all the zeal of the Counter-Reformation, naturally found his greatest support among the Milesians. The Old English, on the other hand, privately deplored the *nuncio*'s unwillingness to seek a realistic accommodation with the king and his supporters. When they blamed him for Confederate disunity, however, Rinuccini dismissed them outright, telling them they were Catholics only in name.

From the safety of Dublin Castle, Lord Ormonde called for the Irish nobility to meet him at Cashel. This was agreed, but when Ormonde rode there with a small escort – a few hundred soldiers in the Lord Lieutenant's personal livery - its hostile citizens refused him admission. He realised he would have to go in person to Dromsicane if he were to rustle up support for his Peace among the Curacy. Not an easy challenge and one he was sorely tempted to duck.

While reflecting on all of this, news reached him that General Owen Roe O'Neill was marching on what the ultramontanes of Dromsicane were calling 'profane' Kilkenny. His route from Ulster would take him through Leinster.

Couriers reached Ormonde and his company two or three times a day. With each up-date the news got worse. When Ormonde heard that General O'Neill and Nuncio Rinuccini were leading the victorious Army of Ulster with its ten thousand men, caution became the better part of valour and Ormonde returned to Dublin.

His evident willingness to retreat from danger impressed nobody.

That September the Confederacy, having pruned its moderates and conceded much of its power to its clergy, formally annulled Ormonde's Peace. Mountgarrett resigned from the Supreme Council in anger and disgust. The generals' combined army – twenty thousand men – was free to march on Dublin. It was the largest force the Confederates had ever fielded, indeed the largest army ever fielded in Ireland.

Their target was less easily identifiable. Rinuccini's war was now against Protestants, Royalists and Parliamentarians alike.

The Dublin campaign continued through the winter of 1646, was into the early spring. It was neither effective nor well run. The Confederates' difficulties were manifold. The Anglo-Irish and the Gaels disagreed, O'Neill and Preston publicly quarrelled, and growing tension between them sapped the resolve of the whole Confederacy. Even in the open country supplies were hard to secure. If the Irish had difficulties securing their own supply lines, relief to a beleaguered Dublin was still if only occasionally arriving by sea.

The Lord Lieutenant could not know the Irish had such internal problems. With the enemy knocking at Dublin's gates, the Marquess of Ormonde felt he had no choice but to open negotiations with the English Parliament. Dublin was in terrible shape: the inevitable famine that came with a siege was exacting its bitter wages of death, especially among the poor. The price of food had quadrupled. Wicklow's wolves were heard again, this time closer and louder.

Ormonde knew he was sitting on a time bomb. He knew that he could not hold Dublin against the Confederates indefinitely. He actually offered to resign as Lord Lieutenant of Ireland and to surrender Dublin to Parliament. Anything but allow its Anglican churches to fall into Catholic hands and Anglicanism itself into desuetude.

The Irish had underestimated Ormonde's loyalty to his particular brand of Protestantism.

*

Lieutenant-General Cromwell had rapidly distinguished himself as one of the most able captains of the Parliamentary 'roundheads'. For good reason; between 1643 and 1646 he fought in battles all across England. He was more than a competent captain-of-horse. He had led charges, critical to victory, at the two of the greatest battles of the war, at Marston Moor in July 1644 and Naseby in June 1645.

He was approached by the Westminster Parliament. Would he consider reinforcing Dublin's Protestants?

His spirits soared but still he hesitated. Parliament's offer had not awarded him overall command of the army, nor even of the cavalry, which he felt he richly deserved. The best they would come up with was a sequence of forty day contracts. It was not enough.

Even though the king was safely confined to Hampton Court, General Cromwell had been busy and active, recruiting men to his Eastern Region. His advertisements enticed 'honest, godly men, prepared to serve under a plain russet-coated captain who loves what he fights for and loves what he knows' to apply.

Whenever his model recruits were accused of excess zeal or 'requisitioning' goods from 'delinquents'[9], he acted swiftly. He would either fiercely spring to the man's defence or hang him. As for his overall purpose, he boasted his tolerance. He would take any man, provided only he was not Catholic. He even protested against the religious intolerance of the Scots and their Presbyterian allies, who were determined to replace a narrow Anglican conformity with an even narrower and specifically Presbyterian one.

Parliament chose to call his bluff. He was refused absolute command. Cromwell replied that he regretted that on this occasion he could not help. Sadly, he had contracted some sort of infection. He would be indisposed for a while.

In his place, the Long Parliament chose Colonel Michael Jones. They awarded the colonel a force of more than four thousand foot and six hundred horse, commandeered directly from the eastern wing of the New Model Army that Cromwell had recruited and commanded.

'Jones is an inspired choice,' the Lord Deputy remarked. 'I know him well. After the Rebellion he fought for the king, here in Ireland, reporting

---

[9] Cavaliers

to me. Only when the English Civil War began did he recross the Irish Sea to join the Parliamentary Army. As a cavalry officer he eventually commanded the siege of Chester.'

'A Parliamentary victory?'

'Of course. He was also conspicuously gallant at the Battle of Rowton Heath.'

'Does he know Ireland well?'

'Certainly. He was schooled by clerics in our kingdom; his Welsh father was the Anglican Bishop of Killaloe and Jones was articled as a lawyer in Dublin. Perhaps it was our emerald lure that brought him home?'

On his arrival, Dublin Castle received Colonel Jones with all appropriate ceremony. He was briefed that Lord Ormonde controlled all of Ireland except for the harassed Parliamentarian enclaves around Dublin and Cork and the Covenanter outpost in Carrickfergus.

'Be aware that the Confederate General Tomás Preston's Leinster Army is currently besieging the Plunkets' seat at Trim, which we took from the Papists a month ago. That fortress is less than a day's forced march from Dublin.'

Colonel Jones decided to relieve his fellow Parliamentarians, and marched to Trim. There he raised the siege.

Unfortunately, he took so many troops with him that Dublin was exposed to attack.

Tomás Preston was as keen as mustard to wrest Dublin from Michael Jones's Parliamentarian garrison and while Jones' army was distracted at Trim he marched on the capital.

The Catholic army had covered a third of the forty-odd miles when it discovered it had been outwitted. At Dungan's Hill it was intercepted.

Preston had marched his men into a classic ambush.

*

Preston may have been a veteran of the Thirty Years' War but, unfortunately for the Confederacy, he had only been a commander of the Spanish garrison at Louvain. He had little experience of either open warfare or cavalry.

Jones, on the other hand, had acquired a painful knowledge of both.

This must have been the reason why Preston tried to take his horse along a narrow covered lane beneath the hill. It was here that Jones's musketeers subjected them to a lethal fusillade. The Irish were unable to respond. Some died instantly. The less lucky died very slowly, where they had fallen, their journey to Valhalla celebrated by crows, who took their eyes as shiny souvenirs, and wild boars, notoriously unfastidious as to their diet.

Even less forgivable was Preston's decision to station half his foot in fields where the wheat was over seven feet tall. His troops didn't even see their Parliamentarian enemy until far too late. When Jones' troops fell in amongst them, the Confederate army spread out in confusion. What was left of the Irish cavalry, which should have protected them, simply fled. Preston's foot was unsupported.

Preston's infantry was equipped with pikes and muskets and had been trained to stand in squares. A square was difficult to break but, without cavalry support, their awkward formations were almost immobile. Worse yet, Preston had positioned them in a large walled field and, when their cavalry ran, the Parliamentarians saw a once-in-a-lifetime chance to surround and entrap the Irish.

Some of the Irish infantry were actually Scottish; Catholic Highlanders brought over to Ireland by Alasdair MacColla. These saw an opportunity to charge and break through Jones' lines. A nearby bog, where no English cavalry could follow, saved Preston and two or three thousand of his regular infantry, who managed to follow the Highlanders to safety. The stragglers were ordered to stand firm and prevent the English from giving chase. These unlucky Irishmen would hold off several assaults, before they could safely follow their comrades through the quagmire.

That was the plan at least.

Under the remorseless pressure, however, they lost their formation. Jones seized the opportunity to surround them and, when the Irish tried to surrender, their rearguard was massacred.

Altogether, some three thousand Confederate troops and a few Parliamentarians were killed at Dungan's Hill. Most of the dead were Irish foot, rounded up and slaughtered in the last moments of the battle. A handful of officers were taken prisoner, mainly for ransom.

Richard 'Mad Dick' Talbot was among these lucky few, but the loss of Confederate manpower and equipment was a body blow to the Irish.

Back in Dublin, Jones would waste little precious time. Preston's Confederates had already captured the garrisons at Carlow, Naas and Maynooth. Jones's army - now ten thousand strong - found them ready and willing to welcome their liberation from Irish oppression.

When news of the defeat and its aftermath was relayed to Owen Roe, he swore vengeance to the archangel who had expelled Adam and Eve from Eden. His Ulster Army marched through Portlester Mill pass. Outmanoeuvring Jones' expeditionary vanguard, sent to crush him, he routed it and made it possible for the survivors of the Leinster army to escape. Jones, cowed by O'Neill's army, retreated to Dublin.

O'Neill and his Ulstermen returned to rescue the wounded at Dungan's Hill and to bury their dead compatriots. They found no one whose life could still be saved. They found only corpses. They were appalled to discover that many slain foot soldiers had their hands tied behind their backs.

After Dungans Hill, the Confederates found themselves forced to ally themselves with the Royalists in a Coalition brokered by Lord Ormonde.

Jones, emboldened by his victory, reported to the English Parliament that he was now in a position to re-conquer Ireland. This was a little hyperbolic. He was still confined to Dublin and was systematically raided by the combined forces of O'Neill, Preston, Castlehaven and Inchiquin. He was suffering badly, moreover, from a lack of food and munitions.

*

Ormonde, who had three thousand men garrisoned in Dublin, was besought by his own administration to give way. Dublin had enough problems already, brought on them by the Confederates. Add to that a murderous legion of Roundheads, jostling for power with Ormonde's reluctant Royalists within the walls of the capital? It would have brought the Civil War onto the very streets of Dublin.

This was a *cul-de-sac*; there was only one way out.

Lord Ormonde agreed to meet his one-time comrade-in-arms, Colonel Jones, on the north bank of the Liffey. There, on June 19, 1647, the Marquess of Ormonde surrendered the City of Dublin to the English Parliament.

Four weeks later, at a formal ceremony in the Castle, Ormonde handed over his sword of office over to the Parliamentary Commissioners. His surrender, which delivered his three thousand troops to Jones's command, was on typically Ormondish terms. It endeared him neither to Catholics nor Royalists. His claim was that it was the only way the interests of both (if they had not actually 'rebelled') could be served and protected.

He dismissed his critics with a throwaway line. He declared that he 'preferred English rebels to Irish ones'.

The Dubliners only reluctantly accepted Parliamentarian rule. All of them were tired of having additional troops billeted on them. The forced destruction of houses at the edge of town had made many homeless. Others had been ruined by their compulsory, wageless digging of trenches, which deprived them of what they might ordinarily have earned. Shopkeepers bitterly resented the collapse in their trade. Only exhaustion persuaded them not to rebel, but they were sorely tempted.

If they had not seen from their rooftops two hundred great fires, all started by Owen Roe O'Neill, they surely would have. The suburbs around Dublin, from Howth to Castleknock, were burning in a gaudy semicircle.

*

Ormonde, his marchioness and his children took ship for England. His plan was wait on his sovereign in Hampton Court. He would be there inside the month.

Preston's disastrous defeat at Dungan's Hill effectively allowed Lord Inchiquin and his army, now hugely reinforced with Parliamentary troops and supplies, to overrun Munster. He felt he had a free hand, now that Ormonde had departed. He had little to fear from the ineffectual Theobald Taaffe.

Inchiquin turned his attention to Royalist Cashel, home to a Confederate garrison. His enemy was in disarray.

Inchiquin had a free hand. His implacable foe, Ormonde, would wait on King Charles for as long as the king liked. During that time would seldom leave Hampton Court, the great palace in which the king was so comfortably quartered.

Now was the time to strike.

*

The same realisation had occurred to the King and his Irish courtier.

Their conversations were also strategic.

There was the 'best case scenario', when the shires would rise for their sovereign prince and evict the ranters and proselytisers from the Houses of Parliament. In that one, Ormonde would command His Majesty's loyal armies and would be given a dukedom. The worst case was also discussed. In that one, an endless civil war would play like a plague of boils upon the yeomen of England, with the Church of England banned, its bishops hanged, and the Anabaptists battling for the streets with the Ranters, and the Levellers with the Unitarians. In that

270

nightmare, the king said gaily, he himself would be hanged as a common felon at Tyburn Hill. Somehow the idea seemed to strike him as preposterous.

Ormonde would always steer such conversations towards the positive but, as winter arrived, he began to see that royal dystopian vision might be realised. Had he hitched his destiny to a worm-eaten mooring? Where did he belong?

*

The Rock of Cashel sits on a rocky plateau three hundred feet above the Golden Vale of Tipperary, in the heart of Munster. The word 'cashel' is a slightly anglicised version of the Irish *caiseal*, meaning 'castle.' The English and Irish languages are not always so very far apart.

The Irish had realised centuries if not millennia before that the rock on which the castle sits was an ideal place for a fort. On a clear day, almost all of County Tipperary can be seen from its peak. Defenders could therefore see an enemy approaching from any direction. That fact, by itself, would be enough to explain why it has been occupied since before the fall of the Roman Empire, even before the arrival of St Patrick himself.

When that saint visited the Rock he converted the last pagan King of Munster, Aengus MacMutfraich. That was in 450 AD.

Only a few years later, a King of Munster, Cormac MacCarthy, built himself a palace there. King Cormac had recruited an architect and his stonemasons from the wreckage of the Roman Empire, while studying his faith and destiny in the Abbey of St James[xli] - Regensburg, Bavaria - a place of pilgrimage that had been founded by Irish missionaries during the chaos that descended on Europe after the fall of Rome. It was not that comfortable. The monastery was small, dark and boasted few windows.

For six centuries the Rock of Cashel was to remain the seat of the Kings of Munster. The last and greatest of these was Brian Boru, who had reunified all of Ireland and became its High King. He ruled the other kingdoms from Cashel for no less than twenty-four years. His was a great reign; he brought his Irish subjects wealth, peace and law.

This should have heralded a golden age, but all things must pass. In the 24th year of his reign, in the early 11th century, marauding Vikings began to assert themselves. They raided Irish settlements and enjoyed their traditional sports; rape, loot and pillage.

The Irish, in desperation, looked to their king to rid them of this menace. Brian Boru rose to the challenge. He defeated them at Clontarf, just outside Dublin, in 1014. So sure were Brian Boru's forces of their superiority and their king's invulnerability that they left the eighty-four year old monarch almost unprotected. Brian and his son, Murchad, were slain during the final hours of the battle, even while the Norsemen were in retreat.

From then on the Vikings thought it best to remain within their coastal settlements of Dublin, Waterford, Limerick, Wexford and Cork.

Like the later Normans, they would marry into the Gaelic race. Two centuries after King Cormac came King Muircheartach O'Brien, who awarded the fortress on the rock to the Bishop of Limerick who, between 1235 and 1270, built a Cathedral on the site of an earlier and smaller church.

In 1101, Cashel's skyline was pierced by a splendid round tower of fitted stones, built without mortar. It served as a watch tower and as a shelter from raiders for the centuries to come and Cashel, along with Tara, is an epicentre of Irishness.

When Lord Inchiquin's Protestant troopers arrived, the stone city was in good condition. Lord Inchiquin was no antiquarian, no lover of architecture. He sent a favourite, the fanatical Puritan Colonel Bridges, to punish the city and its countryfolk for having repeatedly adopted the Royalist, Confederate option.

When the local people heard that Inchiquin and his colonel were ravaging and devastating the land, they feared for their lives. They made their way into the city and sought refuge in the cathedral's venerable sanctuary, believing that there they would be safe from Christian soldiers. They should have been. Tradition had long allowed everyone, even felons and reprobates, to seek sanctuary in such holy places.

Inchiquin was unimpressed. He ordered his men to pile peat around the remarkable cathedral. He then set a flaming torch to the fuel, and encouraged Bridges and his Parliamentarians to do the same. Slow heat and small windows turned the cathedral into a giant bread oven, one that roasted three thousand men, women and children alive. It burned everything within, vestments, wooden statues, holy relics. All that was combustible within the *campo santo's* stone walls was lost forever.

Lord Inchiquin, or 'Murrough of the Burnings' as he that day became, was passionately anti-Catholic. He saw it as denying the simple immutable primacy of the Scriptures in favour of scholarship, interpretation, wisdom, revelation and, especially, digression. He had also read of Catherine de Medici's persecution of the Huguenots in France,

272

the dreadful bloodshed on the Feast day of St Bartholomew. He associated Catholicism and Monarchy with persecution.

Inchiquin was not given to mercy. He ordered his troops to slaughter Cashel's survivors. His men obliged and destroyed every living thing they startled or disturbed in their path.

*

If, that November, 1647, the epic Thirty Years War on the Continent still had another year to run, the English Parliament appeared to have already won its Civil War. In Ireland, however, the Confederate War was in its sixth year and looked set to continue.

Over the previous forty years the science of war had evolved. The use of small arms – notably muskets and pistols - had become widespread. With the arrival of star forts, fortifications had been improved beyond measure. Field artillery and its mounted support – the dragoons - were being introduced everywhere. If archers had faded from memory, the armour worn by the officer class, once needed to deflect a bolt or lance, now needed to be toughened enough to resist a musket ball. The blacksmiths of Sheffield, Saxony and Toledo were busy and rich.

Yet Ireland was not France or Spain. Its entire population in 1647, a quarter of England's, knew terrible and endemic poverty, epidemics were commonplace and physicians who knew what they were doing were as rare as hens' teeth. The few roads were mostly beaten tracks without bridges, with fewer fences. Impenetrable Irish bogs and woods were everywhere. Aside from churches and 'mass-houses', municipal buildings scarcely existed. Nonetheless, no other European country could boast such a proliferation of castles, many of which were heart-breakingly beautiful.

Despite everything, things still looked good for the Catholic Irish. It had been twelve months since, excluding Dublin and a few ports still held by a dogged adversary, the Confederacy had effectively taken control of the country.

Unfortunately, 1648 looked unlikely to be another comfortable year. As always, petty jealousy, opportunism, local rivalry and naked ambition were the true enemies. Confederate attempts to take Dublin had not succeeded and a recent decision by Rinuccini - to send O'Neill to Connacht - was looking to be another serious mistake.

Rinuccini had promoted Lord Taaffe to Command the Confederate Army of Munster, on the non-military basis of being the candidate who would offend the smallest number. He ordered Taaffe to destroy Inchiquin, author of all their troubles.

As directed, Taaffe marched with the Confederate army of Munster against Inchiquin, reinforced by Alasdair MacColla, a veteran of the Marquess of Montrose's campaigns in Scotland.

In the mysterious way of these things, the two enemies settled on a location for their duel. It would be in the Barony of Duhallow.

Inchiquin's army, swollen by enthusiasts from all his garrisons, gathered at Mallow. He had been there before. He remembered the walled town and its handsome castle with something approaching affection. From there he had led a successful sortie against General Barry, five years before.

This time he had four thousand foot and twelve hundred horse, organised in six infantry and two cavalry regiments. His foot were two thirds shot to one third pike and they could field two pieces of heavy artillery.

On both sides the cavalry was armed with rapiers, pistolets, carbines,[xlii] muskets and lances and Inchiquin's and Taaffe's regiments were similarly supplied by baggage trains.

Taaffe ordered his Confederate Army of Munster to assemble at Dromalour, just two miles south of Kanturk. He had more than seven thousand foot and more than a thousand horse. His commanders included General Purcell and the Catholic Scot Lieutenant-General Alistair MacDonnell, who had served Montrose's Royalists with distinction.

Reporting to MacDonnell was the local landowner, the widower Colonel Dermod Oge MacDonogh. Since the death of his wife, Cliona, the year before, an intense and murderous loathing of Lord Inchiquin had festered in his heart. Nor was his hatred confined to Inchiquin. It had now extended to all settlers, planters, undertakers, adventurers, Protestants, Puritans and Parliamentarians.

When Castlehaven retook Liscarroll for the Confederates, he had sought a commission from the Supreme Council. He brought every man in Duhallow that answered his call. Scarcely an adult refused him. Only a handful of his army did not carry the names O'Keeffe, O'Callaghan, MacAuliffe or MacDonogh. Probably four thousand of his men-at-arms were cousins, kin or clansmen.

*

On Wednesday November 10, Dermod Oge and Bryen received at their Court in Kanturk some clothes and personal effects that had belonged to Donogh, the young negotiator who had been in Oxford to discuss the future of Ireland. An accompanying note explained that he had been lynched by a Parliamentary militia which, while scouring the University City for Catholics, or Royalists, or with any luck, both, had found him hiding in an attic.

Tears, designed by God to assuage calamity, were insufficient to their task. Soon the spirit of resentment overtook that of grief. That day father and son were angry, far beyond despair. They were of warrior stock and that dawn a blood-red Celtic mist had risen in the east.

*

CHAPTER TWENTY
KNOCKNANUSS

Taaffe had organised his men into nine regiments of foot and two of horse. A third of the foot – a high proportion - had firearms. There was no artillery. The rest had pikes, swords, farmyard tools and slingshots. All were effective weapons; in the right hands, a pitchfork could be wielded like a trident.

An exception to this peaceful model was General MacDonnell.

Wherever the great Scotsman rode a soldier-servant rode behind, carrying his master's broadsword on his back. This was no ordinary claymore. It was a huge weapon, fully seven feet from the end of his hilt to the tip of its blade.

The sword was ingeniously made, and to MacDonnell's own design. It was hollow. Inside it, a lead weight could move easily up and down its length. When Alistair MacDonnell swung it around his head, the weight moved to the tip. Nothing could then stop it. It would dismember or behead anyone within a nine-foot radius.

'You wanted to see me, Sir?' MacDonnell had sent for Dermod Oge.

'Yes, Colonel. No one on earth knows this country better than you. Lord Taaffe wants to pitch camp closer to Mallow. He wants to tempt Inchiquin from his lair.'

'Then perhaps you should discourage him, my lord. My scouts tell me the enemy has already left Mallow and is reinforcing his position at Garryduff.'

'He expects us to come to him, does he? Where would a suitable place for our battle, MacDonogh? Where would you choose?'

'There is a hill, about three miles from Garryduff, called Knocknanuss. The hill is significant in our legends. There is an enigmatic prophesy, penned centuries ago, that our infantry remember.

> MacDonogh future age shall see
> A Man of thy Posterity,
> By whom the English Lord shall fall,
> Blood shall ascend to the Legges small,[10]
> The place we Knocknanuss do call.

---

[10] Blood shall rise to the knees.

'I shall inform Taaffe. Like yours, his people descend from the chiefs of Duhallow. He is an honorary MacDonogh, he says.'

'Yes, Sir. I have already had the privilege of being informed of his theory.'

'Well, take your men there directly. Have them defend the hill, dig trenches, place some sharpened stakes in strategic places. We should expect to hear from Lord Inchiquin very soon. By the sound of it, it could even be later this morning.'

As it happened, Lord Inchiquin did make contact with Lord Taaffe and, yes, it was that same morning.

'Yes, what is it?' Taaffe snapped at the young officer who had come into his tent at Knocknanuss unexpectedly.

'There is an English officer and his soldier-servant riding towards us from Garryduff,' replied Major Bryen MacDonogh.

'Really? That is good. Let's hear what he has to say. You, Major, find yourself a voice trumpet. We may well want to respond to the rascal's scurrilous nonsense.'

The general and his retinue walked to the entrance to their camp, where they readied themselves to welcome the enemy delegation.

'Lord Taaffe,' declared Inchiquin's messenger through his loudhailer. 'My Lord Inchiquin presents his compliments and requests that you do him the courtesy of joining him in combat at your earliest convenience.'

'Major, be so good as to tell the English captain we accept Lord Inchiquin's kind invitation. Tell him we challenge him to pitch two thousand infantrymen against the same number of ours for our shared recreation.' He smiled. Then he added, 'tell him that if he has men to rival ours he must have seduced them from the service of His Majesty.'

Bryen did as he was ordered.

Hearing him, the English Captain frowned.

'Lord Taaffe,' his man replied, repeating his Captain's softly spoken words, 'be assured I shall convey your message to Lord Inchiquin. I shall return with his response within the hour.'

With that the Englishmen wheeled about and were off at the gallop.

'Well said, Taaffe,' said a smiling General MacDonnell. 'Recreation? Snappy phrase. 'Twas well said!'

It was less than an hour later when the English Captain Courtropp reappeared with Lord Inchiquin's response, the ink fresh, the general's seal clumsily applied.

Murrough O'Brien, Viscount Inchiquin, thanks the Lord Taaffe for his kind invitation to a recreation but regrets he cannot accept. The matter is too important for jousting. I shall defer our dispute until we meet in the morning, when I believe the gentlemen whom you suppose to be seduced or deluded by me, will with God's help use a form of rhetoric that will better conduce to that end, to which I shall refer your lordship for satisfaction, being resolved to contribute therein to the endeavours of your servant, Inchiquin.

'I think your gentle remarks may have pierced his armour-plated carapace, my lord,' chuckled MacDonnell. 'Now we know he will meet us on our ground, and on this sloping hill where we have the advantage.'

'I shall turn in. Have my men do likewise,' said General Purcell.

'Good idea. I shall send the chaplains to ready the men. Those ruins of an ancient oratory surely mean the ground is consecrated. Not even infamy can deconsecrate hallowed turf. Let us celebrate Holy Mass. Some of us may have a troubling interview with the Judge tomorrow.'

Lord Taaffe discovered Dermod Oge at prayer.

'Well, Colonel, this will be a cracking adventure!'

'No doubt.'

'No need to be so negative, MacDonogh. Thanks to you we have a superior position and a greater army. What can go wrong?'

'The answer to that is 'irrepressibility'. Our men believe that their officers are Olympians, that God fights with them, that their little prayers, supplemented with an occasional javelin, will protect them from Satan, and that our numbers and the terrain makes us invincible.'

'That's what I think, too. What's wrong with that?'

'It's hubristic, Sir. It's a notion built upon complacency. A sense of moral and military superiority can undermine our men and our officers. I should like it better if the odds were less even.'

'Dermod Oge MacDonogh Carty of Duhallow! You are talking nonsense. The day is ours. Please confine your damnable pessimism to yourself. That, and prepare to eat your words.'

As darkness came, owls hooted a welcome to the tremulous luminance of a brilliant moon. A nervous landscape knew it was destined to become one of history's great pages.

Passwords for the foot and the horse were given out. On both sides there was a risk that one might be mistaken for the other. The ferns in every Irishman's hat would often fall out in the heat of battle, particularly if the road from the battlefield were clear of witnesses. Taaffe decided that his men would wear a woven straw band around their hats; a 'sugán ribbon'.

His senior officers debated their defence. They had the advantage, knew the lie of the land and had numerical superiority. There was that prophesy, too.

'The English Lord shall fall. That can only be Inchiquin,' said Taaffe. 'I am a MacDonogh, too. I may not be chief, but I am of the ancient clan who took Duhallow by conquest a dozen generations ago. The prophesy is of my victory.'

'Well,' said General Purcell, 'it will not be long before it's fulfilled.'

That November 13 both armies were ready well before dawn.

On the Parliamentary side, Inchiquin worried about the ground and the wind, both of which suited Taaffe better than him.

'I shall write to him again,' he told Courtropp. He scribbled a short letter, folded it and sealed it in wax, this time with great care.

'Take this to our fearless Irish warrior. It will play upon his medieval tastes, I am confident.'

Twenty minutes later, Captain Courtropp was again outside the Irish camp. He arrived as the rim of the sun appeared as if a forest fire above the eastern horizon.

Taaffe took the letter, promising to return directly with a spoken reply.

> My Lord,
> There is a very fair piece of ground between your lordship's army and ours, on our side of the brook; wither if you please to advance, we shall do the like; we do not so much doubt your gallantry, as to think you will not come, but give you this notice, to the end you may see we do stand upon no advantage of ground, and are willing to dispute our quarrel upon indifferent terms; being confident that justice of our cause will be this day made manifest by the Lord, and that your Lordship's judgement will be rectified concerning your servant, Inchiquin.

Taaffe snapped his verbal response. 'Tell my Lord Inchiquin that...'

> I am not so little a soldier as to ignore any advantage I have of ground or wind, which I doubt not the President would do in like case.

When the soldier delivered the response as instructed. Inchiquin realised that Taaffe would have to be engaged and defeated in battle. The hillside at Knocknanuss seemed scheduled for history.

Inchiquin's commanders were brought into their general's big tent. Did they sanction their chief's plan? They were unsure. They advised that prayers should be offered for guidance.

Inchiquin decided to play devil's advocate.

'That's not really good enough, Gentlemen. Yes, we shall pray, but let us also consider the odds. Taaffe has nearly 9,000 men against our 5,000. The wind will blow our own musket smoke back into our faces. Even worse, we will be attacking up hill.'

'Sir, we are better armed. We have field artillery. Our cavalry is several hundred more than theirs.'

'Thank you. We too believe we should attack. The motion is hereby carried. Gentlemen, look about. The broom is in flower everywhere. Considering that few of our men have uniforms, we think our soldiers should display a piece of blossom, rue perhaps, in their headgear.'

'Capital idea, my Lord. A battle cry?'

'What would you suggest?'

'"Victory", my Lord. We think it should be 'victory'.'

'Very good. 'Victory' it is.'

Inchiquin gave the order to advance. As his Protestant army approached the Catholic position, they saw that the Irish had put straw around their hats. They heard their cry, shouted to the heavens. It was 'God and St Patrick'.

Now the fates were ready to take possession of the moment.

Inchiquin deployed his army as a Roman would. He ranged his regiments three to six ranks deep. To either side lay muskets and pikes, flanked by cavalry. Every so often a gap was made to allow the artillery to have the clear sight it needed. The guns themselves were covered by a second line of infantry.

Fifty yards before all these men was the unenviable front line of musketeers, the so-called 'forlorn'. At least musketeers stood a better chance than infantry.

'Come on, men,' their captain told them. 'We have all had to serve in a forlorn at one time or other. No one ever does so twice.'

Inchiquin brought his baggage train as close as he dared, about half a mile from his front line. A party of horse was assigned to guard it.

Over on Knocknanuss hill, Taaffe was equally ready. He had ordered the right wing to remain behind and took personal command of his left wing – three thousand foot. The entire line overlooked Inchiquin's.

The wind continued to blow towards the English.

Five hundred yards separated the two armies. Inchiquin's best troops and his two pieces of artillery were opposite MacDonnell. The infamous Colonel Bridges, he who had supervised the stacking of peat against Cashel's cathedral walls, commanded the English left flank. Inchiquin took the right.

Then began a phoney war until, at three o'clock that afternoon, Inchiquin moved his whole line to the left.

'He intends to surround our right flank,' said Lord Taaffe. 'Soldier, tell General Purcell to take a regiment and reinforce our position on the hill.'

It was done. Taaffe's right flank was strengthened at the expense of his left.

Now was the time to begin in earnest.

Inchiquin directed his artillery to fire on MacDonnell and his company, while the infantry on his left flank set off to protect his line against an advance on that side. Inchiquin ordered his right wing and centre to return to their original positions, effectively creating a pivot on the field of battle.

'We're being outflanked on the left,' cried Taaffe. 'You, soldier, tell that regiment of horse to attack Murrough of the Burnings's moving columns.'

The Prophesy was still praying on Taaffe's mind.

'Men, fall to. Our horse is to attack the English muskets,' barked his Sergeant-Major, O'Keeffe.

Inchiquin's muskets were ready to repel Taaffe's cavalry. The Catholic cavalry turned and had to plough through their own foot soldiers behind them.

Inchiquin saw this and laughed.

'The man's an idiot! He should have restricted his soldierly ambitions to playing with his tin soldiers in his nursery!'

He ordered his own horse to charge the Irish who, already frightened, now panicked. The centre soon joined in the flight, pursued by Inchiquin's right wing.

The cavalry on Taaffe's right inched forward. Inchiquin ordered their opposite numbers to advance, swords drawn.

'Push where it is most likely to give,' Inchiquin told their officers. 'In life, and in every conflict, it's always good advice.'

It was indeed; baffled and outwitted, Taaffe's horse fled.

The nearby English foot, elated, broke cover and advanced over the open ground onto the Irish.

MacDonnell, for the Irish, had been expecting such a key moment. His regiments advanced, fired and charged down on the enemy's left.

MacColla, for the Catholic Highlanders, led a charge against the Parliamentarians, smashing through their lines. Unfortunately, his wilder clansmen had spotted Inchiquin's payroll and baggage train and their Scottish hearts were suddenly set on plunder.

MacDonnell was appalled. Thundering forward without any apparent sense of danger, he brought his men rolling down the hill like a torrent. His infamous broadsword was revolving around his head and his clansmen, having fired their muskets, threw their firearms down and used their claymores to scythe their enemy like corn. Any foot soldiers who had the misfortune to be in their path were overwhelmed. MacDonnell's momentum had soon engulfed Inchiquin's artillery and also found his baggage train.

Understandably, if regrettably, these Catholic Scots deceived themselves into thinking the battle was won. From where they were they had good reason to think that way. The English had apparently fled, and the wagons they had taken were filled with food and drink. When they found the whiskey casks the Scots settled down to an impromptu picnic. Perhaps they thought they had died and gone to heaven? If they did they were close to being right.

When MacDonnell came among them it was too late to deprive them of their spoils. A single glance told him the soldiers would be unfit for the foreseeable future.

He rode away to seek further support from Theobald Taaffe.

Inchiquin, while he could see only too plainly how his enemy had cut his men to pieces and overturned his wagons, was not prepared to cut his losses and retire.

Taaffe called Colonel Dermod Oge MacDonogh to help him press his attack onto Inchiquin's right wing.

Dermod Oge wheeled his horse around.

'Gentlemen, this is not the time for the gentler arts of soft persuasion. If the enemy comes at you, your swords should sweep to the side, aiming always for the neck. A direct thrust to the torso is good but you may lose your weapon. If your enemy retreats, then again aim for the neck, from the side. A slash to the ribs may injure our man but may leave him fit enough to return the favour. No half measures; this is a matter of life or death. Your life, his death.'

Meanwhile, MacDonnell fought his way back towards Taaffe, with only his sword-bearer by his side.

He didn't get there. A company of Inchiquin's horse set about him. He turned to call for his sword, but his faithful friend had already been cut down with sabres. The enemy horse recognised MacDonnell; he wore a breastplate but no helmet, and a kilt like his men. He was effectively unarmed. The enemy had a prize indeed.

An appalled Dermod Oge did what he could. He managed to find a way of shielding his commander with his horse and, when he brandished his flintlocks, the English did draw back for an instant, but not even the greatest warrior could protect his commander from an entire company of cavalry. Dermod Oge took out a captain with a pistol ball, but was himself so badly injured by sabres to his unprotected legs and arms that he soon became faint through loss of blood.

Inevitably, at last, he fell.

Some English soldiers dismounted, pulled his head up by the hair and laughed. Then one of them casually cut off the Irishman's head. Another kicked the grisly relic into touch, as if it were a football.

Major Bryen MacDonogh, notionally attached to General Purcell, found himself beside Major Richard Butler.

'We have to rescue General MacDonnell,' Butler told him.

'How?'

'Lord Taaffe needs to order his army into the English camp. Any decision is better than none. The army needs a purpose. Just look at them!'

At this moment Taaffe himself rode up, surrounded by his household guard. The Commander looked terrified.

'My Lord,' shouted Major Butler. 'You know me. Butler! I beg you, give me a company to rescue General MacDonnell.'

'He is taken captive?'

'Yes sir. If we leave him, he will surely be hanged or shot.'

'MacDonnell gone? My God, why have you forsaken me? A company, Butler? You want to engage a lion in hand-to-hand combat? You pitiable idiot. Get out of my way. It matters not a jot to me if you are Lord Ormonde's brother.'

'Sir,' Butler persisted, 'I implore you. Forget the company. Let me and this major ride out.'

'Major, you are mad. Any more of this and I shall pistol you myself.' He drew his flintlock.

'My Lord, I will go to the aid of General MacDonnell.' Butler had likewise drawn his pistol. 'If you try to stop me *I* shall bullet *you.*'

The two Confederate officers had their handguns levelled at each other.

Bryen had no choice. Only the lack if witnesses prevented Butler from being charged with outright mutiny. If he shot his commanding officer, leaving him dead or harmed, no matter how illustrious his birth, he would be brought before a firing squad.

'Lord Taaffe, leave this man to me,' Bryen told the Commander of the Confederate Army. 'This battle has left him distracted.' With that he rode between the two men and took Butler's horse by the bridle.

Glancing behind him, he saw Taaffe tuck his pistol into his doublet, turn his horse and ride away from the battle.

'Come with me, Butler,' Bryen said. 'MacDonnell is already dead, or as good as dead. Nothing can save him now. We can still bring some succour to his Antrim men.'

By the time they regrouped, the Confederate cavalry and Taaffe himself had been driven from the field. MacColla had been stabbed in the back by one of Inchiquin's officers while negotiating a surrender. His followers had then been massacred.

The setting sun flashed on the blades of the victorious English as they set off in murderous pursuit of the fleeing Irish.

Butler and MacDonogh found that the English had given MacDonnell's regiments no quarter. The two Irishmen saw the casualties of the battle were too numerous to count. It had to be more than two thousand. Walking through the ghastly scene, Butler guessed there were three Irish left on the field for every one of the enemy. They stopped frequently. The two majors' hasty tourniquets ensured that a handful would survive.

They came across some dead Parliamentarian officers, among them General Craig.

Then, horror upon horror, they discovered the headless body of Dermod Oge MacDonogh. Bryen recognised him immediately from his breastplate and from the signet ring that somehow had not yet been taken from his finger. His son removed it and placed it on his own finger. Hw was now Chief of his Name. Tears sprang silently from his eyes.

'Where is his head? Butler, help me find my father's head!'

'Be practical! It could be anywhere in this carnage. Leave the funerary matters alone, their souls are already in heaven. When we can we'll give them a Christian burial. MacDonogh, the Confederate Army of Munster has been defeated. Someone needs to ride to Kilkenny and tell Nuncio Rinuccini.'

'We shall both go. The Parliamentarians will spend the next few days hunting down our survivors. Come with me now. We need to rest and my father's house is barely three miles from here. Trust me; I know the way well enough to ride home in the dark.'

'Your house may have been slighted. Or razed.'

'It's not likely. It hadn't been before the battle. Tomorrow the English will be more interested in finishing off the remaining stragglers. Come, follow me.'

Unopposed, the two young men made their way cross country to the grand Old Court at Kanturk, the mansion improperly called Kanturk Castle.

The Confederate defeat at Knocknanuss left Inchiquin and his Parliamentarians in control of most of Munster. Of the major cities, only Kilkenny, Limerick, Waterford and Clonmel remained in Confederate hands. Mercifully, Jones and Inchiquin were unable to continue their onslaught. Another round of vicious Civil War had broken out in England and Parliament's resources of men and supplies were urgently needed at home. They left Ireland reluctantly. War in Ireeland was great sport.

The MacDonogh clan had been annihilated in this battle. When the dust settled there were just twenty of that name left in Kanturk. Overall, the clan, like most others, had been mostly composed of, valiant smallholders, hardworking tenants, butchers, sawbones' assistants and barkeepers. All the usual trades. Some had been wastrels who had sought redemption on the field of battle. All fought for their faith, and all who died were martyrs, their priests had told them; their sins most certainly forgiven, their indulgencies plenary.

The sword knew no such piety, thought Bryen. Its horrid punishment was indiscriminate. The death it inflicted came slowly, painfully, casting its victim into an agonising awareness of his will to live and his unreadiness for death.

After the battle, it would be some time before any of the dead could be buried. Weeks passed before surviving local gentry could order their reluctant tenants to the task. The gory business – three thousand corrupted Confederates and twelve hundred putrefying Parliamentarians

– needed a final resting place. The Duhallow women heaped the fallen one upon another until they had built a steep hill. Then they covered it in turf.

Never before had such a ghastly earthwork been raised in Ireland, nor would it ever be again. The whole sad chore took a month to perform, and that in a harsh mid-winter. The resulting mound would not subside in the next three hundred and fifty years[xliii].

Among the visitors to the scene, where 'blood had ascended to the legges small', was Bryen MacDonogh Carty.

Bryen came at sun-up every day. He stayed until the light failed. He searched for his father's head. His father deserved a Christian burial and his son had resolved to take what remained of his frame to Lough Arrow, to the Abbey Church at Ballindoon in County Sligo, where the MacDonoghs had been buried since man had first built houses for God. Dermod Oge had done it for his father Dermod. It was Bryen's sacred duty to do the same.

The Confederacy debated how best to further the war.

In Dromsicane, the clergy, and many Gaels, wanted Ireland returned to the Holy Church; to this end they were prepared to abandon the Anglican King Charles to his fate and invite King Philip IV of Spain to become Ireland's protector. They only ruled out the King of France on the grounds he was still too young. Embassies were sent to beg the great Catholic powers of Europe for military intervention.

On the other hand, the Anglo-Irish lords in Kilkenny, always loyal to their Scoto-Hibernian king, simply wanted the Confederacy to support the Royalists and begin a third round of the Civil War with Parliament.

The split within the Confederates, between Gaelic Irish and Old English, at first appeared to be along traditional lines. Since 1641, the Milesians had every year lost land and power. Of course they did when the Vikings or the Geraldines had first conquered Ireland, but nothing like this. Recent aggression on such a scale at last provoked an acquiescent race to make radical demands.

There were, however, members of every race on every side. Phelim O'Neill, the instigator of the 1641 Rebellion, sided with the moderates, whereas the predominantly Old English Wexford area rejected Ormonde's Peace. Ormonde, of course, was in England.

Some Irish gentry, like Dermod Oge MacDonogh, had been willing to compromise with the Royalists as long as their lands and civil rights were guaranteed and immune. Others, such as Owen Roe O'Neill, wanted to overthrow all foreign presence in the country, wanting a wholly independent and Catholic Ireland. They had no place within it for English or Scottish settlers of any kind. Many were more concerned with recovering their former landholdings, small or large, that their families had lost in the terrible times of the plantations.

The matter had no easy resolution. Infighting would hamper the efforts of the Confederate-Royalist alliance to deter for long any concerted invasion by the English Parliamentarian army.

The Roundheads' general behaviour convinced most Confederates to reach an agreement with the Royalists, and negotiations were re-opened. Improved terms with the Supreme Council were agreed.

These confirmed (again) the need for public toleration of the Catholic religion, but Dublin Castle had not been involved in their discussions.

The restoration of lands taken by Irish Catholics during the war and a commitment to at least a partial reversal of the Plantation of Ulster were also demanded.

In addition, the king was asked for an Act of Oblivion, or amnesty for all acts committed during the Rebellion and subsequent Confederate wars - in particular the notorious killing of Protestant settlers in 1641 - and the Confederate armies would be allowed to remain in existence, but under Royalist command.

Most importantly, Poynings' Law was to be repealed.

News of these resolutions came fast enough to Lord Inchiquin. Sickened by the appalling decisions he and his enemy had taken, he was as keen as anyone to see an end to the conflict. He reflected long and hard. Magnanimity is the duty of the victor, he thought. The Confederate terms were enough to persuade him to seek an audience of the king, in Hampton Court, as was his right as a Peer of the Realm. The war might continue in Ulster, he had a little time. In Munster, at least, there was a peace of sorts.

He sailed from Dublin, arriving in Bristol two days later where, ironically, he was met and made welcome by a troop of Ironsides, put at his disposal by Parliament. They accompanied him to the king's riverside palace, while Inchiquin remembered who owed what to whom.

'Ormonde tells us he wishes to capitulate to the Confederacy, noble cousin,' the king delivered. 'He maybe on our side, as ever he was, but no longer has an army. Only in our desperation did we agree to his terms.'

287

'When the war is won, Your Majesty may be able to repudiate them,' said Inchiquin. 'I admit to being unsure of the constitutional hangover of Your Majesty's royal pragmatism.'

'Eh? Is that possible? Can we do that?' The king was equally uncertain.

'Sire, not only can you do that, but you must.' Inchiquin was now decisive.

'And you, dear cousin, do you still intend to fight on the side of Parliament in this terrible war?'

'No, Sire; with your permission I shall henceforward be your most loyal liegeman, as I was in the Bishops War. I shall embrace the Royalist cause in Ireland, a cause I should never have abandoned, and I pray that I shall be welcomed as was the Prodigal Son on his return to the fold.'

'Let us grasp that noble hand, trusty cousin. Welcome home.'

'Your Majesty does me too much honour.'

*

CHAPTER TWENTY-ONE
RINUCCINI LOSES HIS GRIP

Rinuccini thought of looking to France but discovered, to his consternation, that Cardinal Mazarin supported the Anglo-Irish faction. For the cardinal the issue was simplicity itself. He put French interests in his scales and found that King Charles' restoration to the throne outweighed the Protestant Parliament. He had not forgotten the heretic rising in La Rochelle and how the English Parliament's had supported it.

Rinuccini's hold on his Assembly had slackened but he was never anything less than an archbishop. He insisted that no religious settlement could be negotiated without papal sanction.

1647 bore slowly on. It was becoming clear that Rinuccini's 'interim' presidency was failing. His favouring of Lord Taaffe and the disastrous consequences had dismayed Catholic Europe. His decision, early in '47, to sack Tomás Preston had met unconcealed derision. Commentators began to blame the deteriorating military situation on him.

The Supreme Council, which the *nuncio* now chaired, attempted to suggest more moderate, tolerant, policies but Rinuccini, with his bishops and Owen Roe O'Neill, continued to repudiate Mountgarrett's peace overtures.

The *nuncio*, still hoping to rally the Confederate cause with further funding from the Vatican, sent Bishop French and the eminent lawyer Nicholas Plunkett to Rome.

They had some success, but it came too late. In any case the pontifical largesse was far too beggarly to turn the tide of history. Everyone had been waiting a long time, only to see a disappointing result.

Rinuccini found himself in an untenable position. Proud as he was, he could see that his credibility was holed beneath the waterline.

In January, 1648, at a plenary session of the General Assembly, Archbishop Rinuccini resigned his Presidency of the Supreme Council. He continued to reside at Dromsicane, however; an Irish *'emminence grise'* if you will.

While the country was cautiously celebrating the New Year, Ireland had come to a crossroads. Some even suggested a strategic murder here and there, Borgia-style, remembering that relatively small acts of force could overturn political fashions. Brutus had proved that. Assassinations were powerful tools of 'regime change'; economical and not automatically a *casus belli*.

A pity for the Irish, then, that such a useful device was forbidden by the Augustinian Rules of War.

Still reeling from the military disasters of Dungan's Hill and Knocknanuss, the Anglo-Irish lords on the Assembly, loyal as ever to the king, now wanted the Confederacy to declare for the Royalists against Parliament.

This, of course, had been Ormonde's proposal all along. Unfortunately Parliament, with the king under a comfortable house arrest in Hampton Court, with only his Lord Lieutenant of Ireland for company, speculated on this Irish stratagem. At this stage, the Commons had not realised the significance of Lord Inchiquin's audience with his sovereign.

In March, 1648, the Westminster Parliament finally issued their inevitable warrant for Ormonde's arrest, in the same nebulous terms as they had arrested the king so recently and Lord Strafford long before. Clearly, his English holiday could not continue indefinitely.

Aware that he needed to avoid impeachment, he walked his family calmly through Hampton Court's great River Gate and hired a bargee to take them downstream to Tilbury. There he found a sea captain and paid him handsomely to take the Ormonde family to France.

He carried a letter from the king. He presented it to the queen and the Prince of Wales when he arrived in St-Germain-en-Laye that May. In it was the king's command that the Ormondes should enjoy the protection of the court in exile, and a regal request that the young Majesty of France, King Louis XIV should be equally kind o his beloved exiles.

Those who had once been so confident of the way forward were now quite baffled. Confederate diplomats were sent to France to seek common ground with Queen Henrietta-Maria, Ormonde and other leading Royalists. There they found a considerable Irish community; one that grew every day. It was not parliamentarian.

Some of these Irish exiles were well connected. Cormac MacDonogh, a general in the King's Guard, had the ear of Cardinal Mazarin, new to his pink hat and, for most commentators, an unfamiliar successor of the better-known and more powerful Richelieu.

MacDonogh talked Mazarin into giving a reception for the Irish, led by Lord Ormonde, in the former's handsome riverside palace.

'With our support, dear Marquess, you could return to Ireland,' the Cardinal opined. 'There, we think, you will be able to convince the warring factions to rally and unite for a grand assault on Dublin.'

'And once Dublin has fallen to the Irish, Eminence?'

'Then, Noble Marquess, our mutual friend the Prince of Wales will arrive and occupy the Castle as king. He will then lead an allied army of Royalists and Confederates in an invasion of England. The House of Stuart will be restored and, incidentally, so will your estates.'

'The Puritans?'

'Ormonde, you could waste a great deal of time, treasure and blood looking for someone to care for them. They don't even care for each other. They are too fractious even to share a common cause. It's only a matter of time before the Presbyterians in Parliament and the Covenanters in Scotland turn on them, or each lother. Just ignore them.'

'Yes, I see that. Your Eminence's plan will need vigour and time to implement, but I believe it will work. The Confederate Supreme Council once agreed to my Peace and it's still a force to be counted on.'

*

Ireland was not of one mind, however. On June 11, 1648, Owen Roe led his Army of Ulster into battle against both Royalists and Confederates. He declared war on the Supreme Council and led the Army of Ulster against Kilkenny. Although he failed to capture the Confederate capital, O'Neill's troops spent most of that summer laying waste to the surrounding country. Only when they were finally driven back by the combined forces of Inchiquin and Preston, driven by events to ally, would they back down.

If, on the one hand, General O'Neill lacked the resources to achieve a decisive victory, on the other Rinuccini was no longer in a position to unite the clergy against the Supreme Council. The Confederate Supreme Council would ignore Richelieu and agree to negotiate a new treaty with Ormonde, whom they still recognised as Lord Lieutenant, even if temporarily to Paris. The Council's imperative was to present a united front against the English Parliament.

Push came to shove, as it always does. The Council condemned the followers of Archbishop Rinuccini. They declared Owen Roe O'Neill a traitor, for good measure.

Rinuccini finally took it on board that he was neither serving the people of Ireland nor the Prince of Peace. When the Council appealed to Rome, on September 30, Rinuccini withdrew to Galway, from where he planned to return to Italy.

If Ormonde were happy to dedicate his life and career to the king, the *nuncio* was not. He had been convinced that the Royalist cause was lost which, to some extent, was true. Not one of the three kingdoms had an occupied throne.

One of the *nuncio*'s last executive decisions, before taking ship, was to award the future command of the Irish Ulster Army, hitherto commanded by Owen Roe O'Neill, to a Catholic bishop, Heber MacMahon of Clogher. MacMahon had no real military experience but the *nuncio* hoped he would stem the political infighting that threatened to unbalance the war.

Despite such an optimistic objective, Rinuccini knew in his heart his time was up.

He rode with only the company of a small troop of horse and two Irish Franciscans, Richard O'Farrell and Robert O'Connell, to Galway City, whence he departed for Ostia.

It would be a difficult homecoming.

An angry Pope told him his conduct in Ireland had been 'unworthy'. He authorised the absolution of those the *nuncio* had excommunicated. The pious Rinuccini spent many months in Rome as an object of derision before being granted leave to return to his archdiocese in Fermo.

He had brought two Irish friars came with him. They were employed to listen and compile a riveting if self-serving account of his mission to Ireland, the *Commentarius Rinuccinianus*.

As for the archbishop, his health, always fragile, finally broke down. Within five years he would be dead.

In 1647, Parliament ordered the commander of their Army in the East of England, Oliver Cromwell, to award his army to his colonels Robert Venables and Theophilus Jones, and prepare them for a mission to Ulster.

He bitterly resented this and declined the invitation. He explained that he had hand-picked his own men. He had even given them all a copy of the scriptures, out of his own pocket. They reported to him and to no one else.

Parliament overlooked his objections, and Jones and Venables (who was promoted general) cherry-picked the more useful of the East Anglian general's army for their expedition to Ireland. Cromwell found his command much reduced and though (in England at least) another battle was not expected, Parliament had left him too little negotiating strength to reverse the rulings of the War Cabinet.

That was where he needed to be seen and heard. He had learned, to his great annoyance, that the Scots were ready to ally with the Royalists. His spies had told him of a powerful Scottish lobby to crown the Prince of Wales 'King of Scots' at Scone Palace, should some 'misfortune' overtake the present monarch. If that happened, they said, they were ready to declare the youngster their king.

Meanwhile, Owen Roe besieged Coote in Derry. Coote was no easy target. He had held out for a year before the Parliamentary General Venables could rout O'Neill's army. That gave the Parliamentarians command of the war against Ulster's Catholics.

*

The Parliamentarians, always jealous of the Presbytarian domination of the Houses of Parliament, had decided it was time to dispense with the tedious and mostly unnecessary deliberations of the Westminster machine. When their army evicted the Presbyterians from the Houses of Parliament the Puritans would henceforward hold every lever of power.

The House of Lords was immediately sent 'to the country'. As for the Commons, the New Model Army, under Colonel Pride, had evicted all but its most zealous members. Members of the 'Rump Parliament' were now renamed 'Commissioners'. Each of them had been approved by the Puritan High Command.

This was all that was left of the historic and noble chamber, and now it performed the ultimate treason. It asked Pride to find a large number of judges of sufficient distinction to try, convict and sentence the king.

Those with the courage to ask what precise charge the king would face were given no answer. It was enough that they had the reason for the trial. Pride spelled it out.

> It is for his wicked Design to erect and uphold in himself an unlimited and tyrannical Power to rule according to his Will and to overthrow the Rights and Liberties of the People.

This elaborate turn of phrase reflected the fact that nothing existed in Roman, Statute or Common Law that could invalidate the role and will of an anointed monarch. How could there be? Every law in the land was in the name of the king.

Colonel Pride was not going to find his 'trial' easy to legitimate. Deep in the Dutch Republic, the City of Breda had long belonged to the House of Orange-Nassau. Aside from a vast gothic confection of a church, Breda's grandest building was the palace built by the Italian architect Tomaso Vincidor de Bologna for the first Dutch prince. North of the Alps it was the earliest renaissance building and was now the residence of Mary, the holder of two important titles. She was the English Princess Royal and, already, the widow of Prince William II of Orange. Her stately and majestic palace had long encouraged grandees to sprinkle Breda with their own magnificent residences.

After the outbreak of the Thirty Years War, Spinola had taken the ancient *residenzstadt*[11] of Breda for Spain. A decade later, after a four-month siege, the town had been recaptured by Frederick Henry of Orange. By May, 1648, it had been ceded to the Dutch Republic under the terms of the Treaty of Westphalia. All that flag changing made its people pragmatic.

Mary's brother, Charles Prince of Wales, heir to the English throne, realised the fortified and moated town would make it a safe and attractive haven. He rented a suitable mansion and was quickly surrounded by Irish and British Royalists. Their principle motives were to avoid Parliament's attentions and second, to gamble their fortunes and futures on a successful restoration, following the dismal but probable outcome of the trial, now scheduled for early in the New Year.

One of their number was James, Duke of York, the Prince of Wales's younger brother.

Despite its Spanish connections, Breda was a Protestant town. Its churchgoers tolerated the English princes' religion, even if they did not really understand their English brand of Lutheranism. While its merchants welcomed the stream of exiled big-spending Royalists who brought the Prince of Wales news of England and his father's other kingdoms.

The Royalists had seen that so long as the Prince of Wales's father, King Charles, was confined to Hampton Court, the royalist cause in England was not completely defeated. Insurrection against Parliament's High Commission was erupting all over the British Isles. A purposeful if uncoordinated renewal of the Civil War was progressively looking more likely.

---

[11] Citystate

Mary, Princess Royal, received her brother with full pomp in her lovely mansion. She lived alone, if one ignores her hundred servants and her mother-in-law, Princess Amelia. The long period of mourning occasioned by her husband's premature death had deprived her both of suitable company and the gaiety of the court. It was never that much in Calvinist Holland, but was absolutely denied her while in mourning.

Her father, the King of England, had initially wanted her to marry a son of Philip IV, King of Spain, even though her first cousin, Karl Ludwig, the Elector Palatine, had also been a suitor. Both such arrangements fell through. When that happened there was nothing for it. On her ninth birthday King Charles had betrothed her to Willem, the son and heir of Frederick Henry, Prince of Orange and *Stadtholder* of the United Provinces. The marriage had taken place five years later, on May 2, 1641, in the Chapel Royal of Whitehall Palace. A year later, she moved to the Dutch Republic with her mother, Queen Henrietta Maria, who acted for a while as a royal 'duenna'.

Their only child, Willem[xliv], was born in 1644. A few months later, her much older husband died. She was now seventeen and Dowager Princess of Orange. Her royal mother moved back to Paris and she was obliged to share the guardianship of her infant son with his grandmother.

Married life was not a bed of roses. The Dutch branch of her new family disapproved of her sympathies with the 'headstrong, spendthrift' Stuarts. Public opinion was outraged by the lavish hospitality that she showered upon her family. For the moment, however, there was nothing the Dutch royals could do.

*

A deputation of Royalists was received by the Prince of Wales in the Grand Salon of the Residence, Mary's Breda palace. While she sat on the throne and received the bows and curtseys of the English courtiers and their wives who had come to pay their respects, her son remained standing on her right.

As they stepped forward in order of precedence, the Prince of Wales broke a little with protocol. He stepped forward to take the leading visitor by the shoulders and raise him from his deep bow.

'Dear old Newcastle. You have come all the way from Paris to see my mother and me. You must have something of great import to tell.'

'I am delighted to report a number of uprisings, Sir, Ma'am, in England, Scotland and Wales. The political climate at home looks more favourable.'

'Does it indeed? Excellent. Yet you do not mention Ireland. Is that intended? Have you not yet heard that Archbishop Rinuccini has returned to Rome? That may be good news, but the only man I ever really trusted from that strange country, Lord Ormonde, has abandoned the Hibernian Kingdom and is currently skulking in Paris.'

'We have heard that Ormonde is trying to unite everyone there behind their king.'

The prince had been suffering from depression which sometimes manifested itself as defeatism.

'Newcastle, face facts. The king my father is to endure a mock trial. The Civil War is lost. England's destiny is to become a plebeian republic run by ill-educated bigots.'

'Sire, we believe the war may resume!'

'Really? With my father the king confined in Hampton Court?'

'The Navy, or part of it, has come out for your anointed father, Sir. Ten warships have just dropped anchor at Veere, a harbour to the north of here, in Zealand. They need a commander. You, Sir, or your brother Prince James? If this fleet were to sail into the Thames, we have evidence that Essex and Kent will both rise.'

'That's more like it.' The Prince of Wales smiled for the first time in many months. 'Ma'am, Gentlemen, this time justice, and the traditions that define nationhood these last millennia, shall win.'

*

In the event, Prince Charles had needed little persuasion to take command. In September, he took ten warships across the German Ocean, or the North Sea as Parliament preferred to call it, into the Thames estuary.

Informers, however, were everywhere and news of his adventure had reached the 'generals' of the English 'sea-army'.

A Parliamentarian fleet sailed from Chatham to confront and confine him. The two fleets began to find their battle positions but, as luck would have it, were driven apart by a providential storm which took them all back out to sea.

The royalist fleet eventually regrouped but the Prince of Wales's attempts to support the uprisings in East Anglia and Kent had been thwarted.

The prince returned to the Netherlands, where he decided not to try that again. He handed control of his fleet to his favourite cousin, Prince Rupert of the Palatinate.

*

Chapter Twenty-Two
Royal Nemesis

Nothing in either statute or common law existed in all of England's history that could deal with the trial of a monarch. That did not unduly trouble Colonel Pride, the ferociously Parliamentarian High Commissioner. In early January 1649 he unearthed a Dutch lawyer, another arch-Protestant called Isaac Dorislaus. He diagnosed that this God-fearing fellow would suffer neither aversion nor reluctance to inventing a crime, even in retrospect, and one that would apply to one man alone. Nor did it bother him that the king would be found to have committed it, and that the trial already knew its verdict. Perhaps his fee, ten thousand golden guineas, influenced his judgement?

Blood allowed him a week to complete this work.

'I will find a precedent,' said Dorislaus. 'It may not be modern. I will find it in either in the Old Testament or in ancient Rome.'

'And if neither, you will just have to conjure one up from scratch,' Pride replied.

Westminster Hall was to be set up as Parliament's 'Court of Justice'. Its presidency was awarded to John Bradshaw, a man whose earlier career never had never risen above the ranks of those jobbing lawyers who petitioned for business outside the courts. This was his lucky beak. While he agreed to the enormous fee, he still feared for his life. He had his hat lined with steel.

Every one of the four hundred judges in England, from Penzance to Berwick, from Carlisle to Rochester, was summoned to London to serve as a jury. In the event, fewer than seventy turned up, even for the initial swearing-in. Half of them complained it was a travesty of justice. Their point was that the supposed 'crime' was drafted *ad hominem*, contrary to every principle of law. Monarchy as such was not a crime, they said.

Such protests were ruled inadmissible by Pride and Bradshaw.

Westminster Hall had been booked for a week. The king would be present throughout. He would be permitted to plead and hear his sentence pronounced, but there could not be any prospect of an acquittal.

Bradshaw began the formal process by reading out the charge, that the king had 'traitorously and maliciously levied war against the present Parliament and the people therein represented'. Some thought this ironic, given that the army had abolished elections to the Commons and that every member of the Rump was now an army appointee.

The king's war on the Puritans and their fellow-travellers was, Bradshaw continued, 'born out of wicked design'.

Colonel Pride prevented any Commissioners, formerly known as 'Members of Parliament', from entering Westminster Hall unless they had privately sworn to vote for the king's execution. In the end, of the forty-six 'jurors' allowed in, just twenty-six agreed to Pride's line. That would have to do. At least it was more than the twelve of a regular jury.

'Stuart renewed the Civil War', Bradshaw told them, 'even after his military defeat. His objective was and always has been to uphold a personal interest in Will, Power and Prerogative that he and his family have had against the public interest, common right, liberty, justice and peace of the people of this nation'.

His tone was smooth and persuasive.

'I ask you, noble jurors, on behalf of the yeomen and freeholders of England, to impeach the king as a tyrant, a traitor, a murderer, and a public and implacable enemy to the Commonwealth.'

The king was now invited to plead innocent or guilty. Instead, he asked if might first ask the Commissioners a question. Bradshaw conferred with his fellows.

'Yes. Charles Stuart may address the court.'

Still seated, the king addressed the hearing in the first person singular. He had dropped the royal 'we'. 'It is not a style that suits a divided nation,' he had said earlier.

'As I do not recognise this court,' he began, 'I will not defend myself. Nor shall I take off my hat for these 'judges' who sit over me.'

This seemed to confirm that the king was as arrogant as ever and, therefore, as much a danger as before.

'May I know by what lawful power I am here?' he continued from the dock. 'There are many unlawful authorities in the world. Thieves and robbers on the highways are one. This one is not dissimilar.'

He stood and addressed Bradshaw directly.

'I am your lawful king. You bring sins upon your heads and the judgement of God upon this land. Think on this before you progress from the lesser sin to the greater. God, with my old legitimate and documented descent, have singled me out for divine purpose. I hold the kingship not as a man but as a line, in an eternal trust, and I will not betray that trust to answer an illegitimate authority.'

Charles was said to have a pronounced stammer but that day no one in that great hall heard a hint of it. The king stood and waited while it became slowly clear to the paying crowd that the Commissioners had no ready answer.

After a long pause the king pressed on. 'I do not submit to this Court. I stand as much for the privilege of the House of Commons, rightly understood, as any man here. Without the House of Lords, this is no Parliament. Show me a legal authority, warranted by the Word of God, the Scriptures, or by the constitutions of these kingdoms and I will answer my accusers.'

He took a long and steely look around Westminster Hall. The gallery was packed with soldiers. Were they there to protect the judges from loyal subjects in the pews?

Charles waited. As none of his accusers spoke, he resumed.

'Be warned that what you do is not slight. My duty to God and my country is to keep the peace. That I will do, until my last gasp. You might consider satisfying first God and then the country, and tell these witnesses by what authority you proceed.'

Again, no one stirred.

'If it were only my own case, a protest against this Court would have satisfied me. The fact that a king cannot be tried by any superior jurisdiction on earth would have been defence enough. However, the freedom and liberty of the people of England are in this dock beside me, and I stand more for their liberties than you do. Power outside law may make 'laws', may even alter the fundamental basis of the kingdom, but when that happens no subject in England can be sure of his life or anything else he calls his own.

'My plea is for the people of England. I have never imposed a belief upon any man and, for that matter, the Commons of England was never a Court of Jurisprudence; I would fain know how it comes to be so today.'

Among the many witnesses of the trial was General Cromwell. Colonel Pride caught his eye. The general snorted but signalled the accused's statement should be allowed to stand.

The king resumed.

'I took up arms for the people's laws, liberty, and freedom. For the charge, and as a man, I value it not a jot. As your king, I ask all the people of England to uphold justice and maintain the old laws.'

The sheer bravura of the king's statement had taken the court's breath away but Bradshaw, knowing of the outcome of the trial, rose easily to the occasion.

'Charles Stuart, the court still hears you, but you are taking advantage of our patience. Please bring your speech to a conclusion and sit, Sir.'

'So be it,' said the king. 'I have little more to say in any case. All that I hold dearer than life has been taken from me already, except my conscience and my honour. If I had respected my life more than the peace and liberty of the kingdom, then I should have defended myself. Perhaps I might have rebutted the ugly sentence which you will pass upon me. However, the reverse applies.'

He looked Bradshaw straight in the eye.

'That hasty sentence may sooner be repented than recalled. If I cannot have English justice, I protest that these shows of 'liberty and peace' are mere pretence and that you will not hear from your king again.'

When the king sat down, Bradshaw stood.

'Charles Stuart, this is not a common Court of Law. This is the highest Court of Justice of the land,' he said. 'We need not call a meeting of the Lords and the Commons to hear what the former king has to say. We have all heard, seen and suffered in his war on the Protestant Commoners of England. We shall proceed directly to sentence.'

The king, seated, seemed unaffected. He had long known the 'assembly' was not to determine his innocence or guilt.

He did not have long to wait. Still seated, the jobbing lawyer addressed the king directly.

'There is a contract, a bargain made between a king and his people. His coronation oath is central to it,' he said. 'The bond is reciprocal, for as you are the liege lord, your people are liege subjects. This tie, this bond, is the one due from a sovereign, that of protection. Likewise so is the bond of subjection that is due from the subject. Sir, if this bond be broken, farewell sovereignty! These things may not be denied. Whether you have been, by your office, a protector or a destroyer of England, let all England, or all the world, judge that hath looked upon us. You say you disavow us as a Court. Therefore for you to address yourself to us, while not acknowledging us as a Court, is paradoxical. The truth is, all along, from the moment you were pleased to disown us, this Court did not need to listen to one single word from you.' He glanced at Oliver Cromwell. 'This Court adjudges that the present Charles Stuart be Tyrant, Traitor, Murderer and Public Enemy to the good people of this

Nation. Sir, you shall be put to death, by the severing of your head from your body.'

'May I speak, Sir, now that you have pronounced a sentence without even asking the jurors for their verdict?'

'No, Sir, you may not. In law you are already dead. Take him away.'

The King of England was bundled out of the court by Cromwell's model soldiery.

'If your king is not suffered to speak,' he was heard to say, 'imagine the justice lesser people will have.'

The death warrant was circulated for signature among the Commissioners. Bradshaw wanted a unanimous verdict, but by the end of the week - January 27 – only fifty-eight of them had sealed it. Nine refused and a certain John Downes was one. He argued that Parliament should have been called to hear the king's final negotiation.

It was ruled that there was to be no clemency of any kind.

Downes, much later, recalled that he had done his best.

'I could do no more. I was single, alone. Indeed I ought not to have been there in the first place.'

*

King Charles's execution would take place on the Tuesday. Monday night had been frosty and, as dawn broke, the king was allowed to go for a last walk in St James's Park with his faithful spaniel. When he returned he found his execution had been delayed. No one knew until when. He spent what was left of the morning discussing eschatological issues with the Anglican Bishop of London, Dr Juxon.

At last, the roundhead Colonel Hacker presented himself and led King Charles towards his martyrdom. They walked through the park. A regiment of foot accompanied them, some in front, some behind, flying their colours, beating their drums.

The lifeguards and some of his gentlemen walked bareheaded with him. Dr Juxon followed his king half-a-pace behind, as did his jailer, Colonel Tomlinson. They accompanied their king from the park, up the stairs into Whitehall Palace, passing through a gallery into the Banqueting House. There he was ordered to wait.

The king, *fidei defensor*, had asked for an overshirt before his execution. He was worried that if he shivered in the cold, the crowd might think him frightened. It was January, after all, and it had been snowing.

It was impossible not to notice the scaffold outside. It was covered in black cloth.

Though he had been expecting to meet his Maker shortly after dawn, it was nearly two o'clock in the afternoon before King of England, Ireland and the Scots (and pretender to the Kingdom of France) was led out onto the fatal platform.

The 'Tyrant, Traitor and Murderer; a Public and Implacable Enemy to the Commonwealth of England' now knelt on the platform in prayer.

He had refused to dine before receiving the Sacrament of Extreme Unction but, at noon, his gaolers had brought him a last meal of bread and claret. The fitness and poetry of this gesture had never occurred to them.

The Frenchman who had been commissioned to execute the king had refused to do so. So did several other candidates. It wasn't until the early afternoon, and for the huge fee of £100, a headsman and his assistant were found. The executioner was a pork butcher, a member of the Blake tribe, who had declared he would use the fee to buy a public house in faraway Galway City. He had a long and substantial curved cleaver which served him well in his abattoir. Despite the celebrity that he would otherwise have attained, he and his assistant wisely donned masks.

Out on the scaffold, outside the new Banqueting House, the king looked very seriously at the block.

'Does it have to be so low,' he asked Colonel Hacker.

'It will do its task well enough,' replied the Puritan colonel. He indicated the crowd. 'You are permitted to speak.'

Charles turned to the hundreds of thousands of his subjects gathered in the great thoroughfare that led through the royal palace of Whitehall. Several companies of the New Model Army were shepherding the masses. Companies of horse corralled the crowds on the King's Street and Charing Cross sides.

Parliament knew it was taking a risk – the king spoke well – but they also knew that the crowd's shushing, the rustle of their Sunday best and their coughing, wheezing and commentating meant that His Majesty's voice would carry little distance.

'I know,' the king told those subjects within earshot, 'that the liberty and freedom of a people is celebrated by Parliament, but it is the Law that protects that people's lives and property. If I had surrendered, allowing the Law to be changed to suit the Power of the Sword, I would have survived. My refusal, therefore, makes me the people's martyr.'

The block was in the middle of the platform. By it stood the headsman with his strange axe. After a brief glance at it the king continued.

'I shall be very little heard by anybody here. I shall therefore direct my words to those of you nearest to me. I speak, only because if not, some men might think that I accepted guilt as well as punishment. I do not. I do not need to insist long upon my innocence, for all the world knows that I never did begin the war with Parliament. God, to whom I must shortly make an account, knows that I never meant to encroach upon their privileges. Guilt began when Parliament, protesting that the army was mine, thought it right to take it from me. So, as guilt is laid against me, I know that God will acquit me. At that heavenly court I shall not blame the Houses of Parliament; other than to say that they must free themselves. God forbid I am so poor a Christian as to claim God's judgment falls only on me. So many times is justice repaid with an unjust sentence that it is almost a commonplace. I will only say this, that as Lord Strafford was unjustly served, I am equally so.'

The officers on the scaffold bowed to the king. They meant to say that he might continue his speech to the crowd, a silent crowd, its tears running freely. Far more heard his words than anyone might have predicted.

The king turned a little, raising his hand in the direction of Bishop Juxon. Those closest cradled their ears to hear his words.

'This venerable man will bear witness that I have forgiven all the world, even those that have been the chief causes of my death. I pray that they too repent, for they commit a great sin. Let not God, with St Stephen, put this too early to their charge. They may still take the right way to the Peace of the Kingdom of Heaven.'

He paused. He had noticed a figure standing behind Bradshaw, a brooding, ugly, warted Parliamentarian. Nothing about him suggested compassion.

The king turned to the headsman, who was testing the sharpness of the blade with his finger.

'Ne pas faire mal à la hache qui pourrait me faire du mal.' He continued in French, believing it to be the man's native tongue. 'Hurt not the axe, that may hurt me. The laws of the land should have told you that. Because it concerns myself, I only allow you that one touch of it.'

An astonished laugh rippled the multitude, but as it was born it died.

The headsman was puzzled. It seemed that but no one had told the king that his nemesis would not come from France but from Galway.

The Bishop of London saw that the king was ready for his transition.

'Will Your Majesty,' he said in a shaking voice, 'whose affections to religion are well known, say something Godly for the world's satisfaction?'

'I thank you heartily, my lord. I declare before you all that I die a Christian, according to the profession of the Church of England, as I found it left me by my father. I go from a corruptible to an incorruptible Crown.'

The king then turned to the executioner.

'Faites attention de ne me faire pas du mal.'

Then Colonel Hacker came too close to the axe and broke the king's chain of thought.

'Take heed of the axe,' the king told him angrily. 'Stand away, sir. Mind that axe.'

He turned to the executioner.

'Je ne dirai que des prières courtes. Coupez quand je mets les mains comme ça. Juxon, my night-cap, if you please. *Monsieur le bourreau, les cheveux vous dérangent?'*

The executioner seemed not to understand. Was he deaf?

'It would be best to put your hair into your bonnet, Sire,' said Dr Juxon.

The king tucked his luxurious locks into his woven cap.

'Good Dr Juxon, mine is a life spent in the service of a gracious God.'

'Sire, there is but one stage more, a turbulent and troublesome one but it is short. It will carry you a very great way. It will carry you from Earth to Heaven. There you shall find infinite joy and comfort.'

'Where there is neither disturbance nor corruption.'

'A good exchange, Your Majesty.'

'Les cheveux vont bien?'

The headsman again said nothing but Dr Juxon reassured the king that his hair would not obstruct the passage of the axe.

Dr Juxon helped the king with his cloak. He gave Juxon his 'george'. Several people heard him say, 'remember'[xlv].

The king removed his doublet, unaided. He was in his waistcoat. Looking at the block, he turned to the executioner.

'Ça ne bougera pas?'

'It's as steady as the rock of Calvary, Your Majesty,' the Bishop of London replied on behalf of the executioner.

'C'aurait dû être plus élevé.' It was so low the king would almost have to lie on the ground.

304

'*Ça n'était pas pratique, majesté.*' A taller one would not have been practical.

Still talking to an apparently mute executioner, the king pressed a gold ducat into his hand.

'*Quand je mets les mains comme ça,*' he said, spreading his hands out, '*Faites votre devoir.*'

The king then murmured a few words. He then stooped and laid his neck on the block.

'*Attendez mon signe.*'

'Wait for His Majesty's sign, good fellow,' Hacker told the Galwayman.

The executioner heard the king address his Maker for the last time.

'Into Thy hands, O Lord, I commend my spirit,' were the words he murmured.

After the shortest of pauses, the king stretched out his hands and, with one expert blow, the executioner severed his head from his body.

What a horrible, terrible cry welled from the crowd! Gasp and moan combined in three hundred thousand throats. They had witnessed the fall of the last of the line of sovereigns that had begun with King Arthur, if not King David. History itself had been fractured.

They had been told that England was to be a 'Republic'. It was an alien word, one that only scholars had used before. It was also a Godless word, in that it severed the connection between the monarch and the Creator. By removing the limitations of the throne, it unleashed ambition, fear and envy in equal measure, suggesting that the man on your left, or your right, might seek the power to make laws and sentence his neighbours to prison or death. Perhaps in a Republic, that man might be your neighbour, even yourself?

The headsman then stooped, picked the royal head from its basket and held it high. It still bled. He had been ordered to show the crowd that their monarchy, that institution that had built a unified nation out of a few remaining Romano-British, and many Saxons, Jutes, Angles, Celts, Vikings and Normans – once simply warring tribes before the monarchs of the kingdom had engineered their integration - was at last extinct.

Or was it? The king's eyelids still fluttered in his supposedly lifeless head.

Charles would not find dignity, even in death. The New Model Army allowed spectators to go up to, even under the scaffold and, after handing the sergeants a silver coin, dip their handkerchiefs into the royal blood. The public was still, after all this time and all that their preachers and pastors had told them, idolatrous enough to believe the sacred blood of an anointed king would cure a wound or illness.

If the Parliamentarians believed that the regicide had resolved the issues that underlay the Civil War they were mistaken. History would argue for all time if the crowd had witnessed the death of a tyrant or merely an act of treason and impiety.

The king's body and head were reunited in a black velvet covered coffin. The Palace Guard carried the royal remains in silence to his lodgings of the night before.

The coffin would be buried at Windsor, rather than Westminster Abbey, to avoid public disorder. To prevent the proclamation of the Prince of Wales, the Commissioners passed a Bill (or ordinance) that very day forever forbidding the succession of another monarch. It was 'enacted' by the High Commissioners a week later.

England was now a Republic. One where Parliament ignored the implicit hubris and styled itself 'sovereign'.[xlvi]

'The office of the king in this nation is unnecessary, burdensome and dangerous to society, the public interest and the liberty of the people,' Bradshaw had declared.

A 'Council of State' replaced the Crown. Commissioner Oliver Cromwell was elected one of its number.

Of course, Charles I's execution did not end the conflict. The English and Scottish Protestant forces in Ulster, only ever in an uneasy alliance, now filed for divorce. Up to the execution the Ulster Protestants had been led by the Scottish Covenanters, based in Carrickfergus and supported by an informal settler army based around the town they liked to call Londonderry. Now they divided into Royalist and Parliamentary factions.

Many English settlers, like Sir Charles Coote, had sided with Parliament, mostly because they disliked the Royalists' conciliatory overtures to Irish Catholics. That, and the fewer people who shared Ireland's wealth, the better.

The 'king-in-exile', the former Prince of Wales, had powerful allies in France and Spain. No Royalists would accept that the war was over; instead, they needed to prepare for the return of a King of England.

*

As the news of the regicide reached Paris, Ormonde sought an immediate audience of the young King of France. He discovered Cardinal Mazarin already in attendance, wholly aware of the shocking news from London.

'If England sees fit to depose its anointed rulers in a brutal display of *grand guignol*, Your Majesty,' the cardinal advised the eleven-year-old monarch, 'then we should act now. We should take the case to the Regency Council.'

Ormonde was still on one knee when began to put the kernel of his plan to the two princes. He rose.

'May I beg leave to advise Your Majesty and Your Eminence to proclaim the Prince of Wales to be King Charles II of England, Ireland and the Scots?'

'If our ministers have no objection,' the boy-king replied, 'that is exactly what we shall do. Stand up, Lord Ormonde. With this regicide, England has done a grave thing. Every nation in the world will notice their safest institutions, those that bind them and offer them the laws that make them secure, have been undermined by this savagery. What displeases us most is that this royal murder was disguised as a legal process. We have quite enough hot heads in our beloved nation of France. Unless the repudiation is immediate and effective, they might even begin to nurse similar ideas.'

Cardinal Mazarin addressed Lord Ormonde directly.

'Our princely predecessor[12] had ideas of overturning the English administration of Ireland when he sent General O'Neill there with such immense provisions. Is it your belief that you could assist in the restoration of the Stuart dynasty?'

'Yes, Eminence, it is. Without the old king, the Irish Confederates will now be far more amenable to compromise. I shall try to unite everyone behind King Charles II.'

'Well, *mon cher marquis*,' said the king, 'allow us a little time for our Regency Council to deliberate. We firmly suspect that the Council will vote you a sufficient supply of arms and ammunition.'

'But the cost, Sire?' the Cardinal queried.

'Eminence, you must be easily the richest man in France,' replied the boy-king. 'We are confident that your patronage will extend to the defence of the system of government that we have enjoyed in France even before the time of Saint Louis. Those poor languishing idiots in England, who have committed the worst crime imaginable - even by the

---

[12] He meant Richelieu.

standards of the Old Testament – will, in the end, rejoice at the restoration of their monarchy.'

*

With the support of king and cardinal ringing in his ears, Lord Ormonde returned immediately to Ireland. Sailing so early in spring was hard, but in March he landed at Cobh, near Cork.

He was met by Lord Mountgarrett, and the cousins returned to Kilkenny to negotiate. Ormonde began intelligently, by noting who, in the tectonic shifts within the Confederacy, had emerged as a leader. The Damascene conversion of Lord Inchiquin amazed him, everyone, but by Easter Ormonde had invited Lord Inchiquin to merge his forces with the Confederacy.

Holy Week saw his new treaty concluded. It ensured the unfettered practice of Catholicism. Terms of the new Ormonde Peace were amended to allow Catholics to practice their rite quite openly, even in churches, to which, at long last, Ormonde attached his seal. This had been a major stumbling block on the road to peace.

He held a Privy Council in one of Kilkenny Castle's four towers. He had a surprise but very welcome guest. Admiral and lieutenant-general Prince Rupert of the Palatinate had been formally commissioned chief of Charles II's naval forces in March 1649.

When Prince Rupert of the Palatinate arrived in Kinsale harbour, he had learned of the judicial murder of the king and the declaration of the Commonwealth of England. Rupert swore vengeance on the regicides, whom he regarded as common murderers.

He made his way at some speed to Kilkenny, leaving a substantial fleet in Kinsale harbour.

Prince Rupert had secured a significant fleet, which carried a considerable number of Irish Royalist troops with him from Helvoetsluys. His flagship was the 40-gun *Constant Reformation,* whose captain was the Royalist veteran Richard Fielding. Moored alongside was the 40-gun *Convertine,* which housed as vice-admiral his brother Prince Maurice. In the 36-gun Swallow was his rear-admiral Sir John Mennes. Other ships in the squadron included the 30-gun *Guinea,* sometimes called the *Charles,* the 34-gun *James,* the *Thomas,* the ketch *Mary* and the *Elizabeth.*

Two other ships, the 14-gun *Roebuck* and the 18-gun *Blackamoor Lady* had already been diverted to search for prizes, as had the three large

Dutch Indiamen which had sailed with the squadron to protect it from pirates and privateers.

It had been an exciting voyage. During their voyage down the English Channel, the Royalists had driven off Vice-Admiral Moulton's squadron near Dover and captured five English merchantmen as prizes.

Rupert' soldiers were now housed in the Confederate castle yard and Ormonde planned to merge them with Confederate army, now (at least in theory) under his command.

After some further debate, and in the absence of the unlamented *nuncio*, all agreed to Ormonde's plans. The Confederacy was dissolved and replaced with a Confederate-Royalist alliance. It agreed to supply the Restoration Cause with 18,000 Confederate troops. That, having been Ormonde's sole aim, concluded the business of the meeting.

As the retiring President and the titular Lord Lieutenant were now on the same team, the war between them was ended. The need for the separate government evaporated as if it had never been fought over.

Nine years of Confederacy were history.

In England, news of Ormonde's treaty and Prince Rupert's arrival in Kinsale with half the Royal Navy, greatly alarmed the Commissioners. The more so after it had disbanded the victorious New Model Army and the 'adventurers' army' it had wanted to invade Ireland. A rash of Puritan uprisings at home – notably those of the Levellers – had thrust the Irish issue into the background.

Still, the news of Ormonde's aggregated army as it advanced on Dublin was hard to ignore. The first task facing the military rulers of England was to pacify its soldiers. While due back pay, many of them could be let go to fend for themselves. That done, the High Commissioner could engage a trusted officer to initiate a final and thorough subjugation of Ireland. They already had one in mind.

His name was Oliver Cromwell, the recently promoted Commissioner for War.

He was just the man, filled with righteous Puritan anger. He believed that Roman Catholics were Satan's spawn. Just the man for the job.

*

In Kilkenny Castle, Lord Lieutenant Ormonde, recently confirmed in his old title by the king-in-exile, looked magnificent, every inch the unreformed, unrepentant cavalier. He was forty years old. His head bore a grand wig, in a youthful auburn colour, which flowed down his chest. Over his shoulders he wore the blue garter robes that King Charles II had awarded him in Paris. He wore a soft, cream chemise, whose baggy sleeves finished in limp but lavish Belgian lace cuffs. Italian craftsmen had illuminated his waistcoat with designs in pearls and filigree gold. His voluminous pantaloons, descending only halfway down his thighs, were in the same decorated silk as his waistcoat. Beneath them, silk hose passed under his noble garter and continued to his well-heeled court shoes; no buckles, no leather - these slippers, made in damask, were never meant to experience the open air.

His appearance told both of authority and its rewards.

'Since I will not entertain an assault on the capital with heavy artillery, it is to our disadvantage that Dublin's walls are quite beyond repair,' Ormonde patiently explained to his councillors. At first, not all of them quite understood.

Everyone had to stand; there were no chairs. On a long table were Speed's celebrated maps, easily the best in Ireland, published as recently as 1610 and meticulously accurate.

'While our siege is relatively effective, the breaks in the city walls allow Parliamentarian rebels to find some food and water. To think,' Ormonde mused, 'while I was resident I made such efforts to restore them? My wife even organised a phalanx of fashionable ladies to carry baskets of earth and hods of bricks. How they helped the labourers on the ramparts! Few men will ever again see such a sight! Yet, despite their patriotic efforts, repairs proceeded with extreme *lenteur*. The Parliamentarians should be grateful to me.'

'I don't quite understand, my lord. Surely we should attack without further ado?' suggested Lord Castlehaven, a leading member of Ormonde's war cabinet.

'When we take Dublin the rest of Ireland will fall like a set of skittles,' Major-General Purcell agreed. 'Would the young king consider having his throne in Ireland? Perhaps he'll reign from Dublin as King of Ireland?'

'You must believe how hard I tried to persuade Her Majesty the Queen to allow her son to come to Ireland. There is something of an Irish community in Paris and I was a member of it. It was as keen as mustard to help but, despite our eloquence and pleading, it came to nothing. Henrietta-Maria was far too concerned for her son's safety to permit such a risky venture. Instead, the young king himself ordered me home to command his people against the rebel lackeys of the 'Commonwealth'.'

'We have second best, though!'

'Do you mean me?' Ormonde was momentarily wrong-footed. 'No, of course, I am a dolt. You intend His Serene Highness Prince Rupert, Count Palatine of the Rhine, Duke of Bavaria, Duke of Cumberland, Earl of Holderness and the king's nephew. The great gentleman quietly standing behind my right shoulder.'

He was right. Rupert was the very epitome of a cavalier. He was impossibly handsome. His claret red hair was long and unconfined, his eyes dark and seductive. At this meeting his crimson gown was draped across his shoulders, fastened with gold buttons halfway down his chest beneath an ample cravat. Resting on his shoulders, around his neck, was the elaborate gold chain of a Count Palatine.

The more observant in the chamber would also have seen that he wore his princely seal, an enormous thing on a golden rope, over his red satin overshirt, which fastened at his waist. Beneath, the crimson theme continued in blood-red damask as far as his gold slippers. In his right hand he carried a riding crop, a piece of flawless craft in varnished rosewood. He wore no other jewellery, no signet ring, no diamonds. Not even a sword.

Rupert was, of course, the grandson of James I. His very blood owed the Stuarts its bluish strain. Everyone in Kilkenny had been formally presented to discover his exquisite manners. They were left in awe.

'What delightful and providential wind brought you to us, dear Prince?' Lord Ormonde continued unctuously. 'Your landing at Kinsale with your fleet of warships may yet turn the tide!'

'Yes. How did you manage that, Highness?' asked Sir William Vaughan. 'Where did they come from?'

'They are what's left of the Royal Navy,' the prince answered, a subtle German accent lending colour to his faultless English. 'We are the beneficiaries of last year's naval revolt, when half the Royal Navy defected to the Royalist cause. My plan is to take the fleet to Wexford and join the Irish privateers against England's merchant shipping. We can starve the Protestants out of Dublin. Lord Lieutenant?'

The Marquess of Ormonde leant forward. He rested his hands on the table to speak more forcibly.

'I must inform you all that the so-called Commonwealth of England is already in secure communication with Dublin. Keeping the Irish Sea free of Commonwealth shipping for long will not be easy. The English have freely and authoratively patrolled the Irish Sea since the beginning of the year, despite having lost most of the loyal Royal Navy. They may call the remnant a 'Sea Army' but what's in a name? It's smaller, true, but still a lethal menace. Their fleet, under General-at-Sea Robert Blake, comprises ten brand new battleships, mostly built in Woodbridge. They own the shipping lanes and defend them very thoroughly. Our privateers are useless against them, but would regain the seas were we to reinforce them.'

Rupert simply nodded.

'Woodbridge? That's in Suffolk!' exclaimed Lord Castlehaven. 'Isn't that on the wrong coast?'

'It's on the east coast, quite right, but at the moment the Commissioners' greatest fear is an invasion from France. King Louis has just declared the King-in-Exile to be England's rightful Head of State.'

'If we can't have command of the sea', continued Ormonde, 'we can still make life uncomfortable for the Saxons. Over here our Coalition looks very likely to overwhelm the Parliamentarian rebels. We have successfully wrested surrender from Sir Charles Coote's garrisons at Derry and Sligo. Our new Scottish friends in south-east Ulster have blockaded the enemy Colonel Monck in Dundalk. The biggest fly in our ointment is home-grown. The great Colonel-General Owen Roe O'Neill still refuses to join us. He's holding out for a purely Catholic Ireland. I have sent Inchiquin to talk some sense into him, as we speak. Castlehaven, you are to join forces with Inchiquin, and for the same reason.'

*

The town of Kilkenny lies on the Nore, which flows beneath its walls. Where the river laps its banks, across the John Street Bridge from the Castle, there is a fine tavern.

That sundown, Lord Castlehaven and his ADC, Major Bryen MacDonogh, were in it, sipping at their mugs of stout.

'It seems we're going north, Bryen. Lord Inchiquin will join us there. We are ordered to persuade Owen Roe to join our party.'

'Ah. Is that so? I'd been hoping we might be staying on here a little longer. I hate being far from little Sorcha. Presumably this is Lord Ormonde's idea? Anyway, why bother with O'Neill? He's a good man, if a little too pious. He'll come around. Everyone says Dublin is in too poor a condition to survive a prolonged siege. Why don't we just take Dublin without him? An assault would give us the capital tomorrow!'

'Even within these four walls, I must disagree.'

'Disagree? I've heard the town is completely threadbare?' It had been a while since Bryen had been in the capital. 'Is it not true? Could it withstand an assault? You've been there more recently than I. What do you think?'

312

'I was there a month ago. You are right, at least in part. You're correct that the walls are mostly ruined and the town's close to starving. Nevertheless, an assault with artillery would kill many hundreds and would breed resentment for countless generations. Much better that they surrender of their own accord, and very soon they will. They are actually hunting wolves along Dame Street. If Ormonde lets the siege do its work, in the long term he'll save many Irish lives. The Castle itself is out of provisions. Ordnance, too. When I was there it was said to be down to seven barrels of gunpowder. A thorough siege would bring a bloodless surrender and the people would come rejoicing to our side.'

'Parliament's new man? Colonel What's-his-name? The Welshman'.

'Michael Jones, Theophilus's brother. He complains non-stop that his chalice has been poisoned. Even though he has 7,500 men in the garrison he says the capital is for practical purposes defenceless– '

' – but that's an incredible increase since Lord Strafford's time – '

'Yes, but they are poorly fed, irregularly paid and close to mutiny. Parliament's hold is weak.' Castlehaven put his empty tankard down. He caught the serving girl's eye and circled his finger over the empty mugs. 'Dublin, Trim, Drogheda, Dundalk and Derry; that's all Jones has left.'

'Colonel Jones celebrated our Royalist Lord Lieutenant's departure from Ireland by expelling all Catholics from the capital.'

'Hardly all. Only those in office.'

The Anglicans next?'

'Perhaps. Away from Dublin, most of the country is Royalist. Except O'Neill, it seems. He's as stubborn as ever. He won't forgive the royal family for being Anglican. He says they are apostate!'

'Why didn't Ormonde act sooner?' asked Bryen. 'He was in England for months.'

'He had to see the late king. Only through a private audience might he learn how he could help his king *in extremis*.'

'But he didn't come home after his audience. He sailed for France. Was it to avoid impeachment?'

'I don't suppose his time in Parisian exile was unpleasant, but when the monarch was murdered it left Ormonde no choice. In the terrible circumstances, he had to return to Ireland and undo the damage he had done by abandoning its capital.'

'He's already done quite a lot to put things right, hasn't he? He lost no time in recognising the Prince of Wales as King Charles II, even in exile. The prince made him a Knight of the Garter by way of thanks. Murrough 'of the Burnings' abandoned the Parliamentary cause and threw his lot in with us. He's dissolved the Confederacy and united the

313

Royalists with the Catholics. Lord Inchiquin has brought his Protestant Army of Munster into our fold.'

'But Jones is still in Dublin and O'Neill is still a loose cannon.'

'This war is far from over, isn't it? I'd like some action. That or home to Duhallow.'

'Patience, Bryen. It's only a couple of months since the marquess finished negotiating a new 'Ormonde Peace'. Now we all believe in toleration, religious freedom. This new coalition has found 18,000 troops ready to wear the king's colours against the Rump Parliament. Rebuilding Royalist power in Ireland will take time but you'll be in Dublin when the capital falls into our hands. That will end the war. Then you'll be free to go home and play 'happy families'.'

In mid-March, 1649, Lord Castlehaven and his ADC took their army onto the Leinster Road for the far north. They had not travelled long before a messenger in Ormonde's livery drew level with Castlehaven, reared his horse dramatically and gave him vital news.

'Lord Inchiquin has brought his Munster army to Cashel, Sir. He plans to continue his march all the way to Athlone. He has orders to intercept O'Neill and prevent him from moving west into Connacht.'

'It seems', said Bryen, 'that O'Neill is threatened by Inchiquin's army. The Lord Lieutenant thinks their meeting will be 'energetic'.'

'Thank you, Major.' Castlehaven rode his horse alongside the envoy's. Here's a guinea for your trouble.'

Ormonde's emissary reared his horse in salute and wheeled around. He would regain Lord Ormonde in less than a day if he hurried.

'MacDonogh, we had best make speed if we are to prevent Inchiquin from beating too much sense into O'Neill.'

O'Neill had posted scouts with mirrors in a number of churches *en route*. The news that Castlehaven and Inchiquin were converging on him was sent him by heliophore. He promptly decided against the road to Connacht.

'Have they completely forgotten whose side they are on,' he asked angrily. '17,000 men? Do they really want another civil war? I won't let that happen.'

'But where can we go,' asked his ADC.

'Ulster.'

'Ulster, Sir? Are you serious?'

'Dundalk, to be exact. We'll sue for peace with Colonel Monck. In alliance we shall outnumber Ormonde.'

O'Neill's plan worked perfectly. His messengers reached the Presbyterian Colonel Monck and made him the most friendly and generous overtures. They negotiated a three-month truce and exchanged food and water for Monck's pledge not to embrace the Parliamentarian Army.

Castlehaven and Inchiquin, as they marched their separate roads, secured countless townlands, if not yet Dublin, for the Coalition.

Ormonde, meanwhile, would only focus on the capital itself. The City of the Fairs was still held by Colonel Jones's Parliamentary garrison, made up of thousands of English Roundheads.

The marquess speculated quite accurately as to the serious plight of the city. Unfortunately, he could not know how effectively Jones's delivery of supplies and reinforcements from England was being effected. In fact, the beleaguered garrison was able to strengthen its fortifications. Jones was using his time to prepare for an assault all of his own.

Ormonde, busy with his strategising, made no decisions until the end of the month.

With the Pale subdued, Ormonde's Confederate-Royalists could confidently march on Rathmines, where they encamped on the high ground. He then cut off the water supply (the old city watercourse which starts from the Dodder at Firhouse Weir), thereby depriving Dublin of at least half its drinking water and stopping its corn mills.

While O'Neill kept Ulster quiet with his strange alliance with the Scottish Presbyterians, the king-in-exile's Lord-Lieutenant, the Marquess of Ormonde, attempted to order the Parliamentarian governor of Dublin, Colonel Michael Jones, to surrender. When Jones refused, Ormonde prepared to advance on Dublin itself. His powers of persuasion ought to have been good; on June 1, 1649, he had 11,000 foot and 3,000 horse. His Coalition took up a position at Finglas, on the northern outskirts of the capital.

The Coalition armies' successes inspired the Marquess of Ormonde to write to Colonel Jones.

To the Parliamentarian Governor of Dublin   In Castris, Aestivus,
MLCXXXXIX

May it please Your Excellency, rumours of your skill in battle, Colonel Jones, provoke all Ireland to direct her attention to the City of Dublin and ask for the withdrawal of your Castle Garrison to England. To impress on you, Sir, the importance of your agreement to this request, I have gathered two great armies, under generals Inchiquin and Castlehaven, whose reputation, like yours, carries their standards unaided. We are aware of the condition of the citizens of Dublin, held there by your continuing presence, the shortage of munitions your garrison suffers, and the general superiority in numbers our well-nourished armies can boast.

There has never been support for your cause in Ireland, save in the hearts of a few Englishmen who discover themselves unwilling participants in a rebellious war against our lawful king. Your surrender, by responding to this message to your undersigned servant Ormonde, will demonstrate to us and to history your nobility in the face of overwhelming odds.

Ormonde did not have long to wait. A Parliamentary messenger was with him within the same morning. The message he bore was nothing if not terse.

Colonel Jones presents his compliments to the Marquess of Ormonde but regrets he is unable to accommodate the noble marquess's request.

'Oh well, it's only to be expected. My Lords, Gentlemen, we are to advance against Dublin itself.'

What Jones knew, which as yet Ormonde did not, was that the English 'sea-army' had crossed the Irish Sea to Kinsale where it had blockaded Prince Rupert's fleet in its pretty harbour.

Excepting only a few Irish pirates in Wexford, the sea lanes of the Irish Sea were again under untrammelled English control.

A flaming June blended effortlessly into the blaze of early July. In every sense the heat was on.

'It's well and truly summer,' said Bryen MacDonogh, mopping his brow.

At his Council, Ormonde seemed otherwise unruffled. After all, his Coalition controlled most of the country. The war, one commentator observed, felt a little like a joust. Ormonde and Jones were going to clash. Which one would get out of the other's way in time?

'I have gathered 11,000 foot and 3,000 horse, at Clogrennan, near Carlow, about sixty miles from Dublin. That place will be familiar to you. It's where the Celtic Church used to determine Easter's date. As for the march on the capital, we must wait.'

'What are your plans, Sir?' Impatience coloured Lord Castlehaven's tone. 'There will be a reason why we don't take advantage of our numbers and strike?'

'First, I want the army to occupy Finglas, on Dublin's northern outskirts. Then we'll hold a Council of War to decide whether to attack Dublin immediately or whether we should first take the outlying garrisons of Drogheda, Trim and Dundalk.'

'Have we already concluded, Lord Castlehaven, that Dublin is too well-fortified for a direct assault?' asked Lord Inchiquin.

'Yes. A lengthy siege all around the city's perimeter will stretch our lines too thin. We will leave our armies at risk of attack from any number of the outlying Pale forts.'

'Could we not hold back some of our men? Combine the exercise. Part assault, part siege?' Castlehaven was restless.

Lord Inchiquin, too, seemed to have a plan of his own.

'If you, Lord Ormonde, were to hold back, say, 5,000 foot and 1,800 horse to blockade Dublin, I could advance as far as Drogheda. I could be there in a couple of weeks, give the walls a stern bombardment and demand its surrender.'

'You had better hope they don't return your fire for too long.'

That was Inchiquin's signal to proceed.

Ormonde kept back 5,000 foot and 1,800 horse, quite enough to blockade Dublin, while Lord Inchiquin took the balance and advanced north to Drogheda to lay siege to the picturesque port, now in Parliamentary hands.

It took Inchiquin just ten days to bring his army to Drogheda's gates. Once his field guns were close to the walls he began his cannonade.

After a sustained and dramatic bombardment, Inchiquin's first attempt to scale the walls was repelled. If Inchiquin were disappointed he was patient. The parliamentary garrison returned fire for a while, but when it ran out of ammunition it surrendered. A lethal assault was avoided. Its Protestant defenders were disarmed.

There were terms; most importantly the Protestant soldiers were granted safe conduct as far as Dublin's walls.

Inchiquin called a Council of his senior staff. He was joined by an old and distinguished soldier, seemingly unhampered by a wooden leg, to whom he paid particular and courteous attention.

'Sir Arthur Aston? I know you, Sir, and I welcome you to my command. We've been through much together, you and I.'

'That's right, milord. We share some pleasant memories from the time we fought side by side in the Second Bishops' War,' said Sir Arthur.

'That's it! So we did! You were a lot younger then!' Inchiquin volunteered incautiously.

'That's right. Now I have twice the years and half the legs!'

'What have you done since then?' asked Inchiquin.

'Fought for the Crown, Sir. Gave the king this leg at Marston Moor. A Colonel-General of Dragoons, I was then.'

'Well, Sir, I should like to appoint you to be Drogheda's Governor. What do you say, Sir?

'I shall need a garrison…'

'And you shall have one. We will lend you two thousand of these men. That should ensure your little town is invulnerable.'

'Sir, I accept. Can you spare a couple of officers? One of horse and one of foot?'

'Captain Talbot? Major MacDonogh?'

The two young officers saluted in agreement. Mad Dick Talbot reared his horse in the classical gesture.

Bryen was pleased to be relieved of Lord Inchiquin command. He hadn't forgotten the threats the viscount had made before he saw the light.

'Thank you, Lord Inchiquin,' said Sir Arthur. 'An honour to serve you and His Majesty the king.'

'Of course it is. Enough talk. Sir Arthur, there is your new home. Major MacDonogh, march your men to Drogheda, and Captain Talbot, form a mounted escort for the incoming governor. The rest of you, we're going to Trim. Let's see if they want a fight.'

Trim, barely an hour's ride away, took one look at the force investing their town and hoisted a white flag.

Not even a shot was fired, and it's garrison was given directions to Dublin.

'Now that Trim has surrendered without a fight, Inchiquin has been so kind as to retrieve our artillery back from Drogheda and advance on Dundalk.' Ormonde told his Council. 'Owen Roe O'Neill's unlikely deal with Colonel Monck will prove ineffective. Inchiquin thinks he can talk sense into O'Neill but he will fail. When he and his Catholics return, I shall be ready to make a determined effort to capture Dublin. Not before time, I know. With Inchiquin, I shall take most of my army to Rathmines. You are puzzled, Lord Castlehaven? Rathmines is close to the rotten walls of the capital. It's a charming location for those affected by the new fashion for landscape painting. It's laid out in fields, pastures and tillage, punctuated with cottages and farm houses, and with patches of furze all lying about the castle. From its ramparts, if you look north, you can see into Dublin itself.'

'Charming?' muttered Lord Castlehaven. 'I cab see why painters like it.'

'From there we can and will deny the Parliamentarians access to Dublin's best grazing. Though it will deplete my forces, I shall leave Lord Dillon two thousand foot and five hundred horse to cover the northern approaches to the capital.'

'And if your lordship looks to the south?'

'Then I shall see an unbroken panorama of unfriendly Wicklow hills. That's where 'mountainy' men dwell, my daughter tells me, savages from rude hovels. Gentlemen, learn from her. Never underestimate them; they have for centuries exacted spoils in their all-too-frequent raids on the low-lying fields between them and Dublin.'

'Aren't they a little too close to Colonel Jones?'

'You wouldn't even ask if you saw the roads. Just a few rough lanes and tracks across the fields. The only way of reaching our camp at Rathmines is along a small number of easily defensible lanes.'

Prince Rupert had something to add.

'Rathmines is at most three miles from the coast. Raise our pieces to the battlements, and Parliament's warships should come into range of our cannons.'

Meanwhile. Lord Inchiquin was advancing on the Catholic garrison of Dundalk. He was too late. The implausible alliance between Colonel Monck and Owen Roe O'Neill had already collapsed.

Inchiquin easily corralled most of Colonel Monck's troops, andaccepted the Scot's surrender. Most of his men, more concerned with survival than ideology, now joined Inchiquin's royalists. God alone knew where O'Neill had gone.

'Come on you men,' Inchiquin declared to his victorious commanders. 'Let's get this swollen army back to Rathfarnham, where Lord Ormonde has pitched camp.'

'Rathfarnham?

'Rathfarnham. Three miles south of Dublin Castle, a short mile from Rathmines.'

'Isn't that a fort held by the Parliamentarians?'

'It used to be. Lord Castlehaven delivered it to us last Monday. His army overwhelmingly outnumbered it, and it offered little resistance. Now Lord Ormonde is using it to convene a new Council.'

'I mean to destroy their horse,' Ormonde explained to his generals. 'Starve them out. The English rebels in Dublin Castle graze their cattle and horses on the pastures near Dublin.'

'You want to hamper their cavalry?'

'Hamper it? I mean to eradicate it. Bring me the hero of the hour, Lord Castlehaven. Meanwhile, in his absence, Colonel Armstrong, as Lord Castlehaven's officer commanding, take a regiment of horse, round up and bring back all the livestock you find in those fields and meadows.'

'Of course, my lord. Sir, I should like my ADC to accompany me. He is Colonel Michael Jones's nephew – his sister's son – but has recently come over to our cause.'

'Of course, Colonel. Let us pray that the Holy Ghost will encourage Jones to shoot at you only sparingly.'

The colonel managed a smile.

'Inaccurately will suffice,' he said as he saluted and withdrew.

*

During the spring of 1649, the reinstated General Preston's Lagan Army had laid siege to Sir Charles Coote's garrisons at Derry and Sligo, while Owen Roe O'Neill – now in south-east Ulster - declined all Ormonde's overtures to bring his independent Ulster Army into the Lord Lieutenant's Royalist tent. The Lord Lieutenant reluctantly decided it would be better to leave him to his own devices.

Nor was Colonel Jones a pushover. He was mounting ever more daring and murderous raids on Ormonde's Coalition. Every attempt the Lord Lieutenant made to tighten his hold on Dublin, Jones would frustrate, usually by ambushing Ormonde's squadrons of hunter-killers.

With Prince Rupert's fleet trapped in Kinsale, the Coalition could do nothing to prevent the Parliamentarians from importing supplies and reinforcements from Bristol and Pembroke. Even Wexford's friendly pirates could do little to make the Roundheads less comfortable.

Ormonde's series of assaults on the Pale were taking far too long, especially so when his lookouts spotted the arrival of several 'sea army' battleships, each towing ominously large transports – almost certainly filled with reinforcements of cavalry and infantry, as well as arms and ammunition. With sinking hearts the Irish realised that Jones and Dublin Castle had been relieved.

On 25 July, Ormonde held another Council of War, this time at Rathmines.

'Not one of you will be surprised to learn,' Ormonde began, 'that we have intelligence that an invasion force under High Commissioner Cromwell is preparing, as we speak, to embark from England. Unfortunately our intelligencers don't yet know where the general intends to land. Nevertheless we must act before he arrives.'

'Will Cromwell land in Dublin or in Munster?' Inchiquin asked his chief. 'It won't be Ulster. O'Neill owns the entire province. Even though he mistrusts what he calls your 'pragmatic alliance' of Catholics and Protestants, he will remain in the north and deny the Saxons any chance of landing. Ulster is safe. I should like to take three regiments of horse south into Munster and would appreciate your blessing. From there I can organise Co. Cork's defences. Without my guidance, some of those coastal towns might return to Parliament. If that should happen, Cromwell would have an easy landing.'

'See to it, Lord Inchiquin.'

On July 27, Lord Inchiquin – with his requested regiments of horse – headed south for Youghal, Kinsale and Cork to galvanise the province's defences and prevent the defection of the coastal ports of County Cork.

The summer heat enflamed Ormonde's enthusiasm. At his next Council he ordered Castlehaven to clear the area around Rathmines of any opposition. His own vast army pitched camp in the fields beside the old castle.

Ormonde made an odd decision. 'I have decided we should fortify and occupy Baggotrath Castle[xlvii].'

'Baggotrath? I know it. Sir, it's very small,' Colonel Armstrong observed. 'It's merely a tower house. What in heaven's name can your purpose be?'

'It has a small footprint, it's true, but it's very tall. From its battlements there is line of sight to Ringsend[13], where an English battleship could usefully be moored. Now, Lord Castlehaven, you have already earned my congratulations on taking Rathfarnham. How does Baggotrath Castle look to you?'

---

[13] Ringsend is a port on the south side of the Liffey, close to Dublin.

'It would be well suited to our purposes, Lord Ormonde, being between our camp here at Rathmines and Dublin City,' Lord Castlehaven replied, 'but Armstrong has already been there. Colonel, tell the Lord Lieutenant what you saw.'

'My Lord, I saw that Colonel Jones has almost demolished it. He must have thought he could render it useless to us.'

'Can it be made defensible again? His damage can be undone?'

'I believe it can, Sir.'

'Then we shall use it as an artillery battery. We can build some defences to protect the guns. Our pieces, once on the parapets, will be in range of Ringsend. A few judicious balls should dissuade the Saxons from supplying the Parliamentarians and their remaining allies. General Purcell, you've raised a vast number of engineers - home builders, road layers and the like - for our cause. Take a party of masons and kindred toilers to fortify Baggotrath. How many such men do we have?'

'Perhaps eight hundred, My Lord. Enough to repair the castle overnight in any case.'

'I sincerely hope that's not a vain boast. Have fifteen hundred fusiliers watch their backs. The light is failing now and it's a cloudy sky. It will soon be very dark indeed. You may need a local guide.'

'Sir? Baggotrath is no more than a mile from here.'

'I would still counsel a guide. These lanes are baffling. When I get there tomorrow morning I want to see you in residence and your fortifications well-advanced if not complete. Eight hundred workmen should make good progress through a balmy summer's night. General, I have every confidence in you.'

Ormonde was right about the roads. Major-General Purcell had fifteen hundred men to fortify and secure Baggotrath Castle but, while barely a mile away, there was no direct route. To make matters worse, it was a moonless night. When the narrow lanes – in reality little more than field boundaries - turned north, south, east, west without apparent reason, the challenge was made still harder.

Purcell did employ a local guide, one who claimed to know the way like the back of his hand, but soon he too was lost. It took several hours to cover the mile! Unbelievably, General Purcell only took possession of the ruined castle at sunrise. Work on the fortifications has hardly begun when Lord Castlehaven arrived. General Castlehaven was soon joined by Sir William Vaughan with another two thousand horse – a very welcome sight.

The mood would change a few hours later when Lord Ormonde rode over to see the progress of the work.

He was apoplectic.

'What the hell have you been up to, Purcell? You have had eight hundred sappers here all night! What were they doing? Playing cards?'

'My men arrived here barely an hour before daybreak, My Lord, having been misled by the guide. Stupid or dishonest it matters not; he has since been hanged. Since the distance is so short, treachery must have played its part.'

In the early light the Coalition officers could plainly see that the Welsh Colonel Jones had anticipated the Anglo-Irish marquess. He had dismantled the castle some days before, leaving it in such a sorry state that it was scarcely worth fortifying.

It got worse. Obviously, Jones was well ahead of the game. From the ramparts of Dublin Castle, the English colonel had watched the Irish deploy around the ruins of Baggotrath. He had deduced Ormonde's plan, coming to the conclusion that the Irish could make the castle usable. He realised that if the Royalists set up their guns overlooking Dublin Port then all was lost for his garrison.

He mobilised his entire army and ordered them to march on Baggotrath.

'Now,' he snapped. 'That means this instant!'

When the news of Jones's advance reached Ormonde, the marquess sent a messenger to Lord Dillon at Finglas, desperately ordering him to march his 2,500 soldiers across the Liffey and attack the rear of the advancing Parliamentarians.

Dillon did not reply. He was far too aware that there were several thousand fresh Parliamentarian troops in Dublin who were likely to fall upon his own flank and rear if he tried to march to Rathmines. He would end up being culled.

Yet when he ignored, or pretended not to hear the Lord Lieutenant's cry for help, his decision ended any hope of preventing a complete rout of Ormonde's army.

To be fair, Ormonde was not completely unready. He had already given Castlehaven orders that his whole army should stand to arms to support Purcell and Vaughan at Baggotrath.

Jones, moreover, knew that any delay could prejudice Dublin's future. That was why he decided to strike immediately, although at a superior force, always the best means of defence. He ordered four thousand foot and twelve hundred horse to assemble well beyond Ormonde's most southerly fortifications, at a place called Lowsy Hill.

Lord Castlehaven's intelligencers watched this movement through their spyglasses. They relayed the news to Lord Ormonde, who replied that the Alliance should stand to arms.

The greater part went towards Baggotrath's slighted castle. Some were ordered to plant artillery on nearby Gallows Hill from there they could support Purcell and Vaughan in the event of a Parliamentarian attack.

All Ormonde's regiments were battle ready.

'I'm tired, God help me,' said Ormonde told his commanders, stifling a yawn. 'It's been forty-eight hours since I slept. I've been up all night writing dispatches and assigning positions to my officers. They can spare me forty winks.'

He rode back to his camp to take a catnap.

In doing this he had seriously underestimated Colonel Jones' determination, for this was when Colonel Jones began his attack, intent on disputing Ormonde's occupation of Rathmines and Baggotrath Castles.

Some time after seven in the morning, Jones' entire force crossed the meadows towards Baggotrath. His men were fed, refreshed and ready to put their every sinew into their attack.

The English horse routed Sir William Vaughan's cavalry in its first charge. Vaughan himself was killed, skewered through his armour with a lance and left grotesquely impaled, in the air, as crow bait.

The Parliamentarians then engaged Major-General Purcell's forces. Having the advantage of audacity and surprise, Jones was able to push them back.

As the Roundhead cavalry attacked the Coalition flanks it already looked as if the Irish had lost.

Purcell's infantry held its positions for a while but eventually they were overwhelmed; some were taken prisoner or fled and, of those who ran, most were killed. It is easy work for a mounted man with a sabre to dispatch a man on foot whose terror prevents his self-defence. Being taken prisoner was no guarantee of safety either. The English interviewed their captives. They were told they could join the Parliamentary army if they chose to do so freely. Those that did not do so immediately, some with righteous obstinacy, were hanged on the spot. Jones did not intend to strengthen his regiments with traitors.

Colonel Armstrong's troopers were attacked by a party of Parliamentarian cavalry, who took a number of them prisoner, among them, the young ADC - Colonel Jones' sister's son - who had defected to the Royalists.

The lad would later be hanged as a deserter, in Dublin Castle's Yard, on his uncle's personal orders.

Armstrong quickly regrouped and retreated. He knew that in the absence of Royalist cavalry, there was nothing to stop the Parliamentarian horse from working around to attack the flank and rear of any infantry unit that tried to make a stand. It was better, he opted, to cut his losses at Baggotrath and protect the main camp at Rathmines.

General Purcell woke Ormonde from a deep and exhausted sleep.

'That's cannon fire, Sir!' he said. Ormonde had slept fully dressed. Now he was standing, reaching for his sword.

'It's close! Where the hell is it coming from?' asked Ormonde. His soldier-servant was already helping him don his breast plate.

'Baggotrath, Sir.'

'Our guns are set up, then? We are firing on the enemy?'

'They're not our guns, Sir.'

It dawned on Ormonde he had been caught napping.

'Purcell, order the men to shell the Parliamentarian forces anyway!'

'Our cannons are poorly positioned, Sir. The artillery will have little accuracy.'

'Just do it. Stop fussing. That will do, Paco.' He was impatient with his valet. 'Get out of the way, man.'

Now that he was ready for battle, Ormonde rushed from his tent. Before he could even mount his horse, however, General Purcell, hard on his heels, told him that his vanguard had been beaten out of the ruined castle.

'Colonel Jones, Your Excellency' - Purcell was telling him – 'the English colonel surprised and utterly routed the right wing of our army!'

Ormonde, not needing details, was already on his warhorse. He applied his spurs and rode straight into the fray.

Bravely, though unsuccessfully, he attempted to rally his terrified troops as they ran for their lives. The Parliamentarian advance had been too swift to allow a coherent rearguard to be formed.

Baggotrath had fallen and the Irish retreated towards Rathmines and Ormonde's camp. The English foot advanced on them in squares of pikes and muskets, the cavalry with dripping steel swirling above their heads.

An Irish bombardier fired a last ball at the advancing Parliamentarians before he too ran.

His ball struck ground a few yards away from Jones. The Colonel was unharmed but it blew an English NCO apart, his severed arm knocking Jones from his armoured battle horse.

One of the men who saw it cried that Colonel Jones was dead. This was the sort of disaster that can change the course of history but Jones climbed to his feet.

He had fallen heavily and thought for a moment that he had broken his leg. He yelled at his men to get him back on his horse – in breastplate, backplate and basinet it was hard to do this without help – and then to get back to their deadly work. This they did.

Some of the Royalist army, the closest to Ormonde's camp, had become totally demoralised. When they saw the others in retreat they ran without any attempt to engage the enemy.

At that difficult moment, a large part of Lord Inchiquin's Munster foot appeared, under Colonel Gifford's command. There was time to order it to form a defensive line between Rathmines and Baggotrath. That should deny Jones any opportunity to attack the main Royalist camp.

Meanwhile, the Parliamentary troops were still advancing, field after field. Only when they reached Ormonde's artillery did they halt.

Here Ormonde, with two steadfast regiments, and with Colonel Gifford's infantry, made a determined stand. Unhappily, a squadron of Jones's cavalry had ridden across the country, remaining somehow unseen in the confusion. They outflanked Ormonde.

Now they attacked the Royalists in the rear. A legion of pikes advanced in front towards Ormonde, while muskets and horse protected the march of the Parliamentary squares. Surprised and unable to hear the shouted orders of their officers, the Irish infantry took to its heels.

The Parliamentary juggernaut was relentless, overpowering. Some of Ormonde's men called for quarter, throwing down their arms, while others continued shooting. Someone issued an order to quit the field while Ormonde, contrarily, endeavoured to rally the horse. It was all in vain. All around, Royalists fell from musket ball, pike, sabre and horse's hoof, if not parted from their limbs and lives by cannon ball. Ormonde himself was struck by a musket ball but was saved from injury by his famous armour.

The marquess galloped after his cavalry for twelve miles, always hoping to halt its retreat, but found himself attacked by infantry ahead and cavalry on his flanks and rear. His Royalist infantry fought back, gallantly enough, but after two hours, was forced to surrender. Ormonde realised that he had no longer any alternative but to make good his own escape. He retreated south-west with his squadron of lifeguards, not stopping until he reached Kilkenny.

He left behind more than two thousand lifeless Confederates and Royalists, lying where they had fallen upon the field of battle like so many rag dolls.

In the absence of their commander-in-chief, terrified soldiers, madly hoping to save their lives, ran to Rathmines or Rathgar, or to the Wicklow hills. Jones's well-trained cavalry overtook them and slew them, usually with a sabre cut to the neck. Their semi-decapitated corpses, scattered like litter over the countryside, were a heart-breaking epitaph to countless beer-swilling and loveable lads, whose pleasures heretofore were confined to loving their wives and siring children. Now they were folded untidily over hedges or buckled into unrecognisable shapes. English swords had not always killed outright. They had taken a hand here, a slice of skull there; the cause of death had often been shock or loss of blood. The air smelled of blood and excreta, a sweet if sickly farmyard scent, familiar to every battlefield through history.

Jones's forces were well both disciplined and skilfully handled. Ormonde's were worm-eaten with treachery and dissent, commanded by inexperienced officers who lacked the vital enthusiasm necessary for success.

A dispassionate observer could have foreseen the outcome.

Only when Murrough O'Brien, the first Earl of Inchiquin, sent a brave squadron back to the front in a rearguard action, creating a backdoor for the rest to escape with their lives, did the fighting stop. His squadron's captain proved a courageous man. In the past he had served Parliament. He knew better than most his enemy's purpose. Now he had to defend Ormonde's rear.

'Do not surrender to the Saxon locusts. They must be beaten, for if not they will despoil your land, dishonour your wives, defile your churches. When Jones's men arrive,' he told his frightened squadron, 'we will charge them, head on. We will do it for Ireland!'

With good discipline, the troops formed themselves into a line across the Puritan's murderous path.

Minutes later they heard the hooves of the Parliamentarian cavalry, before seeing the dust their chargers were kicking up.

'Draw your pistols,' the Irish captain ordered.

As the first of the English horse crested the hill, the Roundhead officer's face barely had time to register the shock of seeing Inchiquin's horse, coolly lined up to receive an assault. He had believed that he was there to cut down the stragglers and the wounded. A fraction of a second later, Inchiquin's captain had fired his pistolet. His bullet blew his would-be assailant's head apart.

The Irish captain now held his second pistol in his left hand, his sword in the other. Roaring with all his strength he galloped straight into the confusion, hoping his men would follow.

They did.

An Englishman charged at him, his sword above his head, only to catch a round in the chest. Another dismounted to use his pistol more accurately, but the Irishman slashed at his neck with his sword. The blow left him a twitching, dying heap.

From what seemed like nowhere, the captain sustained a glancing blow to his side. His furious counter swipe took the Roundhead's head clean off.

One of the English horse made a wild swing, almost unseating himself in his saddle, but the Irish captain was able to block and return it. Unfortunately, at that moment a loose horse reared and kicked at his mount, dislodging him. He desperately rolled away from his horse and crawled away from the carnage.

The Ironsides had been caught by surprise. They were already tired after the long engagement. They retreated with a few aimless shots over their shoulders.

Only then did the Irish captain realise that he was shaking like a leaf in a storm. A warm crimson stream ran down his legs.

He reclaimed his charger, taking him by his reins and remounted.

'Good boy,' he told his mount. Then, addressing his men, he shouted out. 'Carry the wounded and leave the dead'.

Then he and his troop were gone.

With that, the last organised resistance to the Parliamentarian advance ended. The remaining Royalists fled as the Parliamentarians overran their main camp at Rathmines. Ormonde's artillery and baggage train were captured, as well as his private papers and correspondence.

When the victorious Parliamentarians regathered, they left the dead bodies of their enemy where they were. Eventually, in accordance with the practice of the times, the local peasantry would strip the bloodstained clothes from their countrymen and burn them, before burying the naked soldiers wherever the earth was soft enough to harbour their remains.

Jones was now outside the walls of Rathmines Castle. The curtilage was about sixteen feet high and contained around ten acres. Many Royalist foot had shut themselves up inside. Jones had his blacksmith beat at the door. Believing their army to be entirely routed and their general fled, the refugees unlocked the gate and gave themselves up as prisoners. Their officers were dealt with summarily, in the shameless expediency of civil war, while nearly a thousand men were again offered the poisoned choice between life and death.

Elsewhere, Colonel Jones' men discovered a number of Irish survivors, notionally under Lord Inchiquin's command, who had managed to hide in the open. On being offered clemency they too surrendered and, after instantly promising 'faithfulness', they turned coats, gratefully taking up arms on Parliament's side.

Jones' men continued their hot pursuit of the retreating Irish. Before long they found a large party, almost two thousand strong, in a grove in the grounds of Rathgar Castle. The Irish put up a spirited defence for a while, but at last, and after negotiating terms, they too surrendered. These Irishmen were quick learners. The next day most of them took up arms again, but this time in a Parliamentary regiment.

The Irish had retreated. The gallant representation of an ancient nation had been cut down. As the English rode the battlefield – half a mile wide and many miles long – surveying with elation and pride their victory - the true extent of the slaughter was all around.

Jones had killed around 4000 Royalist or Confederate soldiers and taken 2500 prisoners, losing only a handful himself. This one-sided result was common in war. If an army was put to flight and pursued, it would always sustain huge casualties, while the pursuers would suffer very few.

Every few yards lay a horse, on its back more often than not, its neck twisted around as if hoping its owner would rescue it. For ever fallen mount lay eight or nine men. Logic alone suggested they might have been soldiers. At such awkward angles, the defeated army resembled a chess game after a spoilt child had upturned the board. On green and red soil the impossibly contorted remains told an indecipherable story, though its themes were of cruelty and ferocity, of courage and sacrifice; it told of mutually opposed schools of thought that differed so much that each felt the other should die.

The blood on their clothes had already turned black, rancid, its cloying smell provoking a wave of nausea amongst the English troops, even as they rode their triumphant, celebratory pageant.

Nonetheless they were cheerful. They were alive, after all, and these crumpled corpses were not. That Ormonde had also lost his entire artillery train and all his baggage and supplies amused them even more.

That night the officers mess in Dublin Castle toasted their success in fine wine. In every pub, alehouse and tavern that Dublin possessed, the soldiers did the same.

Colonel Jones' spectacular victory on the Bloody Fields of Rathmines had secured Dublin for Parliament, and news of it shattered Ormonde's main field army.

A shaken Lord Ormonde, safely re-established in Kilkenny, heard unreliable estimates of the number of his soldiers killed at Rathmines. He claimed he had lost less than a thousand men. A more likely figure is the one Colonel Jones reported. Out of the prisoners the English colonel had taken, around 1,250 had seen a hard-working Parliamentary noose in action. A few of the walking wounded were treated to Parliamentary 'clemency'. Stripped of arms and any money they might possess, they were set on the road to Kilkenny.

'Time for the Papists to see for themselves what a long friendless walk is like,' said Jones.

Colonel Jones's victory at Rathmines prepared the way for a new invasion. Two weeks later, it landed, unopposed, in Ringsend. It was to be led by a general who had served Parliament and his Puritan God so well in the Civil War, especially at Naseby and Marston Moor. His name was Oliver Cromwell.

In a manner of speaking, Cromwell had won the Bloody Fields of Rathmines himself, despite not yet being in Ireland. Such was his reputation that Ormonde's men had been terrified by the mere rumour that he had already landed. This, despite Ormonde repeatedly telling them he was not yet even on his way.

'The story is baseless,' he had repeatedly declared. 'It has been circulated by the Castle in the hope of demoralising you.'

Some of the defecting Royalists may not even have really wanted a truly resounding victory. This may be the explanation of the many desertions, cowardice and acts of treachery that came to light in connection with the engagement at Rathmines. Later commentators correctly observed that many in Ormonde's army had fought against the marquess in the battles that immediately followed the 1641 Rebellion, eight years before.

However it is analysed, Parliament's victory was decisive. The Royalist army was broken up, the siege of Dublin raised.

Ormonde sent orders for his remaining troops to retreat from around Dublin. This was another poor decision, since it allowed Oliver Cromwell to land unopposed with 15,000 veteran troops. This he did, on 15 August. Cromwell called the Bloody Fields 'an astonishing mercy', taking it as a sign that God had approved of the Puritan conquest of Ireland.

Without Jones' victory, the New Model Army would have had no port in Ireland to land in. The Cromwellian conquest of Ireland would have been impossible.

*

CHAPTER SEVENTEEN
DROGHEDA

Even if the Battle of Rathmines had been lost, no one thought the war for Ireland was over. Every common soldiery had heard that General Cromwell was either on his way to Dublin with an enormous army, or indeed had already arrived. Some Irishmen went so far as to believe that if they donned a Parliamentarian coat they would be treated as adventurers and rewarded with confiscated land.

A greater number held Cromwell to be altogether less generous. Surely, they argued, he would merely hang any foolish turncoats. Details of his bigotry had been widely circulated. There would be no quarter for Catholics. The English general, they said, saw papists as a race in need of eradication.

Lord Ormonde knew the truth. He saw the Adventurers Act as nothing less than licensed robbery. Without the means to pay a soldier's wage, Parliament was planning to settle his back pay with confiscated land, but at the expense of every Irish landowner, smallholder or great aristocrat. Since this was a racial transfer from Celt to Saxon, it would permanently change the natural composition of the island, and no native Irishmen was meant to prosper.

He regathered his army, now reduced by war and desertion, and encamped in Tircroghan, Co Westmeath, not far from Drogheda.

From there he would hold a Council of War. He sent for Sir Arthur Aston, Drogheda's military commander, suggesting he assemble a bodyguard from his most trusted officers and attend his Council.

Governor Aston, Major Bryen MacDonogh and Captain Dick Talbot made the journey from Drogheda to Tircroghan after dark. When they arrived, all three immediately sought somewhere to sleep. It was the small hours, still dark, and none of them had had time to rest. MacDonogh wasted no time in finding a pallet and, when his eye lids closed, they fell like portcullises.

'Wake up, Bryen.' Dick Talbot was rattling his cot. 'The marquess wants us all. Now, Major!'

Bryen struggled to his senses, while Talbot's face swum into focus.

'He may want us to tell his men what life is like in Drogheda,' suggested Dick. 'Stir them up a bit, perhaps? Put the fear of God into them? I worry that Colonel Jones rather took the wind out of his men's sails. Maybe he wants some puff put back in?'

'More likely he'll want us all to return to our homes and raise more troops from our tenants. That's not good for me. The little that's left of my clan is here with me. Since Knocknanuss there are no fighting men left in Duhallow. Even our name there hangs by a thread.'

'There's only one way to find out. Come along, look lively. Perhaps Lord Castlehaven will offer us breakfast!' The general was famous for his appetite.

Bryen and Dick strode through the earthen fort that Owen Roe had caused to be raised beside the old ruined castle. They wove their way though four thousand Confederate and Royalist troops; stretching, sharpening the blades of their pikes, buckling on their swords, cleaning their firearms, grumpily testing the early morning air. As the two young officers passed through them, the men saluted them informally with a wave. Some barked '*Dia duit*'. God bless you.

Bryen replied, '*Dia is Muire duit*' to every such greeting and some of the men muttered the more pious '*go mbeannaí Dia is Muire duit*' even to that. May God and Mary bless you.

Neither his nor Talbot's pace would slacken.

Despite his defeat at Rathmines, the military force he had secured in his Second Peace – the Coalition of the Catholic Confederates with the Royalists – had become the single biggest threat to the recently announced Commonwealth of England. While divided, Ireland had been easy to rule, but now the Coalition and the Ulster Army controlled most of Ireland. Ormonde's alliance had created what many English considered an indomitable nation. The might of the English military government might not be enough.

Even so, Ormonde knew he would be hard put to restrain the Commonwealth's newly appointed High Commissioner for War. Ormonde had wanted to re-take County Dublin before Cromwell arrived but in the circumstances he determined to confine the Saxon Scourge to the capital by holding the line of castles and fortified towns that contained the Pale.

Even Oliver Cromwell, in a speech he gave to his Army Council in Westminster, allowed himself to voice some concern.

> There is a danger that too small a force might be inadequate to the task, but I had rather be overthrown by a Cavalierish interest than a Scotch one; I had rather be overthrown by a Scotch interest than an Irish one and I think of all this, the last is the most dangerous.

Ormonde's Council of War was vital to the success of the Irish cause. His defeat at Rathmines meant his troops' morale had to be lifted. It would be hard. Cromwell's ambitions were unknown and predicting the Saxon general's first move was little more than guesswork.

Bryen looked about. Some faces he recognised. Over there was the Earl of Westmeath, on whose land they were. Westmeath had been a guest of his father in happier times. On Ormonde's right hand was Sir Thomas Armstrong, the Lord Lieutenant's Quartermaster-General of Horse. He used to be a stalwart of the hunt. There will have been a dozen of the most senior grandees of the Coalition. On the marquess's left was his current chief, the distinguished Governor of Drogheda, Sir Arthur Aston. In this very Irish company Sir Arthur might have linguistic problems, not having a word of Irish, Bryen thought, but then, the Englishman was in the same monoglot boat as Lord Ormonde himself.

'Gentlemen,' began Lord Ormonde. 'Thank you all for coming, especially those of you who have just arrived from Drogheda. Before we begin, let us briefly bow our heads and invite the intercession of Our Lady.'

He outstretched his arms in prayer and his 'congregation' bared its head.

'We turn to you for protection, holy mother of God. Listen to our prayers and help us in our hour of need. Save us from every danger, glorious and blessed Virgin. Amen.'

He lowered his arms to his side.

'I apologise, gentlemen, if I have interrupted your breakfasts. Now that the sun has cleared the horizon we should not casually waste precious daylight. Keen as you all are, however, please be patient. I should like you all to hear Sir Arthur tell us of the situation in his garrison town of Drogheda.'

Aston carefully raised himself to his feet, the effort clearly costing him pain. He cleared his throat. He had no armour and wore a scholarly Erasmus Cap; more professor than soldier. That limp, Bryen had learned, was owed to a wooden leg.

'Gallant friends,' the Governor began. 'Since Colonel Jones teased us at Rathmines, an even more murderous Englishman has just arrived in Dublin. His name, as if you needed telling, is Cromwell. The High Commissioner has been with us these three weeks. His brief was at first only to report the state of our nation to his masters, the Commonwealth, his nice Saxon friends who killed our king. His role has now expanded into replicating the duties he so bloodily discharged at Marston Moor and again at Naseby.'

He sipped at his glass of buttermilk. Perhaps he had not had time for breakfast either?

Sir Arthur took a popular engraving of General Cromwell from the table and gave it to Talbot to hold up.

'Gentlemen, this is our enemy. Mark him well,' Aston continued. 'He is Parliament's most senior general. He established his reputation in '46, annihilating the English Royalists in battle. Even the Puritans believe it dangerous to harness the force of darkness itself. They retain him on forty-day contracts, one after another, not daring to make his commission permanent. He was second-in-command of the New Model Army and, now that General Fairfax has retired, Cromwell is their top man. Yes, that's right. He calls his murderous Roundheads a 'model' army. Of course, Parliament's High Commissioner for War is free to call them whatever he wants. You may think of more suitable names.

'Parliament wants Ireland subjugated, converted into a Saxon colony. Their plan is analogous to Spain's bold plan for the Americas. You all remember meeting Colonel Jones. Cromwell's army is larger and angrier. With the Civil War in England apparently over, and given his control of the Irish Sea, he can be regularly reinforced and re-supplied. We have no idea how long the Commonwealth will allow him, nor how long he will take, but be assured he will not quit until what he calls 'Popery' is a fading memory; with every remaining believer in England and Ireland condemned to what he believes will be eternal flames.' He laughed. 'We, of course, know differently.'

Aston pointed at the etching.

'As you can see, this man is truly ugly. If you want your women or children to sleep by night, don't let them see him. His face, embellished with huge and fearsome warts, is not the only reason to steer clear of him. He has founded his reputation on being the most ruthless, most unforgiving, most ambitious soldier over there. Now he's over here. His roots are barely those of a gentleman; he rose from smallholding stock, what we would call a peasant. An inheritance, five years ago, let him become a farming member of the House of Commons. At that time he had no previous military experience. None at all. Now he is the senior commander of the Parliamentary Army. Parliament loves him and his neatly dressed savages.'

Aston went to the entrance to Ormonde's big tent and pulled the flap aside. Light from the rising sun flooded in. Dawn contrived - as always - to be both symbolic and magnificent.

'Since the general's arrival on our once peaceful shores he has wasted no time. Last Monday he made a powerful speech in Dublin Castle, celebrating Colonel Jones's victory against us. Gentlemen, none of us knows for certain what he is planning but my blood ran cold when my scouts told me that he'd sent a squadron of fighting ships to the Boyne, which dropped anchor a mile between us and the sea. His fleet has been there now for three days and nights. Surely, gentlemen, it can only mean one thing? He is preparing to lay siege to our Royal Garrison. He already prevents provisions from reaching us from the sea but we don't believe he has a siege in mind. His character, established in England's Civil War, says he plans an assault. I have accepted the Lord Lieutenant's invitation to come to this Council to beg for your help. I speak on behalf of the three thousand men, women and children that form my city and garrison.'

He sat. The Irish applauded while Lord Ormonde rose slowly to his feet.

'Thank you, Sir Arthur. Gentlemen, who does not feel for poor old Drogheda? Over the years that garrison has had more than its fair share of sieges. After the Rebellion, Sir Phelim O'Neill and Rory O'More paid it some attention. Even they failed to take the town. Those brave Confederates were minded to follow the rules of war and, after a while, they realised the town could not be taken without undue loss of life. They backed off like the Christian gentlemen they are.'

Ormonde put his hands on the table in front of him and leaned forward, the better to project his voice to the assembled officers and underline his urgency.

'Cromwell does not respect such rules and we are yet to recover from our setback at Rathmines. I have not the manpower to confront twelve thousand Roundheads. Not yet, in any case. Nevertheless, Drogheda must be held. In due course I shall allot two further regiments to its defence but those men have yet to be mustered.

He turned to address the governor directly.

'Sir Arthur, if we include the men MacDonogh and Talbot brought with them, you now have two thousand men at arms. Lord Castlehaven, may I confirm you will leave those companies in place?'

Castlehaven nodded his assent.

Ormonde continued.

'Sir Arthur, you have two brave, lucky and capable commanding officers, Major MacDonogh and Captain Talbot. You have already assured me your supplies can last a month without causing you crippling discomfort. Cromwell's siege will scarcely have started by then. All you will have to do is lock the gates, hold out for a few short weeks, a month at most, until we can relieve you.'

He turned to his Council.

'Gentlemen, we do this because we must. Drogheda is merely one of many tough fortresses surrounding Dublin. Logic suggests that Cromwell will break through the ring of paleforts. He will start with the weakest, and pick us off, fort by fort, before gaining access to the interior of this kingdom. That is why I shall reinforce every one of these forts. Cromwell confined and feeding his ravenous horde is harmless; Cerebus enchained. Cromwell on the loose, however, becomes Polyphemus, the cruel Cyclops whose murderous vision will have to be blinded by an Irish Odysseus. Before we face such a challenge, we should lock him in Dublin Castle and call on our old friends, hunger and sickness, to defeat him there.'

He turned again to Aston.

'Three thousand men, women and children, you said?'

'That number includes our soldiers.'

'Their kind and condition?'

'All sorts. The citizens are mostly fit. The best part of our soldiers are Catholic, including some English recusants. The rest are English or Irish Protestants, but all are loyal to their king. All believe in a Royal Confederate Ireland, and all are willing to confront General Cromwell's peculiar military talents, on which the Parliamentary imperialists stake their claim to Ireland.'

Ormonde redirected his gaze to the Governor of Drogheda.

'We will protect you and your garrison, Sir Arthur. Rest assured.'

General Cromwell's main camp had been pitched a mile to the north of Dublin. Together with Colonel Jones, he passed the days training and assembling a model Parliamentary army, issuing them uniforms that would guarantee no desertions, confirming or changing his officers' military grades and establishing enforceable chains of command.

It was September when Sea-General Deane brought his siege guns - eleven 48-pounders - along the coast by sea and up the Boyne estuary almost as far as Drogheda.

The High Commissioner for War arrived in person just two days later.

Much like Ormonde, Cromwell found speechifying irresistible.

Gentlemen, the future of our Commonwealth faces an unhealthy enemy, Ormonde's nostalgic alliance of Royalists and Papists. Unhealthy, in that they refuse to face the facts, but not threatening. The so-called Lord Lieutenant's army is in disarray; many of his men have deserted, others have sought and found

337

comfort under our standard. In the meantime, their Laudian marquess tours the Pale, vainly trying to rally a dispersed Popish rabble. He guesses which one of his forts we will attack first, yet in his heart he knows that he lost his authority over the Coalition when he ran to France. It was lost a second time when Jones defeated him at Rathmines. Twice is enough. Ormonde is not only a useless general, he is a spent force.

Our purpose in Ireland is both religious and political. We are not driven by greed; our noblest purpose is to extirpate heresy. True, those soldiers who help us achieve these Godly ends will be rewarded with land, but remember, we are not here just to plant their soil with honest Saxons like you. Their Roman Church is our enemy, since it denies the primacy of the Scriptures in favour of clerical edicts. In imposing that view, everywhere in Christendom, the Church of Rome is to blame for the murder of righteous Protestants.

Some Papists accuse our Model Army of ignoring their vaunted 'Augustinian rules of war'. To my mind it is an oxymoron to suggest that war should submit to rules. All any civilised man can ever want is peace and for all wars to end as quickly as possible. Courtly bows and hat-raising do not bring peace. Cato showed us the way at Carthage in the third Punic War. The 'rules' of war are mere folly. When I landed in Ireland a few weeks ago I brought purpose to this God-forsaken island. When I leave I shall take a conquered Kingdom of Ireland into the protection of the Commonwealth of England.

The walls of his big tent rattled with the wind like a drum roll.

Drogheda has come out for the Royal Pretender. The Garrison's troops are English, Anglo-Irish and Confederate; Royalist from their lice-infested hair down to their soiled fundaments. Unfortunately for the garrison's commander, Sir Arthur Aston, an English Catholic who has made Ireland his home, the only life form more despicable to me than a native Irishman is a Catholic Englishman.

Cromwell's dark armour gleamed in the early light as if wet.

My New Model Army must have frequent and regular supplies from England. We will begin our adventure by liberating the port towns on Ireland's east coast. The campaigning season in Ireland, when armies can live off the land, runs only from spring to autumn. This is September. There is little choice for us but to secure a constant supply from the sea. Drogheda has artillery that can target the approaches to Dublin Bay. That is why we will dismantle Drogheda's Garrison.

The general's hand gripped the hilt of his sword.

I readily admit my knowledge of siege warfare is not profound. Have I the patience that a long siege requires? I know not. Neither have I never built siege entrenchments nor lingered in them over a cruel winter, and nor do I propose to do so now. I am not in the slightest interested in teasing out an honourable surrender. My policy is to shock them and in the process deliver the awe they owe God. My recipe for Drogheda will consist of heavy bombardment and an assault so fierce that it will recall the fall of Jericho.

*

While the famous English general organised his camp out of sight of the city, his comings-and-goings were continually reported to Aston.

'Men,' Sir Arthur Aston told his officers, 'Cromwell means business. He probably means to starve us out, but as yet, we have no trustworthy intelligence as to how many they are or what they are planning. I just pray he does not plan to invade Ireland through us. We need a scouting party to go over St John's Hill and bring back an opinion. Who's up for it?'

Bryen MacDonogh's company of dragoons – musketeers but for this exercise armed only with sabres and pistolets[xlviii] rode out of Drogheda's Dublin Gate. Their intention was not simply to gather information; if there were half a chance they would affront the English general and order him to disperse.

As MacDonogh of Duhallow's company crested the hill they suddenly became aware of the scale of the English offensive. Cromwell was not going to obey any order to desist. What they saw was an army, an enormous one of twelve thousand men, bivouacked as far as comprehension would allow, an ocean of canvas cleared only for pikemen to exercise their squares. There were several thousand musketeers alone. The army was dressed in brown and black, enhanced with yellow sashes. They carried colours and the cavalry wore helmets and breastplates. Most terrifying of all were the eleven siege pieces.

MacDonogh's lieutenants watched with mounting horror as the Parliamentarians hauled them to the summit of the hill, from which Drogheda would be within easy range.

Bryen's men would not remain undetected for long. A hail of musket fire told him to return his men to their safe haven. As the balls whistled by, the Royalist company turned and rode back like the wind. Drogheda was impregnable to the west and defended by the Boyne to the east. The company went through the southern Dublin Gate, which slammed behind them. Praise be to the Lord Almighty, they were safe.

Cromwell couldn't care less. He wasn't going to besiege the little city. He was going to destroy it. He had seen the medieval spire of St Mary's rising above its walls. It was a perfect target, and his artillery was well trained in ballistics.

At midday, the Puritan general opened fire. Eleven cannons fired their 48-pound balls into the town. Unerringly the ordnance found the church and its spire. Then they were reloaded and fired again. And again.

The general and his officers had the self-righteous satisfaction of watching the spire fall slowly back to the ground from where it had sprung three hundred years before.

'Cromwell, of course, is making a point,' said an appalled Sir Arthur. 'Our defences consist of medieval curtain walls. They are high but uncomfortably frail. Their builders never imagined such cannonry.'

'The general is on the south bank of the Boyne.'

'Both the Dublin and Duleek gates are across the river in the southern part of the city. That's where the Parliamentarian army will concentrate its fire. Our forces should be massed there, to welcome and receive with the courtesy appropriate to any enemy soldier who has the impertinence to enter our town through a breach.'

'Should I direct my men there, Sir?' MacDonogh was eager to help.

'No, Major. Take your men to the northern walls. While we concentrate on the south gates, we will still need to deter General Cromwell from attacking the north. Your job will be to make yourself and your horse look as numerous as you can.'

Bryen saluted. He ordered his men into the part of Drogheda that lay to the north of the Boyne. There he had them ride outside the walls, coming in and out through the north gate as frequently as could be managed. Cromwell's scouts needed to gather that Aston's garrison was concentrated on the north side of town.

'What is Cromwell doing now?' Aston asked his new ADC.

'His forces have almost reached the south walls, Sir. He is making ready for an assault.'

'Just as I predicted.'

'Exactly, Sir. His dragoons have hauled his field guns close to the Duleek Gate. From there they will have an interlocking field of fire.'

This charged atmosphere was penetrated by a Parliamentarian messenger. The brave soldier carried a white flag. Admitted through the gate under escort, he carried a letter from the enemy general.

> Ex Campo
>
> Sir, having brought the army of the Parliament of England before this place, to reduce it to obedience, to the end that the effusion of blood may be prevented, I thought fit to summon you to deliver the same into my hands to their use. If this be refused, you will have no cause to blame me. I await your answer and remain your servant,
>
> O. Cromwell

'The saints preserve us!' Sir Arthur was for a moment quite beside himself. Then he collected his wits.

His soldiers had to strain to hear to him speak while Cromwell's cannons roared, their ball crashing into the town.

'We are short of gunpowder and ammunition,' he persisted. 'Our best hope is to lock down the gates and wait. Ormonde must have at least four thousand men at nearby Tircroghan. He'll come to our relief as soon as he is aware of this assault. That's right. Drogheda need not surrender to this Godless maniac. You there, fetch me pen and paper. I have two letters to write. The first will tell that heretic Roundhead that we will never give up. The second will implore Lord Ormonde to make God's speed.'

Cromwell was unmoved by Sir Arthur's response.

'We have demonstrated what we are capable of. If he won't surrender, in the face of such overwhelming odds, then the man is not merely a pagan, he is an idiot. Colonel, let the games begin. Take the gates down.'

'Sir!'

'The moment the walls are broken I want to know.'

'Sir!'

There was not long to wait. Cromwell's siege pieces punched holes in the town's medieval walls in a matter of minutes and then, as night must follow day, came the assault.

'Christian Soldiers,' the general told his Roundheads, 'the gaps in the south and east walls of Drogheda are wide enough to allow a coach and horses in. In you go. Be sure to let me know if you meet any significant resistance.'

341

The Royalists only managed to repel two attacks before the Puritan 'forlorn' had successfully fought its way into the town. By five o'clock, Cromwell knew that three of his twelve regiments had gained a foothold.

To the north, Bryen diverted his men eastwards, where in a bloody skirmish they defeated a small detachment of Cromwell's cavalry.

Cromwell watched this unexpected action take place.

'Reinforce the eastern attack with two more regiments,' he barked.

Bryen and his men had no choice but to find shelter inside the city walls. One of Drogheda's bravest Royalists, Colonel Wall, saw a chance to counterattack but was shot dead as soon as he came into range of the Parliamentarian sharpshooters. Headless, his troops fell back.

In the south of Drogheda, across the Boyne, Aston's men killed around a hundred invading New Model Army troops while they scrambled over fallen masonry. A Puritan Colonel Castle was one who fell, his chin having somehow caught the business end of a Royalist pike.

Another fearless Roundhead officer, seizing his chance, ordered a second company of the Parliamentary forlorn into the break. Mostly these men would die in hand-to-hand fighting.

It took a second wave of Cromwell's men to penetrate the City of Drogheda. They had the dismal task of climbing over the heap of comrades' hacked and mangled corpses.

The sight of this melancholy barrier enraged them.

'No priest or anyone in arms in the town is to be spared,' came the orders from on high.

The Model Army was well disposed to obey.

'You are not to surrender,' were Sir Arthur Aston's corresponding orders to the Royalists. 'Don't even consider desertion. Cromwell not spare you.'

Yet even as he issued this command he will have realised that the garrison was lost.

The New Model Army was now pursuing the defenders through the streets, into their houses, sacking any defensible position. Some zealots broke into the churches, pushing the terrified children who guarded their doors out of the way. They were bent on defacing the paintings, frescos and sculptures that the Papists had erected to their pagan God and this satanic rite. Smashing the windows would let some clear Protestant light in.

Any priest who tried to bar their way was summarily dispatched.

Terrified children who witnessed these pitiless murders from outside the doors wondered what they should do.

A drawbridge could have blocked access to the northern side of the town but the defenders were panicking. They had too little time to pull it up behind them. The Grim Reaper, whose name was legion, advanced across the river into Bryen's side of the town.

More and more parliamentary soldiers were streaming into Drogheda, over the collapsed walls. While the Parliamentarians busied themselves in the sack, Sir Arthur Aston and two hundred and fifty others had barricaded themselves in Millmount, a fort inside the walls that overlooked the south-eastern gate.

Wary of trying to storm the fort, which Cromwell later described as a place 'very strong, and of difficult access, being exceeding high, having a good graft, and strongly palisaded', the Parliamentary Colonel Axtell offered 'to spare the lives of the governor and the men with him if they surrendered on the promise of their lives'.

A great and welcome sense of relief floated into the mayhem and carnage, but history would show they were unwise to have accepted.

Cromwell rode into the town at the head of another five thousand men. As infuriated as his men by the sight of Parliamentarian dead, he gave the ultimate hateful order; 'no quarter'.

Cromwell, later writing of the incident, claimed proudly that…

> …our men, getting up to them, were ordered by me to put them all to the sword.

The New Model Army disarmed the governor and some other officers and took them to a windmill. There they clubbed them to death, fully an hour after they had surrendered. The Governor, Aston, had his brains beaten out with his own wooden leg. Cromwell's soldiers apparently thought the leg had gold hidden in it. Aston's ruined head was later sent to Dublin on a pole.

Elsewhere a group of about eighty Royalist soldiers cowered in St Peter's church, while some priests hid in its tower.

It would prove to be no sanctuary.

Cromwell had allowed or ordered his men to use Catholic children as shields against the Irish fusiliers who tried to rescue the church and his involuntary congregation.

Once inside the his soldiers held the inmates at sword point in the chancel. The church furniture was heaped by the altar rail before John Hewson, a zealot, set it alight. While the Puritans withdrew, the half-timbered church caught light. Its inmates were burned alive.

343

One priest, whose cassock had caught fire, threw himself from the tower. Somehow he landed well, breaking a leg but not his back. Cromwell saw the incident and ordered his troops to stay his dispatch.

'He must have gained the Almighty's favour,' he said. 'Providence moves in mysterious ways indeed!'

Another curious incident was reported. During the sack, thirty Protestant citizens of Drogheda were sheltering in their pastor's house. Parliamentarian troops fired in through the windows killing one civilian and wounding another. They then broke into the house, still firing their weapons, but were stopped from killing those they found inside when a Protestant officer identified them by their dress as coreligionists. Had it not been for that observant officer the fate of Drogheda's civilians might have been even worse.

The last concentration of Royalist soldiers was a group of two hundred young men who had been stranded in two towers along the town walls. They stayed there during the night of the sack but the following day they were deceitfully allowed to believe their surrender had been negotiated. When they surrendered to Cromwell they were disarmed.

Any officers of English extraction were singled out for the most ruthless treatment. Directly after being taken prisoner they were hanged, drawn and quartered. Their heads were publicly put onto pikes. The remainder of the officers and one in every ten private soldiers were then clubbed to death. The rest were chained, prior to transportation to Barbados as slaves. The money they made at auction was needed by the Commonwealth.

Their crime? They had refused to accept 'the judgement of God' in opting for war.

> I believe we put to the sword the whole number of the defenders. I do not think thirty of the whole number escaped with their lives, and those that did are in safe custody for the Barbados.

Sixteen heads of Royalist officers were cut off and sent to join Aston's in Dublin. They were not even given pride of place. Instead they were stuck on pikes on the capital's approach roads.

Every single Catholic priest found within the town was beaten to death. 'Knocked on the head', was how Cromwell's orders put it. Two of them were briefly granted a stay of execution, however. They were executed the following day. 'Polythemus' had wanted them to witness the extinction of their race.

An enormous number of men, women and children were butchered, or worse. Fr Denis Murphy wrote to the Irish community in Paris about the Catholic maidens violated and then killed by Protestant soldiers. He told of the Jesuit priests impaled on stakes in the market place.

> Perhaps four hundred Royalists were killed in honest warfare. Beyond that, the New 'Model' Army massacred over 2,700 men, women and children in cold blood. Possibly many more.

Cromwell himself listed the dead as including 'many inhabitants' of Drogheda in his report to Parliament. Hugh Peters, an officer on Cromwell's Council of War, gave the total loss of life as 3,552, of whom some 2,800 were soldiers, implying that between seven or eight hundred civilians were killed.

Cromwell's 'Christian' conscience was untroubled.

General Cromwell lost a hundred and fifty Parliamentarians in his attack. On learning the final toll, his single observation was pithy and to the point.

Let God arise and His enemies be scattered.[xlix]

*

Only at the last minute did Bryen MacDonogh and Richard Talbot escape with their lives, over the northern wall, taking around fifty of MacDonogh's dragoon-musketeers with them. They galloped for the coastal town of Arklow.

*

Bryen MacDonogh and Dick Talbot rode all night. By dawn they had reached Arklow, *en route* for New Ross where they thought they would rejoin Lord Ormonde and his army. The Lord Lieutenant would predict that Cromwell was selecting the coastal cities one by one.

Lord Inchiquin formally welcomed Major MacDonogh, Captain Talbot and their mounted musketeers to his garrison.

'Bryen, I'm very glad to see you again. I hope you will forgive me for some of the messages I sent you when we were on opposite sides in this bloody war?'

'Forgive you, Murrough? It's what we Catholics do best.' He held out his hand. After the briefest of pauses it was taken.

'I am thrilled that you and your sharpshooting musketeers are joining us. We have intelligence that Cromwell's army is coming this way and I have devised an ambush. We could use your support.'

The musketeers and their two young officers gratefully submitted to Inchiquin's authority.

Nearly fifty of Bryen's sharpshooters – forty-seven of them to be precise - had survived the Drogheda massacre when they had escaped through the breaches in that town's north walls. With Bryen and Dick in command they were quite a hunting party.

What terrible things they had seen in the ruined garrison town. Cadavers hanging like sacks from rows of improvised gibbets, lashed by wind and rain. Children cut in half, lying where they fell, in the mud, the squares, the streets. Mothers, having braved impossible odds to save them, speared on Parliamentarian pikes – looking like spit-roasted oxen at Satan's banquet.

Before their adventure in Drogheda, Bryen had scarcely known Richard Talbot. A friendship was indissolubly forged in the heat of war.

If Talbot were highly strung, Bryen had witnessed some extraordinary acts of reckless courage. Widely known as 'Mad Dick', though not too often to his face; he also had a reputation as a duellist.

In Arklow they soon found they were right about Ormonde's plans. The marquess had indeed parked his army in New Ross, on the Kilkenny Road, some twenty-five miles inland. From there he could protect the Port of Wexford's supply lines, to and from the interior. Though he had to abandon his recently acquired castles at Trim and Dundalk to the enemy, he had brought their soldiers and artillery with him. Even with these extra men, however, and after his losses at Rathmines and Drogheda, Ormonde could no longer muster a strong enough army to challenge Cromwell head on.

He was all too aware that it would take time to collect his scattered forces.

'When done', he declared, 'our Union will be stronger.'

Ormonde had concluded it was Wexford that Cromwell would head for next. He sent its castle a thousand foot and three hundred horse under Colonel David Synnot, 'a courageous and noble Catholic of the old school'.

If Wexford's militia was pleased, the predominantly Old English citizens were less so. They had lost faith in their marquess. They remembered that he had surrendered Dublin, and not so long ago; they knew he had recently made common cause with Lord Inchiquin, once the scourge of Irish Catholicism. They remembered how Inchiquin had set his fellow heretics on the Corkonians, and how he had burned Cashel

Cathedral with the faithful still inside. They refused Ormonde's men entry, only to relent when their look-outs saw, through their field glasses, the Parliamentary sea-army off their coast.

Ormonde, as diplomatic and generous as ever, rewarded their new found warmth with powder, ball and a hundred cannons.

'If Ormonde has gone to earth in New Ross, it will be music to Cromwell's ears, old friend,' Murrough Inchiquin told Bryen. 'The Puritan general certainly moves at speed. It took him a mere fortnight since Drogheda to reorganise. Look at the facts. He began his march south on September 23, taking the east coast route. Twenty warships accompanied him off shore. General-at-Sea Richard Deane's fleet carries his supplies and siege artillery in perfect safety.'

'That's because winter is approaching, and all too fast,' said Bryen. 'He can't waste time.'

'No. All too soon he'll have to find winter quarters for his soldiers.'

'Has he still, what is it, fifteen thousand men?'

'A little fewer. He lent General Venables' Ulster expedition three regiments to discover where Owen Roe is hiding. He has had to reinforce the Castle garrison in Dublin. He has even posted a new one in blood-stained Drogheda. As a result, he is now reduced to a mere nine thousand.

'Still a sizable figure, however.'

'Very possibly.' Inchiquin was thoughtful. 'My guess is he means to march them south, along the Wicklow coast, capturing our principal seaports *en route*. He has already closed the Irish Sea to us. He us many things but not stupid. His 'sea-army' will patrol the Bristol Channel and close our lines of communications with France and Spain. It will be essential to stop him, and it will be hard. The roads southwest from Dublin are already safe for the Parliamentarians.'

'Yes. I see what you mean. From here, the nearest 'Papist' port is Wexford.'

'Quite. It is also the base for our privateers.'

'Murrough, you will excuse us, I hope, from any charge of ingratitude but my men are essentially tories. We like to raid. We will take them off, early tomorrow, to New Ross. I shall convey to Lord Ormonde your good wishes, but we should like to show My Lord High Cromwell a thing or two before we leave.'

'You would? I am again amazed. What do you intend? Of, course, you have my blessing. Since we fought side-by-side in Newcastle, I know you to be a fine soldier. But your personal company is just fifty men.

Against nine thousand? On reflection, the enemy would need more than that to stand a chance against you! My warmest regards to the marquess when you meet up.'

*

Bryen, Dick and their squadron of musketeers had recrossed the Avoca, Arklow's river, over Relly's Ford. It was almost dawn. They calculated that Cromwell would have recommenced his march well before sun-up, and they wanted to anticipate the English.

'Come on, Dick. Some of Cromwell's horse are bound to come over the Avoca in an hour or so. They will only be a little behind is. After they cross they will still have forty or so miles to Wexford. That's two, maybe three nights in the open air. If we steal their packhorses we may hinder them a little.'

'Our issue is with their mules, is it, Bryen? Not the general himself?'

'Listen Dick. We should go for the packhorses, even though his ships will have his payroll and ordnance. Whatever's in his baggage train must have a military purpose of some kind, otherwise it wouldn't be there at all. The packhorses will be last in the tail of his column and, therefore, easier to pick off. Winter is on its way; even if all we capture are tents it will still delay them.'

'We may capture a volley of musket balls,' said Dick, doubtfully. Then he relented a little. 'Or some blankets.'

'That will be even better. He won't halt an army to defend his bedding and we can use his packhorses ourselves. And so can Ormonde's dragoons.' Bryen was set on his plan.

'I'm not convinced that Inchiquin's ambush will work,' said Dick. 'Nine to one against, with his thousand men already scared out of their limited wits. They think a glance from a Roundhead is fatal.'

'I no longer bear a grudge against Inchiquin. I hope he succeeds,' said Bryen, slightly implausibly. He had certainly not forgotten the inconstant Inchiquin's promise to hang him. 'If he can force them into the sea or over the slobs[1] he stands a chance. As for us, we'll manage well enough. We'll attack the column here, on the north side of the Avoca, just as soon as the dangerous bits of their army have crossed the ford. We'll break their column like so' - he struck the palm of his left hand with the edge of his right – 'and under covering fire we'll ride his packhorses on to New Ross. Relax, Dick, my musketeers are true marksmen!'

'And the Arklow garrison?'

348

'What d'you think? One of two things. Cromwell will summon it, and if he does it will surrender. Or Inchiquin will engage his men and they will be defeated in open battle. Remember, the heretic has nine thousand men, Inchiquin one. No one has ever won against those odds. It's just the way things are.'

'Cromwell will hang them all.'

'I don't think so. That would take a good few hours. Many of them fought for the English cause anyway. He wants Wexford and he wants it yesterday. He'll just disarm them and send them on their way half-naked. Now, let's find somewhere to lie flat, well out of sight. The sun has cleared the horizon. General bloody Cromwell will soon be here.'

It was not too long before Bryen and Dick first heard the distant pounding drumbeat of the horses' hooves. Soon after, they saw a great cloud of dust, unmistakably raised by a cavalry train. It announced the imminent arrival of the New Model Army.

Their spy glasses revealed that a division of cavalry was riding alongside the Parliamentarian infantry.

'Who the devil is leading the English? Can it be…?'

'Whoever it is, he's in full steel armour. He's out in front by two lengths clear of his second-in-command.'

'Can it really be true that none other than the Roundhead general himself is leading his army, all nine thousand men?'

Oliver Cromwell walked on at a comfortable pace, staring straight ahead. Like his offivers, around his waist he wore an orange sash. His stare was so intense he could easily have been in a trance.

As he grew nearer, the Irishmen could see that his breastplate was fluted, the better to deflect an ambitious mustketball. They deduced and that the similarly attired general behind him would have to be Major-General Ireton. Behind him had to be Major Nelson, in command of the infantry, also in armour.

Dick was staring at the incredible sight of nine thousand foot marching in file.

'They're in uniform,' he gasped. It was true. Most of Cromwell's men were in red or dark-brown woollen clothes. Many wore a steel helmet, and some had a small steel breastplate. They all wore knee-high boots. 'Why does he go to all that expense?'

'It's good for the English wool industry, I expect,' Bryen whispered.

'No, that's not it,' said Dick thoughtfully. 'The uniforms will be to stop his men from running off. They can go nowhere dressed like that.'

Already the Cromwellians were marching by. The tories watched in awe from just a few hundred yards away. The Roundheads threw up so much dust that they almost disappeared. The pounding of iron hooves and leather boots on the packed roadway was almost deafening.

The English were singing! Not a marching song; they were singing a psalm!

'*God, Your worshippers have come marching into view.* [ii]

The Irish watched, horrified, as if Satan himself were riding by. Almost without a pause the enemy began to cross the treacherous ford. They approached it as if it weren't there at all.

'*Your followers are in the sacred tent.*'

The water was high, and it came over their knees. The vast army steadily marched its way across the Avoca, their boots filling with water, not pausing in their holy song.

'*God, show us Your power. Show us Your strength. God, do as You have done before.*'

'At this rate they'll take all day to get across,' Dick observed. It was already well past noon.

'*He rides in the age-old skies above. He thunders with His mighty voice.*'

'Look! They're crossing in threes.' Bryen passed Dick his field glass. 'This crossing may be centuries old but it's still only just a wagon's width wide. I'll remind the men to keep down and out of sight. We may be here for some time.'

'*Tell how powerful God is. He rules as king over Israel.*'

It took eight long hours for Cromwell's army to ford the river. Dick and Bryen, like their men, crouched low in the gorse, a stone's throw away.

'*The skies show how powerful He is.*'

After a long, long time, the tail end of the column could just be made out. It was made up of a number of colourfully clad soldiers, mostly unarmed, some barefoot. These had to be the Irish who had joined the Parliamentarians for the sake of the purity of the scriptures or, just possibly, for a shilling a day.

Scarcely daring to think, let alone talk, the tories would wait until Cromwell's uniformed army was safely on the south side.

At the very rear of his column was indeed a baggage train, but what made Bryen and Dick's eyes light up was that the senior cavalry officers' second horses were being led unprotected at the end. Cromwell had clearly expected no resistance on the march south.

The sun was now setting. Every soldier, except the muleteers, had either crossed or were still wading the river. They could not turn around, even if they wanted to, not on that narrow ford with the others coming behind. The soldiers were easy targets for his Royalist musketeers.

'Men', shouted Bryen. 'Take your positions!'

Only then did the rebels emerge from the gorse where they had been hiding.

As in a dream, fifty horses rose to their full height. Their riders led them to where they had the best view of their enemy and formed four rows. The horses now sank again to the ground, the men resting their charged muskets on their saddles.

'Fire!' Bryen gave his squadron the order they had waited for.

If some of his horses had once been startled by gunfire, the training had had made them passive.

Twelve Roundhead auxiliaries fell back into the slow moving river.

'Second row, fire again,' cried Bryen. The order was obeyed.

'All of you, reload and fire at will!'

The tail of Cromwell's column, now in the water, panicked. Their horses reared and threw their riders into the river. Spurts of river-water sprung up where they fell; the river turned pink and the ford began to clog with the dead and the dying.

'That's enough. We've made our point. Cease fire! Dick, take some men with you and bring those loose horses back.'

He watched with some well-deserved satisfaction as Dick Talbot captured forty good horses and twenty mules.

'Well done, men. Now rope up the horses and mules. Fire only if a Cromwellian turns around to come after us. The Parliamentarians will have learned a little about Irish hospitality today.'

'Yes. Get back to England!' Dick shouted after the English. He was in his usual high spirits. 'Where to now, Major Bryen? Arklow will be a bit difficult.'

'New Ross. We'll find Lord Ormonde there. He'll think these horses a great prize. I wonder what they're carrying.'

As it happened they were mostly loaded with bedding and fodder. A little disappointing but they were sturdy horses, nonetheless.

Bryen, Dick and their little troop of musketeers took off to greet the Marquess of Ormonde. They had done a good day's work and anticipated praise.

*

Bryen had been right, both about Lord Inchiquin and Arklow.

Cromwell, furious, was swift to inflict his revenge. Before arriving in Wexford, he paused just long enough to slight the Royalist forts at Arklow, Ferns and Enniscorthy. His artillery quickly made them uninhabitable.

Cromwell's appetite, however, was unsated.

Inchiquin prepared an ambush for Nelson's infantry a little to Arklow's south. The hills there forced the road onto the beach.

The Parliamentary General, Ireton, however, had paid a useful-looking idiot a penny for his news. Nelson was duly warned and took his foot on a more roundabout route. Ireton's horse took advantage of the tide and used the coastal strand as a road.

Inchiquin realised what was happening soon enough. He abandoned his plan 'A' and ordered his own horse to make God's speed to intercept the Ironsides, gambling on surprise.

When Inchiquin's Irish Army came into view, the English had organised themselves on the beach, their backs to the sea. While Inchiquin still was forming up his troops, three hundred and fifty English horse charged into them. Twice Inchiquin repelled them and then, to Nelson's pretended amazement, the Irishman launched a full cavalry counter-assault on his English opposite numbers. The English horse fled back towards the foot, the Irish in hot pursuit.

The truth was, however, that the New Model Army was well prepared for such a well-known Irish manoeuvre. They had planned the feint. The ranks opened up to allow the Irish horse to pass through. Then they closed ranks behind. Inchiquin's charging cavalry now found that they were facing a mass of pike-heads and levelled musket barrels. The close range musket fire tore into the Irish cavalry, whose survivors retreated in disorder, leaving the beach littered with corpses, their tunics marked with flowers, red petalled and black hearted, waiting silently for the tide to clear the sand and bury them.

The day was Ireton's.

*

CHAPTER TWENTY-FOUR
WEXFORD AND CARRICK

Major Nelson rejoined General Cromwell's great army, now camped a hundred yards or so across the River Slaney from Wexford's walls. It was October 1, 1649.

The general saw before him a future battlefield. He saw a walled city on the Slaney's south side, its medieval church spires rising far above its curtilage, its natural harbour formed by gnarled fingers of land to the north and south. Seaward, the elegant mass of Rosslare Fort proudly guarded its coastal approaches.

That was not at all how High Commissioner Cromwell saw it. If it had to, it could all go to blazes.

Cromwell was nothing if not single-minded. Wexford's capture was essential. It was the port through which the Coalition imported not just its weaponry and provender but also freebooting mercenaries from France and Spain.

As long as anyone could remember, Wexford had been Catholic. These days what was left of its profitable privateering business was licensed by Kilkenny. As many as forty vessels, some large, most small, still operated from the harbour. Their 'corresponding' bases were in Dunkirk, or Calais, or Dieppe, or Honfleur, or St Malo, but it was Wexford that offered them useful shelter and rich rewards. They raided the shipping between Dublin, Chester and Bristol, paying a tithe of their plunder to the Confederacy.

Some years previously, Parliament's 'sea-army' had adopted the ugly practice of throwing captured Irish crew into the sea, their hands tied behind their backs. Desperate, the Wexford garrison kept a few English prisoners of its own and periodically threatened Parliament with their death if such drownings continued. None, of these captives however, were ever executed; the English bought them back for small sums.

General Cromwell sat down with his ADC, Colonel Cook.

'I only became aware of the existence of the Papist stronghold of Wexford last year, when the Confederates and Royalists signed their 'Ormonde Peace' and joined forces against our Commonwealth,' he told his comrade-in-arms. 'Mountgarrett, as Commander of the Confederacy, ordered all English Protestants to quit the town by ship. About eighty of them drowned when the boat evacuating them from Rosslare sank. Since then Wexford has been among my key pupils for a lesson in manners.'

'It appears to me that Wexford is both pleasantly seated and strong', said Colonel Cook. 'A pity its people have long been seduced by Rome's scarlet whore.'

'Yes, it is, but be assured, their meddling with the Word of God has no future. Soon we shall plant some New English here, men who actually fear the Almighty; above all, men who don't believe they command Him.'

An unlucky Catholic soldier, unaware of the gathering storm, had been captured while returning to his Wexford garrison from his village. Under irresistible pressure he disclosed that his city boasted more than two thousand men in the fort and that, parked nearby, were Ormonde's cannons as yet unmounted. In the port, his interrogators learned, three of Ormonde's warships were at anchor, one with thirty-four guns and two with twenty. Another turn of the wheel and he revealed they were currently unmanned.

'Ask him about the walls,' Cromwell persisted.

The soldier soon revealed that Wexford's strength came from a rampart of earth, fifteen feet thick at the base, against and behind the walls. It greatly enhanced the town's chances of withstanding an assault, even if delivered by cannon.

On October 3, Cromwell his issued terms for the town's surrender. His short letter, carried by a terrified messenger over no-man's land, expressed what were becoming his habitual requirements.

1. The soldiers should abandon their arms and leave the city.
2. All Catholic women and children should do the same. They will be allowed to walk to Kilkenny without untoward interference. Any remaining will be hanged.

Was he hoping that he could secure Wexford intact? He may have wanted to use it as winter quarters for his troops. Certainly, the mayor, aldermen and many citizens of Wexford were prepared to surrender. They thought they would be safe. Parliament may have been their enemy but it was at least Christian. Its word was surely good and Kilkenny was only fifty miles away. They could be fed at New Ross; exactly halfway. A walk that the fittest among them could manage in the short hours of daylight.

Colonel Synnot, believing Wexford to be effectively impregnable, played for time. He decided to wait for disease to weaken the

Parliamentarians in their camp. While attrition fought for Ireland, the Coalition was steadily being rebuilt.

Two weeks had passed and it was now well into October. An Irish winter was on its way. Sickness would soon take its toll on any troops camped out in the open. The recently stretched soldier revealed that the Marquess of Ormonde was camped only twenty-five miles away at New Ross, waiting (the soldier said) for a favourable moment to attack Cromwell's army.

There is an English saying – 'strike while the iron is hot'. Nothing if not a brilliant strategist, Cromwell knew it well. He marched upstream, hoping to cross the river at Enniscorthy. The great castle there cost him a precious twenty-four hours, but its partial destruction and surrender allowed him to cross the river and advance on Wexford from the south.

His approach took the Royalist and Catholic Alliance by surprise.

Michael Jones, now a Lieutenant-General, had been sent on ahead to surprise the Rosslare garrison which, at the mere sight of the Protestant dragoons, fled. With Rosslare neutralised and the Irish mariners feeling no pain in some quayside hostelry, Cromwell's army was free to enter Wexford Harbour quite safely. His army-at-sea would now land its provisions.

General-at-Sea Deane unloaded Cromwell's siege artillery on the quays. Cromwell set them up as batteries, concentrating their aim on Wexford Castle, a handsome Norman fort built in cut stone, which had dominated the south-eastern corner of the defences for half a millennium.[lii]

In New Ross, Ormonde, understanding the issues in Wexford, thought he should send Synnot another thousand infantrymen. He was about to give this order when he heard that some Protestants in Youghal had seized the town and declared for Parliament. After some soul-searching, Ormonde sent Lord Inchiquin south with a regiment to subdue the uprising. Regrettably, this had to be at the cost of Synnot's promised reinforcements.

Despite all this, the negotiations between Cromwell and Synnot still had legs. Cromwell felt the city was not taking him seriously. To make himself more convincing, the English general ordered his artillery to bombard Wexford Castle. A storm of cannonballs fell on it all day and well into the night. The effect of this was appalling.

The next day, Synnot and the aldermen of Wexford sent a note, conditionally agreeing to Cromwell's terms.

General Cromwell still had nine thousand men; cavalry, infantry, dragoons, bombardiers, pikemen, artillery and fusiliers. He had eight substantial guns and two mortars. He also had, he believed, a stern Protestant God on his side.

The odds incontrovertibly favoured Cromwell. Many of the civilians in Wexford had begged Synnot to allow them an honourable surrender, hoping to remain in their homes and run their businesses. Synnot therefore suggested that the soldiers of the garrison should be disarmed and allowed to march away. The officers, on the other hand, thought that they would be imprisoned or executed would only obey on condition that the town would not be plundered. Synnot then demanded that provisions be made for the protection of the town's Catholic clergy, and suggested that the garrison be allowed to withdraw to New Ross. This Cromwell would not agree and negotiations broke down again.

Four days in fruitless to-ing and fro-ing passed until the general lost his patience, delivering a furious salvo from the heights overlooking the southern end of the town. Housewives and servants, fetching water and rationed bread, scattered for cover. Some not fast enough. One maid, seeing a fellow servant injured, sat beside her while her life ebbed slowly away. It takes a long time to lose eight pints of blood and her best friend, frightened beyond the wits of man, was lucid throughout. She managed to recite two rosaries and say the *nunc dimittis* - which surely helped.

Wexford's garrison consisted of two thousand Catholic soldiers. They had always been fiercely independent of the Pale, but now they took their orders from David Synnot, whom Ormonde had appointed the town's governor. The town's morale had been low since they first had news of the fall of Drogheda. Now it reached rock bottom.

Ormonde, despite the diversion to reinforce Youghal, was now bound to strengthen Synnot and his garrison. In the dead of night, Wexford opened its East Gate long enough to admit three thousand more troops. With Synnot's strength now up to nearly five thousand, the governor felt confident enough to string out his negotiations. The town's walls were stout and, thanks to Ormonde, the citizens were no longer quite so acutely short of food.

Synnot's newest terms for the city's surrender included the free practice of the Catholic religion, the evacuation of the garrison *with their arms* and the free passage of the privateer fleet to a friendly foreign port; Honfleur, or St Malo, for example.

As he replied to Synnot, Cromwell may have secretly laughed. If so, no one saw him smile, nor did a flicker of emotion cross his face.

> Sir, I have had the patience to peruse your latest propositions; to which I might have returned an answer with some disdain. To be short, I shall give the soldiers and non-commissioned officers quarter for life and leave to go to their several habitations. As for the townsmen, I shall engage myself that no violence shall be offered to their goods, and that I shall protect their town from plunder.
> I remain your servant,
> O. Cromwell

If Cromwell meant any of this is a matter of conjecture, for he immediately ordered Wexford's walls to be mined. This involved tunnelling and laying a new form of mine; terracotta water pipes were dug up – they had led from the springs outside Wexford into the city's pumps and fountains – and were packed with black powder. Work had hardly begun, however, when the Constable of the Castle, a Captain Stafford, acted on his own initiative. For reasons that have never been determined, he elected, single-handedly, to surrender the castle.

*

Wexword Castle lay on the heights to the south west of the city walls, which lent the Commonwealth artillery a magnificent platform to eradicate the city they saw beneath them.

As Stafford must have expected, Cromwell claimed the fort for Parliament. Then he turned its guns on the town. The Royalists guarding the south wall of the town lost heart. As they turned and ran, they will have seen the Parliamentarian infantry using ladders to scale the unmanned walls, open the gates from the inside and usher in the New Model Army. All this while their Commander was still trying to agree terms.

In the afternoon of October 11, Cromwell's gunners opened two wide breaches in the walls. An assault on the town was now inevitable.

Cromwell's officers made no attempt at restraint. Delighted Model Soldiers, once inside, replayed the Drogheda massacre. Three hundred women, in prayer beside the market cross, were slaughtered, some where they knelt, the rest as they fled. Ironically, they had been counting on their closeness to the cross to soften the hearts of Christian soldiers but, alas, it identified them as superstitious pagans, needing to be put to the sword or the club. Cromwell's Model Army did not differentiate between men, children or women, soldiers or civilians, priests or laity. They were treated alike. Those slaughtered that day included many Catholic priests, including seven Franciscans.

Cromwell would later calculate that some two thousand of Synnot's soldiers were killed, compared with just twenty of his own. His report neglected to mention that a thousand citizens were hacked to death with clubs and swords. The Parliamentarians murdered and looted the town like the Vikings who had founded it, pursuing its people into the streets, down its narrow lanes, killing them as they tried to reach their own front doors.

Colonel David Synnot was among those who fell. His head was severed and paraded on a pike, the sight of which caused his men to flee in blind panic. Yet more civilians were shot or drowned as they tried to escape the carnage by crossing the river. Cromwell soon had more deaths of women and children to account for, even than at Drogheda.

Once the bloodlust was finally sated, the half-timbered and thatched town was torched. Its beautiful harbour was destroyed. Its ancient churches were razed.

Most of its medieval housing was razed by fire or burst by cannonball.

So complete was the destruction of Wexford that one indiscreet Parliamentarian source described the sack as 'incommodious to us'. Cromwell reported to the Commission[liii] that of the survivors, perhaps two thousand were unaccounted for. Most likely they had 'run off'. He needed labourers, therefore, to be sent from England to rebuild, re-populate and re-open the town and its port.

The bloated bodies of these unaccounted for citizens would wash ashore, months later and in their hundreds, on the Welsh coast. At first they were mistaken for long dead whales.

The Sack of Wexford is remembered in Ireland as an infamy.

*

As with his taking of Drogheda, Cromwell ignored the fate of Wexford. He would admit he had been angered by Synnot's last-minute attempt to ameliorate the terms of surrender in his subsequent report to Parliament, but he expressed no remorse for the eradication of Wexford's civilians.

'It was God's judgment upon the perpetrators of the Rebellion of '41. My only regret was that an admittedly 'handsome' town was so badly damaged during the sack that it is no longer fit for use either as a port or as winter quarters, even for Parliament's model and victorious army.'

*

'My conscience is clear,' he would later tell his fellow commissioners. 'By any scriptural definition the townsfolk were not true Christians, faithful to the Word. They were so far removed from Christ's simplicity that they might have been Africans, Chinamen or Red Indians. The charity they merited was the same.'

Of course, he was preaching to the converted.

'Charity is not always appropriate,' he continued. 'These men were made to answer for the cruelties they had exercised upon diverse Protestants with their blood. From their unfortunate birth they were destined to horrors in this world and the next. If God had not intended their fate, it would never have come to pass.'

In his written report to the Commonwealth, Cromwell failed to dwell on such trivial matters at all.[liv]

> May it please your Excellencies; you will be pleased to hear that I have captured three Ships, a hundred Field Guns, chests of Powder and Ammunition and tons of Supplies. This magnificent treasure has cost the Commonwealth just Twenty Lives.

*

Ormonde's army had fewer than three thousand men when Wexford fell.

The marquess was desperate to win over O'Neill and his Ulster army. He was well aware of the redoubtable warrior's intransigence.

He decided to visit the famous Irishman in Cloughoughter, an island three hundred feet in diameter, wholly dominated by O'Reilly's stone fortress. The castle's walls were immensely thick, round, massive and hoary, boasting embrasures and coved windows. The island it stood on was scarcely sufficient to share the immense pile and the small margin of rock around it.

How it was ever built – how the stone was brought there – remained a blend of myth and conjecture.

The island stood in very deep water; the shores are a mile distant. The neighbouring mainland was wild and thickly wooded. Cloughoughter was effectively impregnable.[lv]

Ormonde was only accompanied by his household, whose horses had to be trusted to a landsman while the marquess and two faithful *garda* made the crossing.

Once they were seated the Lord Lieutenant spoke plainly.

'Our situation is bleak, General,' he said. 'Recently you have remained aloof from the Confederate-Royalist Coalition, but more than ever Ireland needs you.'

'I'm not sure that Ireland needs you, Lord Lieutenant. You seem to be more in retreat than advance.'

'Surely the bloodbaths at Drogheda and Wexford have persuaded you that a Coalition is your only hope of restoring the Catholic Church and Irish rule to Ulster?'

The urgency in the Lord Lieutenant's voce was tangible.

'While my army grows daily stronger, I still have not the numbers to oppose General Cromwell head on. If you were on my side the course of this war would change. How many men could you raise?'

'There are fifteen thousand Irishmen who have sworn allegiance to a Catholic Ireland and who have asked me to deliver it to them.'

'All Ultonians?'

'All true Ulstermen, indeed. Kinsmen, mostly,'

The to-and-fro of debate kept them busy for some time. Servants brought logs to heat the fire and refreshments to cool the mood. Lamps were lit and curtains were drawn. As the hours passed Ormonde knew with gathering certainty that he needed to make O'Neill some kind of offer.

'General Owen Roe, I solemnly swear on behalf of the king to restore your soldiers' land and to evict the settlers from your province.'

'Their right to practice their faith openly? In churches restored to the Universal Church?'

'You have my word.'

'Well, Lord Lieutenant, when this filthy weather breaks in the New Year, you may add my fifteen thousand to your five. Even before then I can spare a few. We could start with Munster. My Ulstermen like a walk. They face few challenges here. Only that madman Charles Coote at Castle Cuffe.'

'He's as mad as his father ever was, they tell me.'

'Worse, if that's possible. Now, I'll have my secretary fetch paper and ink. We'll set down your promises in writing. These matters we have discussed are worthy of a treaty.'

After far too much acrimony, Ormonde and Owen Roe O'Neill were reconciled, and the Commander of the Irish Ulster army was willing to reinforce the Lord Lieutenant, at least throughout the winter.

After the reconciliation several thousand Ulstermen would join him in the south. Some were dispatched to New Ross, which controlled the roads to the south., and a larger number were sent to swell the Irish ranks in Waterford, a port which more than any other was crucial to the Irish cause. Ormonde's military might was almost completely restored.

For Cromwell, the story told differently. While he had suffered few losses, he had had to leave a large number of men behind in Wexford. It was an uncomfortable billet but it would not do at all if Ormonde were able to take the port back for Ireland.

He was rescued by the English Parliament, whose love affair with their general was still in high honeymoon. It voted him reinforcements and an enormous sum of money, to be deployed at the High Commissioner's discretion but intended to let him buy off any amenable enemy.

Parliament sent a smouldering Wexford the thousand builders that Cromwell had asked for. Even better, they also sent a great many more loyal Protestant soldiers, under Colonel Cook. Cromwell's cup was running over. He allowed around half of them to man the garrison, while the rest were suborned into his army.

Only then did the High Commissioner for War head for New Ross.

The taking of Wexford had broken up the Irish privateering business. That left only Prince Rupert's landlocked squadron at Kinsale; a toothless threat to Commonwealth shipping and Cromwell's supply lines. Rupert knew that his fleet had no further prospect of success. One dark night he took his fleet out of Kinsale, into the Atlantic, and did not stop until he reached Portugal.

*

Despite everything, Lord Ormonde was still hopeful that Cromwell's relentless advance could be halted. He had learned that the Parliamentarian field army numbered but five thousand, after strategic postings in captured towns or garrisons, or expeditions to strategic outposts.

The climate, moreover, was worsening. Ireland was still to emerge from its 'little ice age'.Sickness would take a disproportionate toll on those unused to the Irish weather. This was especially the case in Ulster. By October, it had turned so foul that even Owen Roe O'Neill decided to remain with his immediate guard at Cloughoughter Castle, the picturesque medieval island fortress in County Cavan as yet unmolested by Parliamentarians. The balance of his Ulster Army went south, to help Ormonde contain Cromwell's inexorable advance.

Despite the loss of Wexford and many other garrisons in Leinster, the Marquess of Ormonde was still confident that Cromwell could be halted before he crossed into Munster. Everywhere the Parliamentarian field army went it had to leave large numbers of soldiers behind to man the conquered garrisons. That reduced its strength, quite as much as the worsening weather.

Ormonde planned to control Carrick, a walled town he knew all too well. His country house was nearby.

O'Neill's promises proved good. Ormonde's army swelled with companies of O'Neill's Ulstermen, and for the most part under their own officers. With these fresh men the marquess felt secure enough to menace the Parliamentarian vanguard, but when he saw the sheer scale of Jones's army, however, he quickly retreated.

Seeing he was still massively outnumbered was a great disappointment; the more so when the Parliamentarians rode after the Royalists at full speed. They were only shaken off when Ormonde crossed the River Nore at Thomastown and, once over it, burned the ancient wooden bridge behind him, preventing Jones from advancing any further west.

Ormonde's first concern was now for Waterford, both the greatest port in Munster and arguably the heart of Catholic Ireland.

It was now becoming the apple in Cromwell's crossbow sights. He too had realised that the City of Waterford was the most important major port still held by the former Confederacy.

Cromwell appointed Jones to command his Munster army, and the Welshman was no dullard. He knew that to take Waterford he would need to control both the Barrow estuary and the Suir River. He would have to land his heavy artillery on its banks in order to breach Waterford's walls.

There were two problems. He was on the wrong side of the river Suir, the north side, and was also short of food. His men, tired from the abortive chase they had given Ormonde and Jones, decided to withdraw to New Ross and use it as a base from where they could raid the local farms for live cattle and their barns for winter stores.

This was hard for the Irish. They too had little food of their own. General Jones, calculating that Carrick - an Ormonde stronghold - would prove hostile, assigned his captain of horse, Colonel Reynolds and seven hundred men, to take, garrison and retain the walled Royalist townland of Carrick and, most importantly for Parliament, its bridge,.

Reynolds was flattered and impressed by his orders, the more so as he already had a plan of his own.

From the south, Carrick could only be approached by a long, medieval bridge over the fast flowing Suir. Once that bridge was taken, the flow of armies into and out of Munster would be controlled by Parliament. Once liberated, the bridge could conduct the Roundheads the twenty further miles to the city of Waterford itself. From every other direction, Carrick's walls protected the hamlet, Ormonde's castle and the marquess's unfortified Elizabethan manor

Reynolds surprised a sleepy, unsuspecting Carrick-on-Suir in the early morning of November 19. His artillery smashed a path through the main gate while the rest marched into town to meet an unprepared and complacent Royalist garrison. It had no hope of resistance and fled over the bridge into County Waterford.

Reynolds captured Carrick without the loss of a single man.

Cromwell learned of the taking of Carrick at his daily 'breakfast' meeting, held at such an early hour that few had any appetite. His army was swollen with defecting Royalist Protestants, appalled by Ormonde's promises of religious freedom and his pragmatic treaty with Owen Roe O'Neill.

It was time to re-establish communications with his most senior commander in Munster, Lord Broghill, the Earl of Cork's third son. Kinsale, Youghal and Dungarvan had already declared for Broghill. Cromwell's message to his lordship was that he should deploy his eloquence and persuade every one of Lord Inchiquin's former garrisons to declare for the Commonwealth.

For his part, Lord Ormonde was determined to confront the Parliamentarians, especially in Carrick where his grandfather had converted an ancient fortress into a lovely country house. Unfortunately it was winter and there were 'differences of opinion' amongst his officers on the best way to proceed. O'Neill's Ulster Army also thought that strategic Carrick should be taken back.

Reynold's handful of Roundheads – no one knew how many - should be an easy target. A considerable majority of his officers also thought it vital to retake Carrick before their march on Waterford City, for an easy victory would boost their Catholic armies' self-esteem.

Carrick would be no pushover.

Ormonde divided his forces. He led a Royalist column downstream to the Abbey at Ferrybank, from where it could be shipped across to reinforce Waterford, leaving Lords Inchiquin and Castlehaven to direct a Royalist assault on Carrick and regain control of its bridge.

*

Bryen MacDonogh and Dick Talbot and their men were headed for Waterford from their little victory at the ford. The only route they knew of was over Carrick-on-Suir's ancient bridge but, just as they caught sight of the town walls on the horizon, they found that they had strayed into Lord Castlehaven's camp, outside its walls, and that the town was occupied by the enemy.

'My Lord Castlehaven,' said Major MacDonogh, dismounting and sweeping his hat low and bowing from the waist, 'Captain Talbot and my clansmen would like to join your little party.'

'Bryen, Dick, you and your sharpshooters are most welcome. Have your men graze your horses with the others and go to the canteen, they will find food and drink.' He indicated a large tent surrounded by smaller ones. 'You two stay with me here a few minutes. We have an issue. The heretic Colonel Reynolds has bolstered the wrecked north gate with oak beams from the church and has very successfully barricaded himself into the town. Some hundreds of his fellow schismatics are in there with him, I was going to say found sanctuary which would have been an unhappy phrase for such apostates, and we have no artillery. Neither Inchiquin nor I can think how to get in, and the bridge can only be reached from within the town.'

'Then you'll be talking about a siege. That may take many weeks. We would love to stay but we are on our way to join Lord Ormonde and defend Waterford City. We will have to head upstream and find another crossing into Waterford, if there is one. Musketeers are no use in a siege, I'm afraid.'

'Reynolds may accept terms. He may think we have powder and shot.'

'And if he doesn't surrender, an assault?'

'Precisely. Can we count on you and your men?'

'Well, what d'you think, Dick?'

'I say we join in the fun.'

Lord Castlehaven shook their hands.

'Well said. I never doubted you. Presuming they don't give up, we'll burn down the town gate tomorrow before storming the town. After the liberation you may cross the bridge and join Lord Ormonde with our heartiest blessing.'

'My marksmen have little experience in taking a town.'

'Reynolds' garrison is even shorter of ammunition than we are. They will submit directly, don't you worry.'

It was not true, however.

Colonel Reynolds refused to give way to the Catholics in terms both bold and rude.

It had begun to rain. The battered old oak gate, as hard as iron, proved fireproof.

Castlehaven and Inchiquin had their men assemble ladders and string them together. They leaned these rickety structures against the walls and Owen Roe's brave Ulstermen climbed them, planning on storming Carrick's battlements.

Bryen's men fired an occasional shot but the defending Parliamentarians sustained only limited injury. Meanwhile, Colonel Reynold's men discovered some pikes and used them to push the fragile ladders away from the walls. When they fell it was far enough for the leading assailant to be broken by the cobbled ground below. After four long, deadly and ultimately futile hours, Castlehaven and Inchiquin were forced to stand down. Even then, Major Geoghegan, one of Owen Roe's gentlemen, would not accept defeat and insisted on mounting a second wave of the attack.

Like the concerted attempt that had preceded it, it too was successfully repulsed. Worse, Reynolds seemed utterly unmoved by Irish heroics.

Castlehaven looked likely to have to admit defeat. As his men searched for swords and firearms among the fallen, they counted forty Ulstermen, dead or fatally injured, beneath the walls. Every one of these unfortunate men had joined the war to serve Owen Roe. Reynolds later boasted he had lost just one, a feckless Protestant whose silly face had been taken off his neck by a musket ball. The Catholic assault had been a disaster.

A messenger arrived with a letter and approached Lord Castlehaven.

'Gentlemen,' announced his lordship, 'I have just received orders from Lord Ormonde. He wants O'Neill's Ulstermen to reinforce Waterford. Cromwell has arrived at its walls.'

Of course, neither Inchiquin nor Castlehaven could know how many Parliamentarians defended Ormonde's home turf.

In fact there were very few. Cromwell's sights had always been set on Waterford. He had directed Reynolds to leave a 'forlorn' to protect the bridge. Less than forty men in all.

It was Captain Talbot, sharing a supper with MacDonogh in Castlehaven's 'big tent' who worked it out.

'I don't accept there is a great army inside the walls,' he told Bryen. 'Why would Cromwell want to abandon more than the minimum number possible to deny us access to that infernal bridge. The walls are stout and his model soldiers are on their way to Waterford.'

'I see what you mean. I wonder what that minimum might be. What do you think? Thirty or forty men?'

'We need to use our sharp-shooters. If we take out ten or so of Reynold's men, he will abandon the town. He is not on a suicide mission, after all.'

'Attempting to storm the place was a mistake. We should place as many cartouches as Castlehaven can spare in the cracks in the gate and have half our men train our weapons on it, but wait. The other half should be ready to shoot any Saxon who sticks his head over the parapet. Then, a red herring. Let's have some fit infantrymen begin to attack the gate with a battering ram. Reynold's soldiers will appear on the walls to report and shoot at us, but we are better shots than they are. Finally, at dawn, we blow the gate into eternity. When our men can see the enemy, we will open fire. We shall bring down say a dozen men and then Reynolds will run for it. Then, my lord Castlehaven will take his men into town in a victorious rush,'

'I love it. It's how you sprung Castlehaven from Dublin, after all, which gives you moral leverage over him. He's sure to agree.'

Castlehaven did.

Pragmatically, he ordered the dead beside the walls to be left unburied.

'Leave that to the townspeople. They will do it soon enough. Once inside we must cross the river immediately. Waterford needs us.'

Dick and Bryen's plan worked like a dream. Shortly after dawn, Lords Castlehaven and Inchiquin, their subalterns and ADCs, not to ignore an army of fearless Ulstermen, marched across Carrick Bridge to the south bank of the Suir and onto the road to Waterford, hot on the heels of Reynolds who had preceded them with only fifteen surviving troopers.

As for Dick, Bryen and their company, they remounted and headed for Duncannon - on the north bank of the Barrow Estuary. Ordinarily they would have hired boats to take them across at New Ross, but they had heard that Ireton, Cromwell's son-in-law, had plans to put the place to siege. Maybe he already had?'

'I think our merry band of freebooting tories may have to cross the river further downstream. Come on, Talbot, if we ride hard and if we find a helpful boatman or two, we'll in Duncannon while it's still light.'

*

CHAPTER TWENTY-FIVE
TORIES

The revered if incalcitrant General Owen Roe O'Neill was miles away to the north, at his adopted home on his fortress island of Cloughoughter, deep in territory supposedly ruled by the Provost-Marshall of Connacht, Sir Charles Coote the Younger, bart. When Coote heard from an informant that his arch-enemy O'Neill was sheltering a detachment of his army quite safely at the island fortress, a blood-red tide rose before his eyes. Nevertheless, an outright assault on the castle would be wholly impossible. The width of the river that served Cloughoughter as a moat would keep any cannon well out of range. Coote would need landing craft, simply unavailable inland.

He had a more radical solution, however.

Sir Richard Blake, now a prosperous citizen of Galway City and one of its 'tribesmen',[lvi] was the son of an infamous assassin. It had been Blake's father who had dispatched Philip O'Sullevan Beare in Madrid and had made it look like an accident. Perhaps the scion of such an illustrious secret agent could do the necessary for Owen Roe.

Blake was invited to Coote's seat at Castle Cuffe, where he was asked whether he could rid his nation of a turbulent Papist.

'I can probably gain admission into Owen Roe's presence, Lord Provost. It's getting out again that is the problem.'

'Are you afraid to die for your country, Sir Richard?'

'No. Yet I feel the fee for such terminal service is not yet correctly priced.'

'Well, what would your fee be?'

'I will need £1,000. Payable half now and half when I succeed.'

There was a silence, shocked on one side, ambitious on the other.

'Very well. I had anticipated something of the kind. I agree. How will you achieve your task?'

'It will have to be poison, Sir Charles; one that takes a few hours to take effect. Owen Roe will have to appear fit as I leave his island, or his guards will, how shall I put it, detain me.'

'I see that. What have you in mind? Henblane? Strychnine?'

'The Greek philosopher Plato revealed there is a potion to serve our purpose. He called it 'conium'[lvii]. We call it 'hemlock'. Here in Ireland, that select brotherhood admitted into the secrets of sorcerers call it 'the Devil's Porridge'. You will have seen it many times without guessing its terrible secret. The plant is about my height when fully grown and has a smooth green stem, spotted or streaked with red or purple. Its huge lacy leaves are triangular and in summer its flowers form white clusters of umbels. When crushed, its leaves and root have an unpleasant odour sometimes compared to that of parsnips. Or mice.'

'Hmm. You will be able to persuade Owen Roe O'Neill to drink this unappetising infusion?'

'I will. I shall distract him. He'll think our meeting has some other purpose.'

'Its effect? Should you get away with it?'

'It paralyses the limbs, slowly and painlessly. He won't even call out. If I can get him to take it at sundown he will wake up dead. The world will believe it was natural causes and England will lose a dangerous enemy.'

'Where do we find this hemlock? It won't be available from any ordinary apothecary.'

'Some veterinarians have it. In this country it is thought a humane way to put a sick animal down.'

'How appropriate. The Irish should think that what we do is born of kindness.'

If Cromwell had hoped to surprise Lord Ormonde, he was out of luck. Ormonde had quit New Ross, before making for Waterford. He had left New Ross's garrison to Sir Lucas Taaffe, a loyal royalist whom he installed as the city's governor.

Sir Lucas woke up one unhappy morning to see Cromwell's army camped outside his walls. Taaffe knew the fate of Wexford. He had already gained the Marquess of Ormonde's permission to surrender the town on terms, should the Parliamentarians ever breach the walls.

Cromwell now sent his customary demand for surrender. At first, Taaffe did not even reply. While he was widely seen as a stern general, when the Puritan general fired his cannons at the town walls, on the morning of October 19, destruction was soon achieved, and Taaffe saw that the Saxon foot was preparing to storm their way in.

In accordance with Ormonde's orders, Taaffe finally responded to the summon and asked for terms.

It was a good call. Cromwell wanted to show the remaining Irish garrisons that, if they surrendered, they would enjoy lenient terms.

'Let the citizens collect their possessions. Take your time, you will not be harmed, your town will not be plundered. Those not in arms can remain there unmolested, or depart, as they see fit.'

He refused, however, to allow Taaffe to remove artillery or powder from the town. He did allow the soldiers to march away, taking their muskets, pikes and swords with them.

There is always a catch, however. Henceforward, the practice of Catholicism would neither be tolerated nor would any church or mass-house be allowed to stand.

With the fall of New Ross, General Cromwell had to march his army inland. There was no bridge, however, so he commandeered every fishing vessel that Waterford could provide. He used them to create a pontoon and planks were laid across them to create a road across the river. His field guns were hauled over it by teams of oxen while dragoons pulled sleds piled high with ordnance of every kind.

Deane's squadron, or 'sea-regiment', sailed up the River Barrow almost as far as Passage East, on the west bank of the river. They carried supplies, three brigades and yet more artillery, but could go no further. Passage East was almost opposite Duncannon, and these two star forts effectively prevented the sea-army from coming any further upstream.

Deane disembarked Lord Broghill's and Colonel Phayre's regiments on the west bank of the Barrow. He had orders to secure Cork, Youghal and Bandon for Parliament and carried the resources to reward further defections to the Parliamentary cause.

Cromwell, meanwhile, had ordered his son-in-law, Major-General Ireton, to take a detachment and reduce the Royalist garrison at Duncannon, the star fort that commanded the eastern bank of the estuary.

Bryen, Dick and their fifty dragoons, or musketeers, after their success at Carrick, had stayed on the north side of the Suir. It was a long march, thirty-two miles in all, but they had at last reached the Royalist garrison at Duncannon. The huge fort was at a wide point of the estuary, out on a promontory, and they sought shelter there.

Bryen was only too aware of Duncannon's importance. It was pivotal to the defence of Waterford City. Ormonde had already sent the garrison reinforcements, including a hundred and twenty utterly loyal and well-trained men of his own lifeguard. Their captain, a Welshman called Edward Wogan, was a charismatic fellow, easily able to handle the mounting hostility, even raids, which emanated from Irish Protestants. Having to strengthen the defence of Duncannon, Captain Wogan found the unexpected arrival of Bryen and Dick, and their company of sharpshooters, most welcome.

'Lads,' he said, bringing Bryen, Dick and their band well into the fort, 'our defence of Duncannon needs to be more aggressive. Major-General Ireton would seem to be on his way. Presumably he will bombard us. Mining these walls would seem pointless – they're thirty feet thick. When he arrives, perhaps you could be persuaded to mount a little surprise party for the Protestant gunners? It needn't be too elaborate.'

'That would be grand,' said Bryen. 'In the meantime, is there any chance of a little supper for us, our horses and our brave lads?'

Ireton was indeed on his way.

Duncannon and Passage East - the two fortresses on the Barrow – completely hindered Parliament's naval ambitions from the coast. Cromwell's sea-army would need to control of the estuary before he could turn his attention to Waterford, the most important port still held by the Confederacy. To break its walls he would have to land his heaviest artillery, which meant bringing English warships miles up stream.

Major-General Ireton, with a detachment of the Parliamentarian Army, arrived under at Duncannon, under a white flag, and demanded immediate surrender.

Wogan listened to Ireton's loudspeaker, not dignifying him with the courtesy of a response, but if he thought he was out of danger, he was wrong. On October 27, the newly promoted Lieutenant-General Jones made an unwelcome appearance with two thousand troops and field guns to match. Happily the walls of the renaissance fort were strong, based on the model pioneered by Leonardo da Vinci for the Dukes of Milan, and Jones' cannons were quickly seen to be too puny to achieve a breach.

To make things even more difficult for Ireton and Jones, every time they tried to send in a bombardier or two, Bryen's musketeers would pick off their enemy from the safety of the battlements. It was clear to Wogan that the Parliamentary threat could be safely ignored.

For their part, Ireton and Jones also saw that the garrison was too strong to risk a direct assault. They retreated a little to discuss strategy.

So too Captain Wogan. He wanted now was to send the Protestants packing.

'Any ideas?' he asked his guests.

'Let's see what we can do, Sir.'

Dick had already been thinking long and hard.

'Bryen, you've seen where they've set up their field guns. If we go out of the south gate after dark, we might be able to capture them.'

'I agree.'

'You do? You are aware that there are several thousand of them?' said Wogan.

Bryen simply smiled.

Wogan pushed.

'All right. What would you need, Major MacDonogh?'

'Ten stout men to haul each gun. My marksmen will cover from them from the battlements. It will be a doddle. One thing, Captain. We can do this, but it won't be at night. My musketeers would not be able to see their targets. Besides, the enemy will expect something of the kind. No, our raid should be at sunrise.'

'Brilliant,' said Dick. 'I agree.'

'Well then', said Wogan, 'I admit this sounds promising. Tomorrow too soon for you?'

Bryen, Dick and their forty-seven musketeers were biddable, alert, fed, rested, and ready for action well before dawn. The marksmen were on the battlements, where they had propped up their long firearms with practiced skill.

Two Parliamentarian work parties were advancing on the fort, even before dawn had formally announced itself to an impatient world.

'What d'you think they're up to, Dick,' asked Bryen.

'Jesus, Mary and Joseph, you blithering idiot, they're about to retrieve their sodding guns. What are we waiting for?'

Bryen raised his hand and brought it down sharply. It was a signal. Forty musketeers delivered a volley, every round lethal.

The birds had been typically noisy at daybreak, but the crack of the rifles silenced them.

The doors to the fort's south east wall opened and Wogan's dragoons emerged. They hauled the two Parliamentarian field guns inside. After a few minutes, pulleys had hoisted them onto the battlements. The Puritans' destructive purpose had ironically made Duncannon stronger.

Jones and Ireton had to abandon their assault. They still needed somewhere to cross the river. They set off towards Ferry Port, across the Suir from Waterford. Ormonde, too, they calculated, would have to go there or to the bridge at Carrick-on-Suir, to cross into Waterford, and they were confident that they could defeat Ormonde in a single confrontation.

Only after watching the Protestants withdraw did Bryen and Dick decline Captain Wogan's invitation to celebrate. Instead they took their leave. In Carrick they had heard that Ormonde had been heading for New Ross. If so, their auxiliaries would be needed more than ever and they would be happy to rejoin Ormonde's army.

When Bryen and Dick arrived in New Ross, fifteen miles away to the north, they were amazed to find the town deserted, its gates opened to the wind. Torn tents and flattened pastures strongly suggested that both Castlehaven's and Cromwell's armies had been there.

The town had once been famous for its abbeys. Nowhere in Ireland had heard or enjoyed a sweeter sound of chant than in New Ross's Tintern Abbey[lviii]. It had once been as lovely as any flamboyant or perpendicular monastery in Europe. That is, until the heretic queen had enforced her father's destructive dissolution overseas.

The musketeers were tired, but the abandoned town would could serve as shelter from the elements. Clearly its Catholic soldiers had retreated.

'We can be sure there will be water or small beer in the kitchens,' said Dick. 'For the time being, our men should forage - we'll be able to supply our further deficiencies across the river in Waterford,'

'I agree. It's late in any case. Never despair,' Bryen offered. 'This area is famous for golden plovers, teal, white-fronted geese. Our sharpshooters can earn their breakfast.'

When they stepped into the fort, however, they had the most extraordinary surprise.

A harassed figure in a greatcoat run through with gold thread was directing his personal guards. They were struggling with trunks, presumably filled with valuable possessions, carrying them clumsily down a great flight of stairs.

This august personage drew himself to a halt. Seeing the way in which his unexpected visitors bore themselves he bowed, raising an eyebrow to indicate he was, at the very least, expecting the minimal courtesy of an introduction.

'Who are you?' he demanded curtly.

'This, Sir, is Captain Richard Talbot. I am Major Bryen MacDonogh.' They dismounted and bowed. 'You have to be Sir Lucas Taaffe, the governor of this city?'

'At your service.' He bent down to retrieve a book from the hall's floor. It was *Eikon Basilike*[ix], the late king's own story, penned while he was captive in Hampton Court. He put it into the pocket of his coat.

'What business can you and your men have here, Major, Captain?'

'We came to offer our arms and men to Lord Ormonde. He has gone?' Bryen asked.

'You missed him. He set off for Waterford some time ago, leaving me and the garrison behind. Commissioner Cromwell arrived the day before yesterday. My remaining men, most of the original garrison in fact, surrendered on terms. Cromwell let them march away with their arms, baggage, drums and colours. Two thousand men set off with squared shoulders to rejoin Ormonde's main army.'

'Every man jack of your garrison has left for Waterford?' asked Dick.

'Almost every man.'

'That makes sense. The heretic general believes the weather will do his dirty work.'

'He may be disappointed. The season is not yet deadly. Most will survive.' Dick was used to the cold.

'You said *almost* every man.'

'Around five hundred, mostly Englishmen, went over to the enemy.'

'They wanted Cromwell's shilling, I suppose.' Bryen had concluded that money played the role of god to some Protestants.

'But you remain?' asked Bryen.

'The men were given letters of safe conduct. When I have removed such personal chattels as I had here I shall join them.'

'The Puritan general had the better of you, Sir Lucas?' asked Bryen tactlessly.

'Are you mad, Major?' Sir Lucas snapped angrily. 'When Cromwell turned his murderous attentions on my fortress he had nine thousand men, many of them fresh English conscripts. He had three siege guns, drawn by vast teams of oxen. A naval squadron had accompanied him almost all the way along the Barrow, groaning with supplies and artillery. Don't tell me you hadn't heard he killed everyone in Drogheda and Wexford? The most noble Marquess of Ormonde had graciously allowed me to surrender the town on terms, if the Parliamentarians succeeded in breaking through. That's what we did; surrender on terms. Good terms.'

'Where is the Puritan general going now, Sir Lucas?'

'Do you think we swapped military banter over a pint of milk stout? Take a look at the river! It's two hundred yards across! General

Cromwell's sappers turned every fishing boat in the Barrow into that pontoon. They built a door into County Waterford.' He gestured at the floating bridge and across the expanse of river before them. 'That's where he went.'

'We have just had a brush with his second-in-command, Major-General Ireton,' Bryen admitted.

'In Duncannon', added Dick.

'Did you? I'm surprised you're both alive.'

'Our lady's protection, and that of the angels and saints, saw us through.'

'We had no such luck. When those angels and saints came to your rescue, they deserted us here. Come, come and see how Cromwell makes his presence known.'

Taaffe took his kinsman's arm and led him to the door to the keep. Outside, the damage to either side of the main gate was plain to see.

'When at first I failed to respond to Cromwell's overtures, he trained his mortars on the town walls. Look at the mess they made! Just as his infantry was about to storm us, I answered his summons. I was gambling that Cromwell would want Ireland to see he could be lenient if he got his own way.'

'A good call, Sir Lucas.'

'Yes, God be praised. He allowed my men to march away. I was allowed to remove my personal possessions and maintain my personal cavalry. Cromwell promised the town and garrison would not be plundered, and that the civilian population could remain unmolested or depart with their goods.'

'Why then did they choose to leave?'

Major-General Sir Lucas Taaffe fished around in a pocket. He handed Bryen a letter. Beyond the usual courtesies it read,

> In response to your request, Sir Lucas, I meddle not with any man's conscience. But if you intend a liberty to exercise the Mass, that will not be allowed of.
>
> Your servant, O Cromwell.

'I see.'

'The people were frightened witless. Without their faith or their priests to protect them they followed Cromwell across his pontoon. The boats veered wildly in the wind and the tide. Many stumbled, including mothers with babes in arms. Even some soldiers found the crossing fatal. It was pathetic.'

'The priests had abandoned them?'

'If English troops had entered the town, they would have cut down every priest or monk they saw. They knew that. Every Irish priest has a bounty on his head, you know. The going rate is twenty pounds for a dead or captured priest. One of ours wrote a poem in hope for a better future. A fine poem in the Irish idiom. I have tried to translate it. My Gaelic is not good, but here you are.'

He fished a paper out of his greatcoat pocket.

The Gaels are wasted, a redundant race
Subjugated, slain, and crushed, by
Plague, famine, war, and persecution.
Yet one day, Erin will free herself.
That day will perish the English tongue.
The Gaels in arms shall triumph
Over the crafty, thieving false rite of Calvin.

'A poor translation I readily admit; Erse's metrical, rhyming structure mostly defeats me, but here you have the gist of it. I'm afraid the loss of New Ross will only aggravate the ancient enmities between Catholics and Protestants in the Coalition.'

'Well, Sir Lucas, in the morning we too shall cross that pontoon and find Lord Ormonde in Waterford. Cromwell must be restrained.'

Dick pulled a clay from his pocket and lit it slowly while the governor of New Ross drew his sorry tale to a close.

'No doubt this empty city will soon be planted; Parliamentarians, adventurers, undertakers – the New English, in other words. They will inherit some of Ireland's finest medieval buildings, a prize they will care little for. I and my guardsmen are headed for Waterford, too. With your indulgence we shall ride beside you.'

*

'So, Sir Richard, you have sought and I have granted you an audience. In your letter you said you had to tell me, in person, of a service you could usefully render me.'

Owen Roe's ferryman had brought Blake to Cloughoughter a few hours before. His reputation had preceded him. The nefarious adventures of his secret agent father were the stuff of legend while the son was merely a successful merchant and banker. There was, Owen Roe felt, no need to brand the son with his father's sins. Nevertheless, it is always wise to take precautions. Blake had been searched very thoroughly for a dagger or a pistol when he had disembarked from the little barque that had brought him to the island. No weapon of any kind had been

376

discovered and he was allowed to keep the harmless leather flask of *potín* he carried – for courage, he had said.

'My father did this country a great disservice, General. Nevertheless, since he died I have turned my inheritance into a substantial fortune. It would be, how shall I put it, an *amende honorable* if I could ease some of the financial issues that you face.'

Owen Roe did not trust this polished financier. Two of his guards remained in the parlour where their conversation was taking place. The general was a soldiers' soldier and he disliked bankers and politicians with impartial loathing.

'I can underwrite a bond you might issue to other Catholic landowners. I suggest a return on their investment of fully 5%. For my part, I shall issue an indemnity against my own fortune that, should the Catholic cause be lost, their money will still be safe.'

'I see. Or I think I do. In the words I believe you favour, what's in it for me?'

'You will raise a great deal of money. £10,000? Perhaps more. I shall receive £500 for my troubles, for every year the debt is outstanding. We will both prosper and your cause will be reinforced. Perhaps the balance of the war will shift irreversibly towards you. If, per misadventure, you or I should die, the loans will still be good. Come Sir, what d'you say?'

'What do I say? I have never understood the motives of a businessman, but I do respect courage. To come here to Cloughoughter, you have plenty of that. I think, Sir Richard, we have ourselves a deal. Let us shake hands on it!'

'With your indulgence, Sir, the hour is late and my barque is waiting to take me back across the river. Let us raise a toast to our project, before the lure of the night takes us both to our beds.'

'By all means. I have a passable whiskey?'

'And in this flask I have the most remarkable *potín,* the like of which you will never have tasted. Here, let me, General. These horsehair vessels[ix] are made for our purpose.'

He poured two small measures.

'I shall have all the papers drawn up tomorrow, and sent to you here that evening. You and your secretary will have the time you need to peruse them at leisure. Your good health! *Codladh sámh duit!*'

'Sir Richard, I give you back a toast to the so-called Gunpowder Plot, whose anniversary it is today. To think we might have ended all our problems forty-odd years ago. *Sláinte!*'

They both drained their cups, one truly, the other into the adsorbent lint tucked into his sleeve.

Owen Roe died on 6 November 1649, in his bed at Cloughoughter castle in the County Cavan.

Some suspected he was poisoned by the English. The English version was that the epidemic scourging Ireland at the time must have killed him.

'It may be true,' said Bryen to Dick Talbot, 'but I hear he was alive and in good spirits just the night before he died.'

'A fast-acting plague. Can't say I've heard of one of those.'

'What are the English, then?'

'You have a point.'

The Constable of Cloughoughter arranged for General O'Neill to be buried in an unmarked grave in Cavan's Franciscan cemetery, under cover of darkness. There was a fear that if his remains were discovered, the Provost-Marshall would disinter them and hoist them on a gibbet.

In Castle Cuffe his death, a major blow to the Irish of Ulster, was celebrated.

Sir Charles Coote was particularly cheerful.

'No one is to enter or leave that fortress again. Have muskets posted at ten yard intervals where the river runs closest. Anyone who attempts to leave it or to find its garrison food is to be shot down. Leave it a month. Then bring in our heaviest artillery. The castle is to be used for target practice until it has gone, disappeared, vanished from the history of Ireland. By the end of the year I want its very existence to have been forgotten.'

As with most things the Provost-Marshall of Connacht had his way.

*

Despite the loss of the Royalists garrisons of Drogheda, Wexford, Carrick and New Ross, the Marquess of Ormonde still believed that Cromwell's juggernaut could be halted. Cromwell had posted squadrons of the New Model Army in so many captured towns and fortresses that Ormonde calculated that, combined with the oncoming winter, the Parliamentarian army would daily reduce in force. The weather would always ally with the Irish.

Ormonde configured that Cromwell's gaze would have to be focussed on Waterford, even though the city was strongly defended and held by Royalists under the Confederate General Tomás Preston.

He was right. Cromwell would indeed invest the city, and he did so in person. He set out for the *Urbs Intacta*[xi], as the Irish called Waterford, on November 18 and began operations three days later. He had determined it would not remain 'undefeated' for long.

Waterford was a very Catholic place. Its townsmen knew that General Cromwell wanted to punish them for what he believed was Ireland's cruel treatment of the country's Protestants in 1641. Hadn't he said in a speech in Dublin after he landed on Ireland's shores…

…the sanction of my fellow Puritans will follow the extermination of Irish Papists.

Like most other towns in Ireland's south-east, Waterford had supported the Irish cause from the opening salvos of the Rebellion in 1641.

That was the year when a growing number of dishevelled Protestant refugees began to arrive at the town gates, begging for shelter and food. It greatly troubled the Catholic townspeople. The Mayor wanted to accommodate them but the Recorder, with several Aldermen, were of a differing opinion. They even wanted to strip Waterford's long-resident but 'parasitical' Protestants of their possessions and let the Catholic 'rebels' in to award them the Protestants' former property. If at first the Mayor's faction refused, by March most of his municipal government prevailed. The Protestant citizens were duly dispossessed, put on ships with the refugees and deported, penniless and with only such possessions as they could carry, to England.

Cromwell had already isolated Waterford from the east and north but, before he could take the city, he had to silence the surrounding garrisons and guarantee his lines of communication and supply.

Henry Ireton, Cromwell's son-in-law, had renewed his siege of Duncannon. Edward Wogan's stubborn defence was holding out, mainly because his captured cannons were swiftly trained on any infantry or sappers that came too close. Wogan's artillery divided their time between deterring Ireton and Deane's sea-army as it brought Parliament's siege engines ever closer to Waterford.

Clearly, Cromwell had to gain control of the Barrow estuary. Duncannon was only one of the two star forts that hindered the Parliamentarian navy.

Lieutenant-General Jones was sent to capture the other one, Passage East, a vast stone and earthwork star fort, a mile or so downstream from Duncannon, but on the far bank.

Jones sent a regiment of horse and three of dragoons across the river at Carrick to attack it. Although the fort was well-manned they were able to storm the walls, set fire to the gate and slay its resident Papists. Two hundred of them died in the assault. Jones promised the remaining three hundred their lives. They could even keep the clothes they wore if they surrendered without further ado. The garrison took one look at the sheer scale of their enemy and did what it was told.

The fall of the fort at Passage East effectively gave Cromwell's sea-army the river or, at least, its west bank. Its capture allowed English ships to sail safely up to the city itself and unload their siege guns. It should have guaranteed victory but constant rain had left the ground so wet and boggy, the weight of the guns doomed all Jones's attempts to bring the cannons on shore into range.

Another problem was that many of O'Neill's veterans, now commanded by Richard Farrell, found their way into the city under cover of darkness; three thousand of them, and that in a single week.

What's more, it was growing very cold. The 'little ice age', which had begun fifty years before, still unrelented. As Mad Dick had predicted, the Parliamentarians suffered heavily. Time was against them. Without being able to bring his cannons to bear, Cromwell's only hope could be that Waterford would surrender on terms.

After all, it was quite possible that Waterford's will to resist would collapse. Everyone in Waterford had seen the scale of the enemy. They could all see that that the general had dug in for the duration. Again they wrote to Ormonde. This time he sent fifteen hundred furious Ulstermen, missing their hero-general, to defend them. They would need a few days to get there.

Only a few days remained of that cold and wet November, but it would get worse. In early December the bogs and streams froze over. It was too cold to work or fight outside. Of the four thousand foot, two thousand horse and five hundred Puritan dragoons who had begun the siege of Waterford, Cromwell's combined force was now down to three thousand. Sickness, particularly dysentery, was rife among his soldiers. What choice did he have? He agreed to a parley with Colonel Lyvett, Waterford's mayor. It came to nothing; Lyvett was clearly in a better position to negotiate than the High Commissioner for War.

At this delicate time, Ormonde's relief column arrived. It had to wait until dark to enter the city but, when they came close, Waterford's gates were joyfully thrown open, letting the Catholic soldiers swarm into the city to be greeted with kisses and embraces from its citizens, male and female alike.

Cromwell digested the news. His campaign had, in political and military terms, been a resounding success – so far, and until this setback.

From his big tent, Cromwell could see little possibility of taking the city by force. True, the capture of Passage Fort had let him bring up his siege guns by sea but the terrible weather made it impossible to bring them close enough to the city walls. While it occurred to him that the freezing bogs might help him break his cannons out of the frozen mud and bring them even closer to the walls, the sheer severity of the winter saw his men dropping like flies.

There was no longer any hope that the town would surrender, or even that it might be taken by storm and, on December 2, 1649, Cromwell abandoned his siege.

*

Despite Cromwell's reversal of fortunes at Waterford, the Marquess of Ormonde wrote to the King-in-Exile in Breda. King Charles II read and accepted Ormonde's advice. Ormonde had wisely suggested the plans to use Ireland as a platform for an invasion of England should be postponed or even abandoned. The King-in-Exile should go instead to Scotland. The Scots had issued an invitation and there they would crown him Kings of Scots in Scone Palace, in keeping with time-honoured immemorial tradition.

All round, it had been a disappointing year for the Marquess of Ormonde. While he had managed a rapport with the King-in-Exile, in Ireland the only ray of light was Waterford's stiff resistance to Parliament, holding out against seemingly unbearable odds.

If only the king and his Lord-Lieutenant had known how exhausted Cromwell's army was, how short of supplies and how gripped it was by dysentery, Ormonde might have been less circumspect.

When Cromwell decided to abandon his siege, he meant to resume it in the spring. By then the weather should have become a little more clement. The general marched his army into County Cork, into territories already secured by Lord Broghill. He billeted his army in Cork and Youghal, and made Dungarvan his private winter quarters. That fortress might protect him from the 'tories', but not from the epidemic.

Commissioner Cromwell was very sick that December and January.

Cromwell's plight was truly desperate. With sinister accuracy, he had predicted a thousand of his Ironsides would die that winter. Of course, he had no idea that the fatalities would include Lieutenant-General Michael Jones, the 'hero' of Rathmines. All who contracted the awful disease were unceremoniously heaved into in a lime pit and covered. *Sic transit Gloria mundi.*

The subjugation of Ulster was also turning bloody. After Owen Roe's untimely decease, Colonel Robert Venables and Sir Charles Coote the Younger, commander of the Londonderry garrison, successfully recovered the north in the bloodiest of campaigns. Rory O'More, who had command of the Royalist Scots in King's and Queen's Counties, and who had been helpful in arranging an alliance with Inchiquin in 1647 and another with Ormonde the following year, had thought it best to bring his men to Waterford, leaving Ulster denuded. He too had become something of a folk hero. Soldiers often prayed that 'God and Our Lady be our help, and Rory O'More'.[lxii]

Then disaster. The remainder of the Royalist Scots were cut to pieces at Lisburn, and General Tam Dalyell was forced to surrender Carrickfergus castle to Parliament.

If Cromwell were not so ill he might even have thought that things were going well.

*

CHAPTER TWENTY-SIX
CHRISTMAS IN KANTURK

December, 1649, delivered such a blanket of snow that the parterres surrounding the Court at Kanturk were lost to sight. Its famous gardens resembled little more than an Esquimau's fantasy. As Bryen rode up to his front door, back from the war, his charger Caliban kicked up a train of dry white powder. His master had always said he would be home for Christmas, but as he dismounted and handed the reins to his groom, his brogues sank fully eight inches into the drift. He will have wished he could have returned a little earlier. Before the blizzard, perhaps?

Curiously, the smooth white lawn was littered with great cubes of boxes. Bryen immediately deduced that the long ordered glazed blue roof tiles from Venice had finally been delivered. It would not be long before the house would look the way his father and grandfather had always planned.

Once inside, Bryen was happy to discover a warm castle, its fires lit. The mansion bustled with scurrying maids, all of whom curtseyed as they saw him. Alas, there were no footmen. They had fallen at Knocknanuss.

His elder girl, Aodhamair, rushed up to her father, expecting and receiving a great big hug even before he had time to hand O'Grady his greatcoat. Bébhinn, the younger, was in her wetnurse's arms, gurgling happily.

Behind them, their mother Sorcha waited patiently before she put her arms around Bryen's neck and kissed him slowly on his cheeks, on his lips, on his neck. She didn't even notice the applause she had from her family and guests.

'What will you do with them?' she asked, after he had renewed his affection for her, in the way that sailors and soldiers always do on homecoming.

Sorcha meant the tiles.

'I shall realise my father's dreams, my darling. The war is over, at least for the winter. We shall spend the rest of the season roofing this lovely house. It need only take a couple of months.'

Sorcha snuggled closer to him in their great bed.

'But need this war go on for ever? You'll have to go away again?'

'All wars end. This one will probably end by the summer. Then, at long last, it will be history. The English can't take our climate and are

383

dying like flies. Cromwell himself is sick in Dungarvan. He'll either die or go home. With him gone, His Majesty the King can come to Ireland and we'll help him get his other crowns back.'

'Do you intend to invade England?'

'Perhaps. Whatever Lord Ormonde thinks best.'

'The king's in France, isn't he? I wonder if he's met your uncle Cormac?'

'The king's not in Catholic France. He's in Protestant Holland. Breda, to be exact. He is the Supreme Governor of the Church of England, which he defends with his every fibre. That's what it says on the coins, at least.'

'You must mean *fidei defensor*? I thought that title was given to King Henry by Pope Leo X, in recognition of his book *Assertio Septem Sacramentorum*, which argued the sacramental nature of marriage and the supremacy of the Pope?'

Bryen laughed. His manner had been teasing, but his tone had humour in it.

'The roofless Augustinian nuns of Ballymacadane Abbey taught you something, then.'

'The royal family, they taught us, still call it the 'Henrician Affirmation'. It was an important opposition to the Protestant Reformation, especially Martin Luther's schismatic ideas.'

'I'm impressed. Remind be to put some more money the nuns' way.'

*

Early that December, Ireland's Catholic clergy met in Clonmacnoise. They talked for the month, and then they talked some more. Not before late January did they write down their words in the form of a manifesto. It called on the entire Catholic Irish nation, whether old English or old Irish, new English or Scots or, for that matter, interlopers of any origin whatsoever, to unite against the common enemy in defence of their religion, lives, and fortunes.

As it threatened to extend the war, this clerical posturing greatly angered a recovering General Cromwell. He had decided to go home. Now, from his sickbed, he reversed his decision.

*

Not until the end of January 1650 did Cromwell receive fresh supplies and reinforcements. Then, in a relatively mild February, the Model Army began to sharpen its blades, stretch its legs. Soon Cromwell himself was fit enough to venture out from his winter quarters. His immediate intention was to occupy the Confederate counties of Kilkenny and Tipperary. From there he could easily dismantle most of the remaining Royalist strongholds.

The High Commissioner's first expedition of the year proved the start of a very good few months for the Roundheads. The general took every Popish castle and Papist townland that lay in his way. Ireton compared his swathe through Tipperary to a hot knife through butter. Fethard was the first to capitulate, without a shot being fired. Similarly, Cromwell bloodlessly accepted the keys of Cashel. This, for the survivors of Murrough of the Burnings, was bitter news indeed.

The Confederates surrendered several other citadels without resistance of any sort. It was a surprise, therefore, when Cromwell's progress met a significant challenge. That came at Callan.

For some reason, this almost insignificant little town refused to lie down and die. When it decided against terms, Cromwell attacked it. Sadly, its stand was short-lived. It fell after three days of intense hand-to-hand fighting. Captain Mark Geoghegan, who had led the defence of Skerry's Castle in Callan's West Street, died defending the town. The remaining members of the garrison and most of the civilians were awarded 'exemplary' executions.

The Cromwellians were skilled in mass hangings. Except they weren't really hangings. The victims were hauled six inches from the ground on a noose. For the lucky ones, such a stretching of the neck would break the spinal column but, since most of these lads were farmers or farmhands, their necks were strong. For these, the punishment was asphyxiation. Most of these unfortunate wretches would try to provoke their own extinction in an elaborate dance, always a source of amusement to a victorious Model Army.

One ray of light in an otherwise Puritan gloom; Geoghegan's redoubtable wife escaped with her life after killing at least a dozen enemy troops with her late husband's sword.

*

Eight weeks had passed at Kanturk Court and, despite Knocknanuss, the mood was light. It was Sorcha's birthday; she had turned twenty-three. As a birthday present the midwife had confirmed her mistress was pregnant a third time. Bryen was noisily thrilled, while Sorcha was quietly delighted.

'A boy, this time, if you wouldn't mind,' her husband whispered gently, as if such a thing were in human hands.

Kanturk was to host a double celebration. Sorcha's pregnancy was the best news ever. Running a close second was the fact that the roof was complete, the scaffolding down and the Court 'topped out'. Bryen and Sorcha's long guest list included her distinguished parents, Lord and Lady Muskerry. Dick Talbot was Bryen's honoured guest. Father Boetheus had ridden over from Dromsicane to ensure the joyous event would have a suitably spiritual dimension. He would bless the cook, sprinkle the kitchen with holy water, say grace and praise the Inspiration that commanded the creation of the dishes. Thady MacCarthy had agreed to come, by return of courier. Dermod Oge's old friend and one-time secretary, Fineen O'Driscoll - no longer a youngster - brought his lovely wife Aoife. Captain Millot and Anya had accepted but failed to appear. Their children, when they arrived, told a sad account; how they had both contracted dysentery. Two grim weeks later they both had died. Their children had discovered them in bed, hand-in-hand.

'That is how the angels will have found them, before taking their souls to heaven,' said Sorcha.

Bryen had ordered a new great coat before he had gone to war. This would be the perfect occasion to try it out. He took it from its paper wrapping and put it on. Its stuff was fawn - the latest fashion – and ample cuffs folded back over the sleeves, three gold buttons on each. It had vast pockets over each hip, each with two more buttons. Twenty buttons pretended to fasten it on the front – as if they all could - and its borders were elaborately trimmed with filigree Celtic designs in gold thread. A matching tricorn accompanied it. It was almost impossible not to swank in it.

Despite Mallow, Sir Philip de Perceval, had magnanimously been included in the party. His coat was of cerise damask. After lengthily expressing his sadness at Dermod Oge and Cliona's heroic passing, he was the first to compliment Bryen on the wonderful appearance of the castle. The magnificent roof, at last in its Cobalt livery, bled reflected blue light back into an azure sky.

The attic storey of the mansion had at last become the family's private quarters. Intricate carving and fine plasterwork had made it as grand as the palace of a renaissance prince. Bryen had finished the outer walls in a terracotta render that had been infused with pyrites, giving it an almost golden aspect. The elevated *piano nobile* was mostly given to its 'gallery', a grand reception chamber eighty feet by twenty, elaborately panelled in linenfold oak and heated by two vast fires, set in limestone chimneypieces to either end.

Two flights of stairs were needed to link the kitchen below with the dining parlour. That kitchen, that day, prepared its greatest meal.

Dinner had been called for a half-hour before noon. Dermod Oge, Bryen's late father, had always wanted to import the French way of eating, but his son delivered his guests a more traditional banquet. The groaning table had countless dishes, all served together. The guests were brought helpings of any number of savoury and sweet dishes. There was, of course, a traditional lamb stew. There was also spiced beef, Limerick ham, Colcannon, white pudding, bacon and egg pie, boxty, crubeens, mackerel rolls, 'Brigid's bread', mussel broth with fennel, clapshot, oatmeal and onion soup, skirlie, champ potato cakes with smoked salmon, cabbage pie with bacon, fish chowder and both potato and soda farls. Rhubarb and gooseberries, preserved in syrup, provided crumble and fools for those with a sweet tooth. For those with more savoury tastes, there were plates of cheese; Ardrahan and Munster predominating. No one needed to go hungry.

Nor thirsty.

The shipping company of *Hennessey et Cie* had sent them French wines; Châteaux Brane-Cantenac, O'Brien[14], MacCarthy and Lynch-Bages. The guests felt their palates were a conduit to paradise.

Following dinner the ladies repaired to the Grand Gallery, where a travelling band had been engaged to play some curious 'planxties', songs composed for the Irish harp, accompanied by a bodhrán, a pipe and three fiddles. Before the band struck up, they settled down to what their husbands liked to dismiss as idle gossip, a showy exchange of the names of dress- and saddle-makers, spiced with mildly lurid social tattle. Yet their menfolk would not be entirely right in such casual assumptions.

'I can ride as well as any of our men,' Lady Muskerry declared, her tone exasperated. 'I'm as sorry as anyone for the wicked fate that took Cliona from us, but why can't we women join this war? It would double our strength at a stroke. Why not, I ask?'

'Is it because,' asked Sorcha, 'we haven't studied Caesar, Appian or Florus?'

'Nor have most of the men,' replied the matriarch. 'I can wield a sword or shoot a pistolet with the best of them.'

---

[14] Château Haut Brion

'I could charge the enemy. But it would have to be sidesaddle,' said Lady Perceval. Despite the ghostly presence of Cliona, everyone smiled at the absurd vision of her gentle coterie at war.

'I do wonder if soldiers would ever take orders from a mere woman?' said Aoife. 'If I thought they would, I too would give it a go. Cliona did not teach us a lesson, she set us an example.'

While the ladies became more and more bellicose, their men upstairs explored the solar and loggias, the mellowing smoke from their clays and meerschaums mingling with the smell of fresh paint.

The post-prandial cheer was only a little interrupted when Lord Muskerry took Bryen aside and spoke urgently to him.

'May I barge into this happy moment with a little intelligence that has just come my way? Cromwell has asked Ireton to transfer his efforts to Waterford, just as soon as the weather permits,' he said. 'He is to take what the country fever has spared of Cromwell's army with him. I had this news barely two days ago.'

'That's not a serious army. Not any more. It's already had one try at Waterford and been forced to call it off. Waterford would need the collected armies of Genghis Khan to break it.'

'Ireton's not in any hurry. I think he intends to come through here. Now that the English towns have declared for Parliament, Lord Broghill is to leave the coast and make his own way to Limerick, calling in at any Coalition stronghold he may pass.'

'So, what do you propose, Sir?'

'That you raise your clans and ride with me to add our numbers to General Preston's.'

'We are not what we were, Sir. We took a terrible hit at Knocknanuss. My musketeers are reduced to fifty. We sent but never saw return a squadron of our finest horse to regain Dungarvan. All gone. We have to thank Lord Broghill for that.'

'How many men could you raise, Major MacDonogh?'

'No more than a hundred. A hundred and one, if you include my father's constable, Seamus O'Callaghan. He celebrates his sixtieth birthday this year. Given the circumstances, he may be immortal.'

'Let him enjoy his dotage in peace. It's your younger and mouldable men we need.'

'Of course. I'll have them ready and trained by April.'

'Well done, Major. Or perhaps I should call you Colonel?'

'Colonel?'

'Yes, Bryen. Lord Ormonde has ratified your promotion.'

It was now almost four o'clock. The views from the Court's ramparts were almost sumptuous as they faded into the glow of the setting sun.

Sir Philip voiced what everyone was thinking.

'Is there anywhere in the world as beautiful as this?'

The silence seemed to agree with him. At last Fineen O'Driscoll offered an alternative.

'Perhaps you've never seen the lands around Sherkin Island?'

Dick Talbot would not accept this challenge.

'Obviously you've never been to Ulster,' he said. 'We have the Causeway, the Mountains of Morne, the inland ocean of Lough Ney.'

'It will be Carlow that none of you have seen from its castle's ramparts.'

'What about the countless estuaries of County Cork?' an amused Lord Muskerry volunteered. 'Visit Kilbrittan if you want a view.'

'Glendalough houses the beacon that brings the saints to our shores,' said Fr Boetheus.

'I'd say the sternness of our countenance, the resolution on our people's faces; they are our most pleasant sight,' said Bryen.

The whiskey had been a fine one.

By the time the sexes rejoined, each had already enjoyed the best of each other. Their vinous cheeriness would now push them to know the best of themselves.

The orchestra played a planxty of the greatest wistfulness. Then, perhaps more wisely, it played a jig.

As the month of March progressed, the arctic winter relaxed its grip. Cromwell celebrated by storming Thomastown. The defenders were unarmed, so to save powder and ammunition the 'Ironsides' were encouraged to use clubs. The defenders' heads were crushed like ripe tomatoes.

Next came Cahir. Offered terms by Cromwell, the terrified garrison surrendered with minimal resistance.

After that, a more stubborn Kiltinan Castle had to be bombarded into submission.

With gathering confidence, Cromwell put the fear of an Old Testament God into the hearts of every jittery, panic-stricken city in Royalist Ireland.

Above Gowran, on the northern edge of the Walsh Mountains, stood Castle Howel.[lxiii] Howel Walsh had built it in the 13th century, and

Walshs had proudly lived in the fortress ever since. It was perched on mountainous land and its occupants had a wide panoramic view across the county's Central Plain. For the people of Gowran, just beneath its walls, it was a stone sentinel. For the Cromwellians, its hill-top location was of the utmost strategic importance.

High Commissioner Cromwell decided to take both town and castle for Parliament. He sent in his troops, swords drawn, with *carte blanche*. Personally, he stayed aloof in his tent, burying himself in maps, charts and *De Bello Gallico*, his constant companions.

The Roundheads went up that hill with a spring in their step; like foxhounds with the scent of their quarry in their nostrils. When they reached the townland they went as had their Viking forebears - berserk. They killed men, women, and children on sight. Their methods of dispatching their enemy were varied; imaginative even, but always brutal. Since the Irish were unarmed, his infantry again found clubs to be the most satisfying and economical weapons to use on labourers and peasants. Women and children, as they were easier to lift, were thrown over the walls to break on the rocks a hundred feet beneath. There they were eaten by wolves. The luckier ones were already dead.

As the castle's owner, Sir Nicholas Walsh, had already been killed in a skirmish in Waterford's defence, his elder brother, Walter, had to defend his Old English family's patrimony. He was so totally outnumbered that it would have been kinder and simpler had he put himself, his wife and children into a weighted sack and toppled it into the moat. Instead, he chose to go down fighting. After witnessing the butchery of his wife, children, servants, soldiers, tutors and chaplain, their dismembered corpses thrown into a cesspit, Walter himself was cut to pieces in his dining room while attempting to reason with a deranged sergeant.

Then his castle was razed.

Somehow, no one had told the New Model Army that victory would suffice. Not one inhabitant of Gowran, nor indeed at Castlehale, survived.

Leaving Gowran behind, Cromwell led his forces to the semi-deserted townland of Bennettsbridge. The inhabitants, having heard of Cromwell's victory at Gowran, had abandoned their town. Most of them laid low in the hills, yet Bennettsbridge was on the long list of victories that Cromwell reported to the High Commission in Westminster in his Easter submission. As he put it in his submission to his Commonwealth paymasters, he had at last completed the isolation of Kilkenny, the second city of Ireland. Grateful Puritans back home voted him a magnificent London house in gratitude.

Thus he took another step on his road to becoming the richest man in the three former kingdoms of the United Commonwealth.

Taking the town and castle of Kilkenny - the capital of the Catholic Confederacy – was the *ne plus ultra* of Cromwell's objectives.

The name for Kilkenny derives from the Gaelic *Cill Chainnigh*. It means 'Church of Cainneach', or St Canice. The town had grown up around the sixth century church, whose superb round tower was still erect a thousand years later. The town owed much of its grandeur and reputation to its famous quarries of black and white marble.

In its long history, Kilkenny had faced many terrible challenges but its darkest hour had now come.

The mere fact of the Commissioner for Wars' imminent arrival sapped the town's morale. This, combined with a local outbreak of cholera and dysentery, had severely weakened Kilkenny's Royalist garrison. Lord Castlehaven had reinforced it with a thousand foot and two hundred horse but, by the eve of the siege, half of these had died of these lethal scourges. Of the survivors, barely three hundred were fighting fit. The earl was powerless to prevent Cromwell and his enormous war machine from approaching the walls.

The countdown began on a frosty March 22, in 1650, when a frightened city woke to witness Oliver Cromwell pitching camp beneath its walls.

Lord Castlehaven, now the Royalist military commander of Leinster, in conjunction with Kilkenny's town council, agreed to appoint James Walsh Constable. Sir Walter Butler remained governor of the city.

Cromwell sent Walsh a message, offering terms for Kilkenny's immediate surrender.

> It does not please your servant to have to warn the citizens who beg your protection and their lives that their town will be sacked if my Godly army has to carry it by storm.
>
> £2,000 in compensation to my troops for forfeiting their right of plunder must be paid by return. Once done, the citizens may either remain where they are unmolested or will be free to depart with their goods.
>
> The garrison and priests may march safely away. The Commonwealth of England presumes to recommend Connacht.

That same day, after Butler rejected Cromwell's summons, Parliamentary troops began the grim business of cleansing the outlying suburbs of

Royalists and Catholics. In reality, that was everyone. They might have harboured potential saboteurs, their commander said, but what followed was truly brutish. The English general was aware that an infantry assault on the walls and city would have to be through these townlands and, if they were still inhabited it, it would be hard fought. His artillery also ignored the general's gentler concerns, if there were any; it was already battering the town's walls.

The three districts of Kilkenny City were strongly fortified. The High Town, by the castle, was bounded by a strong tall wall. To the east, the River Nore served as another wall. Irish Town, proudly Catholic, stood close to High Town on its north side. Its walls were only slightly lower. Across the Nore, to the east, lay the walled suburb of St John's. It connected to High Town over a single narrow Bridge.

Then there was the plague. All generals know disease is more dangerous in town than in the country. While it depletes the strength of a defending garrison, the contagion also deters any general from sending a force inside a city's walls. Cromwell saw that Kilkenny was badly afflicted. The municipal graveyard, with its eight hundred freshly dug graves, sent Parliament's general a clear warning.

The threat caused a divided town to join its forces. The mayor and aldermen of Kilkenny defended the large Irish Town, down by the river. Butler and his reduced garrison guarded both the castle and the small Anglican High Town on the hill.

Lord Dillon, the man that King James had tried to appoint to the duumvirate in Dublin Castle in 1632, had an army of fifteen hundred foot and six hundred horse. They were at Kilderry – not that far away. They would have greatly improved the lot of the defenders but their commander flatly refused to come to Kilkenny's defence. He saw resistance as hopeless and was not afraid to tell Lord Ormonde so.

> While my evaluation of the circumstance into which Kilkenny has fallen is clear to you, it follows that the noble City will fall quickly into Parliament's hands. As I have explained, I see at the head of a well-disciplined machine, a ruthless Puritan with 17,000 crack troops, all men trained to the pitch of military perfection. Immediately behind their iron-sided general are four horsemen, Plague, Famine, War and Death, who have collectively trampled Drogheda, Wexford and New Ross into the dust. Your most noble lordship saw them capture your manor at Carrick-on-Suir on November 23. You saw them brook no opposition.

There was Captain Tickell, an officer of the Kilkenny's city garrison. This gentleman, thinking it better to be a rich man on the winning side than a holy martyr on the other, sent Cromwell letters offering vital information about weakness in the walls that might have led to a bloodless, Puritan victory. Cromwell also learned from Tickell how much of the town's former strength had bled away.

This correspondence allowed Cromwell to believe he could take Kilkenny without a siege.

> If your Excellency will draw before this town I will send a messenger unto you upon your first approach who shall give an account of the weakest part of the town and the force within exactly. The proximate gate shall be opened.

Cromwell replied with an offer of £4,000, a high command in his army and the governorship of Kilkenny in exchange for the city's betrayal.

Yet the inevitable assault still did not happen. Within the walls the burghers speculated that a lack of firepower was one factor in the Puritan's continuing postponing of his big push. The truth was that Cromwell had put too much trust in Tickell's treason.

Nevertheless, his investment in the turncoat looked set to pay off, especially if the captain opened the city gates as agreed. Unfortunately for Cromwell, and even more so for Tickell, one of his treasonable missives was intercepted. Walsh ordered Tickell to be hung, drawn and quartered. What was left of his body was left on a gibbet, overhanging the walls, where the crows would screech while they dined.

Governor Butler's reaction to Cromwell's renewed summons was dismissive.

> I am commanded to maintain this city for His Majesty, which, by the power of God, I am resolved to do.

He would not give in and, with Tickell dead, battle was joined.

*

The Royalists had to fight on two fronts; one against Parliament and one against Mother Nature. The terrible sickness that raged within the city's walls would cut down as many, if not more, of its brave defenders, than Cromwell's cannons, bullets and industrious nooses.

At last, Cromwell began his assault. He sent a regiment of dragoons to storm the great gate into Irish Town. Its Gaelic-speaking Catholics held firm, firmly repulsing the Puritan attack.

An angry Cromwell then sent his soldiers to seize St Patrick's Church, just outside the south-western walls of High Town. Once the church was taken, Cromwell's gunners used pulleys to haul an artillery battery onto its battlements.

At dawn, the next day, those guns began their destruction of the southern wall of High Town. By noon that day, he had opened a breach and by that evening much of the wall was down.

Cromwell's Colonel Hewson led his men through the break while Colonel Ewer led a simultaneous attack on Irish Town, hoping to burn or batter down Dean's Gate. It did not take long before Ewer's regiment had forced its way in and seized Saint Canice which, like all early Irish churches, had been built on high ground.

Governor Butler had ordered earthwork defences to be built behind the breach, palisading and lining them with fusiliers. He drove Hewson's men back but suffered forty casualties.

Hewson himself took a ball in the thigh, Despite the efforts of the model army's most talented field surgeon, the fracture, blood loss and shock proved fatal.

Cromwell renewed his offer of terms. His artillery was as yet not in a commanding position. While pretending to be negotiating for a peaceful outcome, he was secretly planning to storm the city.

Butler, unsure, asked for time to reflect. This Cromwell granted.

In the meantime, General Cromwell ordered his Colonel Giffard, who had gained a foothold in Irish Town, to abandon all caution and cross the River Nore into the eastern suburb of St John's. It was a shrewd move; Giffard's men captured the townland, while only sustaining token losses themselves. Now they made ready to return and assault High Town across the bridge.

Butler, however, anticipated the Puritan manoeuvre and reinforced High Town's defences.

It was then that he discovered that Cromwell, while the town was distracted, had built a second battery. On the morning of March 27, 1650, Cromwell's artillery demolished a wide stretch of Kilkenny's walls.

The situation was now hopeless. Butler let himself be persuaded by the townspeople to agree to Cromwell's terms. Kilkenny surrendered that very evening.

Cromwell allowed the defending soldiers to march out with their colours flying. It was an empty honour. Two miles beyond the town, well out of sight of the townspeople, they were ordered to lay down their arms and lay flat upon the earth. They were summarily butchered. Swords are quieter and cheaper than pistols. Their remains were interred in a pit, and lime and turf were laid on top. The exact location of this mass burial has never been revealed for fear of making it a centre of veneration.

Oliver Cromwell had come to the well-fortified city of Kilkenny to suppress its Papists. In the process he damaged many of its churches and abbeys, leaving many slighted beyond repair, sometimes beyond recognition. With its landmarks all destroyed, castles levelled, walls demolished, a familiar ancient Ireland would never be seen by the generations to come.[lxiv]

Everywhere, he confiscated private property, sending captured leaders of the Confederation and Catholic landowners to the most barren parts of western Connacht. Cromwell presented them with a stark choice. 'To Hell or Connacht,' was how he wittily put it.

In the meantime, the High Commissioner had problems of his own. Not least he needed somewhere to shelter his horses. St Canice's Cathedral fitted the bill nicely.

Its round tower, built to watch for Viking invaders, had been of no use against the might of General Cromwell. In its nave, the tombs of Butlers, Walshs and Fitzgeralds, righteous beneath their effigies, stood as stalwart memorials to Ireland's past. Now they bore silent witness to the fall of their country and the erasure of its traditions.

> Side by side, their faces blurred,
> The earl and countess lie in stone
> Their proper habits vaguely shown
> As jointed armour, stiffened pleat,
> And that faint hint of the absurd, stirred
> The little dogs beneath their feet.

Cromwell's 'model' army was not restrained from literally defacing these tombs. Within hours, the magnificent relics had no faces, just vague shapes, with gashes for eyes. The Puritans, with their axes and swords, accompanied by laughter fuelled with either malice or ale, sliced off their noses and ears. A little alabaster dog, symbolising faithfulness and upon which a knight's dames's feet rested, was angrily beheaded. One poor knight not only lost his face. A Cromwellian chose to plunge a pike into the gentleman's stone codpiece, but found the blade impossible to withdraw.[15]

The building itself, even with its altar stripped, might yet inspire the faithful. Cromwell began its 'reform' by ordering its great stained glass windows to be smashed. Ropes were needed to hurl the primitive baptismal font to the ground. The five thirteenth century brass bells were

---

[15] It's still there.

carefully removed, as they were destined for the Puritans' new foundry, heated as it was by burning the pews and panelling. The lead from the roof was melted there and then, on the spot, and carefully poured from the battlements into large tubs of water. The resulting shot turned ploughshares into swords.

Cromwell was a religious man. Only when nothing remained of its sacred purpose would he consent to put the cathedral's shell to use as his stables.

In Cromwell's Puritan mind, God would never admit an Catholic to the Protectorate of Heaven. His soldiers were sent into the churchyard to destroy the graves they found there, some of which predated the arrival of the Normans in Ireland. The bones of the traitorous and impious pagans they found there were hurled into a common pit, previously used for cess.

Cromwell's New Model Army was waging the first ideological war since the Crusades. It was its duty to root out and destroy its enemy's traditions and identity.

The Parliament of England had passed a decree for the absolute suppression of the Catholic religion in Ireland. No graven images were to remain.

*

Sorcha was at a window seat in Carrigadrohid, a spectacular three storey fortified towerhouse. Somehow it had been built on a rocky outcrop halfway across the River Lee. The MacCarthys of Muskerry had built this wonderful place in 1455 and over the years had modernised and extended it. In her hand she held a copy of the notice that had been nailed to trees in the province, perhaps all over Ireland.

It was May, 1650, and the swell of her pregnancy was already obvious.

Only a few feet from her, the fast moving river crashed against the castle walls and gurgled over the boulders. Occasionally an ambitious trout would leap at a low-flying insect, barely a yard beneath the lowest stone mullion.

She had been in that panelled chamber for hours, sitting in the twelve foot oriel, Bryen's latest letter was beside her and an uncontainable tear had splashed it.

She stared out, but not over the Lee. Her mind was on the bridge, over which she hoped to see her husband coming in his armour, his visor raised, sporting the same smile she had seen him wear after his return from the Battle of Cappoquin.

ADVERTISEMENT

THE COMMISSIONERS OF THE COMMONWEALTH
REQUEST AND REQUIRE

WANTED

the Delivery of wanted Tories or Brigands
to be made to any Governor or Provost
of any Province County or Precinct in Ireland

DEAD OR ALIVE

upon which 40 shillings shall be paid without question.

*Local Countrymen should be advised that
these Persons are Dangerous and Desperate*

For Particular Tories the Rewards may be higher.

exempla Gratis

For 'Mad Dick' Talbot   £40

For Brian MacCarthy alias MacDonogh   £30

For Jenny Ryan   £20

For Dermot Ryan   £20

For James Leigh   £5

She wore a plain calico day dress. Her maid had made her hair look lovely but it was not for anyone's benefit but her own.

Bryen had sent her instructions. In his absence she was to seek shelter – with twelve other guests and twenty soldiers - in her father's garrison at Carrigadrohid. The Constable, the Royalist Felix O'Leary, was a loyal friend of Lord Muskerry. His orders, and he was confident he could protect her, were to keep her safe in such picturesque captivity. After all, the mansion's entrance was on the first floor and the fort was could only be reached by the road bridge which joined the eastern wall.

Her prayers and confession were to be heard by Fr Ignazio ffrench, a stern Jesuit.

Almost every day another letter came from her husband.

The latest one, the one onto which that tear had fallen, read:

397

My dearest little thing, as a good soldier I salute you. But, as a father and lover, but let me tell you how much I miss my duties at home – kissing my beautiful daughters goodnight, and putting my arms around you to protect you from a chill in the night air. At least I know Constable O'Leary would die rather than see you threatened by some impertinent castle mouse.

God in His infinite wisdom has seen fit to keep me alive and unscathed in this soulful conflict. Equally fortunate is Dick Talbot, with whom I share my good fortune. Our fates have been somehow conjoined.

That winning smile of yours is all that's needed to persuade Thady and the others, like last year and the year before that, to keep an eye on the Duhallow harvest and to help our people to manage their *sorrens* and tribute. I am drawing down quite hard on our patrimony at present, with fifty private soldiers and Dick's modest needs (and prodigious appetite) to accommodate. Oh well, my darling, patience! As my father liked to say, it's a case of *force majeure*.

The news across the Irish Sea is that the Scottish Royalists have risen, this time for the king-in-exile. As a consequence we expect General Cromwell to be recalled very soon. My prayer, to St Francis who wants us to be an instrument of His peace, is that this war will soon come to some form of a close. Dick, the men and I will be in Clonmel tomorrow; beating Cromwell to it, God willing. The garrison there is commanded by Black Hugh O'Neill. Have I mentioned his name before? He served with his cousin Owen Roe in the Spanish Legion. We shall be safe there, for a night or two, before we journey on to Waterford and join Lord Ormonde in a more formal capacity. Being a 'rover', or 'tory' as they call us is great fun but not a responsible life for a family man.

You will be a mother again quite soon. I have decided on your present. Our son will be as heroic as Aodhamair and Bébhinn are beautiful. He, and the end of the war, will mark a new beginning, for your and my entwined hearts. Whatever befalls us, he will always remind you that your most ardent lover is your husband, Bryen.

*

Bryen and Sorcha had been married for nine years. Never in that time had they grown tired of each other. Rather the contrary; Sorcha had given her husband two beautiful girls. The elder had been conceived at around midnight on the eve of Cappoquin, the younger when Bryen had visited Carrigadrohid for a single night on his way to defend Cashel against Lord Inchiquin, who at that time was on the side of Parliament.

They were her spitting image, though many would say they were portraits of their father. That may have been meant to make her love them more, but the ambition was unnecessary. No woman could have loved her daughters more than Sorcha did, and with reason; both were curious, as bright as buttons and justifiably adored.

'Bébhinn, though barely one year old, is walking, talking and already a little lady,' Sorcha happily but excusably exaggerated.

Even in beautiful Carrigadrohid the war could not be escaped. Her father, Lord Muskerry, when from time to time she saw him, brought her heroic and optimistic tales from the front. Constable O'Leary's account was rather grittier.

A few evenings before, O'Leary had sat down with her in that same window seat. He had patted her hand while telling her that Oliver Cromwell was advancing on Clonmel.

'Do not worry. Your husband will be fine. The town is well defended and Cromwell's troops are plague-ridden.'

He took a lace handkerchief from his sleeve and offered it to his charge. Sorcha duly dried her eyes with it.

'What's more,' he added, 'Fr Boetheus has commissioned David Roche to raise an Irish army for the town's defence. Two thousand men, no less.'

'Fr Boetheus? That bad-tempered and old Franciscan from Dromsicane?' She gave him back his handkerchief.

O'Leary laughed uneasily.

'I don't think there can be too many Father Boetheuses, Sorcha. With Lord Muskerry and your husband away he is effectively my chief. In my opinion he's also one of the best soldiers we have.'

Sorcha smiled bravely.

'Is it not unusual for a priest to earn that compliment? Or even fight a war, Colonel? Where is he now, anyway?'

'Not so far, Sorcha. Macroom. Five miles or so to the west of here.'

'Macroom? Uncle Thady's castle? What can he be doing there? Thady is an Anglican!'

'How well do you know Fr Boetheus?'

'He was my father-in-law's chaplain for a time. Perhaps I don't really know him? What sort of man is he, this warrior priest?'

'An important one. A local man, a fellow Duhallovian. At thirteen or so he found his way to Spain to complete his education. It's many years since he returned to Ireland. That was when he began to confess

399

the Lords of Duhallow and their clansmen. Since then he has had many positions of importance.'

'I bet he's a tub-thumper with no time for sinners.'

The colonel laughed a little more readily.

'Tub-thumper, yes, and an able one. That's why he went to Kerry to help Colonel Roche raise an army of young men. Depend on it, his enthusiasm for our war is infectious. Young Irishmen are signing up in droves.'

'Dare I ask if it's respectable for a Franciscan to be a warrior? It seems contrary to the spirit of what I thought was a pacifist Order.'

'These are martial times. St Francis himself was a soldier. He fought in an even greater Crusade. Fr Boetheus is in good standing with his Order. He was proposed as Bishop of Ross by the *nuncio* himself and was consecrated at Waterford a few years back. He was always a loyal supporter of Archbishop Rinuccini. The *nuncio* saw his talent straight away, making him Chaplain General of Owen Roe's Ulster Army. He accompanied the army on many campaigns, most notably at Benburb.'

'My husband was there, you know.'

'I do. No one knows or trusts our bellicose Franciscan better than your husband.'

'Can we infer that God is on our side?'

'Who can say? No one can know how God moves, but I do know this. From the moment that Cromwell landed at Ringsend last August, Fr Boetheus threw himself into the war with all his terrific energy. You ought to have seen him with the clergy at the Clonmacnoise Congregation!'

'I don't trust those priests with wars. At the Jamestown Synod in County Leitrim they rejected Ormonde's authority and urged him to leave the country.'

'I know. The great Lord Ormonde was deserted by Protestants and Catholics.'

'If I were Ormonde I'd make plans to leave Ireland for good.'

Outside, the castle bell tolled the hour. Felix O'Leary rose to his feet.

'It is later than I thought. I must leave you some peace and bid you a good night. May God bless and save you.'

'Thank you, Constable. I shall ask St Michael to intercede for you, as well as for Fr Boetheus and my husband.'

As the O'Leary left, Sorcha took herself to her *prie-dieu*. Her longest prayer was to the Holy Virgin, that Victory might desert the English standard.

A week later, none other than the mighty Protestant Lord Broghill, in his black steel armour, rode up to the bridge that crossed the Lee beside Carrigadrohid Castle. He was accompanied by a household guard of forty uniformed Roundheads, all wearing a orange sash. He looked at the magnificent river fortress ahead and saw that it was unassailable. That, and its walls were strong and well defended.

Its ramparts bristled with idolater troops. Broghill could see no weakness. Its large mullions faced away from the bridge, overlooking the mudflats of the river and the valley beyond. They would provide magnificent views but were out of range of any artillery.

'One hundred men, at most two,' he told his ADC. 'There won't be more than that. Let's begin by scaring the living daylights out of them and then starve them into surrender. Assign a thousand to the bridge, and in shifts; we don't want them to run away under cover of night. The rest of our men are to come with me to Macroom. That's where their soldier-bishop is, I rather think. We'll engage the holy warrior there. When we come back here, those wretched Papists will think Satan himself is in command of a legion of goblins and slubberdegulions.'

He wheeled his stallion around and his personal guard followed him to the west.

Weeks before, Thady MacCarthy had handed his great urban fortress at Macroom over to the bishop and his entourage. Thady, had had to choose between one front and another. He chose the warrior's path. Fr Boetheus could look after the spiritual, physical and even the military needs of Macroom's mostly Catholic garrison.

Possibly Boetheus may have hoped to remain undetected by the enemy in Anglican Thady's huge castle? If so, he did not remain inconspicuous for long.

Shortly after Thady's departure for Clonmel, Roche's child army arrived at the gates. Boetheus was ecstatic and the whole garrison welcomed the schoolboys as heroes in the making. Tears of gratitude were in the Franciscan's eyes. The youngsters had swollen his garrison's numbers to four thousand foot and three hundred horse.

Boetheus's joy, however, was both misplaced and short-lived.

Broghill had marched to the strongly garrisoned Kilcrea Castle, just twenty miles from Macroom. He had more than two thousand horse, the same number of foot, and Roche and Boetheus's combined force was untrained, unshod and poorly equipped.

Boetheus suggested that Roche's regiment, many of whose voices had not yet broken, should form up in the park surrounding the castle. Some had armed themselves with slingshots and pitchforks. It made for an uncomfortable sight. The boys chattered nervously and excitedly, and Boetheus MacEgan saw at a glance they lacked the discipline that the Roundheads had in such abundant supply.

He knew then with a terrible certainty that Broghill would want to use Macroom to control Munster. Proof, if he needed it, came from another courier. At Kilcrea, Broghill engaged the Royalists housed there. His campaign was characteristic; immediate and merciless. His army had proved irresistible; brutalised as to the lives and deaths of its enemies.

The Parliamentarians were on their way.

There was nothing for it. Macroom would serve Broghill as a base to rule the whole of Munster. Roche asked the bishop for permission to torch the old place. Boetheus wearily agreed. He would explain to Thady what had happened to his castle when the time came.

It was far too late for discussion in any case.

As he advanced on Macroom, Broghill admitted to his captains he was concerned.

'Boy soldiers have two qualities which make them more dangerous than adults,' he said. 'They have no fear of death and our soldiers do not enjoy killing them.'

When he was brought the intelligence, however, that the Catholic lads were drilling in the castle's park he relaxed. There they would look more like an enemy, less like a playground. That would make his ugly task much easier.

Wanting to surprise the enemy, Broghill began his assault by sending in his cavalry.

The Catholics were amazed to see a vast army coming at them at full tilt. They had no time to flee. The fast-moving English horse rode into Roche's young troopers, skewering them on their lances.

Surprise, as ever, had given Broghill the advantage. His manoeuvre gave neither Colonel Roche nor Fr Boetheus time to form defensive squares or lines. Nor would Roche risk an open encounter between his raw recruits and the seasoned Roundheads; it would have been a slaughter of the innocents. He ordered his boys and men to run for the woods. Only his veterans were asked to engage the enemy.

Broghill threw his seasoned troops at them. The lances had had their turn. Now was the time for English sabres.

They cut through Roche's forlorn as Sheffield steel does through leather. Most of the survivors took to their heels.

Six hundred behind were left, confused, wounded or both. Most of these were disarmed and dispatched where they lay.

Twenty of them, identified by their dress, were taken prisoner. Among them were the High Sheriff of Kerry and the notorious Bishop of Ross himself, Fr Boetheus.

Never mind that so many had escaped into the hills and bogs where the English cavalry could not follow, the priest was a great prize.

Broghill was delighted. Now he had a lever to prise open Carrigadrohid castle. He offered Fr Boetheus full pardon 'on a number of conditions'.

'Do you want me to repudiate the Holy Catholic and Apostolic Church?'

'Good heavens, no!' To the astonishment of his men, Broghill actually laughed. 'We are not Mohammedans, most reverend sir. Your enlightenment alone would earn the joy of all in the pure faith, as attested in the scriptures. We just want you to carry a message to Carrigadrohid. You will be our prodigal son. If you can induce the garrison to surrender, to come out peacefully, your own life shall be spared and you and your priests may depart with them.'

'Strike while the iron is hot, as my general says!' Broghill thought outloud.

While Carrigadrohid was garrisoned by Irish troops, other than confining them, Broghill had ignored it. Now, with his victory at Macroom behind him, Lord Broghill wanted to go north. He reached the castle on the bridge. He sent a major with some horse and foot soldiers to summon the castle garrison. Fr Boetheus was to accompany Major Nelson and, to add flesh to the bones of his message, Broghill authorised the major to threaten to hang the bishop if the garrison did not surrender.

'This land will make some honest God-fearing Protestant Englishman a fine barony, I rather think,' he told Major Nelson.

It was true. The land around Carrigadrohid was generally good and well sheltered, particularly towards the southern boundary of its demesne. Most of it was well cultivated, if what was not was rough pasture or bog. Disused quarries, from which the stones that built the castle and its bridge had been hewn, were everywhere. The bridge connected the church on one side with the pretty village of Killinardrish on the other.

He knew, what's more, that the incumbents had long been awarded the patent for a fair, or market, held in a field in the parish every Wednesday. This too was valuable; the merchants would pay handsomely to auction their sheep, ducks, geese, cattle and horses. It made the capture of the castle intact even more appealing.

It added up to a valuable property and, if taken by conquest, it would be legally his to sell

Carrigadrohid was in fact quite beautiful. The castle proper was a massive structure, twelve great chambers, built onto a stone outcrop halfway across the river Lee. It boasted a loggia and a solar. Many of the windows - those that faced away from the bridge - had mullions in local stone. A princely prize, if only the natives could be persuaded to abandon it without damaging its fabric.

Perhaps the castle should be sold to a studious pastor, or preacher, of substantial means, Lord Broghill mused. He had noted in its glebe the remains of a cromlech and several nearby standing stones. The new owner would be able to meditate on the supremacy of his Reformed Church as he took the morning air.

Inside the castle, in its famous solar, Constable O'Leary, his ADC, Fr Ignazio, Sorcha, her younger sister Rioghnagh and her maid had gathered.

'I've never seen so many soldiers, Constable,' said the younger girl. 'Do they mean to destroy the castle with us all in it?'

'No, Mistress Rioghnagh. The castle has too great a strategic purpose. I think they'll ask us to leave.'

'And if we refuse?' asked Sorcha.

'They will think of some way of persuading us.'

Lord Broghill could see – and not to his particular surprise - that the castle was still holding out.

'Time to act. Produce the Franciscan bishop.'

Major Nelson rode to the castle gate, halfway across the Lee. Boetheus MacEgan, whose hands had been tied behind his back, rode uncomfortably behind him. Boetheus felt as Regulus had, when the Carthaginians had carried him to Rome.

Fr Ignazio, from the battlements, shouted an instruction to the bishop, mounted and trussed, all alone in the world.

'Trust in God, His Son and in the Holy Ghost. Accept your crown at His hands.'

Boetheus turned his head the better to address the castle's soldiers. The only problem was that he didn't say the words that Broghill and Nelson had drafted.

Instead, what he shouted was:

'Hold out to the end, for your religion and your country!'

He knew full well that he had signed his own death warrant. Of course, he knew there was only one outcome. His 'antics', as General Lord Broghill would call them, would further enrage that savage heart.

Boetheus then addressed his maker, and in Latin.

Broghill turned to his sergeant-at-arms.

'Tell Major Nelson to do his worst.'

Boetheus's last prayer, or 'spell' as the Puritans would call it, was heard by all. Catholics heard every word, and many of them understood that he was comparing the fall of Ireland with the fall of Jerusalem.

Jesu Christi, Filii Dei vivi, illumina me, benedicta mater Dei, Gubernatrix angelorum et totius mundi, ora pro me ad benedictum Filium tuum floram, angelorum ad coronam, crelorum et confessorum, affligentium civitatis suso Jerusalem.'

The 'language of idolatry' infuriated the Puritan soldiers. They set upon him. In the Roman legend that Boetheus had recalled, Regulus's eyelids had been cut off. In Ireland, the soldiers were not so refined in their cruelty. They knocked the priest from his horse, his hands still tied behind his back. Then they broke his legs and arms with their clubs.

The priest's defiant courage upset Broghill. He ordered his portable gallows to be erected on the spot. The reins of the bishop's horse would serve as a rope. They were put round the clerical neck and he was hanged there and then.

The Roundheads had to be restrained until his macabre dance of death was over. Then they cut him down, cut off his head, put it on a pike and held it up, taunting the Irish in the solar with this ghastly sight.

Broghill did not bother to witness the passing of the priest. Another ruse, an ingenious stratagem, had occurred to him.

Carrigadrohid was strong, and Broghill's men had no artillery to break in. The Protestant general directed his men to cut down some trees whose trunks could be readily fashioned to resemble great cannons. Broghill had teams of oxen drag them close to the castle, but only to where O'Leary's spyglasses could not make out any detail. The Irish constable saw, or thought he saw, wagons struggling with the weight of substantial ordnance, bent on bombarding the castle's walls.

Everyone in the solar was similarly taken in.

'What shall become of us?' gasped a terrified Sorcha. 'When they finish battering these walls, we'll be seized and hanged! My girls are here!'

All in Carrigadrohid had seen what the Parliamentarians were capable of, even to a man of the cloth.

Fr Ignazio's brow puckered, its furrows deepened.

'God serves the righteous. We should pray that the Holy Sprit possesses their blasphemous souls and that they see the Light.'

'I'm sorry. Pray by all means, but know that up against weapons of that calibre we have no hope of holding out,' Constable O'Leary said aloud.

'What'll you do?'

'I intend to surrender the castle, on the conditions we previously refused.'

'The martyred priest?'

'We'll ensure the Franciscan's is the pre-eminent name, even in an era of outstanding names. He was a trusted friend not just to me but to all true Christians, self-sacrificing and indefatigable, fearless to the end and unswerving in his devotion to religion and his country.'

'His name will be put before the Sacred Congregation of Rites in Rome as one who made the ultimate sacrifice,' added Fr Ignazio.

'He wears his laurels in heaven,' said Sorcha through her tears.

'Amen,' concluded the Jesuit.

When O'Leary raised the white flag from Carrigadrohid's battlements, Roundhead squaddies were allowed to amuse themselves for a few hours - plundering the nearby village of Killinardrish and leaving it uninhabitable – while their officers met O'Leary to renegotiate terms.

In the event, Carrigadrohid's little garrison, with its constable and priest, were all allowed to leave, unarmed of course, but for where? Since Broghill was on the south bank, they set off north, taking with them as much in the way of private possessions as they could carry. In the mêlée, the priest and constable were separated. Fr Ignazio found himself on the north side of the Lee, surrounded by Irish soldiers, while Constable O'Leary stood by the palings of a cattle enclosure, on the south bank, into which the civilians, servants and family were shepherded.

Pressed through the field's five bar gate, Sorcha held her daughters's hands. Aodhamair and Bébhinn were trusting and quiet, but Sorcha's little sister Rioghnagh was inconsolable.

Sorcha murmured words of comfort but looked around. All around her were the fitter female servants and villagers. Many, most, were in tears. They had no idea of what was in store for them and naturally they suspected the worst. O'Leary was shouting something at the English soldiers. Sorcha heard him say her father's name, but could not hear the rest through the wailing.

Now the soldiers forcibly divided the older men and women from the rest.

In the lee of the castle, the portable gallows that had been erected on the bridge for Fr Boetheus had three new victims, twitching, swinging. Twenty elderly or infirm men and women awaited their turn in tears of fear. The Lee was in full flood and escape that way was impossible. Fifty soldiers blocked any foolhardy escape along the bridge. Clearly the victors had no need of the elderly.

Sorcha had known them all. She meant to pray for their souls but a nearby voice penetrated her distress.

A detail of soldiers was at hand to escort some of the surviving prisoners to Cobh. Without feeling the need for tact, Major Nelson told them that they were to be loaded into ships for the Caribbean. There they would to be sold at auction to plantation owners in the business of tobacco, cotton and sugar cane. Sugar, especially, was heavily reliant on indentured labour – slavery - and the money they made would swell General Cromwell's depleted coffers.

'Oh good. Pretty girls. Nice and tall. They'll fetch a good price.'

Of course, women were not needed for hard labour. They would serve another purpose.

An English soldier came over to inspect the girls.

'These Irish tarts will make a few Ibo tribesmen happy, eh, Martin?' He rolled his hips.

The Barbadians had been providing Parliament with cash for slaves and had been doing so for some time. Their needs were inexhaustible and the Puritans sent them prisoners of war, some that had simply been kidnapped, and released some amenable prisoners from England's crowded gaols. The Commonwealth needed the money and was not over-concerned with giving the slaves a good reference.

They also sent them women, especially Irish women. The Ibo warriors, shipped from West Africa to work the plantations, were short people while the Irish were tall. Provided they were nubile, captured females were sent as breeding stock. Soon the imported Africans would soon be bearing children two inches taller than their grandparents.

Two soldiers came over to Sorcha and pulled at Bébhinn.

'Let go of her, wench. She's no use to anyone. She won't be going where you are.'

Sorcha clasped her daughter even harder.

'Then have it your own way.'

One soldier drew back, raised his musket and impaled the toddler on its bayonet. With a practiced action, he flicked the dead little girl from the narrow pointed blade.

'Always best to obey an Englishman,' he said.

'What about this one?' The other was looking at the very pregnant Sorcha. 'She looks as if she will drop a nipper any day soon.'

'Let her be. The slavers will toss the child overboard when the time comes, but mum is a sexy bitch. How old are you, darling? Not even twenty-five I'll wager. Five foot eight? They'll love you in the New World. Might love you a bit in this one, what d'you say, Bill? Give her a test run?'

Sorcha, through her agony, grew dimly aware that Constable O'Leary was still there, pleading with Lord Broghill.

'My Lord, let me take these ladies to Kanturk, I beg you in the name of all that's sacred. These two are Lord Muskerry's daughters, and that one is his granddaughter. They deserve better than the fate you have in mind for them.'

'Irishman, do you take me for a fool? That one is the wife of the notorious tory Bryen MacDonogh. Pity is too valuable a resource to waste on such people. Come on, sir, you have negotiated your own escape. Take to the road and be off with you or I shall hang you with the others.'

O'Leary had no choice. Though he knew it was a vain hope that she might hear him over the soldiers' jeering and the captive women's sobbing ululation, he shouted at Sorcha.

'Pray for me and that this war is soon over. Adieu, brave Sorcha.'

The Lord President of Munster declared the voided Carrigadrohid Castle forfeit to Lord Broghill. He would eventually sell it to the Bowens, a prosperous family of Welsh origin.

The village and castle had lost its people and land to settlers. It would never revert.

O'Leary knew the country well. Clonmel was almost a hundred miles away to the north-east. It was a five day walk.

He and Fr Ignazio would do it in four.

*

Chapter Twenty-Seven
An English Court in Exile

When, in January 1649, he succeeded to his father's throne, Charles II was a striking lad of nineteen. While his schooling was of a high standard, his mother's court at Breda bored him. Distracted by every appetite a young man can be heir to, he gradually replaced his *tête-à-têtes* with a very young King Louis, his royal mother, even with the Cardinal, with rather more intimate conversations with his own followers. In particular, he sought out the engaging company of exiled Englishwomen.

Had he been a monarch like any other he would, undoubtedly, have been married to some suitable European princess. Unfortunately, in darkest Breda, he was in no position to negotiate an advantageous match.

One of the first to lend him a sympathetic ear was Lucy Walter. She was more than willing to help the king in his further education and to graduate in the ways of the world. She certainly enjoyed his company and in due course she bore him a son. Perhaps she was too generous with her tuition? The young king 'recognised' the infant and ennobled him a duke, even though neither priest nor lawyer had sanctioned the affair. Was Miss Walter too unsparing in her affections? She was unselfish, that's for certain; many other exiled courtiers were also on her list and, sadly, she would die a few months later of a venereal disease.

Charles was not quite heartbroken; Lucy was not his only extravaganza. While the Stuart line was by no means extinct, more and more of its latest members were illegitimate.

His lovely little boy amply compensated for Lucy's loss and the king resolved to provide the Duke of Monmouth with the lands and income he would eventually need.

Forming like planets are said to do around a star, the dust of his courts began to cluster.

A 'Louvre Faction' turned like a planet around the queen. Its moons were the effeminate Lord Jermyn and the flamboyant Lord Bristol, the former and recently elevate Lord Digby. Catholics both, their passionate belief was that English and Irish recusants were prey to an intrusive tyranny, by name the Commonwealth, which presumed to have title to their consciences.

They sought links with friendly potentates, even suggesting concessions to unfriendly ones and included, here and there, an occasional Presbyterian or Lutheran. It was always in the mostly vain hope that such men would sanction a Restoration at the earliest opportunity.

Opposing them, Sir Edward Hyde's 'Old Royalists' argued it better to rely exclusively upon those proven Royalists. Their loyalty could be guaranteed. Given Cromwell's extreme asceticism, which showed most recently in his abolition of all feast days, including Christmas, opinion in England would surely swing over to the king? Hyde's principal supporters were the Anglican courtiers Sir Edward Nicholas and Lord Hopton.

Then there were the 'Swordsmen', pragmatists all, who orbited Prince Rupert. When Rupert had taken his fleet to Ireland, intending to prevent the Protectorate's 'sea-army' from putting into port, they had been left leaderless. In the prince's absence they had no policies, other than a shared, visceral and, frequently, a lethal dislike of Puritans. Now that Rupert had rejoined his acolytes, after being outmanoeuvred in Ireland, and having conspicuously failed to gain the support of the Portuguese, they still enthusiastically welcomed him back. His infinite charm had reinvigorated them.

Not so, the 'Louvriste' Lord Bristol. He took great exception to the prince. When Rupert challenged him to a duel, the queen herself had to intervene. Rupert was a prince, she pointed out. He was not to duel with mere lords. Rupert's second, Lord Wilmot, then called Bristol out himself. Kildare Bristol was a remarkable shot and Wilmot was badly injured.

When she first met the king, Mrs Palmer was twenty-nine years old. She was of English county stock and was already married to a royalist. Barbara had arrived in Breda with a shrewd and loyal delegation. The English had chosen her well and her radiant beauty made her an instant star.

Exactly nine months after her presentation to the king-in-exile, who was ten years her junior, she bore him a daughter. The little girl was ennobled Countess of Sussex at her baptism. Her mother's cuckolded husband was difficult to pacify, until Charles made him Earl of Castlemaine in exchange for what His Majesty called 'visiting rights'. The arrangement was satisfactory all round until she gave birth to a son, whom the king created Duke of Southampton. Enough was enough. Castlemaine deserted his wife and rather caddishly refused her the divorce she begged him for.

*

In Ireland, and on a rocky road, two worried tories were leading a troop of fifty musketeers.

'Dick,' said Bryen, *à propos* very little, 'if we're going to survive at all we must find somewhere where neither defections nor betrayals are possible. Is there such a place?'

'Of course not. General Cromwell's war engine will run us down like rabbits. He commands it from some hellish place where neither divine pity nor common humanity is allowed to hold sway.'

'Wait. Let me think. There may be a place we can put ourselves and our men up for a while. Have you ever heard of a little place called Clonmel, a few miles upstream from Carrick?'

'Of course I have. It's in darkest Tipperary. The Confederates held their Parliament in Clonmel, I forget how many times. More than once, anyway. It's easily the most pious town in Ireland. They say its monastery somehow escaped the Dissolution. It's where the Franciscan Bonavventura Baron is from and there are some Capuchins still there, in their habits, in public, just as they were a hundred years ago.'

'Is all that true? Then hell will freeze over before such a place turns Puritan. They will welcome our musketeers. I presume it has a garrison?'

In war, it sometimes takes very little to make a decision. Two days later two officers and a squadron of tories rode through Clonmel's north gate into the ancient borough. They were met and welcomed by its military commander Black Hugh O'Neill, a cousin of the late Owen Roe's, who immediately invited the two tories to share his princely quarters.

They had, unfortunately, chosen absolutely the worst place in Ireland to lay low. Wholly unknown to them, General Cromwell had heard it was the most Papist city in that accursed nation.

A red rag to a Puritan bull. The general was on his way.

That afternoon the tourists looked around the town, parting here and there with a little gold in exchange for food, cartouches and comfortable lodgings for their men. All these things were villainously expensive. The war was ruinous enough but greedy merchants had stocked Clonmel's warehouses well and were already reaping the rewards of their far-sightedness.

Bryen and Dick could not avoid observing that even if Clonmel was not exactly the marvel it once had been, it retained a sad, nostalgic beauty. The abbey church of St Mary's was in surprisingly good repair, and its surrounding Norman monastery was picturesque and commanding, only a little dented by the Tudor iconoclasts. It was built inside in a corner of the city and not in open country which, perversely, may have helped preserve it. It is easier to desecrate an abbey when it's out of sight of its congregation.

Inside St Mary's, an astonished Bryen and Dick found unstripped altars in the side-chapels.[lxv] In the chancel was a handsome group of marble sarcophagi, each topped with an alabaster replica of a knight or his lady, eternally reviving the memory of the nobles buried within the abbey's precincts. They were particularly struck by a terrifying statue of the order's founder, St Francis himself, in the sacristy, somehow unseen and unmolested. No one, it was said, could tell a lie in the presence of this statue without having the unadorned truth brought to light by the direct interposition of Heaven. Any perjurer would be punished by sudden death.

Counter-intuitively, a fractious, even vicious, dispute between the Jesuits, Franciscans and secular clergy had helped preserve the precious thatched church. The Jesuits alleged that Pope Paul V had confirmed their claim to it. Bryen and Dick soon learned that the townspeople, on two occasions, had banned the Franciscans from their town. The brotherhood had begged the Lord Lieutenant, then merely an earl, to restore their monastery's ancient endowments to them. Predictably, their pleas fell on deaf ears. The abbey's lands, mills, weirs, palaces and fish-ponds had long ago been escheated and a fuller restoration was no longer possible.

Bryen and Dick learned that the friars had been forcibly dispossessed of those lands that Clonmel's Old English lords, the de Burgos and the Grandisons, had long ago endowed them. If so, it made it even more remarkable that the faithful of that city had maintained the church, cemetery and sacristy of their abbey, and at their own expense.

The current Provincial was as stubborn, as persistent as any of his predecessors. He had taken every measure available in cannon law to re-establish his claim. At last there came a pragmatic solution - by papal indult, no less - that they should repossess their ancient church, despite the intelligent objections of the Jesuits and the romantic ones of the secular priests.

The monastic infirmary, a fine Romanesque edifice, had remodelled by an even earlier Lord Ormonde who had converted it into a mansion which he renamed the *Aula Comitis*[16]. He awarded it, as a dowry, to Lady Helen de Barry, whose great aunt Isobel had married Sir Owen

---

[16] Earls' Hall

MacDonogh. That fortunate fellow was Bryen's great-grandfather. Her second husband was Thomas, Earl of Somerset. Standing outside it, Bryen could hear the ghostly echoes of his ancestors.

The little town took credit for the birth and early education of Dick Talbot's hero, Fr Bonavventura Baron. In 1636 the great scholar had gone up to the Irish College of St Isidoro, in Rome. His uncle, Fr Luke Wadding, when he founded the school just eleven years before, had spared nothing in promoting the education of his kinsman and protégé. Eventually the two of them would pool their wits and concentrate all their energies on two splendid ends.

Their first was to revive the literary glory of those early Christians who had so beautifully immunised the words of scholarship's early heroes from the entropic force of oblivion. From the fall of the Roman Empire to the rise of Charlemagne, the world had endured a long and dismal era, one when knowledge and civilisation could find no sanctuary beyond a few cloisters. The greatest of these was at Montecassino[lxvi], said to hold the only copies of Aristotle's comedies and Plutonius's satires. Such Monastic libraries rendered all mankind a signal service.

Their second, if for Black Hugh, Bryen and Dick it would have been the first, was the liberation of Ireland from any uninvited, or unwarranted promotion of the Gospels and their contemporary Scriptures – the Word of God – over the Church's centuries of scholarship, revelation and mysticism. The English were determined to expunge all eschatological analysis and metaphysical poetry from the Land of Saints and Scholars, in short, to treat the Bible as merely a work to be read literally.

Bryen and Dick found themselves at Black Hugh O'Neill's table, early that same evening. A table had been set up in one of the newer towers, one which overlooked the river. They were joined by the Mayor, John Fitzgerald White. No women were there to soften or refine the mood; which meant that matters of life and, more importantly, death could be talked of without passion.

'Neither the antiquity nor the beauty of this handsome town will restrain the New Model Army,' Black Hugh soberly told his guests. 'Cromwell and his vandal hordes will arrive any day soon. At that point our lives are over. Until then, our merchants have ensured our warehouses are full and we have pumps to deliver us fresh water from the Suir.'

'Our swords and muskets are at your service, General.'

'Good. Well said. Clonmel thanks you, Colonel. When I came here I had fifteen hundred men under arms, fine fighting Ulstermen. My first care, of course, was to strengthen the defences of the place. Let me tell you it has not all been plain sailing. After I was proclaimed Governor, I sent a detachment to Fethard, and another eighty men to Cahir Castle, to keep them safe from Parliament. Cahir was strong, well supplied with provisions and ammunition and strengthened by two strong gates, a draw-bridge, a fair-sized bawn and a strong-walled bass-court. Its people gave my Ulstermen a cordial welcome.'

'You're trying to tell us that Cahir has fallen?'

'You didn't know? Our men troops stuck it out for a while. When they saw the enemy's ordnance being readied to break Cahir's walls they knew that only Death would welcome them if they remained. At first the Constable refused to let my men take shelter in the keep, thinking it would jeopardise the castle, but when Cromwell demanded a parley, he was forced to capitulate. My men marched out, standards held high. God be praised, the Saxon General treated them honourably, even made a fuss of them, trying to seduce them into to joining him. When they unanimously refused he allowed them to rejoin us here in Clonmel.'

'I see. Cromwell wants to concentrate his enemy into one place, and that's here. He has a reasonable army, but it will need a lot of firepower to get through these walls.'

'True, but we are short of men and ordnance, things he has in plenty. I depleted our wherewithal when I sent reinforcements to Clonmel's satellite fortifications, Ballydine, Kilcash and Castle Caonagh. Finding powder and ball is a problem. Our Lord Lieutenant is too busy watching the walled cities of Munster fall to Cromwell like ninepins.'

The mood had taken a brittle turn.

'I wrote again to Ormonde. Here is a draft of my letter. Go on, take it, read it.'

Bryen took it and unfolded it.

> May it please your Lordship,
> This day I received your letter of the 25th instant. Since my last letter to your Lordship I have learned that Cahir was yielded without shot or blows upon what terms I know not. Kilteenan likewise was besieged ere yesternight and yielded yesterday morn about nyne of the clock. An army is within a myle of the town and the rest are coming to them in great haste. They have sent a number of horse and oxen for more cannons. We expect nothing else but to be besieged every hour now that they no other place to aym at but this. Your Lordship may know in what condition we

are and the consequence of this place to the kingdom which requires most speedy succour. All which I humbly refer to your Lordship's grave consideration and humbly take leave to remain

Your Lordship's most humble servt,

Hugo O'Neill

'Did you get a reply?'

'By return. Here it is.'

Bryen took the letter and read it aloud.

Sir

Your letter intimating your expectation of being suddenly besieged I received not till about nine of the clock this morning. In answer whereunto I think fit to assure you that rather than the town should fall into the hands of the rebels[lxvii] I shall draw all the forces of the kingdom into a body for its relief which I shall endeavour so to effect as in ten days to be in a readiness to advance to towards you, relying on your uttermost endeavours to defend that place during that tyme though you should as you expect be closely besieged and so desiring to hear as frequently from you as possibly you may.

I remain

Your very affectionate friend, Ormonde.

*

It was time to talk defence.

'I'm fairly strong on pikes,' said Black Hugh. 'We have fusiliers, though none with the legendary reputation of your tories. Saying that, our numbers are good. The garrison has been reduced by the general sickness but the men have been reinforced with troops evicted from Cashel and Kilkenny. We are bracing ourselves for a long siege. Sadly, I'm all too familiar with that kind of warfare. I spent too long in the Spanish service.'

'The town would seem defensible,' Dick remarked.

'Yes. It is. You will have seen that it's protected on three sides by a circuit of walls, twenty feet high, six feet thick. The Suir, and some defensive towers, protect us to the south. My earthen reinforcements can also resist artillery.'

'Not just that, General. That moat that runs around the town will stop Cromwell from laying mines.'

'You keep your eyes well open, I observe, Colonel.'

*

415

The following morning, at five o'clock, two men walked up to Clonmel's North Gate and struck rudely, even insolently on its brass filion. One of them wore the *escapulae* of the Jesuit Order. His black eyes burned fiercely at the frightened soldier who opened the portal. Both men at the doorway showed the dust of the road and the soldier was clearly sad and exhausted. The leader of the two, also a soldier but one of the counter-reformation, looked more angry than tired.

'*Cad dhe seogh?*' the porter croaked. What's this?

'*Druis ish an doras!*' growled the priest. Open the door!

The porter hurriedly complied, cowed by the authoritarian tone. That, or by the air of menace that seeped into the vapours of a frosty morning. Once admitted, the two strode through the gate. When a nervous gatekeeper skipped around them, trying to stutter a repeated enquiry as to who or what or why, the sight of Ignazio ffrench's black cross choked off his questions.

'Enough of this mongrel gibberish. Speak again to me and I'll feed you your own tongue. Take us before the O'Neill at once', barked the Jesuit. 'You will announce us. I am Ignazio ffrench of Cilcormac and this is Constable Felix O'Leary of Carrigadrohid. Have the MacDonogh immediately brought into the sacristy, before its sacred statue. Yes, vermin, that statue! Constable O'Leary will address him there once the good Fathers are assembled. This is a matter of the *spiritu sancti*. You had best remember that, or the wrath of St Michael will break over your head like a tureen of boiling pigs blood. Go!'

The man scurried off. Felix O'Leary did not even allow himself a melancholy smile, but he did say a few rough words to the Jesuit.

'Well said, Fr Ignazio. That should put the wind up their collective arses. They will need to be galvanised in time for the coming siege. Yet what I have to tell Colonel MacDonogh fills me with dread.'

Black Hugh, disturbed at his dawn devotions, arrived adjusting his *phailtere* belt, nodded uneasily toward O'Leary, and knelt before the Priest.

The Jesuit extended his hand and O'Neill fervently brought the priest's hard pewter ring to his lips.

'Bless me, Father, for I have sinned', he began to intone, but ffrench reversed his hand, and tapped him a light blow on the cheek, commanding his silence and attention.

'No need to beg my or His pardon this day of all days, *Dubh Aodh Ó Néill*. Of all men, you are blessed. Here in your fief great things shall be spoken and you are bidden to the feast. I say to you, friend, brother, go higher. Thou art worthy that the Blessed Virgin Mary, Mother of Mothers, Queen of Heaven, who standeth together with His angels and His saints, calls you now. She calls out to you, Black Hugh, miserable sinner and ordure of swine, to come unto Her, in all of Her glory and Her Radiance. Just as you have honoured and protected one who sought shelter and protection 'neath your battlements, so now the blue cloak of Our Blessed Lady envelops you, in the Holy Name of Her Son Jesus Christ. Come! Will you come? Mary, Mother of God, cries out to you! Will you come unto Her? Speak now!'

O'Neill was shaking with emotion, trembling on his knees. His mouth was dry, his voice cracking as he falteringly answered.

'Lord,' he gasped, 'I am not worthy…that thou should enter under my roof! Say but the word and thy servant shall be healed!'

'Excellent!' said the Jesuit. 'Jesus shall wipe away those tears. *Ego te absolvo.*' He made a reflexive Sign of the Cross.

Fr Ignazio ffrench reached down and lifted Black Hugh's face up from under his chin, glaring at him.

'Get up, man. Your sins they are forgiven! Well done, thou good and faithful servant. Enter thee into the joys of thy master. Stand up, man!'

O'Neill struggled to his feet, stunned by ffrench's fierce onslaught; yet it seemed that he might still be in the Priest's good books. Years of service in many wars had taught him to keep his mouth firmly shut at times like these. He did so, bewildered.

Suddenly ffrench was all affability and grace. He surrendered little of his control, however.

'Black Hugh O'Neill, Captain of the North, before you stands O'Leary of Carrigadrohid. He greets you in the name of His Holiness, and his Embassy to you bears the Seal of the Lateran, which I myself appended. His silence is anointed, for he may not address you or any other for a while. Presently, all shall be known unto you and yours. Enough! You are host I believe to the MacDonogh of Duhallow?'

'Yes, and I am proud to be so, Father'.

'And a fine upstanding man yourself, you are! Happy is he who can say as much on this hallowed day. O'Leary shall speak to him before the Statue and tell his sad tale. That is his mission. Even now the good labourers of the vineyard, verily our brethren, meet in the Chapel, and we shall hear a terrible tale, witnessed by the servant of the soldier of Christ, St Francis. Arise. Let us go. *Dominus nobiscum.*'

'*Et cum spiritu tuo,*' answered O'Neill, his eyes cast downward.

'*Amen*', said ffrench, darting a glance at his friend.

417

O'Leary seemed to bare his teeth like a cornered cat. He stayed silent.

'I know, O'Leary,' persisted ffrench, 'you are reluctant to tell your terrible story of Carrigadrohid, but tell you must. Every single word of your narrative will be weighed in the balance of your telling. Should any one of them be less or greater than the unvarnished truth, the dark shadows in this room will elongate like sea serpents as far as your person, there to take you by your limbs, their hellish purpose to wither them away as if you were already dead. Be sure to tell MacDonogh your story directly. He'll be here momentarily. Make certain of your words, for however skilful you are, they will break his great and noble heart.'

The priests had assembled before the Statue and now, like the unwitting host at a surprise party, MacDonogh came into the sacristy. To his great surprise, he saw his Constable, to whom he had entrusted his wife, his niece and his children. He saw O'Leary fall to his knees and let welling tears flow freely down his face in anguish. His sobs prevented him from speaking.

It was MacDonogh of Duhallow, therefore, who spoke first.

'My family, O'Leary, where are they?' MacDonogh asked, his voice not unreasonable. 'I left them in your charge. Are they here with you?'

At last, O'Leary began his horrid history. He told the statue of St Francis, he who had been so traumatised by battle so long ago, of how dear Sorcha had piteously addressed her daughter's murderer, saying that she forgave him his sins 'with all of her heart'. That the man's arm, the one that had wielded the great two-handed sword and had cleaved little Bébhinn in two, had shrivelled and withered away, his flesh corrupting to the bones, first from the hand and all the way to his heart; this while he screamed skeletally for mercy.

'No less a force than Satan incarnate came for your family, Sir. There was nothing I could do.'

'Satan? Do you mean Lord Broghill? Or even General Cromwell?' Bryen's face had emptied of blood. His hand was on the hilt of his sword. His racing mind was already painting a thousand nightmarish pictures.

'I mean that the Prince of Darkness had found a way to possess poor Broghill's soul. He hanged Fr Boetheus before our very eyes and then obtained our surrender by hauling logs up to the bridge, making believe that they were heavy artillery. We were promised clemency, which we took to mean all of us, but which in fact only attached to our soldiers. The old, the infirm; they were simply hanged. We soldiers were disarmed and sent on our way. I had no choice but to come straight here to warn you that Broghill was on his way too. I beg you to forgive me. At least your wife is alive.'

'Yes, yes. But the rest of my family; my daughters, my sister-n-law? What of them?'

'The luckiest was little Bébhinn. She is already in heaven, carried there by angels. She was too young to be of any use, they said.'

Bryen needed to support himself against the statue.

'The others are to be 'wild geese', Sir.'

'Wild geese? Like exported game?'

'It's the name we give to such ladies. They are to be sent to the American colonies, Sir, and forcibly mated with Ibo slaves. They are to be breeding stock. It was their height that spared them the sword or the noose.'

'That fate is far worse than death. The sentence that Lord Broghill will receive will be before St Peter will be eternal torment.'

Bryen focussed on O'Leary. The old man was still on his knees. Bryen took him by the shoulders.

'Stand up, man. You did all you could, but I can do more. Broghill's master, Beelzebub, he of the killing fields and their plagues of flies; he is on his way. We shall confront him here. My men will give him the lesson in chivalry he needs. Each of them will give him a private tutorial. We will fight to our last man. Let his vile and murderous heresy end here.'

'Broghill, the sorcerer's apprentice, is also on his way.'

'So much the better. Let them all come. They will all rot in hell.'

The colour that had so recently drained away now returned to Bryen's cheeks. Was it more than that? A quality that no one had ever seen before, one that eclipsed his easy sense of humour, became disturbingly visible.

'No Cromwellian will leave here alive. While my sword arm still has strength I shall kill as many as I can. I shall hound Cromwell to his grave. All my men will follow me, this I vow. We shall not leave Clonmel until Satan turns tail and runs.'

*

Outside the sacristy, freakish winds repainted the rainy sky. Then, in the middle of its colourless desmesne a window, lit in pure blue, opened wide.

'It is the blue of Our Lady's mantle,' a soldier told another, who passed the message on. Soon everyone knew that the Mother of God had appeared in the heavens over Clonmel. Some even saw her hold little Bébhinn by the hand.

419

In County Cork, an army of marauding English soldiers was 'turned back and vanquished' when the dead infant daughter turned up in a ghostly grotto. Dozens bore witness to the miracle.

General Cromwell was widely reported to 'lie at point of death', tortured by unassuageable guilt. Fr Ignazio passed this last on to MacDonogh and O'Neill.

'Cromwell has been discovered by the avenging angel,' he explained.

In the midst of all this, Felix O'Leary rolled in pent up agony on the sacristy floor, confessing in his pain that he 'had a moment of doubt' that Ireland would be saved! Fr Ignazio reached out to him.

'I pardon you your doubt, for thou art only flesh and a sinner.'

MacDonogh, however, had left the cloister to exchange a few words with Dick and with his men.

'Parliament's heretic machine is rolling towards us. Unwittingly, I seem to have been its first victim. My family has been taken from me, in ways too terrible to list. When Beelzebub arrives, I shall be happy. I intend to turn the monster back. Friends, will you help me do this? Will you help me free Ireland from the darkness its shadows are made of?'

'I will,' came his answer, and in unison.

*

When Beelzebub, or Cromwell, arrived outside Clonmel, with eight thousand infantry, six hundred cavalry and twelve small field guns, it was clear that his army had been horribly reduced by hypothermia, cholera and dysentery. Unfortunately for the Catholics, those that had survived were the fittest of all.

Advance units of his elite forces now began to surround Clonmel with a blockade. No one would leave the city without the High Commissioner's express permission.

The Englishman was anxious to conclude operations in Munster before returning home. Without his personal intervention, sieges took too long. He had had a secret message from his 'rump' Parliament. His fellow 'Commissioners' wanted him home. A third round of the Civil War had broken out and the general was needed to subjugate Scotland.

In the circumstances, Cromwell's only option was to storm the city and garrison.

Lord Broghill had hurried from the 'liberation' of Carrigadrohid to Clonmel to reinforce his commander. He now arrived.

Pleased, Cromwell was unusually effusive. He embraced him and, in a speech to his troops, he listed the newcomer's recent exploits.

The Roundheads cried out, 'Ah Broghill! Ah Broghill!' It sounded for all the world like an Irish war cry.

Now his enthusiastic army was more than ready for the assault.

*

In Clonmel, Black Hugh's resolution was about to be put to the test. The gates were closed and would shortly be bolted from the inside. The prayers that arose from this lovely little city, on the verge of extinction, must have been heard by every saint in heaven.

Black Hugh always kept his troops under his closest watch. He had their cooperation, even their affection, and the mayor and townsmen of Clonmel were impressed. They rewarded him with their full support.

'I believe that Ormonde is raising another army, this time in Ulster, to challenge Cromwell,' Black Hugh told His Honour Mayor White. 'That is why I am determined to defend this place, everything it stands for, until the marquess can get here.'

But how long would that take? That unspoken question occurred to every one of them.

*

The Parliamentarians' assault on Clonmel began with a bombardment of the northern wall. Black Hugh O'Neill, determined to resist with his every fibre, was fully aware of the demonic vengeance with which the Puritans would repay such valour. Cromwell's efforts had to be repulsed.

Roundhead infantry tried to scale the outer wall but they were easily repelled by O'Neill's Ulstermen. Cromwell's artillery was not yet powerful enough to make a large enough gap to allow a concerted assault. The Saxon general commanded his siege artillery – some very big guns - to be hauled overland.

Dragoons brought the Commissioner's massive cannons into play, hauling them to the top of Gallows Hill, about two hundred yards from the North Gate. It was the only place which would support the weight of these impressive weapons; the ground to the east and west was too boggy. As they were put in place, all Clonmel's defenders saw exactly where he was training his cannons. It was at their weakest point: a few yards east of the North Gate.

O'Neill maintained an aggressive defence. Bryen and Dick took their musketeers to the battlements, from where they could disrupt any Parliamentarian work party.

Bryen's musketeers' extraordinary accuracy caused the enemy enough losses for the otherwise unflappable Cromwell to grow concerned.

Cromwell donned his most merciless carapace. Arguably he always wore it. Black Hugh and his officers watched grimly as the Parliamentarian bombardiers made ready to hurl stone balls at Clonmel's walls. Weapons like these would not take long to break through them.

'We have very little time. Cromwell will send his foot to storm the first breach,' said Bryen. 'Once in, his soldiers will throw open the nearby North Gate and admit his horse. Gentlemen, you have a few hours at most. Get your sappers on the case. Our *coupure* must be ready before dawn.'

'A *coupure*, Colonel?' Black Hugh had never heard of such a thing.

'It's a strategy I learned from my uncle. He fought in the recent European War. It's a V-shaped inner fortification of earth and timber. Its walls should be about six feet high and converge to a point about eighty yards from the breach. Post two field pieces and arm them with chainshot.'

This, thought Black Hugh, was not the time to remind Bryen who commanded whom. In fact, the contrary applied.

'Our shot, Colonel? Any use?'

'Your fusiliers should take their positions in the houses to either side of the broken wall. They will open fire on the Cromwellians as they advance. Since only one fracture is being attempted, I will concentrate on the point of attack. General, my musketeers will line the walls of the *coupure*, firing rapidly, and at close range. Your pikemen will defend us.'

'My men will fire on your command, Colonel.'

'Good. Cromwell's men will have no shelter. It will mean slaughter, General.'

'Repayment in kind for Drogheda, Colonel?'

'Nothing so grand. Only a token payment for the murder of my infant daughter Bébhinn and for the squalid infamy he has inflicted on my beautiful Sorcha, her sister and for my elder girl.'

A very angry man had nothing more to say. Bryen and Dick saluted their chief with a brief bow and withdrew. There was no more time to lose.

Cromwell's guns soon began their task of forcing their uninvited entrance. They never bothered to aim at the gate itself. Their first round had crashed noisily into the walls, to the left of the town gate, displacing a few stones. The second round had come less than thirty seconds later. Then it continued, every twenty seconds or so.

No one could sleep that night. By the morning the cavity in the town's curtain walls was wide enough to let a few brave men in.

Cromwell mustered a forlorn of English footsoldiers and ordered them through the gap. To their astonishment and despair, they found themselves trapped in an enclosed wooden palisade, with no shelter from a rain of musketball and chainshot. The Puritans could neither advance nor retreat, trapped by the sheer numbers swarming through the broken wall behind them. For fully four hours they were mowed down without mercy. A thousand infantrymen of the Cromwellian forlorn would die before Cromwell allowed his bugler to sound the retreat.

Bryen signalled to his musketeers they should not permit the few survivors to escape with their lives.

'Murderers should explain themselves directly to the Almighty. It is not for us to treat them gently. Let them explain themselves at the bar of the heavenly court.'

Cromwell, however, rallied his troops for a second assault, but the infantry refused to enter the fissure a second time. Instead, they called on the Lord General to send in his elite cavalry, his Ironsides, so-called after their body armour. His commanders immediately volunteered to lead the assault. If they had any questions about the tactic they were left unasked. Desertion, cowardice and mutiny were all punishable by death, and on the battlefield there were no 'soldiers' friends' to plead their case.

Once the Ironsides had readied themselves for battle, Cromwell had directed them to dismount and make their assault on foot. They were unhappy with this – their battle armour made them clumsy on the ground – but, at around 3 pm, the Protestatnt Colonels Culme and Sankey led a column of dismounted but armoured cavalrymen into the fatal opening.

Quickly they drove the Irish infantry back from the principal hole and into the inner fortification. The Irish could not fire their cannons as too many of Black Hugh's men were struggling in hand-to-hand fighting with the English. Neither could Bryen's marksmen fire that many good shots into the morass for the same reasons.

If both sides took casualties, in the end it was the English who suffered most. For three dreadful hours the fatal scythe swung between life and death, but the English shot were unable to silence the musketeers without being impaled on Irish pikes. In the end they retreated, but only after all their officers and another thousand troopers had died.

By the end of that awful night, the Irish had beaten back their assailants three times, but at horrendous cost. So determined was their gallant resistance that no more of Cromwell's reinforcements could be persuaded to enter the yawning breach.

Indeed, the soldier-general was unable to conceal his professional respect for the Irish. He declared Black Hugh 'invincible' and by dawn he had called off the assault.

To lose to the Irish might be a set-back, but better to lose a battle than a war.

Believing that Cromwell would try a fourth time and that relief from Ormonde was far from imminent, O'Neill had called the Mayor, John White, and Colonel MacDonogh to his campaign office.

'I have decided to evacuate my troops. Colonel MacDonogh. You should do the same. We will do so under cover of darkness. Tomorrow, Mayor White, I suggest you send a message to Cromwell asking for terms. He is bound to accept. He cannot afford to be seen to be defeated by the Irish after all he has promised Parliament.'

'I understand. What will you do, general?' Bryen asked.

'We'll cross the old bridge over Suir Island, Colonel. The only access to the bridge is from the walled town, so we shall be safe. You may keep the remaining rations; without us they will go a lot further.'

'I shall do as you suggest. Thank you, General O'Neill, for your heroic kindness.'

Black Hugh had been right. The next day, anxious to bring the costly siege to an end and not realising that O'Neill and his freebooting auxiliaries had already gone, Cromwell offered the defenders more generous terms. He guaranteed to respect the lives and property of the townspeople, including its clergy. No mention was made of any soldier found in arms.

These terms were acceptable to John White. Shortly after daybreak he raised the white flag from the battlements and threw open the gate. Cromwell led his cavalry into the town, followed by the rest of his great army. He soon discovered that the garrison was gone and the town defenceless.

Although he was furious when he saw how he had been outwitted, and aside from considerable vandalism to the monastery and to St Mary's church, Cromwell did not allow his soldiers to abuse the terms of the surrender.

'Whatever you may think of me,' he told White, 'my word is good.'

What the Parliamentarian General did not know, and if he had he would not have cared, was that while O'Neill had resisted his attack, several hundred of the Irishman's best troops had fallen. Their ammunition had been exhausted. Bryen's tories, while had been none killed, were reduced to using their muskets as bayonets.

Cromwell had sent his terms, and it was time to go. Bryen and Dick mustered their musketeers and left Clonmel over the old bridge. Once over Suir Island the marksmen and their chiefs parted ways, most making for Tipperary while Bryen retained a few as a bodyguard on his journey back to Carrigadrohid, there to search for any remains of his daughter Bébhinn that the wolves might have spared, and thence to Kanturk to mourn his losses.

Cromwell sent a squadron of cavalry after Black Hugh's column. Waterford City was still in Coalition hands. The Cromwellian horse managed to overtake and cut down some walking wounded and their carers - usually fathers and brothers - but the main Confederate body escaped.

When they arrived at Waterford's walls, however, O'Neill and his troops were refused entry into the town by the governor, Tomás Preston, the former Confederate general and rival of Owen Roe O'Neill. He claimed that he did not have enough food to spare for the Ulsterman and his men.

Instead, Preston advised him to relieve Limerick, where he promised O'Neill he would be welcomed.

'With greater civility than here', replied Black Hugh. 'Men, Ireton has Limerick City under siege. There is no time to lose. We shall go there directly, and at a forced march.'

Parliament's demands for Cromwell's return home were every day more strident. The King-in-Exile had been invited by the Scots to return to Scotland and be crowned. He was a Stuart, after all. This *volte-face* required the Caledonians to be subdued. After a hard debate with himself and with Providence, his god, Cromwell submitted to the pressure. He transferred the command of his army to Ireton. On May 20 the 'Scourge of Ireland' sailed from Youghal, leaving behind a legacy that his name would thereafter be only repeated in curses.

Cromwell would address the High Commission.

In the assault on Clonmel, I lost 2,500 soldiers. It was my New Model Army's first defeat and was certainly the greatest loss of life it has sustained in any single action. By some considerable margin, I will admit. Yet I will remind you that it remains my only defeat. If I had attempted to renew the siege, to starve O'Neill into submission, my return to England would have had to be delayed. That would have been contrary to every missive you have sent me for the last month. Scotland might have reverted to monarchy.

Parliament was assuaged. It voted him a substantial country house and celebrated his skills and gallantry. 'The stain of defeat need not discolour his breastplate', it declared.

Irish miseries must have seemed incapable of increase, yet they were. The Irish clergy prayed for peace, and their supplications to the Almighty besought the heavens to intercede for their unfortunate country. Even Ormonde's bright star had become occluded. Limerick and Galway both refused to receive him. On August 6, the clergy congregated in Jamestown from where they sent him a formal message, requesting his withdrawal from the kingdom and asking for the appointment of someone in whom the people might again trust.

Beneath its courtly surface, Ormonde's pride was badly damaged. He refused to retire but the Irish bishops published a declaration, denouncing his rule as Lord Lieutenant and threatening to impeach him before the new king.

*

CHAPTER TWENTY-EIGHT
CROMWELL PROTECTS ALL

Almost as the sound of the Galwayman's fatal cleaver ricocheted around the courts of Europe, Prince Charles, or better, the King-in-Exile as he was widely known, wrote to every European monarch, appealing or even begging for military help against the regicidal High Commission of the Protectorate of the Commonwealth. His eloquence, at least at first, came to nothing.

In his home territories, however, he fared a little better.

In Kilkenny, he was immediately proclaimed King of Ireland. It was, of course, an heroic but empty gesture. Ireland was still fiercely engaged against Lord Ireton.

Charles calculated that the support of the Scottish army was his best hope for regaining the English throne. In Scotland, the Scots had many reasons to resent the execution of King Charles I, reasons that Parliament seemed not to have anticipated. They they too proclaimed the King-in-Exile Scotland's lawful ruler, *in absentia*, and pretender to the thrones of England, France and Ireland.

The Scots attached a precondition, however; he would have to sign the National Covenant and promise to enforce Presbyterianism as the official religion in England. This would be a hard call. Moderate English Royalists were almost uniformly opposed to Presbyterianism and any deal with the Covenanters.

The king invited the Scottish Commissioners to send a team to Breda and negotiate terms. They accepted by return. In March, a party of ten arrived, including Brodie of Brodie, the Provost of Aberdeen, Sir John Smith and Mssrs Livingstone, Wood and Hutcheson. There were also two Scottish peers, neither of whom the king could constitutionally refuse an audience.

'Noble friends,' the King-in-Exile told the Earls of Cassilis and Lothian and their delegation, 'gentlemen and fellow Scots, we have arranged our ballroom as a debating chamber. We shall join you in the morning for prayers and will attend each day for an hour in the early afternoon, before we dine. At this last, we shall listen to a summary of the daily discussions and submit or disagree as we see fit.'

If the King-in-Exile had thought that the Scots' demands would be moderate he was destined to be disappointed. They were very tough. He had thought they needed him more than the other way round, but the Covenanters had a contrary view. Even on the first day, when he asked them to abbreviate their long list of conditions, they countered that he had to swear to the Covenant and impose Presbyterianism not just on Scotland but also on England and Ireland before they could countenance a coronation.

'Your Majesty,' Alexander Jaffray, the Provost told him at two o'clock that first day, 'God's truth is not for bartering. We have further decided that if you are to accept your throne at our hands, you must also impose and enforce penal laws against the Papists.'

For the king the next five weeks passed like an endurance test. He sought solace in his usual way – many English gentlewomen were only too ready to accommodate his 'bawdy carousing', as John Livingstone put it - and when he attended morning prayers he pointedly took the Book of Common Prayer in his hand, a work reviled by Presbyterians. During those weeks he sought ceaselessly to mitigate the worst conditions, but in the end he gave way and signed a draft agreement.

The king, penniless, surrounded by enemies, badly advised by his Council - such as it was - and unable to seek refuge anywhere else concluded there was little or no chance of help from Europe. Scotland was the only game in town.

The king's uneasy capitulation was good enough for most of the delegation but, exceptionally, Livingstone concluded that the Scottish mission was on course for disaster. He argued for an extension, less to impress the king, more to bring his own team round to his way of thinking.

'While the King-in-Exile has accepted the Covenant', he told his Scottish fellows, 'if there is no real change in his heart, then he is merely hypocritical. Since he has not forsworn his former principles, counsels and company, I suggest that is the case.'

'The ugly fact is, we have sinfully entangled and engaged ourselves,' said Alexander Jaffray, apparently taking the king's side, 'with that poor young Prince to whom we have been sent. We have made him sign and swear a Covenant which we know from clear and demonstrable reasons that he abhors in his heart. Yet knowing that only upon these terms could he be admitted to rule over us - all other means having failed him - he sinfully complied with what we equally sinfully pressed upon him. Brethren, I must confess, to my mind our sin is greater than his.'

Jaffray, with his Highland compatriots Alexander Brodie and Hutcheson, saw that the king had, effectively, been forced to accept to the deal on offer.

'I find myself hoping,' said Brodie of Brodie, 'that the King-in-Exile will reject this largely specious 'agreement' we have forced on him.'

'I shall counsel the king that he must not sign the Covenant, unless he truly believes what he says,' said Jaffray.

With a sad heart the king gave way. On May 1, 1650, he flourished a quill, imprinted his seal, abandoned his loyal Marquess of Montrose and repudiated the Marquess of Ormonde's peace treaty with the Irish Confederacy.

In exchange, he had been reassured, the Scots would return and crown him king.

On June 2, believing he was home and dry, Charles, King of Scots, accompanied by an enthusiastic entourage, and set off from Holland for Scotland. Three weeks later, he landed in Speyside.

The Lord Protector heard immediately. He assembled a brigade and moved like the wind to catch the king and arrest him.

The king should have known better. At Dunbar, the inevitable battle between his Royalists and Cromwell's English Commission was joined. The Royalists were roundly defeated. Charles only just escaped, riding for his life with his officers to the safety of Dunfermline Castle. His lifeguard vanished into the hills and nearby forests.

Only now did Charles, King of Scots, discover that he had no real power. Actually, less than that. On August 16, Presbyterian zealots on the ruling Committee of Estates blamed his defeat at Dunbar on his lack of serious religious commitment. They demanded he remove all 'ungodly' Cavaliers from his army and retinue.

Royal revenge was delayed by a period of regal deliberation. Not until the winter would it bear fruit. His plan, known as 'The Start', would in the end be a failure, but at least it prised the Presbyterian grasp apart. Their rivals in the power struggle, the Royalists and a new faction, the 'Engagers', were able to crown the Duke of Rothesay – the king's most senior Scottish title – at Scone Palace on January 1, 1651.

Cromwell's army stayed north of the border, which allowed King Charles II of the Scots, England, France and Ireland the chance to lead his freshly recruited Scoto-Royalist army across the border into England. When he crossed the border he expected a series of loyal uprisings. They failed to materialise. What's more, Cromwell steadily closed on him.

At Worcester, two old enemies confronted each other.

After the battle, in which the king was again defeated, there was no handy royalist castle nearby. Charles was forced to escape through a succession of rural England's cottages and inns. For six desperate weeks he avoided capture, thinly disguised, hiding in hovels and cellars, bearing in place of a crown a huge price on his head. At one point he hid from Roundheads in an oak tree at Boscobel, later to be the famous Royal Oak, all the time running for his life. Not until mid-October was he able to take ship for France.

It was a crowned king, however, who rejoined his mother, this time at the palace of the Louvre. Somewhat regrettably, the counsellors who gathered around him were quarrelsome, which left him gloomy and withdrawn. At least the French king was generous financially and found time to lend the Scot a sympathetic hearing.

*

In June, 1651, Bishop Heber MacMahon, O'Neill's successor, assembled his Ulster Army - four thousand foot and six hundred horse - in Loughall, South Armagh. This was a real threat to the Ulster settlers,. It was, however, very short of ammunition and half his men were obliged to carry pikes rather than muskets.

'Brave Irishmen all,' he addressed them, 'we have determined that we shall march through the heart of Ulster. I have already billeted a string of garrisons across the centre of the province. I will continue to post men until we reach Ballycastle, on the north coast. Some of you will find yourselves housed in forts, others in country houses. Our aim is to drive a wedge between Coote's 'Londonderry' garrison in the west and Venables's, in Carrickfergus, to the east.'

He smiled affectionately at his warriors.

'You will of course know that the Parliamentarians are not merely divided amongst themselves, they are also tied down by our noble 'tories'. The Ulster Army will engage Coote's army in Lifford, near Derry, where Venables's men cannot reinforce them.'

MacMahon adroitly fended off the English cavalry as they crossed the river Finn, to camp on the side of a mountain at Scarrifholis, just south of *Leitir Ceanainn*, or Letterkenny. He was at the first downstream crossing point of the river Swilly, on the road to Donegal Town.

Coote's Protestants retreated to their fortified towns as soon as they heard of the Catholic mobilisation, believing the exaggerated atrocities of the 1641 Rebellion unquestioningly. Their caution seemed to predict that the Catholic Army would be victorious.

MacMahon, however, began to see his officers, who were still counselling a more defensive strategy, as defeatist, and in turn, they found the Bishop-General stubborn and unmoveable.

Their loyalty was sorely tested when they came him to with dreadful news.

'Your lordship should know,' said one, 'that Parliament has managed to reinforce Coote and raise his strength to some three thousand. We may have garrisoned many forts but the Protestants have far more ammunition, more troops and many more horses.'

'Please, your lordship,' begged another, 'do not abandon our strong defensive position. Do not even consider risking battle. Parliament's army is superior to ours. We should stay put and wait for the enemy's supplies to run out. Only then, my lord bishop, should we march back to our strongholds along the border with Leinster.'

MacMahon listened gracelessly.

'What are you? Are you the noble instruments of a righteous war or are you base cowards? Your counsel would only guarantee a long and drawn out confrontation. No, gentlemen, no. I shall order my troops down from their mountain camp. We shall engage the Parliamentarian army head on. This field, marked on this map as Scarrifhollis, will henceforward be forever remembered as an Apostolic victory.'

All too soon it was apparent that the bishop's impatience for battle was reckless. When he formed up his troops he stationed a very small vanguard in front. Behind, a huge block of squares was marched at a fierce pace. The soldiers found this formation difficult. It would permit only a few units to engage the enemy at any time. Most of their soldiers would be uselessly trapped within their own ranks.

For Parliament, Sir Charles Coote the Younger's squares were smaller. They could far more easily reinforce each other and move around a battlefield with ease.

When the baronet sent an infantry detachment to confront the Irish advance party, all hell broke loose. First the two sides exchanged musket volleys. Then they fought hand-to-hand with pikes and the butts of their unloaded muskets.

Whereas Coote could steadily reinforce his infantry, MacMahon could do no such thing. In the end Coote drove the Irish back onto their old positions, and there they stuck. Coote was able to send in yet more infantry. The Irish were trapped between his men, the river and the mountain side, and Coote was free to attack their flanks.

MacMahon's army may have outnumbered its enemy but now it was tied up in one great, unmanageable mass. Its condition, horribly obvious, was that it could no longer defend itself. Panic turned a once disciplined Irish army into a mob, and the Parliamentarian fusiliers were able to load and pour their volleys into it at will. The Irish could not return fire and were cut down from a safe distance.

Inevitably, the Irish horse turned tail. Parliamentarian cavalry pursued it in a loose league with blood-thirsty local settlers, all with scores of their own to settle. A cornered and doomed infantry fought and fought, until all were stilled. Two thirds of them had fallen on the battlefield, the rest along the path of pursuit.

The battle was an immense, impressive, absolute victory for Coote and his Parliamentarians. Three thousand Ulster Catholics were killed; three quarters of their total number. Parliament lost just a hundred. Coote, true to his family's tradition, ordered the captured to be executed. The roll of the fallen included Henry O'Neill, Owen Roe's son, who had surrendered on terms and believed himself safe. A week later Venables found Bishop MacMahon hiding in a looted Catholic church in Enniskillen, in which he had sought sanctuary. Venables had him hanged outside the west door.

Scarrifhollis marked the end of the Ulster Army. The loss of common soldiers could, perhaps, be made up, given time, but the death of so many experienced officers, with almost all their weapons, could not. The roll call was voiced in the darkest melancholy. The Irish lost nine colonels, four lieutenant-colonels, three majors, twenty captains and hundreds of junior officers. It was a cull of what little remained of the Ulster Irish Catholic land-owning class, far more devastating than the famous Flight of the Earls of 1607. It marked the extermination of the province's native aristocracy and it assured the Protestant settler ascendancy for centuries to come.

News of the defeat had England, Scotland and Wales rejoicing. All that was now needed was another army, pure in faith, purpose and thought, to finish the job. Parliament decided on a competition to see which soldier of means could offer the Commonwealth the best deal. Plenty of feathers in one's cap were on offer.

In the event, it was Major-General Ireton's regiment that won.

It had the clear advantage of being there already.

General Ireton had first arrived in Dublin just days after General Cromwell, back in August, 1649. He had brought seventy-seven warships with him, overflowing with troops and supplies.

After Cromwell's return to England, to prepare his Roundheads for their invasion of Scotland, Ireton assumed command of the New Model Army in Ireland. The Commissioners congratulated him with the venerable title and powers of Lord President of Munster.

In England, 'sea-troopers' were pressed. The Sea-Army stacked them into their battleships, into hammocks that allowed four inches between one marine and the trooper above.

Far more comfortably, since he ravelled in the state quarters of Sea-General Deane's flagship, was the austere Solicitor-General John Cooke. No one could have been more anti-royalist than this man; he was one of the few 'judges' who had had the courage to sign the king's death warrant. His brief was now to reform the laws of Ireland, anglicise them and, of course, make them amenable to peaceable rule. This required the massive use of capital punishment. Permanent gallows were erected in every Irish hamlet, ready to do their God-given duty.

Ireton had been ordered to complete Parliament's subjugation of the third kingdom. Ireton became the heir to Sir Walter Raleigh, Humphrey Gilbert, Sir George Carew, and all such ilk.

He read and reread the last's *Pacata Hibernia*.

In the event, Ireton modelled himself on his famous father-in-law, both in the retribution he meted out to his men at the faintest hint of disobedience and in the violence of his oppression of the natives.

He wrote to his wife's father, the High Commissioner for War.

> As I see it, I am faced with a pair challenges. One is the capture of the remaining cities held by the Irish. The 'tories' are the other, who seek every opportunity to attack my supply lines. We are short enough of food and water as it is – let alone the wherewithal to build siege engines. Ireland is a country where there is not enough water to drown a man, wood enough to hang one, nor earth enough to bury him. Dear Sir, may I appeal to you to supplicate the Parliament of England to publish lenient terms for any Irish surrender? If you fail your son-in-law, he shall no choice but to subdue the Papists with irresistible force.

Poring over Steed's map of Munster, Ireton saw at once that he could cut the Irish-held City of Waterford off from the rest of Ireland. He had no need to reinstate his father-in-law's siege. All would depend on Sir Hardress Waller, then engaged at Carlow. If that townland fell, Waterford's food could no longer be supplied via the River Barrow and The parliamentarian general's siege would then be irresistible.

'So gentlemen', he told his officers, 'we wait upon Sir Hardress's victory. That may take some time but the delay will free up a few days. We shall put them to good use. Let us adopt the Hibernian taste for hunting, but this time not foxes. High Commissioner Cromwell wants foxhunting banned in England and we shall eschew it here. Instead, let us hunt 'tories'.'

He casually waved a gauntleted arm in the direction of the hills to the north.

'Out there is our sports field, gentlemen, the Wicklow Mountains. They are rustling with vermin. England expects them rooted out, quickly, mercilessly, and it's our job to do it before they go to earth.'

Ireton's vast army had a happy season in Wicklow, ruthlessly suppressing countless bands of tories, destroying the barns and warehouses that may (or may not) have belonged to Catholics or fellow travellers, torching the province's crops as they went. The people were already destitute; now they could only starve.

It was a sad, repetitive story. One after another, each little town stood out for a while against him, but against such numbers it was forced to open its gates to the English. When news of the fall of the Irish garrison at Carlow reached him, which had surrendered on terms, the Lord President of Munster was free for a duller purpose; the blockade of Waterford.

Having barely survived Oliver Cromwell's predations, the inhabitants of the ancient port now found that his successor and son-in-law, Henry Ireton, had ordered his Roundheads to isolate the place. This was for ther second time.

Inside the town, typhoid joined dysentery in a plot devised by Lucifer himself. Diseases stalked its citizens, concentrating their evil venom on the old, the women and their children. Food was scarce; the little that remained commanded the price of a ransom. Tumbrels, drawn by emaciated mules, rattled along the cobbled streets, collecting men, women and children, every day, all day, each dead through hunger or plague. Pathetic remains, once the mortal engines of immortal souls, were piled into a common grave, under a blanket of flies.

It got worse, much worse. By late July starvation and disease were killing four hundred people a week. Soon the Reaper had claimed his thousands; everyone's dreadful misery would only end in tragedy. Terror lurked behind every front door.

Henry Ireton directed Lord Broghill to prevent any attempt to relieve Waterford from the north west. He posted a regiment of horse at nearby Carrick-on-Suir - a highly mobile reserve, designed to resist any Irish incursion into central Munster. Waterford was now wholly isolated by land and sea, and Ireton brought up additional regiments of foot and some heavy artillery to finish the job, once and for all.

Waterford, under the Irish general Tomás Preston, recently elevated Viscount Tara by the King-in-Exile, refused Ireton's summons to surrender. Even so, the Irishman knew it was a futile gesture; the fall of the city was merely a matter of time. After three months of renewed siege, the garrison had been reduced to just seven hundred not-very-fit troops. They gallantly manned its extensive walls, knowing that its store of gunpowder could not maintain its defence. Preston, or Tara, watched impotently while Ireton's gunners calmly set up their artillery batteries. At first he wondered why this lethal work was so unhurried, but then he deduced that even more Parliamentarians must be on their way. Having taken Carlow, they had been freed up for a grander assault.

'Lord Tara!'

The unfamiliar address came from the Mayor of Waterford. He and his aldermen had sought an audience with their famous general, formerly known as Tomás Preston. 'Lord Tara, we have heard of the lenient terms that were granted to the defenders of Carlow. We beg you to abandon this hopeless struggle. Negotiate, Sir, we implore you.'

Tara seemed to waver.

'Gentlemen,' he said, 'if Carlow was a sprat to catch a mackerel, we are that mackerel. If this city falls, as Cromwell demonstrated at Drogheda, Wexford and elsewhere, the lives and property of Ireland's defenders will be forfeit. Sir,' the mayor continued, 'Ireton's Parliamentary fleet is now blockading the port, just off the city. Considered opinion is that relief by sea is impossible.'

'Nor by land, not even if a rescue were mounted from Munster,' added an alderman. 'Ireton has raided every farm for a hundred square miles - every cow, pig, sheep and horse has been stolen and slaughtered, smoked, soused in brine, wind-dried I know not what. Now the English have our meat, enough to feed their troops for months, maybe years. My wife says the Commonwealth has banned Sunday dinner.'

Still Preston, or Tara, hesitated.

'Lord General,' said one alderman, 'Ireton's capture of our cattle has provided him with an immense quantity of intestines. We have had intelligence that his kitchens have painstakingly cleaned them out and, on Ireton's orders, inflated them into balloons to be attached under the palettes that his carpenters are assembling.'

Tara has never heard anything so proposterous. He began to worry about his own sanity.

'My Lord,' began another, 'Ireton has dug trenches between his siege guns and our walls. The English will put their huge field pieces onto their makeshift rafts and tow them close to the city.'

'Enough, Gentlemen, I know, I know.' Preston had heard enough. 'But you must realise that Waterford, and the fortress at Duncannon, are among the last of our strongholds left in Munster. Limerick is also holding out, under Black Hugh O'Neill. Beyond that, Lord Inchiquin commands a small force around Kerry in the west while the Marquess of Ormonde commands an army based somewhere, anywhere, in County Limerick.'

This last gave the company little comfort.

'Sir, everyone knows the Lord Lieutenant is holed beneath the water-line; neither the Catholics nor the Royalists like the cut of his jib.'

'An alliance with Lord Inchiquin would be a pact with the devil. He is the monster who burned the cathedral at Cashel.'

'With five thousand good men and women inside!'

Inchiquin would never be forgiven.

Preston, or Tara, sighed. If the Catholics of Waterford were ill-disposed to support Ormonde or Inchiquin, even when Ormonde and Inchiquin were attempting to rally forces to march to their relief, then he had no alternative.

It surprised few people, therefore, when Tomás Preston opted to let those he protected live, rather than die. He agreed to surrender the town of Waterford on August 10, 1650.

In an unprecedented act of chivalry, Lord President Ireton graciously consented to allow Waterford's soldiers to live. They would have to march away, the men to Galway, their officers to Athlone, both of which were still in Irish Catholic hands. There was a proviso, however. They had to leave behind all their possessions, especially their artillery and ordnance. Non-military citizens of the town could depart or stay as they wished. Ireton issued a pledge that their property would not be plundered.

Duncannon saw the town surrender. It had been built to protect Waterford, and the moment the toen abandoned its fight the fort become quite pointless. Just a week later, it too hoisted the white flag.

Waterford's fall forced the Irish to redirect their efforts. Limerick had become their capital, and Galway stood solidly behind them.

As thunder follows lightning, Henry Ireton marched his forces north, determined to lay siege to Limerick. His threat to that great city was short-lived. The intensely wet and cold October weather would compel him to abandon the siege well before the onset of winter. It had been ineffective in any case; flag, semaphore and heliograph, at which arcane arts the Irish had developed a proficiency, conspired to let the city to open one of its gates to let in an overladen wagon whenever the need arose.

Ireton would have to wait for good weather before returning to the siege.

Topologically, the City of Tipperary was split in two. The great Abbey River separated its unequal halves. The smaller but grander English Town, which included King John's citadel, was encircled by the Abbey on three sides and by the Shannon on the other. Only one fortified bridge gave access – the Thomond Bridge. Irish town was larger, and more roads let into it, but it was also more heavily fortified. Its even older walls had been buttressed with twenty feet of solid earth, making them impossible to break. Moreover, the walls had bastions every hundred yards or so, each surmounted with cannon, powder, ball and an impatient bombardier. Every approach to the city was covered by musket loops. Inside, the English would have met a city garrison of two thousand, mainly composed of veterans from the Ulster Army. It was commanded by Black Hugh O'Neill, who had had some useful tuition in how to resist an English siege at Clonmel.

Beautiful Limerick would not be an easy conquest, but Ireton was resolute and well-provisioned.

Ireton had brought eight thousand men, twenty-eight siege pieces and four mortars with him. His first act was of course to summons Black Hugh O'Neill to surrender and, equally predictably, O'Neill refused.

Ireton's investment began as it might have in a textbook. He secured the approaches to the city, cutting off the town's supplies. He threw up his own earthworks and topped them with artillery. He made himself conspicuously ready to rain death upon the defenders.

Before long, the Englishman had a result: his men stormed and took the fort on Thomond Bridge. From there the Roundheads swarmed towards English Town but, unfortunately for them, Black Hugh had mined the bridge. Its destruction killed a very large number of Parliamentarians and cut off the road. Some very unfortunate Saxons were caught on the wrong side of the bridge.

After that, the English general had been left no choice but to attack the city in small boats. Black Hugh counter-attacked. The English were easily beaten off.

O'Neill had pointed out to Ireton that he could not take the town by storm. Any direct assault on its walls was pointless.

Ireton had no choice but to starve the city out. He built two forts on a nearby hill. The earth walls broke the wind and, inside, a canvas city sheltered his men. The siege was on and it looked set to last.

Black Hugh needed help from the outside, and it was not so far away. Two Irish chiefs, related by marriage, were determined to help. Lord Muskerry, quartered in Dromagh Castle, was joined there by the young Lord of Duhallow. They had taken it upon themselves to raise an army from the hedgrows and villages for Limerick's relief.

Unfortunately, if inevitably, some of the men they wanted to recruit had already been retained by Broghill as spies. In the summer of 1651 the small coins Lord Broghill had promised those desperate men was paying off. One of them informed Lord Broghill that Lord Muskerry was leading a substantial company of horse and foot from Dromagh, along the Blackwater, determined to surprise Ireton in his rear. The spy also gave him the interesting news that Lord Muskerry's Captain of Horse was Colonel Bryen MacDonogh, the notorious tory, and that as well as Muskerry's horse he was commanding at least twenty well-trained and mounted musketeers.

Broghill decided to intercept the Royalist relief column in person. He led eleven squadrons of horse and fifteen of foot. They crossed the river at a place called Knocknaclashy, where to their astonishment they met ninety Irishmen walking easily along the path. They were clearly not soldiers; they were unarmed and clothed in rags. They had a modest escort but, on seeing Broghill's men, their mounted guards evaporated like a mist for the safety of the woods.

Broghill did not shoot from the hip. If these wanderers were innocent they could live. Even go about their business.

'What are you doing here?' he asked their elderly leader, reasonably enough.

'We've come to see the battle,' the man replied.

The Irishman seemed utterly unimpressed by a great English army. He was powerfully built. He had probably been a blacksmith or armourer in his day, Broghill thought.

He had replied in English and, as Broghill took his measure, his lordship saw the man's clothes were in a slightly better state of repair than his companions'. He wore a great green fern in his cap, but then many did. One thing was sure; this blacksmith was too old for a fight.

'What makes you think there will be a battle?' The intelligence that Broghill already had was supposed to be the latest.

'There is a prophecy we Duhallow men have repeated for many years. One will be fought here, sooner or later, and we thought no time more likely than the present.'

'A battle? I don't suppose you can remember how that prophecy goes?'

'A rough translation from our language would be, 'Thou wouldst fain talk a victory at Knocknaclashy and praise him next to the God of mercy,' my lord.'

'I see. How very Delphic. Do you think it means a Royalist victory?'

The Irishman shook his head.

'The Godless will have the day,' the elderly blacksmith said resignedly.

Broghill let them go. In all probability their escort had already gained the shelter of their countrymen's hovels in the woods. The forests were a danger to the English. There were few marked paths. Somehow the Irish navigated without them. Everywhere one looked, in any thicket or woodpile, there were threadbare tories ready for a scrap. If they drew their compatriots out of the woods, the plain would briefly become a bloody and disorderly battlefield.

Broghill marched on, taking the road between the woods. The plain was straight ahead.

His left wing had eighty musketeers and they marched with their weapons loaded. He halted his army just where the plain opened up and directed his men to fire a lethal volley into the woods to either side. If there were tories hidden there they did not immediately answer.

'Ha! The bogtrotters are beaten already', a soldier cried out. The cry was taken up by the soldiers.

'The bogtrotters are beaten!'

'Yes,' said Broghill, laughing with affected confidence, 'and they shall be beaten rather worse in a few short moments.'

The truth was that Broghill had doubts. He had misgivings about the Irish. Were they really insouciant, simple idiots? Had they led him into a trap?

He created two pincer armies, each of five horse squadrons, three to charge and two to second. A central troop would pursue any rout, while the crab's claws would execute the attack. His foot, consisting of five battalions, was similarly disposed. It was an elegant arrangement, as one would expect. It had first been demonstrated by Julius Caesar.

Broghill's caution was well founded. Even before Broghill could complete his battle formation a great Irish army came at them out of the woods to either side, and at speed. It quickly outflanked Broghill's army, which drew to the right. Lord Broghill rode with them, bellowing his orders over the thunderous drumbeat of his horses' hooves.

Broghill's infantry had not yet been mobilised, and Lord Muskerry had seen a standing target. The Irishman stationed his musketeers; a thousand of them. They were ready for action but were told to hold their fire until his cavalry had scattered their Protestant counterparts.

At his signal, his horse attacked Broghill's, head to head. As they rode passed each other, the English and Irish hacked at each other with their swords. The battleground was soon a bloody quagmire; severed limbs littering the awful scene. It was not wholesale slaughter, however. The armies were so intermixed that the musketeers could not shoot.

Nevertheless, the victory seemed to be with the Irish. So much so, in fact, that Captain Banister, who had been fighting on the English left wing, turned and rode off to Cork with news of an English defeat. The Irish had never fought more bravely, he would report.

The carnage lasted a dismal hour. The Irish horse feinted a withdrawal but, when they turned and charged a second time, Broghill managed to rout their left wing.

It was not yet over. Just when Broghill thought the day was his, a squadron of a hundred and forty horse appeared from nowhere, focussing its terrible energy on the English rearguard. Broghill turned around. He saw they were led by a young officer whose brown coat was brocaded in gold. He was unstoppable, cutting through the English like a *skean* through a fillet. This had to be Bryen MacDonogh Carty, Lord of

Duhallow, leading his charge for his Irish horse. Broghill was impressed. The young man was fighting like a wild boar.

Until his horse was shot from under him, that is.

Broghill's cavalry charged through the Irish again and again but, as the English charged, the Irish parted to let them through, only to strike the English tail in each pass.

In was all threatening to end in a horrible disaster for the English, when Broghill had a daring idea. He ordered his men to shout out 'they run, they run'.

When the first Irish rank heard this cry, they looked back to see if it were true. They saw faces radiating fear and panic, thinking their comrades were about to turn and run. It was enough. They fled.

Bryen MacDonogh, unhurt but on the ground, found himself directly beneath the hooves of a rearing Parliamentarian cavalryman. His sword rose vertically to penetrate the horse's heart, but as it fell it trapped the Irishman's leg. Its rider dismounted and took his pistolet from its holster. Its round was not intended for Bryen however. The soldier calmly dispatched the hurt animal.

'Irishman, this sword has already dispatched six rebels like you.' Bryen was still on the ground, struggling to gain his feet. The Parliamentarian looked him up and down.

'I must say, you are my best dressed one yet.'

While his sword was held over Bryen's shirt, he still hesitated.

'Come, men,' he shouted out as he was joined by other Ironsides, their reddened sabres similarly drawn. 'Here's a rebel gentleman, keen to meet his Maker. Let's not rush this. Let's send him to heaven in Christmas parcels.'

'We failed to damage the Irish cavalry at all, with the exception of one exceptional horseman who was slain,' Lord Broghill would report to Ireton. 'It turned out to be the infamous tory MacCarthy, the one they call MacDonogh. Unfortunately, his musketeers must have skills or weapons we do not – despite the confusion they took out the first rank of my squadron, hardly losing any of their own in the mêlée. Thirty-three of my best men were either killed or wounded by their first volley and it got worse. The whole affair made me a little angry and I ordered my men to give no quarter, neither during nor after the battle.'

In the fray Lord Muskerry's own horse had also been wounded. This time the general shot it. Then he ran to where a group of frightened horses had gathered but, before he could seize one and remount, Broghill's men closed in and captured him. A prize indeed.

Some way from Knocknaclashy, an elderly spectator limped slowly home towards Kanturk. His heart was broken. His name? It was no secret. If anyone cared to ask, he was 'O'Callaghan of the Ferns', or *Baith-na Ui Ceallachan*, perhaps in commemoration of the green fern he had worn so proudly for nine long years. Seamus O'Callaghan, now without a master, knew now, in his heart, that the Irish defeat would put Ireland beyond repair for the rest of time.

In Limerick, Black Hugh O'Neill's only remaining hope was to hold out until bad weather, or hunger, or both, would force Ireton to raise his siege. To this end, O'Neill sent the town's old men, women and children out of the city. They were obviously no one's enemy and without them his supplies would last a little longer. Ireton, however, rounded them up, hanged forty of them and sent the rest back whence they had come.

It would not need a military scholar to see Limerick's case was hopeless. Now the mayor and his civic dignitaries put Black Hugh under pressure to surrender. Food was rationed and a round of dysentery had broken out.

While O'Neill was trying to calm a panicky City Hall, Ireton's informants had discovered a weakness in the walls of Irish Town. The Englishman immediately blasted a gap in them. With sudden horror the town realised that they were in for an all out assault. Mortal fear overtook them. An English Royalist - Colonel Fennell – mutinied. He turned his cannon around and threatened to fire on O'Neill's men unless they surrendered.

Muskerry and his famous colonel's valiant attempt to reverse the tide of history had only hastened Limerick's capitulation.

After Lord Broghill had returned to Limerick with news of his crushing victory at Knocknaclashy, Ireton awarded him a military salute. His shot fired three volleys. The war was all but over.

Limerick itself formally surrendered on October 27, 1651. The terms required the inhabitants' lives and property to be respected but the householders were warned that they might still be evicted in the future, should 'appropriate Protestants deserving of reward' approach the Commonwealth authorities. As for the common soldiers of the garrison, they were offered Cromwell's choice of 'Hell or Connacht'. County Galway was still holding out for the Coalition. The soldiers weapons were to be left behind but when they arrived on the Atlantic coast they could at least enjoy the muted consolation of a hero's welcome.

Limerick's officers were not treated with such gallant magnanimity. They, including the mutinous Colonel Fennell, were hanged with neither trial nor absolution.

A sick and not entirely rational Ireton put Black Hugh before a court martial which sentenced him to death. The day before his hanging, however, General Ludlow (the new Commander-in-Chief) commuted his sentence. Black Hugh was to be sent to the Tower of London, in chains, and for indefinite safekeeping.

The lives of the civilian leaders of Limerick had not been included in Ireton's 'generous' terms. The Catholic Bishop Terence Albert O'Brien and a sympathetic Alderman were simply hanged. The mayor, he who had for so long counselled surrender, was hung, drawn, quartered and decapitated. His head was mounted over St John's Gate. It would stay there for fully twenty years.

Of the original Irish garrison some seven hundred had died. Civilian casualties weren't counted by the occupying forces but were by the churches entrusted with their graves. The total came to five thousand.

More than two thousand Parliamentary soldiers died at Limerick, mostly from disease. Among them was the Lord Protector's famous son-in-law who died a month after the fall of the city. General Ireton succumbed to the feverish dysentery that had been plaguing his men.

His loss 'struck a great sadness into me', said the High Commissioner for War.

Ireton left a son and three daughters by his wife, Bridget Cromwell.

Limerick was one of the last in a dispiriting litany of defeats. It extinguished in the Irish any residual traces of loyalty among them towards the king's Lord Lieutenant, the Marquess of Ormonde.

At Scarrifhollis, the remnants of the Ulster Army had been destroyed. There was no opposition left.

In English salons, an often asked question was as to why the Catholics had fought to the bitter end. During the war, elsewhere in Ireland, 'innocent' Catholics were offered land – usually in Connacht - to compensate for their forfeited estates. The typical English hostess thought all Irish land was equally poor; undrained bog for the most part. She would not have realised that in Limerick and Waterford they were not even offered that. That was why they had held on.

After Limerick's fall the 'tories' would carry on their skirmishing warfare against the Parliamentarians. In the end even they too would surrender. Some were allowed to go into exile as soldiers 'of fortune'. The number who agreed to go surprised some English commentators. Thirty-five thousand Irish soldiers signed up to fight for foreign armies.

Lord Muskerry was also tried for his life, and found guilty on all counts. He was pardoned on condition he quit Ireland. He had a choice. That or be beheaded.

He saved some lands and most of his more liquid assets by dint of a gift of £1,000 a year to Lord Broghill and by going into exile, taking ship for Spain. Blarney Castle, alas, he could not save. Broghill had already expropriated it.

Despite her husband's 'nocence', or guilt, Lady Muskerry was permitted to enjoy the residue of the estate during her lifetime. After that, it was not to revert to the rebel earl. Instead, his estates would be settled on the Earl of Cork.

In Spain, Muskerry met O'Sullivan Beare, the author nephew of the assassinated chief. He unsuccessfully petitioned the Spanish monarch for money to carry on the war. Lord Muskerry was greatly saddened when he left Madrid.

His itinerary now took him to the Continent, where he had an idea that his late son-in-law's Parisian brother might help him with Cardinal Mazarin. His hope was to obtain the office of *Maitre de Camp*.

For his part, Lord Inchiquin also attempted to recruit a new Irish army. This time the Irish froze him out. Murrough 'of the Burnings' had massacred the priests and congregation at Cashel. He could never be forgiven.

In a letter to the Speaker of the Westminster Parliament, sent from his recently acquired palace at Blarney Castle, the residence that Queen Elizabeth had coveted for her Irish seat, Lord Broghill wrote,

> May it please your Excellency, with the defeat of Lords Inchiquin and Ormonde at Limerick, and an unexpected triumph over Lord Muskerry at Knocknaclashy, I believe I may confirm that our Heroic Conquest of Ireland is complete. My last gave details of the great siege. All I need to add is that we captured the Irish generals Lord Muskerry and Hugo O'Neill, but released the first into exile, chastened but free, and the second is available for your inspection in the Tower. Let it not be said that we are barbarians. As for the battle on the plain beside the Clonmeen, we had a very fair execution for above three miles and, indeed, it was bloody, for I gave orders to kill all, though some few prisoners, of

good quality, were saved. All their foot field-officers charged on foot with pikes in their hands, so that few of them got off. That was so far from any bogs or woods I believe was deliberate, so that their men might have no fall-back but their courage. We relied on a better strength than the arm of flesh, and when their strength failed them ours did not. Their priests, all the way before they came to fight, encouraged them by speeches, but especially by sprinkling holy water on them, and by charms, of which I herewith send you a copy. We found many such spells quilted into the doublets of the dead.

Certainly the Irish are a people strangely given over to destruction. Though otherwise understanding enough, they let themselves be deluded by ridiculous things and by more ridiculous persons. Had I been one of them, I would have told the priest who gave me a spell to protect me to try it himself first.

Our signal was a white feather in our hats, theirs was a fern. Our word was 'Prosperity!', theirs 'St James!' We chose prosperity over the saint. There is a lesson there, perhaps, for our Commonwealth.

Trusting to find your Excellency in good health. That he may continue to enjoy the favour and confidence of His Highness the Lord Protector is the happy wish of your obedient servant, Broghill.

Sir Charles Coote the Younger, following his father's footsteps no matter where they led, was appointed Provost-Marshall of Connacht. He had the charge of leading the local Parliamentarians. He was a member of Lord President Clanrickarde's cabinet but he seldom indulged such civil niceties. When he heard that Limerick was under siege he simply marched his army south, hoping to lend Ireton a hand. On the way he stormed Sligo and its attractive castle. Neither lasted long. His gallows earned their living that winter.

When news reached him, in November, that Limerick had already fallen, he merely changed direction.

Galway was a fiercely defended Catholic city and, as Commonwealth Armies strengthened their hold over the province of Connacht, it was to become the very last fortified city under Irish control. Its Confederate Army was now under the leadership of Tomás Preston, Viscount Tara.

The town had long been controlled by fourteen merchant families, or 'tribes', all of whom were Catholic and Royalist. Athy, Blake, Bodkin, Browne, d'Arcy, Dean, ffont, ffrench, Joyce, Kirwan, Lynch, Martyn, Morris and Skerret were their names. Their stock was mixed; Old

English, Milesian, French, Welsh and Anglo-Irish blood circulated in their veins.

Over centuries, these devout families had greatly strengthened their city's defences. Recently, since Parliament had so enthusiastically embraced heavy artillery and was using it to destroy every Irish town, they had reinforced the walls with earthworks. All this, coupled with Galway's position between Lough Atalia to the east, Lough Corrib to the north and the Atlantic to the west, made it a difficult nut to crack.

Preston had two thousand soldiers and civilians. Not a lot, but Lord Clanrickarde had almost three thousand fresh troops nearby.

Coote was all too aware of this. Rather than have his six or seven thousand Ulster Scots be caught by the enemy in some obscure mountain pass, he decided on a lengthy siege and sent his men to surround the City by every road, from every direction. He would 'protect' Galway's citizens' interests in the name of the Parliament and the Protectorate.

Preston closed the city gates and took stock. The enemy was spread around the coastal city and its port. Thinly, perhaps, but nothing was going in or out over land.

Coote, uncharacteristically, had doubts. It would be hard to prevent Galway City from eating and surviving. There was a highway in; the sea.

He was to be pleasantly surprised. That same November, Ludlow ordered his Roundheads, who otherwise would have been at a loose end, to reinforce Coote. Suddenly Sir Charles found himself in charge of a greatly swollen Parliamentarian army, ready to add the town to his list of victories.

When Clanrickarde rode up to Galway's walls, he found Coote's army well entrenched. There were only a limited number of approaches to the city and the Provost-Marshall had well-defended them with musketeers. The President mounted a number of raids but was driven back every time.

While Coote consolidated his isolation of Galway, Ulick Burke – Marquess of Clanrickarde and Lord President of Connacht - set off to assemble a force of Irish Catholics in County Leitrim. He would do everything in his power to relieve Galway City.

To make matters worse, the Parliamentary fleet now arrived to prevent food and ordnance from reaching the port.

The stalemate lasted for many long months. It demoralised the Irish soldiers. Clanrickarde was forced to recommend that Galway surrender; he knew how dire the situation was within the walls. Widespread hunger and an outbreak of plague didn't help.

Not until May, 1652, however, did Preston seek terms for the surrender of the city. He sent Sir Charles a letter detailing his demands.

Coote replied positively. He would allow Preston and his troops to take ship for Spain. Civilians could remain but would have to attend services in Anglican Churches. The merchant 'tribes' would pay exorbitant fines for their long-standing insolence and abandon in perpetuity their ancient plutocracy.

The fall of Galway marked the end.

Irish resistance to the English was pointless. Thousands of Irish soldiers left for service in Continental armies. Those that remained were rounded up. The Parliamentarians sold many thousands of them into slavery in the West Indies.

At long last the war had drawn to a close. Bitter retaliations guaranteed that the entire country would soon be racked by skirmishing, hunger and plague, but that Ireland was subjugated could not be gainsaid.

Except, that is, by the handful of tories who continued to harry their English masters.

For most Irishmen, however, the ceasefire was a blessing. After nine long miserable years, a people that had been praying so long for peace could breathe again, if shallowly.

Oliver Cromwell was now the President of the Council of State. He let his ministers know that he wanted to be addressed as 'Oliver', suggesting it less 'formal' than 'Lord High Commissioner' or even 'General'. Coins were ordered to be struck and, on the obverse, the dictator's name would be given as 'Oliver', *sic*, where before it had been 'Carolus', the Latin for Charles.

English conquerors were keen to divide the spoils, in Royalist England, in Scotland and in Ireland. A Parliamentary Committee was convened. Its duties were to value and assign every rebel landowner's possessions to deserving Protestants.

Even so, it proved a fractious business. With such spoils on offer the Committee fought for the plums in the pudding. At last, at a General Council, Lord Broghill proposed that the entire Protectorate might be formally surveyed and each acre given a valuation. The land would then be awarded to the victorious soldiers to pay off their back-pay. His suggestion, that the best land in the Kingdom of Ireland was valued at four shillings an acre, the poorest at a penny, was accepted by the Commissioners of the Commonwealth.

Now the soldiers and adventurers could draw lots for their portions, as all the forfeited land was to be divided among them. As for the recusants, they were marched under guard into Connacht where the hardness of the land so shattered them that many were never seen again.

Captured tories (real or merely suspected) were summarily hanged.

The Boyle family added square miles to their already immense estates. The Commonwealth conquest of Ireland made them the richest family in that country, outstripping Ormonde by a huge margin.

Nor did Oliver, Lord Protector and President of the Council of State neglect his generals and friends. General Venables was awarded a hundred thousand acres in County Cavan. Sir William Penn[lxviii], the most famous 'sea-general' of the Commonwealth, had defended Youghal in 1645 while it was besieged by Lord Castlehaven. Penn, the 'father' of the Quakers, was rewarded for his good and faithful services to the Commonwealth with land worth £300 a year. It was stipulated that his grant was to be on good soil and had to include a fortress.

The Commissioners selected an appropriate castle for him; the manor and castle of Macroom.

The Rebellion was over, the Confederacy long gone. There was no strength left in Irish arms. The war was over, the dust settled. The human cost of the war had been terrible. Between 1641 and 1653, almost half Ireland's two million people had died from war, pestilence and famine.[lxix]

Parliament rejoiced. In celebration the Lord Protector assented to an Act of Settlement. It declared that any Catholic who could not prove his innocence would lose his land. The Parliamentarians had ensured that a new Protestant landowning class would dominate the country, presumably for ever.

*

Terence O'Rourke, whose family had been close to the MacDonoghs for a millennium, was moved to write a letter to Cormac in Paris.

Sherkin Island, Co Cork

Fineen O'Driscoll has implored me to write to you, my dear General, and pass on some terrible news from Ireland. Only his wounds prevent him from writing himself.

Now that you are without educated kinsmen in Ireland, the unhappy task falls to me to report the extinction of your Name in Duhallow.

We had been trying to relieve Ireton's siege of Limerick. Donogh MacCarthy, better known as Lord Muskerry, commanded our forces. A relief column from Dublin came upon us at a miserable place called Knocknaclashy and we faced the New Model Army in a pitched battle. It was at this battle where what was left of your line after the calamity of Knocknanuss was slain, all MacDonogh clansmen, soldiers, foster children, servants and hirelings. Your nephew, Bryen MacDonogh, Chief of his Name, raged against Broghill who had evicted everyone of your proud and ancient Name from their plots, shops and businesses in Kanturk. Your Old Court was given to Sir Nicholas Chinnery, as were Dromsicane, Lohort and your other seats. The blue glass tiles that Bryen had used to provide the Old Court with a magnificent roof like none other were all broken down by the Roundheads and thrown into the river. This was done to make the Court in Kanturk uninhabitable. The townspeople are already calling that stretch of the Blackwater the 'Bluepool'.

Those few MacDonoghs that still remained in Duhallow were declared 'tory'. Within a month the English gallows had done their terrible worst. A price was put on the heads of those who could not be found, some of whom you had trained as musketeers. I know of none who survived, but there is a rumour that some did. If it is true they will have gone west to join their distant cousins in the wilds of Roscommon and Sligo.

As for your nephew, in the furnace of that ill-fated day, Bryen was wounded many times over. He fought furiously, refusing to die. He moved about on his knees after his lower limbs had been broken by pikemen. Cromwellian horsemen teased him for a while, as a cat will tease a mouse, until he too was finally dispatched, this time with cold steel. At least he was spared the gallows.

Should you want it, Sir, you are unquestionably the Chief of your Name, but it is today a reduced name, dispossessed and vagrant. That its time will come again is beyond question, its line being so studded with courage and purpose. The Ireland which the MacDonoghs have ornamented for so many centuries is gone. So is General Cromwell, returned to England to the Parliament he supposedly protects, there to rule the three kingdoms as Caesar governed Rome.

He has chosen to be styled His Highness Oliver, Lord Protector of the Commonwealth of England and Ireland and, most ironically, by Grace of God.

Your brother will have told you, Sir, with the characteristic pride of their race, of the gaiety and sparkle of those dinners after hunting in Duhallow, the beauty of Cliona and of his children, the resolute and pious purpose of that great chief which made all that had the privilege to have met him slightly magnified, especially your servant,

Terence O'Rourke

*

Sir Philip de Perceval was standing in the parterres before the 'Roman' door to Kanturk Castle. Sir Nicholas Chinnery stood beside him.

'So do you intend to live here, Sir Nicholas?' the banker asked, glancing at the open roof where the blue-tiled roof had lain for just a single year.

'No. The award was appreciated, but when Ireton ordered the house to be unroofed he made the prospect of settling here very unattractive.'

'Yes. I know just how much those blue tiles cost.'

'Thousands, I imagine? No, Sir Philip, I shall sell this place. In its present condition it has little value. Someone is bound to want it. A warehouse, perhaps? It served the old chiefs as a hunting lodge I believe.'

'Yes. If you are amenable I shall make you a generous offer. I shall use the place as its late occupants did. We shall keep the Duhallow going. At least over here, fox-hunting will become an Englishman's sport.'

'You will have lost a great deal in the settlement?'

'Not really. What I have gained from the forfeited estates is a great deal of land and the tribute of as many as three or four thousand cabins. An academic figure, presently, as they have been emptied of their occupants. Kanturk will become a God fearing and loyal townland, and the memory of its chiefs, the MacDonoghs, will fade from its memory. My name, not theirs, will be the one that posterity recollects, the one that Kanturk retains. All in all, a good return on investment.'

'Surely the Lord Deputy will require the lands to be parcelled out, Sir Philip?'

'Not in this case. I am an Anglican and have repossessed the MacDonogh demesnes by mortgage contract. There is no one left to repay them. I shall continue to live at Burton Park, as I do now. I may even enlarge it. The Helvetic Kingdom of Egmont, Dermod Oge once called it. Terrible enemy but great friend. He had a sense of humour. To speak frankly, I miss them all.'

*

FINIS

450

If Cormac's first-born son was barely a babe, he was healthy and alert. He may have taken his time to arrive – there had been several false starts - but his father was already claiming he could detect a nascent soldier in his arms. What was indisputable was that the lad's life had started well, even before his birth.

The exiled King of England had come to Paris, and the King of France housed him in the Palais Royal. Cormac and Isobel had found an opportunity to pay homage to His Britannic Majesty at Queen Henrietta Maria's court.

'They tell us that you are an exiled subject of ours, General.' The King of England was all charm. He looked Cormac up and down. 'Judging from appearances the Kings of France have been kind to you.'

Cormac drew in his stomach.

'I am your servant, Sire,' he said. 'I heartily embrace that fact, but I was educated here. I have neither friends nor, any longer, family in any of your kingdoms.'

'It pleases us to contradict you, General. You have at least one friend. You may count on us and our patronage.' Cormac bowed in recognition of the royal compliment. 'Your wife is with child, we infer from her figure?'

'She is indeed, I am delighted to say.'

'We are advised that the late King of France attended your wedding. Your first wedding, that is. In the Sainte Chapelle, no less! We cannot allow the fleur-de-lys have all the fun. Perhaps you will allow our lion and unicorn to support your child's Christening?'

'I am a committed Catholic, Sire.'

'So, dear sir, is our mother. We are not debating the Eucharist, General. The baptism service is almost exactly the same in our Anglican rite as it is in your Roman one, and in any case I am not proposing to conduct it. Why do we not beg His Eminence the Cardinal Mazarin to introduce your boy to Christianity in the Louvre and grant us special dispensation to sponsor him?'

'Sire, you honour me so much that I can scarcely speak.'

'Then we'll take that as a 'yes', then? In around a month's time, if our eyes do not deceive us?'

'They do not, Sire. The child is due at the beginning of May.'

Cormac had had an idea, but now he contrived to make it look like a recollection. 'Sire, if he's a boy, my wife wants me to ask your permission to call him Charles?'

'Of course. And if he's a girl?'

Cormac smiled.

'Then, again with your permission, we should like to call him Henrietta-Maria.'

The king laughed generously.

'Good choice, General. We have every confidence that he will inherit your virtues of piety, honour, valour, courtesy, gallantry and, we presume, chastity – at least outside the duties of wedlock. You will inculcate in him the loyalty due to God and to his temporal master, the King of France. When he grows, be sure his heart is dedicated either to a nubile virgin or to the blessèd one.'

*

From His Highness the Lord Protector of the Commonwealth of England, Scotland and Ireland to His Eminence, Monseigneur le Cardinal Mazarini.

The Commonwealth wishes, Monseigneur, to learn your intentions relating to the existing state of affairs in England. We are so near that France must be as interested in our situation as we are interested in that of France. The English are of one mind in contending the tyranny of Charles Stuart, the so-called King-in-Exile, and his adherents. Placed by popular confidence at the head of that country, I can appreciate better than any other its significance and its probable outcomes. I am at present engaged in the aftermath of a war fought bitterly for freedom from royal tyranny. The hope of the nation and the Spirit of the Lord are with me. Charles Stuart, the one you shelter, has no further resources in England or in Scotland; if he returns he will be captured or killed. I understand his mission in France is to recruit soldiers and to furnish himself with arms and money. France has already received Queen Henrietta, and, unintentionally, doubtless, maintains a centre of the defeated party in your country. But Madame Henrietta is a daughter of France and is entitled to your kingdom's hospitality. As to Charles Stuart, the question must be viewed differently; in receiving and aiding him, France censures the acts of the English nation, and thus harms England, and especially the well-being of the government that such a proceeding will be equivalent to pronounced hostilities.

It is important, therefore, Monseigneur, that I should be informed as to France's intentions. The interests of that kingdom and those of England, while taking now diverse directions, are very nearly the same. England needs tranquillity at home; France needs tranquillity to put the throne of her young monarch on solid foundations. You need, as much as we do, that interior condition of repose which, thanks to the energy of our government, we shall soon attain.

Your quarrels with the Parlement, your noisy dissensions with the princes, who fight for you today and tomorrow will fight against you, the popular following directed by the coadjutor, President Blancmesnil, and Councillor Broussel - all that disorder, in short, which pervades the several estates - must lead you to view with uneasiness the possibility of a foreign war; for in that event England, exalted by the enthusiasm of new ideas, will ally herself with Spain, already seeking that alliance[lxx]. I have therefore believed, Monseigneur, knowing your prudence and your personal relation to the events of the present time, that you will choose to hold your forces concentrated in the interior of the French kingdom and leave to her own the new government of England. That neutrality consists simply in excluding Charles Stuart from the territory of France, and in refraining from helping him - a stranger to your country - with arms, money or troops.

My letter is private and confidential, and for that reason I send it to you by a man who shares my most intimate counsels. It anticipates, through a sentiment which Your Eminence will appreciate, measures to be taken after the events. As Protector, I considered it more expedient to declare myself to a mind as intelligent as Mazarini's than to the Queen-Regent, admirable for her firmness, no doubt, but too much guided by vain prejudices of birth and of divine right.

Farewell, Monseigneur; should I not receive a reply in the space of fifteen days, I shall presume my letter will have miscarried.

Oliver P

*

1654 had arrived. Cormac and Isobel MacDonogh were sitting in the library in their townhouse in the rue des Deux Ponts. A fire blazed; it was a cold beginning to the year. The household had arisen to hoar frost and rimed windows. The master was reading Ben Jonson's Volpone, an unsparing satire of lust and greed, while, more demurely, the mistress embroidered some table napkins with her and her husband's conjoined initials.

The pleasant domestic silence, however, was not to last. Rupturing the domestic idyll, a servant burst into the room, nodded briskly and announced that they had a guest, waiting in the petit cabinet, or little parlour, by the front door.

'*C'est le compte Digby, sieur-dame,*' the servant revealed.

Cormac closed the slim volume and put it onto an occasional table.

'*Veuillez m'excuser cette interruption inattendue, Isobelita.*' While, or because, he was a good few years older than her, he treated her with a curious blend of affection, courtesy and formality. 'I am glad he has come, however. I have to break some sad news to him. His time in France should come to an end.'

He liked keeping his wife informed and enjoyed hearing her opinion on affairs of state. She was an intelligent woman and her conclusions steered his judgement.

'Lord Bristol? What can he have done?' she asked, genuinely surprised.

'There are now more than ten thousand Irishmen here in Paris. Digby has persuaded some three thousand of them to declare that they will fight as Royalist soldiers if called home. Bristol, however, despite the fact that the king's brother James York has consented to command them, has offered these restless souls to the Spanish, presumably to build the case for another Spanish invasion.'

'I can see why King Louis would hardly be best pleased, but then I suppose the King-in-Exile hides any discourtesy to the King of France by hiding himself behind Lord Bristol?' She put her embroidery down. 'I do think it a little strange, however, that the Lord Protector, who so publicly despises all Catholics, should even consider allying with a French cardinal.'

'As always, it's a question of greater and lesser evils. The Lord Protector will see an alliance with France as his best way of keeping Spain in check. Many remember Kinsale. There may even be a few still alive who can remember the Armada.'

'So, in such circumstances, Kildare Bristol can't really stay in France?'

'No. I'll warn him he's in trouble and will invite Lord Bristol to my afternoon audience with Mazarin. The cardinal can tell him himself. The best I can do is prepare the poor lamb!'

Bristol was an extremely distinguished and handsome old man. When, much younger, as Lord Digby, he had been James I's ambassador to Spain. After the regicide, five years ago, he had become both an ornament to the Irish in exile and to the French king, whom he had served as a Lieutenant-General.

As the statesman was shown into the library, he bowed to Isobel and her general, and casually tossed his tricorn onto a chaise longue. It landed exactly where Cormac had been sitting. He then and took the general's arm.

'I need your help, General du Halloa, if I am to be restored to Queen Anne's[lxxi] sympathy. She has turned against me, shut me out. Now rumour reaches me that Mazarin wants to send me to some godforsaken outpost in the provinces. Lisieux, it's called.'

'Lisieux is not a hardship posting, Bristol. It's a charming spot in Normandy, full of healthy dairy cattle and apple trees. You can almost see England from there. You'll love it.'

'You wouldn't say that unless you have turned against me too.'

'I have not, but I must question your judgement. When you disappeared from France on some secret mission, you let no one know your plans. You should have known that the new cardinal and the Queen-Dowager would take exception - even suspect you of being a double-agent.'

Lord Bristol's thoughts were elsewhere.

'Just what sort of a man is this Mazarin?'

'Wait and see for yourself. We'll attend Palais Mazarin this afternoon.'

Mazarin, small and dapper prelate that he was, was an unusual figure to have been elevated to such heights. Tormented by fear, and thirsty for counsel and information, he had to keep himself accessible. There was, however, a problem: the French. Many if not most of his untrustworthy acquaintances were trying to kill him. He engaged 'secretaries' - armed guardsmen - who controlled access to their master, and who were insusceptible to gold, sword, charm or wand.

Mazarin's uneasiness was justified. If just one of his servants turned *frondeur*, downfall would come knocking at his door.

In Cormac, however, Mazarin saw a portal to a loyal constituency. Please, he told himself, just don't let the Irish realise that France was prepared to conspire with the Lord Protector.

Paris loathed the cardinal's Parisian ministry. An insurrection, colloquially known as the *Fronde*[17], broke out. Frondeurs had attacked the *corps du roy*, whose lieutenant, yet another Irishman called Cummings, was badly wounded. The king, a boy, was kept out of harm's way but adequately free from public scrutiny. It was cries of *à bas Mazarin* that rang in the cardinal's ears everywhere he went.

Mazarin may have been many things but he was no coward. He spent much time touring the city, if always in disguise. Everywhere he turned, he discovered *frondeurs* in full cry, protesting that the power of the Church and Crown should be limited. The rabble, believing that the liberty of the people included the right to be insubordinate, even to criticise the powers of a Prince of the Church, had been stirred to fever pitch.

'The English are to blame for the mood in France,' Mazarin would say, once back in his palace. 'They have opened Pandora's Box by executing their king, and for all time. From now on, revolutionaries everywhere will feel free to execute whomsoever stands between them and the ill-considered vision of some power-crazed demagogue, one happy to feed the rabble's greedy imaginations on a diet of cakes and ale. That sinful English regicide has licensed them, and their descendants, to slaughter princes, aristocrats, Jews, priests - all who stand in their way. Not even schoolmasters and the educated will ever be safe again. Some child, contaminated by Albion's perfidious legacy, will some day use the precedent to cull a population of its adults. I, if permitted, would pack the Bastille with these idiots and throw the keys into the Seine.'

MacDonogh was having a preparatory chinwag with Lord Bristol, before the latters's presentation.

'Let me share with a little history with you. Some time ago, our cardinal opened negotiations with the Calvinists of the South of France. He has long kept them from boiling over with shallow promises and profound prevarication. For six long years they have believed themselves to be on the point of recovering their heretic privileges! Their optimism is wildly ill-founded. They should have realised that the cardinal knows only too well how to retain useful Protestants, like Turenne or Gassion, in His Majesty's service.'

'He is a Prince of the Church! What can the Pope make of such cynical alliances?'

---

[17] 'slingshot'.

'My money says his personal relations with the Holy See will not be cordial.'

'Mazarin hates me. He hates me for trying to involve Spain in our Royalist cause.'

'Not necessarily, Kildare. He's less of a priest than a politician. Don't quote me, but I'm not sure he has any beliefs at all.'

'I went to Fuenterrabía, you know.'

'Fuenterrabía?'

'It's a Spanish townland. In the Basque contry. On the border between Spain and France. *'Muy noble, muy leal, muy valerosa y muy siempre fiel'* [18], the King of Spain called it in 1638, after the siege.'

'Yes. Now I recall. So I should; it's not even twenty years ago. Memories fade with age. Yes, a huge French army of tens of thousands of men and countless warships was commanded by Henri Bourbon de Condé and Henri de Sourdis to besiege the city for two long months. They fired so many thousands of balls into the walled city that only a few hundred citizens survived. Though the city was almost destroyed, it would never surrender. It stayed fast, always waiting, until at last Juan Alfonso Enríquez de Cabrera's army relieved the city and defeated the French.'[lxxii]

'Quite. Every year they arrange a memorial parade, the *Alarde*. It gave me cover.'

'Of course. Please do not think me rudely inquisitive, but why on earth did you go? During these *fronde* disorders, it must have seemed perilously close to desertion for a serving military man. At least to some.'

'Yes. I see that. I mean, I see that now, Cormac. I wanted to persuade the Spanish to invade England from what little is left of their Netherlands. In the event I was forced to conclude that Spain is no longer the power it was. I think their king has run out of money.'

'You were right to call on me, Kildare. I will help you. How could I not? You enjoy the confidence of Paris's Irishmen. Indeed, you are their spokesman.'

'I used to be, MacDonogh of Duhallow. Now I am all washed up.'

'I will explain your situation to His Eminence, of course, but you may be wise to consider re-joining King Charles's court in Breda. To do so you would have to resign your commission here, but your perfect Spanish coupled with your skills in the subtleties of diplomacy could well prove useful to King Charles in his negotiations with Spain.'

---

[18] Most noble, most loyal, most valiant and most always faithful.

'Is that it?' Kildare Bristol was utterly crestfallen. 'I am to leave the French Army? France?'

'You could do far better than serving the French military if you publicly transferred your loyalty to the King-in-Exile, that's all I am saying.'

'Does not the King-in-Exile negotiate directly with Spain?'

'That need not imply he need no further help, Kildare.'

'What I really want, Cormac, more than anything, is to be reappointed to my old duties, those I had under the king's grandfather. Perhaps that's why I feel obliged to keep the Spanish sweet, almost as much as the King-in-Exile. King Charles must know that everything I have done has been for him and for Ireland.'

'I'm sure he does. Good. Excellent. So steel yourself. We are off to Palais Mazarin right now.'

It had been through Queen Henrietta-Maria that Mazarin had first heard of Cormac MacDonogh. In turn, it had been that general who had recommended Viscount Digby, who now was styled Earl of Bristol, following his uncle's death. The cardinal was not, however, quite sure of him. He chose the introductory audience to tell Lord Bristol that he was to be installed as Commander of Normandy, a great honour so long as he kept well out of harm's way.

Some of MacDonogh's other recommendations were considerably safer. At du Halloa's suggestion, for example, the Count de Rochefort was brought blinking into the sunlight outside in the Bastile.

Despite his new friends, however, Mazarin told the Queen Dowager of France that his worst fear was that 'the whole world is conspiring to break its bonds of loyalty'.

*

At the same time, across the channel, the Protector steered a difficult meeting in St James's Palace, his preferred London residence.

Baron de Baas, Cardinal Mazarin's special envoy to the Commonwealth, was cordially received by its Lord Protector. Cromwell knew the baron had been tasked with reconciling England with France.

Baas found the Protector in a vast and opulent hall, hung with tapestries, buried in vast charts of Ireland.

'Still trying to seduce the Irish into your Protectorate, Your Highness,' the Frenchman asked in his excellent English.

'Catholics, Baron, are the bane of my life, more even than Anglicans, whose church doors we have bolted shut[lxxiii]. Our orders are that the Irish transplantations be complete by the summer. Permit me to explain. We incorporate that ungrateful and intemperate nation into the Commonwealth, and what happens?' He picked up a letter from where he had angrily thrown it. 'Of all people, our trusted servant Ludlow objects!'

Cromwell's Council of State had met in the Painted Chamber of Whitehall Palace, where they had just passed an Ordinance finalising the Commonwealth. England, Scotland and Ireland were no more. Henceforward the 'British Isles' were all one country, and the Lord Protector was to rule it - the United Commonwealth - as might a Roman Emperor.

'Our son tells us that in Ireland, Ludlow still resists our Protection!' Cromwell told the Council. 'We hereby recall Ludlow. Our son Henry will take his place. He will overhaul Dublin Castle, reform its administration. The Commission has already formally attached Ireland to the Charter by addendum. One Republic, one set of laws, one set of customs. Every Irishman due for transportation to Clare or Connacht has at last been dispatched. Disappointingly, Lieutenant-General Henry Cromwell reports that many still claim exemption. He is ordered to remind General Fleetwood that our soldiers have swords and they're not simply for decoration. Henry will order the Commissioners in the Castle to announce the allocation of confiscated land to any of our disbanded soldiers who have helped in this operation.'

'Your standing abroad grows daily, Sir. Our ambassador, Monsieur de Bordeaux-Neufville, has been directed by *son eminence le cardinal* Mazarin to recognise you as Head of State. That will imply that our young King of France recognises you, too.'

'Yes. Tell your royal master we're grateful. We are also recognised by the States General of the Netherlands. Of course, theirs was a diplomatic move designed to prevent us from invading their American settlement of New Amsterdam.'

Bass bowed.

'Being no longer distracted with that expedition will liberate your 'sea-army', Your Highness,' he said. 'His Eminence commands me to request that you join us in an attack on Spanish Dunkirk. Once retaken, we would consent to your administration of that port until Calais, perhaps, can be returned into its historic English fold.'

'Dunkirk? We will consider the offer.' He turned his back, his attention fixed again on his Irish charts. Baas, bowing, reversed from the room, hat in hand almost wiping the floor.

The very second the Frenchman had left the chamber, Cromwell shouted at his Secretary of State for Ireland.

'Show our son Henry in. Is he here or in some godless tavern?'

'He is here, Sir.'

Henry Cromwell was issued into the chamber. Always uncomfortable, he looked especially uneasy in his father's presence.

'Cromwell!' the Protector exclaimed. It suited him to address his son in this way. 'Cromwell, you are to make for Dublin directly. You are to have the Castle. We need you to report on the religious allegiances of our army in Ireland. You will remember how to write? You should, your education cost me enough. Remind Ludlow, yet again, that every godless Catholic in Kilkenny, Wexford and Clonmel is to be expelled to Connacht. Give them a choice: go, or be put down. That's all. Go now, forthwith, and hurry, for the love of God!'

Henry bowed and clumsily retreated, grovelling like a frightened dog. His father scared him rigid, always had. If Lord Deputy Henry Cromwell had actually whimpered it would have made the simile exact.

It was the turn of the Spanish Ambassador to step forward. Both his gait and the flicker in his eye revealed a hint of nervousness.

'Ah.' The Protector acknowledged him, fairly graciously. 'Señor Alonso de Cárdenas. Let us talk privately.'

He waved his audience away with the back of his hand. Officials and soldiers in the great chamber all drew well back to allow Cromwell to speak quietly to the Ambassador.

'Thank you, Your Excellency,' he began, 'for reporting your king's proposal to ally his kingdom with our Commonwealth, but we deduce this royal gesture has little to do with recognising our role as Protector. It is more a cry for help in his war on France.'

The Spanish Envoy said nothing. He didn't have to. He knew that if Cromwell were truly opposed to the idea he would not have been granted an audience.

After a calculated pause, Cromwell purred that 'England is minded to agree, Excellency.'

'Perhaps you have conditions, Highness?'

'Spain may be the richest country in the world. Our treasury in England has been emptied by a feckless monarch and a long Civil War.'

'Perhaps if His Most Catholic Majesty were to supply your navy with ships and ordnance?'

'Our price for declaring war on our nearest foreign neighbour is that Spain will pay the entire cost of the adventure.'

462

'The Archduke Leopold has already seen that might be your fee. He has authorised me to offer you £120,000 a year.'

'Please convey the Protectorate's heartfelt thanks to His Serene Highness the Archduke.'

Cromwell stood back from the Spaniard. The private audience was over. The Ambassador withdrew, backing through the doors, to return to his ancient embassy in Ely Place[lxxiv].

Cromwell turned to his confidential Secretary, Mordaunt. 'Let the French ambassador approach. We may be able to extract an even better offer if we turn the tables on Catholic Spain.'

*

A baptism is, in effect, an exorcism. It is quite separate, at least in theory, from a Christening, in which an onomastic saint is besought to conduct the child from the Church Militant into the Church Triumphant at the end of days.

Holy water, laboriously blessed by a consecrated bishop and carried from the River Jordan, would assist the priest drive the impiety of original sin from a child's otherwise blameless life.

The ceremony would be in the Louvre, the King of France's palace in Paris. As the day came closer, Cormac could not help recalling the grandeur of his first wedding.

'It's a beautiful place, the Chapel of the Louvre,' Cormac told Isobel, 'and you need not worry about crowds. It's also far more discreet than the Sainte Chapelle. Mazarin will restrict the faithful to the French court and half-a-dozen of the most senior members of the English court-in-exile. He would feel safer that way.'

'Why has he consented to this honour?'

'Isobel, there are 10,000 Irishmen in Paris. The king-in-exile wants them to join his constituency, to help him secure a restoration. The cardinal wanted their loyalty, and believes that this elaborate baptism will secure him the Irish community in Paris. The king and his Council see the Irish as a tool with which new alliances can be forged. We have a mighty reputation as a fighting force.'

*

'Is Baron de Baas here?' the Lord Protector asked his Confidential Secretary, Mordaunt, without looking up.

The French baron advanced.

'We have sent a letter to your master, King Louis XIV of France and Navarre, announcing our willingness to pursue negotiations for an alliance. You should know that Señor Cardenas has offered us £300,000 a year for a military alliance. You should also know that our Council of State regards this as inadequate. We are currently advised to accept this Spanish offer of £300,000 and declare war on the Kingdom of France. Relax, dear baron, for a year at least, this will be a naval war. Our wars in Ireland and Scotland have left our army weary.'

'May I be permitted to make a suggestion, Your Highness?' Baas knew well that Cromwell was merely negotiating a price. 'Your Commissioners are even now suggesting, with our envoy's support, that the port of Brest be ceded immediately to England as security, until Dunkirk can be taken from the Spanish.'

'Very well. We shall pursue a purely commercial treaty with France, not a military alliance against Spain. Any idea our generals may have of intervening in another European war will be suppressed forthwith. Be sure to advise your people that the Commonwealth will not lose financially by switching sides. We look forward to learning your revised terms.'

That seemed to conclude the matter and Cromwell turned away.

*

Even before Cormac's and Isobel's baby was allowed into the Royal Chapel, the cardinal turned solemnly to bar the way inside with outstretched arms. He forced Cormac, Isobel and the godparents, the King of Scots and his mother, Madame Royale to a halt.

'*Quid petis ab Ecclesia Dei?*' he asked of them. What do you demand of the Church of God?

'*Fidem*', the parents and godparents replied. Faith. Amazingly the King-in-Exile spoke the tridentine response in Latin with the others. He must have learned the words from his mother.

'*Fides, quid tibi præstat?*' And what does Faith offer you? The Cardinal still barred their way.

'*Vitam æternam.*' Life everlasting.

The cardinal had a good tenor voice, in which he sang the ancient rite in its familiar Church Latin.

'*Si igitur vis ad vitam ingredi, serva mandata. Diligis Dominum Deum tuum ex toto corde tuo, et ex tota anima tua, et ex tota mente tua, et proximum tuum sicut teipsum.*' If then you desire to enter into life, keep the commandments, especially the first: 'Thou shalt love the Lord thy God with all they heart, with thy whole soul and with thy whole mind; and love thy neighbour as thyself'.'

The cardinal then performed the exsufflation, breathing three times on Charles MacDonogh in the shape of the Cross. The gesture represented the Spirit - breath, wind, *ruach* - of God.

'Go forth from him, unclean spirit, and yield your place to the Holy Spirit, the Paraclete,' he intoned, never departing from the old tongue.

Cardinal Mazarin now made the Sign of the Cross on Charles' forehead and chest. He then laid his hands on the infant's head.

'Drive out from him all blindness of heart; break all the toils of Satan wherein he was held: open unto him, O Lord, Thy loving kindness, Thy wisdom, that he may be free from foul and wicked desires and dwell in the sweet odour of Thy precepts to serve Thee joyfully in Thy Church and grow in grace from day to day.'

Now Mazarin put a little blessed salt in Charles's mouth.

'Salt,' he explained, 'symbolises the wisdom in which is relished the sweetness of divine nourishment; it preserves, through the Gospel, man from the corruption of sin and prevents evil passions from growing in his soul.

They were almost ready to enter the chapel but before they could the infant had to be exorcised.

The cardinal focussed closely on the baby.

'Unclean spirit, in the name of the Father, of the Son and of the Holy Spirit', he declaimed, always in Latin, 'depart from this servant of God for we, Jules Mazarin, Prince of the Church, command thee, accursed devil, to give honour to the living and true God; give honour to Jesus Christ His Son, and to the Holy Spirit; depart from this servant of God, Charles, because God and our Lord Jesus Christ hath vouchsafed to call him to His holy grace, benediction and to the font of Baptism.'

The cardinal laid the end of his stole on little Charles. At last he could be carried, tenderly, into the Holy Chapel of the Louvre, that long unaltered relic[lxxv] of Christ's particular relationship with the Kings of Lutèce.

A succession of royal French dynasties, while modernising their fortress-cum-palace, had left this little place alone. A marvellous fan vault began over the altar and descended to the floor in a semicircle of gothic columns, as might an old beech. Its ceiling was dark blue with golden stars. The fanciful could have thought themselves in a forest glade, admiring the handicraft of God, just as the primitive church had gazed in wonder upon the firmament.

Blind arcades lined the chapel walls. Ordinarily the infirm might sit in them, resting against a wall or a barleycorn column. The majesty of this holy place was so overwhelming, some may have simply felt overawed and the need to sit. 'Faith through beauty', the controversial Laudian rubric to which Dr Duppa and the king so doggedly adhered, was amplified here by an order of magnitude.

Once inside, even though not yet in the sanctuary, there came a second exorcism, followed by an ephpheta. For this, Mazarin had to cough into a silk handkerchief and touch the ears and nostrils of the candidate for membership of the Universal Church. Supplementing the mucus with a little spittle, the cardinal was emulating the moment when Jesus had healed the deaf-mute.

'And taking him from the multitude apart,' the cardinal intoned 'he put his fingers into his ears: and spitting, he touched his tongue. And looking up to heaven, he groaned and said to him: Ephpheta, which is, be thou opened. And immediately his ears were opened and the string of his tongue was loosed and he spoke right.'

At last, the renunciation of Satan and all his works. The cardinal anointed the boys heart and shoulders with the sacred oil of catechumens in the shape of a cross.

The sponsors were invited to approach the font, an octagonal essay in alabaster, supported by four angels and four evangelists. Mazarin replaced his violet stole with a white one and the child was given to his godparents to carry, suggesting they do this all the boy's life.

Each professed their faith, including Dr Brian Duppa, the King-in-Exile and his mother Queen Henrietta Maria. The king and queen carried the lad to the font where the queen held him in her arms and his royal godfather held the baby's shoulder with his right hand.

Mazarin re-anointed the baby held out to him. Then, taking a white linen cloth - symbolising the purity of a soul cleansed of all sin - he placed it on Charles' head. The new-born child would wear it for eight days.

In his magnificent Christening robe, the infant seemed to find the whole business amusing. He gurgled throughout.

The stirring service was almost over. Cardinal Mazarin gave Cormac a lighted candle to hold upright and make sure his son's face was lit.

'*Accipe lampadem ardentem,*' intoned the cardinal, '*et irreprehensibilis custodi Baptismum tuum:* Receive this burning light and keep thy Baptism so as to be without blame: keep the commandments of God, that when the Lord shall come to the nuptials, thou mayest meet Him together with all the Saints in the heavenly court and mayest have eternal life and live for ever and ever.'

The cardinal turned to face the godparents. Cormac MacDonogh and his wife Isobel Nassau de MacDonogh stood a pace or so behind. Then Mazarin delivered the all too familiar words of dismissal.

'Vade in pace et Dominus sit vobiscum omnes. Amen.'

Charles had passed through the first great gate of Christendom into the Church Militant.

'This young Christian,' Cormac, much moved, murmured to his wife, 'will always be Charles, never Cathal as in our Irish language. This moment is meant to be recalled while all of us live.'

*

The Lord Protector of the Commonwealth had come to Paris to negotiate in person with Cardinal Mazarin. His object was the containment of Spain through an alliance with France.

In the circumstances, the Royalists-in-Exile found Paris suddenly disagreeble. If the regicide-dictator were to attend court, which he surely would as a visiting head of state, their paths would inevitably cross. Everybody, especially Queen Henrietta-Maria and her personal entourage, felt obliged to quit the capital while the Protector was there.

For the Henrietta-Maria, Cromwell was the epitome of evil. She knew that it mattered not a jot to the Protector whether the monarchical principle were respected or condemned abroad. Despite his care to protest the contrary, in her heart she was certain he would ally with the devil to gain a permanent dynastic shift – a hereditary Protectorate.

She was only a little wrong. As it happened, there were more immediate things on the Protector's mind than his sons' succession.

The king-in-exile took his court to the free city of Cologne. As a sovereign state within the Holy Roman Empire, it had the right (and obligation) to maintain its own military force. More than that, Cologne was one of very few places to hold out an open hand of welcome to the Pretender. Cologne had witnessed the signing of the Peace of Westphalia, a few years before, ending thirty years of violence and death. Its ruler was pleased with his reputation as a tolerant peacemaker. He outlawed the incessant evangelising of the Reformed Church and ordered Cologne's Catholic archbishops, appointed by the Wittelsbach dynasty, out of the city. They took up residence in Bonn and Brühl, from where they furiously challenged and threatened the free status of Cologne. It took diplomacy, propaganda and frequent use of the Holy Roman Empire's supreme courts to keep them at bay.

In that sense at least, the ruler was a rare European potentate, taking kindly to a young and stateless king. He forgave him his rattling empty coffers and welcomed his threadbare court of money-lenders and royal concubines.

King Charles was safe. He would not be betrayed to the Commonwealth. If parts of Westphalia had come under Brandenburg control during the century, most of it was still divided into duchies and baronies. There was no dominant religion in Westphalia. The ancient and the reformed churches had more-or-less equal footing. Perhaps Lutheranism was stronger in the east and north, but Münster and especially Paderborn were mostly Catholic. Osnabrück was undecided. This accidental 'tolerance' gave the King-in-Exile much comfort.

As for the seditious (if accurate) commentaries that accompanied the king, tales of a score of mistresses and countless children, made him unpopular in many royal circles. Not so with Cologne's ruler, who was rumoured to have similar tastes.

Not that his enemy, the Commonwealth, was itself secure. An uprising occurred in Britain every month. That summer three came in quick succession; Glencairn in Scotland, Penruddock in Cornwall and Booth in Cheshire. All declared for the king-in-exile. Their protests did not reverberate for long - Cromwell's military machine had no difficulty in identifying and 'suppressing' each and every one of them.

The Lord Protector's spy network had almost completely infiltrated every monarchist circle. The Commonwealth was always one step ahead of the Royalists. Following the discovery of the 'Ship Tavern Conspiracy', named after a long-closed inn where a rhythmical knock would admit the thirsty or rowdy to drinks and revels, those loyal to the Crown had been goading the apprentices who drank there to riot as a prelude, even an incitement, to a general uprising. The Protectorate imprisoned large numbers of them. The 'conspiracy' showed there was a growing number of people who saw that their nation had made a terrible mistake.

Lord Digby, now Earl of Bristol, was reconciled with his king.

He had found his way back into royal affection by promoting the Spanish interest against a cynical alliance of Cardinal and Protector. What he really wanted, and in his ambition was supported by the entire Irish community in France, was for the Spanish to put his Stuart master onto a single British throne.

Bristol was about to fall out of favour yet again, however. It emerged that he had secretly converted to Catholicism.

This was an embarrassment for Charles. The king was striving to distance himself from Catholicism in order not to lose favour with English Protestants. He felt obliged to dismiss Lord Bristol from his new office.

If Bristol lost much political influence as a result, the king graciously invited him to explain his 'apostasy' in private. When he did, Bristol spoke from his heart. He was surprisingly eloquent. He gave the king much food for thought.

Studying reports from England, Charles concluded that the English throne was his for the taking. The only proviso was that a great politician should be found to harness and direct the daily mounting dissatisfaction with the Puritans. His advisors settled on Lord Ormonde for this role. The marquess would be disguised and, at great personal risk, sent secretly into England to test and prepare the Royalists for revolt and reestablishment.

Ormonde soon discovered a small group of leading noblemen. They suited his purposes exactly. They liked to swear to restore the monarchy in an elaborate ceremony, which they called the 'Sealed Knot'. Wonderful news indeed! Ormonde sent an excited but coded message back to the king, before heading back to Europe. He took the first boat from Tilbury.

Waiting on His Majesty, he found the king so overjoyed that Ormonde worried about Charles' discretion.

'The omens are good but many a slip falls twixt cup and lip,' Ormonde warned.

Charles behaved reasonably and rationally. He sent Ormonde on to Paris, to engage with Mazarin, divert that pragmatic alliance with Cromwell and plan for the Restoration of the Stuarts.

Paris? Ormonde thought he might find a useful ally in the Irish general Cormac MacDonogh. Were there not three thousand Jacobite soldiers in Paris, desperate for a chance to support their king in battle?

*

In the great chamber of St James's Palace the Lord Protector received his Irish envoy.

'What of the Limerick issue? Speak!'

'The Limerick issue, Your Highness?' The emissary from Dublin trembled. What could the Protector mean? 'We have expelled soldiers, even tories, but many Papist civilians are reluctant to leave of their own accord.'

'Just how clearly do I have to make my orders? Yes. Liberate that town from the Idolaters. Round them up, throw them out. For goodness sake, that's enough. Leave us.'

Seeing a beckoning finger, the Protector's discreet emissary came close.

'Mordaunt, any intelligence from France?'

'They still believe you are likely to attack them, Sir.'

'Ah, yes. Baas gave us a stormy interview, reproaching us for encouraging the Spanish.'

Did Cromwell smile? Or was it indigestion?

'Our dealings with the Huguenots? Are they compromised?'

'Mazarin also deals with them. In fact, all the time.'

Mordaunt stood silently, waiting for his instructions.

'We believe an alliance with France against Spain is in our best interest, despite the loss of trade.'

The oracle had pronounced. Cromwell dismissed his private secretary with a wave of his hand.

'Woodbridge continues to furnish our sea-army. £300,000, Calais and from there we may draw up terms.'

*

In Paris, Isobel positively tripped into her salon in the île de la Cité. She loved to see her gallant husband with his old and her new Irish friends. Her English was coming on well, thanks to a terrific and sustained effort and, she was the first to admit, a talented tutor and consort. It was not so hard. It was structurally similar to Flemish, the language she had long used to speak to her servants, nuns and some of the priests in Arras.

Cormac had never particularly warmed to the new king or cardinal. He found the former charming but a keenly ambitious boy, addicted to protocol, determined to be old before his time. The latter struck him as suspicious, devious, unpopular and scheming. Clearly the cardinal reciprocated his distrust. Cormac found himself having ever less to do with the decision makers of France. He was reduced to his ceremonial duties.

Seven years had passed since the execution of the King of England. Paris swarmed with Royalists - English, Irish and Scottish. Isobel had launched her own salon; not the grandest in Paris, and by some considerable margin, but it was greatly favoured by those with an interest in matters martial.

This afternoon, however, her salon would be like no other. She had invited every exiled Irishman she knew in Paris. Lord Ormonde, Lord Taaffe, Lord Bristol, 'Mad' Dick Talbot – recently escaped from the Tower of London and a great new friend of Cormac's – and all these and many more had accepted.

Few French socialites had.

Her French friends preferred a literary salon. They knew Isobel's guests would talk of War, Peace and Restoration. That, and hunting and country matters. Few of these desperate men had the necessary time for literature or music. Their masculine boorishness, however, was considerably palliated by their delightful wives, always full of vim. Irish ladies seemed to have a heightened awareness, not just of what made people tick, but of the value of life; far beyond that of mere men. Perhaps they had seen death too often to treat it as a commonplace?

Her political salon did not favour the harpsichord recitals or dancing all the rage by other distinguished Parisiennes. Her conversazioni, as she called them, were becoming sought-after events in the Parisian social calendar, but this one had not been widely advertised. Its lingua franca was more likely to be English, or even Irish, than French.

And then there was Isobel herself, fast becoming a fulfilled woman. Even if the journey were not completed, her son's birth had been the making of her. It had taken her from a timid and insecure child into an outgoing and spirited woman. Like so many mothers before and since, in the company of other mothers she celebrated his every little achievement. Only the fact that all the others did exactly the same prevented her from being thought tedious.

The first of her guests to arrive was Lord Muskerry. He seemed a little more interested in the two-year-old than in his mother.

'Et qui est ce petit garçon?' Lord Muskerry had asked Isobel when he arrived at the door. 'Madame, faites-moi l'honneur de me présenter à ce petit guerrier, s'il vous plaît.'

'Charles, sois le gentleman. Dis bonjour au général Irlandais.'

The toddler said 'bonjour, monsieur'. Never mind that he had clearly been coached – it was a charming moment.

'Tu t'appelles Charles?' Lord Muskerry smiled at the infant. *'Moi aussi. Quelle coïncidence! Et Isobel, désormais vous aussi devez m'adresser 'Charles'.'*

It was clear that Muskerry, despite his great tragedies in the war, was willing to adapt and adore this little token of Continuance. His family was intermarried with this infant. Not only had the boy's uncle married his daughter – now lost in Jamaica - Dermod Oge's daughter Caitlín had married a MacCarthy Reagh.

While his daughter Sorcha had been sold into infamy, to be bred with Ibo slaves, too many of his kin had died in battle. He knew too well that Cormac's clan had been exterminated in the slaughter at Knocknanuss. All that survived of the MacDonoghs in Duhallow was a man-made hill, built of the fallen, covered in turf. True, meagre pockets of the once princely tribe, now leaderless, lived off their wits in the west. If some were reduced to tinkers, this lad was a true MacDonogh Carty.

*

Other guests began to arrive at Isobel's levée. She ordered Charles to be taken to his nursery. Muskerry said *'au revoir'* and again the child replied correctly.

As the party renewed old acquaintances and accepted glasses of wine, there was much kissing,. Soon the salon was filled. Footmen pushed their way through the throng while the guests took wine or a 'liqueur', an infusion of fruit, herbs and a little alcohol. Servants served the guests to the best of their ability, despite the fact that the guests were speaking English, if not the far older tongue, Erse.

As Isobel drew close a bearded officer was talking livelily to Cormac. It turned out to be Theobald Taaffe.

'But, General,' she heard him say, 'will you tell me how we can justify to the Spanish our support for the claims of an excommunicated monarchy?'

Her husband's answer was direct enough.

'Only Queen Bess was actually excommunicated, my lord. That and the Stuarts are very nearly Catholics. If King James I and King Charles I were Anglicans, it will only have been for practical reasons. Actually they have one more saint than we do, for they have canonised their martyr king. They adhere to the doctrines of forgiveness and redemption. Like us, they reject the Protector's heretical notion of predestination. Were it not for the Anglican Martyr, England and probably Ireland would have become as humourless and perpetually damned as Geneva is today, filled with exiled Puritans writing and rewriting the Bible time after time,

472

always determined to refine their preposterous case. Their seriousness travels well. I have been told that these days laughter is seldom heard in either Westminster or Edinburgh.'

'Darling, may I present Fr Maginn?' she asked, interrupting her husband's all too familiar exposition. 'Fr Maginn is bent on establishing an Irish College here in Paris, now that there are so many of you in exile.'

The priest raised his biretta in a salute.

'The savagery of the suppression that followed our Rebellion has given me a cause,' the priest declared.

'Well, we have a candidate for you to educate in a few years' time. We are parents now and will not under-equip our children for the Struggle.'

'Your clan survived the Rebellion and all that followed?'

'The clan did not, Father, but I did.'

Fr Maginn laughed uneasily.

'That's because you were in Paris, my son.'

Lord Taaffe broke into the conversation.

'Given the history of your clan, it surprises me a little how unconditional is your loyalty to the House of Stuart,' he said, 'I recall hearing, back in '41, how the newly crowned king stepped up the pace of his father's settlement on our old lands.'

Before Cormac could defend his royalism, Lord Dillon – now the commander of a regiment of exiled Irishmen – came into the conversation.

'Is it true, General,' he asked, 'that you support the claims of a foreign monarchy? The Stuarts are Scots. Should not the O'Neills be High Kings of Ireland? Owen Roe would have been an ideal candidate for the revival of this ancient honour, had he lived.'

'He did he call on my brother Dermod Oge and his sword.'

'Yet neither he nor your brother could defeat the Cromwellian hordes?'

'There was a time when the war went well for us all. Owen Roe's victory on the banks of the Blackwater at Benburg in '46 was one. My nephew Bryen was there. He told us that Archbishop Rinuccini had carried the old Earl of Tyrone's sword from Rome to Kilkenny, passing as it should from chief to tanist. Unfortunately Owen Roe missed his chance to finish the business. Instead of driving the remnants of settler forces into the sea, he diverted his attention to the north.'

'Where he was murdered,' Fr Maginn added sadly.

'The late King Charles continued his father's shameful practice of planting Ulster with Protestant Scots,' said Taaffe. 'I don't see Ireland

473

ever recovering from the ill-will that came of it. The English seem to favour people of low birth and pietistic faiths; you know, Presbyterians, Calvinists, Baptists, Adventists, Covenanters, all the rest. It's difficult to understand. Before anyone spoke of 'reforming the church' we all got on like a house on fire.'

'After the Flight of the Earls,' said Rory Enniskillen, 'they settled in droves on our tribal lands, unopposed, knowing full well that the men supposed to defend them were in exile.'

'That was fifty years ago,' mused Theobald Taaffe. 'Just about a lifetime. Over that half-century the character of Ireland's people has irreversibly changed.'

'Irreversibly? Not necessarily, gentlemen,' said Fr Maginn. 'I would have you all remember that King Charles II is king by Grace of God, and Defender of the True Faith.'

'Even more importantly,' said Cormac with a weary smile, 'he is of Irish stock.' He had heard this line of argument too many times before.

'Irish?' laughed Lord Dillon. 'The Stuarts are Dalriadan. Their ancestry may be Irish but their throne is in Westminster and the king looks mainly to London. I think that makes them English.'

A footman, struggling to squeeze through the crowded room, lost his balance and two charged glasses fell from his tray.

'Before the Scottish god raised his finger to admonish us, where were we?' Taaffe asked, after a moment. 'In any case, I do not believe the Irish have the heart for another war against heresy.'

'There we differ. I believe they do,' said the Earl of Bristol. 'I think a million souls, the remaining population in fact, would hear the call to arms. The more so if they were supported by English Catholics. There are plenty of those who would find for us if we only asked.'

'The chiefly remnant of the old order is overseas. We have to prevent Ireland from imploding,' said Rory Enniskillen. 'Some or all of us must return.'

'Our hearts are beating like a bodhràn orchestra,' commented Lord Bristol. 'That alone gives me hope. There is a chance. Especially if the Spanish can be coaxed into supporting us.'

'Or the French. Please, Lord,' prayed Fr Maginn, 'let Cromwell's and Mazarin's scheming fail.'

'Well, you have certainly persuaded me. Clearly we Milesians still have a purpose.'

Isobel drew Dick Talbot and Rory Enniskillen aside for her particular attention. She brought them to an occasional table and indicated that they should sit beside her.

'You were particularly close to my nephew, Captain Talbot; everyone tells me so. Was Bryen really as brave as they all say?'

'Any story you have heard will have understated his courage, Madam MacDonogh. The pair of lions on your family's shield underestimates his courage, while the boar tells of the tenacity of his race. His flaw, if he had one, was that his courage knew no bounds at all. The fact that I had the privilege to fight alongside him is my greatest, my only claim to merit or fame.'

'I wish I could have known him,' Rory Enniskillen, dressed in the uniform of Lally's regiment, broke in.lxxvi

Isobel suggested he sit.

'I wish I had known him better. Everyone has told me he was of the stuff of legend,' said Isobel. 'My son will hear of him, and so will his younger brothers and sisters, if God favours us. Death alone is not enough to still his voice.'

'Gentlemen, I have been in exile since I was six.' The newcomer to the conversation was the banker Muirgheas Brannagh. 'You may have thought that I watched you all from a safe distance, but I have followed your every adventure, and how great they all have been. How I envy you. When Parliament declared war on the king, you formed your own government, the Confederacy of the Clans at Kilkenny. You brought Owen Roe O'Neill and Tomás Preston back to Ireland to command your armed forces. Most of you swore an Oath of Association to reunite Ireland under the king and the Catholic Church. Some of you have served the Confederacy for all of its nine years. What a story! Now it needs a writer to do it justice.'

'It will never be written. Only victors write history.'

'It was a close run thing. Had it not been for General Cromwell we would have won.'

'You may be right, Lord Castlehaven,' said Brannagh. 'Cromwell is unquestionably a great general, but his opposition to the Church borders on the lunatic. I have always suspected that when he heard of Catherine de Medicis' persecution of the Huguenots, his mind may have forged a permanent association between Catholic Monarchy and persecution.'

'That, absurd as it is, rings true,' said Taaffe. 'When reports of our Rebellion reached him in England, back in '41, he heard hyperbolic tales of killings of Protestant settlers at the hand of Irish Catholics. Anyone with a level head should have known the reports to be wildly exaggerated, in Parliamentarian circles at least, but Cromwell was convinced. He must have thought us savages. He since has downgraded his opinion. He has now concluded we are less than human.'

Cormac nodded in agreement.

'It didn't take long,' he said, 'for the man we now dignify with the outlandish title of 'Lord Protector' to begin his murderous campaign. My father, then an officer in the King's Guard, received letters from home almost daily. He read them with mounting horror.'

Fr Maginn's sad voice came in. Isobel's 'conversation within a conversazione' drew Madam MacDonogh's guests in like magnets.

'It's worse even than that,' said the priest. 'Cromwell wrote to every Catholic Bishop, every one mark you, that 'you are part of the anti-Christ and before long you must have, all of you, blood to drink.' He is of course mad. Delusional and mad, but this is the man whom the English have as a ruler!'

'More of an emperor,' said Lord Dillon. 'Oliver Cromwell grants a united England, Scotland and Ireland 'protection'. The Commonwealth is to have a single Parliament, a single Council of State, a single commitment to the achievement of a single code of law. All national characteristics are to be consigned to history. Only in religion will he countenance dissent, provided always that none of his subjects be Anglican or Catholic.'

'Both scripture and history show all too clearly that unbridled force never leads to permanent peace,' said Fr Maginn.

'His empire was conceived in blood,' Lord Taaffe remarked. 'In conquering Ireland, beyond his denial of quarter to the garrisons of Drogheda and Wexford, he licensed his Roundheads to kill. Dick and Bryen were actually at Drogheda. There, better than anyone, they saw how he launched a cycle of fratricidal violence.'

'For years, since '41 in fact, we have had to endure the most terrible news,' Cormac confirmed. 'First from Ireland, then from England. The trial and execution of the king – a monarch who appeared at least willing to hear our arguments – broke our backs. We were not the only people to be shocked. In France, in all of Christendom, news of the regicide disturbed and undermined the centuries-old easy assumptions of custom and tradition. I am proud to say that France immediately offered sanctuary to the late king's son, our king-in-exile, then running for his life.'

Brannagh, who was reputed to have made an immense fortune in clever financial speculation, permitted himself another comment.

'So, ironically, we now find Cromwell here in our wonderful city, closeted with a Catholic cardinal. King Charles and his immediate entourage have left Paris. Spain has gone to war against an alliance of the Commonwealth and France, while King Charles secretly negotiates with Spain for military assistance in restoring the throne of England. Lord knows what will become of it all. What advice can he be getting?'

'His entourage now includes Lord Massereene.'

'Yes, I heard that too,' said Brannagh. Everyone knew his immense fortune derived from such rumours and their invariable reliability. 'Strange but apparently true.'

'The Ulster Puritan?' Fr Maginn was amazed. 'Now those two are queer bedfellows.'

'Massereene was one of the dark forces that overthrew the throne. He has since seen the light and come over to us,' said Kildare Bristol.

'I remember him too.' Lord Dillon had been in England at the time. 'He was an outspoken opponent of the Earl of Strafford, the king's favourite. Why should he turn coat?'

'He also played a big part in the prosecution of Archbishop Laud' offered Fr Maginn. 'I too find it baffling that he and the king are reconciled, but it may just be that since he fell out with Parliament. It could be a case of my enemy's enemy being my friend.'

'Yes. The Arab saw. It would explain such an epistemological alliance', Taaffe volunteered.

'Can it be true? Massereene has fallen out with Parliament?' asked Brannagh.

'Yes. Unlikely as it seems, during the Confederate Wars he tried to prevent Ormonde from surrendering Dublin to Parliament. Cromwell was beside himself. He accused Massereene of intentional betrayal of scriptural purity and threw in a charge of embezzlement for good measure. Massereene fled to the Continent.'

'But he returned?'

'Yes, a year later, but only after the late king's arrest. Cromwell was newly in charge and still very angry. Massereene's standing was nothing like enough to prevent his arrest. I don't remember a trial, but he went to prison for three or four years. As he came out he joined our court-in-exile.'

'The king has offered him a position? In the court-in-exile? It beggars belief!'

'You may be forgetting that Massereene is probably the richest man in Ulster,' Brannagh volunteered. 'In exchange for a slice of his immense fortune, a restored king has promised to redeploy him in

Ireland. He is needed to plan and manage the affairs of the soldiers, settlers and other adventurers over there.'

'Yet he still detest us Papists?'

'Absolutely. The Laudians, even more. The king has pragmatically chosen to overlook his questionable views.'

Fr Maginn found a moment to exchange a quiet word with his hostess's husband.

'General, might you find a way to inter your brother, Cliona, Bryen and Brébhinn at your family mausoleum at Balindoon? Would it not be a shame if their souls could not hear, while their ears await the last trump, the sweet polyphony of the Franciscans?'

'Father, I would happily do so. I sent good men to Knocknanuss. At least my niece Cliona's relics are buried behind Drishane. Nothing of the others' mortal frames have ever been recovered. Bryen was buried where he fell at Knocknaclashy. He's in that great hill, most likely.'

'Then a monument at Balindoon? There is one already there to your father.'

'Perhaps. One day. Travel to Ireland is not currently possible. There is a price on the head of any member of my clan. When the king-in-exile takes his rightful throne, then perhaps. We can but pray.'

'In the meantime, therefore, we shall have to make sure that every Irishmen here in France has reason to hear your family's story. It is my intention to build an Irish College here, somewhere in among the other colleges of the University of Paris19. May I count on your support for its foundation?'

'Utterly. But, please, I am merely a soldier; my contribution will be relatively modest. Let me present you to Count Brannagh. Frankly, he has more money than is good for him.'

Now it was Lord Muskerry's turn to lead Cormac by the arm. Out of the others' earshot he spoke urgently and quietly.

'General, I am desperate for an introduction to Cardinal Mazarin. All Paris has heard he baptised your son. Like you, I am a soldier, if not such a great one. I need a position in the King of France's army and your sponsorship would carry the day.'

'You surprise me, General. Is not your leadership needed in Ireland?'

'Not now. Not yet. We did mount a little sporadic raiding for a while, after our defeat, but Philip O'Reilly formally capitulated, back in

---

[19] It still exists. It is to be found in the heart of the Latin Quarter.

'53, after Venables's murderous assault on his tories at Lough Oughter. The two saddest words. At home the Irish will need much time to recover. They have no strength, no taste for the fight, no soldiers. We will have to wait a dozen years for a new generation of boys to turn into men. While we speak their problem is famine. That and scurvy and the typhoid. Wolves have so multiplied that they too have a price on their heads, like you, if not quite as high.'

'The war is either over, or it isn't, Charles?'

'The war is over, Cormac. The English have brought our brave soldiers a cruel season of punishment. Tens of thousands have been executed. In some parts of the country, every tree has had a man at one time hanging from it. Since the 'pacification' another twelve thousand have been transported in chains to the Barbados, or Jamaica, Cromwell's little colonial venturelxxvii. Millions of acres have been confiscated. Only those landowners who could prove 'constant good affection' to Parliament have not been punished.'

'There actually are some of these?'

'Oh yes. Plenty. Lord Broghill swanks unpleasantly in my old seat at Blarney. Lord Cork is at last the richest man in Ireland, this time beyond dispute. Your brother's banker, Sir Philip de Perceval, is wealthy beyond the dreams of Midas. Lord Clanrickarde fares well; despite his efforts in Galway he has somehow proved his innocence, but even he has lost his country seat to Henry Cromwell. Add to a few scores of survivors, hundreds more are presenting their desperate cases in the Courts of Common Plea, in the unlikely hope of securing restitution. The lawyers who represent them will clean the crumbs from the table, while the Irish will fail. Their only hope? The restoration of the monarchy combined with a fair hearing, neither of which looks likely.'

'I shall obtain an audience for you with the cardinal, Charles. Two-faced as he is, he may yet help with that commission. Personally, I will advise him to leap at the chance. Your perfect French will endear you to him far more than your evident piety.'

*

Parliament appointed their Lord Deputy of Ireland. It was Charles Fleetwood, who now bowed low before his Protector. Parliament wanted him to replace Cromwell's son Henry who, uncrowned, already held that office.

The Lord Protector considered it his role alone to appoint Ireland's Lord Deputy. As far as Irish monarchists were involved the Marquess of Ormonde, who believed his appointment had tenure, was that man.

Clearly he stood no chance. In the view of the Royalists, Fleetwood was an illegitimate rival to Ormonde. Then there was Henry, the bibulous boy. The Irish had three Lords Deputy to choose from.

Understandably, Fleetwood was unsure of himself. The title had always been a poisoned chalice. The more so, now that he had been summoned into the presence of the Lord Protector of the Commonwealth.

He was received in the Painted Chamber of Whitehall Palace. He approached the Protector very cautiously. He knew His Highness had no affection for the country Charles Fleetwood liked to call 'home'.

'Fleetwood,' began the Protector, 'God has brought us where we are, to consider the work we may do in the world, as well as at home. As your tête-à-tête with Lieutenant-General Edmund Ludlow has disturbed you, we shall deal plainly with you. Be of no doubt; Government by a single person - and a Parliament - is a fundamental to a people's nationhood. Though we may seem to plead for ourself, we do not; we know that no reasonable man will say we are mistaken. Our actions are for this Commonwealth and all the honest men therein. They Irish need not what they want but what is good for them. Do you agree so far?'

Fleetwood continued to stand to attention. He had not been given leave to stand at ease. He was talking to a man who had destroyed the country, razed twenty-eight towns on or near the east coast and had redistributed only slightly less than half of the land mass to fellow Protestants. Ireland's future government needed a Deputy to Cromwell. Him? If that were not a poisoned chalice, what was?

'I do, Your Highness,' he stuttered.

'Our son Henry, already a Major-General in our Model Army. is to command in Ireland. I task you to help him settle into the Castle. We have issued an Ordinance allowing all good Protestant Irish who mistakenly fought under the traitor Charles Stuart's banner to pay a fine rather than forfeit a proportion of their property, as stipulated in the Act of Settlement. When you are again in Ireland, you and the Irish Council are to ensure that the transplantation of Papists to Clare and Connacht is completed by March 1, next year. Once that is accomplished you may formally resile your office. That will be all.'

The acting Lord Deputy retreated circumspectly from the Lord Protector's presence. It was in his interest to tread carefully. He would not be sad to relinquish the role he had never applied for but his pension had not yet been agreed.

Mordaunt coughed gently. Cromwell swivelled to focus on him.

'Your Highness, Parliament will divide shortly. On the succession of your Protectorate, Commissioner Major-General Lambert has proposed that it should be made hereditary. Our information is that the best part will vote to keep it elective.'

'What?'

'Yes, Your Highness. Our intelligencers suggest that are many so-called Republicans consider that an hereditary Instrument of Government is a step too far. It would give you greater powers, they say, than the Stuart dynasts ever had.'

'Who's responsible for such a calumny? Have him arrested.'

'They are legion. They are called 'Levellers', Your Highness. We have incarcerated many of them already but, like the poor, there are always with us.'

'Of course. Have them share their cells with Anabaptists and Fifth Day Monarchists. Let them talk each other to death.'

*

King Charles II would have to stay in Westphalia's capital, Cologne, for however long it took Cromwell, in Paris, to negotiate the most profitable relations between France and Spain.

Still, Cologne was not proving too wearisome. There were some new ladies at court, wives and daughters, slim and plump, affectionate and stern.

'Sire!' The King-in-Exile's Secretary of State, a reappointed Lord Bristol, interrupted His Majesty's train of thought. 'His Eminence the *nuncio* waits outside.'

'Send him in.'

The Pope had sent an Irish Jesuit to be the king's guest. The missionary turned out to be none other than 'Mad' Dick Talbot's eldest brother, the Professor of Theology in Antwerp University. The king usually avoided contact with Catholics - he was keen to avoid reopening old wounds and was still striving to gain approval from what he presumed was a silent Anglican majority in England – but this particular Jesuit was oddly acceptable to him. Perhaps it was because His Majesty was aware that Dr Talbot was also brother to Sir Robert Talbot, who had himself held a high military rank in Lord Ormonde's Confederacy. There were also the much-travelled tales of the youngest Talbot, Mad Dick, and his many battles and his heroism.

'Good afternoon, Dr Talbot.'

'Your Majesty.'

'Talbot, your knowledge of continental languages is unmatched. Would you consider acting for us? We have to address the courts if Lisbon and Madrid, as well as Paris. We hear you are fluent in all of these languages. We would hope to give abundant proof of the fitness of our House to rule and reinforce fidelity to the cause of monarchy everywhere.'

The king gently took Talbot's arm.

'You might also help us with our reputation,' he said quietly. 'Wags say we are only religious when sober.'

'That is indeed a well travelled libel, sire.'

'Well, it must be corrected or swamped with more helpful ones. Anyway, we are interested in instruction into the Catholic faith.'

If the sound could be sucked from a room, this was when it happened. Only after a while did Talbot recover.

'Sire, the Holy Father would delegate that privilege to me, I am confident.'

'Not that we want piety to extinguish our merrier moods, mind you.'

'Merriness is not incompatible with Faith, Your Majesty. Unfortunately, however, I should have to decline this privilege unless Your Majesty were to promise concessions to those Catholics who would see you regain the throne.'

'Talbot, that will happen. For the present, however, everything that passes between us must remain utterly confidential. Were it made public we should all of us lose everything. It's just that we have been looking under the wrong stone for the Truth.'

'Your Majesty, this Truth is not found under a stone. This Truth shines like the sun in the day and like the stars in the night. It serves to guide soldiers, sailors and princes to distant shores.'

A courtier interrupted this extraordinary moment. Lord Bristol announced that a very distinguished visitor from England had arrived, bearing wonderful news.

'He is an agent of the Sealed Knot. He wishes to announce a revival of the society's activities in England. He believes his company will soon be able to assure your Majesty's Restoration.'

*

In a charming house in the rue des Deux Ponts, on the île de la Cité, Paris, a loud and apparently aggressive knocking at the front door made Cormac start.

'Are you expecting anyone?' Isobel asked him.

'No. Yet a knock with such impatience must be important. I have heard it before; it is a military tattoo.' He turned to the footman who had been standing by the door. 'Bring the soldier in here, Gaston. Let's hear whatever is so important it warrants disturbing us on a Sunday.'

Seconds later Major Talbot was admitted into the salon.

'Dick! You have news for me, I deduce. Should my wife leave or stay?'

'Cormac, old friend, she should stay. Madame, vous allez bien, j'espère ? The news from England is joyous. The Lord Protector is dead! Three days ago! He died on Thursday, of a bout of malaria, they say, a souvenir of Ireland. Parliament has wasted no time. It has already voted £60,000 to his obsequies, more than for any monarch in English history. He is succeeded by his third son, Richard.' lxxviii

'Tumbledown Dick? They kept him out of the tavern long enough to succeed his father? And what of Henry? The Lord Deputy of Ireland?'

'There are no taverns in England, Sir. Henry is safe in Ireland but out of favour in England. Last year he advised his father not to accept the throne.'

'I thought he supported that idea.'

'He changed his mind, Sir.'

'So what does he think of being passed over? Cromwell, at least at the time of his death, was the richest man that England, at any time in that troubled country's history, has ever seen. He lived in Hampton Court and held great estates in every county.'

'When he ordered his son to Dublin with such manifest delight, the Lord Lieutenant and Governor General of Ireland, Henry Cromwell remains in Ireland. He lives as a country gentleman in Portumna, in Lord Clanrickarde's mansion, his ample cellar fuelled from Galway City's Spanish warehouses. He goes to Dublin as infrequently as he can contrive. He is not minded to reside in Dublin Castle.'

'And Richard is about to be crowned Protector in Westminster Abbey, with all due pomp.'

*

Very quietly, Cormac opened the door to his boys' nursery. They would soon be going to bed. When he came in their nursemaid put a book down and bobbed to him. She had been reading them a fairy tale. Isobel and her husband, in the spirit of the times, had made over a suite of rooms for their boys, nursemaid and tutors. The family has long decided that the children would learn to read and write in French, English and Irish.

Charles, the elder, now four years old, was easily seduced with his father's romantic and knightly tales. His younger brother had just turned one year old, was less susceptible either to romance or to scholarship. He had been Christened 'Turlough', but his father, seeing the difficulty the French were having with this curious name, had looked for an equivalent. He settled on Terence.

As usual, Cormac began to improvise a tale.

'Once upon a time, Charles and Terence, your family was one of the mightiest in Ireland. It was a great clan, and its chiefs were paramount to many other chiefs. It could raise thousands of men in times of war and was guided by the twin stars of piety and steadfastness.'

He paused. The door to the room had opened and his wife had silently come into the room.

'Terence will be far too young to understand a word, Husband Cormac,' she said, sotto voce.

'But Charles understands it all. Don't you, Carlotto?'

'Don't stop, Papa,' said Charles. 'Is this the story when you and your brother sailed across the world in that tiny boat in a terrible storm?'

'No, Carlotto. Nor is it the story of how my brother got our castle back from the tinkers. This is a tale of how it fell to a couple of fine boys, brought up in a country far from Ireland, to free the land in which their line was forged from heresy and impiety, from greed and selfishness.'

'Do you mean us to fight the English?'

'No, Carlotto. I want you to outwit them. The English have a new weapon. They call it 'politics'. It is a very powerful one. They use it to put ordinary men on thrones, to rid their people of loyalty and replace it with opportunism, to reward the grasping and greedy with great estates and to impoverish those who have ruled their servants benignly for so many long centuries. This new politics of theirs celebrates sin. You will learn to use it and turn the tables on them. England will soon become a monarchy again and, when it does, you two boys will find a way of serving your forebears.'

'Do I have to grow up first, Papa?'

'Yes. You are to be schooled in all the arts, not just this new one. You will go to La Flèche, the great academy where I and your late uncle went. It will be the making of you. The Jesuits will tell you tales of warriors, of the Romans, of the Spartans of old, who could defeat the armies of Persia with just five hundred men. There you will learn of the moral exhaustion of kings, like Hamlet, who saw his own father usurped and murdered. Above all you will learn of the Kingdom of Heaven, and how forgiveness, courage and learning will take you there.'

'Is it a long way away, that kingdom?'

'It is a long journey, Carlotto. At least La Flèche will set you on the right path.'

A click told Cormac that Isobel had left the bedchamber and closed the door behind her.

'Good night, lads. Always remember, the blood of kings long dead still courses though your veins.'

Then he too quietly left the nursery to allow their nanny to hear their prayers.

Downstairs, Isobel was waiting for him. They would shortly go in to dinner.

'Cormac, you fill their heads with such lofty tales.' Isobel slipped her arm around his waist. 'These romantic tales of Lohort, Dromsicane and Kanturk.'

'Charles sees it all. He is a bright four-year-old. He has told me that he will live in Lohort one day. Perhaps he'll put the roof back on the Court? One thing's for sure, the name of MacDonogh will be heard again in Ireland, one day.'

'Cormac, you encourage all this nonsense. How, or why, would he ever get to Ireland?'

'They both will, Isobelita. Charles will be a soldier, I think. That shrewd look on Terence's face has long told me he will become a lawyer. Perhaps he will argue our case at some Court of Restitution? Whatever they do, wherever they go, they will have the best education that money can buy. They will go to my old school. Who knows? Now that Death has deposed the Lord Protector, I am more than ever convinced the rightful king will be restored.'

'If it is your wish, Husband mine, we can only pray that it will come to pass.'

'Rumours of a strange kind are reaching me. Mad Dick tells me that his saintly eldest brother calls on the king to rehearse the catechism. Isobelita, I have a secret to reveal to you, but no one else, and I tell you this upon the sacred honour of our vows. The King-in-Exile has adopted our Holy Catholic and Apostolic Faith. I have this from Dick. He should know; his eldest brother is the king's confidential confessor. With Cromwell dead and his two idiot sons pretending to rule the 'Commonwealth', Restoration cannot be far away. Imagine, Isobelita, Ireland under a sympathetic monarchy, and this time a Catholic one! Our darkest hours are almost over. Charles and Terence, schooled and grown, will carry our standard home and plant it where it belongs, in County

Cork. It will be a triumph, the reward of all our prayers. It will be that miracle which for so long has been merely a flickering candle at the end of a great disused cathedral. It will become the herald of God-given light, beneath a lavishly illuminated east window.'

*

Author's Notes

[i] Queen's County is now called Laois.

[ii] Much later, and after conflict and treaties between the Dutch, Portuguese and British, the colony became known as British Guyana. It is now called Belize.

[iii] (Mercenary) Irish cavalry, long banned but whose costumes were infrequently tolerated in a romantic or ceremonial context.

[iv] Rum punch

[v] Catholics were 'foreigners'. Their allegiance was said to be to a 'foreign prince', i.e., the 'Bishop of Rome'.

[vi] *Law of the Innocents*. Brehonic rules for a just war, loosely based on St Augustine.

[vii] Sir John Temple, the highly partisan son of the Provost of Trinity College, published his *History of the Rebellion* in 1646. This one-sided book would permanently affect later English attitudes to Ireland. His description of the refugees, however, is probably accurate.

[viii] Here, the word 'English' may simply mean 'Anglican'. More generally it meant those who avoided the natives, their churches or language.

[ix] There are no public documents or private letters, written in Ireland in the last week of October or even in the first days of November that even hint of wholesale murder. Clearly, the stories of blood and horror, afterwards so hungrily swallowed by the English Parliamentarians and their fellow travellers, had yet to be written.

[x] The Puritans refused to refer to Catholics (or even Anglicans) as Christians.

[xi] Such an enormous fee was easily enough to guarantee O'Connolly a repeat appearance in history. He was in no hurry to return to Ireland. He knew he would find that the nation of his birth would be a trifle inhospitable for a few years yet. In due course he would use a little of his fortune to purchase a colonelcy in what would become the New Model Army.

[xii] *Way of working together.* Irish official documents were mostly in Latin at this time.

[xiii] Monk was later made Duke of Albemarle

[xiv] Lord Muskerry's eldest daughter was just fifteen. 'Surkha', or 'Circa', means 'bright' or 'radiant'. In Brethonic law, girls were free to marry after their fourteenth birthday. A boy had to wait until his seventeenth.

[xv] Julius Caesar described these tattoos in Book V of *de Bello Gallico* (54 BC).

[xvi] An alderman and future regicide

[xvii] These words have most recently been added to an ancient melody, today most widely known as 'John Brown's Body'. John Brown was an abolitionist, widely celebrated by African-Americans. Julia Ward Howe's restoration of the battle hymn has given it fame. Her words conjure the original menace and attempt to regain the spirit of the lost original; she took the first line from Matthew 24:30, Mark 13:26, and Luke 21:27. The second and third lines contain the images of treading out a

winepress and a 'terrible swift sword', which are from the Book of Isaiah and the Book of Revelation. Isaiah 27:1 (KJV) states, 'In that day the Lord with his sore and great and strong sword shall punish leviathan the piercing serpent,' and Isaiah 63:3 states, 'I have trodden the winepress alone; and of the people there was none with me: for I will tread them in mine anger, and trample them in my fury.' Revelation 14:19 describes an angel casting grapes into 'the great winepress of the wrath of God' (14:19), and Revelation 19:15 describes the Word of God who wields 'a sharp sword' and 'treadeth the winepress of the fierceness and wrath of Almighty God.'

[xviii] Then an open-air arrangement. It was not covered until the mid-eighteenth century.

[xix] Following the Restoration of the English and Scottish monarchies in 1660, Elizabeth travelled to London to visit her nephew, King Charles II, and died while there. Her youngest daughter, Princess Sophia, had already married Ernst Augustus of Hanover, the future Elector. Sophia became the nearest Protestant heir to the English and Irish crowns (later the British Crown) and, under the Act of Settlement, the succession was settled on Sophia and her issue. All monarchs of Great Britain from George I onward are therefore descendants of Elizabeth Stuart.

[xx] The Royal Spanish name has long been Irished. The town is now 'Daingean', (or Dungeon – fortress - of the Offalys).

[xxi] The courtroom itself stood unused, but served as an admonition until it was demolished in 1806, when some of its materials were salvaged. Its door now hangs in Westminster School. Its historic ceiling, with its bright gold stars, was incorporated in Leasowe Castle, along with four beautiful tapestries depicting the four seasons.

[xxii] Now known as Speakers' Corner.

[xxiii] The Barons of Enniskillen would serve in France, not even returning to Ireland when King James II was crowned. The last of the Enniskillens would be a captain of Lally's regiment at the outbreak of the 'glorious revolution' of 1688.

[xxiv] Both orb and sceptre were melted down by Cromwell to pay for the Protectorate.

[xxv] The mansion withstood the sack but, in 1645, submitted to Lord Castlehaven. Inchiquin took it back the following year and the Parliamentarians recovered it in 1646.

[xxvi] The Knight of Glin, one of several proud titles of the Fitzgerald princes. The Knight of Glin, also known as the Black Knight, has been, since the early 14th century, an hereditary title of the Fitzgeralds of County Limerick. There are several others, the Knight of Kerry and the White Knight are examples. An Irish 'Knight' is addressed as 'Knight'; not, as one might otherwise expect, 'Sir xxxx Fitzgerald'.

[xxvii] From the seventeenth to the nineteenth centuries, must houses in Ireland boasted this shape of window over the front door.

[xxviii] A portion of the east wall fell down in 1636. After the failure at the Battle of the Boyne in 1689, Charles MacDonogh Carty moved from Lohort with the apparent intention of taking the castle. Major-General Scavemore, who was approaching the town from the other direction, sent Colonel Dundas ahead to burn the bridge in an

effort to stop the Jacobite advance. The Williamites then attacked the Irish Forces in the meadow near the bridge and defeated them. Just the same, the mansion was so badly damaged that when the Jephsons returned after that war they decided that the building was too far gone for repair so they settled in what had been the stables and eventually made them into the charming building which is now the modern Mallow Castle. It had been intended to repair the building, but this was never done.

[xxix] The ghosts of Jephson and Miss Norreys still walk on the avenue in the evening. Many have seen them, and have reported seeing lights in the castle mullions. This reputation for its haunting has kept the townspeople out of the mansion since its reduction in the Confederate War *(this story was told to me quite late one evening in O'Keeffe's Bar and Lounge, Kanturk)*.

[xxx] Both sides called the other 'rebels'.

[xxxi] Their final resting place lies beneath a stone plaque in the transept, commemorating the courage of the Burgats that day.

[xxxii] Much of this confiscated land was returned to its legal owners, in the 1660s, and after the restoration of the monarchy.

[xxxiii] Draco, the Athenian judge under whom small offences had disproportionate punishment, has leant his name for the rest of time to legalised cruelty. The emperor Dionysus was infamous for his persecutions of the early church.

[xxxiv] The 'mall' has been relocated outside the old walls, over the north bridge. It is now called the MacDonagh Centre.

[xxxv] Dublin (in reality, Canterbury) had consecrated Archibald Hamilton the incumbent archbishop in Cashel, now that the abbey was 'Church of Ireland'. This Anglican would die in Stockholm in 1659. His Catholic rival, Bishop Butler, was never permitted to celebrate the Eucharist in his own abbey.

[xxxvi] François de Salis, 1567–1622, was the French Catholic priest who became a Doctor of the Faith. He was a member of a grand Savoyard family and was trained for the law but instead, in 1593, he was ordained against his father's wishes becoming a key figure in the Counter Reformation. At first he preached to the Protestants, making many conversions. He became Bishop of Geneva, living in less hostile Annecy in his native Savoy. His fame spread rapidly. From 1600 until his death he delivered Lent and Advent sermons all over France. He set up schools and paid particular attention to the poor and, with with Ste Jeanne-Frances de Chantal, he founded the *Order of the Visitation* for women who could not abide the great established orders. His *Introduction to the Devout Life* and his *Treatise on the Love of God* are widely read classics. Today he is the patron saint of Catholic writers.

[xxxvii] The word 'dragoon' originally meant mounted infantry, trained in riding as well as infantry. The word evolved over time. During the 18th century, dragoons became conventional light cavalry. Most European armies had Dragoon regiments in the late 17th and early 18th centuries. The name may be derived from a field weapon, a *dragon*, pulled or dragged by the French Army.

[xxxviii] After Pope Sixtus V, the Della Rovere Pope who commissioned its decoration.

xxxix It is now the *Institut Français*, home to *les immortels*. These academicians still wear blue gowns and horsehair wigs, just as they did at the time of Louis XIV. It is today the only surviving and unchanged institution of the ancient regime.

xl The MacCarthys were not able to regain the castle from Lord Broghill, whose seat it became, before 1661.

xli The official name of the actual church, the most prominent building within the abbey complex, is *Die Irische Benediktinerklosterkirche St. Jakob und St. Gertrud*, 'The Irish Benedictine Abbey Church of St. James and St. Gertrude'.

xlii The carbine was then very new to Europe. It had a shorter barrel than its unwieldy rival, the musket, making it more useful in mounted warfare. Lighter and shorter, it had been designed to be loaded and fired from the saddle, even if this was rarely done - a moving horse is a very unsteady platform. Soldiers always preferred to halt, dismount, load and fire; that way the soldier became a smaller target. Musketeers could carry full length weapons comfortably enough on a horse, but only if riding from A to B (the practice of the original dragoons and later mounted infantry). A 'regiment of horse' had to ride with agility. Engaging in sword-wielding mêlées with opposing cavalry would turn full-length muskets into dangerous encumbrances. A carbine, the length of a sheathed sabre, usually hung with its hilt clear of the rider's elbows and its business end clear of the horse's legs.

Carbines' shorter sight plane and the lower velocity of their bullets meant they were less accurate and less powerful than the longer muskets of the infantrym bur when fast-burning smokeless powder became available, the muzzle velocity become less of an issue. Carbines continued to be issued and used by many who preferred a lighter, more compact weapon. The Italians maintain to this day a paramilitary regiment of *Carabinieri*.

xliii And nor has it.

xliv Later William III of Orange.

xlv The star of his Order of the Garter. He was reminding Juxon that it was to be passed to the Prince of Wales.

xlvi Can the Civil Wars be dismissed as merely a series of confrontations over the allocation of executive power and the way the kingdom's money was distributed? Certainly, the disagreements were made fatally worse by a progressively Puritan army, an Anglican monarchy, a largely Catholic old ruling class and a Presbyterian Parliament. The Dukes of Norfolk, the Earls of Shrewsbury and Waterford, the Viscounts of Hereford and the Barons Stourton were and remain the premier nobles of England. All of them retained their Catholic faith throughout this terrible period. All of them so remain. Of the premier nobles of England, to this day only the Marquesses of Salisbury have embraced the Anglican Communion.

All four sides claimed that they stood for the rule of law, but did 'law' mean the societal discipline that derives from a frightening sword, a succession of enacted bills, 'a way of life', or the rules of conduct as laid out in Leviticus and derived from the Ten Commandments?

The Civil War was, eventually, an armed discussion on these philosophical matters. Yet war is by definition a matter of force. Charles I, in his unwavering belief that he stood for the constitution – essentially the Common Law - and the right of the people to enjoy the benefits of stable government, fatally failed to negotiate a compromise with Parliament. He paid the price. Even so, and to many, King Charles was a martyr for his Anglican Faith and for his subjects. Wreaths of remembrance are still laid by his supporters on the anniversary of his death at his statue, which faces down Whitehall towards the place of his execution.

[xlvii] This small castle has long been replaced with the Baggot Street Bridge.

[xlviii] Small firearms suited to mounted soldiers.

[xlix] Cromwell's extraordinary ruthlessness was still unfamiliar to the courts of Europe, even given the lengthy blood-stained annals of warfare. His authorisation of the mass execution of its garrison and people appalled every European power, other than the English.

The general's interpretation of the rules of engagement were unusual, to put it generously. He declared that if a garrison were taken by assault, the lives of its defenders were automatically forfeit; if it surrendered after the storming of a break, the lives of the defeated were at the discretion of the aggressor. The only comparable cases in his previous career had been the storming of Basing House in 1645, where a hundred soldiers out of the four hundred defenders were killed after a successful assault. In 1648, when he besieged Pembroke Castle, the 'greatest and the most beautiful mansion' in Wales, not only did he starve out its royalist defenders, he cut off their water supply. The consequences were truly terrible. In a final flourish he trained his artillery on the Norman stronghold. Though it had already surrendered, he blew up the barbican and the fronts of all the towers. It has been a brooding ruin ever since.

After the storming of Drogheda, the English press concluded that two of the three thousand dead were civilians. The Irish had a different figure. They calculated that four thousand civilians had died at Drogheda, The Church refused to arbitrate. It contented itself with denouncing the atrocity as egregious blood-letting, without even the utilitarian purpose of a cattle slaughterhouse.

Cromwell, in a letter to the Speaker of the House of Commons, had justified his actions at Drogheda.

> I am persuaded that this is a righteous judgement of God on these barbarous wretches, who have imbrued their hands with so much innocent blood; and that it will tend to prevent the effusion of blood for the future, which are satisfactory grounds for such actions which cannot otherwise but work remorse and regret.

'The righteous judgement of God'? Civilians aside, could this be the justification for the massacre of Drogheda's garrison? The general left no doubt that his 'barbarous wretches' were Irish Catholics. He willfully ignored that a large number of those who fell to his 'model army' were Anglicans or other Protestants.

Cromwell was all too aware that Drogheda had neither fallen to the Irish rebels in 1641 nor to the Confederacy in the years that followed. He will equally have known that Catholic Irish troops had been admitted to Drogheda after the Great Rebellion. If clubbing priests to death and displays of officers' heads on pikes were meant to discourage others from opposition, it all worked. The neighbouring garrisons of Trim and Dundalk, so recently reclaimed by the Alliance, saw their soldiers flee for their lives when they heard what had happened at Drogheda.

According to the High Commissioner for War, Sir Arthur Aston's refusal to surrender justified the taking not just of his life but that of his entire garrison and its civilian fellow-travellers.

In Paris, Madrid, Rome and Vienna, everyone was shocked by the Drogheda massacre. The citizens of these far flung places gasped at Cromwell's mercilessness, thoroughness, cynical calculation, ruthlessness, his hot- and cold-bloodiness. Its sheer scale was unprecedented in post-classical European history. Even in classical history such barbarity was rare.

In the English Civil War, Cromwell himself had shown a limited degree of mercy to a defeated enemy but Drogheda remains a vile stain on his record. Perhaps, to be generous, in the heat of the moment, he lost his characteristic firm control over his troops? He may have surrendered to an atavistic blood-lust? One thing is sure. At Drogheda, he lost that 'government of himself'' that the Commonwealth's heroic propagandist, Milton, so much admired. His impatience, or anger, tarnished his talents.

Cromwell still had great savagery to perform in Ireland. This time he set his intentions to words.

> So that the people of that nation may know that it is not the intention of Parliament to extirpate that whole nation, but that mercy and pardon, both as to life and estate, may be extended to all husbandmen, ploughmen, labourers, artificers, and others of the inferior sort, in manner as is hereafter declared; they submitting themselves to the Parliament of the Commonwealth of England.

The Protector's personality and political skills were shaped by his deep religious commitment.

> God has brought us where we are, to consider the work we may do in the world, as well as at home.

A grateful Parliament promoted him Lord General of the Army and High Commissioner of the Commonwealth. In England alone he had already led more than thirty successful engagements. By the time of his death, his military achievements would include a new conquest of Scotland and the first complete subjugation of Ireland.

His government of England, however, was the cruellest and the most arbitrary ever known, excepting perhaps King John's. Yet there were (and are) some who described him as gracious and gallant. Few Irishmen share this perception.

> I have rid the Commonwealth of barbarous wretches.

A sympathetic tract, written just months after the Lord Protector's death, when his son Christopher had replaced his father's head on the coins, remarked that it was the dictator's conviction that 'religious belief was the greatest of all liberties. God had conferred it on the English people through its victory over King Charles'. Cromwell had never ceased to plead with his Parliaments to extend and protect freedom of religion 'for every species of Protestant'. Except, presumably, the Anglicans.

The Protector was happy to receive 'good men' from every sect. If he paid for a bible for his soldiers to carry at all times, he pointedly refused to make membership of the Church of England a qualification for office.

Nevertheless, he was not an hero to every sectarian. He may have loathed Catholics, but he also disliked and distrusted such former allies as the Fifth Monarchy Men and other Dissenters sects. The Fifth Monarchists, believing that the Second Coming was a rolling five days away, thought they had persuaded the dictator to establish a system of government that would prepare for it. When Cromwell agreed to become Lord Protector, he proved unable to yield that role to the Lord Jesus Christ. The Fifth Monarchy Men became his bitterest enemies. They declared that

> the king chastised us with whips, but Cromwell chastiseth us with scorpions.

Oddly, ar least to some, he favoured the return of the Jews to England. King John had expelled them in 1290. Of course, this so-called tolerance was born of pragmatism. He had realised that the Jews were a formidable source of foreign intelligence. Not one of them ever achieved a role in Government.

^l replaced: [l] Areas of mud-flats at the estuary of the River Slaney at Wexford Harbour, Ireland. The North Slob, an area of 1,000 hectares, was reclaimed in the mid-19th century by the building of a sea wall.

[li] Psalm 68

[lii] Now renamed 'Cromwellsfort'.

[liii] Parliament's new name (for what remained of it).

[liv] Eleven years later, a request from Wexford Town would be sent to the restored monarchy. It demanded compensation for 1,500 'innocent, unarmed and property-owning survivors who had lost their livelihoods and wherewithal in the sack and were now attempting to find a living on the open road.'

[lv] Cloughoughter is in the historic Kingdom of Breifne, specifically in the part that would later be subdivided into East Breifne and the future County Cavan.

[lvi] The fourteen tribes of Galway are Athy, Blake, Bodkin, Browne, D'Arcy, Deane, Font, French, Joyce, Kirwan, Lynch, Martin, Morris and Skerrett.

[lvii] *Conium* is a sub-genus of the carrot. The Plant List lists four such species, of which, *conium maculatum* is native to the Mediterranean but will thrive on the gulfstream warmed coast of Ireland around Rosslare.

[lviii] A twelfth century Cistercian foundation, confusingly with the same name as an English one.

[lix] The *Eikon Basilike, or Royal Portrait, a Pourtrature of His Sacred Majestie in His Solitudes and Sufferings*, was written in very stylish prose. It deeply observes the solemnity and affecting eloquence of Anglican piety, much as expressed in Cranmer's *Book of Common Prayer*. It depicts a steadfast monarch who, while admitting his weaknesses, declares the truth of his religious principles and the purity of his political motives, trusting in God in the face of any adversity. His greatest sin, it declares, was in yielding to Parliament's demands for the head of the Earl of Strafford. For this, Charles believed he paid with his throne and his life. *Eikon Basilike*'s portrays Charles as a martyr, tacitly inviting comparison of the king to Jesus Christ.

Its elegant pathos made it an instant masterstroke of Royalist propaganda. It went into thirty-six editions in 1649 alone, despite official disapproval.

Parliament retaliated by commissioning John Milton to write a riposte, which he published under the title *Eikonoklastes*, or *The Icon-Breaker*, in 1649. Milton sought to portray the image of Charles, and the absolute monarchy he aspired to, as idols, claiming a share of the reverence due only to God, and therefore justly overthrown to preserve His laws. This theological counterattack failed to dislodge the sentimental narrative of the Eikon itself from public esteem.

The *Eikon Basilike* and its portrait of Charles's execution as a martyrdom were so successful that, at the Restoration, a special commemoration of the king on January 30 was added to the *Book of Common Prayer*, directing that the day be observed as an occasion for fasting and repentance. On May 19, 1660, the Convocation of Canterbury and York canonised King Charles on the urging of Charles II. They added his name to the Prayer Book, and Charles I remains the only saint to have been formally canonised by the Church of England.

This commemoration was removed from the prayer book by Queen Victoria, in 1859. Several Anglican churches and chapels remain dedicated to 'King Charles the Martyr'. The *Society of King Charles the Martyr* was established in 1894 to work for the restoration of the king's name to the *Calendar of Saints* and to encourage the veneration of the Royal Martyr.

[lx] Varnished horsehair flasks and mugs were greatly valued by horsemen as they never broke and weighed almost nothing.

[lxi] The city motto *Urbs Intacta Manet Waterfordia* - Waterford Remains the Untaken City - was granted by Henry VII, first of the Tudors, in 1497. Waterford had refused to recognise either pretender to the English throne, Lambert Simnel or Perkin Warbeck.

[lxii] Rory O'More was no longer as young as he was, and heartbreak for Ireland had prematurely aged him. Within a year or two he fled to the island of Inishbofin, County Galway, after Galway's fall. St Colman's Church, on that island, bears a tablet with the inscription:

> In memory of many valiant Irishmen who were exiled to this Holy Island and in particular Rory O'More a brave chieftain of Leix, who after fighting for Faith and Fatherland, had to disguise as a fisherman to escape to a place of safety. He died shortly afterwards, a martyr to his Religion and his County, about 1653. He was esteemed and loved by his countrymen, who celebrated his many deeds of valour and kindness in their songs and reverenced his memory.

[lxiii] Usually called Castlehale.

[lxiv] Today's visitors to Ireland will see little that survives from before this time, A great shame, for Ireland was as rich in ancient and beautiful buildings as anywhere in Europe, even Italy.

[lxv] Situated in the town of Clonmel, County Tipperary, Old St. Mary's Church is believed to have been built by William de Burgo in 1204. In the late-14th to early-15th century, a fortified church was constructed on the site. The base of the bell tower and the east tower house survive The rest of the church was destroyed in 1650 by Cromwellian troops. In 1805, the structure underwent major renovations and the

25m-high octagonal bell tower was built on the base of the original tower. Old St Mary's is still use, but now by the Church of Ireland.

[lxvi] St. Benedict of Nursia established his first monastery, the source of the Benedictine Order, here around 529 AD. Rome had fallen to the Hun in 460 AD. It housed the greatest library of manuscripts and scrolls from the ancient world ever assembled. At the Battle of Monte Cassino, which raged from January to May, 1944, the Abbey was a section of the 161 kilometre (100 miles) Gustav line, a defensive German line designed to hold the Allied attackers from advancing any further north into Italy. Stretching from coast to coast, the monastery was a key stronghold, overlooking Highway 6, blocking the path to Rome. On 15 February 1944 the abbey, including its library, was almost completely destroyed in a series of heavy American air-raids, conducted because many reports from troops on the ground suggested that Germans were occupying the monastery. It was certainly a key observational post by all those who were fighting in the field. However, actually during the bombing no Germans were present. It is certain from every investigation that followed since the event that the only people killed in the monastery by the bombing were 230 Italian civilians seeking refuge there. The ruins of the monastery were subsequently occupied by German *Fallschirmjäger* (paratroopers), as the ruins provided excellent defensive cover, as would any hilltop ruin. The heavily outnumbered Germans held the position until withdrawing on 17 May 1944, having resisted four offensives by the New Zealanders, British Indian division and the Polish corps. After that the road to Rome was reopened. In December 1942, some 1,400 irreplaceable manuscript codices, chiefly patristic and historical, in addition to a vast number of documents relating to the history of the abbey and the collections of the Keats-Shelley Memorial House in Rome, had been sent to the abbey for safekeeping. Fortunately, German officers Lt. Col. Julius Schlegel (a Catholic) and Capt. Maximilian Becker (a Protestant), both from the Panzer-Division Hermann Göring, had them transferred to the Vatican at the beginning of the battle. More than a hundred German lorries, however, were loaded with monastic assets and art. They left the Abbey for the Fatherland in October 1943. It took 'strenuous' protests before they were turned around and delivered their booty to the Vatican. Fifteen lorryloads, however, containing the property of the Capodimonte Museum in Naples, were delivered to Göring in December 1943, for his birthday.
    They did not survive the war.

[lxvii] Both sides called the other 'rebels'.

[lxviii] Pennsylvania is named after his son.

[lxix] No race or country in classical or modern history has lost so much of its population in ten years from such concentrated aggression, or for any other reason. Not the Potato Famine, the Holocaust, the Suppression of Carthage, the Black Death, the Armenian genocide, the Russian Pogroms, the Great War or the ravages of Genghis Khan. Only the battles between Royalists and Parliament come close.

[lxx] Cromwell is referring to the first Fronde War and (accurately) predicting the second.

[lxxi] Louis XIII's wife and Louis XIV's mother.

lxxii The raising of the siege is celebrated annually on 8 September in a parade, known as 'Alarde'. Enríquez de Cabrara was Hereditary Admiral of Castile, the ninth of his line.

lxxiii The word Anglicanism and its derivatives refer to the *Ecclesia Anglicana*, the (Roman) church in England that St Augustine had founded. In the mid-sixteenth century it would have been more readily known as the Episcopal Church. Cromwell's decision to ban it, in 1649, was not overturned until the Restoration and, in 1662, its buildings were purged of its 2000 Puritan, antivestarian preachers. Today's familiar service owes much to the Oxford Movement and the Gothic Revival of the early nineteenth century.

lxxiv The Spanish acquired the London palace of the bishops of Ely before the Reformation. Under Spanish protection, the Catholic Church in its grounds, now open to the public, is today the only mediaeval church in London that never became Protestant.

lxxv It had been built in the Romanesque period and enlarged in the Flamboyant.

lxxvi Major Isaac Lally (Laly, or Mulally) had created one of the original three Irish regiments in France. Another was Lord Dillon's. Out of these would grow the Irish Brigades, which fought for France throughout the next century. King Louis XIV ennobled Lally *baron de Tollendal, comte de Lally* in the French *noblesse d'épée*, and a Count of Mulally-Tolendal would be beheaded in 1766. The original Irish Brigade was a unit made up only of Irish regiments in the service of the kings of France, made up entirely of exiles. It was formally incorporated in the French army in 1690, and was only dissolved during the Revolution. Units of James II's Irish Army would swell its ranks. Irish exiles at this time liked to be known as Wild Geese, or *Oies Sauvages*, after their ladies who had been sold into slavery. They participated in many Jacobite rebellions.

lxxvii Cromwell sent a military expedition under General Venables and 'Sea-General' William Penn to the Caribbean. His original plan was to wrest Hispaniola from the Spanish, but the assault failed. The expedition then sailed to Jamaica, successfully capturing that island for England - the second overseas possession (excluding Ireland) of a fledgling British Empire. The first was of course Virginia. Jamaica is a large island and needed skill to repopulate it and make it viable. The first idea was either to free the indentured Irish on Barbados, and the second was to round up any rebellious Irish and send them there. Cromwell appealed for planters to come to his new colony, but this met with little success. Cromwell repeated his offer to liberate and offer land to indentured Irish labourers in Barbados. That policy also met with resistance from the plantation owners, short of muscle to work their sugar cane. When Cromwell offered land, many slave owners moved from Barbados to Jamaica, along with their slaves, and were granted land there. Yet still the demand for labour could not be met. Cromwell turned to his 'man-catchers' in Ireland and ordered them to round up and transport several thousand women and 'as many young men as could be lifted out of Ireland' to work on the new plantations as slaves. 2000 children were taken and transported to the colony and put to work. Henry Cromwell, Lord Deputy of Ireland, wrote that it would do them good; it would 'make them Englishmen, I meane rather, Christaines' *[sic]*. This reflected the belief among Puritans that Catholics were not in fact Christians. Conditions in Jamaica for Irish labourers were very poor. They worked long hours in searing heat. Many died and were buried in the sugar fields where they fell. Precise numbers are unknown; the deaths of slave were rarely reported and the fate of many remains unrecorded. Any who attempted to escape were severe punished. First offenders were whipped and a year was added to their term of servitude. Repeated escape attempts were punished with hanging. Slaves who struck their owners were burned alive. One visitor to Jamaica wrote that 'they are nailed to the ground with crooked sticks on every limb and then applying the fires by degrees from the feet, burning them gradually up to the head, whereby their pains are extravagant'.

[lxxviii] Cromwell was buried alongside the English monarchs in Westminster Abbey in a lavish ceremony. Three years later his remains were exhumed and hanged, still in their shroud, at Tyburn. His severed head was later shown on a pike outside Westminster Hall until it was rescued by a well-wisher nearly twenty years later. For those who welcome the State's intrusion into the religion and private thoughts of the people, his radical paternalism and his determination to remove all ornament from society makes him a hero. While he closed both Parliament and every Anglican church in England and Ireland, some Dissenters still favour him as one who was committed to freedom for 'the poorest Christian, the most mistaken Christian' [sic]. 'Christian' when used by Puritans, excludes all Anglicans and Catholics. He was as authoritarian as any dictator before or since. Where some chose to exterminate Jews, or aristocrats, peasants or (in the case of Pol Pot) all who had completed their education, he sought to eliminate Catholicism, wilfully construing it with persecution and modernity. Extraordinarily, Dissenters and dictators still canonise him as a hero and military genius. In Ireland, he transformed a land so studded with churches, abbeys and castles that it was as rich in architecture as Italy, justifying his devastation of the country's people, heritage and traditions in his assertion of a 'pure', 'primitive' and unornamented faith. Since most of the relicts of those Royalists and Catholics who witnessed his gloating massacres in Ireland will demonise him, to hear well of him it may be necessary to travel to Belfast or Londonderry. Thomas Carlyle's edition of his letters and speeches was one of the ten best-selling books of Victorian England, but contemporary attempts to raise a statue to him outside the Palace of Westminster led to bitter debates in both Houses and thunderous leaders in the newspapers. The statue was, nonetheless, erected.

Lightning Source UK Ltd.
Milton Keynes UK
UKOW04f0345060115

244060UK00001B/14/P

9 781784 078126